大学本科翻译研究型系列读本

总主编　张柏然

文学翻译读本

Selected Readings of Literary Translation

主　　编　辛红娟

副主编　廖晶　郭薇

参编人员　汪璧辉　鄢宏福　李文竞

吴琳　唐宏敏　王昱

南京大学出版社

大学本科翻译研究型系列读本
大学翻译学研究型系列教材

总　序

张柏然

　　到了该为翻译学研究型系列教材说几句话的时候了。两年前的炎炎夏日，南京大学出版社责成笔者总揽主编分别针对高等院校翻译学本科生和研究生学习与研究需求的研究型系列读本和导引。俗话说，独木难撑大厦。于是，笔者便千里相邀"招旧部"，网罗昔日在南大攻读翻译学博士学位的"十八罗汉"各主其事。寒来暑往，光阴荏苒，转眼两年过去了。期间，大家意气奋发，不辞辛劳，借助网络"上天"，躲进书馆"入地"，上下求索，查阅浩瀚的文献经典，进而调动自己的学术积累，披沙拣金，辨正证伪，博采众长，字斟句酌，终于成就了这一本本呈现在读者面前的教材。

　　众所周知，教材乃教学之本和知识之源，亦即体现课程教学理念、教学内容、教学要求，甚至教学模式的知识载体，在教学过程中起着引导教学方向、保证教学质量的作用。改革开放以来，我国各类高校组编、出版的翻译教材逐年递增。我们在中国国家图书馆网站上检索主题名含有"翻译"字段的图书，检索结果显示，1980 至 2009 年间，我国引进、出版相关著作 1800 余种，其中，翻译教材占有很大的比重。近些年来，翻译教材更是突飞猛进。根据有关学者的不完全统计，目前，我国正式出版的翻译教材共有 1000 多种。* 这一变化结束了我国相当长一段时间内翻译教材"一枝独秀"的境地，迎来了"百花齐放"的局面，由此也反映了我国高校翻译教学改革的深化。

　　但是，毋庸讳言，虽然教材的品种繁多，但是真正合手称便的、富有特色的教材仍属凤毛麟角。教材数量增多并不足以表明教学理念的深刻转变。其中大多都具有包打翻译学天下的纯体系冲动，并没有打破我国既往翻译教材编写从某一理论预设出发的本质主义思维模式和几大板块的框架结构。从教材建设看，我国翻译理论教材在概念陈设、模式架构、内容安排上存在着比较严重的雷同化现象。这表明，教材建设需要从根本上加以改进，而如何改则取决于我们有什么样的教学理念。

　　有鉴于此，我们组编了"大学翻译学研究型系列教材"和"大学本科翻译研究型系列读本"这两套系列教材。前者系研究生用书，它包括《中国翻译理论研究导引》、《当代西方翻译理论研究导引》、《当代西方文论与翻译研究导引》、《翻译学方法论研究导引》、《语言学与翻译研究导引》、《文学翻译研究导引》、《汉语典籍英译研究导引》、《英汉口译理论研究导引》、《语料库与翻译研究导引》和《术语翻译研究导引》等 10 册；后者则以本科生为主要读者对象，它包括《翻译概论读本》、《文化翻译读本》、《文学翻译读本》、《商务英语翻译读本》、《法律英语翻译读本》、《传媒英语翻译读本》、《科技英语翻译读本》、《英汉口译读本》、《英汉比较与翻译读本》和《翻译资源与工具读本》等 10 册。这两套教材力图综合中西译论、相关学科（如哲学、美学、文学、语

---

　　* 转引自曾剑平、林敏华：《论翻译教材的问题及编写体系》，《中国科技翻译》，2011 年 11 月。

言学、社会学、文化学、心理学、语料库翻译学等)的吸融性研究以及方法论的多层次研究,结合目前高校翻译教学和研究实践的现状进行创造性整合,编写突出问题型结构和理路的读本和导引,以满足翻译学科本科生和研究生教学与研究的需求。这是深化中国翻译学研究型教材编写与研究的一个重要课题,至今尚未引起翻译理论研究界和教材编写界的足够重视。摆在我们面前的这一课题,基本上还是一片多少有些生荒的地带。因此,我们对这一课题的研究,也就多少带有拓荒性质。这样,不仅大量纷繁的文献经典需要我们去发掘、辨别与整理,中西翻译美学思想发展演变的特点与规律需要我们去探讨,而且研究的对象、范畴和方法等问题,都需要我们进行独立的思考与确定。研究这一课题的困难也就可以想见了。然而,这一课题本身的价值和意义却又变为克服困难的巨大动力,策励着我们不揣浅陋,迎难而上,试图在翻译学研究型教材编写这块土地上,作一些力所能及的垦殖。

这两套研究型系列教材的编纂目的和编纂特色主要体现为:不以知识传授为主要目的,而是培养学生发问、好奇、探索、兴趣,即学习的主动性,逐步实现思维方式和学习方式的转变,引导学生及早进入科学研究阶段;不追求知识的完整性、系统性,突破讲授通史、通论知识的教学模式,引入探究学术问题的教学模式;引进国外教材编写理念,填补国内大学翻译学研究型教材的欠缺;所选论著具有权威性、文献性、可读性与引导性。具体而言,和传统的通史通论教材不同,这两套系列教材是以问题结构章节,这个"问题"既可以是这门课(专业方向)的主要问题,也可以是这门课某个章节的主要问题。在每个章节的安排上,则是先由"导论"说明本章的核心问题,指明获得相关知识的途径;接着,通过选文的导言,直接指向"选文"——涉及的知识面很广的范文,这样对学生的论文写作更有示范性;"选文"之后安排"延伸阅读",以拓展和深化知识;最后,通过"研究实践"或"问题与思考",提供实践方案,进行专业训练,希冀用"问题"牵引学生主动学习。这样的结构方式,突出了教材本身的问题型结构和理路,旨在建构以探索和研究为基础的教与学的人才培养模式,让年轻学子有机会接触最新成就、前沿学术和科学方法;强调通识教育、人文教育与科学教育交融,知识传授与能力培养并重,注重培养学生掌握方法,未来能够应对千变万化的翻译教学与研究的发展和需要。

笔者虽说长期从事翻译教学与研究,但对编写教材尤其是研究型教材还是个新手。这两套翻译学研究型教材之所以能够顺利出版,全有赖各册主编的精诚合作和鼎力相助,全有仗一群尽责敬业的编写和校核人员。特别值得一提的是,在这两套系列教材的最后编辑工作中,南京大学出版社外语编辑室主任董颖和责任编辑裴维维两位女士全力以赴,认真校核,一丝不苟,对保证教材的质量起了尤为重要的作用。在此谨向他(她)们致以衷心的感谢!

总而言之,编写大学翻译学研究型教材还是一项尝试性的研究工程。诚如上面所述,我们在进行这项"多少带有拓荒性质"的尝试时,犹如蹒跚学步的孩童,在这过程中留下些许尴尬,亦属在所难免。作为教材的编撰者,我们衷心希望能听到来自各方的意见和建议,以便日后再版修订,进而发展出更好更多翻译学研究型教材来。

是之为序。

二〇一二年三月二十七日
撰于沪上滴水湖畔临港别屋

前　言

自人类文明之初,文化交流的介质就涵盖了物质文化而外的精神文明。文学作为文化的重要组成部分,在构建民族文化形象上起到无可替代的作用。英国的莎士比亚、法国的巴尔扎克、德国的歌德、西班牙的塞万提斯、俄罗斯的托尔斯泰、中国的李白……在展示各自国家尊严的天平上无不占据着很重的分量。古今中外文学巨匠的世界声誉,无不得益于一代又一代翻译人的努力。

从 2005 年起,我国首批高等院校翻译专业获得批准设立。这是在高校外语专业人才培养基础上直接定向培养“翻译”的新专业。但《人民日报》记者 2009 年 11 月对北京外国语大学英语学院首届翻译系学生进行职业意愿调查却发现,这批“明天的翻译家”们把文学翻译作为“第一职业”选择的几乎为零。针对文学翻译人才培养上出现的这一令人堪忧的瓶颈现象,专家、学者们纷纷发表看法,为翻译人才尤其是文学翻译人才的培养献计献策。《中国翻译》杂志常务副主编杨平建议,国家应把对文学翻译现状的关注上升到实现国家文化战略的高度,并从体制机制上加以保证。刘士聪教授则认为,目前我国有人才,也有条件,关键在于应当尽快转变培养翻译人才的模式。优秀的文学翻译人才,较之于其他应用类型的翻译人才,培养周期长,对译者自身的素养要求高,要求翻译者兼具母语、国学、知识面、阅历、文化积淀等方面的综合素质。这些素质的获得绝非一日之功,要求学习者要有研究的宏观视野和能力。加大人才培养和自我培养过程中对于文学的偏重,成为翻译学界的当务之急。

有鉴于此,本教材严格遵循“翻译学研究性课程系列教材”的编纂目的与编纂特色:突出问题型结构和理路,注重学生思维方式的训练和研究能力的培养;突出研究范例性,注重选文的经典性,为学生提供可资借鉴、参考的优秀翻译范本,以引导学生及早进入理论联系实践的科学研究阶段,提高文学翻译的自我培养能力。

该分册共 8 章,每章由“导论”、“选文”、“翻译鉴赏”、“翻译试笔”、“延伸阅读”、“问题与思考”六大部分组成。编者围绕章节“导论”所述相关专题的主要内容,选取翻译学界具有代表性的论述,依循“先易后难,循序渐进”的准则,结构“引文”部分。围绕引文中的主要文学翻译问题,选取国内知名学者经典翻译片断,以典型个案分析引导学生开展"翻译试笔",希冀试笔之后的参考译文可以为学习者指点迷津。"延伸阅读"部分旨在为有志于在翻译理论研究领域进一步深造的学生拓展研究视域,并通过"问题与思考"检验学生对该章主要问题的熟悉程度。本教材主要内容包括:① 文学翻译概貌篇;② 文学翻译风格篇;③ 文学翻译修辞篇;④ 诗歌翻译篇;⑤ 散文翻译篇;⑥ 小说翻译篇;⑦ 戏剧翻译篇;和⑧ 影视译制篇。

　　本教材从整体内容上可划分为两大部分。前三章包括文学翻译概貌、文学翻译风格、文学翻译修辞,主要描述文学翻译框架和文学翻译基本问题,分析文学翻译的本质特征,详述文学翻译研究中诸如风格可译性问题、文学翻译"再创造"问题、文学阐释"度"的问题以及风格传递中的修辞问题。本教材以修辞切入,但并不仅仅停留在修辞格表层,而是将翻译置于修辞的哲学层面展开,分析指出:修辞格所引发的翻译困难,实则是由于不同民族思维习惯、文化传统不同而带来的接受困难,翻译从宏观上而言是一种跨语言、跨文化的修辞接受。后五章依据不同文学体裁,依次探讨诗歌、散文、小说、戏剧和影视作品的翻译,既有对所涉文学体裁的翻译美学研究,又有对文本在异域接受过程中意识形态、诗学等影响因素的深度描画。

　　本教材所选文章严格依据经典性和权威性原则,均为历经时间淘拣积淀而来的翻译学经典定论,涵盖自夏尔·巴托(Charles Batteux)以降诸多西方权威翻译论者的译理阐释和中国现当代著名翻译学人的译笔勾连,力图简洁、全面地为学习者展示相关论题的本相。选文既有投身文学翻译实践数十年的著名翻译家的理论提升,又有结合哲学、现象学、社会学、政治学、传播学、文体学等交叉学科对翻译概念的纯理论剖析。本书既可作为教师课堂教学用书,也可作为有志深入研究翻译理论与实践的年轻学者开展自主学习和研究。

　　本教材在厘定框架、选文审定和编写的整个过程中,无不刻印着导师张柏然教授的学术点拨与指导,诚挚感谢学术成长道路上张柏然教授所给予的教诲与引领。感谢中南大学外国语学院为本书编写提供时间上的保证,感谢中南大学 MTI 教育中心同仁们工作上的支持与配合。同时,感谢南京大学出版社领导与编辑为本书刊印所付出的辛勤劳动。

　　本教材中所引大部分文献已获得原作者的使用授权,对于因种种原因无法与原作者取得联系并获得使用授权的引文,我们在此对原作者深表谢意和歉意。

　　编者学术视野所限,选文偏颇或行文不当之处,还请就教于方家。

辛红娟

2012 年 7 月于湖南长沙

目 录

第一章　文学翻译概貌篇

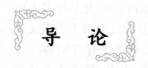

导　论

《圣经》钦定本(1611年)译者在序言中对翻译作了一番形象比喻:"翻译就是把窗户打开,让光线进入房间;翻译就是把贝壳撬开,这样我们便可以品尝里面的肉核;翻译就是撩开窗帘,这样我们便能窥见最圣洁的地方;翻译就是打开井盖,这样我们便可以获得水源。"这一连串生动的比喻,说明人类生存离不开翻译活动,翻译行为是文明与文明之间展开的关于生存的对话。

人类文明史上,知识的传递主要依赖语言为工具,因此,翻译一直是传播外来知识的重要渠道。可以毫不夸张地说,世界上各主要文化系统的发展都和翻译活动有着密切的联系。在西方,自罗马帝国以降,国与国之间的对话与交流大多通过翻译开展。史载罗马最早的翻译家里维乌斯·安德罗尼柯(公元前284?—公元前204)所翻译的大多是文学作品;更有研究者指出,荷马史诗《奥德赛》片断"是第一首拉丁诗,也是第一篇译成拉丁语的文学作品","译文对引导当时罗马青年一代起了不可低估的作用"。由于他和其他同时代乃至后代翻译家的共同努力,古希腊戏剧对后世欧洲的戏剧产生了根本性的影响。在古希腊、拉丁文学方面,荷马史诗、希腊悲剧、喜剧和抒情诗,忒奥克里托斯(约公元前310—公元前250)、卡图卢斯(约公元前87—公元前54)、普卢塔克(约公元46—公元120或127)等的作品也被译成欧洲众多国家的语言。在保存古希腊文艺方面,阿拉伯译者做出了巨大贡献。至于欧洲各国古代和近代的其他大作家,如维吉尔、但丁、莎士比亚、歌德、塞万提斯、安徒生、易卜生、托尔斯泰、陀思妥耶夫斯基、莫里哀等人的作品,也都被多次译成其他国家语言。在东方,阿拉伯的《一千零一夜》、中国的散文与诗歌、印度的《薄伽梵歌》和《沙恭达罗》等都被译成欧洲语言。东方文学作品的译介,不仅弘扬了东方各民族的文化,也极大地促进了东西方文化交融,对于保持东方文明古国的文化身份有着不可估量的意义。

西方翻译史上第一次高潮,带有明显的文学活动性质。从古罗马帝国后期开始,宗教翻译逐渐成为西方翻译的主流。我国的翻译事业有着更加悠久的历史,当许多国家还没有自己的文字时,我国的翻译事业就产生了。据有关史书记载,周朝和秦始皇时代,语言中就已经出现了外来语,说明当时已有翻译活动。大规模的翻译实践始于东汉桓帝建和二年(公元148)开始的佛经翻译,前后历时约1 400多年。从表面上看,宗教翻译和文学翻译似乎没有多大关系。但实际上,由于宗教翻译的主体——《圣经》和佛典经籍本身就是很有文学价值的文学作品,因此其影响就不仅仅局限于宗教翻译本身,也进入了文学翻译的领域。在《圣经》被译成欧洲各民族语言的过程中,《圣经》的翻译对这些民族书面语言的最终形成起到了巨大的作用。

对很多民族来说,《圣经》译本就是该民族的第一部书面文学作品,与欧洲各民族文学的创作和发展关系极其密切。佛经的翻译则对中华民族的思想和文化传统产生巨大的影响。在文化上的影响有语言、文学、学术思想等,尤其在语言方面非常显著:词汇(增加了 35 000 个词汇),音韵(四声的发明和诗歌韵律上的变化),句法和文体(倒装句增多,反诘句增多等);对中国文学传统的影响则主要体现在新意境和新材料的输入方面,开辟了唐以降格律诗词新体裁,催生六朝志怪小说,激发浪漫主义文学,使古代文学获得解放。

　　丰富的文学翻译实践,催生了人类历史上丰富的文学翻译理论。东西方历史上都多次出现文化典籍的翻译高潮,如阿拉伯人对古代欧洲文化的翻译和传播、西方传教士对于中国文化典籍的翻译工作。各个民族的文化典籍从其根本上而言都属于各自民族关于存在的诗意言说,因而大多属于文学翻译范畴。经过 2 000 年的积淀和淘拣,20 世纪 70 年代,随着人文社会科学认识的深入和发展,文学翻译研究也取得了突破性进展,极大地拓展了人们对于翻译学的认识:首先,从语言性质上来看,文学翻译处理的是具有想象性、审美性和高度创造性的文学语言,决定了文学翻译的创造性和审美性特质;其次,文学翻译必定发生在特定的文化语境内,文化系统的结构、意识形态和诗学决定了文学翻译的文化性和社会性特质;最后,译者的个人学养和气质不可避免地印刻在原文理解和译文生产过程中,决定了文学翻译的阐释性和主体性。文学翻译是将一种相对陌生的表达方式转换成相对熟悉的表达方式的过程,是增强、促进人们社会交流发展的重要手段。其内容有语言、文字、图形、符号的翻译,所有与语言相关的事物基本上都可以进行翻译,包括小说、电影、诗歌、演讲等,但不同的领域,翻译困难度也不同。例如,诗歌几乎是不可能准确翻译的,因为诗歌的形式、音韵等都是组成其含义的重要分子。出于美学的考量,文学翻译不能仅仅注重字对字、词对词的翻译,尤其不能忽略文化间的不同,否则会导致译文在语意、美感、风格上的流失,优秀的翻译人员必须在准确性和可读性之间找到很好的平衡。

　　“文学”一词的概念有广义和狭义之分。广义的文学泛指一切口头或书面作品;狭义的文学指诗歌、散文、小说、戏剧,以及文学性较强的杂文、传记、儿童文学等创作题材。文学翻译,顾名思义就是对文学作品进行的翻译,是对文学作品的语言形式、艺术手法、情节内容、形象意境等的再现,要求译者具有作家的文学修养和表现力,以便在深刻理解原作、把握原作精神实质的基础上,把原作的内容和艺术魅力在译作中传达出来。文学翻译必须是文学——翻译文学,因为大凡文学都是一门语言艺术,而艺术需要创造性,因此文学翻译也需要创造性。但文学翻译毕竟是翻译而非原创,因此准确说来,文学翻译属于再创造的艺术。翻译的作用在于将原语中体现的文化移植到陌生的目的语文化中去,是不同文化之间进行交流的媒介。由于不同语言文化之间存在着显著差异,不同语言系统之间不存在完全对应的关系,因此,用一种语言文化再现另一种语言文化时,译文不可避免地会反映出两种语言、文化的特征。

　　本章选文主要围绕文学翻译的定义、文学翻译的本质特征、翻译的简单分类以及文学翻译的再创造特质等方面展开,力图使学习者对文学翻译的基本概念有较全面的了解,构建初步的翻译理论图谱。

选文一 文学翻译的本质特征

郑海凌

导　言

本文选自《中国翻译》，1998 年第 6 期。

选文通过简单回溯东西方对于"文学翻译"的界定历史，发现在中外翻译史里，混淆翻译文体的现象很常见，讨论翻译时往往不加分类，不区别对待，把文学翻译与非文学翻译熔于一炉，甚至拿文学翻译的理论来对待一切文体。基于这一现实，作者指出，学界必须要正确认识文学翻译的性质，让其与非文学翻译划清界限，才能名正言顺地显示文学翻译的独立性和特殊性。通过与艺术本质的对比，不难发现，文学翻译的本质特征首先在于其审美本质及其在审美创造上的局限性。文学翻译本身是在"信"与"美"、束缚与自由的矛盾和统一中生存与发展的，这种矛盾和统一就是文学翻译本身，离开其中任何一方，文学翻译就不存在了。文学翻译与艺术相通，但又有较大差异，它具有艺术的创造性，又有自身的局限性和依附性，只能算做一种特殊的准艺术形式。

文学翻译的本质是什么，究竟应该怎样描述它的本质特征，至今仍是一个有争议的问题。当前较为流行的说法是：文学翻译是一门艺术。那么，文学翻译果真是艺术吗？如果它是艺术，为什么它没有像其他艺术形式那样得到普遍的、持久的承认？如果它不是艺术，为什么人们给它冠以艺术的美名？如此追问下去，我们便会发现，求证这一命题并不那么简单。在翻译领域里，由于对文学翻译的本质特征认识模糊，人们有时陷入重艺术轻语言，或者重语言轻艺术的倾向，造成翻译实践的随意性和翻译批评的极端化。本文拟对文学翻译的本质特征问题作初步探讨，同时求教于翻译界同行和前辈。

一

文学翻译作为一个独立的概念，最早出现在西方译论里。古罗马修辞学家西塞罗关于"演说家式的翻译"的主张对后世产生了较大影响。我国传统的翻译理论，并没有单独提出文学翻译的概念，尽管大诗人谢灵运、李白都曾涉足翻译活动，刘禹锡也曾有诗句："勿谓翻译徒，不为文雅雄。"从汉末佛经译者的文质之争，到严复的"信达雅"理论，都涉及文学翻译的本质问题，却没有旗帜鲜明地标举它的名目。也许先辈们要寻找一种能涵盖一切的翻译原则，忽略了翻译的对象。在中外翻译史里,混淆翻译文体的现象很常见,讨论翻译时往往不加分类,不区别待遇,把文学翻译与非文学翻译熔于一炉,甚至拿文学翻译的理论来对待一切文体。严复的"信达雅"理论,指导文学翻译实践最为贴切。严复却用来指导社会科学著作的翻译,还在"尔雅"上大做文章,岂不画蛇添足!这种误会在当代也不鲜见。美国翻译理论家尤金·奈达一度认为翻译是科学也是艺术,后来又说翻译不是科学只是艺术,强调翻译才能是天赋。他并没有把翻译分门别类。科技翻译机器人即将问世,哪里需要什么"天赋"。德国翻译理论家沃尔夫拉姆·威尔斯在其《翻译学:问题与方法》一书中指出文学翻译的特殊性,却仍然把它和其他文体的翻译放在一起研究,试图建立包容一切文体的翻译学。俄国的翻译家们似乎明智一些,很早就分成语言学派和文艺学派,森严壁垒地相互对峙,但他们往往各自强调一个极端,甚至把语言和文学隔离起来。当然,这些现象与当时当地的译学风气或文化传统分不开,不能妄加批评。各国翻译家的理论无疑得到他们本国人的认同,在本国文坛上独领风骚,我们列举这些无非是指出人们以往在研究方法上的疏漏或者个性。

西方提出文学翻译的概念虽早,其界说却显出自发的天真。从西塞罗、贺拉斯到当代的列维、加切奇拉泽,都强调文学翻译是一种文学创作,注重它的创造性、随意性,忽视它的局限性。我国提出文学翻译的概念较晚,但其内涵透视出自觉的严谨,有师法:"文学的翻译是用另一种语言,把原作的艺术意境传达出来,使读者在读译文的时候能够像读原作时一样得到启发、感动和美的享受。"(引自茅盾于1954年8月在全国文学翻译工作会议上的讲话)我国翻译界对文学翻译的界定,注重传达原作的艺术意境,把读者的反映作为衡量翻译效果的依据,其审美原则与我国传统文论中的"意境说"一脉相传,并呼应清末马建忠的"善译说"。意境是文学作品通过形象描写表现出来的境界与情调,是作家审美理想的最高层次。要求译作传达原作的艺术意境,准确揭示了文学翻译的本质;让读者参与翻译活动,更把文学翻译提高到一个新的层次。在接受美学理论尚未流行的50年代,提出这样的见解尤为难得。

正确认识文学翻译的性质,就能让它和非文学翻译划清界限,名正言顺地显示自己的独立性和特殊性。文学翻译与非文学翻译的区别,首先表现于对象的不同。文学翻译的对象是文学作品,具体地说,就是小说、散文、诗歌、纪实文学、戏剧和影视作品。而非文学翻译的对象是文学作品以外的各种文体,如各种理论著作、学术著作、教科书、报刊政论作品、公文合同等。其次表现于语言形式的不同。文学翻译采用的是文学语言,而非文学翻译采用的是非文学语言。第三是翻译手段不同。文学翻译采用的是文学艺术手段,带有主体性、创造性,而非文学翻译采用的是技术性手段,有较强的可操纵性。鉴于文学翻译与非文学翻译的区别,我们对二者的要求也大不相同。如果说,我们要求非文学翻译要以明白畅达的合乎该文体习惯的语言准确地传达原作的内容,那么对于文学翻译,这样的要求就远远不够了。文学作品是用特殊的语言创造的艺术品,具有形象性、艺术性,体现着作家独特的艺术风格,并且具有能够引人入胜的艺术意境。所以,文学翻译要求译者具有作家的文学修养和表现力,以便在深刻理解原作、把握原作精神实质的基础上,把内容与形式浑然一体的原作的艺术意境传达出来。

二

文学翻译的本质特征,在与艺术本质的对比中显得更为明晰。文学翻译相对于非文学翻译的特殊性,并不能说明它是一门艺术。要判定它是不是艺术,还得把它同艺术本身做对照。

谈到艺术,人们往往会联想到具有感性形象的绘画、雕塑、舞蹈、音乐和诗歌等艺术作品,或者把它们与艺术等同起来。其实这是一种误解。艺术与艺术作品是两个不同的概念。艺术是人类的一项活动,而艺术作品则是这项活动的产物。那么艺术究竟是一项什么样的活动呢?关于艺术的定义,自古以来说法很多,比如"艺术即模仿"(柏拉图,亚里士多德)、"艺术是一种愿望的想象性表现"(弗洛伊德)、"艺术即表现;表现即直觉"(克罗齐)、"艺术即情感语言"(杜卡斯)、"艺术是对真理的直感的观察,或者说是用形象思维"(别林斯基)等。尽管说法不同,但有一点是一致的,即艺术是一种创造、具有审美的属性,也就是说,是艺术家对现实生活的审美的把握。

我们再来看文学翻译与艺术的异同。首先,文学翻译是审美的翻译,其审美特征表现在两个方面:其一,文学翻译再现原作的艺术美;其二,文学翻译是一种创造性的活动,具有鲜明的主体性,其创造性的程度是衡量它的审美价值的尺度。从文学翻译活动的内涵看,它是一个由阅读、体会、沟通到表现的审美创造过程。在这一过程中,译者通过视觉器官认识原作的语言符号,这些语言符号反映到译者的大脑转化为概念,由概念组合成完整的思想,然后发展成为更复杂的思维活动,如联想、评价、想象等。译者阅读原作时,头脑中储存的思想材料与原作的语义信息遇合,达到理解和沟通,同时他的主观评价和情感参与其中。所以,通过译语最终表现出来的东西可能正确,也可能谬误。然而,不管译作正确与否,翻译活动本身无疑是一种创造,因为它涉及译者的想象、情感、联想等审美心理因素。

文学翻译的审美本质,我们还可以从译者与原作的审美关系来理解。以往研究文学翻译,人们偏重于从哲学认识论的角度看待翻译过程,注意力往往集中于译者的正确理解与表达。译者作为翻译主体,在翻译过程中是被动的,只能亦步亦趋地跟在原作后面爬行。这种以理性为中心,以语言学原理为基础的翻译模式对于非文学翻译无疑是正确的,但对于文学作品来说就未免过于简单了。文学作品是一个复杂的艺术整体,它的内容丰富多彩,可以是一个人的内心独白,可以是一个人的瞬间感受,可以是一幅宏伟壮烈的战争画卷,可以是一段富有诗意的爱情故事,可以是整个社会的缩影,也可以是某一段奇特生活的写照。总之,文学作品容量极大,并且处处流露着艺术美。在文学翻译过程中,译者与原作之间是审美关系。译者的审美趣味、审美体验和审美感受,直接关系着能否准确传达原作的艺术美。在翻译活动中,译者既是原作艺术美的欣赏和接受者,同时又是它的表现者。从欣赏、接受到表现,有一个重要环节,即译者的审美再创造,或者叫做心灵的再创造、情感形式的再创造。从国外接受美学的观点看,文学作品要体现自身的价值,必须通过读者阅读。不然,它就是一叠印满文字符号的纸。艺术作品为人们提供一个多层次的未定点,人们通过阅读和理解填补空白,将其具体化,最终使作品的意义从语言符号里浮现出来。译者凭着超出常人的文学修养和审美力阅读、透视和体会原作的方方面面,再以他的创造能力把自己的体会和理解表现出来,最终完成翻译过程。译者的审美视角、审美力和表现力因人而异,所以一部原作有多部不同的译本。

三

当人们广泛运用对话理论来揭示艺术的本质规律时,我们看待文学翻译的结构模式,也会发现它的对话性。实际上,翻译产生于对话,它本身就是一种对话活动,是一种由隔膜、误解引起的对话。在文学翻译活动中,译者通过阅读原作同原作者对话,通过建构译作同原作对话,并且通过译作与读者对话。译者的这种多重对话也是中外两种文化的对话与交流。对话中包含着创造,创造中包含着误解,最终在误解与创造中达到沟通。所以,文学翻译离不开误译,它传达原作的艺术意境只能是相对的。

我们具体分析这种对话结构中的关系,首先会发现,文学翻译的创造性来自译者的主体性。就是说,译者的主观参与行为是文学翻译的艺术创造的关键。文学翻译活动的第一层次是译者对原作的阅读。这种阅读不同于一般读者的读书活动,也不同于文学研究者阅读他所要研究的某个作家的作品,不能够一目十行地只欣赏故事情节或者只探索某种思想倾向的艺术手法。译者对原作的阅读比他们认真得多。正如马建忠所说,"一书到手,经营反复,确知其意旨之所在,而又摹写其神情,仿佛其语气",最终达到"心悟神解"。对译者来说,原作里没有一个字可以滑过、溜过,没有一处困难可以支吾扯淡。这种阅读就其本质而言就是文艺学里所说的"阐释"和"解读",是主客体之间的"对话"。在译者与原作的对话交流中,译者的主观评价和个人情感必定参与其中。译者的想象力、直觉力和感悟力在原作内容的激发下活跃起来,自觉或不自觉地参与对原作文本的解释和建构,把原作者所创造的艺术形象所包含的丰富内容复现出来,加以理解和体悟,同时不由自主地掺入自己的体会和理解。译者对原作的解读不可避免地带有主观性。同一句话,不同的译者有不同的理解;同一个形象,不同的译者有不同的体会。鲁迅曾指出,不同的人读《红楼梦》所见不同,"经学家看见'易',道学家看见淫,才子看见缠绵……"莎士比亚所创造的哈姆雷特的形象,在歌德、赫尔岑、托尔斯泰看来性格截然不同。因此,文学翻译活动从一开始就和原作者拉开了一定距离。

文学翻译的对话结构的第二层次,是译者通过建构译作与原作对话。文学翻译以传达原作的艺术意境为宗旨,实际上给译者规定了极为艰难的任务。我们说到某种玄妙虚无的事物时,常说"只可意会,不可言传"。而文学作品的艺术意境就是一种极玄妙的东西,正如王国维所说,其妙处如空中之音,相中之色,水中之影,镜中之像,言有尽而意无穷,实际上是只可意会,不可言传。翻译的任务往往是不可为而为之,文学翻译尤为如此。译者在"意会"的基础上,开始通过译语同原作对话。译语是一种特殊的语言,是译者的审美创造表现出来的一种形式,是译者在原作语言的土壤之上,在同原作对话的艺术氛围和文化语境里生成的新的语言。从形态上看,译语具有原作语言的某些特征,但又与原作的语言形式有很大差异,它接近于汉语文学语言,但又与之略有不同。译语在译者与原作的对话中生成,体现着译者对原作艺术美的再创造。译者在这一层次的对话里,把原作者的一切化为我有,同时把我有的东西奉献给原作者,恰如初交的朋友赠送礼物,有时因为不了解对方,难免强加于人。例如,在我们的译作里,把中国特有的成语、俗话和方言赠送的最多。再就是把原作者的东西拿过来,涂上中国色彩讨好读者。比如,把外国大诗人的诗作译为顺口溜,充做艺术精品,中国读者蒙在鼓里,还以为外国的精品都是顺口溜的水平。总之,这一层次的对话有创造,也有误解,创造中包含着误解,误解里产生着创造,相辅相成。传统观念把误译看得很重,实际上也是一种误解。由于中外语言和文化的差异,译者的"意会"同原作之间必然有距离,他的"意会"与"言传"的能力之间必然有距离,所以译者与原作者之间的对话难免产生误解。当然,我们不能因为误解难免而放纵自己,译者的责任是在对话中慎之又慎,尽量减少误解,增进理解,使对话充满精彩而又恰如其分的艺术创造。译者审美创造的关键在于把握的适度,在于译者的分寸感。把握的适度取决于译者的分寸感,而分寸感是译者的审美能力和艺术表现力的集中体现,是译者实践经验的结晶,也是译者成熟的标志。一个译者,只有经过大量的翻译实践,经过反反复复的成功与失败的教训,才能产生一定的艺术直觉和把握这种艺术直觉的能力。在对话过程中,一方面,译者的分寸感左右他的审美能力。译者对原作的审美接受,是由原作发出的感染,引起译者原有的认知结构的同化而做出积极的反映。译者不可能百分之百地接受原作包含的信息,而接受部分也经过译者的理解加工。不同的译者,认知结构和审美趣味不同,对原作艺术价值的理解和接受程度也就不同。而分寸感则是译者把握适度的审美准则和内应力。另一方面,分寸感同时左右着译者的艺术表现力,使他在创作激情的冲动之下不至于放纵自己。译者受分寸感的制约,才能不偏不倚,恰如其分地表现原作的艺术整体,从心所欲而不逾矩。

译作的出版还不是翻译的完成,而是译者对话的新层次的开始。当一个译本出现在读者面前时,原作以新的存在形式与读者对话与交流,同时开始了译者与读者的对话。这时的原作者已改变了原来的面貌,带上了译者的色彩,而译作也带来了原作者的色彩,以一种全新的文学现象的姿态,以一个具有译者的创造性内涵的文本与读者对话。好的译本使读者忘记译者,藏拙的译本使读者误解原作。可见译者责任重大,弄得不好,就会由原来的媒人变为离间者,干扰两国文化的对话与交流。

四

文学翻译在审美创造上的局限性,是它同艺术的最大差异,也是它的本质特征的一个方面。这种差异表明,原作与译者之间是主仆关系,译者在对话中不能喧宾夺主,更不能自作主张、自行其是。

艺术的对象是现实生活,而文学翻译的对象是文学作品,是艺术家运用艺术手段表现出来的现实生活。如果说文学作品是一面镜子或者一幅画,那么文学翻译就是把镜子里或者画里反映的生活临摹下来。在我们的传统观念里,临摹是算不上艺术的。再逼真的临摹作品也登不得大雅之堂。虽然有的临摹作品达到乱真的境界,蒙混了鉴赏家的眼睛,也能登堂入室,但它毕竟是赝品,不敢亮出真实身份。美国当代哲学家杜卡斯曾为那种可以乱真的摹品说好话,说它在供人研究和供人观赏审美方面跟原作等值。可是在人的心目中,临摹终归是二流艺术,因为它有原作作为依托。

文学翻译对原作的依赖性和从属性限制了译者的艺术创造的自由度。译者不能像画家、诗人、音乐家、舞蹈家那样,可以凭着激情天马行空独来独往,自由驰骋于广阔的艺术空间。相比之下,译者发挥创造的余地很有限度,他的创造必须以忠实于原作为前提。离开了对原作的忠实,译者的任何创造都是对原作艺术价值的背离和毁坏。"忠实"作为文学翻译的基本原则,像一条锁链束缚着译者。译者既要忠实原作,又要发挥自己的创造,戴着锁链去追求表现的自由。其次,原作语言行为的不可重复性也是对文学翻译的艺术创造的束缚。构成原作艺术美的语言是活的语言,处处闪烁着作家的思想火花,流露出诗意,具有顽强的抗译性和免译力。克罗齐在其《美学原理》中指出,语言凭直觉产生,言语行为受潜在的思维支配,并对思维加以扩展和修正,所以每一个语言行为都是创新的、不可重复的。这种不可重复性构成译语对原作语言的背离,约束着译者的创造力。当然,对待这些约束,译者并非束手无策。西方人对待文学翻译的局限性往往不大认真,尤其是具有创作能力的翻译家,总想抛开原作而自行其是,去追求译作的优美。英国 17 世纪著名作家德莱登把依附于原作的翻译比做"戴着镣铐走钢丝"。他认为,表演的人也许不至于中途摔下来,但这样的翻译没有优美可言。他主张翻译摆脱原作语言形式的束缚。当代法国诗人瓦勒利也坦白承认,他在翻译桓吉尔的《牧歌》时,往往心痒痒地想修改原作。比较起来,我国翻译家则不反对"戴着镣铐跳舞",认为戴着镣铐并不影响翻译的优美,关键在于译者的功夫。在翻译实践中,有的译者更多地照顾中国读者的口味,尽量把原作的形式化为我有,争取艺术创造的自由。对待抗译性较强的言语行为做变通处理,得其意而忘其言,离形得似。有的译者注重言与意、形与神的和谐统一,在有限的艺术空间里发挥创造,同时最大限度地贴近原作,尽量再现原作的艺术意境和风格。文学翻译在艺术创造上的局限性,是它的审美特质所决定的,同时也是它的审美特质的组成部分。成熟的译者在翻译中并不感到"镣铐"的约束,正如闻一多论诗词格律时所说:"越有魄力的作家,越是要戴着脚镣才能跳得痛快。只有不会跳舞的人才怪脚镣碍事。"文学翻译本身就是在"信"与"美"、束缚与自由的矛盾和统一中生存与发展的。也可以说,这种矛盾和统一就是文学翻译本身,离开其中任何一方,文学翻译就不存在了。

文学翻译对原作的依赖,使译者享受不到平等对话的自由和洒脱。译者在对话中往往如履薄冰,小心翼翼,尽量做到不露声色,把自我融化于译语的创造,但又不可避免地流露出自我的痕迹。译作的审美价值,应该体现在译者个性的藏而不露,体现在有我和无我的融合之中。

综上所述,我们可以看出,文学翻译与艺术相通,但又有较大差异。它具有艺术的创造性,又有自身的局限性和依附性,只能算做一种特殊的准艺术形式。它之所以不能像其他艺术形式那样得到普遍的、持久的承认,是因为它不能个性鲜明地显露自己的艺术特征。另一方面,翻译质量不高,平庸的译作充斥书市,也是社会误解文学翻译,使之不能跻身艺术之林的重要原因。应该看到,文学翻译的潜力是很大的,它与创作是紧邻,像画与诗一样的亲密无间,在与创作的对话和交流当中它会不断提高自己。我们坚信,总有一天,它会像诗与画那样在艺术的殿堂里受到人们的承认和尊重。

选文二　阐释、接受与再创造的循环

杨武能

导　言

本文选自杨武能著,《三叶集——德语文学·文学翻译·比较文学》,巴蜀书社(成都),2005 年版。

选文立足"文学翻译必须是文学"这一定论,剖析文学翻译工作模式,在对"阐释"一词作广义的现代理解的基础上提出:文学翻译家首先是阐释家。文学翻译要求对原著多重意义的追寻,对原著从内容到形式的全面的把握,以期最终以相对等值的形式,尽可能不多也不少地再创原著的多重意义。文学作品的审美意义由表及里,与其他几种意义融和、渗透,相辅相成,相得益彰。因此,在文学翻译的整个创造性活动中,翻译家始终处于中心的枢纽地位,发挥着最积极的作用。基于 20 世纪 70 年代以来兴起于联邦德国的接受美学,选文指出,对于原著及其作者而言,翻译家也是读者,而且是最积极、最主动、最富于创造意识和钻研精神的读者。全文分析了处于中心地位的翻译家的活动——作为读者兼作者、学者兼作家,翻译家的责任在于时时考虑读者的接受,完成原著的阐释、接受和再创造,使包括"审美意义"在内的种种意义都尽可能地重现于译本中。

文学翻译必须是文学。文学作品的译本必须和原著一样,具备文学所有的各种功能和特性,即除了一般地传递信息和完成交际任务,还要具备诸如审美功能、教育感化功能等多种功能,在可以实际把握的语言文字背后,还会有丰富的言外之意、弦外之音。而这些,就决定了文学翻译的复杂性和艰巨性,就决定了文学翻译在各类翻译活动以及各类文学活动中的特定地位,就要求文学翻译家是一些具有特殊禀赋和素养的人。

一、文学翻译家首先是阐释者

过去人们常常简单地将文学翻译工作的模式归结为:原著—译者—译本,而忽视了在此之前创作原著的作家,特别是在这之后阅读译本的读者。在我看来,全面而如实地反映文学翻译特性的图形应该是:

作家—原著—翻译家—译本—读者

与其他文学活动一样,文学翻译的主体同样是人,即作家、翻译家和读者;原著和译本都不过是他们之间进行思想和感情交流的工具或载体,都是他们创造的客体。而在这整个的创造性的活动中,翻译家无疑处于中心的枢纽地位,发挥着最积极的作用。在前,对原著及其作者来说,他是读者;在后,对于译本及其读者来说,他又成了作者。至于原著的作者,自然是居于主导地位,因为是他提供了整个活动的基础,限定了它的范围;而译本的读者也并非处于消极被动的无足轻重的地位,因为他们实际上也参与了译本和原著的价值的创造。因此,在上面的图形中,没有指示单一方向的"→",只有表明相互关系的"—"。

当然,对于原著及其作者来说,翻译家绝非一般意义的读者,绝不能满足于只对它和他有大致的把握和了解,而必须将其读深钻透、充分理解、全面接受。只有这样,翻译家才能出色地完成自己的任务,实现原著的价值与功能的再创造。对于这个问题,兴起和成熟于德国的传统阐释学和现代阐释学都提供了许多有益的启示。

传统阐释学视作者如上帝或天神,因为他同样是光荣的创造者:上帝创造了世界,作家创造了作品,创造了作品中的世界。而追寻和揭示作品深义的阐释者,就犹如传达天神旨意的神使 Hermes,因而在希腊文中动词"阐释"为 Hermeneuo,阐释学便叫 hermeneutics。然而,hermeneuo 以及相应的拉丁语动词 interpretari 乃至现代英语动词 interpret,都在"阐释"、"解释"之外,还同时有"翻译"的意义。这便从词源学的角度证明,翻译家就是阐释者。而事实上,古代的阐释者主要起着翻译家的作用,例如荷马史诗的阐释家和《圣经》诠释家(也许还有我国的古文今译家),他们的主要工作就是将原著翻译给不再使用那些古老语言的听众或读者,力图跨越原著创作的时代与读者生活的时代之间的历史鸿沟。也就是说,从历史看,翻译家即阐

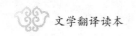

释者。

显然,这儿所说的相当于翻译的阐释,其内涵是十分丰富的,不能作一般字面的机械的理解。古罗马神学家圣奥古斯丁在《基督教教义》一书中,曾引用下面这首中世纪流行的小诗,来说明《圣经》注释工作的繁难:

> 字面意义多明了,
> 寓言意义细分晓,
> 道德意义辨善恶,
> 神秘意义藏奥妙。①

事实上,在古今中外的文学佳作中,不只是那些伟大的传世巨著如《红楼梦》、《水浒传》、《西游记》抑或荷马史诗、但丁的《神曲》、阿拉伯的《一千零一夜》、莎士比亚的悲剧以及歌德的《浮士德》,而且就连一些杰出的短篇小说和诗歌,都无不同时蕴含着上述多层次的意义。例如,笔者译过德国诗人海涅的小说《佛罗伦萨之夜》的一个片断《帕格尼尼》②,它虽说只有七八千字,却明显地具有多重意义:① 它描绘了作者海涅听帕格尼尼演奏时眼前出现的各种幻象场景,即钱钟书先生所谓的"通感"和现代科学家所谓的"联觉"现象③,此系小说的"字面意义";② 通过这些联觉现象的描绘,展示了作为被压迫的意大利民族代言人帕格尼尼富于传奇色彩的一生,借他的音乐对囚禁在海底的"牛鬼蛇神"发出了解放的呼号,这是小说的"道德意义";③ 通过对幻象中崇高圣洁如天神的帕格尼尼及其庄严雄壮的琴音的赞颂,宣扬了人为宇宙中心的人道主义理想,讴歌了人类的光明前景,此为小说的"寓言意义";④ 对音乐的神奇力量的宣示,如结尾说"这样的妙音啊,你可永远不能用耳朵去听;它只让你在与爱人心贴着心的静静的夜里,用自己的心去梦……",如此这般的非理性的内容,都暗示着小说的"神秘意义"。更有甚者:在传统的阐释家看来,不仅任何一部或一篇成功的文学作品,甚至就连某些单个的词语,都可能蕴含着多重意义,他们常以"耶路撒冷"为例子来说明问题④。

笔者对圣奥古斯丁所引的小诗和他企图证明阐释之繁难的观点详加分析,只是为了说明作为阐释者的翻译家的任务同样艰巨,他必须具备阐释家一样的精神、素养和本领,才能真正吃透原著,追索出其中多层次的深藏着的意义。

这儿笔者觉得必须作两点说明或补充,就是:

1. 上引小诗中所说的四重意义,在平庸的作品如一般通俗小说中不会全都存在;在具有这些意义的多数杰作中,它们又并不都那么容易地明显分开,特别是"寓言意义"和"神秘意义",常常是紧密地联系在一起的。

2. 在翻译或阐释文学作品时,还必须看到并足够地重视作品的审美意义、哲学意义等。如果说哲学意义仍属于作品的思想内涵,可以勉强纳入寓言意义的范畴之中的话,那么,既关系内涵又关系形式(或者说主要关系着形式)的审美意义,就是必须补充进去的至关重要的第五重意义了。文学作品的审美意义由表及里,与其他几种意义融和、渗透,相辅相成,相得益彰。

---

① 李郊等译:《当代西方文学理论导引》,四川文艺出版社 1986 年版,第 199 页。
② 杨武能选编:《德语国家短篇小说选》,人民文学出版社 1980 年版。
③ 钱钟书:《旧文四篇》,上海古籍出版社 1979 年版。
④ 详见《当代西方文学理论导引》第 200 页。

由上面的论述尤其是第二点说明引申开来，我们便可划定文学翻译与一般意义的阐释或一般翻译的界线，指出其间的差异。一般说来，后两者都只要求思想内容的准确传达。在翻译科技资料、政治文献乃至关系日常生活的实用书籍时，没有"寓言意义"、"神秘意义"等需要追寻，对"审美意义"也用不着特别重视，译文以畅达为上。在对文学作品作一般阐释时，就相当于进行分析和评论，以说理的精深透辟为重，形式不必计较。对任何作品的阐释都既是一篇论文，也是一部专著乃至于一首诗。而文学翻译则要求对原著多重意义的追寻，对原著从内容到形式的全面的把握，以期最终以相对等值的形式，尽可能不多也不少地再创原著的多重意义。因此，本文所谓文学翻译家即阐释者这个命题，又是在对"阐释"一词作广义的现代理解的基础上提出的。

二、文学翻译家同时是接受者

70年代以来兴起于联邦德国的接受美学（Rezeptionsaesthetik），将作品在读者中引起的反应和读者的阅读活动收进了文学及文学史研究的视野，认为读者作为文学活动的又一主体，同时积极地参与了作品价值的创造。前文说过，对于原著及其作者而言，翻译家也是读者，而且是最积极、最主动、最富于创造意识和钻研精神的读者。他应该是自觉地力求对原著的多重含义以及隐藏于原著背后的作者的创作本意，作全面的把握和充分的接受。这意味着，他不仅要在思想意义上把原著读懂、读深、读透，领会其精神要旨，而且还要完成对它的审美鉴赏，在表现形式上也能细致地把握。很难设想，一部连自己都不能深刻理解和衷心喜爱的作品，会翻译得异常出色、成功；很难设想，一部作为直接的第一读者的翻译家都未充分接受的作品，它的译本会为更多的间接的读者所接受。

要作全面的把握和充分的接受绝非易事。掌握外文和起码的背景知识，仅仅能帮助你理解原著的表层意义如"字面意义"或者明显的"道德意义"。为了达到更高的要求，译者就必须研究和学习，研究作者的生平、著作和思想，研究作品产生的时代，研究他们的民族文化传统，等等。从这个意义上讲，翻译家又同时必须是研究者；不预先进行研究就从事翻译，特别是翻译杰作名著，多半是不可能成功的。

现代文艺阐释学认为，先有（Vorhabe）、先见（Vorsicht）、先把握（Vorgriff）等构成了我们意识中的所谓"先结构"，而阐释总是在"先结构"的基础上进行的，因此说"成见是理解的前提"。我们译者意识中的"先结构"，必定是十分复杂的，无疑会受到本身所处的时代和民族文化传统乃至个人经历、修养、性格的影响。这种情况，不可避免地会干扰我们对原著的理解，使我们的阐释总是或多或少偏离原著，打上译者自己时代、历史、民族乃至译者个人风格的烙印。客观地、严格地讲，文学翻译的绝对等值实不可能；一部原著在不同时代必然有不同的译本，再成功的译本也只能"各领风骚"数十年甚至只有几年，所以重译就成了时代的需要；而另一方面，同一原著又可能同时有一个以上的出色译本。从总体上看，文学翻译的标准是不易掌握的，在这儿更难找到"绝对真理"和等值，而只能力求尽可能的近似。

为此目的，翻译家一方面要研究学习，提高自己的文化素养和审美能力，特别增加对一切与原著有关的知识和学问的了解把握，以完善自己的"先结构"；另一方面，还要学习有关翻译的理论，加深对自己的工作性质和任务的理解，以便在实际做翻译时，适当地、自觉地运用意识中的"先有"、"先见"、"先把握"，特别是排除其中的"干扰"，从而尽可能地使译文贴近原著，尽

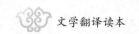

量避免偏离,使原文失去的东西尽量地少,译文尽量不添加进新的东西。

至此,作为阐释者、接受者和研究者,翻译家仍处于他活动的第一个阶段,做的是一种学术性很强的工作。工作成绩的好坏,对原著的理解是否深,接受是否充分,主要取决于他的外文水平、研究能力和理解能力等构成的学术修养。因此,在活动的第一阶段,翻译家在很大程度上又是学者。前些年,王蒙同志曾在《读书》上撰文谈"非学者化"现象对作家创作的影响,指出它是当今文坛难于产生鲁迅、郭沫若、茅盾似的大师和划时代的巨著的原因。在我们文学翻译界,这个问题应该说更加突出,更值得引起注意。因为,文学翻译家相比一般的作家来,更有必要同时,或者更确切地说首先是学者。特别是名著和文艺理论的翻译,都将考验翻译家的学术水平;无论在序、跋或是译文中,都会融进他作为学者的心得和成果。

翻译家当然不是一般意义的学者,或仅仅是学者,他还必须同时是作家。这不只是就本文一开头已指出的他与译本及其读者的关系而言,也指他的素质、修养、能力等。文学翻译已被公认为一种艺术、一种再创造。文学翻译必须是文学。从事这一艺术和文学再创造的人,他除了无须像作家似的选取提炼素材、谋篇布局和进行构思以外,工作的性质应该说是与作者差不多的。他在这方面的条件,绝不限于我们一般讲的"外文好中文好"。过去,我们从事文学翻译的人出于自谦和自卑,不便谈这个问题,多数作家同行出于对我们工作的不了解,无从谈这个问题。事实是,为了完成原著的再创造,使它包括"审美意义"在内的种种意义都尽可能等值地重现于译本中,文学翻译家不只需要有作家的文学修养和笔力,还必须有作家一样对人生的体验、对艺术的敏感,必须具备较高的审美鉴赏力和形象思维能力,在最理想的情况下,甚至也有文学家的气质和灵感。实践证明,并非所有"外文好,中文也好,又有广博知识"的人都能成为好的文学翻译工作者,更别说成为真正的文学翻译家。著名诗人兼译诗家卞之琳教授要求他的弟子裘小龙在译诗之前先学写诗,那意思就是译诗者最好同时是诗人。由翻译家而作家,或由作家而翻译家,或同时兼而为之,是我们无数杰出的先辈走过的路。今天,在我们的作家协会中,可惜中青年的文学翻译家还不够多,而且未受到应有的重视。究其原因,恐怕是我们不少人忽视了自己作家素质的提高。近几年大量出版的缺少文学味儿的"文学翻译",也从另一个方面说明了问题。

综上所述,真正的文学翻译家,应该同时是学者和作家。在他的整个活动过程中,学者和作家都同时发挥作用,只不过在不同阶段,有时这个的作用突出一些,有时那个的作用突出一些。很难设想,一个缺少作家素养的一流学者能成为一流的文学翻译家;反之亦然。事实常常是,二三流学者加上二三流作家,倒可以成为第一流的文学翻译家。从这个意义上讲,做文学翻译的人有些不伦不类,是一种处境尴尬的"两栖"乃至"三栖"动物。然而文学翻译的任务和性质决定了他的地位就该如此。要摆脱尴尬处境,一是使自己成为傅雷等少数先辈那样的大家;二是建立新的、科学的评判标准,在学术界和公众中形成一种新的、合理的价值观。对我们整个文学翻译事业的发展来说,当然第二个办法更加可取。为此,我们必须加强对文学翻译的研究和评价,指出它特殊的性质、巨大的困难,而本文便是一个尝试。

最后,笔者还想重提一下本文开始时画的那个表示文学翻译特性的图形:

作家—原著—翻译家—译本—读者

全文只分析了处于中心地位的翻译家的活动。他作为读者兼作者、学者兼作家,完成阐释、接受和再创造的任务,将原著转换成译本。在此过程中,他经常想到贴近原著及作者的同时,还要经常想到他的广大读者。因为在拿到译本以后,读者们同样要完成一个阐释、接受和再创造的过程,只不过这个过程的结果不形诸文字,不进行两种文字之间的转换罢了。广大读者能不能很好地实现对作品的阐释、接受和再创造,或如现代阐释学所说的很好地与原著及其作者进行对话,同样有一个"先结构"问题。翻译家还有责任改善他的读者的"先结构",常用而可行的办法就是认真负责地为译本作序跋、加注释、写评价赏析文章等。现时不在少数的无序或无跋或序跋十分简单的文学作品译本,其译者应该还未完全尽到应尽的职责。因为归根到底,文学翻译活动的全过程,包括译者→作者以及读者→译者→作者的阐释、接受和再创造的循环。心中没有自己的读者,即使你身兼学者、作家且懂翻译理论,仍不能成为优秀的翻译家。反之,你如果在翻译时经常考虑到读者的接受——这在修辞造句上表现得格外明显——就可以说你的读者已无形地参与了译本的创造……

这里写下了一个文学翻译工作者的感想,浮光掠影,支离破碎,难免有所偏颇,权作引玉之砖吧。

选文三　Translating Literature/Translated Literature: The State of the Art

André Lefevere

导　言

本文选自 Ortrun Zuber, *The Languages of Theatre*, Oxford & New York: Pergamon Press, 1980.

传统的翻译活动一直被认为是两种语言之间的转换过程,因而翻译研究一直停留在语言分析和文本对照上。20 世纪 70 年代后期,翻译研究呈现多元化的趋势,并上升为一种文化上的反思,探讨译文的产生与作用的"翻译研究学派"因此得以出现。作为文化学派代表的安德鲁·勒弗维尔原为比利时学者,后移民美国,任德克萨斯州大学奥斯汀分校德语系和比较文学系教授,国际著名文论家、比较文学家和翻译理论家,是当代西方比较文学与翻译领域十分重要的理论人物。作者在文中肯定了语言学派、语用学派翻译理论的建设性作用,但也同时令人信服地分析了两种理论的偏颇与不足,明确指出,翻译研究应当跳出传统的语言学研究窠臼,以充分检视翻译在文学演进和阐释中所起的作用。

For a long time the study of translation has meant little more than the study of translating. How should one translate? How does one train good translators? Until the beginning of the 20th century this type of translation study centred mainly on literary texts. It tried to answer a certain type of questions related to what might be called "stylistic aesthetics" (How "good", how "apt" is a language at expressing what it expresses, what does it lose in translation?) and to the "genius" of languages and literatures (Why is literature X so much "better" than literature Y?). It also dabbled in linguistic philosophy and in linguistic psychology, producing many an analysis of "A as translator of B", in which a few memorable things might be said about either A, or B, or both, but not too many about translation.

Linguists would have us believe that modern linguistics has changed all that. The questions asked above, so deliciously speculative in nature and thus admitting of endless speculation, are still being answered to the present day. They are no longer central questions in the study of literary translation, which is shifting more and more from the study of translating literature to the study of how translated literature functions inside the system of a given native literature, thus effectively establishing a long postulated link with comparative literature.

The advent of a mainly linguistically inspired analysis of translating has contributed to the exclusion of the study of translating/translated literature from translation studies as a whole. It was considered that literary texts were too complex for the type of analysis based on linguistics. Alternatively, the specificity of literary translation could not be analysed by means of modern linguistics. This exclusion, elegant or not, of the study of translating/translated literature was also undertaken for practical reasons, especially in the late 50s when the impending triumph of machine translation necessitated the construction of relatively simple programmes that could be fed into machines. Now that the machine translation euphoria has subsided, there appears to be less reason to exclude more "complex" texts from the construction of such a programme. Consequently, the latest development in modern linguistics, text linguistics, tries to make statements about both literary and non-literary texts. To a student of literature, however, some statements about literary texts sound suspiciously trivial, because they are dressed up in the garb of extremely complicated and unnecessary formalisation. But the important new phenomenon is that the dividing line seems to be disappearing. The rare pronouncements textlinguistics has seen fit to devote to the study of translation try to encompass all kinds of translated texts.

It would be wrong to write off most, if not all, of the results of about 50 years of translation study undertaken mainly from the linguistic point of view as "irrelevant" for the study of translating/translated literature. Literary scholars who are interested in the phenomenon of translated literature could use some of the instrumentation developed by linguistic translation analysis. By doing this they would render their own statements on translated literature less vague and less subjective. It might also help to standardise the language of translation studies as a whole.

Linguistic definitions of translation tend no longer to be normative. The old translation should render the information that is available in the source text into an acceptable text in the target language, preferably by using features in the target language equivalent to features used in the source text. This, however, has proven to be untenable. Instead translation is seen as a text which shows certain correspondences with the original and also certain deviations from it. The ideal of optimal translation is thus being tacitly abandoned. A distinction is made between the informational function of a translation and the linguistic features used to achieve this informational function. This distinction admits that the informational content remains invariant (or as nearly invariant as possible), whereas the form in which the information is "processed", so to speak, can change considerably. Moreover, during the last ten years, linguistics has devoted more and more attention to the pragmatics of the text, and the ways in which pragmatic features (what the old philologies used to call "realia", and what is still called by that name in Soviet and East European translation studies) are transposed from source text into target text. All in all, a much more flexible definition of translation has emerged, which could be formulated as follows. Translation is the result of an activity which derives from a text in the source language to a text in the target language which corresponds with the text in the source language in certain relevant features and can be substituted for it under certain circumstances. This type of definition is also, in practice, applied to texts on the basis of the concept of "family resemblances", i. e. not all features of the definition of translation need occur in a given text for that text to be treated or identified as a translation.

Seen from this angle, the concept of equivalence, launched in the mid-60s, has also lost much of its stringency. Some linguists propose abolishing it altogether. Others would tend to relativise it to a great extent. They would point out that other correspondences are also possible between source text and target text and that equivalence is not the only type of correspondence. They would further advocate restricting its use to the level of conceptual meaning only, or else to use it merely to denote the arbitrary permutability of texts on the basis of an intuitively accepted "identity" which would be semantic or pragmatic in nature. Adequacy seems, as a concept for use in translation studies, to have a brighter future than equivalence.

Deviations from the source text tend to be called "shifts" more and more, and a distinction is made between substantial and formal shifts. Substantial shifts have to do with the semantics, the communicative value of the source text. They often result in modulations, e. g. from general to particular, or from abstract to concrete, or from cause to effect. The result of modulation is often either an "explicitation" (the translator "explains" what is explicit in the source text) or a levelling of the source text (the translator reduces stylistic differences). Formal shifts are of less fundamental importance. Obligatory shifts are made necessary by the very difference in languages, but optional shifts are of great interest to the student of translated literature. They depend on the translator only, who may use them as stylistic features in order to influence the text he is producing, depending on whether the shifts his work shows have been motivated or unmotivated.

Much of the "realignment" in linguistic thinking about the phenomenon of translation has been caused by the move, which took place in linguistics at the end of the 60s, "beyond the sentence". Texts were seen as the basic units of communication, and it was soon admitted that texts were inextricably bound up with contexts. This kind of statement many a rhetorician in imperial Rome or even many a sophist in Socratic Greece would have put aside as trivial. Still, it became generally accepted that generating texts was not just a matter of linguistic conventions only, but of linguistic and other semiotic conventions, mainly socio-cultural ones. It was even posited that aesthetic and moral constraints dominate all others during the process of text generation with the proviso that structural-expressive constraints dominate cultural-semantic ones. They in their turn dominate structural-syntactic constraints. Effectively the discovery of text and context has freed the linguistic study of translation from its fixation on word and/or sentence and has enabled it to take many other factors into account. It has, of course, also greatly complicated its task.

In attempting to deal with these new complications, attempts to make the pragmatics of texts more manageable by drawing up typologies of texts have been disappointing. The old bipolar opposition literary-non-literary tends to surface again, and it is often overlooked that the cultural focus through which the reader approaches the text decides on its being literary or not. For it is not the actual features of the text which decide whether it is literary or not, but the way the reader relates to it.

On the other hand, pragmatics has influenced semantics to the extent that a typology of meanings has emerged, which is much more operational than the abortive typology of texts. Distinctions are made (and could profitably be made by students of translated literature) between

    (a) conceptual meaning, in which the identity of Semantic Representation as opposed to the difference in semantic expression makes possible the transfer of meaning from source text to target text;

    (b) stylistic meaning, which also says something about the relationship between the participants in a text; and

    (c) the way the speaker/hearer sees himself playing his part, or establishes himself inside the cultural conventions regulating a text.

It is important then to make a distinction between stylistic category, being the social meaning expressed, and stylistic function, being the phonological, syntactic or semantic way in which that category is expressed. The former remains relatively invariant in different languages, the latter does not. Associative meaning consists of connotative, affective, collocative variants of meaning, and thematic meaning contains certain elements of sentences (for example, it is "responsible" for the difference between active and passive sentences).

Linguistic models of the translation process have also not tended to be very successful. They have been either too vague or too inapplicable. These models should explain how a text came into being (not a sentence), on what linguistic, contextual and intertextual basis, and why each particular translation realises only one possibility among many. It would therefore seem more profitable to operate with a certain concept of "norm", which is looser than that of "model". One would distinguish between the following norms:

(1) preliminary norms: the translator asks himself what kind of a translation he wants to produce.

(2) initial norms: the translator decides on whether to adopt the code of the source text or that of the target text.

(3) operational norms: the translator makes use of the linguistic, contextual and intertextual instrumentation described above.

The area in which research done in contemporary linguistics tends to overlap most with the traditional research done in the study of literature is that of "text processing". In textlinguistics the concept can be said to cover all operations by means of which texts are derived from other texts. It is plain to see that both translated literature and all intertextual components of works may be subsumed under this concept as well.

It would be advisable though, for the study of translating/translated literature to abandon its own definitions of what a translation "ought" to be, and to accept the definition(s) proposed by linguistics in more recent years. Past literature oriented theories of translation have rather uniformly and depressingly tended to be normative in outlook. That is, they have been written mostly to justify a certain kind of practice and a certain manner of translating. Moreover, they have often been based on one kind of literary text (for example, the Bible). And they have been widened to include other texts in a manner not always warranted.

It could be argued that normative theories of translating literature have been formulated for so long because translated literature has always been the Achilles heel of a certain concept of comparative literature. One could not do without translations, but on the other hand one did not feel too inclined to admit this. Hence the desire to "ensure" the "best possible" translations which, in practice, meant that the standards defining the "best possible" tended to change about every 20 years or so. It would seem most appropriate to avoid the continuation of this rather sterile succession of post-factum ukases and to banish the giving of rules for translating literature from the scientific study of translated literature altogether. This does not mean that from now on "anything goes" in the production of translations of literature. It does mean, however, that the giving of rules is limited to a field called "praxiology" or "didactics", and not seen as the central, and eternally unproductive problem a theory of literary translation has to solve.

If we accept that the definition of translation should not be determined by a certain practice limited to a certain place and time (even though each of these definitions has taken great pains to pass themselves off as "eternal" or "unchangeable"), we can look at the role translated literary texts play inside the literary system of a given language. We could widen the scope even more, if we looked at all the different kinds of "processing" which a given text is subjected to in the receiving literary and cultural system. In doing this we would consider what place it is given in handbooks of (world) literature written in the target culture, e. g. in what manner it is summarized, what "image" of it arises in the receiving culture, how this image changes, etc.

Translated literature is the channel through which most interliterary communication passes, or even has to pass. It is therefore of great importance that one should ascertain who translates, and with what goal in mind. To put it in "linguistic" terms, one should pay due attention to the preliminary and initial norms certain translators, or version writers, or imitators select.

Roughly speaking, we can distinguish between two kinds of translators, those who wish to influence the evolution of their native literature and those who do not, or do not primarily have that wish. In order to make this clear, it seems advisable to introduce here the notion of "polysystem" for the description of a given literature.

The polysystem can be described as a canonised system, which is the leading "fashion" of a given day. It is vindicated and defended by a number of writers and critics and is taught as the literary standard to emulate in schools. In addition, it influences the writing of "timeless" handbooks of poetics by its proponents. The polysystem also contains countercurrents, which try to displace the canonised system and replace it.

In this struggle between the canonised and the non-canonised systems, text processing plays an important part. Both canonised and non-canonised concepts of literature will look outside their own literature for support for their own claims. They will look for foreign models made available by text processing, and first and foremost by translation. If translators of literature want to promote either the canonised or the non-canonised concept, their choice of primary and initial norms, which dictates their choice of shifts and of processing contextual and pragmatic factors, is likely to be radically different.

Foreign models need not be limited to the literary domain. New philosophical, sociological and other doctrines, in so far as they are expressed in works of literature, will also make an impact on the target culture, without necessarily affecting the balance between canonised and non-canonised inside the literary polysystem.

Let us, for the sake of argument, call those translators who want their translations to take part in the struggle between canonised and non-canonised systems, "literary translators" pure and simple. Yet there are also those translators who do not, as "literary translators" do, limit their endeavours to the defense or advancement of a certain "poetic concept", i. e. a number of rules, a literary "fashion" on which either the canonised or the non-canonised systems are built. These translators are concerned not with changing and eventually ephemeral (even though they sometimes last two hundred years in Western literature) poetic concepts, but with "poetics" themselves. They want to show how a literary polysystem evolves, how it changes, what factors make it behave the way it does, etc. They are also concerned with the interaction between different literary polysystems.

Part of their work may be taken up with the production of translations of literary works which are not intended to function as models, manifestoes, or calls to arms, but simply as information. Those translators might be called "metaliterary" translators, because their choice of initial and preliminary norms, as well as the shifts their work will show, will be based on insights gained from the scientific study of literature, not on critical convictions. It will also be clear that the divisions between both types of translations produced by both types of translators may run rather deep, while the metaliterary translator can never completely escape from the literary taste of his own time. It would, therefore, not be unwise for the study of translated literature to spend some time trying to ascertain what the initial and preliminary norms are a certain translator has selected, and why.

Whether linguistically oriented or not, the study of translated dramatic literature has been treated extremely superficially by translation studies. It is easy to see that a linguistics which had not discovered the central notion of pragmatics could not devote too much energy to one of the most important aspects of drama, whereas literary analyses of translated dramatic texts very often were confined to its textual dimension, to what was on the page. Neither discipline developed the necessary tools to deal with other dimensions in a satisfactory way.

It would seem, for reasons described above, that the study of translated dramatic literature would do well to eschew all normative pretensions. It might productively concentrate on two main fields:

(1) the pragmatics of production, in which the way a play is produced can also be seen as a type of text processing, and

(2) the way in which certain productions influence the target dramatic literature.

Next to these two fields, there will also always be a need for the production of "metaliterary" translations of dramatic literary texts.

Finally, what is it all good for? We shall not, as a result of the "state" which the "art" has attained at this moment, be able to say what "good" translations are and what not, or how "good" translators should be trained and how not. What we shall be able to do, however, is to show how literature operates, through the study of translated literature, and we shall be able to do so without recourse to speculation, criticism or propaganda. In other words, the study of translated literature will be one of the angles from which light may be shed on the study of human communication in general, whereas the study of translating literature would represent only the description of one, usually short lived, attempt to influence that communication in a certain way.

选文四 The Translation of Serious Literature and Authoritative Statements

Peter Newmark

导 言

本文选自 Peter Newmark, *A Textbook of Translation*, Harlow: Pearson Education Ltd., 2003.

英国著名翻译理论家彼得·纽马克根据布勒的语言功能理论将文本划分为三大范畴,即表达型文本、信息型文本及呼唤型文本。同时,他提出了交际翻译和语义翻译这两种翻译方法。在此基础上,他指出表达型文本主要使用语义翻译的方法,信息型文本和呼唤型文本主要使用交际翻译的方法。对于表达型文本而言,语言表达功能的核心在于说话者或作者运用这些话语表达其思想感情,主要包括严肃的文学作品(抒情诗、短篇小说、长篇小说、戏剧等)、权威性言论和自传、散文及个人信函等。翻译严肃的文学作品、散文、权威性言论及自传等表达型文本时,由于作者的地位是至高无上的,在翻译时应采用语义翻译的方法,忠实地翻译原作的思想内容,同时还应保留原作中带有作者个人风格"印记"的独特搭配、创造性比喻、新奇的句型等。原作中带有文化色彩的成分也应忠实地移植过来,以保留原作独特的异域情调。

Introduction

Theorists sometimes maintain that cognitive translation (the transfer of cold information) is perfectly possible and may be possibly perfect—it is the hard core, the invariant factor; the only snag comes when: (a) there is an emphasis on the form as well as the content of the message or; (b) there is a cultural gap between SL and TL readers (different ways of thinking or feeling, material objects) or there is a tricky pragmatic relation, i. e. between on the one hand the writer and on the other the translator and/or reader. There is a certain truth in these generalisations, though they miss one point, that the adequacy of a translation basically depends on the degree of difficulty, complexity, obscurity of the whole passage, rather than the one or the other aspect. Further, any passage that stresses SL form can be perfectly explained and therefore over-translated into the TL, though it will not have the naked impact of the original. However, if one must make generalisations, I can say that normally the translation of serious literature and authoritative statements is the most testing type of translation, because the first, basic articulation of meaning (the word) is as important as the second (the sentence or, in poetry, the line) and the effort to make word, sentence and text cohere requires continuous compromise and readjustment.

Bühler's expressive function of language, where content and form are on the whole equally and indissolubly important, informs two broad text-categories: serious imaginative literature and authoritative statements of any kind, whether political, scientific, philosophical or legal.

The two categories have obvious differences: (a) authoritative statements are more openly addressed to a readership than is literature; (b) literature is allegorical in some degree; authoritative statements are often literal and denotative and figurative only in exceptional passages, as in broad popular appeals ("islands" amongst the literal language), such as "The wind of change is blowing"—*Un grand courant d'air souffle* (both stock metaphors); "I have nothing to offer but blood, toil, tears and sweat" (Churchill, 13 May 1940)—*Je n'ai à vous offrir que du sang, de la sueur, du travail, des larmes* (figurative language, but these are symbols, to be understood literally as well as figuratively); "the underbelly of the Axis" (Churchill, January 1943)—*le bas-ventre de l'Axe*—not *le point vulnérable* (an original metaphor). Further, the element of self-expression in authoritative statements is only incidental but the translator has to pay the same respect to bizarreries of idiolect as in fantastic literature: *La France y voit un renfort decisif de notre latinité à l'avantage de tous les hommes*—"France sees it as a decisive strengthening of our Latinity benefiting all men" (De Gaulle).

A further generalisation for the translator: literature broadly runs along a four-point scale from lyrical poetry through the short story and the novel to drama.

Poetry

Poetry is the most personal and concentrated of the four forms, no redundancy, no phatic language, where, as a unit, the word has greater importance than in any other type of text. And again, if the word is the first unit of meaning, the second is not the sentence or the proposition, but usually the line, thereby again demonstrating a unique double concentration of units. Thus in:

> ... But Man, proud man
> Drest in a little brief authority,
> Most ignorant of what he's most assured
> His glassy essence, like an angry ape,
> Plays such fantastic tricks before high heaven
> As make the angels weep...
>
> (Shakespeare, *Measure for Measure*, II. II. 117)

The integrity of both the lexical units and the lines has to be preserved within a context

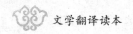

of: (a) corresponding punctuation, which essentially reproduces the tone of the original; and (b) accurate translation of metaphor. Consider Tieck's version:

> ... *doch der Mensch, der stolze Mensch,*
> *In kleine kurze Majestät gekleidet,*
> *Vergessend, was am mind'sten zu bezweifeln,*
> *Sein gläsern Element—wie zorn'ge Affen,*
> *Spielt solchen Wahnsinn gaukelnd vor dem Himmel,*
> *Daβ Engel weinen ...*
>
> (trans. Tieck and Schlegel, *Maβ für Ma*)

Here the word—and line—units have been preserved with the punctuation; the image "plays such fantastic tricks" becomes "plays such madness, conjuring" but the other images are preserved, whilst "most ignorant of" becomes "forgetting" and the positive "most assured" becomes the double negative "least to be doubted", which is a common modulation. The greatest and unnecessary loss here is the "fantastic tricks" metaphor. Original metaphor is the controlling element in all creative language, evoking through a visual image—even abstract images such as justice or mercy become people or objects—not only sight but the four other senses (e.g. fur as touch, food as taste, flowers as smell, bells or birds as sound) as well as the concomitant human qualities, good or evil, pleasure or pain, that these images (sensory, sensuous, sensual, sensitive, perhaps even sensational, to liven up language) can produce. Poetry presents the thing in order to convey the feeling, in particular, and however concrete the language, each represents something else—a feeling, a behaviour, a view of life as well as itself. Original metaphors the translator has to reproduce scrupulously, even if they are likely to cause cultural shock. Shakespeare's "Shall I compare thee to a summer's day" (Sonnet 18), as Neubert has commented, will leave Arabic or Eskimo readers cold, but the Arabic or Eskimo reader must make the effort to find out the truth of the simile, which is at least half-revealed in the next line: "Thou art more lovely and more temperate." A cultural metaphor (e.g. the technical term "(Summer's) lease") is not so important.

The translator can boldly transfer the image of any metaphor where it is known in the TL culture. But for lines such as Walter de la Mare's:

> And even the thought of her when she is far
> Narcissus is, and they the waters are
>
> (*Reflections*)

> or Kingsley Amis':
> Should poets bicycle-pump the heart
> Or squash it flat?
>
> (*Something Nasty in the Bookshop*)

Faced with literal translations in cultures where Narcissus and the bicycle-pump are not known, the reader is not so much culturally shocked as baffled. In such poems there is a case for creating a culturally equivalent TL metaphor, or converting the SL metaphor to sense or, where there is space, adding sense to the metaphor; but if the translator regards the metaphor as important, it is his duty to carry it across to launch it on the target language and its culture.

Whilst I think that all images have universal, cultural and personal sources, the translator of poetry cannot make any concession to the reader such as transferring the foreign culture to a native equivalent—If autumn in China is the season not of Keats' "mists and mellow fruitfulness" but of high clear skies and transparent waters, and the sound of clothes laundered for the cold weather pounded on the washing blocks, then the reader must simply accept this background and, if he wants to feel it, repeated reading is more likely to make it his possession than are detailed background, explanation of allusions and so on. Nevertheless, the European must be aware that, for the Chinese culture, jade is not jade-coloured but white ("jade snow", "jade beads", "jade moon"), that comparisons with eyebrows assume the custom of painting women's eyebrows green, that the phoenix has no myth of resurrection, that dragons are close and kindly, that cypresses suggest grave-yards, as in the West (see Graham, *Poems of the Late Tang*).

The transition from Chinese to English culture is made easier because all the images mentioned are not unfamiliar to an English reader. The difficulty comes when and if local flowers and grasses are used as metaphors.

I am sceptical about the idea that a translator of poetry is primarily communicating—that he is, to his readers in the conventional definition of communicative translation, trying to create the same effect on the target language readers as was created by the poet on his own readers; his main endeavour is to "translate" the effect the poem made on himself. A translator can hardly achieve even a parallel effect in poetry—the two languages, since all their resources are being used here as in no other literary or non-literary medium, are, at their widest, poles apart. Syntax, lexis, sound, culture, but not image—clash with each other. Valéry wrote: "My aim is *not* literary. It is not to produce an effect on others so much as on myself—the *Self* in so far as it may be treated as a work... of the mind. I am not interested in writing poetry without a view to its function. "

Compare John Cairncross, who was not trying to disprove that French, or poetry, or French poetry, or Racine, was untranslatable, or to present Racine to his English readers, or to present his English readers with Racine, but set about translating simply because the English words started forming themselves in his ear, and so he quotes Racine again: *Ce que j'ai fait, Abner, j'ai cru le devoir faire*—"What I have done, Abner? I had to do" (*Athalie*, 1. 467), which is itself an echo of γεγραΦα, γεγραΦα—Pontius Pilate's "What I have written I have written". Take it or leave it.

Now I think that in most examples of poetry translation, the translator first decides to choose a TL poetic form (viz. sonnet, ballad, quatrain, blank verse, etc.) as close as possible to that of the SL. Although the rhyming scheme is part of the form, its precise order may have to be dropped. Secondly, he will reproduce the figurative meaning, the concrete images of the poem. Lastly the setting, the thought-words, often the various techniques of sound-effect which produce the individual impact I have mentioned have to be worked in at later stages during the rewriting (as Beaugrande has stated in his fine translation of Rilke). Emotionally, different sounds create different meanings, based not on the sounds of nature, nor on the seductive noises in the streams and the forests, but on the common sounds of the human throat: *Sein oder nicht sein—das ist hier die Frage* appears to have a ring of confidence and challenge in it which is foreign to Hamlet's character—is it the redoubled *ei* sound? —that opens up the whole question of the universal symbolism of sounds. All this plangency, this openness is missing in "To be or not to be—that is the question" which is almost a word-for-word translation, though the German *hier*—"that is here the question"—appears to underline the challenge which is not in Shakespeare. The fact is that, however good as a translation, its meaning will differ in many ways from the original—it will, in Borrow's phrase, be a mere echo of the original, not through Gogol's glass pane—and it will have its own independent strength. A successfully translated poem is always another poem.

Whether a translator gives priority to content or manner, and, within manner, what aspect—metre, rhyme, sound, structure—is to have priority, must depend not only on the values of the particular poem, but also on the translator's theory of poetry. Therefore no general theory of poetic translation is possible and all a translation theorist can do is to draw attention to the variety of possibilities and point to successful practice, unless he rashly wants to incorporate his theory of translation into his own theory of poetry. Deliberately or intuitively, the translator has to decide whether the expressive or the aesthetic function of language in a poem or in one place in a poem is more important. Crudely this renews Keats' argument concerning Truth and Beauty: "Beauty is Truth, Truth, Beauty—that is all you know, and all you need to know," when he maintains that they define and are equivalent to each other, as well as the later argument between art as a criticism of life (Matthew Arnold) and art for art's sake (Theophile Gautier) which characterised two French poetic movements as well as much turn-of-the-century literature—"All art is useless," wrote Oscar Wilde, whose own art belies the statement. Clearly Keats, who was not thinking of translation, oversimplified the argument. If Truth stands for the literal translation and Beauty for the elegant version in the translator's idiom, Truth is ugly and Beauty is always a lie. "That's life," many would say. But a translation theorist would point out that both these versions, the literal and the elegant poem, would normally be equally unsatisfactory as translations of a poem or of anything else. Some fusion, some approximation, between the expressive and the aesthetic function of language is required, where in any event the personal language of the poet which deviates from the norms of the source language is likely to deviate even more from those of the target language. Thus Karl Kraus complained that Stefan George, by "doing violence to the English sense of Shakespeare's sonnets and to German verbal and grammatical usage, had produced la unique abortion!" But, in my belief, George is the closest and most successful of all translators.

Thus:

> *Lebwohl! zu teuer ist dein besitz für mich*
> *Und du weißt wohl wie schwer du bist zu kaufen*
> *Der freibrief deines werts entbindet dich*
> *Mein recht auf dich ist völlig abgelaufen.*

which is:

> Farewell! too dear is your possession for me
> And you well know how hard you are to buy
> The charter of your worth releases you
> My claim to you has fully run its course.

which becomes:

> Farewell! thou art too dear for my possessing,
> And like enough thou know'st thy estimate:
> The Charter of thy worth gives thee releasing;
> My bonds in thee are all determinate.
>
> (Sonnet 87)

George's translation is notable for its tautness and flexibility, and particularly for its emphasis on the corresponding theme-words ("dear", "charter", "releasing", "bonds", "determinate"). Where he is unable to reach Shakespeare is in the polysemy of "estimate", "releasing", "bonds", and "determinate", and thus he restricts the meaning of the quatrain—and above all in the splendid logical statement of Shakespeare's opening with its communicative dynamism on "possessing", where George is forced into an inversion.

Angus Graham, in his discussion on the translation of Chinese poetry, says that the element in poetry which travels best is concrete imagery. A crib or trot of Chinese such as:

> Kuang Heng write-frankly memorial.
> Success slight Liu Hsiang transmit classic.
> Plan miss.

could be rewritten as:

> A disdained K'uang Heng, as a critic of policy,
> As promoter of learning, a Liu Hsiang who failed.

Here the poet is miserably contrasting his failures with the success of two statesmen, but contrast this with:

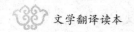

> Tartar horn tug North wind,
> Thistle Gate whiter than water
> Sky, hold-in-mouth Koknor Road
> Wall lop moon thousand mile

I note that, even in a *Times Literary Supplement* review, Erich Segal comments on most translators "metarophobia", their unease in the presence of metaphor, Pindar speaks of man being *skias onar*—"the dream of a shadow" but Richmond Lattimore turns it round to the conventional "shadow of a dream". According to Aeschylus, Prometheus *stole the anthos/pyros*, the "blossom of fire", but according to half the translators he merely "plucked the blossom", because, like Hippolyte, I am continuously looking for and failing to find even the condensare', Pound wrote, mistakenly thinking that *dichten* is related to dicht, "dense" or "narrow", but stating a truth. Original poetry itself has no redundancy, no phatic language, but the translator usually needs a little extra space, he relies on redundancy in over-translating, say, *veule* as "flabby" or "weak and soft" and here he is often hemmed in by the metre. Racine's wonderful line *Le jour n'est pas plus pur que le fond de mon coeur* may become: "My heart is candid as the light of day" (Dillon) or: "The daylight is not purer than my heart" (Cairncross) and whilst the second translation is closer and more successful, it cannot match the fullness and softness of the original; the alliteration, the monosyllables, the repeated r's, the emotive *fond* are missing.

I have said that original metaphors have to be translated accurately, even if in the target language culture the image is strange and the sense it conveys may only be guessed. *Und jener, der "du" zu ihm sagte träumt mit ihm: Wir* (Celan, In *Memoriam Paul Eluard*): "And he who addressed him as 'thou' will dream with him: We." The translator Michael Hamburger has to use "thou", although the connotations of friendship and love—what I would call *le plaisir de te tutoyer*—will be lost on the reader of the translation or perhaps soon on the reader of the original, now that the intimate *du, tu* has been taken over by the Left and all the under-thirties. *Le plaisir de te tutoyer* has almost gone, unless you are old, but so, thankfully, has *das erste Du stammelte auf ihren keuschen Lippen.*

Sound-effects are bound to come last for the translator, except for lovely minor poetry such as Swinburne's. Inevitably, he must try to do something about them and, if not, compensate either by putting them elsewhere or substituting another sound. German, the *Brudersprache* to English, often finds its adjectives and nouns—*fremde Frau*, "alien woman": *laue Luft*, "tepid air"—unreproduced, but longer alliterations.

> Und schwölle mit und schauerte und triefte
> (G. Benn, *Untergrundbahn*)

can usually find a modest, suggestive equivalence:

> To swell in unison and stream and shudder
> (trans. M. Hamburger)

John Weightman has stated that French poetry is untranslatable into English. I cannot accept this. Firstly, because a lot of French poetry (Villon, Rimbaud, Valéry) has been more or less successfully translated into English; secondly, because although there are obvious minuses—the syntactical differences; the huge English vocabulary compared with the small French vocabulary, so that many French words appear to be generic words covering many English specific words that themselves lack a generic word (e. g. humide, mouillé: "humid, damp, dank, moist, wet, clammy, undried"; noir: "black, dark, dim, dull, dusky, deep, gloomy, murky"), making French "abstract" and intellectual whilst English is concrete and real—yet in the actual particular of a text, English has infinite creative resources. English has the disyllables as well as the monosyllables. English in the eighteenth century got close to all the so-called French properties and, given empathy, given sympathy, there is no reason why, one day, even Racine should not find his inadequate but challenging English translator.

John Cairncross sets out three considerations for the translation of Racine: ① the translator must adopt ten-syllable blank verse; ② Racine must be translated accurately; ③ Racine's verse is particularly difficult owing to his capacity of evoking music from the most unpromising material—I could think of more.

Hippolyte's confession of love—I would not call it that, it is too restless and feverish—to Aricie (*Phèdre*, 11. 524 – 60) is often considered to be *precieux*, i. e. affected, conventional, too polished, sophisticated, class-bound, with too many stock metaphors, but for me they have always been Racine's most beautiful lines, crystallising the neurotic exposed mental and nervous obsession which is the essence of the Racine character. Taking the critical lines 539 – 48, it appears to me that in any modern version, the language must be kept modern and formal, the polar oppositions (*fuir, trouver, suivre, éviter, lumière, ombre*) retained, the stresses and repetitions preserved, the image of the hunted, haunted animal (Hippolyte) kept dear, and some attempt made to keep the simple language, the soft sounds with occasional alliteration.

Consider first the version of John Caircross. In general it is accurate, though a new image is unnecessarily created ("Cut from my moorings by a surging swell1") and some oppositions blurred:

> Present I flee you, absent you are near
> *Présente je vans fuis—absente, je vous trouve*

and the stresses often changed. The translation, written in 1945, has a few old-fashioned phrases: "in thrall", "a single blow has quelled". With all this, lines such as

> Before you stands a pitiable prince...
> Who, pitying the shipwrecks of the weak...
> Deep in the woods, your image follows me.

> *Dans le fond des forêts votre image me suit*

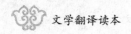

The light of day, the shadowy of the night.
La lumière du jour, les ombres de la nuit.

(the latter a one-to-one translation)

Everything conjures up the charms I flee
I seek but cannot find myself again—
Maintenant je me cherche, et ne me trouve plus

(note the unusual number of French monosyllables) are close to the original and successful.

George Dillon, like Cairncross, uses blank verse, and prefers formal accuracy to musicality. His translation is closer than Cairncross', so that lexical inaccuracies such as "surprise" for *trouble* and "hurt"for *déchirer* are disconcerting, as is the weak line: "Your image moves with me in the deep forests" (the alliteration is compensatory). Some stresses and contrasts are more clearly rendered than Cairncross':

With you and with myself, vainly I strive
　　　　　　　　　　　　　　(1. 545)
All summon to my eyes what I avoid
　　　　　　　　　　　　　　(1. 545)
I seek myself and find myself no more
　　　　　　　　　　　　　　(1. 548)

(the latter the most successful line)—such lines show how simply and precisely Racine can be translated. Both Dillon and Cairncross hit on the same translation for line 544 and there are occasions where one or two lines of Dillon's could improve Cairncross' rather better overall version; Dillon's

Only my deep sighs echo in the wood;
My idle couriers have forgotten my voice.

is better than Cairncross'

My idle steeds no longer know my voice
And only to my cries the woods resound.

(I do not know why Cairncross has reversed the lines.)

Robert Lowell's "imitation" of *Phèdre* is another matter. These rhymed pentameters attempt to explicate the image of the speech:

Six months now, bounding like a wounded stag
I've tried to shake this poisoned dart, and drag
Myself to safety from your eyes that blind
When present, and when absent leave behind

Volleys of burning arrows in my mind.

I do not know how such lines would strike a reader or spectator new to *Phédre*. For myself, with Racine's images burned into my mind, I find them unsatisfying, because, like Hippolyte, I am continuously looking for and failing to find even the simplest images which Lowell would have had no difficulty in retaining or recapturing. In fact I find the greatest loss in Racine translations is the resonance of the only 1,800 words that are used in the twelve plays.

The Short Story/Novel

From a translator's point of view, the short story is, of literary forms, the second most difficult, but here he is released from the obvious constraints of poetry—metre and rhyme—whilst the varieties of sound-effect are likely to play a minor role. Further, since the line is no longer a unit of meaning, he can spread himself a little —his version is likely to be somewhat longer than the original though, always, the shorter the better. He can supply cultural glosses within the text—not, as in poetry or drama, delete or banish them to some note or glossary: *L'ascenseur ne fonctionnait pas, en raison des économies de courant*— "With the war-time electricity cuts, the lift wasn't working."

Since formal and thematic concentration and unity may distinguish the short story from the novel, the translator has to be careful to preserve certain cohesive effects.

I use Thomas Mann's *Tonio Kröger* to illustrate two types of key-words I propose to define: leitmotifs are peculiar to a short story, characterising a character or a situation. When they are repeated, they should be appropriately foregrounded and repeated in the translation; *Zigeuner im grünen Wagen*—"gypsies in green wagons" for the artists; *die Blonden und Blauäugigen*—"the blond and blue-eyed ones" for the ordinary people; *die Feldblume im Knopfloch*—"the wild flowers in his buttonhole" for the respectable bourgeois Knaak with his *gedämpfte Stimme*—"muffled or subdued voice", or for Magdalena: the clumsy ones, *die immer hinfallen*—"who always fall down". Descriptive leitmotifs were used in Romantic short stories before Wagner invented the term, e. g. in Gotthelf's *Dark Spider*, giftig glotzend—"gaping poisonously", where the alliteration is moderately compensated. As dialogue becomes more important in fiction, certain phrases become attached to characters (Grev's billiard remarks in *The Cherry Orchard*, the numerous tags for Dickens's characters, Holden Coulfield's "phoney", Esmé's "extremely" in Salinger (now it is "totally" for anyone) and these have to be foregrounded.

The second type of key-word is the word or phrase that typifies the writer rather than the particular text: *sich verirren, jagen, beirrt, nämlich, beengen* and all the *Beamte* words may be said to typify Kafka, as powerful verbs like *entraîner, épier, agir, frémir, exiger, grelotter, tressaillir, obséder* may typify Mauriac. Some of these words go into a ready one-to-one translation into English, and get their connotational significance from repetition and context (situational and linguistic) which can more or less be reproduced by the translator.

Words like *jagen* and *entraîner* are difficult: *jagen* suggests "hectic chase" and *entraîner* (*Quelle force m' entraîne?*), "impel irresistibly".

For key-words, translators have to assess their texts critically; they have to decide which lexical units are central, and have the more important function, and which are peripheral, so that the relative gains and losses in a translation may correspond to their assessment. (I realise that many translators will claim they do all these intuitively, by instinct, or by common sense, and they do not need translation theory to make them aware of relative importance.)

There is no advantage in making generalisations about the translation of serious novels. The obvious problems: the relative importance of the SL culture and the author's moral purpose to the reader—it may be exemplified in the translation of proper names; of the SL conventions and the author's idiolect; the translation of dialect; the distinction between personal style, literary convention of period and/or movement; and the norms of the SL— these problems have to be settled for each text.

The signal importance of the translation of some novels has been the introduction of a new vision injecting a different literary style into another language culture, and when one looks at *Weltliteratur* translations in this sense—I think of Proust, Camus, Kafka, Mann, Pavese—it is clear that the translators have often not been bold, which means not literal, enough: these are the million cases where a literal translation is aesthetically not inferior to a free translation, fashionably justified as "sub-text", formerly the "spirit" or the "genius" of the language or the author.

Drama

The main purpose of translating a play is normally to have it performed successfully. Therefore a translator of drama inevitably has to bear the potential spectator in mind though, here again, the better written and more significant the text, the fewer compromises he can make in favour of the reader. Further, he works under certain constraints: unlike the translator of fiction, he cannot gloss, explain puns or ambiguities or cultural references, nor transcribe words for the sake of local colour; his text is dramatic, with emphasis on verbs, rather than descriptive and explanatory. Michael Meyer, in a little noticed article in *Twentieth Century Studies*, quoting T. Rattigan, states that the spoken word is five times as potent as the written word—what a novelist would say in 30 lines, the playwright must say in five. The arithmetic is faulty and so, I believe, is the sentiment, but it shows that a translation of a play must be concise—it must not be an over-translation.

Meyer makes a distinction between dramatic text and sub-text, the literal meaning and the "real point": i. e. what is implied but not said, the meaning between the lines. He believes that if a person is questioned on a subject about which he has complex feelings, he will reply evasively (and in a circumlocutory manner). Ibsen's characters say one thing and mean another. The translator must word the sentences in such a way that this, the sub-text, is equally clear in English. Unfortunately, Meyer gives no examples. Normally one would expect a semantic translation of a line, which may be close to a literal translation, to reveal its implications more clearly than a communicative translation, that simply makes the dialogue easy to speak. Lines such as "Aren't you feeling the cold"? and "I think your husband is faithful to you" have potential implications of escape and suspicion respectively in any language, provided there is cultural overlap between them. (They would not have the same implication if the climate or the sexual morality respectively differed considerably in the SL and the TL culture.)

Finally a translator of drama in particular must translate into the modern target language if he wants his characters to "live", bearing in mind that the modern language covers a span of, say, 70 years, and that if one character speaks in a bookish or old-fashioned way in the original, written 500 years ago, he must speak in an equally bookish and old-fashioned way in the translation, but as he would today, therefore with a corresponding time-gap—differences of register, social class, education, temperament in particular must be preserved between one character and another. Thus the dialogue remains dramatic, and though the translator cannot forget the potential spectators, he does not make concessions to them. Given the emphasis on linguistic form, and the subtlety of the SL, his version is inevitably inferior but also simpler and a kind of one-sided introduction to the original. Kant is easier to read in French than in German, perhaps even for a German.

Whilst a great play may be translated for the reading public's enjoyment and for scholarly study as well as for performance on stage, the translator should always assume the latter as his main purpose—there should be no difference between an acting and a reading version—and he should look after readers and scholars only in his notes. Nevertheless, he should where possible amplify cultural metaphors, allusions, proper names, in the text itself, rather than replace the allusion with the sense. ("Hyperion to a satyr" becomes "a sun god to a monster" in Chinese.)

When a play is transferred from the SL to the TL culture it is usually no longer a translation, but an adaptation.

Conclusion

Finally in discussing the translation of serious literature, I must make it clear that I am trying to look at the future. There is no question that translators such as Stuart Gilbert, who translated Malraux and Camus into English and Joyce into French, had a quickening effect on translation: possibly reacting against the stiff and literary translation style which so fouled up the translation of Russian literature at the turn of the century. Profoundly influenced by Hemingway who was mainly responsible for bringing fiction closer to normal speech, Gilbert produced a lively enough equivalence: *Aujourd'hui, maman est morte ou peut-être hier*, *je ne sais pas* becomes "Mother died today, or maybe yesterday, I can't be sure"; *Je prendrai l'autobus à deux heures et j'arriverai dans l'après-midi.* —"With the two o'clock bus I should get there well before nightfall" (examples from Camus, *L'Etranger*). You can see that half the time Gilbert is trying to be more colloquial than the original, yet every time he might have said that the further colloquialism was in the sub-text, i. e. implied or implicated in the original. Nevertheless it is hard to see how one can justify translating *Il faisait très chaud* as "It was a blazing hot afternoon", and there are a thousand other examples of such "deviations" which show that these translators may have been aiming at "intuitive truth", an instinctive naturalness (there is no question usually of ignorance, of carelessness, such as is so common in translations from the German) rather than accuracy at any level. I am suggesting that some kind of accuracy must be the only criterion of a good translation in the future—what kind of accuracy depending first on the type and then the particular text that has been translated—and that the word "sub-text" with its Gricean implications and implicatures can be made to cover a multitude of inaccuracies.

【翻译鉴赏】

《圣经》佳句赏析

[1] What has come into being in him was life, and the life was the light of all people. The light shines in the darkness, and the darkness did not overcome it.

译文:生命在他里头,这生命就是人的光。光照在黑暗里,黑暗却不接受光。(《新约·约翰福音》第1章)

评析:这是基督教神学思想的核心。这里的"光"指的是耶稣基督,"生命"指的是永生——战胜死亡,获得真理。

[2] Enter through the narrow gate; for the gate is wide and the road is easy that leads to destruction, and there are many who take it. For the gate is narrow and the road is hard that leads to life, and there are few who find it.

译文:你们要进窄门,因为引到灭亡,那门是宽的,路是大的,进去的人也多;引到永生,那门是窄的,路是小的,找着的人少。(《新约·马太福音》第7章)

评析:这是耶稣"登山宝训"中最短的一段,是整个新教精神的核心。对于清教徒而言,人生意味着无尽艰险,意味着走窄门。

[3] Love is patient; love is kind; love is not envious or boastful or arrogant or rude. It does not insist on its own way; it is not irritable or resentful; it does not rejoice in wrongdoing, but rejoices in the truth. It bears all things, hopes all things, endures all things. Love never ends.

译文:爱是恒久忍耐,又有恩慈;爱是不嫉妒,爱是不自夸,不张狂,不做害羞的事,不求自己的益处,不轻易发怒,不计算人的恶,不喜欢不义,只喜欢真理;凡事包容,凡事相信,凡事盼望,凡事忍耐;爱是永不止息。(《新约·哥林多前书》第13章)

评析:基督教是"爱的宗教",该段是使徒保罗对爱的诠释。

[4] Where, O death, is your victory? Where, O death, is your sting? the sting of death is

sin, and the power of sin is the law. But thanks to God, who gives us the victory through our Lord Jesus Christ.

译文:死啊,你得胜的权势在哪里?死啊,你的毒钩在哪里?死的毒钩就是罪,罪的权势就是律法。感谢上帝,使我们借着我们的主耶稣基督得胜。(《新约·哥林多前书》第15章)

评析:使徒保罗用优美的语言阐明了基督教的脉络:原罪与堕落,牺牲与救赎,胜利与永生。总体说来就是"用爱战胜死亡"。

[5] The grass withers, the flower fades, when the breath of the LORD blows upon it; surely the people are grass. The grass withers, the flower fades; but the word of our God will stand forever.

译文:草必枯干,花必凋残,因为耶和华的气吹在其上;百姓诚然是草。草必枯干,花必凋残;唯有我们上帝的话,必永远立定!(《旧约·以赛亚书》第40章)

评析:旧约的最大特点是"信念"。这句话就是无比坚定的信念,既相信上帝,又相信作为上帝选民的自己。以色列人的辉煌,大半缘自信念。

[6] For I know that my Redeemer lives, and that at the last he will stand up on the earth; and after my skin has been thus destroyed, then in my flesh I shall see God.

译文:我知道我的救赎主活着,末了必站在地上。我这皮肉灭绝之后,我必在肉体之外得见上帝。(《旧约·约伯记》第19章)

评析:这是约伯的信念。无论承受多么巨大的打击、多么绝望的境遇,都不放弃希望、放弃信仰。亨德尔为此句作的咏叹调也极为感人。

[7] Do not seal up the words of the prophecy of this book, for the time is near. Let the evildoer still do evil, and the filthy still be filthy, and the righteous still do right, and the holy still be holy.

译文:不可封了这书上的预言,因为日期近了。不义的,叫他仍旧不义;污秽的,叫他仍旧污秽;为义的,叫他仍旧为义;圣洁的,叫他仍旧圣洁。(《新约·启示录》第22章)

评析:这一句是《启示录》中众多让人不能不动容的话之一,通过一系列对比,强调为义、圣洁的终极教义。

[8] Who will separate us from the love of Christ? Will hardship, or distress, or persecution, or famine, or nakedness, or peril, or sword? No, in all these things we are more than conquerors through him who loved us.

译文:谁能使我们与基督的爱隔绝呢?难道是患难吗?是困苦吗?是逼迫吗?是饥饿吗?是赤身裸体吗?是危险吗?是刀剑吗……然而,靠着爱我们的主,我们在这一切的事上已经得胜有余了。(《新约·罗马书》第8章)

评析:圣保罗是无与伦比的传道者,他讲道如此气势磅礴且发人深省。这段话继承了旧约的信心,增加了新约的爱,完美地体现了基督教精神。

[9] And I applied my mind to know wisdom and to know madness and folly. I perceived that this also is but a chasing after wind. For in much wisdom is much vexation, and those who increase knowledge increase sorrow.

译文:我又专心察明智慧、狂妄和愚昧,乃知这也是捕风。因为多有智慧,就多有愁烦;加增知识的,就加增忧伤。(《旧约·传道书》第1章)

评析：《传道书》中传道者的话虽低沉消极，却蕴涵着希望，能够用来战胜愁烦和忧伤的只有一件事——信仰。

[10] Hallelujah! For the Lord our God the Almighty reigns. The kingdom of the world has become the kingdom of our Lord and of his Messiah, and he will reign forever and ever.

译文：哈利路亚！因为主我们的上帝，全能者作王了。……世上的国成了我主和主基督的国；他要作王，直到永永远远。……万王之王，万主之主。（《启示录》第11、19章）

评析：这也是亨德尔歌剧《弥赛亚》中大合唱《哈利路亚》的歌词，从这短短的几句话中可以看到无穷的胜利喜悦。

《论语学而篇·第一》

子曰[1]："学而时习之[2]，不亦说乎[3]？有朋自远方来[4]，不亦乐乎[5]？人不知而不愠[6]，不亦君子乎[7]？"

【背景介绍】

这是《论语》"学而篇·第一"中的首篇。要译好古籍经典，关键的问题是吃透对原文的理解。文言文中既有实词，又有虚词，还有令人费解的文言句式。翻译工作者的任务是，在正确理解原文的基础上，首先要把原文译成浅显的现代汉语，然后再译成英文。此段中的关键词是虚词"而"，实词"时"、"习"、"之"、"说"、"乐"、"人"、"不知"、"不愠"、"君子"等，还有古汉语句式"不亦……乎"。把握了对这些词的理解就抓住了全段的精髓。

本段今译 孔子说："学了知识并且经常复习，不也是令人愉快的事吗？有志同道合的人从远方来，不也是值得高兴的事吗？别人不了解自己，但自己不恼怒，这不也是君子的风度吗？"

【六种不同的译文】

1. **James Legge 译：**The Master said, "Is it not pleasant to learn with a constant perseverance and application? Is it not delightful to have friends coming from distant quarters? Is it not a man of complete virtue, who feels no discomposure though men may take no note of him?"

2. **Arthur Waley 译：**The Master said, "To learn and at due times to repeat what one has learnt, is that not after all a pleasure? That friends should come to one from afar, is this not after all delightful? To remain unsoured even though one's merits are unrecognized by others, is that not after all what is expected of a gentleman?"

3. **王福林译：**Confucius said, "Isn't it a pleasure for one to learn and then constantly review and practise what he has already learned? Isn't it a pleasure for one to have like-minded people coming from faraway places? If others don't know him, he doesn't feel displeased. Isn't it a superior person's bearing?"

4. **赖波、夏玉和译：**Confucius said, "Is it not a pleasure after all to practice in due time what one has learnt? Is it not a delight after all to have friends come from afar? Is it not a gentleman after all who will not take offence when others fail to appreciate him?"

5. **潘富恩、温少霞译：**The Master said, "Is it not pleasant to learn and to review constantly what one has learned? Is it not delightful to have friends coming afar? Is he not a superior man, who feels no discontent though others do not know him?"

6. **丁往道译**：Confucius said, "Is it not a pleasure to learn and practise from time to time what is learned? Is it not a joy to see a friend who has come from a faraway place? Is it not gentlemanly to have no resentment when one is not properly understood?"

【译文评析】

[1] 子曰："子"是古代人对男子的尊称，常写在姓的后面。这里称孔子为"子"而讳其名，是孔子的学生对孔子的尊称。直呼孔子为 Confucius 是符合西方传统的，西方对学者一般直呼其名，而不加表示职称、身份等的词语。王译、赖译、丁译用 Confucius 显然是为了点明"子"指的是谁。而威译、潘译为了传达中文的含义，用了 The Master 表示"先师"之意，这就尽可能地保留了原文中的人际关系和文化特征，这样做虽然会使西方读者感到不习惯，但有利于他们了解原文的内容、风格及原作者的意图。

[2] 学而时习之："学"意为"学习"。此段中两个"而"都是连词，第一个"而"表递进关系，相当于"并且"and，第二个"而"表转折关系，相当于"但是"。"时"意为"经常"constantly; at due times; from time to time。"习"意为"复习，练习"review and practise; repeat。"之"是代词，指学过的知识 what one has already learned。

[3] 不亦说乎："不亦……乎？"是古汉语中一种常用句式，表示委婉的反问语气，相当于"不也是……的吗？""说"（yuè），同"悦"，意即"高兴，快乐"。此句译成 Isn't it a pleasure for one to do...? 或 Is it not pleasant to do...?

[4] 有朋自远方来："有朋"的旧注为"同门曰朋"。这里"朋"当指"弟子"解，王福林解做"志同道合的人"。多数译者译做 friends；王译为 like-minded people，比 friends 有更深一层的意义，比较贴近原文。"自远方来"有不同的译法：coming from distant quarters; come to one from afar; coming from faraway places。

[5] 不亦乐乎："乐"意为"快乐"delightful; pleasure; a delight; a joy。

[6] 人不知而不愠："人"意为"别人"others; men。"人不知"中"知"字无宾语，解做"别人不了解自己，不欣赏自己"，译法有：don't know; take no note of; one's merits are unrecognized by; fail to appreciate; is not properly understood。"愠"（yùn）：恼怒，feel displeased; discomposure; take offence; feel no discontent。

[7] 不亦君子乎："君子"意为"道德高尚，有修养的人"。译法有：a man of complete virtue; a gentleman; a superior person (man)等。a man of complete virtue 译出了"君子"一词的内涵。

【翻译试笔】

【英译汉】

The Creation of the World

When God made heaven and earth, the earth was a mass of whirling clouds and vapour without form and it was dark all over. God said, "Let there be light, let there be light." And there was light, god saw that the light was good, and he separated light from darkness. He called the light day, and the darkness night. So evening came, and morning came. It was the first day.

God said, "Let there be a vault between the waters, to separate water from water." So God made the vault, and separated the water under the vault from the water above it; and

God called the vault the heavens. Evening came, and morning came, a second day.

God said, "Let the waters under heaven be gathered into one place, so that dry land may appear." And so it was. God called the dry land earth, and the gathering of the waters he called seas; and God saw that it was quite good. Then God said, "Let the earth produce flesh growth, let there be on the earth plants bearing seed." So it was. Plants bearing seed grew on the earth, and God saw that it was good. Evening came, and morning came, a third day.

God said, "Let there be lights in the vault of heaven to separate day from night, and let them serve as signs both for festivals and for seasons and years. Let them also shine in the vault of heaven to give light on the earth." So it was. God made the two great lights, the bigger is called the Sun to govern the day and the smaller is called the Moon to govern the night; and with them he made the stars. God put these lights in the vault of heaven to give light on the earth, to separate light from darkness; and God saw that it was good. Evening came, and morning came, a fourth day.

God said, "Let the waters be filled with countless living creatures, and let birds fly in the heavens." God then created all living creatures that move and live in the waters, and every kind of bird; and God saw that it was good. So he blessed them and said, "Be fruitful and become more and more, fill the waters of the seas; and let more and more birds on the land." Evening came, and morning came, a fifth day.

God said, "Let the earth filled with such living creatures, as cattle, sheep and wild animals..." So it was. God made wild animals, cattle, sheep and all reptiles. And he saw that it was good. Then God said, "Let us make man in our image and likeness to rule the fish in the sea, the birds of heaven, the cattle, all wild animals on the earth. That crawl upon the earth." So God created man in his own image: male and female. God blessed them and said to them, "Be fruitful and increase, fill the earth, rule over the fish in the sea, the birds of heaven, and every living thing that moves upon the earth." God also said, "I give you all plants that bear seed everywhere on the earth, and every tree bearing fruit, they shall be yours for food. All green plants I give for food to the wild animals on the earth, to all the birds of heaven, every living creature." So it was. God saw all that he had made, and it was very good. Evening came, and morning came, a sixth day.

Thus heaven and earth were completed. On the sixth day God completed all the work he had been doing, and on the seventh day he stopped his work. God blessed the seventh day and made it holy, because on that day he did not need to do any work.

This is the story of the making of heaven and earth when they were created.

【汉译英】

《荀子·劝学》

君子曰:学不可以已。

青,取之于蓝,而青于蓝;冰,水为之,而寒于水。木直中绳,輮以为轮,其曲中规。虽有槁暴,不复挺者,輮使之然也。故木受绳则直,金就砺则利,君子博学而日参省乎己,则知明而行无过矣。

......

故不积跬步,无以至千里;不积小流,无以成江海。

【参考译文】

创世之初

上帝创造天地时,地球还是一团尚未成形的旋转云块和雾,到处一片黑暗。上帝说:"光明到! 光明到!"天地间随即就有了光明。上帝视"光"为祥物,于是他就把光明与黑暗分开,光明之时为白天,黑暗之时为夜晚。晨曦送走长夜,这就是第一天。

上帝说:"要有苍穹将茫茫之水上下分隔。"说罢,他就动手造就苍穹,苍穹之上有水,苍穹之下有水,上帝称分隔的穹顶为天空。晨曦送走长夜,这就是第二天。

上帝说:"将普天之水汇集成域,显露出干涸的土地!"土地马上就露出水面之上。上帝称大块干涸之地为陆,称聚集的水域为海。上帝见水陆之分甚好,接着说:"让大地繁衍生机,树木结籽,万物生长。"于是,大地上各种瓜果树木,参差生长,带籽丛生。上帝觉得这是件好事。晨曦送走长夜,这就是第三天。

上帝说:"让苍穹中有光来区分昼与夜,让光来作为标志,表示节日、年月、季节的更替,让它们在苍穹之中发光,照亮大地。"说罢,上帝就创造了两个大型发光体,较大的天体称日,主宰白昼;较小的天体称月,主宰黑夜。在日月之间,上帝又创造了满天繁星。上帝在苍穹里撒下光明,照亮海洋陆地,划分光明与黑暗。上帝觉得这样不错,晨曦送走长夜,这就是第四天。

上帝说:"让水中生长无数鱼类,让鸟儿在天上飞翔。"上帝当即就创造了游弋的鱼类,栖息于水中,并创造了万千飞鸟。上帝感到这是件好事,就赐福于它们,祝愿说:"愿海中鱼儿繁衍,愿天上众多鸟儿飞。"晨曦送走长夜,这就是第五天。

上帝说:"地球上应有千虫百兽,诸如牛羊、野兽……"上帝就随心所愿创造了走兽、牛羊和爬行动物。上帝觉得这是件好事。他说:"要按我们自己的形象和喜好来塑造人类,来监管约束海洋之中的繁多鱼类、空中飞鸟、牛以及地上爬行的牲畜野兽。"因此,上帝就按照他的形象创造了人类,有男与女。上帝为他们祝福:"多多繁衍子孙后代,让人类遍布地球的每一个角落,成为海洋、空中、陆地的主宰,驾驭鱼类、鸟类、爬虫走兽。"上帝还说:"我要赐予你们结籽类植物,播种根植于整个地球,让每棵树都挂满沉甸甸的果子,赐予你们为食——野兽、飞鸟以及一切生物。"上帝就这样行随所愿,创造了一切,并感到一切非常美好。夜晚来临,很快晨曦初露,这就是第六天。

天地万物皆已成形,在第六天,上帝完成了全部工作,第七天他停止工作,就赐福于第七天,并称之万圣日,因为这一天他无需工作。

这就是上帝创世的故事。

Master Xun·Persuasion and Study

"Never stop learning," said by a saint.

The indigo, though extracted from cyan, is deeper in color than the cyan;

The ice, though formed by water, is colder in temperature than the water.

A timber, as straight as an unbent rope, can be made into a wheel by broiling; the incurvate degree of the wheel nearly equals that of a compass. Even though insolated dry, the already bent timber cannot be unbent any more due to the outward force of transformation. Therefore, A wooden timber becomes straight if processed with an unbent rope；A metal knife becomes sharp if whetted on a stone.

Similarly，if a man keeps learning avidly and reflecting daily，he will be wise both in thought and action. This is the significance of keeping learning.

A place a thousand miles away can never be reached without an addition of small paces；A deep ocean can never come into being without the convergence of small streams.

【延伸阅读】

[1] Baker，M. *In Other Words：A Coursebook on Translation* [M]. London & New York：Routledge，1992.

[2] Baker，M. *Routledge Encyclopedia of Translation Studies* [M]. Shanghai：Shanghai Foreign Language Education Press，2004.

[3] Bell，R. T. *Translation and Translating：Theory and Practice* [M]. New York：Longman Inc，1991.

[4] Flotow，L. V. *Translation and Gender：Translating in the "Era of Feminism"* [M]. Shanghai：Shanghai Foreign Language Education Press，2004.

[5] Hermans，T. *The Manipulation of Literature* [M]. Worcester：Billing & Sons Limited，1985.

[6] Landers，C. E. *Literary Translation：A Practical Guide* [M]. Clevedon & Buffalo & Toronto & Sydney：Multilingual Matters Limited，2001.

[7] Munday，J. *Introducing Translation Studies：Theories and Applications* [M]. London and New York：Routledge，2001.

[8] Newmark，P. *A Textbook of Translation* [M]. Shanghai：Shanghai Foreign Languages Education Press，2001.

[9] Snell-Hornby，M. *Turns of Translation Studies：New Paradigms or Shifting Viewpoints？* [M] Amsterdam/Philadelphia：John Benjamins Publishing Company，2006.

[10] Tytler，A. *Essay on the Principles of Translation* [M]（1907）. Digitized for Microsoft Corporation by the Internet Archive from University of Toronto，2008.

[11] 蔡新乐. 文学翻译的艺术哲学[M]. 开封:河南大学出版社,2004.

[12] 韩子满. 文学翻译杂合研究[M]. 上海:上海译文出版社,2005.

[13] 姜秋霞. 文学翻译中的审美过程:格式塔意象再造[M]. 北京:商务印书馆,2002.

[14] 金圣华. 桥畔译谈——翻译散论八十篇[M]. 北京:中国对外翻译出版公司,1997.

[15] 刘宓庆. 翻译美学导论[M]. 北京:中国对外翻译出版公司,2005.

[16] 罗新璋. 翻译论集[C]. 北京:商务印书馆,1984.

[17] 孟昭毅,李载道. 中国翻译文学史[C]. 北京:北京大学出版社,2005.

[18] 钱歌川. 翻译的基本知识[M]. 北京:世界图书出版公司,2011.

[19] 沈苏儒. 论信达雅——严复翻译理论研究[M]. 北京:商务印书馆,1998.

[20] 沈苏儒. 翻译的最高境界——"信达雅"漫谈[M]. 北京:中国对外翻译出版公司,2006.

[21] 王宏志. 翻译与文学之间[M]. 南京:南京大学出版社,2010.

[22] 王向远. 翻译文学导论[M]. 北京:北京师范大学出版社,2004.

[23] 杨平. 名作精译——《中国翻译》英译汉选萃[C]. 青岛:青岛出版社,1999.

[24] 杨平. 名作精译——《中国翻译》汉译英选萃[C]. 青岛:青岛出版社,2003.

[25] 杨全红. 翻译史另写[M]. 武汉:武汉大学出版社,2010.

[26] 张柏然,许钧. 面向 21 世纪的译学研究[C]. 北京:商务印书馆,2002.

[27] 周克希. 译边草[M]. 上海:百家出版社,2001.

【问题与思考】

1. 什么是文学翻译?

2. 文学翻译与非文学翻译的区别是什么?

3. 文学翻译的本质特征是什么?

4. "文学翻译是决定世界文化发展方向的主要影响力量"这句话言过其辞了吗?

5. 文学翻译是一门艺术还是技术?

6. 文学译品在哪些方面必须与原文一样?

7. 请查找人类历史上关于文学翻译的比喻,你认同这些看法吗?

8. 为什么说"翻译即是阐释"?

9. 文学翻译语言与接受国作家的语言有哪些区别?

10. 文学翻译与翻译文学属于同一概念吗? 区别与联系是什么?

第二章　文学翻译风格篇

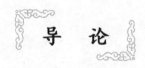

导　论

　　《现代汉语词典》将"风格"定义为,一个时代、一个民族、一个流派或一个人的文艺作品所表现的主要的思想特点和艺术特点。徐有志在关于"文体学"的阐述中将众说纷纭的风格定义从文本角度上分归四大类:一是指个人运用语言的特征,即个人的语言习惯。所谓"莎士比亚风格"、"鲁迅风格"即指此。它常常强调个人表现出的特有的或首创的语言特点,所以广而言之,它可以指一个作家对常规用法的"变异"。二是指集体运用语言的特征,即众人在特定的时间、地点、场合等情景下表现出的类似的语言习惯,诸如"建安风骨"、"美国式幽默"、"公众演讲风格"、"民谣风格"等。这个定义的重心不在于发话人的个人特点,而在于他们在特定场合表现出的类似特征。三是指有效的表达方式,即所谓"以最有效的方式讲适切的话",如大部分写作教程所提倡的那种"明白的"或"优雅的"风格。四是单指"好"的文学作品的一种特点,文学批评家们广泛运用的诸如"庄严"、"华美"、"清丽"、"平淡"等风格。(杨自俭,2002:204)

　　风格是一个作家的标志,尤其是他们之所以成为大作家的标志。讽刺而不辛辣、幽默而不浮华,洋溢着浪漫动人的诗情的莎士比亚;"风格像水一样清纯,只是常常流入地下,靠着老式的管道传送出去",不役于外物、靠自家朴拙诚实的笔尖流向纸页,流给时间的毛姆;以干净利落、简洁凝练的"电报式"风格著称的海明威;浑厚、雄健、博大又混杂着庞杂、粗疏、用字不够讲究的巴尔扎克……以中国古诗而论,李白的飘逸雄放,杜甫的沉郁顿挫,韩愈的雄肆艰险,白居易的明白晓畅,苏轼的清旷放逸,秦观的婉委清丽,辛弃疾的雄健清壮,姜白石的清淡雅洁……古今中外的大作家之所以成为大作家,无不验证着雨果所说的:"拿走这件简单而微小的东西:风格,那么伏尔泰、帕斯卡尔、拉封丹、莫里哀这些大师身上,还将剩下什么呢?"

　　文学风格是文学作品思想内容和艺术形式上的各种特点的综合表现,是作家的思想修养、审美意识、艺术情趣、艺术素养和语言特质构成的艺术个性在文学作品中的集中反映。风格的传达,是文学翻译中最敏感而最复杂的问题之一。风格与语言紧紧联系在一起,语言的不同,必然会使风格产生变化。加之,不同语言文字系统所固化的文化差异的现实存在,给翻译者带来不可克服的困难。百分之百地译出原作的风格是很难做到的事,译文也永远无法跟原文完全"重合",甚至有一些具有民族特色的内容,根本就无法用另一种语言表达出来。然而,对于一部文学作品来说,风格就是生命,风格翻译是否成功是决定一部译著是否具有生命力的关键。翻译作为整体的艺术,个别不能或较难翻译的成分并不妨碍整体的表达。对文学风格的翻译,译者的责任是尽量扩大其可译性,尽可能最大限度地在总体上再现原作的风格。译者可以通过自己的不懈努力,译文总是可能"无限地"接近原作。

许多人写文章讨论翻译中的风格问题,对于风格是否能译,大体上有两种意见。一种意见认为风格是能译的。1790 年英国著名翻译理论家亚历山大·弗雷泽·泰特勒在他著作《论翻译原则》中指出:"我想这样描述好的翻译:原作的长处应完全无损地移入另一种语言,使移入语所属国的本地人能够明白地领悟、鲜明地感受,如同使用原作语言的人所领悟、所感受一样。"进而,在此基础上,泰特勒提出三原则为:"① That the Translation should give a complete transcript of the ideas of the original work;② That the style and manner of writing should be of the same character with that of the original;③ That the Translation should have all the ease of original composition".(意即:① 译作应完全复写出原作思想;② 译作风格和手法应和原作属于同一性质;③ 译作应具备原作所具有的通顺。——参见谭载喜,2006:129)英国诗人兼文学批评家 Matthew Arnold(阿诺德)也提出类似的见解,即要创造性地传达原作的风格,虽然困难,但并不是不可能。他认为不能把传达原作的风格排斥在"信实"概念之外,并且翻译必须保持语言的自然性。我国古代译论中的"文质之争"、"信达雅三难说"、"神韵说"、"神似论"、"化境说"等,无不以翻译标准的形式确认风格传达的必要性和可能性。举凡有关翻译标准的论述,大多涉及文学翻译的本质——风格翻译问题,这展现了风格在文学翻译中的重要性。但对于文学语言风格的翻译方法和策略至今仍是译界争论的热点,出现了直译与意译、形式与内容等二元对立的翻译观点。

　　风格是作品内容与形式的有机统一。西方一位美学史家对风格瑰丽动人而又迷离恍惚的特征作了贴切的比拟:风格有如彩虹,五彩缤纷、虚幻漂渺,当你想探求其奥秘前往觅寻时,一切光色便消失得无影无踪。然而,觅寻不见彩虹并不证明彩虹的子虚乌有;相反,这只能证明你对彩虹独特的存在方式认识不足(McMullen,1974:123)。与彩虹一样,风格也有其独特的存在方式。它是实在的,因而是可感的。美国著名作家詹姆斯曼衍的长句、繁芜的修饰和隐晦的措辞曲折地反映出他的内心深处所蕴藉的深邃、复杂的思绪,以及他对人类含混微妙的动机的意识。海明威清新、简洁、洗练的风格,句短词精,萧散简远,意在笔墨之外的风格深受他小说的题材和人物的塑造所制约。从这个意义上说,风格即人,莎士比亚对帝王将相、豪门贵族的描绘,巴尔扎克对封建贵族和资产阶级的刻画,与他们的风格有莫大关系,至少他们的雄浑气势是由此而来的,这种风格特点总能在译品中表现出来,不同的译者一般都可以传达出这种特点。换句话说,风格是可以部分或基本上传达出来的,这就是为什么不同国家的读者都可以从译作体会到别国作家的风格。

　　但是,翻译作品并不会出现"千人一面"的雷同结果,在很大程度上是因为译者也有自己的文字风格,不同的译者有不同的译品。1979 年罗新璋在《读傅雷作品随感》一文中说过这样一句话:"服尔德的机警尖刻,巴尔扎克的健拔雄快,梅里美的俊爽简括,罗曼·罗兰的朴质流动,在原文上色彩鲜明,各具面貌,译文固然对各家的特色和韵味有相称体现,拿《诚实人》的译文和《约翰·克利斯朵夫》一比,就能看出文风上的差异,但贯穿于这些译作的,不免有一种傅雷风格。"可见即使是名家的译作也难免既有原作的风格,又有译者的风格,而不可能是单纯的原作的风格。译者必须从哲学思辨充分认识到"自我"风格发挥的有度性,通过风格调整的翻译策略,"动态忠信"于原作语言风格,从而达到语言风格的"和谐翻译"。

　　本单元所选文章围绕风格翻译的必要、困难、可能与必然展开,分析中西语言文化风格差异,并结合现代文体学的核心概念,从语音、语法、词义三方面具体阐发风格翻译的可能性极其效度。

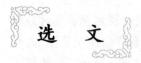

选文一　风格的翻译：必要、困难、可能与必然

冯世则

导　言

本文选自冯世则著，《翻译匠语》，文汇出版社（上海），2005年版。

选文率先分析风格及其构成，明确指出，文章之有风格，是普遍性的，不限于文艺也不限于优秀之作，因此，翻译中对原著风格的追求便是对忠实原则的信守。文章直接切中"风格难译"的要害问题，并以诗的格律和双关这两种极端抗拒翻译的文学表达方法的翻译为例，说明原著的风格一定会透过两种语言两种文化之间的隔阂，在相当的程度上顽强地复现于译文之中。风格翻译的根本条件就是忠实——首先要忠实于原著的或正确或错误或兼而有之的思想内容，同时必须尽量贴近原文的因言语而异的表达方式而又不损害归宿语言的规范，把握一词一句的修辞方式、捕捉原文的特色。翻译力求忠实，是译者主观上必须信守的译德；但要求绝对的等值，客观上却不可能做到。因此，风格的翻译不但必要和可能，甚至必然，但却不免局限。

风格的翻译是否必要，有否可能，已有不少论说。本文拟就风格本身试作考察，看看它无论就一般或就具体而论能否认识，能否在翻译中复现。

一、根据：风格及其构成

按辞典和理论书籍所言，风格的定义和构成似均有宽窄之分。

窄派认为风格仅见于文艺著作，且限于优秀的作家和作品；风格所指无非写作方式。宽派认为文章之有风格，是普遍性的，不限于文艺也不限于优秀之作；四人帮的"帮八股"风格——例如见之于梁效的那种南霸天北霸天的蛮不讲理、自说自话、颠倒事实、逻辑混乱——也很突出。至于风格的构成，宽派认为诚然主要在于语言表现的特点，但又与作品的题材、主题和作者的思想感情息息相关。有的还列举了主题、思想、形象、情节、结构语言和表现手法等构成因素。[①]

[①]　以上综述的论点，分见 Concise Oxford Dictionary、《现代汉语词典》以及下列各书：蔡仪主编《文学概论》，176－181页；以群主编《文学的基本原理》，397页；山东大学中文系文艺理论教研室编著《文艺学新论》，429页。

本文取宽派的说法。这是因为恰如文艺而外也还要译其他著作、文章一样，兼听则明，我们原就不能专挑被认为优秀健康之作来翻译。而尤其重要的是，宽派的提法乃是风格翻译的必要性和可能性的理论基础。

二、必要性

既然文章之有风格是普遍性的，则对原著风格的追求便是对忠实原则的信守，概无例外。而所谓普遍性还有一层意思：风格作者有，译者也有；原著有，译文也有。按忠实原则，译者便须撇下自己的风格，译文处处紧跟原著，而尤其要注意行文。因为因言语而异的表达方式之具体运用，不完全字字句句出于自觉，长期的思维和表达习惯自然而然发挥着相当的作用。多人合译的著作，虽然通常有一两人负责统一文风，却仍然往往前后笔调不一。经过有意识的努力尚且如此，少了这一层自觉，译者势必会听任自己的文字特色取代原著的特色，造成若干若肯留意便原可避免的损失。

风格翻译的必要性还有一项根据：风格学早已成为一个专门学科，而它所考察的显然不能止于母语著作。以外译汉而论，许多世界名著和名家的风格早已通过各种译本而相当地为广大读者所认识，成为学术界研究讨论、学者和作家参考借鉴的对象。这说明风格的可译性早已由实践证明，所需的不过是从理论上做出解释；同时也说明风格的介绍是文化交流的一项内容，因而也是翻译的任务。

三、困难

风格难译。风格的可译性之所以长期有争论，一方面诚然是由于传统上有时把一些名诗名著的风格说得神乎其神，"神来之笔"、"妙手偶得"等，给风格涂上了一层神秘的色调，令人肃然起敬乃至望而生畏——你这个寻常的翻译者居然自以为也有作者的丹青妙手、也能够神来而偶得之么？另一方面，有些原著的风格确实难以捕捉。而其所以难，则是由于客观上两种语言、两种文化之间横亘着一道天然的鸿沟。这其间的种种问题非笔者和本文所能遍及，因此只就较受注意的两个方面举两个例子加以探讨。一是诗的格律，二是双关语。

（1）格律 诗人入于格律之中而优游自得，不仅没有束手束脚，反而从中取得更大的自由、更为得心应手地抒情表意。翻译时不顾格律，所译便不成其为诗，而要顾及格律便立即遇见一重天然的障碍：原诗格律的诸多内容——字数、行数、平仄或轻重音等所形成的节奏以及韵律，无不植根于母语之中，以母语为基础、为根据，托身形象以出，与形象浑然一体。而母语虽然给诗人提出了种种限制，同时却也提供了突破乃至利用这些限制的条件。译者用的是另一种语言，它虽然也具有形成自己的格律的种种条件，却与出发语言具备的条件南辕北辙，未必恰好得以假借。

限于能力且图方便，下面姑且以两种方式试译近代英国诗人豪斯曼（A. E. Housman，1859—1936）的一首诗为例——

Could man be drunk for ever
With liquor, love, or fights,
Lief should I rouse at morning

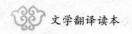

And Lief lie down of nights.

But men at whiles are sober
And think by fits and starts,
And if they think, they fasten
Their hands upon their hearts. ①

译文一:

> 如果人真能够永远酩酊
> 于酒、于爱情、或于战争,
> 每天早晨我都将怡然起身,
> 每天夜晚都怡然就寝。
>
> 但人啊总不免有几时清醒,
> 一阵阵一阵阵蓦地思忖;
> 而一思忖,他们便赶紧
> 把双手掩住自己的心。

译文二:

> 如果酒、或爱情、或战争
> 真令人能永远沉醉,
> 每早晨我都将怡然起身,
> 每夜晚又怡然入睡。
>
> 但人啊总不免有几时清醒,
> 一阵阵一阵阵蓦地思量;
> 而一思量,他们便赶紧
> 把双手掩在心上。

两条假定:姑且假定二者都大致不失原旨,此处只论韵律而且译文多少算得上合辙押韵,那就也许可以说它们得失互见。原诗双行一韵,两节所押者不同。译文一一韵到底,不如译文二之跟着原诗换韵以反映诗意的转折;这就比较符合原诗在韵律上的具体安排:不仅追求音乐性,而且追求以韵表情的特色。但另一方面,末行谓以手掩心,原是为了不思量、停止思量,以按捺住由于蓦地思量而猛然迸发出来的对人生的绝大苦闷,其形象有如受创者用手紧紧捂住喷血的伤口而终于无济于事。原诗以 heart 一词结尾,用它押韵,就突出了这个词也突出了这个形象(痛苦的心和以手掩心),突出了这种感情,从而突出了人生的不堪思量这个主题。译文一在末行以"心"成韵,复现了这一修辞特色。译文二的末行为了和"思量"押韵,在"心"字后边加了个"上"字。而"心上"所指其实是心的位置,不是心的本身,立体的形象于是成为平面图,力量

---

① A. E. Housman: *Selected Verses*; Verse 9, "Last Poems".

于是顿减；心不再是韵脚所落之处，因而不再重点突出。虽然，从用词看，"思忖"却不如"思量"。得失相权，以哪一种译法较为适宜呢？言语上的这种顾此失彼，显然是由于语言的差异所致。

再如拜伦的这两行——

> Maid of Athens，ere we part，
> Give，oh，give me back my heart！

其中 part 和 heart 两词，一个是典型场合：离别；一个是典型形象：因离别而痛苦的心。原诗用它们押韵，突出了重点，抒情叙事，情景交融，内容和形式达到高度统一。因此，如果译为——

> 雅典的姑娘，我们离别之前，
> 请，啊，请把我的心儿交还！

意思是出来了，也押上了韵，抒情色调却远不如原句浓烈，因为丢失了原来的修辞特色。但译文要照原文原样来押韵恐怕是办不到的。part 和 heart 之能成韵，一方面固然是诗人善于驾驭语言，另一方面也是英语本身提供的条件，即二者都以[aːt]为韵母；而这一条我以为尤其重要。诗人固然是"妙手偶得之"，但首先还是得助于"文章本天成"吧。只因为有这个先天性的条件，诗人才有可能在离愁别意、思绪万千之际甚至不假思索脱口而出，但汉语却没有这个条件。"离别"不与"心"同韵，一些同义词如分离、分别、分手……也都不成，唯有某些唱词中听见过的"离分"似属例外。但它本身便违背构词习惯，且因此种违背规范的构词法之常见于诸如此类的俗文学而俗气逼人，用来翻译拜伦，岂非不伦不类？

（2）双关语　修辞格中的双关语，运用并不为广，但或则妙趣横生，或则寓意深远，有时用以点明典型人物或环境的特征，作用尤其重要，例如甄贾宝玉。这种表达方式音义双关，译音则失义，译意则不仅失音，尤其把作者不过是暗示的意思说破，便索然无味。虽不能因此说凡属语带双关便绝对妙处不传，大多数双关语之毕竟不可译也是大家都熟悉的。遇见这种情况，便只能求助于注解。但修辞方式既未能保存下来，风格便受损伤。显然，双关语之译不出纵属翻译的缺欠，根源既然在于语言的性质，就算不得翻译的过失。

一方面，各种语言中虽然都有一词多义或同音词的现象，在具体的上下文中一词只能以一音一形表示一义一性，因此才不致引起误解，语言才有其社会性，才能尽其社会的功能。另一方面，就总体来说，两种语言中表达同一义的词的音（形）必然不同，否则便无所谓两种语言，也就无所用于翻译。这两条应当说是语言的根本性质或规律。翻译之设，以第二条为其必要性的根据，而以头一条为其可能性的范围。实践证明，翻译应当做到、也只能做到的是或则译义（绝大多数情况），即以归宿语言中含义相同的词语取代原文中相应的词语，从而表达同一个意思；或则译音（少数情况），即以同音词取代原文中相应的词，从而表达同一个（其实不过是大致相似的）音，例如地名或姓氏。个别还有译形的，例如把"工字钢"与"I-Steel"互译。译音时难以存义，译义时难以顾音。音义或两义双全，殆不可能。双关语实际上是把一个词当做两个词来用，所根据的是出发语言中某些一词两义（严格说是两个词）或两词同音现象，而且有赖于在上下文中做出相应的安排。归宿语言既然是用不同的音表达这两种不同的意思，它的一词多义和两词同音便极不易与出发语言相重合。因此，翻译中音义二者得兼或两义得兼，这种情况即使有也是巧合，可以得之于偶然，无法求之于经常。于是往往只得加注。所以说这译不出是由于两种语言之间的差异、由于语言本身的性质，势有必至。

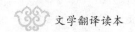

诗之难译或竟不可译,部分原因与此相同,译意的同时必须押韵,即兼顾某种程度的译音,而有关的词在归宿语言中未必恰好同韵,于是顾此失彼。这同样是由语言本身的性质所规定的。

窃以为"表达方式"一语,有两种不同的含义:同一个意思,不同的语言分别用自己的词汇和句型来表达,我谓之"因语言而异的表达方式";而同一语言的不同的人则可能就此同一语言选择不同的词汇和句型来表达,我谓之"因言语而异的表达方式"①。二者互为区别,同时又有不能分割的联系:言语以语言为根据,不能不受到语言的制约。译文和原文立足于不同的语言,当然不可能无所遗漏地复现原文言语的巧妙之处,这不仅不能责备翻译,而且从总体上看也不至于完全掩住原文的风格。例如 Uriah Heep 只得音译为"尤利亚·希泼",而人们仍然能从《大卫·科波菲尔》或《块肉余生述》中窥见狄更斯的风貌。

四、可能与必然

具体分析风格的构成因素,是为了提出风格可译性的理论基础。如果这些构成因素大体可译或基本可译,风格的翻译便有了根据。

由于上面举出的诸如韵律和双关语之难译或竟不可译,风格的翻译确实受到限制。但局部毕竟不是全局。即使仅就修辞来说,事实证明,不可译者终归是少数,绝大多数修辞手段,例如比喻、借代、设问、排比等的运用,各种语言之间还是共通的,因而也就可译。而就构成风格的其余因素来说,似都不难翻译,夸张一点,也许可说是不译自出。因为思想、主题、题材、情节、结构早由作者安排停妥,拆成零件搬入异国重新安装,不至于走样。尽管译文的语言运用时有不足之处,因此影响到表现手法和形象铸造,毕竟无损于全局。这里的关键是力求忠实,不要自作主张另起炉灶,而要从思想感情到行文用语步步紧跟原文。抓住了这一点,则缀词成句,积段成章,全书既出,主题思想、情节结构等便都不劳经营而自成,风格便也在其中。

这样看来,关于风格的翻译也许应作另一种提法:不是能否翻译出来,而是会否都翻译不出来。换句话说,原著的风格一定会透过两种语言、两种文化之间的隔阂,在相当的程度上顽强地复现于译文之中。

五、关键在于忠实

必须重复:风格的翻译有一个根本条件,就是忠实;首先要忠实于原著的或正确或错误或兼而有之的思想内容(丢了这一条,例如"宁顺而不信",翻译便成撒谎,其他无从也不必谈起),同时必须尽量贴近原文的因言语而异的表达方式而又不损害归宿语言的规范。这就涉及直译或意译视情况择善而从的问题,涉及把握住一词一句的修辞方式、捕捉原文特色的问题。

词汇的选择,一般讨论甚多,例子也多,不去多说。此处仅就一句之中如何选择语序的安排试举一例——

At some dramatic moment in the story, the terrible secret becomes known and

---

① 参见冯世则:《意译、直译、逐字译》,《翻译匠语》,文汇出版社 2005 年版。

a reputation is ruined. The reader's hair stands on end when he reads in the final pages of the novel that the heroine, a dear old lady who had always been so kind to everybody, had, in her youth, poisoned every one of her five husbands("A skeleton in the cupboard"). ①

（译文一）：……读者在小说的最后几页念到书中的女主角、一位和蔼的老太太，待人一向那么慈祥，年轻时却曾接二连三毒死了她的五位丈夫，这时不禁毛发倒竖。

（译文二）：……书中的女主角、一位和蔼的老太太，待人一向那么慈祥，年轻时却曾接二连三毒死了她的五位丈夫；读者在小说的最后几页念到这个情节，不禁毛发倒竖。

（译文三）：……读者念到小说的最后几页，不禁毛发倒竖；原来书中的女主角、一位和蔼可亲的老太太，待人一向那么慈祥，年轻时竟曾接二连三毒死了她的五位丈夫。

三种译法都用同样的词汇表达同样的意思，而效果不一，原因在于语序即句型结构。首先是一不如二；一中的"毛发倒竖"及其主语"读者"之间插进 50 多个字，文气不接。其次则一和二又都不如三，因为它们都颠倒了原文的先果后因的语序，破坏了它特有的表达方式。

叙事先果后因，在汉语也是常见的文章作法，并无何出奇之处。英语则状语和定语从句或经常后置或永远后置，因语言而异的这种表达方式，为因言语而异的表达方式提供了方便条件，此种句法语序于是较汉语为多。例如这一句：She was too excited to do any housework that morning, for in the evening she would be going to a fancy dress party with her husband ("It's only me")②. 叙事顺序与事发过程相反，有两个优点。其一，它恰恰符合人们感知事物的客观过程：先是注意到某种现象，感兴趣——主妇无心家务；这才寻根究底，探索原因——原来是一心挂念着晚间的化装舞会。其二，它有助于抓住读者的好奇心理，增加文字的吸引力。前一例原句所取，也属于这种笔法；先讲"骇人听闻的秘密"一经泄露，读者"毛发倒竖"，最后才讲秘密如何；中间插以老太太的"和蔼"与"慈祥"，故作跌宕。译文三之强于前两者，便在于它在汉语规范之内复现原文的因言语而异的表达方式，而没有煞风景地把作者有意留作结尾的惊人之笔挪到前边，抢先揭穿了谜底。当然，文章这样写是否当真惊人，又当别论。

忠实的一面是不使好的原文减色，另一面则是也不给原来不怎么高明的原文润色——

The last tax I shall mention is the poll-tax. Every male Christian, from birth to death, must pay the poll-tax for exemption from the military conscription. It amounts to thirty piastres a head, and every male Christian is bound to pay it, from the new-born babe to decrepit beggar. It is supposed to be a fine paid for exemption from military service... ③

---

① 引自 *New Concept English*。20 世纪 70 年代末期"复课闹革命"，大学英语均从 ABCD 起步，黑龙江大学英语系曾以此书为精读课教本，翻译课为节约时间且配合乃至补充精读课，因势利导，练习作业就中取材。下面的汉译例句多半取自学生的翻译而加整理，以免枝蔓。于今观之，不免浅显。虽然，此所谓时代的烙印，铅华固不必也难以尽洗者也。

② 同上。

③ 引自 Stanley G. Evans: *A Short History of Bulgaria*, p. 96。汉译《保加利亚简史》，有黑龙江人民出版社 20 世纪 90 年代出的版本。

The last tax I shall mention is the poll-tax，which amounts to thirty piastres a head，and which，supposedly a fine for exemption from military service；every male Christian，from the new-born babe to the decrepit beggar，is bound to pay ...

前一段引文是新闻报道,转引自《保加利亚简史》英文版,后一段是笔者对前一段的缩写,以资说明问题。缩写没有漏掉前者的任何内容,字数却减少了三分之一。两段英文分别译成汉语,差别也相仿佛,原文的啰嗦和重复于此可见。但既称为翻译而不是译述、节译或改作,便不可用后者的译文去顶替前者的译文,只能听其自然,原文的哕嗦和重复于是复现于译文之中,无可避免。作者未必不识得简洁为风格的生命,但他是在引用当年的新闻报道,借以见证保加利亚人民当年遭到的奥斯曼帝国的苛政,而新闻报道的风格向来如此。由此可见,但凡译文忠实,则可取与不甚可取的文风都是会复现出来的;但凡忠实,则风格的翻译便不仅可能,而且总体上属于必然。

一本书的风格,前后大体一致。但由于在书中的不同部分题材会有变化,作者的思想感情会有起伏,风格也会发生起伏变化。例如历史著作虽以不动声色的平铺直叙为常规或主调,历史学者却毕竟也有自己的喜怒爱憎;于是每逢国家兴亡、民族盛衰、英雄人物有所作为或因病死去之际,作者文以情生,各种积极的修辞方式便会纷至沓来,文风也就为之一变。再一个例子:学术著作的序言似有一种通常的格式,即前一部分是学术性的论述,内容有一定深度,行文斐然成章;后一部分则往往像记账,因为需要对给予作者种种帮助的前辈学者、同事、或学术机构一一致谢。无论作者如何极力腾挪变化,这后一部分总是无法跳出此种格式,风格于是随之而变,前后迥然不同。同一本书同一篇文章中风格的这种变化,在译文中同样表现得清清楚楚,是风格必能译出的一种旁证,尽管由于主客观条件的限制,译起来多半要打折扣。

六、外国味：译文风格的共性

文章也有国籍:是创作或是译著、是译自东洋或西洋,往往一望可知。使译著迥然区别于创作的这种特色,我想称之为外国味。

泄露文字的客籍的,首先自然是外国特有的人、地、文物、制度等的名称。但这些只是皮相的符号,未必总靠得住:中国人,例如驻外记者写报道文章,也会用到的。外国味之由来,重要的根源是外国的文化传统——

They（the dolphins）are constantly after the turtles，the Ferdinands of marine life，who peacefully submit to all sorts of indignities（Window in the Sea）[1].
　　它们(海豚)总是不断捉弄海龟,而海洋生物中的这种裴迪南式的角色,也总是老老实实地忍受种种有损尊严的戏谑。

裴迪南是莎士比亚戏剧《暴风雨》中一个人物、那波利王的儿子,这句译文的外国味主要便来自这个外国典故。如是中国人写作,外国典故虽不能说绝不会用,却往往避开,因为中国读者不

---

　　[1] 引自 *New Concept English*。20 世纪 70 年代末期"复课闹革命",大学英语均从 ABCD 起步,黑龙江大学英语系曾以此书为精读课教本,翻译课为节约时间且配合乃至补充精读课,因势利导,练习作业就中取材。下面的汉译例句多半取自学生的翻译而加整理,以免枝蔓。于今观之,不免浅显。虽然,此所谓时代的烙印,铅华固不必以尽洗者也。

熟悉,掉这样的书袋子吃力不讨好。在翻译,这也属于"不易懂"之列,但却顾不得,只好加注,尽管并不能因此掩盖其外国味。有时,文中一个外国名字也没有,外国味还是跃然纸上——

> Such birds (ducks, pigeons and swallows) do us good, though we no longer take omens from their flight on this side and that, and even the most superstitious villagers no longer take off their hats to the magpie and wish it good morning (A Countryman's Creed)[1].

> 这些鸟儿(鸭子、鸽子、燕子)叫人心情愉快,虽然我们不再把它们在这边或那边飞当做某种兆头,而且即令是最迷信的乡下人,也不会向喜鹊脱帽致敬、祝它早安了。

"喜上梅梢"的刺绣和"今日里喜鹊闹门墙"的唱词,说明中国人民也曾同样苦难深重,因此巴不得从毫不相干的事情中找到一点儿吉祥的兆头自我安慰,也算"人民的鸦片"吧?但"向喜鹊脱帽致敬、祝它早安"却是地地道道的外国做法。而且,尾上以"而且"引起的状语从句后置,也原是外国的句法,虽然如今已随处可见、不再显得那么外国味十足了。

可见外国味并不限于行文用语,深一层的根源在于译文中反映的外国生活方式和外国文化。

从表达方式看,情况也是如此。例如文艺创作中的对话,中国的传统方式是先交代谁讲话,再交代他讲了什么。西方的记述顺序有时却恰好相反。照此翻译,便显出了外国味,曾引起非议;引入创作之中,尤其曾引起更多的非议——例如对鲁迅——尽管这种办法其实是可取的,实际上也已为绝大多数创作所取:让读者先闻其言、再见其人,符合人们感知的过程而且生动。但就翻译而论,要点不在于这种记叙顺序有或没有某种优点,而在于它不是因语言而异的表达方式、不属于应在翻译过程中以归宿语言特有的表达方式加以替换的范围;它属于因言语而异的表达方式,恰恰是"能直译时便应直译"之处。有时由于两种语言之间的差距而未能完全保存,反而遗憾。

说到头来,既称为翻译,可知原是外国人在讲外国事,至少是外国人在讲中国事;内容是外国人的思想行为,说法是外国人的习惯说法,虽然和中国的有若干共通,却总有自己的特色。外国味蕴藏其中,表现为各自的民族风格。翻译只要忠实,便不可能全然漏掉。

因此说外国味是译文风格的共性,不仅正常,而且正当:中国人说话作文有中国作风、中国气派,为中国人所喜闻乐见,外国人说话作文,岂不也当如是?风格的翻译之可能与必然,于此又得一个佐证。

风格的翻译不但必要和可能,甚至必然,但却不免局限。为之奈何?我以为不必失望。翻译力求忠实,是译者主观上必须信守的译德;但要求绝对的等值,客观上却不可能做到。想想几于无日或无的人际交流本身吧:思想反映现实而语言表达思想,都应当实事求是。但大千世界、万事万物,如何能概无遗漏?"Only bores want to express everything, but even bores find it impossible to express everything."[2]而我们并不因此认为语言无用,更不能极而言之,认为人们根本无法互相了解。风格翻译的局限乃至翻译本身的局限无非如此。翻译工作者知其艰难,唯有努力而已。

---

① 同上。

② O. Jespersen: *Essentbls of English Grammar*, p. 19:"唯啰嗦精才想事事说周全,但即使啰嗦精也会发现无法事事说周全。"

选文二　从现代文体学看文学风格与翻译

张英进

导　言

本文选自《外国语》,1986 年第 1 期。

选文开篇即借助李白的飘逸雄放,杜甫的沉郁顿挫,韩愈的雄肆艰险,白居易的明白晓畅,苏轼清旷放逸,秦观婉委清丽,辛弃疾雄健清壮,姜白石清淡雅洁等具体、可感的风格特质,为下文利用现代文体学展开文学风格翻译剖析定下可持续探讨的基调。文学风格的多样性和独特性,使其成为翻译无法回避的一个重大美学问题。翻译首先应该通过客观的分析这个科学手段,把握作品的各种风格特征,然后运用综合的创造这个艺术手段,在译作中再现原作风格,使其具有同等的艺术感染力。根据语言学家 Ullmann 的观点,选文从语音、词法和词义三个方面展开对风格翻译的具体研究。由韵的作用、音的象征及书面表达开始,推及句式长短、词序变化、变异与重复在翻译中的具体处理方式,进而分析因语域混淆、陈词滥调和古词古语等造成的原作风格变化。例证丰富,层层推演,充分揭示了现代文体学视域中的文学风格与翻译的关系,为风格翻译研究提供了新方法。

文学风格的实在性与可感性

文学风格一词焕耀着奇光异彩,令人仰羡、令人神往。西方一位美学史家对风格瑰丽动人而又迷离恍惚的特征作了贴切的比拟:风格有如彩虹,五彩缤纷、虚幻缥缈,当你想探求其奥秘前往觅寻时,一切光色便消失得无影无踪。然而,觅寻不见彩虹并不证明彩虹的子虚乌有,相反,这只能证明你对彩虹独特的存在方式认识不足(McMullen:123)。

与彩虹一样,风格也有其独特的存在方式。它是实在的,因而是可感的。评唐诗必提李白飘逸雄放,杜甫沉郁顿挫,韩愈雄肆艰险,白居易明白晓畅,而论宋词须辨苏轼清旷放逸,秦观婉委清丽,辛弃疾雄健清壮,姜白石清淡雅洁……(严迪昌:《文学风格漫说》)。这些表面上不可捉摸的抽象概括原本来自诗人实实在在的具体感受。以姜白石为例,代表他精神本质的最隐秘、最深沉的心声,往往在凝神握管的刹那间有意无意地流露出来——

　　　　"数峰清苦,商略黄昏雨",

　　　　"二十四桥仍在,波心荡,冷月无声",

　　　　"千树压西湖寒碧",

　　　　"嫣然摇动,冷香飞上诗句……"

诗人所疾爱的这些字眼("清"、"苦"、"寒"、"冷"),简直是他空灵诗境的评语,决定了他清雅诗风的基调(梁宗岱:《诗与真、诗与真二集》)。

应该承认,揭开变幻莫测的迷雾,文学风格即是具体可感的,是可以从语言分析入手而感知的。现代文体学(modern stylistics)的发展为风格的感知提供了良好的条件,因为文体学研究的正是语言形式与文学功能之间的关系(Leech & Short:4)。个性语言(idiolect)的分析,如上所述,颇能揭示一位作家的风格特征。姜白石的"清雅"风格证实了这一点,苏轼评孟郊、贾岛两人风格的"郊寒岛瘦"也可以证实这一点。举外国文学家为例,美国的詹姆斯以其曼衍的长句、繁芜的修饰和隐晦的措辞为风格的外部特征,而这些复沓、重叠的词语结构曲折地反映出他的内心深处所蕴藉的深邃、复杂的思绪,以及他对人类含浑微妙的动机的意识。与他形成强烈对照的是海明威的清新、简洁、洗练的风格,句短词精,萧散简远,意在笔墨之外;而海明威简约、含蓄的风格又是受他小说的题材和人物的塑造所制约的。从这个意义上说,风格即人,风格是作品内容与形式的有机统一。

文学风格的独特性与其翻译的必要性

风格的重要性决定了文学翻译必须尽可能再现原作的风格,使译作的读者感受到的是作者其人,而不是译者其人。李白的飘逸不同于杜甫的沉郁,詹姆斯的繁芜不同于海明威的简练。文学风格既有多样性,亦有独特性,翻译无法回避这个重大的美学问题。

文学是语言的艺术,文学翻译自然应该、也只能是语言的艺术。如何从语言学角度探讨文学风格与翻译这个美学问题呢?现代文体学在此架设了沟通文学和语言学之间的桥梁。近几十年来,作为语言学一个分支的文体学已广泛应用于文学作品的分析与评论(Chapman:1-4)。诚然,美学的风格概念有别于语言学的风格概念:美学强调从作家的生活经历、心理功能、艺术修养、道德标准等方面入手,在时代、民族、阶级的高度上整体把握风格(吴功正:《文学风格七讲》),语言学注重作品的客观剖析,从作家的选词造句、音韵节奏、篇章结构等方面具体探求风格的主要特征。语言学家一致认为,选择是风格的基本概念(Turner:21)。但是,某一特定的词句、意象、乃至题材与主题的选择,最终都与作家的主观因素和社会的客观因素的制约有关。孟郊在《苦寒吟》"天色寒青苍,北风叫枯桑……调苦竟何言,冻吟成此章"一诗中创造的凄寒苦涩的基调与清淡萧瑟的意象,一方面凝练地状写了诗人穷愁失意的生活际遇,另一方面典型地反映出那个时代特定的知识阶层的情思。诗人所进行的选择(所谓"两句三年得,一吟双泪流"),其效果远远超越了语言的界限。不难看出,语言学家的选择概念与美学家的风格概念是有内在联系的,虽然二者有微观与宏观的明显差别。

文学翻译中也有一个重要的选择过程。从理论上说,翻译的过程既是分析的过程,又是综合的过程,既是科学的过程,又是艺术的过程(库勒拉:《美学原理》)。翻译首先应该通过客观的分析这个科学手段,把握作品的各种风格特征,然后运用综合的创造这个艺术手段,在译作中再现原作风格,使其具有同等的艺术感染力。这里有一个部分与整体的关系问题:部分为整体服务,整体由部分组成。拘泥部分而失去整体是不容许的,但抛弃部分而另求一个整体亦是不可取的。传统的诗论,如:"神韵说"重视作品的整体印象,行之于翻译易于凭译者的主观印象在译入语中进行"再创造",其极端结果可能产生一个"新的表现品",如美学家克罗齐所言,或一个"新的、但属派生的作品",如语言学家 Robins 所称。① 现代文体学分析构成整体的各种风格因素,用之于翻译则应在译入语中选择具有同等功能的风格手段,使译文与原文在整体效果上一致或趋于一致。显然,翻译的选择过程不是一个简单的对比过程,而是一个创造性的过程。正因为是艺术的创造,忠实再现原作风格的翻译常常成为富于生命力的优秀作品,在译入语国家中深受读者与批评界的喜爱。②

现代文体学与翻译研究

如何从现代文体学角度看待文学翻译中的选择与风格的相互关系呢? 不同的选择固然表达不同的情思,形成不同的风格,但与风格密切相关的不同情境(context or situation)和不同题材或文学种类(literary genre)又会直接影响风格因素的选择。根据语言学家 Ullmann 的观点,风格的研究可以从语音、词法和词义三个方面进行(Turner:30)。具体运用于文学作品的分析,语音方面则可以探讨诗的韵律节奏,音的象征意义,以及有关的书面表达方法;句法方面可以剖析句式的长短,词序的意义,和句法的变异与重复,而词义方面可以研究语域混淆,陈词滥调,及古词古语的联想意义。文学作品是一个有机的整体,风格因素的分析研究绝不是为了拆散这个有机体,而是为了更好地理解作品的风格内涵。正确的理解是翻译的必要前提,翻译中每个风格因素的选择必须顾及作品的整体效果。下面就分三个方面浅析文学风格及其在翻译过程中的再现。

语音方面:韵的作用、音的象征及书面表达

韵无疑是诗的一个主要风格因素:诗人可以根据不同情况选择是否用韵,用什么音的韵(Turner:65-66)。沈德潜在《说诗晬语》中强调:"诗中韵脚,如大厦之有柱石。此处不牢,倾折立见。"韵对律诗的重要性由此可见一斑。韵的重要性不仅在于它加强了语言旋宕而进的运动,使读者(或听众)产生欲知下文的期待心理,而且还在于它增强了诗的内在联系,一环紧套一环,如音乐主题的反复丰富了诗的艺术表现力。鉴于此因,韵这个风格要素应该在翻译中得以再现,尤其当原诗是以音乐性为其主要特征时。法国象征派诗人魏尔伦有一首抒情小诗"Il pleut doucement sur la ville",这首诗以"pleut","pleure"("下雨"、"哭泣")和"coeur","s'écoeure"("心"、"伤心")以及"langueur"("疲困")等词中的/oe:/音的尾韵、腹韵往复回环,造成一种莫可名状的悲哀氛围,使诗具有强烈的艺术感染力。这首诗的许多译者注意到魏诗的这个风格特征,在各自的翻译中较理想地再现了原作的艺术魅力。③

要再现诗的音乐性,不能不考虑音的象征意义。美国诗人爱伦·坡认为,人类语言中最能表现悲哀心情的是"o"音,于是在他"The Raven"一诗中大量使用包含这个音的词。反映到翻

---

① Robins:"... in those cases in which the translation is said to be better work than the original ... one is dealing with a new, though derived, work, not just a translation".

② 举例说,格雷戈里·拉巴萨翻译的《百年孤独》1970 年成为美国畅销书。原书作者马奎茨系哥伦比亚诺贝尔文学奖获得者,他对拉巴萨的英译评价极高。

③ 魏尔伦这首诗的成功译者及译文有:闻家驷与葛雷(载《国外文学》1983 年第 4 期),范希衡(载《法国近代名家诗选》237-238 页),飞白(载《翻译通讯》1984 年第 2 期),以及英译 Ernest Dowson(*An Anthology of World Poetry*, ed. by M. V. Doren, p. 783)

译,音韵的联想意义也应该考虑。江枫译雪莱的《悲歌》时就有意识地采用汉语的"怀来"韵,以模仿原诗"No more,oh,never more!"中唤起凄戚之感的哦哦叹息——

> 你青春的绚丽何时再来,
> 不再,哦,永远不再!

凄楚的惋惜之情跃然纸上,理想地再现了悲怆的气氛。在类似例子中,"音"已不仅仅是"意"的一种回声(如蒲柏所谓"The sound must seem an echo to the sense"),而简直是"意义"的具体表现(Leech & Short:233-236)。

按语言学家分析,不同的辅音或元音具有不同的联想意义(associative effect)。以英语为例,l音和s音较为轻柔舒缓,德拉玛尔诗句"Silence and sleep like fields of amaranth lie"婉转徘徊,余音缭绕,给人一种恬静而虚幻的感觉。相反,爆破音p,t和k则迅猛强烈,哈姆雷特对克劳底斯的严厉谴责激昂排宕,力重千钧——

> A cutpurse of the empire and the rule,
> That from a shelf the precious diadem stole,
> And put it in his pocket.

字里行间充溢着无可抑制的愤怒(Chapman:38-39)。中国文学中亦不乏此例。袁可嘉的《沉钟》以洪亮的"中东"韵一押到底,全诗音节嘹亮,音调铿锵,音域宽广:"让我沉默于时空,/ 如古寺锈绿的洪钟,/ 负驮三千载沉重,/ 听窗外风雨匆匆。刀把波澜掷给大海,/ 把无限还诸苍穹……",诗风刚健遒劲,气度非凡。艾青的《祝酒》诗效果别致,清如朔雪,明若春日:"杯子和杯子,/轻轻地相碰,/ 发出轻轻的声音,/ '亲亲'、'亲亲'、'亲亲'。你的心,我的心,/ 也轻轻地相碰……",富于深蕴淡出的情味。"亲亲"在意大利语中意为"干杯",谐以汉语的"轻轻"、"心"饶有一番情趣。英译以 clink 译"轻轻"元音相同,悦耳动听,诚属匠心独运之举——

> One glass and another glass
> Are clinking together,
> Making a "clink-clink" sound,
> "Chin-chin", "chin-chin", "chin-chin".
> (trans. by Eugene Chen Eo yang)

然而,艾青诗中的"亲亲"原是一语双关,既表达"干杯",又暗示"亲吻"与"爱情",英译 clink 忍痛割爱,只取词的象声(onomatopoeia),而其余联想,便不得不求诸于注解说明了。

翻译中,不单谐音双关(pun)难译,小说人物的不标准发音也很难处理。在小说《大卫·科波菲尔》中,狄更斯为表现辟果提见识鲜寡、口齿木讷,让她将 exactly 说成 azackly。董秋斯的译文为反映辟果提的这个特点,师心独见,选择了"十风"一词,借与"十分"相对,颇为精彩。但是,汉语毕竟是象形文字,要表现其他语言中发音的细微变化有时是几乎不可能的。英译托尔斯泰的《复活》有这么一段话:

> Kitaeva spoke with a strong German accent:
> "Zee young voman is etucated and elecant. She vas prought up in a coot family
> and can reat French … … A fery coot girl."

英译者运用表音的书写手段来再现说话者的德语口音,可谓煞费苦心。仔细分析一下,其实上述英译也不是绝对正确的标音,girl 没有拼写成 kirl,原因是译文首先必须能够理解,然后才能产生修辞效果。至于汉语,对一连串的语音差别实在束手无策。这种不标准发音的不可译性源于两种语言的不同特点。幸好,文学作品中这类描述尚不多,倘有亦属风格的次要部分(Leech & Short:131);所以,翻译时个别地方的缺漏并不影响整体风格。

句法方面:句式长短、词序变化、变异与重复

句法的变化是作品很重要的风格特征。海明威简洁明快的短句符合他笔下"硬汉"的性格,直截了当,充满活力;詹姆斯锋款精密的长句刻画出人物错综细腻的心理活动,缠绵悱恻,难以尽言。短句给文章以力量、以运动,长句给文章以庄严、以凝重。翻译应该注意这两种句式带来的不同风格特征。

陶渊明的《桃花源记》"文体省净",质朴自然:"……缘溪行,忘路之远近。忽逢桃花林。夹岸数百步,中无杂树,芳草鲜美,落英缤纷。渔人甚异之。"John Turner 的英译将整段纳入一个长句,叠床架屋,层次繁多,使读者如入迷宫,效果欠佳。方重先生选择了短句句式,译文迂缓中见顿挫,潇洒中见自然,很能传达原作的风格:"... One day he rowed up a stream, and soon forgot how far he had gone. All of a sudden he came upon a peach grove... "

词序(word order),有如句式,也是风格研究中值得重视的问题。词序的不同不仅带来意义上的不同,也会带来风格色彩上的不同。杜甫常欲以颜色字置于句首,如"红入桃花嫩,青归柳叶新",又如"绿垂风折笋,红绽雨肥梅"。色彩位于句首,既鲜艳夺目,引人去读下文,又真实可信,符合认识过程:"青惜峰峦过,黄知橘柚来",先见黄色而后知是橘柚。倘调回词序,作"峰峦惜青过,橘柚知黄来",则语弱气馁,情味不足(周振甫:《诗词例话》)。

词序,除着重状物绘景之外,还可以细致入微地描述人物心理。在莎士比亚笔下,奥菲妮亚这样悲怆地哀叹哈姆雷特的精神失常——

> O what a noble mind is here o'erthrown!
> The courtier's, soldier's, scholar's, eye, tongue, sword.

这里,词序上的倒置(eye, tongue, sword 三个词的顺序与其各自的所有者 courtier, soldier, scholar 的顺序不相配对),加上句法上的变异(所有格名词与所有物名词被截然分隔于两地),令人信服地揭示出奥菲妮亚在极度的痛苦中已失去常规语言的逻辑性。这惟妙惟肖的传神之笔理应在译文中保存下来。但是,有一种中译本将莎翁有意的句法变异做了修正,译成"好一个高贵人品就这样完了呀! / 亲臣,才子,军人,那眼神,那舌锋,那剑芒"。奥菲妮亚难以形容的凄楚哀叹变成了相当理智的人物评判,风格有别于原作。另一种中译本力求保持原词序,"哦,这里毁掉了一个多么高贵的心胸! / 重臣的,军人的,学者的,眼神,辞令与武艺",音情顿挫,风格接近原作。这个例子表明,词序的作用是不可低估的。所谓"文章千古事,得失寸心知",文章的寸心得失,有待译者的潜心研读,悉心品味,细心迻译。

句法上的含混多义,即是对译者才智的一大挑战。杜甫诗曰:"不薄今人爱古人,清词丽句必为邻。"究竟是"不薄今人,但爱古人"呢? 或是"既不薄今人而又爱古人"? 抑或是"不薄今人之爱古人的清词丽句"? "诗无达诂",不同的理解可以产生不同的译文。译者总有其所好,读者亦不妨择其所好。但是,为了不影响原作含蓄的风格,翻译最好应保持原句的多解之义,让

读者再三吟咏而有余味。李商隐《锦瑟》诗句"沧海月明珠有泪,蓝田日暖玉生烟",意蕴深奥,颇难断句,翁显良先生避实就虚,以隐对隐,译成:

> Dark green sea, tears, pearls, moonlight streaming;
> Sunny blue jade field, warm haze shimmering.

这种没有结构词的"脱节译法"[①],其本身即是一种句法的变异。

诚然,对语言常规的变异(deviation from the norm),是文学风格的主要特征,也是分析风格的重要途径(Leech:41-51;Leech & Short:43-51)。一句"翠干危栈竹,红腻小湖莲",豁然醒目,情趣盎然,一词 a grief ago,语出不凡,耐人寻味。然而,变异之外,语言本身的规则性已为作者提供了大量的风格手段。平行结构(parallelism)和反复强调(repetition)在文学作品中最为常见(Leech:62-82),如诗歌的叠字对仗,又如散文的遣词造句。苏轼词中有"多情多感仍多病,多景楼中",又有"莫道狂夫不解狂,狂夫老更狂"。艾略特的《普鲁弗洛克情歌》一诗有——

> The yellow fog that rubs its back upon the window-panes,
> The yellow smoke that rubs its muzzle on the window-panes.

词语的重复与句子的对仗渲染了黄昏懒洋洋的病恹气氛。查良铮的译文:"黄色的雾在窗玻璃上擦着它的背,/黄色的烟在窗玻璃上擦着它的嘴。"字句相对,神形皆备。鲁迅的散文《秋夜》亦有许多重复之例:开篇首句的"一株是枣树,还有一株也是枣树"便敲定全文冷峻幽邃的基调;接着用清淡的冷色烘托出"奇怪而高"的夜空,"然而现在却非常之蓝,闪闪地映着几十个星星的眼,冷眼",给人以突兀的强烈一击。英译 For the moment, though, it is singularly blue; and its scores of starry eyes are blinking coldly 自然不错,但后半句失去原作磊落清壮的韵味,近乎平淡的交代。若仿造原文句式,结尾处突然顿住,重复"冷眼":... and blinking there are its scores of starry eyes, cold eyes,作者压抑的情感便可力透纸背,引起读者的共鸣。

中国律诗的精华在对仗,英译能不能再现这个风格特征?杜甫《登高》诗:"无边落木萧萧下,不尽长江滚滚来",气势磅礴——

> Through endless Space with rustling sound
> The falling leaves are whirled around.
> Beyond my ken a yeasty sea
> The Yangtze's waves are rolling free.

Fletcher 的译文音调铿锵,形象生动,两句皆是"状语＋定语＋主语＋谓语"的结构,与原诗"定语＋主语＋谓语"的对仗句式极其相似。而且,每句内自押尾韵(sound / around, sea / free),以此译"萧萧"、"滚滚"两组叠字,可谓异曲同工的妙笔。事实说明,律诗的对仗是可迻译的。李白《独坐敬亭山》中的"众鸟高飞尽,孤云独去闲",在许渊冲笔下用平行结构译出:"All birds have flown away, so high; / A lonely cloud drifts on, so free."自然而贴切,有

---

① "脱节译法"一词见赵毅衡《意象派与中国古典诗歌》(载《外国文学研究》1979 年第 4 期):如庞德译李白"惊沙乱海日"一句的 Surprised. Desert turmoil. Sea sun.

何不可?

谈到诗,诗行的长短也要考虑。密尔顿辞彩精拔、跌宕昭彰的诗风一部分来自于他无韵体中的连续跨行(enjambement)所取得的气势,惠特曼惊才风逸、壮志烟高的诗情一部分取决于他自由诗中句法重复(syntactic repetition)所带来的节奏。翻译应该反映出原诗的气势与节奏。赵甄陶译毛泽东《十六字令》"山,刺破青天锷未残。天欲堕,赖以柱其间",字数与原诗完全相等——"Mountains! / They pierce the blue, unblunted. / The heaven would give way / But for their mighty stay."形象地再现了原诗豪放的风格。

在文学作品中,有时无须变异、无须重复,句法也可以产生独特的表现力(Chapman:53 - 54)。奥斯汀在著名小说《傲慢与偏见》中开门见山:

"It is a truth universally acknowledged that a single man in possession of a good fortune must be in want of a wife."严谨缜密的句法结构引导读者期待一个不同寻常的"真理";可是,读者的期待(expectation)没有实现,"男大当婚"的常识与郑重其事的句法形成鲜明的对照,富于幽默诙谐的色彩。无疑,高雅风格与庸俗内容的有意并列(juxtaposition),会产生极其滑稽的效果(Leech:178)。狄更斯笔下的密考伯先生之所以可笑,主要是因为他酷爱选择冠冕堂皇的词句表达司空见惯的琐事,而且往往不顾场合与对象(Turner:124)。

句法中的系列(series)同样具有风格色彩。据美国作家 Winston Weathers 分析,两项系列含有肯定的意味,三项系列具有劝说的功能,而四项以上系列暗示了细节的渐递(Turner:106)。培根的著名散文《谈读书》用了大量的三项系列结构(tripartite division):"读书足以怡情,足以傅彩,足以长才";"书有可浅尝者,有可吞食者";亦有"少数须咀嚼消化"者,"读书使人充实,讨论使人机智,笔记使人准确"——王佐良言简意赅的译文,传神地再现了培根劝世箴言式的风格。四项系列既可渐升达到高潮(climax)又可突降落入平庸(bathos)。《威尼斯商人》中的夏洛克以犹太人的愤恨不平责问道:"If you prick us, do we not bleed? if you tickle us, do we not laugh? if you poison us, do we not die? and if you wrong us, shall we not revenge?"在"流血"、"笑"、"死"之后,一词"复仇"具有奇异的感情力量,而用 shall 代替 do("我们难道不会复仇吗?")更增强了第四项 revenge 的感染力。如果将原有系列反过来,整个句子的强烈感人的风格效果则将丧失殆尽(Leech:68)。

词义方面:语域混淆、陈词滥调、古词古语

词义对风格的重要性是不言而喻的。当然,词义词汇的研究无法同语音和句法的研究完全脱离(Turner:110);譬如前述密考伯的滑稽可笑,除了句法上的原因外,还同他滥用俪语的癖性有关。为了说明科波菲尔初进伦敦可能迷路,他在绮丽言辞的迷宫中绕了如此大的一个弯:"Under the impression that your peregrinations in this metro-polis have not as yet been extensive, and that you might have some difficulty in penetrating the arcana of the modern Babylon in the direction of the City Road ..."最后才言归正传,说他很乐意带路:"I shall be happy to... install you in the knowledge of the nearest way."多么迂腐的一位老好先生! 这种滑稽的浮夸文风(comic pomposity)有一个特点,即在应该使用日常口语的场合滥用学究气十足的拉丁词(Turner:123),由此产生"语域混淆"(register mixing)。事实上,语域混淆也是一种变异,指的是在同一文句中使用具有不同语域特点的言辞(Leech:50)。试想一位主人在晚宴上拍着来宾的肩膀说:"有朋自远方来,不亦乐乎!"他的错误,同一个不穿外衣参加婚礼或只

穿网球鞋进入舞厅的冒失青年一样,实在令人啼笑皆非。

"语域"的概念对风格至关重要。文学翻译中有意无意地混淆语域,或多或少都会对原作风格产生不良影响。朗费罗是美国一位温文尔雅的诗人,他的《人生颂》说教味颇浓,劝诫人们在信奉上帝的同时要把握现在、奋力向前、成就伟业——

> Trust no Future, how'er pleasant!
> Let the dead Past bury its dead!
> Act,—act in the living Present!
> Heart within, and God o'erhead!

诗的格调典雅,语气庄严,神情肃穆,颇为读者喜爱。可是有位中译者在选择词语时犯了混淆语域的错误,将第二句写成"让已逝的岁月也去它的蛋吧!"严肃的宗教诗中怎会出现粗野的咒骂? 且不说原诗典雅的风格荡然无存,取而代之的庸俗、鄙陋的笔调本来就不宜于此诗的题材和主题。

诗是语言的精髓。成功的诗人力求在两个方面避开语言的平庸和陈腐(banality):一方面是当今的日常俗语,另一方面是传统的陈言套语(Leech:24)。然而,雅俗之争自古难以均衡。过分口语化易流于浅露,将上引朗费罗诗的第三句译作"干吧,抓住活泼泼的现在干吧!"可为佐证,过分文言化又易流于迂腐,将苏格兰农民诗人彭斯的名诗"O, my luve is like a red, red rose",译作"吾爱吾爱玫瑰红",几近戏谑! 诗的语言有三大忌:一曰陈词滥调(cliche)、二曰抽象概括(abstraction)、三曰古词古语(archaic diction)。王佐良译上述彭斯抒情诗中的比喻"Till a'the sea gang dry, my dear, / And the rocks melt wi' the sun! ",为保持其新鲜感,宁可舍弃"海枯石烂"的成语,而选用"纵使大海干涸水流尽, / 太阳将岩石烧作灰尘"。翻译如此,创作亦然。莎士比亚对诗歌传统中"眼睛比太阳明亮"、"双唇比珊瑚红艳"等千篇一律的比喻深感厌倦,于是在一首十四行诗中反其意而用之:

> My mistress' eyes are nothing like the sun;
> Coral is far more red than her lips' red...

(我的爱人的眼睛绝不像太阳,红珊瑚远远胜过她嘴唇的红色。——屠岸译)

意新而语工,风格奇异,令人耳目一新。

古词古语与古典文学作品有着千丝万缕的联系,慎重选用可使文章语气庄重、格调高雅(Leech:14)。王佐良以浅近文言译培根的《谈读书》,取得良好的效果。然而,古词古语是民族文化的一部分,有极其强烈的文学联想性,用于翻译,对译文风格就有直接影响。戚叔含译莎氏十四行诗中有这么两句:

> And summer's lease hath all too short a date. (好景能有几时,转眼花事阑珊。)
> A bliss in proof, and proved, a very woe. (道是销魂,岂知换来是痛苦。)

"花事阑珊"令人回忆起李煜"帘外雨潺潺,春意阑珊"的清丽意境,"道是销魂"也容易联想到李清照"莫道不消魂,帘卷西风,人比黄花瘦"的凄婉哀叹。由于这些文学联想的作用,戚译莎诗弥漫着浓郁的中国情调[①],莎士比亚的诗风难以捉摸,而他喜欢择用法律词汇(比如 lease

---

① 戚叔含译莎士比亚十四行诗的全文及钱兆明的评论,见《外国文学》1982 年第 12 期。

和 proof)的缘故也无从考证了。

翻译,为了保存原作的风格,应该尽力避免选用时代色彩或地方色彩太浓的词语。英译《诗经》中出现 castle 一词当然不妥,因为古代中国并没有"城堡"建筑,汉译华兹华斯形容"黄水仙花赋禅悦"实在令人迷惑,英国浪漫诗人怎么竟会笃信东方的佛教?长篇小说《飘》的中译本心裁别出,将美国的人名、地名全盘"民族化",改造得非常符合译者的自家口味:Scarlett O'Hara 姓郝名思嘉,Rhea Butler 姓白名瑞德,最显眼的是 Atlanta——"饿狼陀",面目何其狰狞!如此"再创造",不一而足。值得遗憾的是,中国读者并不接受译者精心绘制的幻境,因为在中国的土地上并不曾发生"南北战争"!显而易见,这里牵涉的翻译问题已不仅仅是词语选择的问题,而是历史事实的问题。翻译,应该正确再现原作风格,忠实反映客观现实。

以上试用现代文体学的理论从语音、句法和词义三个方面探讨文学风格与翻译的关系。三个方面的划分不是绝对的,它们之间经常会有交搭重叠处,如诗的节奏既与格律有关,又与句法有关,是二者相互关系的产物(Leech:122;Chapman:93-95)。此外,文学作品还可以在更多的层次上进行分析。lily 作为一个语言符号,指的是一朵白色的小花—— 百合,这是词的指意(denotation)。但是,具有相当文化修养而对语言特别敏感的读者,除百合花之外,还会想起 19 世纪英国拉斐尔前派的绘画,以及与此有关的美学思想,这些是词的联想意义(即connotation)。这样,有了词的指意与联想意义,读者就容易理解济慈的诗句:

> I see a lily on thy brow,
> With anguish moist, and fever dew...

通过比喻 lily 已不再是一朵小百合花,而是一个有色有香的娇弱意象,是一个纯净贞洁的具体象征(Chapman:74)。当然,风格研究也可以在更广的背景内进行,探讨方言、俚语等不同语体,或分析讥讽、幽默等不同笔调。

文学风格像彩虹,焕耀着神秘而妩媚的五光十色。这些炫目耀眼的光色不是彩虹的本身,但它们结合在一起,形成了光彩照人的彩虹。同样,五花八门的风格因素也不是风格的本身,但它们有机地结合在一个作品中,相互作用、相互完善,形成了感人至深的风格。文学风格是可感的,是实在的,因而应该也是可译的。新兴的文体学为风格研究提供了新的方法,开辟了新的领域。这对文学翻译的研究的确大有裨益。

选文三　**Essay on the Principles of Translation（extracts）**

Alexander Fraser Tytler

导　言

　　本文选自 Lefevere André，*Translation/ History/ Culture*，London & New York：Routledge，1992.

　　本选文系 18 世纪末爱丁堡大学历史教授亚历山大·弗雷泽·泰特勒（Alexander Fraser Tytler）《论翻译的原则》一书的摘录，力图展现其核心观点——进行翻译和评判翻译标准的三条基本原则。选文从"何为好的翻译"界定入手，从中提炼出译者从事翻译时所应该遵循的三条原则：① 翻译应是原著思想内容的完整再现；② 翻译应具备原著所具有的通顺；③ 译文的风格和手法应与原著属同一性质。泰特勒的翻译原则主要针对文艺翻译尤其是诗歌的翻译，但他的原则广义地说适应于所有的翻译，他强调原文读者和译文读者反应的一致。为能完全摹写原作思想、风格，译者必须具有完全驾驭原文与原文所涉内容的能力。泰特勒主张译者的责任就是不悖原作和原作者，完全忠实再现原作者的旨意与表达方式。如果想要成功做到这一点，译者在翻译过程中必须时时刻刻提醒自己如果原作者用译入语写作，将会采取何种表达方式。建议将该文与我国近代思想家、翻译家严复的"信达雅"联系起来对比阅读。

I would therefore describe a good translation to be，*That in which the merit of the original work is completely transfused into another language，as to be as distinctly apprehended，and as strongly felt，by a native of the country to which that language belongs，as it is by those who speak the language of the original work.*

Now，supposing this description to be a just one，which I think it is，let us examine what are the laws of translation which may be deduced from it.

It will follow，

（1）That the Translation should give a complete transcript of the ideas of the original work.

（2）That the style and manner of writing should be of the same character with that of the original.

（3）That the Translation should have all the ease of original composition.

In order that a translator may be enabled to give a complete transcript of the ideas of the original work，it is indispensably necessary that he should have a perfect knowledge of the language of the original，and a competent acquaintance with the subject of which it treats.

Where the sense of an author is doubtful, and where more than one meaning can be given to the same passage or expression, (which, by the way, is always a defect in composition), the translator is called upon to exercise his judgement, and to select that meaning which is most consonant to the train of thought in the whole passage, or to the author's usual mode of thinking, and of expressing himself. To imitate the obscurity or ambiguity of the original, is a fault.

If it is necessary that the translator should give a complete transcript of the ideas of the original work, it becomes a question, whether it is allowable in any case to add to the ideas of the original what may appear to give greater force or illustration; or to take from them what may seem to weaken them from redundancy. To give a general answer to this question, I would say, that this liberty may be used, but with the greatest caution. It must be further observed, that the superadded idea shall have the most necessary connection with the original thought, and actually increase its force. And, on the other hand, that whenever an idea is cut off by the translator, it must only be such as is an accessory, and not a principal in the clause or sentence. It must likewise be confessedly redundant, so that its retrenchment shall not impair or weaken the original thought.

Analogous to this liberty of adding to or retrenching from the ideas of the original, is the liberty which a translator may take of correcting what appears to him a careless or inaccurate expression of the original, where that inaccuracy seems materially to affect the sense.

I conceive it to be the duty of a poetical translator, never to suffer his original to fall. He must maintain with him a perpetual contest of genius; he must attend him in his highest flights, and soar, if he can, beyond him: and when he perceives, at any time, a diminution of his powers, when he sees a drooping wing, he must raise him on his own opinions. It is always a fault when the translator adds to the sentiment of the original author, what does not strictly accord with his characteristic mode of thinking, or expressing himself.

Next in importance to a faithful transfusion of the sense and meaning of an author, is an assimilation of the style and manner of writing in the translation to that of the original. This requisite of a good translation, though but secondary in importance, is more difficult to be attained than the former; for the qualities requisite for justly discerning and happily imitating the various characters of style and manner, are much more rare than the ability of simply understanding an author's sense. A good translator must be able to discover at once the true character of his author's style. He must ascertain with precision to what class it belongs; whether to that of the grave, the elevated, the easy, the lively, the florid and ornamented, or the simple and unaffected; and these characteristic qualities he must have the capacity of rendering equally conspicuous in the translation as in the original. If a translator fails in this discernment, and wants this capacity, let him be ever so thoroughly master of the sense of his author, he will present him through a distorting medium, or exhibit him often in a garb that is unsuitable to his character.

But a translator may discern the general character of his author's style, and yet fail remarkably in the imitation of it. Unless he is possessed of the most correct taste, he will be in continual danger of presenting an exaggerated picture or a caricature of his original. The distinction between good and bad writing is often of so very slender a nature, and the shadowing of difference so extremely delicate, that a very nice perception alone can at all times define its limit. Thus, in the hands of some translators, who have the discernment to perceive the general character of their author's style, but want this correctness of taste, the grave style of the original becomes heavy and formal in the translation; the elevated swells into bombast, the lively froths up into the petulant, and the simple and *naif* degenerates into the childish and insipid.

From all the preceding observations respecting the imitation of style, we may derive this precept, that a translator ought always to figure to himself, in what manner the original author would have expressed himself, if he had written in the language of the translation.

This precept leads to the examination, and probably to the decision, of a question which has admitted of some dispute, whether a poem can be well translated into prose?

There are certain species of poetry, of which the chief merit consists in the sweetness and melody of the versification. Of these it is evident, that the very essence must perish in translating them into prose.

But a great deal of the beauty of every regular poem consists in the melody of its numbers. Sensible of this truth, many of the prose translators of poetry have attempted to give a sort of measure to their prose, which removes it from the nature of ordinary language. If this measure is uniform, and its return regular, the composition is no longer prose, but blank verse. If it is not uniform, and does not regularly return upon the ear, the composition will be more unharmonious, than if the measure had been entirely neglected. Of this, Mr. Macpherson's translation of the *Iliad* is a strong example.

But it is not only by the measure that poetry is distinguishable from prose. It is by the character of its thoughts and sentiments, and by the nature of that language in which they are clothed. A boldness of figures, a luxuriancy of imagery, a frequent use of metaphors, a quickness of transition, a liberty of digressing; all these are not only *allowable* in poetry, but to many species of it, *essential*. But they are quite unsuitable to the character of prose. When seen in a *prose translation*, they appear preposterous and out of place, because they are never found in an *original prose composition*.

The difficulty of translating poetry into prose, is different in its degree, according to the nature or species of the poem. Didactic poetry, of which the principal merit consists in the detail of a regular system, or in rational precepts which flow from each other in a connected train of thought, will evidently suffer least by being transfused into prose. But every didactic poet judiciously enriches his work with such ornaments as are not strictly attached to his subject. In a prose translation of such a poem, all that is strictly systematic or receptive may be transfused with propriety; all the rest, which belongs to embellishment, will be found

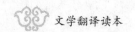

impertinent and out of place.

But there are certain species of poetry, of the merits of which it will be found impossible to convey the smallest idea in a prose translation. Such is Lyric poetry, where a greater degree of irregularity of thought, and a more unrestrained exuberance of fancy, is allowable than in any other species of composition. To attempt, therefore, a translation of a lyric poem into prose, is the most absurd of all undertakings; for those very characters of the original which are essential to it, and which constitute its highest beauties, if transferred to a prose translation, become unpardonable blemishes. The excursive range of the sentiments, and the play of fancy, which we admire in the original, degenerate in the translation into mere raving and impertinence.

We may certainly, from the foregoing observations, conclude that it is impossible to do complete justice to any species of poetical composition in a prose translation; in other words, that none but a poet can translate a poet.

It remains now that we consider the third general law of translation.

In order that the merit of the original work may be so completely transfused as to produce its full effect, it is necessary, not only that the translation should contain a perfect transcript of the sentiments of the original, and present likewise a resemblance of its style and manner; but, that the translation should have all the ease of original composition.

When we consider those restraints within which a translator finds himself necessarily confined, with regard to the sentiments and manner of his original, it will soon appear that this last requisite includes the most difficult part of his task. To one who walks in trammels, it is not easy to exhibit an air of grace and freedom. It is difficult, even for a capital painter, to preserve in a copy of a picture all the ease and spirit of the original; yet the painter employs precisely the same colours, and has no other care than faithfully to imitate the touch and manner of the picture that is before him. If the original is easy and graceful, the copy will have the same qualities, in proportion as the imitation is just and perfect. The translator's task is very different: he uses not the same colours with the original, but is required to give his picture the same force and effect. He is not allowed to copy the touches of the original, yet is required, by touches of his own, to produce a perfect resemblance. The more he studies a scrupulous imitation, the less his copy will reflect the ease and spirit of the original. How then shall a translator accomplish this difficult union of ease with fidelity? To use a bold expression, he must adopt the very soul of his author, which must speak through his own organs.

If the order in which I have classed the three general laws of translation is their just and natural arrangement, which I think will hardly be denied, it will follow, that in all cases where a sacrifice is necessary to be made of one of those laws to another, a due regard ought to be paid to their rank and comparative importance. The different genius of the languages of the original and translation, will often make it necessary to depart from the manner of the original, in order to convey a faithful picture of the sense; but it would be highly preposterous to depart, in any case, from the sense, for the sake of imitating the manner. Equally improper would it be, to sacrifice either the sense or manner of the original, if these can be preserved consistently with purity of expression, to a fancied ease or superior gracefulness of composition.

It may perhaps appear paradoxical to assert, that it is less difficult to give a poetical translation all the ease of original composition, than to give the same degree of ease to a prose translation. Yet the truth of this assertion will be readily admitted, if assent is given to that observation, which I before endeavoured to illustrate, viz. that a superior degree of liberty is allowed to a poetical translator in amplifying, retrenching from, and embellishing his original, than to a prose translator. For without some portion of this liberty, there can be no ease of composition; and where the greatest liberty is allowable, there that ease will be most apparent, as it is less difficult to attain to it.

For the same reason, among the different species of poetical composition, the lyric is that which allows of the greatest liberty in translation, as a freedom both of thought and expression is agreeable to its character. Yet even in this, which is the freest of all species of translation, we must guard against licentiousness; and perhaps the more so, that we are apt to persuade ourselves that the less caution is necessary. The difficulty indeed is, where so much freedom is allowed, to define what is to be accounted licentiousness in poetical translation. While a translator endeavours to give to his work all the ease of original composition, the chief difficulty he has to encounter will be found in the translation of idioms, or those turns of expression which do not belong to universal grammar, but of which every language has its own, that are exclusively proper to it.

If a translator is bound, in general, to adhere with fidelity to the manners of the age and country to which his original belongs, there are some instances in which he will find it necessary to make a slight sacrifice to the manners of his modern readers. The ancients, in the expression of resentment or contempt, made use of many epithets and appellations which sound extremely shocking to our more polished ears, because we never hear them employed but by the meanest and most degraded of the populace. By similar reasoning we must conclude that those expressions conveyed no such mean or shocking ideas to the ancients, since we find them used by the most dignified and exalted characters.

I shall now touch upon several other characteristics of composition, which, in proportion as they are found in original works, serve greatly to enhance the difficulty of doing complete justice to them in translation.

(1) The poets, in all languages, have a license peculiar to themselves, of employing a mode of expression very remote from the diction of prose, and still more from that of ordinary speech. Under this license, it is customary for them to use antiquated terms, to invent new ones, and to employ a glowing and rapturous phraseology.

(2) There is nothing more difficult to imitate successfully in a translation than that species of composition which conveys just simple and natural thoughts in plain, unaffected,

and perfectly appropriate terms; and which rejects all that constitutes what is properly termed *florid writing*. It is much easier to imitate in a translation that kind of composition (provided it be at all intelligible), which is brilliant and rhetorical, which employs frequent antitheses, allusions, similes, metaphors, than it is to give a perfect copy of just, apposite, and natural sentiments, which are clothed in pure and simple language: for the former characters are strong and prominent, and therefore easily caught; whereas the latter have no striking attractions, their merit eludes altogether the general observation, and is discernible only to the most correct and chastened taste.

(3) The union of just and delicate sentiments with simplicity of expression, is more rarely found in poetical composition than in prose; because the enthusiasm of poetry prompts rather to what is brilliant than what is just, and is always led to clothe its conceptions in that species of figurative language which is very opposite to simplicity. It is natural, therefore, to conclude, that in those few instances which are to be found of a chastened simplicity of thought and expression in poetry, the difficulty of transfusing the same character into a translation will be great, in proportion to the difficulty of attaining it in the original.

(4) There is another species of composition, which, possessing the same union of natural sentiments with simplicity of expression, is essentially distinguished from the former by its always partaking, in a considerable degree, of comic humour.

(5) No compositions will be found more difficult to be translated than those descriptions, in which a series of minute distinctions are marked by characteristic terms, each peculiarly appropriated to the thing to be designed, but many of them so nearly synonymous, or so approaching to each other, as to be clearly understood only by those who possess the most critical knowledge of the language of the original, and a very competent skill in the subject treated of.

(6) There is no species of writing so difficult to be translated, as that where the character of the style is florid, and the expression consequently vague, and of indefinite meaning.

选文四　On the Different Methods of Translating
Friedrich Schleiermacher

导　言

本文选自 Lefevere, André, *Translation/ History/ Culture*, London & New York: Routledge, 1992.

本选文系德国学者施莱尔马赫 1813 年在柏林皇家科学院的学术讨论会上宣读的一篇长达 30 多页、题为《论翻译的方法》("Üeber die verschiedenen Methoden des Üebersezens")的论文。施莱尔马赫率先将笔译和口译加以明确区分和阐述,并提出翻译分真正的翻译和机械的翻译两种:前者指文学作品和自然科学作品翻译,后者指实用性翻译;笔译属真正翻译范畴,口译则属机械翻译范畴。施莱尔马赫着重讨论了翻译与理解的关系问题,他通过对笔译与口译、真正的翻译和机械的翻译进行区分,指出翻译可以有两种不同途径:一是尽可能地不扰乱原作者的安宁,让读者去接近作者;另一种是尽可能不扰乱读者的安宁,让作者去接近读者。究其实质,这两种途径所得到的译文也就是西方翻译学界争论了近 2 000 年的"直译"、"意译"之争。20 世纪美国翻译理论家劳伦斯·韦努蒂在此基础上提出"归化"和"异化"的翻译策略,建议作为延伸阅读资料。

We are faced everywhere with the fact that speech is translated from one language into another, and that this happens in many different ways. On the one hand, this allows people who were originally as far apart as the length of the earth's diameter to establish contact, and texts produced in a language that has been dead for many centuries may be incorporated into another. On the other hand, however, we do not even have to go outside the domain of one language to encounter the same phenomenon. The dialects spoken by different tribes belonging to the same nation and the different stages of the same language or dialect in different centuries are different languages in the strict sense of the word, and they often require a complete translation. Even contemporaries who are not separated by dialects, but merely belong to different classes not often linked in social intercourse and far apart in education, can often understand each other only by means of similar mediation. Indeed, are we not often required to translate another's speech for ourselves, even if he is our equal in all respects, but possesses a different frame of mind or feeling? Sometimes we feel that the same words would have a totally different sense in our own mouth, or at least that they would carry more weight here and have a weaker impact there. We also feel that we would make use of totally different words and locutions, more attuned to our own nature, if we wanted to express what he meant. If we define this feeling more closely, and if it becomes a thought for us, we realize we are translating. Indeed, we sometimes have to translate our own words after a while when we want to make them really our own once again. This ability is not only exercised to transplant into foreign soil what a language has produced in the field of scholarship and the arts of speech and to enlarge the radius within which these products of the mind can operate. The same ability is exercised in the domain of trade between different nations and in the diplomatic commerce individual governments engage in: each is accustomed to talking to the other in its own language only if they want to make sure they are treated on a basis of strict equality without having to resort to a dead language.

We shall be able to distinguish two different fields [in translation] as well. They are not totally distinct, of course, since this is very rarely the case, but they are separated by boundaries that overlap and yet are clear enough to the observer who does not lose sight of the goal pursued in each field. The interpreter plies his trade in the field of commerce; the translator operates mainly in the fields of art and scholarship. Those who think of this definition as arbitrary, since interpreting is usually taken to mean what is spoken and translating what is written, will forgive me for using them, I am sure, since they are very conveniently tailored to fit the present need, the more so since the two definitions are by no means far removed from each other. Writing is appropriate to the fields of art and scholarship, because writing alone gives their works endurance, and to interpret scholarly or artistic products by word of mouth would be as useless as it seems impossible. For commerce, on the other hand, writing is but a mechanical tool. Oral bargaining is the original form here and all written interpreting should really be considered the notation of oral interpreting.

Two other fields are joined to this one, and very closely so as regards their nature and spirit, but they are already transitional because of the great multiplicity of objects belonging to them. One makes a transition to the field of art, the other to that of scholarship. If a transaction includes interpreting the development of that fact is perceived in two different languages. But the translation of writings of a purely narrative or descriptive nature, which also merely translates the development of a fact into another language, as already described, can still include much of the interpreter's trade. The less the author himself appears in the original, the more he has merely acted as the perceiving organ of an object, the more he has adhered to the order of space and time, the more the translation depends upon simple interpreting. The translator of newspaper articles and the common literature of travel remains in close proximity to the interpreter and risks becoming ridiculous when his work begins to make larger claims and he wants to be recognized as an artist. Alternatively, the more the author's particular way of seeing and shaping has been dominant in the representation, the more he has followed some freely chosen order, or an order defined by his impression, the more his work is part of the higher field of art. The translator must then bring other powers and abilities to bear on his work and be familiar with his author and that author's language in another way than the interpreter is. Every transaction that involves interpreting is concerned with drawing up a specific case according to certain legal obligations. The translation is made only for participants who are sufficiently familiar with these obligations, and the way these obligations are expressed in the two languages is well defined, either by law or by custom and mutual explanation. But the situation is different in the case of transactions initiating new legal obligations, even though on the formal level it may be very similar to what we have just described. The less these can be subsumed as particular cases covered by a general rule which is sufficiently known, the more scholarly knowledge and circumspection are needed in formulating them and the more scholarly knowledge of both language and fact the translator will need for his trade. On this double scale the translator will, therefore, rise higher and higher above the interpreter until he reaches his proper field, namely those mental products of scholarship and art in which the free idiosyncratic powers of combination vested in the author and the spirit of the language that is the repository of a system of observations and shades of moods are everything. In this field the object no longer dominates in any way, but is dominated by thoughts and emotions. In this field, indeed, the object has become an object through speech only and in which it is present only in conjunction with speech.

What is the basis of this important distinction? Everyone perceives it even in borderline cases, but it strikes the eye most strongly at the outer poles. In the life of commerce one is for the most part faced with obvious objects, or at least with objects defined with the greatest possible precision. All transactions are arithmetical or mathematical in nature, so to speak, and number and measure help out everywhere. Moreover, an established usage of individual words will soon arise through law and custom even in the case of those objects which, as the ancients were wont to say, subsume what is more and what is less into themselves and are referred to by means of a gradation of words that sometimes carry more weight in common life and sometimes less, because their essence is not defined. It follows that if the speaker does not intentionally construct hidden indeterminacies or makes a mistake with intent to deceive or because he is not paying attention, he can be understood by everyone who knows both the language and the field, and at worst only insignificant differences will appear in linguistic usage. Even so there are rarely any doubts that cannot be immediately dispelled as to which expression in one language corresponds to an expression in another. Translating in this field is therefore almost a mechanical activity that can be performed by anyone with a fair to middling knowledge of both languages. It shows little distinction between better and worse as long as the translator manages to avoid obvious mistakes. But when the products of art and scholarship have to be translated from one language into another, two considerations surface that completely change the equation. If one word in one language corresponded exactly to a word in another, if it expressed the same concept to the same extent, if the declensions of both languages represented the same relationships, and if the ways in which they connect sentences matched, so that the languages would indeed be different to the ear only, then all translation would belong in the field of commerce, in so far as it would communicate only the contents of a spoken or written text. Every translation could then be said to put the foreign reader in the same relationship to the author and his work as the native reader, except for effects produced by sound and melody. But this is definitely not the case with all languages that are not so closely related that they can almost be considered different dialects. The farther languages are apart in time and genealogical descent, the less a word in one language will correspond completely to a word in another, or a declension in one language encompass exactly the same multiplicity of relationships as in another. Since this irrationality, if I may call it that, tends to pervade all elements of two languages, it is obviously also bound to make an impact on the domain of social intercourse. Yet it clearly exerts much less pressure there, and its influence is minimal. All words denoting objects and actions that may be of importance have been verified, so to speak, and even if empty, overcautious inventiveness might still wish to guard against a possible unequal value of words, the subject matter itself immediately restores the balance. Matters are completely different in the realms of art and scholarship, and wherever thought—which is one with the word, not the thing of which the word is only a sign, possibly arbitrary but nonetheless fixed—dominates to a greater extent. How endlessly difficult and complex the problem becomes here! It presupposes precise knowledge and mastery of both languages. How often the most expert and best versed in languages, starting from a shared conviction that an equivalent expression cannot be found, differ significantly when they want to show which expression is the closest approximation. This holds true both for the most vivid pictorial expressions in poetical works and for the most abstract terms denoting the innermost and most general components of highest scholarship.

The second consideration that changes true translation into an activity that is radically different from mere interpreting is the following: whenever the word is not completely bound by obvious objects or external facts it merely has to express, wherever the speaker is thinking more or less independently and therefore wants to express himself, he stands in a double relationship to language, and what he says will be understood correctly only in so far as that relationship is perceived correctly. On the one hand every man is in the power of the language he speaks and all thinking is a product thereof. He cannot think anything with great precision that would lie outside the limits of language. The shape of the concepts he uses, the nature and limits of the way in which they can be connected are prescribed for him by the language in which he is born and educated. Both his intellect and his imagination are bound by it. On the other hand every free thinking, mentally self-employed human being shapes his own language. In what other way would it have developed and grown from its first raw state to its most perfect elaboration in art and scholarship, except for precisely these influences? In this sense, then, the living power of the individual creates new forms by means of the plastic material of language. At first he does so only for the immediate purpose of communicating a passing consciousness, but gradually more or less of it stays behind in the language, is taken up by others and reaches out, a shaping power. Any verbal text is bound to die soon if it can be reproduced by a thousand organs in a form that remains the same always. Only those texts can and may endure longer that constitute a new element in the life of a language itself. As a result each free and higher speech needs to be understood twice, once on the basis of the spirit of the language that contains its component elements, as a living representation bound and defined by that spirit and conceived out of it in the speaker, and once on the basis of the speaker's emotions, as his own action, produced and explicable only in terms of his own being. Indeed, any speech of this kind can only be understood, in the higher sense of the term, when these two relationships have been perceived together and in their true relationship to each other, so that we know which of the two dominates the whole, or individual sections. We understand the spoken word as an act of the speaker only when we feel at the same time where and how the power of language has taken hold of him, where the lightning of thought has uncoiled, snake-like in its current, where and how the roving imagination has been held firm in its forms. We only understand the spoken word as a product of language and an expression of its spirit when we feel that only a Greek, to take one example, could think and speak that way, that only this particular language could operate in a human mind in this way and when we feel at the same time that only this man could think and speak in the Greek manner in this way, that only he could seize the language and shape it in this manner, that only his living possession of the riches of the language reveals itself in this way, as an alert sense of measure and euphony that belongs to him alone, a power of thinking and shaping that is specifically his own. This type of understanding is difficult to achieve, even in the same language, since it presupposes a profound and precise penetration into both the author's own nature and the spirit of his language. Imagine, then, what a high art understanding must be when it has to deal with the products of a distant and foreign language! Whoever has mastered this art of understanding through the most diligent cultivation of a language, the most precise knowledge of the whole historical life of a nation, and the living representation of single works and their authors, he and he alone may wish to unlock that same understanding of the masterpieces of art and scholarship for his own contemporaries and compatriots. But the risks increase when he prepares himself for his task, when he wishes to define his goals more accurately and surveys the means at his disposal. Should he decide to bring two people—two people who are so fully separated from each other as the author himself and the man who speaks his own language but not the author's—together into a relationship as immediate as that which exists between the author and his original reader? Or does he merely want to unlock for his readers the same understanding and the same pleasure he himself enjoys, with the traces of hardship it carries and the feeling of strangeness that remains mixed into it? How can he achieve the second goal with the means at his disposal, let alone the first? If his readers are to understand they must be able to perceive the spirit of the language that was the author's and to see his own peculiar way of thinking and feeling. Yet to help them achieve both those aims the translator has nothing more to offer than his own language, which at no point fully corresponds to the other, and his own person, he who understands his author sometimes more clearly and sometimes less so, just as he admires and approves of him to a sometimes greater and sometimes lesser extent. Is translation not a fool's errand if we think about it in this way? That is why people who have fallen prey to despair before they reached this goal or, if you prefer, before they reached the stage at which all of this could be clearly formulated in thought, discover two other methods for becoming acquainted with works in foreign languages, not primarily to gather their real artistic or linguistic sense, but rather to fill a need and contemplate spiritual art. These methods forcibly remove some of the difficulties mentioned here while slyly circumventing others, but they completely abandon the concept of

translation we are dealing with here.

These two methods are called paraphrase and imitation.

Paraphrase tries to overcome the irrationality of languages, but only in a mechanical way. It reasons as follows: even if I do not find a word in my language that corresponds to a word in the original language, I still want to try to penetrate its core by adding definitions, both restrictive and expansive. In this way it laboriously works itself through to an accumulation of empty particulars, caught between a troublesome too much and a painful too little. In doing so, paraphrase may possibly succeed in rendering the content with limited precision, but it totally abandons the impression made by the original, because the living speech has been killed irrevocably since everybody feels it cannot have originally proceeded from the feelings of a human being—and yet it has. The paraphrast treats the elements of the two languages as if they were mathematical signs that may be reduced to the same value by means of addition and subtraction. The spirit of the original language is not allowed to reveal itself where this method is used, and neither is the spirit of the language that is being transformed. Paraphrase often tries to mark the traces of the conjunction of thoughts in a psychological manner. It does so by means of interjected sentences it inserts like so many landmarks, even though the conjunctions themselves are unclear and attempt to obliterate themselves whenever it tries to do so. A paraphrase tends to usurp the place of commentary where difficult compositions are concerned and can, therefore, not be reduced to the concept of translation any longer. Imitation, on the other hand, submits to the irrationality of languages: it grants that it is impossible to render a copy of a verbal artifact into another language, let alone a copy that would correspond precisely to the original in all its parts. Given the difference between languages, with which so many other differences are connected, there is no other option but to produce an imitation, a whole composed of parts obviously different from the parts of the original. Yet, as far as the effect of the text is concerned, that whole would come as close as possible to the original as the difference in material allows. Such an imitation no longer claims to be the work itself, and in no way should the spirit of the original language be represented in it and be active in it. On the contrary, many things are bartered for the foreignness that spirit has produced. A work of this kind should merely be the same thing for its readers as the original was for its own readers, as much as possible and as far as the difference in language, morals, and education allows. The identity of the original is abandoned in favor of analogy of impression. The imitator does not try to bring the two parties concerned, the writer and the reader of the imitation, together in any way because he does not think a direct relationship between them is possible. He merely wants to produce an impression on the reader that is similar to the impression the original must have made on its contemporaries who read it in their own language. Paraphrase is more current in the domain of scholarship, imitation in that of art. Just as everyone confesses that a work of art loses its tone, its brilliance, its whole artistic essence in paraphrase, so too no one has, as yet, undertaken the foolish task of producing an imitation of a scholarly masterpiece that would treat its contents freely. Both methods, however, fail to satisfy the person who, permeated by the value of a foreign masterpiece, wishes to extend its operational radius to those who speak his language and keeps the stricter concept of translation in mind. Neither method will therefore be subjected to closer scrutiny here, since both deviate from this concept. They were discussed only because they mark the boundaries of the field that is our real concern.

What of the genuine translator, who wants to bring those two completely separated persons, his author and his reader, truly together, and who would like to bring the latter to as correct and complete an understanding of the original as possible without inviting him to leave the sphere of his mother tongue? What roads are open to him? In my opinion there are only two. Either the translator leaves the author in peace, as much as possible, and moves the reader toward him. Or he leaves the reader in peace, as much as possible, and moves the author toward him. The two roads are so completely separate that the translator must follow one or the other as assiduously as possible, and any mixture of the two would produce a highly undesirable result, so much so that the fear might arise that author and reader would not meet at all. The difference between the two methods must be immediately obvious, just as obvious as the relationship that exists between them. In the first place the translator, through his work, tries to replace for the reader the understanding of the original language that reader lacks. He tries to communicate to his readers the same image, the same impression his knowledge of the original language has allowed him to acquire of the work as it stands. In so doing he tries to move his readers toward his own point of view, which is essentially foreign to them. Yet if a translation wants to make its Roman author, say, speak the way he would have spoken to Germans if he had been a German, it does not merely move the author to where the translator stands, because the author does not speak German to the translator, but Latin. Rather it drags him directly into the world of the German readers and transforms him into their equal, and that is precisely the case under discussion. The first translation will be perfect in its kind when it can be said that if the author had learned German as well as the translator has learned Latin he would not have translated the work he originally wrote in Latin any differently than the translator has done. But the second translation, which does not show the author as he himself would have translated, but as he would have originally written in German if he had been a German, can have one measure of perfection only. It will be perfect if it could be certified that the original would have meant exactly the same thing as the translation now means to all German readers if those readers could be changed into experts who lived at the same time as the author. In other words, the translation will be perfect if it can be certified that the author has changed himself into a German. This opposition makes it immediately obvious that the procedure must be different in every detail and that everything would become unintelligible as well as unpalatable if the translator tried to switch methods in the course of one and the same project. I would merely like to add that there cannot be a third method with a precisely delimited goal over and above these two. The two parties who are separated must either meet at a certain point in the middle, and that will always be the translator, or else one must join up with the other completely. Only the first of these two possibilities belongs in the field of translation. The other one would be realized if, in our case, the German readers totally mastered Latin, or rather, if that language totally mastered them to the extent of actually transforming them. Much has been said about translations that follow the letter and translations that follow the sense, faithful translation and free translation and whatever other expressions may have become current. Yet these supposedly various methods must all be reduced to the two methods mentioned above, even though the faithful translation that follows the sense or the translation that is too free or too literal will not be the same according to one method as it is according to the other, if we want to talk about merits and mistakes. It is my intention, therefore, to put aside all problems related to this matter, which have been discussed by specialists, and to observe only the most general features of these two methods in order to reveal their particular advantages and disadvantages, the limits of their applicability and the ways in which they best reach the goal of translation. After such a general survey two things would remain to be done, and this essay can be no more than an introduction to them. Matters would be clarified even more if a set of rules could be designed for both methods, taking into consideration the different genres of speech. Furthermore, the best attempts produced according to either method could be judged and compared. But I must leave both of these tasks to others, or at least to another occasion.

The method which tries to give the reader, as a German, the impression he would get from reading the original work in the original language must, of course, first define what kind of understanding of the original language it wants to imitate. There is one kind it should not imitate and one kind it cannot. The first kind is a school-like type of understanding that laboriously bungles itself through separate parts, possessed by an attitude close to loathing, and therefore never acquiring a clear overview of the whole, nor a living comprehension of its connections. When the more educated part of a nation as a whole has no experience of a more intimate penetration of foreign languages, then let those who have progressed beyond this point be saved by their good genius from trying to produce this kind of translation. If they wanted to take their own understanding as a measure they themselves would be little understood and have little impact, but if their translation were to represent common understanding, their ungainly work could not be pushed off the stage fast enough. In such a time free imitations should first awaken and sharpen the desire for the foreign, and paraphrases prepare a more general understanding to open the way for future translations. But there is another kind of understanding no translator is able to imitate. Let us think of such wonderful people as nature produces every so often, as if to show that it is also capable of destroying the barriers of the common in isolated cases: people who feel such a peculiar kinship with foreign existence that they live and think completely in a foreign language and its products, and while they are totally preoccupied with a foreign world they let their own language and their own world become completely foreign. Or let us think of such people who are destined, as it were, to represent the power of language in its totality, and for whom all languages they are able to touch have the same value: in fact, they are in the habit of dressing up in them as if they had been born in them. These people have reached a point at which the value of translation becomes nil since their mother tongue does not even exert the slightest influence on their perception of foreign works. Since they do not become conscious of their understanding in their mother tongue but are immediately and totally at home in the foreign language itself, they do not feel any incommensurability between their own thinking and the language they read in. It is therefore obvious that no translation can achieve their understanding or ever portray it. Just as producing translations for them would be like pouring water into the sea, or into wine, so too they are wont to smile sympathetically from their Olympian height on all attempts made in this field, and rightly so, since we would not have to go through all this trouble if the audience translations are produced for was their equal. Translation therefore relates to a state of affairs between these two extremes and the translator must take it as his aim to give his reader the same image and the same delight that reading the work in the original language would give any reader educated in such a way that we can call him the lover and the expert, in the better sense of the word; the type of reader who is familiar with the foreign language, and yet that language always remains foreign to him. He no longer has to think through every single part in his mother tongue before he can grasp the whole, as schoolboys do, but he is still conscious of the difference between that language and his mother tongue, even where he enjoys the beauty of a foreign work in total peace. Granted, the definition of translation and its operational radius remain unsettled enough even after we have settled this point. We can only observe the following: since the desire to translate can originate only when a certain ability for intercourse with foreign languages is widespread among the educated part of the population, the art of translation will develop and its aim be set higher and higher the more knowledge and love of foreign products of the spirit spread and increase among those elements of the population who have exercised their ears and trained them without specializing in the knowledge of languages. Yet at the same time we cannot be blind to the fact that the more readers are predisposed toward this kind of translation, the larger the difficulties of the enterprise grow, all the more so if efforts are concentrated on the most characteristic products of a nation's art and scholarship—the most important objects for the translator. Since language is a historical fact there can be no right sense for it without a sense of history. Languages have not been invented and all mechanical and arbitrary work in and on them is stupid; they are gradually discovered and art and scholarship promote this discovery and bring it to fulfillment. Some of the ideas of a nation shape themselves in a particular way in one of those two forms in every excellent spirit and he will work in language and influence it to that end. His works must therefore also contain part of that language's history. This fact presents the translator of scholarly works with great, indeed often insurmountable difficulties, for whoever reads an excellent work of that kind in the original language, and is equipped with sufficient knowledge, will not easily overlook its influence on that language. He will notice which words and combinations still appear to him in the first splendor of novelty. He will observe how they insinuate themselves into the language through the special needs of the author's spirit and his expressive power, and this type of observation most essentially determines the impression he gets. It is therefore the task of the translation to transplant that very same impression in its reader. If the translation fails to do so the reader will lose part of what was intended for him, and often a very important part. But how can this be achieved? To start with particulars: how often will a word that is new in the original correspond best with one that is old and used in our language, so that the translator will have to replace it with a foreign content? If he did so he would have to move into the field of imitation if he wanted to reveal the language-shaping aspect of the work. How often, when he can render the new by means of the new, will the word closest in etymology and derivation not render the sense most faithfully, and yet the translator will have to awaken other connotations if he does not want to obscure the immediate connection. He will have to console himself with the thought that he can make good his omissions where the author did use old and well-known words and that he will therefore achieve in general what he is unable to achieve in every particular case. But consider the totality of the word-shaping work a master produces, his use of related words and roots of words in a whole array of inter-related writings. How does the translator propose to find a happy solution here since the system of concepts and their signs in his language is totally different from that of the original language, and since the roots of words do not correspond to each other in a parallel manner, but rather cut through each other in the most amazing directions? It is impossible for the translator's use of language to be as coherent as his author's. In this case he will have to be content with achieving in particular what he cannot achieve in general. He will reach the understanding with his readers that they will not think of the other writings as stringently as readers of the original would, but rather consider each one on its own, and that they should, in fact, praise him if he manages to salvage similarity with regard to the more important objects in particular writings, or even only in parts thereof, so that one single word does not acquire a number of totally different deputies or that a colorful variety does not reign in the translation where the original has strictly related expressions throughout. These difficulties reveal themselves for the most part in the field of scholarship. There are other difficulties of a more artistic nature to be tackled in the field of poetry and prose, and those are by no means smaller in size since the musical element of language that becomes apparent in rhythm and change of tone also carries a specific and higher meaning in this case. When this is not taken into account everybody feels that the finest spirit, the highest magic, or the most perfect products of art are lost, or even destroyed. Our translator will, therefore, also have to translate what a sensible reader of the original perceives as particular in this respect, as intentional, as influencing tone and mood of feeling, as decisive for the mimicking and musical accompaniment of speech. But how often (it is almost a miracle if one does not have to say always!) will rhythmical and melodic infidelity not be locked in irreconcilable combat with dialectic and grammatical fidelity? How difficult it is to avoid sacrificing something, now here, now there, as one swings to and fro, and to avoid what is often exactly the wrong result. How difficult it is even for the translator, when the occasion arises, to restore to his author with impartiality what he has had to take away from him before and not to succumb to a persistent one-sidedness, even unconsciously, because his inclination goes out to one artistic element above all others. If his taste in works of art gravitates more toward the ethical in subject matter and the way in which it is treated, he will be less inclined to notice where he has failed to do justice to the metrical and musical elements of the form. He will not ponder how to replace them; he will be satisfied with a translation that gets more and more diluted into the easy and semi-paraphrastic. If, on the other hand, the translator should happen to be a metrician or a musician he will put the logical elements last in order to grasp the musical elements completely. He will sink deeper and deeper into this one-sided enterprise and his work will become less and less felicitous. A comparison of the total effect of his translation with the original will reveal that he comes closer and closer to that schoolboyish inadequacy that loses the whole in the parts and does not even notice he is doing so. If he changes what is light and naturally expressed in one language into heavy and objectionable expressions in the other merely for love of the material similarity of rhythm and tone, a totally different overall impression will be the result.

Still other difficulties arise when the translator reflects on his relationship with the language he is writing in and on the relationship of his translation with his other works. If we except those miraculous masters for whom one cannot translate, as we said before, for whom many languages are as one, or for whom an acquired language is even more natural than their mother tongue, all others retain a sense of the strange, no matter how fluently they read a foreign language. How should the translator render this feeling of being faced with something foreign to readers to whom he offers a translation in their mother tongue? One might say that the answer to this riddle has been given long ago and that the problem has often been solved more than well enough in our case, since the more closely the translation follows the turns taken by the original, the more foreign it will seem to the reader. That may well be true and it is easy enough to ridicule this position in general. Yet if this joy is not to be bought too cheaply, if the most magisterial is not to be discarded in one and the same bathwater with the most schoolboyish, it will have to be admitted that an indispensable requirement of this method of translation is a feeling for language that is not only not colloquial but also causes us to suspect that it has not grown in total freedom but rather turned toward a foreign likeness. It must be admitted that to achieve this with good measure and in an artful manner, without disadvantage to one's language or oneself, is probably the biggest difficulty our translator has to overcome. The attempt seems to me to be the strangest form of humiliation a writer who is not a bad writer could impose on himself. Who would not like to allow his mother tongue to stand forth everywhere in the most universally appealing beauty each genre is able to give? Who would not rather sire children who are their parents' pure effigy and not bastards? Who would willingly force himself to appear in movements less light and elegant than those he is capable of, to appear stiff and brutal, at least at times, and to shock the reader as much as is necessary to keep him aware of what he is doing? Who would put up with being thought clumsy by trying to stay as close to the foreign language as his own language allows? Who would suffer being accused of bending his mother tongue to foreign and unnatural dislocations instead of skillfully exercising it in its own natural gymnastics—not unlike parents who abandon their children to acrobats? Finally, who would like to be exposed to the compassionate smiles of the greatest masters and experts who would be unable to understand his laborious and ill-considered German if they were unable to supplement it with their Latin and Greek? These are the sacrifices every translator is forced to make, these are the dangers he exposes himself to when he fails to observe the most delicate balance in his attempts to keep the tone of the language foreign. He will never escape from these dangers altogether, of course, because everyone strikes that balance a little differently. If, in addition to this, he also thinks of the inevitable influence exerted by habit, he may well fear that much that is raw and does not really belong will insinuate itself into his free and original production via translation, and that habit will somehow blunt in him the tender sense of his natural feeling for language. If he also ventures to think of both the great host of imitators and the slowness and mediocrity reigning among those of his readers who also write, he will be horrified at the volume of unlawfulness, genuine stiffness and clumsiness, and linguistic corruption of all kinds perpetrated by others. And yet he will probably have to answer for it since there is no doubt that only the best and the worst will not attempt to derive a false advantage from his endeavors. We have often heard this type of complaint, namely that such a translation must of necessity be harmful to the purity of a language and its peaceful development. Even if we want to put it aside with the consolation that there will also be advantages to counterbalance these disadvantages, and that true wisdom would counsel us to acquire as much as possible of the former while taking over as little as possible of the latter, since all good is mixed with evil, we shall nevertheless have to draw some consequences from this difficult task of representing what is foreign in one's own mother tongue. First, this method of translating cannot thrive equally well in all languages, but only in those which are not the captives of too strict a bond of classical expression outside of which all is reprehensible. Such bonded languages should look forward to a broadening of their sphere of influence when they are spoken by foreigners who need more than their mother tongue to express themselves. They will be perfectly suited to this. They may incorporate foreign works by means of imitations, or even translations of the other type, but they must abandon their first type of translation to languages that are freer, in which innovations and deviations are tolerated to a greater extent, to such an extent, in fact, that the accumulation thereof may well generate a certain characteristic mode of expression in certain circumstances. Another obvious consequence is that this type of translation has no value whatsoever if it is practiced only by chance in a given language, and in isolated instances. This would obviously fall short of its stated goal, namely to make a foreign spirit blow toward the reader. On the contrary, if the reader is to be given a notion, albeit a very weak one, of the original language and what the work owes to it, in partial compensation for his failure to understand that language, he must not only be given the totally vague impression that what he reads does not sound completely familiar. He must also be made to feel that it sounds like something different, yet definite, and that will be possible only if he is able to make comparisons on a massive scale. If he has read something he knows has been translated from other modern languages and something else that has been translated from the classical languages he will acquire an ear for distinguishing between what is old and what is not so old, provided the texts have been translated in the way described above. Yet he will have to read much more if he wants to be able to distinguish between works of Greek or Roman origin, say, on the one hand, and works of Italian and Spanish origin on the other. Even this is not the highest goal we try to achieve. On the contrary, the reader of the translation will become the equal of the better reader of the original only when he is able to first acquire an impression of the particular spirit of the author as well as that of the language of the work, and to develop a definite grasp of it by and by. He can do so only by exercising his powers of observation, but if he is to be able to really exercise them he will have to have many more objects of comparison available to him. These objects of comparison will not be available if only isolated works of masters in isolated genres are sporadically translated into his language. In this way translation will allow even the most educated readers to achieve only a very deficient knowledge of what is foreign, and it is inconceivable that they would be able to arrive at any judgment of either the original or the translation. This method of translation should therefore be applied extensively: whole literatures should be transplanted into a given language. The method makes sense only to a nation that has the definite inclination to appropriate what is foreign, and to such a nation only. Isolated works translated in this manner can be of value only as precursors of a more generally evolving desire and willingness to adopt this procedure. If they fail to inspire this willingness, the language and the spirit of the time will begin to work against them, and in that case they will be seen as mistaken attempts only and achieve little or no success. Yet even if this method of translation should prevail, we should not grow complacent and expect a work of this nature, no matter how excellent, to gather general approval. Since many factors have to be considered and many difficulties have to be resolved, it is inevitable that different opinions should develop as to which parts of the task should be considered of primary importance and which should not be considered in this manner. Different schools, so to speak, will therefore arise among the masters, and different parties among the audience that will follow these schools. Even though the method remains basically the same, different translators of the same work undertaken from different points of view will be able to exist side by side and we shall not really be able to say that one is, as a whole, more or less perfect than another. Certain parts of the work will be more successful in one version, others in another. They will not have fulfilled their task exhaustively until they are all taken together and related to each other and until it becomes clear how one translator attaches particular value to this particular approximation of the original, while another attaches particular value to another approximation, or how one translator exercises particular forbearance toward what is native. Until that happens each translation in itself will always be of relative and subjective value only.

These are the difficulties besetting this method and the imperfections essentially inherent in it. Once we have conceded these, however, we must acknowledge the attempt itself and we cannot deny its merit. It is based on two conditions: that a nation should know the importance of understanding foreign works and want to do so, and that its language should be allowed a certain flexibility. Where those conditions are fulfilled this type of translation becomes a natural phenomenon influencing the whole evolution of a culture and giving a certain pleasure as it is given a certain value.

But what of the opposite method that does not expect any labor or exertion on the reader's part since it aspires to bring the foreign author close to him, as if by magic, and to show the work as it would have been if the author himself had originally written it in the reader's language? This requirement has frequently been formulated as the one a true translator would have to fulfill and as being even higher and more perfect in nature when compared to the other one. Isolated attempts have been made, some of them even masterpieces maybe, which have clearly taken this as their goal. Let us now find out what they are like and see whether it would be desirable for this method, that has not been applied as frequently as the other until now, to be adopted, to be applied with greater frequency, and to supplant the other that is of dubious nature and unsatisfactory in many ways.

It is immediately obvious that this method does not threaten the translator's language in any way. Considering the relationship between his work and the foreign language, the first rule the translator must follow is not to allow himself anything that would not also be allowed in an original work of the same genre in his native language. Indeed, it is his duty first and foremost to observe at least the same care for the purity and perfection of language, to strive after the same light and natural style his author is famous for in the original language. If we want to make clear to our compatriots what an author meant to speakers of his language, we cannot think of a better formula than to make him speak in such a way as we imagine he would have spoken in ours, especially when the level of development at which he found his language is similar to the one our own language happens to have reached. We can imagine to some extent how Tacitus would have spoken if he had been a German or, more accurately, how a German would speak who meant the same to speakers of our language as Tacitus did to speakers of his, and good luck to he who is able to imagine this so vividly that he can actually make him speak. Whether this would happen if he let him say the same things the Roman Tacitus said in Latin is a question which cannot easily be answered in the affirmative. It is one thing to correctly grasp the influence a man has exerted on his language and to show it in some way, and quite another thing to seek to know how his thoughts and their expressions would have shaped themselves if he had been used to thinking and expressing himself in another language. The whole art of understanding all speech and hence also of all translation is based on belief in the internal and essential identity of thought and expression. Could a person who believes in this ever really want to sever a man from the language he was born into and think that a man, or even just his train of thought, could be one and the same in two languages? Or if they are different in a certain way could he then presume to dissolve speech to its very core, separate the part played by language from it, and let that core combine with the essence of another language and its power, almost as if by means of a new and almost chemical process?

But we have dealt with what is strange at too great length and it must seem as if we have been talking about writing in foreign languages rather than translating from them. The case, then, is simply this: if it proves to be impossible to write something in a foreign language that is worthy of and in need of translation as an art, or if this is a rare and miraculous exception at least, we cannot set up as a rule for translation that it should imagine how the writer himself would have written precisely what he has written in the translator's language since there are few examples of bilingual authors for the translator to follow. On the contrary, the translator will have to rely almost totally on his own imagination for all works that do not resemble light entertainment or commercial transactions. Indeed, what objection could possibly arise if the translator were to tell the reader: here is the book just as the author would have written it if he had written in German, and if the reader were to reply: I am much obliged to you, just as I would have been if you had brought me a picture of the author just as he would have looked if his mother had conceived him by another father? If the writer's particular spirit is the mother of works of art and scholarship in a higher sense, his national language is the father. Artificial writings, on the other hand, lay claim to secret insights nobody possesses and can be enjoyed without inhibition only as a game.

That the applicability of this method is severely limited, indeed, that it is almost equal to zero in the field of translation, is borne out most obviously when one observes the insuperable difficulties it becomes entangled in where isolated fields of literature and art are concerned. We must admit that there are only very few words in colloquial usage in one language that correspond perfectly to words in another, so that one may be used in all cases in which the other is used and that one would produce exactly the same effect as the other in the same constellation. Imagine the incomparably greater extent to which this must hold true for all concepts, the more a philosophical essence is added to them, and it is therefore most true of genuine philosophy. In spite of differing contemporary and successive opinions, this is the very field in which language contains within itself a system of concepts that constitutes a whole whose isolated parts do not correspond to any in the system of other languages, precisely because they touch each other in the same language, because they connect with each other and complement each other. This observation holds true even for concepts like "God" and "Is", the primeval noun and the primeval verb. Even what is commonly believed to be general is illuminated by language and colored by it, even though it lies outside the boundaries of the particular. The wisdom of every individual must be dissolved in this system of language. Everyone partakes of what is there and everyone helps bring to light what is not yet there but has been prefigured. This is the only way in which the individual's wisdom is alive and able to really rule his existence which he completely summarizes in that language. Imagine that the translator of a philosophical writer does not want to take the decision to bend the language of the translation toward that of the original as far as possible in order to communicate an impression of the system of concepts developed in it, to the extent to which that is possible. Imagine that he would rather try to make his author speak as if he had originally fashioned his thoughts and his speech in another language. What choices are open to him in view of the dis-similarity between the elements of both languages? He must either paraphrase and fail to achieve his aim, since a paraphrase can never be made to look as if it had been originally produced in the same language, or he must transpose his author's entire knowledge and wisdom into the conceptual system of another language and therefore change all isolated parts, in which case it is hard to see how the wildest license might be kept within bounds. Indeed, it should be said that no one who has even the slightest respect for philosophical endeavors can allow himself to be drawn into so loose a game. I leave it to Plato to justify the transition I am now about to make, from the philosopher to the author of comedies. From the linguistic point of view this genre comes closest to the domain of colloquial conversation. The whole representation is alive in the morals of the people and the time and those, in turn, are perfectly mirrored in language, in the most lively manner. Lightness and naturalness in elegance are its prime virtue, which is precisely why the difficulties of translating according to the method just outlined are immense. Any approximation to a foreign language is bound to harm those virtues of diction. If the translation seeks to make a playwright speak as if he had originally written in its language, that translation will not be able to let him show too many things because they are not native to its people and therefore have no symbol in their language. In this case, consequently, the translator must either cut them out completely and destroy the power and the form of the whole in doing so, or else he must replace them. It is obvious that the formula will either lead to pure imitation if it is faithfully followed in this field, or else to an even more repulsive and confusing mixture of translation and imitation that cruelly bounces the reader back and forth like a ball between the foreign world and his own, between the author's wit and imagination and the translator's. The reader is not likely to derive any pure pleasure from this but in the end he is certain to be left with more than enough dizziness and frustration. If he follows the other method the translator is not required to subject himself to such self-willed changes because his reader must always remember that the author lived in a different world and wrote in a different language. He is bound only by the admittedly difficult art of supplying knowledge of this strange world in the shortest and most efficient way while allowing the greater lightness and naturalness of the original to shine through in all places. These two examples taken from the opposite extremes of art and scholarship clearly show how little the real aim of translation, the unadulterated enjoyment of foreign works within the limits of the possible, can be achieved by means of a method that insists on breathing the spirit of an alien language into the translated work. Moreover, every language also has its own rhythmic peculiarities, both in prose and poetry. As soon as the fiction that the author could also have written in the translator's language is established, the translator would be under the obligation to let the author appear in the rhythm of that language, which could disfigure his work even more and limit even further the knowledge of its particular character as provided by translation.

This fiction, which is the sole basis of the theory of translation now under discussion, goes far beyond the aim of that activity. Seen from the first point of view, translation is a matter of necessity for a nation in which only a small minority of people are able to acquire a sufficient knowledge of foreign languages while a greater minority would like to enjoy foreign works. If the latter became completely subsumed under the former all translation would be rendered useless and it would be very difficult to get anyone to take on this thankless labor. This is not the case when translation is seen from the second point of view. In this case translation has nothing to do with necessity. Rather it is a labor of recklessness and lasciviousness. Even if knowledge of foreign languages became as widespread as possible, and even if anyone who is competent had access to their noblest works, anyone who could promise to show us a work of Cicero's or Plato's in the way these authors would have written it directly in German at the present moment, would still be engaging in a miraculous endeavor that would be sure to attract more and more listeners who would be sure to become more and more intrigued. If, further-more, somebody brought us to a point at which we would be doing this not just in our mother tongue, but also in another, foreign language, he would obviously be a master of the difficult and almost impossible art of dissolving the spirits of languages into each other. It soon becomes obvious, however, that this would not be translation, strictly speaking, and that its goal would not be the most precise enjoyment possible of the works themselves. Rather it would develop into more and more of an imitation and only those readers who were already immediately and independently familiar with those authors could truly enjoy such a work of art. The real aim of translation could only be to point out the similar relationships that exist in different languages between many expressions and combinations on the one hand, and certain inner features on the other. This would be translation's more limited aim; its general aim would be to illuminate a language with the particular spirit of a foreign master, as long as it is a master who is completely separated and cut off from his own language. Since the former is only an elegant and artificial game, and since the latter rests on a fiction that can almost definitely never be applied in practice, it is not difficult to understand why this type of translation is only sparingly practiced in a few attempts that serve to demonstrate that it cannot be more widely practiced. It is also not difficult to understand why only excellent masters who may presume the miraculous could work according to this method. Only those who have already done their duty by the world and therefore allow themselves to be drawn into an exciting and somewhat dangerous game are entitled to do so. On the other hand, it is very easy to understand why the masters who feel they are unable to carry out such a task would look down with a certain compassion on the industrious efforts made by translators of the other type. They believe that they alone are engaged in that fine and beautiful art while all others appear to be much closer to the interpreter in so far as they, too, serve a need, albeit of a slightly nobler nature. Such interpreters seem to be all the more deserving of pity since they invest more labor and art than could possibly be justified in such a subordinate and thankless business. That is the reason why the masters will always advise the public to get by with paraphrases as much as possible, as interpreters do in difficult or dubious cases, and it is also the reason why this type of translation should not be produced at all.

Should we share their opinion and follow their advice? The ancients obviously translated little in that most real sense, and most moderns, deterred by the difficulties of true translation, also appear satisfied with imitation and paraphrase. Who would want to contend that nothing has ever been translated into French from either the classical or the Germanic languages? Yet even though we Germans are perfectly willing to listen to this advice we should not heed it. An inner necessity that is the clear expression of our nation's particular calling has compelled us to translate on a large scale. We cannot go back and therefore we must go on. Just as our soil itself has no doubt become richer and more fertile and our climate milder and more pleasant only after much transplantation of foreign flora, so too we sense that our language, which we exercise less than other nations do theirs, because of our Northern sluggishness, can thrive in all its freshness and completely develop its own power only by means of the most many-sided contacts with what is foreign. Coincidentally our nation, which respects what is foreign and is destined for mediation by its very nature, may be called upon to carry all the treasures of foreign art and foreign scholarship in its language, together with its own treasures in those fields and to unite them all into a great historical whole, so to speak, which would be preserved at the very center and heart of Europe. With the help of our language all nations would then be able to enjoy whatever beauty the most different times have brought forth, to the extent that foreigners can succeed in doing this in a pure and perfect manner. Indeed, this appears to be the real historical aim of translation as we have grown used to it now. If we want to attain this goal, however, we should practice only the first method discussed in this essay. Art must try to overcome as much as possible the difficulties besetting that method, which we have not tried to hide. We have made a good start but the larger part of the work still remains to be done. We shall have to go through many exercises and many attempts, in this field as in any other, before a few excellent works will come into being, and much is likely to shine at the outset that will later be supplanted by what is better. We already have many examples of the extent to which individual artists have overcome these difficulties, at least in part, or skirted them in a felicitous manner. Even if some who are working in the field are less able than we would like them to be, we should not be afraid that great harm will come to our language as the result of their endeavors. It must be established at the outset that translators work in a field that is theirs only, in a language in which translation is practiced to such an extent, and much of what should not be permitted to show itself elsewhere ought to be allowed to translators when they work in that field. Whoever tries to further transplant these innovations in an unauthorized manner will find only a few imitators, or none at all, and if we want to close the account after a reasonable period of time we can rely on the process of assimilation that is at work in all languages to discard again whatever has been accepted only because of a passing need and does not really correspond to its nature. On the other hand, we should not fail to acknowledge that much of what is beautiful and powerful in our language has in part either developed by way of translation or been drawn out of obscurity by translation. We are used to speaking too little and making too much conversation. It cannot be denied that our style had evolved too far in that direction over quite a long period of time and that translation has contributed more than a little to the reestablishing of a stricter style. We shall be less in need of translation for the development of our language when and if ever the time comes in which we are blessed with a public life that produces the kind of social behavior that is more meritorious and truer to our language, and gives more scope to the orator's talent. Let us hope that time will come before we have rounded the whole circle of difficulties in translation in a dignified manner.

【翻译鉴赏】

The Old Man and the Sea

(Excerpt)

[1] As the sun set he remembered, to give himself more confidence, the time in the tavern at Casablanca when he had played the handgame with the great Negro from Cienfuegos who was the strongest man on the docks. [2] They had gone one day and one night with their elbows on a chalk line on the table and their forearms straight up and their hands gripped tight. [3] Each one was trying to force the other's hand down onto the table. [4] There was much betting and people went in and out of the room under the kerosene lights and he had looked at the arm and hand of the Negro and at the Negro's face. [5] They changed the referees every four hours after the first eight so that the referees could sleep. [6] Blood came out from under the fingernails of both his and the Negro's hands and they looked each other in the eye and at their hands and forearms and the bettors went in and out of the room and sat on high chairs against the wall and watched. [7] The walls were painted bright blue and wire of wood and the lamps their shadows against them. [8] The Negro's shadow was huge and it moved on the wall as the breeze moved the lamps.

⁹The odds would changed back and forth all night and they fed the Negro rum and lighted cigarettes for him. ¹⁰Then the Negro, after the rum, would try for a tremendous effort and once he had the old man, who was not an old man then but was Santiago El Campeon, nearly three inches off balance. ¹¹But the old man had raised his hand up to dead even again. ¹²He was sure then that he had the Negro, who was a fine man and a great athlete, beaten. ¹³And at daylight when the bettors were asking that it be called a draw and the referee was shaking his head, he had unleashed his effort and forced the hand of the Negro down and down until it rested on the wood. ¹⁴The match had started on a Sunday morning and ended on a Monday morning. ¹⁵Many of the bettors had asked for a draw because they had to work on the docks loading sacks of sugar or at the Havana Coal Company. ¹⁶Otherwise everyone would have wanted it to go to a finish. ¹⁷But he had finished it anyway and before anyone had to go to work.

——from *The Old Man and the Sea*. New York: Charles Scribner's Sons，1980

【背景介绍】

当代欧美作家中,风格朴实之冠,恐怕非海明威莫属。人们誉其风格为"电报式"风格:干净利落,简洁凝练。显而易见,要翻译海明威的作品,译者最重要的工作就是竭尽全力使译文再现原作的这种风格。这两节文字在整篇小说中可谓举足轻重,为老人后来成功地钓到大鱼以及与群鲨搏斗而不屈的惊险情节布下了一个惟妙惟肖的伏笔。细细吟咏原文,人们不难发现,其字里行间无不洋溢着一种平实而朴素的风格美。

【译文】

太阳落下去的时候,为了给自己增强信心,他回想起那回在卡萨布兰卡的一家酒店里,跟那个码头上力气最大的人,从西恩富戈斯来的大个子黑人比手劲的光景。整整一天一夜,他们把手拐儿搁在桌面一道粉笔线上,胳膊朝上伸直,两只手紧握着。双方都竭力将对方的手使劲朝下压到桌面上。好多人在赌谁胜谁负,人们在室内的煤油灯下走出走进,他打量着黑人的胳膊和手,还有这黑人的脸。最初的八小时过后,他们每四小时换一个裁判员,好让裁判员轮流睡觉。他和黑人手上的指甲缝里都渗出血来,他们俩正视着彼此的眼睛,望着手和胳膊,打赌的人在屋里走出走进,坐在靠墙的高椅子上旁观,四壁漆着明亮的蓝色,是木制的板壁,几盏灯把他们的影子投射在墙上。黑人的影子非常大,随着微风吹动挂灯,这影子也在墙上移动着。

一整夜,赌注的比例来回变换着,人们把朗姆酒送到黑人嘴边,还替他点燃香烟。黑人喝了朗姆酒,就拼命地使出劲儿来,有一回把老人的手(他当时还不是个老人,而是"冠军"圣地亚哥)扳下去将近三英寸。但老人又把手扳回来,恢复势均力敌的局面。他当时确信自己能战胜这黑人,这黑人是个好样的,伟大的运动家。天亮时,打赌的人们要求当和局算了,裁判员摇头不同意,老人却使出浑身的力气来,硬是把黑人的手一点点朝下扳,直到压在桌面上。这场比赛是在一个礼拜天的早上开始的,直到礼拜一早上才结束。好多打赌的要求算是和局,因为他们得上码头去干活,把麻袋装的糖装上船,或者上哈瓦那煤行去工作。要不然人人都会要求比赛到底的。但是他反正把它结束了,而且赶在任何人上工之前。

【译文评析】

[1] 原文风格分析 字里行间无不洋溢着一种平实而朴素的风格美,主要表现如下:① 词简。

原文 413 词,其中 398 词为单音节或双音节词,而且皆为口头熟语,无一隐晦冷僻之词。此外虚词甚多,重复率亦高,以介词为例,前后使用了 14 个,其中 for 重复 3 次,of 重复 4 次,at 重复 6 次,on 重复 9 次。② 句易。原文 17 句,初初看去,单句少(5 句),复句多(12 句),颇有叠床架屋之嫌。但一经剖析,便会觉察出这些复句实是平易不过。作者先将短词缀成短语,再将短语扩为短句,而后又用一个个极普通的关联词语(其中以 and 为最,前前后后出现过 28 次),将这些短句密密地"缝"在了一起。使人一看,便觉得这些句子流畅练达、脉络清晰、音调铿锵、节奏明快。③ 适当运用常见修辞手法,一种是反复,如 People went in and out of the room 和 the bettors went in and out of the room 的相继出现,烘托出店堂内熙熙攘攘的热闹场面。又如 he had looked at the arm and hand of the Negro and at the Negro's face 与 they looked each other in the eye and at their hands and forearms 的一再重叠,暗示了两位对手不断相互窥测,以求最后一逞的紧张心理。另一种是排偶,如 he had the old man, who was not an old man but was Santiago El Campeon, nearly three inches off balance(句 10)与 he had the Negro, who was a fine man and a great athlete, beaten(句 12),这种结构上的整齐对称,完全是为了映衬出两位强者的势均力敌。

[2] **译文句法处理** 重视原文的表层结构,采取直译为主的方法,力求做到形似。其具体做法是:① 句数相等。如原文 17 句,译文亦为 17 句。② 句式相同。如原文中以 as, until, before 引导的时间状语从句,so that 引导的目的状语从句,because 引导的原因状语从句以及 that 引导的宾语从句均依原文译出。③ 局部调整。为了保证译文地道,译者并不完全拘泥于原文,而是采用变通的方式对原文的局部稍加调整,做到大体形似。如将 Where was much betting 译为"好多人在赌谁胜谁负",显得入情入理。又如将 Blood came out from under the fingernails of both his and Negro's hands 译为"他和黑人手上的指甲缝里都渗出血来",更符合汉语的说法。尤其值得称道的是对原文中定语从句的灵活处理。如原文第一句中 when 与 who 引导的两个重叠交错的定语从句,译者均译为定语,可谓细针密缕,极工逼肖。而原文句 10 和 12 中 who 引导的非限制定语从句,译者则分别采用括号注释和译为分句,使句式顺序和原文保持了一致。

[3] **译文词汇和短语处理** 注重原文的神韵,采用意译与直译并举的方法,力求达到神似。① 口语化。原文口头熟语甚多,译文也尽量保持这一特色。如:play the handgame——比手劲,the time——光景,elbows——手拐儿,each one——双方,so that——好让,back and forth——来回,a fine man——好样的,down and down——一点点朝下,many of bettors——好多打赌的人,anyway——反正,otherwise——要不然等。② 化宾为主,以动代静。如将原文句 2 中 with 引导的三个复合宾语分别译为三个主谓句:"他们把手拐儿搁在桌面一道粉笔线上,胳膊朝上伸直,两只手紧握着",将介词短语 after the rum 译为动宾词组"喝了朗姆酒"等。这些清新活泼的译文强烈地表现了原文的气氛,与作者的用心完全是一脉相承的。③ 使用汉语把(将)字结构。如:force the other's hand down——将对方的手使劲朝下压,threw their shadows against them——把他们的影子投射在墙上,fed the Negro rum——把朗姆酒送到黑人嘴边,had the old man ... off balance——把老人的手扳下去,forced the hand of the Negro down and down——把黑人的手一点点朝下扳,loading sack of sugar——把麻袋装的糖装上船,had finished it——把它结束了。这样的译法既符合汉语的特点,又再现了原文的情貌风采。

[4] **译文修辞手法处理** 不拘囿于原文,采用保留与舍弃等灵活方法,力求保持艺术效果上的

一致。以"反复"为例,原文中相继出现的 went in and out of the room,均译为"走出走进",而 look 则被分别译做"打量"、"正视"、"望着",great 译做"大个子"、"伟大的",force 译做"使劲"、"硬是把",甚至连重复出现的 as 也各自译为"……的时候"与"随着"。又如 odds 一词,乍一看,恰似"双关"(竞赛者比赛的让步/打赌人赌注的让步),但译者断然译成"赌注的比例",显示了无比的准确性。至于原文中的"排偶"修辞手法,虽然在译文中没有表现出来,但读者仍然可以从中品尝出那种强烈的对比意味。

——参考郑延国,"妙手剪裁 风格再现——《老人与海》新译片断赏析",《中国翻译》,1990年第 3 期

想北平
(老舍)

设若让我写一本小说,以北平作背景,我不至于害怕,因为我可以拣着我知道的写,而躲开我所不知道的。让我单摆浮搁的讲一套北平,我没办法。北平的地方那么大,事情那么多,我知道的真觉太少了,虽然我生在那里,一直到廿七岁才离开。以名胜说,我没到过陶然亭,这多可笑!以此类推,我所知道的那点只是"我的北平",而我的北平大概等于牛的一毛。

可是,我真爱北平。这个爱几乎是要说而说不出的。我爱我的母亲。怎样爱?我说不出。在我想做一件讨她老人家喜欢的时候,我独自微微地笑着;在我想到她的健康而不放心的时候,我欲落泪。言语是不够表现我的心情的,只有独自微笑或落泪才足以把内心揭露在外面一些来。我之爱北平也近乎这个。夸奖这个古城的某一点是容易的,可是那就把北平看得太小了。我所爱的北平不是枝枝节节的一些什么,而是整个儿与我的心灵相粘合的一段历史,一大块地方,多少风景名胜,从雨后什刹海的蜻蜓一直到我梦里的玉泉山的塔影,都积凑到一块,每一小的事件中有个我,我的每一思念中有个北平,这只有说不出而已。

真愿成为诗人,把一切好听好看的字都浸在自己的心血里,象杜鹃似的啼出北平的俊伟。啊!我不是诗人!我将永远道不出我的爱,一种像由音乐与图画所引起的爱。这不但是辜负了北平,也对不住我自己,因为我的最初的知识与印象都得自北平,它是在我的血里,我的性格与脾气里有许多地方是这古城所赐给的。我不能爱上海与天津,因为我心中有个北平。可是我说不出来!

伦敦、巴黎、罗马与堪司坦丁堡,曾被称为欧洲的四大"历史的都城"。我知道一些伦敦的情形;巴黎与罗马只是到过而已;堪司坦丁堡根本没有去过。就伦敦、巴黎、罗马来说,巴黎更近似北平——虽然"近似"两字要拉扯得很远——不过,假使让我"家住巴黎",我一定会和没有家一样地感到寂苦。巴黎,据我看,还太热闹。自然,那里也有空旷静寂的地方,可是又未免太旷;不像北平那样既复杂而又有个边际,使我能摸着——那长着红酸枣的老城墙!面向着积水潭,背后是城墙,坐在石上看水中的小蝌蚪或苇叶上的嫩蜻蜓,我可以快乐的坐一天,心中完全安适,无所求也无可怕,像小儿安睡在摇篮里。是的,北平也有热闹的地方,但是它和太极拳相似,动中有静。巴黎有许多地方使人疲乏,所以咖啡与酒是必要的,以便刺激;在北平,有温和的香片茶就够了。

论说巴黎的布置已比伦敦罗马匀调得多了,可是比上北平还差点事儿。北平在人为之中显出自然,几乎是什么地方既不挤得慌,又不太僻静;最小的胡同里的房子也有院子与树;最空旷的地方也离买卖街与住宅区不远。这种分配法可以算——在我的经验中——天下第一了。北平的好处不在处处设备得完全,而在它处处有空儿,可以使人自由地喘气;不在有好些美丽

的建筑,而在建筑的四围都有空闲的地方,使它们成为美景。每一个城楼,每一个牌楼,都可以从老远就看见。况且在街上还可以看见北山与西山呢!

好学的,爱古物的,人们自然喜欢北平,因为这里书多古物多。我不好学,也没钱买古物。对于物质上,我却喜爱北平的花多菜多果子多。花草是种费钱的玩艺,可是此地的"草花儿"很便宜,而且家家有院子,可以花不多的钱而种一院子花,即使算不了什么,可是到底可爱呀。墙上的牵牛,墙根的靠山竹与草茉莉,是多么省钱省事而也足以招来蝴蝶呀!至于青菜、白菜、扁豆、毛豆角、黄瓜、菠菜等等,大多数是直接由城外担来而送到家门口的。雨后,韭菜叶上还往往带着雨时溅起的泥点。青菜摊子上的红红绿绿几乎有诗似的美丽。果子有不少是由西山与北山来的,西山的沙果、海棠,北山的黑枣、柿子,进了城还带着一层白霜儿呀!哼,美国的橘子包着纸;遇到北平的带霜儿的玉李,还不愧杀!

是的,北平是个都城,而能有好多自己产生的花,菜,水果,这就使人更接近了自然。从它里面说,它没有像伦敦的那些成天冒烟的工厂;从外面说,它紧连着园林、菜圃与农村。采菊东篱下,在这里,确是可以悠然见南山的;大概把"南"字变个"西"或"北",也没有多少了不得的吧。像我这样的一个贫寒的人,或者只有在北平能享受一点清福了。

好,不再说了吧;要落泪了,真想念北平呀!

【背景介绍】

老舍是中国文坛一位知名作家,被誉为语言艺术大师。他的作品《想北平》对乡情作了最好的诠释,作品纯朴的风格通过他的浓郁的北京韵味的语言——体现。他的语言通俗质朴而又典雅精致,简洁凝练而又含蕴丰厚,幽默诙谐而又不失严肃深刻。北京于1930年改称北平,1949年新中国成立时恢复旧名。《想北平》是老舍名篇,写于1936年。约60年前的古都风貌和生活情调,时至今日,已发生巨大变化。当时老舍在山东大学任教,正值日寇入侵,国难当头。文章热情颂扬北平,字里行间洋溢着强烈的爱国主义和民族自豪感。

【译文】

I have no misgivings about writing a novel with Peiping as its background because I can choose to write about what I am most familiar with while shying away from what is less known to me. But I shall be at a complete loss if I should be called upon to write exclusively about Peiping. Peiping is so big and multifaceted that very little of it, I believe, is known to me though I was born and brought up there and never went away until I was 27. Just fancy that I have neglected to visit even Tao Tan Ting, a local scenic attraction! It follows that, in contrast with Peiping in its entirety, what little I know about it is probably a mere drop in the ocean.

I do cherish, however, a genuine love for Peiping—a love that is almost as inexpressible as my love for Mother. I smile by myself when I think of something I can do to please Mother; I feel like crying when I worry about Mother's health. Words fail me where silent smiles and tears well express my innermost feelings. The same is true of my love for Peiping. I shall fail to do justice to this vast ancient city if I should do no more than extol just one certain aspect of it. The Peiping I love is not something in bits and pieces, but a phase of history and a vast tract of land completely bound up with my heart. Numerous scenic spots and historical sites from Shi Sha Hai Lake with its dragonflies after a rain to the

Yu Quan Shan Mountain with the dream pagoda on top—all merge into a single whole. I associate myself with everything in Peiping no matter how trivial it is; Peiping is always in my mind. I can't tell why.

If only I were a poet, so that with all the sweet and beautiful words at my command, I would sing of the grandeur of Peiping in as longing a note as that of a cuckoo! Alas, I am no poet! I shall never be able to express my love—the kind of love as inspired by music or painting. That is quite a letdown to both Peiping and myself, for it is to this ancient city that I owe what I have within me, including my early knowledge and impressions as well as much of my character and temperament. With Peiping possessing my heart, I can never become attached to either Shanghai or Tianjin. I can't tell why.

London, Paris, Rome and Constantinople are known as the four major "historic capitals" of Europe. I know something about London; I have been to Paris and Rome only briefly; I have never visited Constantinople at all. Of all these cities, Paris has the closest affinity with Peiping (The word "affinity" may perhaps sound a bit farfetched). Nevertheless, if I should make my home in Paris, I would feel very lonely as if I had no home at all. As far as I know, Paris is too much of a bustling town. It does have quiet open spaces, but they smack of mere expanses of vacancy. Peiping is complicated and yet tangible. I can feel it by touch. I can feel the red wild jujubes growing on its ancient city wall! I can spend a whole day enjoying myself sitting on a rock to observe tiny tadpoles in the water or tender dragonflies on reeds while facing me lies Ji Shui Tan Pond and right behind me rises the high city wall. I can thus enjoy a perfect inner calm, free from any desire or fear, like a child sleeping peacefully in the cradle. There are also bustling places in Peiping, to be sure, but like the traditional Chinese shadow boxing *Tai Ji Quan*, the city retains its stillness in the midst of motion. While Parisians have to turn to coffee or wine for the relief of boredom caused by so many wearisome places in their city, the mild beverage of jasmine tea will be more than adequate for dwellers of Peiping.

Though Paris has a better layout than London or Rome, it nevertheless cannot compare with Peiping, one always finds the natural in the midst of the artificial. The city as a whole is neither too crowded nor too secluded. Even houses tucked away in very small lanes have their own courtyards and trees. Even the most secluded places are situated within a stone's throw of business or residential districts. Such a layout is, to my mind, without equal all over the world. However, what distinguishes Peiping is not the perfect layout, but the open spaces here and there where people can breathe freely; not the many beautiful buildings, but the open grounds around each building which add to its architectural beauty. Each gate tower of the city wall and each *pailou* (decorated archway) can be seen from afar. And the Northern and Western hills are visible to people in the open streets.

Those who are fond of studying or collecting curios will naturally be drawn to Peiping, which is remarkable for its rich store of books and curios. Personally I am not given to studying, nor do I have spare money to buy curios. But I am keen on the flowers, vegetables and fruit which grow in rich abundance in Peiping. Gardening is something very expensive. But since flowers of herbaceous plants in Peiping are very cheap and each house has a courtyard of its own, it does not cost very much to plant a whole courtyard of such flowers which, though humble, are nevertheless lovely to look at, such as morning glories on the wall, china pinks at the foot of wall and marvels-of-Peru. Yes, cheap as they are, they attract butterflies! Green vegetables, cabbages, hyacinth beans, young soya beans, cucumbers, spinach, etc. are often carried straight from the suburbs to your residential quarters for marketing. Often, leeks from rural farms after a rain still have specks of mud on their leaves. The vegetables stalls are so colorful that they present a scene of poetic charm. Fruits come mainly from the western and northern suburbs, such as crab apples and cherry apples from the Western Hills, and jujubes and persimmons from the Northern Hills.

Look, how they are still covered with frostlike bloom when they are put on the market! Indeed, America's paper-wrapped oranges will pale beside Peiping's plums bearing a thin coating of frostlike bloom!

The city of Peiping brings its residents into closer contact with nature by growing flowers, vegetables and fruit in large quantities. The city proper is not plagued by factory chimneys such as you find in London giving off volumes of smoke all day long. On the outskirts of the city lie numerous flower gardens, vegetables farms and villages. An ancient Chinese poet by the name of Tao Yuanming says aptly in one of his famous poems, "Plucking chrysanthemums under the eastern hedge, I calmly view the southern hills." To adapt it to life in Peiping, I might as well substitute the word "western" or "northern" for the word "southern" in the line. Peiping is probably the only place for a man of limited means like me to live an easy and carefree life in.

Now, let me leave off writing, for I am on the point of shedding tears. How I miss Peiping!

——trans. by Zhang Peiji

【译文评析】

[1] **全文风格分析**：我们都知道汉语重意合，而英语重形合。形合与意合是语言学涉及句法问题的两个重要概念。其相应的英语表达源于希腊语的 Hypotaxis 和 Parataxis。《英语语言学词汇》(中国社会科学出版社，1979 年版)对 Hypotaxis 的释义是：形合法(复句中同等或从属句之间需要一种方式来表达它们之间的句法关系)。对 Parataxis 的释义是：意合法(分句中不用连词)。这两种解释尚有难尽人意之处，在众多的外版辞书中有以下两条释义，深入浅出，扼要简明，并附有例句，现摘录如下：形合(hypotaxis)即 the dependent or subordinate construction or relationship of clauses with connectives. Example：I shall despair if you don't come. (*The American Heritage Dictionary*, p. 649)意合(parataxis)即 the arranging of clauses one after the other without connectives showing the relation between them. Example：The rain fall; the river flooded; the house was washed away. (*The World Book Dictionary*, p. 1513)(毛荣贵，2002)

汉语重意合，故句子多是以意义为枢纽；英语重形合，故句子多以形式或主语为枢纽。

主语在汉语中并不占主要,事实上,汉语句子中有大量的无主语句,甚至在一个复杂句中有多个主语并存的现象。这种以意义为枢纽的句法特点使得汉语中有大量的流水句。相反,没有主语的句子在英语中是不符合语法规则的。这种中英文之间的巨大差异给译者带来了很大的困难和挑战。在中译英时要特别注意从意合到形合的转换。在形合句中,各从句通过连接词(connectives)组成完整的、合语法的句子。而枝枝节节的汉语句子看似零碎独立,实则通过隐含的意义紧密相连,所以它表现的是一种休闲、散落的口语化风格。而那种由多个连接词连接的带有许多从句而组成的复杂句承载的是一种严谨正式的风格。

[2] **原文**:设若让我写一本小说,以北平作背景,我不至于害怕,因为我可以拣着我知道的写,而躲开我所不知道的。

译文:I have no misgivings about writing a novel with Peiping as its background because I can choose to write about what I am most familiar with while shying away from what is less known to me.

评析:原文是个典型的意合句。读着这几个短句,感觉轻闲、自然、放松,似乎在聆听邻家大爷絮叨。由于中英文句法标记的不同,张培基先生把带有四个逗号的句子译成了一个结构紧凑的长句。但译文仍然朗朗上口、轻松自然,因为译者的选词仍然遵循了轻松口语化的风格。譬如译文中连接词 because 和 while,简单、流畅,与原文的句法风格不谋而合,自然贴切。

[3] **原文**:可是,我真爱北平。这个爱几乎是要说而说不出的。我爱我的母亲。怎样爱? 我说不出。

译文:I do cherish, however, a genuine love for Peiping—a love that is almost as inexpressible as my love for Mother.

评析:原文又是几个短句组成的长句,摇身一变,译文成了一个简单的长句。译者巧妙地添加一破折号来解释"爱",有效地回避了一个潜在的复杂复合句,成功地再现了原文简洁的风格。

[4] **原文**:我所爱的北平不是枝枝节节的一些什么,而是整个儿与我的心灵相粘合的一段历史,一大块地方,多少风景名胜,从雨后什刹海的蜻蜓一直到我梦里的玉泉山的塔影,都积凑到一块,每一小的事件中有个我,我的每一思念中有个北平,这只有说不出而已。

译文:The Peiping I love is not something in bits and pieces, but a phase of history and a vast tract of land completely bound up with my heart. Numerous scenic spots and historical sites from Shi Sha Hai Lake with its dragonflies after a rain to the Yu Quan Shan Mountain with the dream pagoda on top—all merge into a single whole. I associate myself with everything in Peiping no matter how trivial it is; Peiping is always in my mind. I can't tell why.

评析:该句原文也是个典型的意合句。原文恰似涓涓细流,顺着作者的思路自然流淌,闲聊似的句子洋溢着对北平的无限热爱。如果按着原文的流水句直译,那连原文的意思都不能完整传达出来。此时,译者张培基先生对原文作了一个整体的分析。他把这个长长的句子译成了五句。原文的前两个短分句在意义上实则是第一层;中间的几个短分句是对第一层含义的详细阐释;后三个短分句可看成是结论,同时也是对前面部分的一个强调。有了对原文分句含义的清楚认识,译者就重塑了原文的句子结构。首先,译者把前两个短分句合二为一成一个完整的句子 The Peiping I love is not something in bits and pieces，but a phase of history and a vast tract of land completely bound up with my heart. 然后借助一个破折号,融合了中间四个短分句 Numerous scenic spots and historical sites from Shi Sha Hai Lake with its dragonflies after a rain to the Yu Quan Shan Mountain with the dream pagoda on top—all merge into a single whole. 最后,译者把这个无主句译成了一个地道的英文句子 I associate myself with everything in Peiping no matter how trivial it is; Peiping is always in my mind. I can't tell why. 其中分号的运用正确地显示了后两个短分句的内在关系。总而言之,张培基先生在句法上运用重构式换码,再现了原文自然流畅的口语化风格。

【翻译试笔】

【英译汉】

The Conquest of Happiness
Bertrand Russell
Chapter 6：Envy (excerpt)

Among average respectable women envy plays an extraordinarily large part. If you are sitting in the underground and a well-dressed woman happens to walk along the car, watch the eyes of the other women. You will see that every one of them, with the possible exception of those who are better dressed, will watch the woman with malevolent glances, and will be struggling to draw inferences derogatory to her. The love of scandal is an expression of this general malevolence：any story against another woman is instantly believed, even on the flimsiest evidence. A lofty morality serves the same purpose：those who have a chance to sin against it are envied, and it is considered virtuous to punish them for their sins. This particular form of virtue is certainly its own reward.

Exactly the same thing, however, is to be observed among men, except that women regard all other women as their competitors, whereas men as a rule only have this feeling towards other men in the same profession. Have you, reader, ever been so imprudent as to praise an artist to another artist? Have you ever praised a politician to another politician of the same party? Have you ever praised an Egyptologist to another Egyptologist? If you have, it is a hundred to one that you will have produced an explosion of jealousy. In the correspondence of Leibniz and Huyghens there are a number of letters lamenting the supposed fact that Newton had become insane. "Is it not sad," they write to each other, "that the incomparable genius of Mr. Newton should have become overclouded by the loss of reason?" And these two eminent men, in one letter after another, wept crocodile tears with obvious relish. As a matter of fact, the event which they were hypocritically lamenting had not taken place, though a few examples of eccentric behaviour had given rise to the rumour.

Of all the characteristics of ordinary human nature envy is the most unfortunate; not only does the envious person wish to inflict misfortune and do so whenever he can with impunity, but he is also himself rendered unhappy by envy. Instead of deriving pleasure from what he has, he derives pain from what others have. If he can, he deprives others of their advantages, which to him is as desirable as it would be to secure the same advantages himself. If this passion is allowed to run riot it becomes fatal to all excellence, and even to the most useful exercise of exceptional skill. Why should a medical man go to see his patients in a car when the labourer has to walk to his work? Why should the scientific investigator be allowed to spend his time in a warm room when others have to face the inclemency of the elements? Why should a man who possesses some rare talent of great importance to the world be saved from the drudgery of his own housework? To such questions envy finds no answer. Fortunately, however, there is in human nature a compensating passion, namely that of admiration. Whoever wishes to increase human happiness must wish to increase admiration and to diminish envy.

...

Chapter 11: Zest (excerpt)

In this chapter I propose to deal with what seems to me the most universal and distinctive mark of happy men, namely zest. Perhaps the best way to understand what is meant by zest will be to consider the different ways in which men behave when they sit down to a meal. There are those to whom a meal is merely a bore; no matter how excellent the food may be, they feel that it is uninteresting. They have had excellent food before, probably at almost every meal they have eaten. They have never known what it was to go without a meal until hunger became a raging passion, but have come to regard meals as merely conventional occurrences, dictated by the fashions of the society in which they live. Like everything else, meals are tiresome, but it is no use to make a fuss, because nothing else will be less tiresome. Then there are the invalids who eat from a sense of duty, because the doctor has told them that it is necessary to take a little nourishment in order to keep up their strength. Then there are the epicures, who start hopefully, but find that nothing has been quite so well cooked as it ought to have been. Then there are the gormandisers, who fall upon their food with eager rapacity, eat too much, and grow plethoric and stertorous. Finally there are those who begin with a sound appetite, are glad of their food, eat until they have had enough, and then stop.

Those who are set down before the feast of life have similar attitudes towards the good things which it offers. The happy man corresponds to the last of our eaters. What hunger is in relation to food, zest is in relation to life. The man who is bored with his meals corresponds to the victim of Byronic unhappiness. The invalid who eats from a sense of duty corresponds to the ascetic, the gormandiser to the voluptuary. The epicure corresponds to the fastidious person who condemns half the pleasures of life as unaesthetic. Oddly enough, all these types, with the possible exception of the gormandiser, feel contempt for the man of healthy appetite and consider themselves his superior. It seems to them vulgar to enjoy food because you are hungry or to enjoy life because it offers a variety of interesting spectacles and surprising experiences. From the height of their disillusionment they look down upon those whom they despise as simple souls. For my part I have no sympathy with this outlook. All disenchantment is to me a malady, which, it is true, certain circumstances may render inevitable, but which none the less, when it occurs, is to be cured as soon as possible, not to be regarded as a higher form of wisdom.

Suppose one man likes strawberries and another does not; in what respect is the latter superior? There is no abstract and impersonal proof either that strawberries are good or that they are not good. To the man who likes them they are good; to the man who dislikes them they are not. But the man who likes them has a pleasure which the other does not have; to that extent his life is more enjoyable and he is better adapted to the world in which both must live. What is true in this trivial instance is equally true in more important matters. The man who enjoys watching football is to that extent superior to the man who does not. The man who enjoys reading is still more superior to the man who does not, since opportunities for reading are more frequent than opportunities for watching football. The more things a man is interested in, the more opportunities of happiness he has, and the less he is at the mercy of fate, since if he loses one thing he can fall back upon another. Life is too short to be interested in everything, but it is good to be interested in as many things as are necessary to fill our days. We are all prone to the malady of the introvert, who, with the manifold spectacle of the world spread out before him, turns away and gazes only upon the emptiness within. But let us not imagine that there is anything grand about the introvert's unhappiness.

【汉译英】

一件小事（鲁迅）

我从乡下跑到京城里,一转眼已经六年了。其间耳闻目睹的所谓国家大事,算起来也很不少;但在我心里,都不留什么痕迹,倘要我寻出这些事的影响来说,便只是增长了我的坏脾气,——老实说,便是教我一天比一天的看不起人。

但有一件小事,却于我有意义,将我从坏脾气里拖开,使我至今忘记不得。

这是民国六年的冬天,大北风刮得正猛,我因为生计关系,不得不一早在路上走。一路几乎遇不见人,好容易才雇定了一辆人力车,叫他拉到S门去。不一会,北风小了,路上浮尘早已刮净,剩下一条洁白的大道来,车夫也跑得更快。刚近S门,忽而车把上带着一个人,慢慢地倒了。

跌倒的是一个女人,花白头发,衣服都很破烂。伊从马路上突然向车前横截过来;车夫已经让开道,但伊的破棉背心没有上扣,微风吹着,向外展开,所以终于兜着车把。幸而车夫早有点停步,否则伊定要栽一个大筋斗,跌到头破血出了。

伊伏在地上;车夫便也立住脚。我料定这老女人并没有伤,又没有别人看见,便很怪他多事,要自己惹出是非,也误了我的路。

我便对他说,"没有什么的。走你的罢!"

车夫毫不理会,——或者并没有听到,——却放下车子,扶那老女人慢慢起来,攌着臂膊立定,问伊说:

"你怎么啦?"

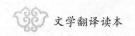
"我摔坏了。"

我想，我眼见你慢慢倒地，怎么会摔坏呢，装腔作势罢了，这真可憎恶。车夫多事，也正是自讨苦吃，现在你自己想法去。

车夫听了这老女人的话，却毫不踌躇，仍然搀着伊的臂膊，便一步一步的向前走。我有些诧异，忙看前面，是一所巡警分驻所，大风之后，外面也不见人。这车夫扶着那老女人，便正是向那大门走去。

我这时突然感到一种异样的感觉，觉得他满身灰尘的后影，刹时高大了，而且愈走愈大，须仰视才见。而且他对于我，渐渐的又几乎变成一种威压，甚而至于要榨出皮袍下面藏着的"小"来。

我的活力这时大约有些凝滞了，坐着没有动，也没有想，直到看见分驻所里走出一个巡警，才下了车。

巡警走近我说，"你自己雇车罢，他不能拉你了。"

我没有思索的从外套袋里抓出一大把铜元，交给巡警，说，"请你给他……"

风全住了，路上还很静。我走着，一面想，几乎怕敢想到自己。以前的事姑且搁起，这一大把铜元又是什么意思？奖他么？我还能裁判车夫么？我不能回答自己。

这事到了现在，还是时时记起。我因此也时时煞了苦痛，努力的要想到我自己。几年来的文治武力，在我早如幼小时候所读过的"子曰诗云"一般，背不上半句了。独有这一件小事，却总是浮在我眼前，有时反更分明，教我惭愧，催我自新，并且增长我的勇气和希望。

一九二〇年七月

【参考译文】

论幸福（罗素）
第六章 嫉妒（节选）

在一般的善良妇女身上，嫉妒具有非常大的作用。要是你坐在地道车内，有一个衣服华丽的女子在车厢旁边走过时，你试试留神旁的女子的目光罢。她们之中，除了比那个女子穿着更华美的以外，都将用着恶意的眼光注视着她，同时争先恐后的寻出贬抑她的说话。喜欢飞短流长的谈论人家的阴私，就是这种一般的恶意的表现：对别一个女人不利的故事，立刻被人相信，哪怕是捕风捉影之谈。一种严峻的道德观也被做着同样的用处：那些有机会背叛道德的人是被嫉妒的，去惩罚这等罪人是被认为有功德的。有功德当然就是道德的酬报了。

同样的情形同样见之于男人，不过女人是把一切旁的女人看作敌手，而男人普通只对同行同业才这样看法。我要一问读者，你曾否冒失到当着一个艺术家去称赞另一艺术家？曾否当着一个政治家去称赞同一政党的另一政治家？曾否当着一个埃及考古家去称赞另一埃及考古家？假如你曾这样做，那么一百次准有九十九次你引起的炉火的爆发。在莱谱尼茨与惠更斯的通讯中，多少封信都替谣传的牛顿发疯这件事悲叹。他们互相在信里写着："这个卓绝的天才牛顿先生居然失掉理性，岂不可悲？"这两位贤者，一封又一封的信，显然是津津有味地流了多少假眼泪。事实上他们假仁假义的怅惜之事并不真实，牛顿不过有了几种古怪的举动，以致引起谣言罢了。

普通的人性的一切特征中，最不幸的莫如嫉妒；嫉妒的人不但希望随时（只要自己能逃法网）给人祸害，抑且他自己也因嫉妒而忧郁不欢。照理他应该在自己的所有中寻快乐，他反而在别人的所有中找痛苦。如果能够，他将剥夺人家的利益；他认为这和他自己占有利益同样需要。倘听任这种情欲放肆，那么非但一切的优秀卓越之士要受其害，连特殊巧艺的最有益的运用也将蒙其祸。为何一个医生可以坐着车子去诊治病人，而劳工只能步行去上工？为何一个科学实验家能在一间温暖的室内消磨时间，而别人却要冒受风寒？为何一个赋有稀有才具的人可毋须躬操井臼？对这些问题，嫉妒找不到答案。幸而人类天性中还有另一宗激情——钦佩——可以作为补偿。凡祝望加增人类的幸福的人，就该祝望加增钦佩，减少嫉妒。

……

第十一章　热情（节选）

在这一章里，我预备讨论我认为快乐人的最普通最显著的标记——兴致。要懂得何谓兴致，最好是把人们入席用餐时的各种态度考察一下。有些人把吃饭当作一件厌事；不问食物如何精美，他们总丝毫不感兴味。从前他们就有过丰盛的饭食，或者几乎每顿都如此精美。他们从未领略过没有饭吃而饿火中烧的滋味，却把吃饭看作纯粹的刻板文章，为社会习俗所规定的。如一切旁的事情一样，吃饭是无聊的，但用不到因此而大惊小怪，因为比起旁的事情来，吃饭的纳闷是最轻的。然后有些病人抱着责任的观念而进食，因为医生告诉他们，为保持体力起见必须吸收一些营养。然后，有些享乐主义者，高高兴兴的开始，却发觉没有一件东西烹调得够精美。然后有些老饕，贪得无厌的扑向食物，吃得太多，以致变得充血而大打其鼾。最后，有些胃口正常的人，对于他们的食物很是满意，吃到足够时便停下。

凡是坐在人生的宴席之前的人，对人生供应的美好之物所取的各种态度，就像坐在饭桌前对食物所取的态度。快乐的人相当于前面所讲的最后一种食客。兴致之与人生正如饥饿之于食物。觉得食物可厌的人，无异受浪漫底克忧郁侵蚀的人。怀着责任心进食的人不啻禁欲主义者，饕餮之徒无殊纵欲主义者。享乐主义者却或向一个吹毛求疵的人，把人生半数的乐事都斥为不够精美。奇怪的是，所有这些典型的人物，除了老饕以外，都瞧不起一个胃口正常的人而自认为比他高一级。在他们心目中，因为饥饿而有口赋之欲是鄙俗的，因人生有赏心悦目的景致，出乎意料的阅历而享受人生，也是不登大雅的。他们在幻灭的高峰上，瞧不起那些他们视为愚蠢的灵魂。以我个人来说，我对这种观点完全不表同情。一切的心灰意懒，我都认为一种病，固然为有些情势所逼而无可避免，但只要它一出现，就该设法治疗而不当视为一种高级的智慧。

假定一个人喜欢杨梅而一个不喜欢；后者又在哪一点上优于前者呢？没有抽象和客观的证据可以说杨梅好或不好。在喜欢的人，杨梅是好的；在不喜欢的人，杨梅是不好的。但爱杨梅的人享有旁人所没有的一种乐趣；在这一点上他的生活更有趣味，对于世界也更适应。在这个琐屑的例子上适用的原则，同样可适用于更重大的事。以观看足球赛为乐的人，在这个限度以内要比无此兴趣的人为优胜。以读书为乐的人要比不以此为乐的人要优胜得多，因为读书的机会较多于观足球赛的机会。一个人感有兴趣的事情越多，快乐的机会也越多，而受命运播弄的可能性也越少，因若他失掉一样，还可亡羊补牢，转到另一样上去。固然，生命太短促，不能对事事都感兴趣，但感到兴趣的事情总是多多益善，以便填补我们的日子。我们却都有内省病的倾向，尽管世界上万千色相罗列眼底，总是掉首不顾而注视着内心的空虚。但切勿以为在内省病者的忧郁里面有何伟大之处。

An Incident

Six years have slipped by since I came from the country to the capital. During that time I have seen and heard quite enough of so-called affairs of state; but none of them made much

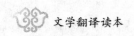

impression on me. If asked to define their influence, I can only say they aggravated my ill temper and made me, frankly speaking, more and more misanthropic.

One incident, however, struck me as significant, and aroused me from my ill temper, so that even now I cannot forget it.

It happened during the winter of 1917. A bitter north wind was blowing, but, to make a living, I had to be up and out early. I met scarcely a soul on the road, and had great difficulty in hiring a rickshaw to take me to S Gate. Presently the wind dropped a little. By now the loose dust had all been blown away, leaving the roadway clean, and the rickshaw man quickened his pace. We were just approaching S Gate when someone crossing the road was entangled in our rickshaw and slowly fell.

It was a woman, with streaks of white in her hair, wearing ragged clothes. She had left the pavement without warning to cut across in front of us, and although the rickshaw man had made way, her tattered jacket, unbuttoned and fluttering in the wind, had caught on the shaft. Luckily the rickshaw man pulled up quickly, otherwise she would certainly have had a bad fall and been seriously injured.

She lay there on the ground, and the rickshaw man stopped. I did not think the old woman was hurt, and there had been no witnesses to what had happened, so I resented this officiousness which might land him in trouble and hold me up.

"It's all right," I said. "Go on."

He paid no attention, however—perhaps he had not heard—for he set down the shafts, and gently helped the old woman to get up. Supporting her by one arm, he asked:

"Are you all right?"

"I'm hurt."

I had seen how slowly she fell, and was sure she could not be hurt. She must be pretending, which was disgusting. The rickshaw man had asked for trouble, and now he had it. He would have to find his own way out.

But the rickshaw man did not hesitate for a minute after the old woman said she was injured. Still holding her arm, he helped her slowly forward. I was surprised. When I looked ahead, I saw a police station. Because of the high wind, there was no one outside, so the rickshaw man helped the old woman towards the gate.

Suddenly I had a strange feeling. His dusty, retreating figure seemed larger at that instant. Indeed, the further he walked the larger he loomed, until I had to look up to him. At the same time he seemed gradually to be exerting a pressure on me, which threatened to overpower the small self under my fur-lined gown.

My vitality seemed sapped as I sat there motionless, my mind a blank, until a policeman came out. Then I got down from the rickshaw.

The policeman came up to me, and said, "Get another rickshaw. He can't pull you anymore."

Without thinking, I pulled a handful of coppers from my coat pocket and handed them to the policeman. "Please give him these," I said.

The wind had dropped completely, but the road was still quiet. I walked along thinking, but I was almost afraid to turn my thoughts on myself. Setting aside what had happened earlier, what had I meant by that handful of coppers? Was it a reward? Who was I to judge the rickshaw man? I could not answer myself.

Even now, this remains fresh in my memory. It often causes me distress, and makes me try to think about myself. The military and political affairs of those years I have forgotten as completely as the classics I read in my childhood. Yet this incident keeps coming back to me, often more vivid than in actual life, teaching me shame, urging me to reform, and giving me fresh courage and hope.

July, 1920

trans. by Yang Hsien-yi and Gladys Yang

【延伸阅读】

[1] Bowie, A. *Aesthetics and Subjectivity*: *from Kant to Nietzsche* [C]. Manchester: Manchester University Press, 1990.

[2] Lefevere, A. *Translation*, *History*, *Culture*: *A Sourcebook* [C]. Shanghai: Shanghai Foreign Language Education Press, 2004.

[3] Lefevere, A. *Translation*, *Rewriting and the Manipulation of Literary Fame* [M]. Shanghai: Shanghai Foreign Language Education Press, 2004.

[4] Rose, M. G. *Translation and Literary Criticism*: *Translation as Analysis* [M]. Manchester: St. Jerome Publishing, 1997.

[5] Shuttleworth, M. & Cowie, M. *Dictionary of Translation Studies* [Z]. Shanghai: Shanghai Foreign Language Education Press, 2004.

[6] Simms, K. *Translating Sensitive Texts*: *Linguistic Aspects* [C]. Amsterdam-Atlanta: Rodopi, 1997.

[7] Wang, Zuoliang. *Articles of Affinity*: *Studies in Comparative Literature* [M]. Beijing: Foreign Language Teaching and Research Press, 1987.

[8] Venuti, L. *The Translator's Invisibility*: *A History of Translation* [M]. Shanghai: Shanghai Foreign Language Education Press, 2004.

[9] 包通法. 文学翻译中译者"本色"的哲学思辨[J]. 外国语,2003 (6).

[10] 陈志杰. 文言语体与文学翻译——文言在外汉翻译中的适用性研究[M]. 上海:上海外语教育出版社,2009.

[11] 冯庆华. 文体翻译论[M]. 上海:上海外语教育出版社,2002.

[12] 胡壮麟. 理论文体学[M]. 北京:外语教学与研究出版社,2000.

[13] 黄忠廉. 翻译变体研究[M]. 北京:中国对外翻译出版公司,2000.

[14] 金兹堡. 陈志华译. 风格与时代[M]. 西安:陕西师范大学出版社,2004.

[15] 黎昌抱. 王佐良翻译风格研究[M]. 北京:光明日报出版社,2009.

[16] 刘宓庆,章艳. 翻译美学理论[M]. 北京:外语教学与研究出版社,2011.

[17] 刘宓庆. 文体与翻译[M]. 北京：中国对外翻译出版公司,2009.

[18] 刘重德. 文学风格翻译问题商榷[J]. 中国翻译,1988（2）.

[19] 罗国林. 风格与译风[J]. 中国翻译，1996(2).

[20] 马红军. 翻译批评散论[M]. 北京：中国对外翻译出版公司,2000.

[21] 许钧. 生命之轻与翻译之重[M]. 北京：文化艺术出版社,2007.

[22] 许渊冲. 文学与翻译[M]. 北京：北京大学出版社,2003.

[23] 严晓江. 梁实秋中庸翻译观研究[M]. 上海：上海译文出版社,2008.

[24] 杨自俭. 语言多学科研究与应用[M]. 南宁：广西教育出版社,2002.

[25] 周仪,罗平. 翻译与批评[M]. 武汉：湖北教育出版社,2005.

【问题与思考】

1. 风格的定义是什么？

2. 翻译学界围绕风格问题的主要讨论有哪些？有无结论？

3. 风格翻译的具体困难是什么？

4. 请结合文体学相关理论,解释"傅雷体华文语言"存在的合理性。

5. 译者风格与作者风格的关系何在？

6. "风格不可译"论者的依据是什么？

7. 翻译非文学作品,是否也有一个如何对待风格的问题？如何具体处理？

8. 能否结合风格研究相关成果,谈一谈你对泰特勒翻译三原则的看法？

9. 在国内二十世纪的风格翻译争论中,能否列举各派主张的主要代表人物及其对于风格翻译的论点？

10. 就文学风格翻译而论,严复"信达雅"三原则的逻辑顺序如何？

第三章 文学翻译修辞篇

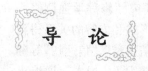

导　论

　　修辞学(Rhetorics)是研究语言表达效果的学问。人们在说话、写作时常使用一些修辞手法来说明问题,描述事物。使用修辞手法可以带来强调、渲染气氛、增加色彩等效果。修辞格是在使用语言的过程中,利用多种语言手段以达到尽可能好的表达效果的一种语言活动。恰当使用修辞格能使语言生动形象、具体活泼,给人以美的享受。要翻译好英语修辞格,首先要弄清其特点、弄清英汉两种语言在文化方面的异同,然后根据具体情况采用恰当的技巧进行翻译。英语较汉语具有更丰富的修辞种类,与汉语的修辞格并非完全对等。英语的修辞格从大类上分有三种:音韵修辞格、词义修辞格和句法修辞格。这三类里包括大约有二十多种修辞格。常用的也有十多种。音韵修辞格(phonological rhetorical devices),是利用词语的语音特点创造出来的修辞手法,主要包括拟声、头韵和脚韵等;词义修辞格(semantic rhetorical devices),是指借助语义联想和语言变化等特点创造出来的修辞手法,主要包括明喻、暗喻、转喻、移就、拟人、夸张、反语、委婉、双关、矛盾修饰法、轭式搭配法、对比等;句法修辞格(syntactical rhetorical devices),则是通过句子结构的均衡布局或突出重点创造出来的修辞手法,主要包括重复、反问、平行结构、倒装等。

　　语言是思维的载体,依附于有声的外壳,因此首先诉之于听觉或内在的听觉。有史以来,人们一直追求语言的交际功能和美学价值的结合。在这个过程中,最重要的发现就是语言的音乐性质。英国作家斯蒂芬·斯彭德(Stephen H. Spender)说:"有时,在写作中我感到遣词造句犹如谱写音乐。这种音乐性对我的吸引,远远超过词语本身。"语言内在的音乐性,要求我们在说话和写作的时候选择具有节奏感和韵律美的词语,以加强语言的渲染力。尽管翻译界对翻译中的基本问题一直争论不休,但大都认同翻译中两个阶段的分法:理解阶段和表达阶段。理解是翻译中的关键,但深透的理解要靠好的译文来体现,翻译能否再现修辞格的原貌是一个很重要的问题。译文若不能正确表现原文的修辞法,就不能准确地表达原文的思想和风格,即使与原文大意差不多,也会使原文的语言力量遭到削弱。对于英汉语言中相似的修辞手法,在翻译中应当尽可能采用直译,即在用词上和修辞结构上都与原文一致,做到形神兼备。但有时单纯用直译的方法还不行,还需使用诸如加注、释义、归化、切分等方法来补充直译的不足。由于两个民族历史发展、生活环境、风俗习惯各不相同,思维方式和美学观念也有所不同,对于双关、幽默等文字游戏修辞而言,保持原文修辞格式常常需要译者另辟蹊径,对原有修辞格进行改造,或者只能放弃。

　　"翻译学中的表达问题,与修辞学关系十分密切,因为两者都是探讨运用语言的技巧。"(刘宓庆,1998:536)随着语用学理论的发展,注重交际效果的语用翻译日益受到关注,译界在翻译领域逐渐走出"语言的牢笼",从修辞、文化、意识形态等层面跨越交流的障碍,而人们也不再会觉得语言的鸿沟足以使交流的"遗憾接近于绝望"。谭学纯在《广义修辞学》开篇说,"人不仅是语言的动物,更是修辞的动物"。人类的交流在语言层面展开,却在修辞的层面实现沟通。张弓在《现代汉语修辞学》中亦明确指出,"修辞学是语言学的一个部门,它和语言学的其他各部门(词汇、语法、语音)密切相关,而又具有一定的独立性"。"它是研究词汇、语法、语音的运用,它研究词汇、语法、语义,是从表达态度、表达方法、表达效果的角度来研究。"修辞学强调修辞应适应题旨情境,结合现实语境,注重交际效果,就其实质而言,语言的形式和内容的关系得到前所未有的重视。翻译界的"直译/意译"、"归化/异化"等的争论以及"信达雅"、"信达切"等翻译准则无不是追求在另一种语言中实现原文内容与形式的最佳契合。翻译,从根本上说追求的是两种语言在广义修辞范畴的对等。

论及翻译,我国译界前辈马建忠说:"夫译之为事难矣。译之将奈何?其平日冥心钩考,必先将所译者与所以译者,两国之文字,深嗜笃好,字栉句比,以考彼此文字孳生之源,同异之故。所有相当之实义,委曲推究,务审其音声之高下,析其字句之繁简,尽其文体之变态,及其义理精深奥折之所由然。夫如是,则一书到手,经营反覆,确知其意旨之所在,而又摹写其神情,仿佛其语气,然后心悟神解,振笔而书,译成之文,适如其所译而止,而曾无毫发出入其间。夫而后能使阅者所得之益与观原文无异,是则为善译也已。"马氏的"务审其音声之高下","夫而后,能使阅者所得之益与观原文无异"强调了文学翻译中修辞手段传递的必要性和审美标准。

修辞不仅研究"美化之艺术"或"美辞",而且是对语辞的形、音、义随时加以注意和利用。修辞学已经逐渐摆脱狭义的消极修辞的藩篱,结合现实语境,研究每一个活的、有根的、有个性的语辞,对双语转换中在所难免的修辞失落进行积极的补偿,使原文的美和蕴含得到最大程度的传递。文学是语言的艺术。文学作品具有意境美、结构美、音韵美等多层次的美感体现,无论中文还是英文,都具有独特的方式构成美的形式和美的音韵,看去赏心悦目,听来和谐悦耳。更为重要的是,作为文学作品,很多完美的形式和音韵正是作者的匠心所在,是表达其作品精神实质的必不可少的符号。因此,文学作品翻译中的由于思维方式不同造成的修辞翻译的困难,不能任其失落而不做补偿的努力,这些蕴含着美的修辞的失落,将会意味着作品翻译的失败和文化交流的失败。

本单元所选文章围绕英汉修辞格的具体特点和差异、文学翻译中修辞格传递的重要性、修辞格表述给翻译造成的障碍和设置的樊篱等方面展开,涉及修辞格中极度抗拒翻译的双关、习用性比喻、隐喻等具体修辞方式在《鲁拜集》等经典诗歌、散文文学体裁中的具体处理方式。本单元通过选取张南峰教授的《Delabastita 的双关语翻译理论在英汉翻译中的应用》一文,着力指出西方翻译理论和微观操作应用理论往往也可以用来解释英汉语言转换过程中的问题,导致西方翻译理论对英汉翻译实践指导力不足的往往不是语言特殊性,而可能是理论背后蕴含的文化特殊性。

选文一 英汉翻译中修辞格的处理

余立三

导 言

本文选自余立三编著,《英汉修辞比较与翻译》,商务印书馆(北京),1985年版。

文章开宗明义,指出"译文中若不能正确表现原文的修辞法,就不能准确地表达原文的思想、精神和风格"。作者分析认为,英汉两种语言在修辞手法上极为相似,绝大多数英语常用修辞格都能找到与之相对应的汉语修辞格,在翻译中应当尽可能采用直译的办法,即在用词上和修辞结构上都与原文一致,做到形神皆似,这种最臻上乘。凡由两个民族历史发展、生活环境、风俗习惯、思维方式和美学观念等差异造成的修辞差异,则可以采取意译的办法,通过增加用词、引申词意、转换修辞格和转换比喻形象等方式进行积极补偿,以求尽可能准确表达原文的思想和精神,保持原文的语言感染力,在不可能做到使译文与原文形神皆似的时候,译者应当牢记形似不如神似。论文通过《致英国人民之歌》、《嘉丽妹妹》、《董贝父子》等大量经典译文,详细分析了对照、设问、借代、借喻、反语、矛盾修辞法、轭式搭配法等修辞手法在作品中的成功再现方式。

正确运用修辞手法,是翻译中一个重要课题。作者使用修辞格,是为了使语言更加生动形象,鲜明突出;或者使语言更加整齐匀称,音调铿锵,显示出前后事物的内在联系;以加强表现力和感染力,更加深入地阐明事件的意义或刻画人物的性格。有时则可以引起读者丰富的联想,发人深省,或者使读者感到意外,引人入胜。因此,译文中若不能正确表现原文的修辞法,就不能准确地表达原文的思想、精神和风格。即使与原文大意差不多,也会使原文的语言力量遭到削弱,不符合"信达雅"的翻译标准。

英语和汉语都有悠久的发展历史,经过成千年劳动人民和文学家的创造,这两种语言都具有极其丰富的修辞手法。而且,绝大多数英语常用修辞格都能找到与之相对应的汉语修辞格,它们无论在结构上,或修辞作用上都彼此十分相似,有几种英语修辞格在分类上与汉语修辞格互有参差,但在本质上双方仍有相同的修辞现象。只有极个别的英语修辞格,如专门涉及音韵的 Alliteration(头韵法)和 Assonance(准押韵),在现代汉语中没有相对应的修辞格,在古汉语中虽然有所谓"双声、叠韵",但主要是一种文字游戏,与英语头韵法和准押韵在结构上近似而修辞作用不同。

根据英汉两种语言在修辞手法上这种极为相似的情况,在翻译中当然应当尽可能采用直译的办法,即在用词上和修辞结构上都与原文一致,做到形神皆似,这种最臻上乘。但是,事实上,许多时候却不能墨守原文的修辞格式,也不能照搬原文的比喻形象。这是因为两个民族的历史发展、生活环境,风俗习惯各不相同,思维方式和美学观念也有所不同。机械地照搬原文修辞法,有时不仅不能保持原文的语言表现力和感染力,反而会弄到词不达意,晦涩难懂,甚至歪曲原意。在这种情况下,就需要采取意译的办法,可以:一、增加用词;二、引申词意;三、转换修辞格;四、转换比喻形象。力求准确表达原文的思想和精神,符合汉语习惯,并且保持原文的语言感染力。也就是说,在不可能做到使译文与原文形神皆似的时候,译者应当牢记形似不如神似。

一

现在我们先举出例子来看一看怎样在翻译中采取直译的办法,使译文在用词和修辞格上与原文一致,以及在什么情况下就必须采取增加用词的意译法:

To the Men of England

1. Men of England, wherefore plough
  For the lords who lay ye low?
  Wherefore weave with toil and care,
  The rich robes your tyrants wear?

2. Wherefore feed, and clothe, and save,
  From the cradle to the grave,
  Those ungrateful drones who would
  Drain your sweat—nay, drink your blood!

3. Wherefore, Bees of England, forge
  Many a weapon, chain and scourge,
  That these stingless drones may spoil
  The forced produce of your toil?

4. Have you leisure, comfort, calm,
  Shelter, food, love's gentle balm?
  Or what is it ye buy so dear
  With your pain and with your fear?

5. The seed ye sow, another reaps;
  The wealth ye find, another keeps;
  The robes ye weave, another wears;
  The arms ye forge, another bears.

6. Sow seed—but let no tyrant reap;
  Find wealth,—let no impostor keep;
  Weave robes,—let no idler wear;
  Forge arms,—in your defence to bear.

7. Shrink to your cellars, holes, and cells;

In halls ye deck, another dwells.
Why shake the chains ye wrought? Ye see
The steel ye tempered glance on ye.

8. With plough and spade, and hoe and loom,
Trace your grave, and build your tomb,
And weave your winding-sheet, till fair
England be your sepulchre.

—P. B. Shelley

致英国人民之歌

1. 英国人民啊，为什么要替老爷们耕种？
   他们把你们踩在脚下。
   为什么要精工织造锦袍，
   向那些暴君交纳？

2. 为什么要把那些忘恩负义的雄蜂，
   从摇篮一直伺候到坟墓里？
   穿衣、吃饭、保驾样样管，
   让他们榨干吸尽你们的血和汗。

3. 为什么，英国的蜜蜂啊，
   要铸造许多武器、钢鞭和枷锁，
   让那些本来没有刺的雄蜂，
   可以强迫你们劳动供他们挥霍？

4. 你们可曾得到过粮食、住房和抚爱？
   你们可曾有过安宁、舒适和闲暇？
   你们整天痛苦又害怕，
   究竟为什么要付这么高的代价？

5. 你们播下的种子别人收；
   你们找到的财富别人留；
   你们织造的锦袍别人穿；
   你们铸成的武器别人握在手。

6. 播下种子吧，可别让暴君收割；
   寻找财富吧，可别让骗子囤积；
   织造锦袍吧，可别让懒汉穿上；
   铸造武器吧，拿起来保卫你们自己。

7. 还是钻进你们的地窖、洞穴和小屋吧，
   你们布置的大厦别人住在里边。
   何必摆脱你们自己铸造的锁链，
   那钢铁的锁链在你们身上闪闪发光多体面。

8. 尽管用耕犁、铁铲、锄头和织机
   挖掘和装饰你们的坟墓。

织造你们自己的尸衣，
直到美丽的英国成为你们的墓地。

在这首诗中，作者使用了多种修辞格。首先，他用 Contrast（对照）贯穿全诗，如人民对老爷、暴君；蜜蜂对雄蜂；一边是饱受压迫、昼夜辛劳，一边是坐享现成、挥霍无度。此外，在前四节，用了 Rhetoric question（设问）；在前三节连问为什么是 Anaphora（首语反复法）；第二节中的摇篮、坟墓是 Metonymy（借代）；第二、第三节中的蜜蜂、雄蜂是 Metaphor（暗喻，对应的汉语修辞格包括隐喻、借喻和拟物，译文用了借喻）；第五、六节用了 Parallelism（排偶），以上这些修辞格在译文中都得到忠实的再现，无论在用词上还是在修辞结构上都与原文一致。

在第七、八两节，主要修辞手法是 Irony（反语）。这是作者痛心于英国人民饱受剥削压迫却不敢奋起革命，抱着恨铁不成钢的感情，说这些反话，打算用激将法来鼓舞人民的斗志。译文保持了原文的修辞格，但在用词上却有所增加。第七节增加了"多体面"三字，第八节增加了"尽管"二字。因为，如果不加这些词，逐字直译，原著中那种说反话的意思就不容易看出来。顺便说一下，采用"多体面"三字而不用别的表现法，也是为了照顾诗歌押韵。

在翻译英语用了修辞格的句子时，需要加词的情况相当多。下面再举一个例子：

The messenger was not long in returning, followed by a pair of heavy boots that came bumping along the passage like boxes. (Dickens)

送信人不久就回来了：后面跟着一个穿着笨重靴子的人，在过道里走得咯噔咯噔乱响，像滚动箱子一样。

这段话中的 a pair of heavy boots（一双笨重靴子）属于修辞格 Metonymy（借代），译文加词为"一个穿着笨重靴子的人"；bumping（碰、撞）属于 Onomatopoeia（拟声）译文增加"咯噔咯噔乱响"；like boxes（像箱子一样）属于 Simile（明喻），根据上文，译文增加"滚动"二字。

加词翻译的原则是所加的词在原文字面上虽然没有，然而却包含了这样一层意思。加词之后能够更清楚地表现原文的思想和韵味，却不能在原文之外增加新的意思。

二

在翻译英语用了某些修辞格的句子时，往往要引申词意。例如英语 Oxymoron（矛盾修饰法，相当于汉语修辞格反映）被运用得很广泛，而汉语反映却相对用得较少。因此翻译时要多加推敲。否则，有时按照字面意义和语法结构直译出来会使人感到别扭，甚至不解。为了使译文流畅易懂，要注意词义的选择和引申，要照顾汉语习惯。举例如下：

The whirling wheels began to sing in a steadily modifying key, until at last they died away in a low buzz. There was *an audible stillness*, in which the common voice sounded strange. (Theodore Dreiser: *Sister Carrie*)

飞速旋转的机轮开始奏出越来越减弱的曲调，终于消失在一片低沉的嗡嗡声中。出现了一种有声音的相对寂静，在这种寂静中普通的谈话声听起来有点古怪。

如果上述例子中的 an audible stillness 直译为"一种听得见的寂静"，就令人费解了。

The Major again pressed to his blue eyes the tips of the fingers that were disposed on the edge of the wheeled chair with *careful carelessness*. （Charles Dickens：*Dombey And Son*）

少校用一种精心做出的漫不经心姿态再次把原来放在轮椅边上的指尖按住自己的蓝眼睛。

这句话中的 careful carelessness 如果直译为"小心翼翼的漫不经心"就显得有些别扭。又例如：

My heart is full of empty.
我满腹凄凉。（不宜译为"我心中充满空虚"。）
jarring concord
时常吵闹的友好关系（不宜译为"冲突的和谐"。）
poor rich guys
可怜的有钱人（不宜译为"贫穷的有钱人"。）

除了 Oxymoron 之外，还有一些英语修辞格在翻译时往往需要注意引申词意。例如 Zeugma（轭式搭配法）虽然与汉语修辞格拈连相似，但因为词的搭配范围不尽相同，有时在翻译中就不能直译。例如：

The summer show at the Lathrop Gallery *was the biggest art exhibit* of the year *in quality*, if not *in size*. （Rude Goldberg：*Art For Heart's Sake*）

莱塞罗普画廊的夏季展览是一年中最重要的艺术展览，即使在规模上并非如此，在质量上也是这样的。

文中的 the biggest（最大的）在翻译时引申为"最重要的"，因为"最大的"可以与"规模"搭配，但却不能与"质量"并用。

Shipowners fear that *saving jobs* in Britain's ailing shipyard comes before *saving its merchant fleet*. （Andrew Neil：*Britainia Rues the Waves*）

船主们担心英国把在一息奄奄的造船厂中保证就业看得比抢救商船队更重要。

文中用 saving（抢救）搭配了 jobs（工作岗位）和 merchant fleet（商船队）两个词，但"商船队"可以"抢救"，"工作岗位"却不能"抢救"，因此引申译为"保证就业"。

You *won a hundred* at the tables, then *lost it* at the bar. （Author Hailey：*Hotel*）

你在赌桌上挣了一百元，然后又在卖酒柜台上花光了。

这句话用了 won（赢）之后又用了它的反义词 lost（输）。但是赌桌上有输赢，卖酒柜台上却不会有输赢的。这种修辞方式是 Zeugma 的变体，相当于汉语拈连中的反拈，尽管汉语有相同的修辞格式，就本句而言，lost it 仍不宜直译为"输光了"，因为那样可能使人误会为卖酒柜台上也进行了一场赌博，所以根据该词的另一词义"丢失"引申为"花光了"。为了尽可能保持原文的修辞风格，又根据前一个动词 won 的另一词义"获得"引申为"挣了"。赌桌上一般说"赢了"，不说"挣了"。正因为如此，才与后文的"花了"构成反拈，而又不致造成误会。

必须说明，这一类句子在翻译中做了词义引申之后，往往失去了原文的修辞风格。语言感

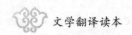

染力和表现力有所削弱。因此,若有可能,可以考虑在译文中运用另一种修辞格,这个问题在下一节再作进一步讨论。

三

原文运用了某些英语修辞格,有时在翻译中需要换用另一种修辞手法,这是正确翻译英语修辞格的重要方法之一。

有些英语修辞格的句子用相对应的汉语修辞格加以直译,会歪曲原文的意思,或不符合汉语习惯。还有个别英语修辞格根本找不到相对应的汉语修辞格。如果按照原文的意思,用平铺直叙的语言来翻译,又会失去原文的生动性和语言表现力。因此,这时就有必要考虑能不能换用另一种汉语修辞格,以准确表达原文的思想和精神,并保持一定的语言感染力。这就是翻译技巧中所谓的"补偿原则"。举例如下:

She was dressed in a maid's cap, a pinafore, and a bright smile.

她戴女仆帽,系白围腰,容光焕发,面带微笑。

上例中的 dressed in(穿戴)可以和帽子、围裙搭配,却不能单独与容光或微笑搭配,这是 Zeugma 修辞格式。如果用对应的汉语修辞格拈连来翻译,就显得牵强,因此改用了四四排比的结构,并且押上了韵,以保持原文引人注目的韵味。

Benjamin Franklin:"If we don't hang together, we shall most assuredly hang separately."(Peter Stone and Sherman Edwards:*1776*)

本杰明·富兰克林:"如果我们不能紧密地团结在一起,那就必然分散地走上绞刑台。"

这句话中用同一个动词 hang 分别搭配两个副词 together 和 seperately,前者意为"团结在一起",后者意为"分散地被绞死"。这是英语修辞格 Syllepsis(异叙)的用法,却无法用与之对应的汉语修辞格异叙来表达。因此译文采用了对偶的形式。

又例如,He made the money fly. 这种修辞格属于 Metaphor(暗喻,相当于汉语修辞格隐喻、借喻或拟物;本句用法相当于拟物)。如果我们也用汉语拟物的方式直译为"他把钱弄飞了",那就难以理解,甚至可能造成误会。不如换用现成的明喻:"他挥金如土。"

以上例句说明,某些用了英语修辞格的句子即使有相对应的汉语修辞格,在翻译时也往往需要换用另一种与之不相对应的汉语修辞格来表达。至于没有对应汉语修辞格的 Alliteration(头韵法),就更有必要采用其他汉语修辞方式来翻译了。所谓 Alliteration,是在一句话或一个诗行中,用了几个以同样字母开头的词。例如:There is zip and zing here. 这句话中的 zip 和 zing 两个词押了头韵。我们可以译为:"这一点既有劲儿又有趣儿。"勉强表现出原文的结构和风格。可惜这种译法不能作为普遍仿效的例子。因为英语 Alliteration 的搭配千变万化,很难碰巧又找到这样既符合原意又以同声字开头的几个词。处理带有这种修辞格的句子,主要办法恐怕就是尽可能换用其他汉语修辞格了。例如:

To Pledger, after three years of walking and waiting, it felt good to be back at his trade again.(Alexander Saxton:*Home Is the Soldier*)

对于普莱杰尔,经过三年的东西奔走,朝夕盼望,现在又回来干自己的本行,真是好极了。

　　上述例子中 walking 和 waiting 两个词押了头韵,译文采用汉语对偶:"东西奔走,朝夕盼望。"

　　It was a splendid population—for all the slow, sleepy, sluggish-brained sloth stayed at home. (Noel Grove: *Mark Twain—Mirrow of America*)

　　这是一批卓越能干的人民——因为所有那些行动迟缓、瞌睡稀稀、呆如树懒的人都留在家乡了。

　　这句话中用 splendid, slow, sleepy, sluggish, sloth 和 stayed 押头韵,译文采用了排比格式:"行动迟缓、瞌睡兮兮、呆如树懒。"

　　(注:sloth:树懒,一种南美洲动物,以行动迟缓著称。)

　　Alliteration 更经常地出现在英语的诗歌之中,怎样翻译才好,要根据具体情况而定。例如:

Song

Sweet and low, sweet and low,

Wind of the western sea,

Low, low, breathe and blow,

Wind of the western sea

Over the rolling waters go,

Come from the dying moon and blow,

Blow him again to me;

While my little one, while my pretty one sleeps.

Sleep and rest, sleep and rest,

Father will come to thee soon;

Rest, rest, on mother's breast,

Father will come to thee soon;

Father will come to his babe in the nest,

Silver sails all out of the west,

Under the silver moon;

Sleep my little one, sleep, my pretty one, sleep.

—Alfred Tennyson

歌

西边海上的风啊,

你多么轻柔,多么安详;

西边海上的风啊,

你轻轻地吹吧,轻轻地唱。

你告别西边低垂的月亮,

又飞过海上起伏的波浪,

伴送小宝的爸爸回家乡，
回家乡把睡着的小宝看望。
睡吧，静静地睡吧，
爸爸就要来到你身旁；
睡吧，在妈妈怀里睡吧，
爸爸就要来到你身旁。
银色的月亮照在他的帆船上，
银色的帆船展翅飞翔向东方，
睡吧，我的小宝宝，睡吧，
同爸爸相见在梦乡。

原诗多处运用了 Repetition（反复），第六行末尾和第七行开始的两处 blow 是 Catchword repetition（联珠）。译文也多处运用反复，并在第七行尾和第八行首用了联珠（回家乡，回家乡）。除此以外，这首诗的一个修辞特点就是 Alliteration 的使用。如第二行（w, w），第三行（b, b），第四行（w, w）和第十四行（s, s）。根据原诗的意境和音韵，译文第二、四、五行用了拟人法（安详，唱，告别），第五、六行用了对偶，而在第十四行则用了拟物（展翅飞翔）。

四

在处理英语修辞格句子的翻译时，另一个值得注意的问题是有时必须更换比喻的形象。这是因为，有许多用做比喻的形象在英语民族心目中的概念与中国人大不相同。例如，兔子的形象在中国人心目中是敏捷的象征。中国人说"静如处子，动如脱兔"，又说"穿兔子鞋"（东北方言，表示跑得极快）。英语民族却认为兔子是胆小的象征，英语常说 as timid as a rabbit。翻译时最好根据汉语习惯译为"胆小如鼠"，不要译成"胆小如兔"。同样，as stupid as a goose 与其译成"笨得像鹅"，就不如译为"蠢得像猪"，因为中国人怎么也想象不出鹅能够象征愚蠢。as stubborn as a mule 与其直译为"顽固得像头骡子"，就不如译为"犟得像头牛"。试看汉字"犟"怎么写，就可以知道中国人心目中代表顽固的是牛，而绝不是骡子。to work like a horse 不应译为"像马一样工作"，因为这没有表达出原文中那种自愿拼命干活的意思，应译为"像老黄牛一样干活"。

这一类例子很多，为了引起翻译工作者注意，现在再列举一些如下：

to swim like a duck
游得像条鱼（不宜直译为"游得像鸭子"。）
like a duck to water
如鱼得水（不宜直译为"如鸭子得水"。）
like a hen on a hot girdle
像热锅上的蚂蚁（不宜直译为"像热锅上的母鸡"。）
like a drowned rat
好像落汤鸡（不宜直译为"像落水的老鼠"。）
industrious as an ant

像蜜蜂一样勤劳（不宜直译为"像蚂蚁一样勤劳"。）

hungry as a bear

饿得像狼（不宜直译为"饿得像熊"。）

dumb as an oyster

守口如瓶（不宜直译为"哑得像牡蛎"。）

thirsty as a camel

像一条渴龙（不宜直译为"渴得像骆驼"。）

以上是翻译 Simile（明喻）句子时应当更换喻体的例子。下面再举一些翻译 Metaphor（暗喻）句子时需要更换喻体的例子：

The crowd moved forward *in a wave*.

群众潮水般向前涌去（不宜直译为"群众波浪般向前涌去"或"群众成一道波浪向前涌去"。因为前者使人误解为分批前进，后者使人误解为成一横排前进，都与原意不符。）

Hs is the black sheep of the family.

他是全家的害群之马。（不宜直译为"他是全家的黑羊"。）

She is really a duck，he thought.

她真是一只可爱的小鸟，他心里想。（不宜直译为"她真是一只鸭子"。）

to be flung to the four winds

抛到九霄云外（不宜直译为"抛给四种风"。）

to cast pearls before the swine

对牛弹琴（不宜直译为"对猪抛珍珠"。）

to kill two birds with one stone

一箭双雕（不宜直译为"一石杀两鸟"。）

以上例子都说明了在翻译某些用了修辞格的英语句子时更换比喻形象的必要性。当然，英语的比喻形象与中国人概念一致、不需要改变喻体的例子也很多，如 cold as ice（冷若冰霜），fresh as a rose（像玫瑰一样鲜艳），a rooted prejudice（根深蒂固的偏见）等，这里就不加赘述了。

五

综上所述，可以归结为两句话：在翻译中处理英语的修辞格，应当尽可能采用结构相同，含意也一致的汉语词句，以保持原文的思想、精神和风格。若做不到这一点，就要采取加词、引申、改变修辞格、或更换比喻形象的办法，尽可能以某种符合汉语习惯的修辞方式，来保持原文的语言表现力和感染力。

但是，这些规律也正如所有的翻译规律一样，只能适用于若干情况，而不能适用于一切情况。

有些英语修辞格的句子就不宜用上述任何一种办法来以某种汉语修辞格表达。例如：

After two centuries of crusades the Crescent defeated the Cross in all

Southwestern Asia. (Daily Worker)

　　经过两个世纪的圣战,在整个西南亚伊斯兰教战胜了基督教。

　　原文用事物的明显标志代替该事物,即用 Crescent(新月)代替"伊斯兰教",用 Cross（十字架)代替基督教,属于修辞格 Metonymy(借代)。但许多中国人对此不太熟悉,不如干脆不用修辞格,意译为"伊斯兰教战胜了基督教"。

　　Give every man thine ear and few thy voice. (Shakespeare)
　　听每一个人讲,自己少讲。

　　这句话以工具代替行为,即用 ear(耳朵)代替"听",用 voice(声音)代替"说",也属于 Metonymy 修辞格。不便采用某种修辞格来翻译,改用普通的说法意译。

　　The year 1871 witnessed the heroic uprising of the Paris Commune.
　　1871 年爆发了英勇的巴黎公社起义。

　　该句用了 Personification (拟人),说 1871 年 witnessed(目睹了)巴黎公社起义。但我国人民不习惯用拟人法来描写抽象的东西,如年代等。因此不用修辞格,意译为"爆发了巴黎公社起义"。

　　此外,前面讲到,对于比喻的形象,在翻译时要考虑它是否符合中国人的概念或习惯。如果不符,就应当更换所用的喻体。该处指的是已经有了固定的汉语说法的情况。至于英语比喻中有些说法是汉语还没有固定搭配的,只要为中国人所能理解和接受,就可以照直翻译,不但不别扭,还能丰富我们民族的语言。例如, to turn swords into ploughs(化剑为犁), a political chameleon(政治上的变色龙)等,都已经移植成为汉语所常用的了。各种语言都是首先通过良好的翻译,然后把另一种语言中极为巧妙生动的说法移植成为自己的常用语。例如汉语中的"保全面子"是用具体事物"脸面"代替抽象概念"尊严"这样一种借代法,现在就已经移植为英语的常用词组 to save one's face。

　　最后,还要谈一谈关于译文必须符合汉语习惯的问题。对这一点,在翻译中要注意防止使用汉语中民族色彩太浓的、为我国所专有的词语。例如,Conan Doyle(柯南道尔)在他的 *The Adventures of Sherlock Holmes*(《福尔摩斯侦探案》)中曾经写道:"He is the Napoleon of crime."(他是罪犯中的拿破仑。)这种修辞方法属于 Antonomasia(专名和普通名词互代法),我们就决不能用同样的汉语修辞法译为"他是罪犯中的楚霸王"。因为这样译,意思虽然相同,又符合汉语习惯,却无益于译文。在一篇外国故事中忽然跑出楚霸王的名字来,会使人感到不伦不类。

　　同样,英语 Allusion 是用典故或某些谚语中的一部分关键词作为比喻。在翻译中却不能运用含意相似的中国典故来代替外国典故。因为这样做不仅会显得本民族色彩太浓,同整个作品不协调,而且各民族文学中的典故所包含的思想或所描写的性格总有一些大同小异之处。例如:

　　It is 7：30 am... The TV set blinks on with the day's first newscast... The latter-day Aladdin, still snugly abed, then presses a button on a bedside box and issues a string of business and personal memos, which appear instantly on the genie screen. (*The Age of Miracle Chips Time*, Feb. 20, 1978)

早上七点半……电视机悄悄地自动闪亮，传来当天的第一次新闻广播……当代的阿拉丁还舒舒服服地躺在床上，他按一按床头柜上的电钮，发布一系列有关业务上和个人事务上的备忘录，这些事项都立即出现在灯神的屏幕上。

上述例子中的 genie(灯神)典故出自 *The Arabian Nights*(《天方夜谭》)，主要说明现代的微型电脑像阿拉伯神话故事中的灯神一样，能够帮助人们实现一切愿望。在翻译时却不能套用中国的典故译为"宝葫芦的屏幕"。因为灯神的故事是讲一个善良的神灵帮助善良的人，而宝葫芦的寓意却是告诫人们不要幻想不劳而获。如果用在译文中正好与原意相反。

这一点之所以值得注意，是因为有些翻译工作者过分强调了要使译文符合汉语习惯，于是在译文中就出现了这样的问题。例如在我国过去出版的翻译小说《续侠隐记》中，译者就把大仲马笔下的一位法国贵族夫人变成了中国人，因为她居然说起"要请张天师收妖"来了。这种译法，恐怕是不妥当的。

选文二　Delabastita 的双关语翻译理论在英汉翻译中的应用

张南峰

导　言

本文选自《中国翻译》2003 年第 1 期。

选文详细介绍了对双关语翻译颇有建树的比利时学者 Delabastita 的研究成果，其因基于《哈姆雷特》多部德语、法语、荷兰语译本中文字游戏的翻译研究，引起西方学界较为广泛的关注。Delabastita 将双关语翻译详细划分为：双关语译为相同的双关语(同类型)，双关语译为相同的双关语(不同类型)，双关语译为不同的双关语，双关语译为类双关语，双关语译为非双关语，双关语译为零，照抄原文，非双关语译为双关语，零译为双关语和通过编辑手段在注释、译序等地方解释原文的双关语或者提供另一种译法等十种方法。本文以多个例子证明，Delabastita 的双关语翻译理论虽然源自西方，但应用于描述英汉翻译现象时，尤其能够揭示译者的翻译观，同时也可用来指导英汉翻译实践。论者高屋建瓴地指出，目前中西译论交流不足，主要原因不在于翻译理论的语言特殊性，而在于其文化特殊性。

一、引　言

尽管 20 世纪 80 年代以来已有越来越多的西方翻译理论被介绍到中国，但直到近来，在中国的翻译界和翻译学界仍能听到一种声音，说西方理论没有什么可借鉴的，其所持理由有二：一是西方理论不比中国理论先进，二是西方理论不适用于语系不同的中国。因此，本文打算介绍 Delabastita 的双关语翻译理论,供大家参考。

无论在东方还是西方,传统译论在双关语的翻译问题上不外持两种态度:一是认为双关语除非有完全对应的词语,否则不可译;二是认为译者虽然有时可以制造另一个双关语以作"补偿",但全凭天赋,没有多少可以传授的技巧。两种态度的结论都是:双关语的翻译没有什么可研究的。[①]

Delabastita 并不同意这种看法。他指出,可以假设任何语言都有制造双关语的能力,所以谁也不能否认,对双关语进行各种各样的跨语处理(interlingual processing)是可能的。但问题是,这些处理方法不一定符合各人心目中的翻译(或者是"好的"或"真正的"翻译)的标准(Delabastita, 1987:151; 1991:146);因此,双关语最能模糊"翻译"与"改编"之间的界线,对译者是很大的考验,迫使他在两极之间做出抉择,暴露自己的翻译观,所以最值得研究(Delabastita, 1996:356; 1997:11,封底)。

二、Delabastita 的双关语翻译策略分类法

Delabastita 是比利时学者,现为那慕尔圣母大学(Facultés Universitaires Notre-Dame de la Paix, Namur)英国文学和文学理论教授。他师从多元系统学派代表人物之一朗贝尔(José Lambert)教授,1990 年在洛文天主教大学(Kathofieke Universiteit Leuven)取得博士学位,其论文以《哈姆雷特》的多部德语、法语、荷兰语译本为例,探讨莎士比亚作品中的文字游戏的翻译问题(Delabastita, 1993)。此外,他曾专门针对双关语的翻译问题,发表过几篇期刊文章(如 Delabastita, 1987, 1994),并编辑过两部论文集(Delabastita, 1996, 1997)。在这些著述里(Delabastita, 1987, 1993, 1996),他提出过三种大同小异的双关语翻译策略的分类法。下面介绍的,是他的三个分类法的结合[②]:

一、双关语译为相同的双关语(同类型):以同类型的双关语[③]保留原文双关语的两层意思。

二、双关语译为相同的双关语(不同类型):以不同类型的双关语保留原文双关语的两层意思。

三、双关语译为不同的双关语:在译文中与原文双关语相近的位置上有双关语,因此可视为对原文双关语的翻译手段;但译文双关语的一层甚至两层意思与原文不同[④]。

---

① Newmark 的这番话也许有一定的代表性:"双关语的翻译问题重要性有限而趣味无限。"(1988: 217)韩迪厚更断言,"'双关语'的问题是任何翻译理论无法解决的"(1969: 134)。

② 1993、1996 年的分类法(Delabastita, 1993: 192-221; 1996:34)把头三种合为一种(双关语译为双关语),另加上第4、第10种。

③ Delabastita 把双关语分为四大类型,即同音同形(homonymy)、同音异形(homophony)、异音同形(homography)、异音异形(paronymy),然后把每一类型再细分为垂直双关语和水平双关语两类,前者的两层意思同时出现(例如"春蚕到死丝方尽"),后者则分开出现(例如"道是无晴却有晴")(Delabastita, 1987: 145-146)。

④ 这个定义的前半部分取自 Delabastita 给"双关语译为双关语"所下的定义(Delabastita, 1993: 192);后半部分为本文作者所加,以区分第一、二种策略和第三种策略。Delabastita 给第三种策略所下的定义,原本是"译文的双关语只有一层意思与原文相同或近似或者两层都与原文近似"(1987: 148)。按照这个定义,译文双关语必须起码有一层意思与原文近似,才能算是把双关语译为双关语——尽管可能是不同的双关语,这显然有欠妥当。(例如下文所举的例 4 就只能视为把双关语译为非双关语,同时又把非双关语译为双关语以作补偿,而不能视为把双关语译为不同的双关语了。)Delabastita 在1993 年修订的分类法,虽然没有明说,但其实已取消了起码有一层意思相近的要求。

四、双关语译为类双关语（punoid）：用某些带有文字游戏性质的修辞手段（例如重复、头韵、脚韵、所指含糊、反语等），以求再造原文双关语的效果。

五、双关语译为非双关语：以非双关语的方式传达原文双关语的一层或两层意思，但也有可能把两层意思都译得"面目全非"。

六、双关语译为零：删去包含双关语的一段文字。

七、照抄原文：把原文双关语原封不动地搬到译文里。

八、非双关语译为双关语：在翻译一段不包含双关语的原文时，自己制造双关语。

九、零译为双关语：在译文里加入一些包含双关语的全新的语篇材料。

十、编辑手段（editorial techniques）：在注释、译序等地方解释原文的双关语或者提供另一种译法，等等。

这些策略是可以结合运用的，例如把双关语译为非双关语（第五种），再用注脚解释原文的双关语（第十种），又在另一个地方自创双关语作为补偿（第八或九种）。

三、双关语翻译策略举例

以下从英汉翻译文学中找一些现成的例子来说明这十种策略：

（一）双关语译为相同的双关语（同类型）

例1

> Most people, of course, found Ulster a dead end, (though there was always the possibility of finishing up there in a blaze of glory.) (Lynn & Jay, 1989：24)
>
> 大部分人都会发觉北爱是条死胡同，（不过还是可能有轰轰烈烈、光芒四射的时刻的。）（张南峰，1993：20）

原文是说，当北爱尔兰事务大臣没有政治前途，甚至可能死于恐怖袭击：dead end, finishing up, blaze of glory 都是双关语。在这个语境里，"死胡同"可说与 dead end 完全对应。

（二）双关语译为相同的双关语（不同类型）

例2

> "I gather," he replied disdainfully, "that he was as drunk as a lord—so after a discreet interval they'll probably make him one. " (Lynn & Jay, 1989：24)
>
> 他轻蔑地答道："我看，既然他喝得那么醉醺醺的，等风平浪静以后，他们会封他做勋爵的。"（张南峰，1993：19）

这里的话题是，内政大臣酒后驾驶，撞了车，因此被迫辞职，政治生命就此完结，但过一段时间之后，他可能会被封为贵族，出任上议院（House of Lords）议员，当个政治花瓶。原文双关语（lord 及其代词 one）同音同形，译文双关语则同音异形，但两层意思都保留了。

（三）双关语译为不同的双关语

例3

> (—Holy Wars, says Joe laughing, that's a good one if old Shylock is landed. So the wife comes out top dog, what?)

——Well，that's a point，says Bloom，for the wife's admirers.

——Whose admirers，says Joe.

——The wife's advisers，I mean，says Bloom.（Joyce，1992：330）

——这个么，布卢姆说，得看打他老婆主意的人了。

——打谁的主意？约说。

——我是说给他老婆出主意的人，布卢姆说。（金隄，1994：477）

译文以"打……主意"和"出主意"来制造双关，但"打主意"和 admire 的意思不尽相同，而且译文的双关语出现在词组而非词的层次上，因此可视为不同的双关语。

例 4

"You see the earth takes twenty-four hours to turn round on its axis—"

"Talking of axes，"said the Duchess，"chop off her head!"（Carroll/赵元任，1972：17 - 18）

"要知道地球绕轴转一圈要用二十四个钟头。"

"说什么头。"公爵夫人说，"把她的头砍掉！"（管绍淳、赵明菲，1981：51）

原文的双关语在 axis/axes，译文的双关语则在"钟头/头"，与原文明显不同。

（四）双关语译为类双关语

例 5

Heart to heart talks.

Bloo... Me? No.

Blood of the lamb.（Joyce，1992：158）

推心置腹的谈话。

羊羔……我？不对。

羊羔的血。（金隄，1994：226）

原文是说，布卢姆（Bloom）看到 Bloo，就以为是他的名字；译文则是说他心虚，以为别人说他是羊羔(Jin，2000：133 - 134)，以所指含糊来代替原文的双关语。

（五）双关语译为非双关语

例 6

（原文同例 3）

"那位老婆的仰慕者们所着眼的，"布卢姆说，"正是这一点。"

"谁的仰慕者？"乔说。

"我指的是给那位老婆出主意的人们。"布卢姆说。（萧乾、文洁若，1994：223）

（六）双关语译为零

例 7

She smiled. "Apparently he's looking forward to reading the New Year's Honours List."

That seemed a fair deal. I asked her how we'd do that. In which section?

Bernard leaned forward confidentially. "How about through the Welsh Office? For services to leaks?" He is irrepressible. (Lynn and Jay, 1989：372)

原文是说一家会计公司的合伙人向首相的顾问泄漏了客户的资料，以求列入英女王的元旦授勋名单；首相觉得这笔交易很公平，但想不出用什么名目给他授勋，他的秘书于是开玩笑地建议经由威尔士事务部，表彰他在 leak 方面的贡献。leak 在英语里是泄漏之意，而在威尔士语里则是一种蔬菜。译文(张南峰,1993：426)把这个双关语连带其上下文(即斜体部分)一起删掉了。

（七）照抄原文＋（十）编辑手段

例 8

"I don't give a stuff about sport! I've got 4,000 tobacco workers in my constituency. What about my seat?"

"What about your lungs?" I said.

"My lungs are fine," he snarled.

"And he doesn't breathe through his seat," said Bernard. (Lynn and Jay, 1989：198)

"体育，我一点也不在乎！要知道在我的选区内有四千烟草工人。我的 seat，怎么样？"

"你的肺部怎么样呢?"我说。

"我的肺很好。"他吼叫起来。

"噢，他呼吸不通过臀部。"伯纳德说。

此处的 seat 一词无法翻译，莱斯利意思是他的职位、席位、位置、地位往哪里搁呢？但 seat 在英语中也是一个婉词，做臀部、屁股讲。哈克为了调侃他，故意曲解，问他肺部怎么样？——译者注(杨立义、娄炳坤,1992：252)

首相说要推行反吸烟运动，但烟不离口的体育部长恐怕失去烟草工人的选票，因而失去国会议员的席位，所以大力反对。译者照抄第一个 seat，然后用脚注解释。

（八）非双关语译为双关语

例 9

Indeed, she had quite a long argument with the Lory, who at last turned sulky, and would only say, "I'm older than you, and must know better." (Carroll/赵元任,1972：17-18)

她竟同那鹦哥争辩了半天，辩到后来，惹得那鹦哥不耐烦了，它就说："我到底是你哥哥，我应该比你知道。"(Carroll/赵元任,1972：17-18)

例 10

Algernon：How are you, my dear Ernest? What brings you up to town?

Jack：Oh, pleasure, pleasure! What else should bring one anywhere? (Wilde, 1979：254)

奥哲能:你好哇，认真。什么风把你吹进城里来啦?

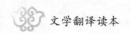

杰克：当然是风流快活的风啦！别的风吹得动人吗？（张南峰，1990：6）

"鹦哥/哥哥"、"风流快活的风"，都是译本里才有的双关语。

（九）零译为双关语

例 11

> It was the White Rabbit. （Carroll/赵元任，1972：24）
> 来的不是别"人"，而就是那位白兔子。（Carroll/赵元任，1972：24）

例 12

> Lady Bracknell：A girl with a simple，unspoiled nature，like Gwendolen，could hardly be expected to reside in the country. （Wilde，1979：267）
> 费：像温黛琳那么天真纯朴的女孩子，可不能住在乡下呀。乡下花太多了，简直是个花花世界。（张南峰，1990：23）

"不是别'人'"、"花花世界"，在原文没有对应部分，纯粹是译者的发明创造。

四、优胜之处

Delabastita 这个分类法的优点，首先是针对翻译研究的实际需要而设计。从理论上来说，双关语翻译策略的分类法可以有许多种。比方说，我们可以从对比语言学或者对比修辞学的角度出发，集中比较译文双关语和原文双关语在结构、语义、修辞手段等方面的异同，例如把同音同形的双关语译成同音同形、同音异形、异音同形、异音异形的双关语，等等。但这类研究，对于我们了解双关语翻译所涉及的主要问题帮助不大（Delabastita，1994：232 - 233），而 Delabastita 的分类法，有助于研究某个译者或者某个文化的翻译观和文学观。譬如说，假如一个译本里同音异形的双关语特别多，也许只能说明某个译者的个人偏好或者某种语言的结构特点；但假如某个译者常常把双关语译为非双关语，却从来不把双关语译为不同的双关语或者把非双关语译成双关语，那就很可能反映出他对翻译的定义比较狭窄，或者说，他的翻译观比较强调字面意义上的忠实，而且不重视译文本身的文学性。

其次，Delabastita 的分类法十分细致、合理。如果用来衡量译者的翻译观，则可把这十种策略大致分为两类：第一类偏重译文的充分性，包括双关语译为非双关语、照抄原文、编辑手段三种；第二类偏重译文的可接受性，[1]包括双关语译为相同的双关语（不同类型）、双关语译为不同的双关语、双关语译为零、非双关语译为双关语、零译为双关语、双关语译为类双关语六种，而双关语译为相同的双关语（同类型）则两者兼顾。[2]

第三，这个分类法相当详尽，几乎可以涵盖一切在译文里能找到的双关语翻译方法。比较传统的译论研究者，向人介绍翻译方法时总要先经过自己的审查（censor），不认可的方法就不

---

① "充分性"与"可接受性"的定义见张南峰 2001：62n。

② 相比之下，笔者在中国译论中唯一所见的双关语翻译分类法，只列出四种，即契合译法、补偿译法、侧重译法和加注法（徐仲炳，1988：31 - 33）。从作者举的例子来看，大致相等于 Delabastita 所说的双关语译为相同的双关语（同类型）、双关语译为不同的双关语或非双关语而大致保留原文双关语的两层意思、双关语译为非双关语而只保留原文双关语的部分意思，以及编辑手段中的一种。其中的补偿译法，涉及两种反映不同翻译观的方法，实在不够细致。

介绍。但 Delabastita 采取中立的立场,不带价值判断地"描述能够采用而且已经有译者采用过的一切可能的策略"(Lefevere,1992：101),因此比较全面、客观。再者,他遵循面向译语系统的研究途径(target-oriented approach),所以能够看到非双关语译为双关语、零译为双关语这类翻译现象;而这类翻译现象,那些以原文为标准来评判译文优劣的研究者就看不到或者不承认为翻译现象了(Toury,1995：81-83)。①

最后,这个分类法所用的名称和定义都十分准确、明晰,没有含混不清的毛病。②

总而言之,这个分类法是描述性的,而且全面、严密、精细,具有很高的科学性。

五、对英汉翻译的适用性

Delabastita 的这个分类法,看来并不具有很大的语言特殊性(language-specificity),就是说,它既适用于描述欧洲语言之间的互译现象,也大致上适用于描述英汉翻译现象,这一点本文所举的例子已经证明。③ 他列举的十种策略,在英汉翻译中都可以采用而且有人采用过;唯一的例外是,"照抄原文"在同属拉丁语系的语言互译之中比较常用,而在英汉翻译中比较少用。反过来说,就笔者所见,在英汉翻译中有人用过的双关语翻译策略,大致上都离不开这十种。④

用这个分类法做框架来研究双关语的翻译现象,我们可以统计一个译本里每种策略的运用次数和比例,从而探视译者的翻译观(如 Chang,1998)。而且,如何处理双关语,在英汉翻译中尤其能够揭示译者的翻译观,原因是:在一方面,英汉语言没有历史和文化联系,所以很难找到结构和意义都相同的双关语;但在另一方面,正如 Newmark 指出,单音节的字词最容易用来制造双关语,所以双关语在英语和汉语最为常见(1988：217)。可以补充一句:因为汉语的基本单位是字,而中文字绝大部分是单音节的,而且汉语的音节结构简单,没有辅音丛(consonant cluster),同音或同韵的字特别多,比英语更容易制造双关语(详见 Chang,1997：163-164)。因此,假如认为必须保留原文双关语的结构和字面意义才算翻译,那么,就英汉翻译而言,双关语的可译性就很低。但假如认为双关语不必译为相同的双关语才算翻译,那么可译性就很高了。换言之,在不同的翻译观之下,双关语的可译性差异极大;反过来说,从译者处理双关语的策略,很容易看出他的翻译观。

此外,我们还可以比较原文和译文的双关语数量,从而大致衡量译文的艺术效果等值度,

---

① 例如,在中国的现有译论中,双关语翻译方法的介绍似乎止于双关语译为不同的双关语(如毛荣贵,1992;欧阳利锋,2000);至于双关语译为零、非双关语译为双关语、零译为双关语,则未见有人介绍。尽管这些方法已有人(包括名家)用过,例如赵元任就用过后两种(例9,11),但译论者往往视而不见,避而不谈,或者不承认为翻译。

② 徐仲炳的分类法、名称和定义都有一些值得商榷之处。例如"补偿译法",读者看了定义——"进行翻译的处理,英语双关语虽然会有部分的损失,但是有可能从汉语的表现方法中得到某种补偿"(1988：32)——之后,大概还是不明所指,得看译例,才知道是把双关语译为不同的双关语或非双关语而大致保留原文双关语的两层意思;而且,把这类策略称为补偿,那么在某处把双关语译为零或非双关语,又在另一处把零或非双关语译为双关语的策略,就无法命名了。顺带一提,起码在西方的译论中,"补偿"(compensation)早已有约定俗成的意思,指的是在译文的某个地方处理某种翻译问题(如笑料、比喻、俚语、文化专有项等)有所损失,而在另一个地方加插该种特征,以补偿损失(参 Shuttleworth and Cowie,1997：25;Toury,1995：83)。

③ 徐仲炳的分类法也不见得只适用于英汉翻译,所以也没有什么语言特殊性。

④ 如果纯粹描述现有的汉英翻译,则第七种"照抄原文"可以删去,因为大概还没有人采用过,而且在可见的将来也不大可能会有人采用。但如果要比较汉英翻译与英汉翻译的规范,找出其相异之处,那么这个类别就十分有用了。

甚至可以调查一些在双关语的处理方面被公认为成功或比较成功的译本,看看哪些策略的使用率比较高,然后向翻译工作者和学生推荐这些策略——尽管这些用途并非 Delabastita 的设计原意。

如果我们接受双关语不必译为相同的双关语才算翻译的观点,那么这个分类法还可以直接应用于翻译技巧的传授,外汉翻译尤其如此。拿前面举的例 8 来说,译者说 seat 这个双关语"无法翻译",其实意思只是说这个双关语在汉语里没有完全对应的项目,而其他的处理方法都不是翻译。但这两位译者的话说得很绝对,就好像世界上只有一种(正确的)翻译(观)①,而这种说法也的确把许多人吓怕了,以致根本不敢想象还有别的解决办法。但假如我们意识到,翻译观只是相对的,不一定有正确错误之分。假如我们愿意参考赵元任、金隄等翻译家采用过的策略,假如我们接受等效论或其他一些观点,认为最重要的是保留原文的修辞效果和语篇完整,而不一定要保留原文双关语的结构和两层意思,不一定要在完全对应的语篇位置上制造双关语,甚至可以改动上下文,以容纳译文的双关语,那么我们就可能想出多种解决办法。例如:

例 13

（原文同例 8）

"体育我才不管呢! 我的选区里有四千个卷烟工人。要是弄得我屁股没地方坐,我可要找个地方出气!"

"你的肺堵住了吗?"我问道。

"我的肺好好的!"他咆哮道。

"他又不是用屁股出气的。"本纳德在旁边插了一句。（张南峰,1993:236）

这段译文改动了上下文,提供了一个新的位置来容纳一个新的双关语"出气",又另觅地方安置原文双关语的两层意思。

原文双关语的两层意思,有时只有一层需要保留,另一层根本无关大局,如鲁迅《阿 Q 正传》中讽刺乡下人不知自由为何物,把"自由党"说成"柿油党"(鲁迅,1976:49)。从文学效果的角度来看,这一对双关语,只有前者的意思是重要的,后者则可视译文语境的需要而改动。假如把"自由党"译成 Liberal Party,则"柿油党"也许可译成 Ribald Party。如果对这个译法的双关效果仍不满意,还可考虑把"自由党"改成"民主党"、"民权党"、"人民党"之类,然后再想办法译"柿油党"。这样改动之后,讽刺效果依然是近似的。这就是说,两层意思都可以改动,下例的双关语就是这样:

例 14

Cecily: This is no time for wearing the shallow mask of manners. When I see a spade I call it a spade.

Gwendolen (satirically): I am glad to say that I have never seen a spade. It is obvious that our social spheres have been widely different. (Wilde, 1979:292)

赛:这种时候可用不着礼貌这种破烂面具喽! 不过,跟你这种人顶牛儿我可没兴趣。

温:[挖苦地]顶牛儿? 我可没跟牛打过交道。看来很明显,你我的社交圈子相差

---

① 不那么绝对的说法可以是"我们(认为)无法翻译"。

很远哪！（张南峰，1990：58 - 59）

原文双关语的作用在于制造吵架的气氛并且提供机会让 Gwendolen 这个住在城里的贵族姑娘嘲笑 Cecily 是粗鄙的乡下人。译文放弃了原文双关语的两层意思，却基本上能起相同的作用，其关键是找一个成语，其中包含一样跟农事有关的事物，让 Gwendolen 借题发挥。

以上几个例子，都是把双关语译为不同的双关语。这样的翻译策略，大大增加了翻译的可能性，想不到某一个办法，通常可以想到另一个。而要是碰巧一个都想不到，那么只要我们接受零翻译和补偿翻译，在翻译较长的语篇时，还可以有多得多的选择。所以 Lefevere 说，翻译难题之所以存在，全因为有规范性的理论存在。如果翻译理论只是描述有人用过的策略，就根本不会有翻译难题（1992：101）。

由此可见，Delabastita 的双关语翻译理论，不单可以指导英汉翻译研究，而且可以指导英汉翻译实践。

六、修改建议

不过，笔者以为，Delabastita 的分类法仍有一些不足之处。比较明显的一点是，既然有一种策略叫做"双关语译为类双关语"，就应该有一种叫做"类双关语译为双关语"，如下例：

例 15

I do not want the Queen to break the law, I merely ask the Prime Minister to bend it. (Lynn and Jay, 1989：350)

我并没有要求女王陛下违背法律，我只是要求首相阁下回避法律罢了。（张南峰，1993：403）

原文里的 break 和 bend 押头韵，是一种类似双关语的修辞手段，而译文里的"违背"和"回避"在语音上的近似程度，大概已足以归类为双关语了[①]。当然，这个例子也可以归为"非双关语译为双关语"。"双关语译为类双关语"和"类双关语译为双关语"两个类别，要么都要，要么都不要，否则就不对称了。

此外，Delabastita 把"编辑手段"限定为在正文之外的解释等，似乎也有点问题，因为编辑手段也有可能在正文里做，例如加插一些解释（而不一定说明是译者引进的），以便在把双关语译成非双关语时保存语篇的完整性，或者改动上下文以便容纳与原文不同的双关语等。后一种手段争议性较大，因此其存在或不存在，是译者翻译观的明显标志。好像下面这个例子，为了容纳双关语而对上下文做如此大幅度的改动，可以想象是不少译者不愿意做的，而且在英汉翻译中也的确不常见。

例 16

Gwendolen：Personally I cannot understand how anybody manages to exist in the country, if anybody who is anybody does. The country always bores me to

---

① 当然，正如 Delabastita 在与笔者的通信中指出，双关语和非双关语只是一个连续体上的两端，中间的灰色地带就叫做类双关语，因此这三个类别没有明确的、固定不变的分界。我们当然也可以把例 15 译文里的修辞手段归为类双关语，甚至在分类法中再增加一种策略，叫做"类双关语译为类双关语"。但这又似乎太复杂化了。

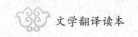

death.

　　Cecily：Ah! This is what the newspapers call agricultural depression，is it not? I believe the aristocracy are suffering very much from it just at present. It is almost an epidemic amongst them，I have been told. May I offer you some tea，Miss Fairfax? (Wilde，1979：293)

　　温：你们乡下地方，到处都是那么湿漉漉的，上哪儿都不方便，闷极了，有名有气的人可住不下去。我要是住上两天哪，肯定就既没名、也没气了。

　　赛：噢，这就是恐水病是吧？你们贵族圈子怎么流行起这种病来啦？真够呛的！费芬斯小姐，您喝点茶大概没关系吧！(张南峰，1990：59-60)

　　由此可见，把"编辑手段"分拆为"文外编辑手段"和"文内编辑手段"两种，也许有些好处。但是，对上下文做细微的改动其实比较普遍，却不易察觉，甚至难以界定，所以这也许是个见仁见智的问题。

　　必须指出，笔者提出这些修改建议，主要并非基于英汉翻译现象的特点，因此也没有语言特殊性。

七、Delabastita 理论的文化特殊性

　　前面说过，Delabastita 的双关语翻译理论基本上没有语言特殊性，但要补充的是，这套理论有颇高的文化特殊性。

　　首先，它是作为一套纯理论而提出来的，只是客观地总结、归纳研究者所观察到的现象，而不对这些现象加以价值判断。这种研究态度，在西方的学术界早已成为主流之一。Delabastita 所属的学派甚至认为，与研究对象保持距离，不喜不恶，不偏不倚，才能得到正确、可信的研究结果，才是真正的学术研究。所以，身为翻译学者，他们不会、也不屑于提倡某些翻译标准或者规范。正是基于这种立场，Delabastita 才把照抄原文与零译为双关语这样极端对立的方法都列为翻译策略。

　　但是，这种描述主义的纯学术研究是与中国甚至东方的文化传统相违背的。在东方，改造客观世界是学者的天职，作价值判断是学者的特权。因此，东方的翻译学者，主要任务是培养翻译人员，提高翻译水平。应用导向的翻译研究，至今仍是主流。Delabastita 的分类法中的某些类别，在东方一定会遇到这样的质疑："这怎么能算是翻译呢？"西方的学者，当然也各有自己的翻译观，但是他们中的许多人会意识到纯学术研究和应用研究的分别，不会以学者的身份提出这样的质疑。

　　此外，Delabastita 的分类法，是对西方翻译现象的归纳，其中有一些类别，在西方比较常见，而在中国则不常见。前面说过，"照抄原文"就是这样，那是语言对（language pair）的性质不同而造成的。另外有一些类别，使用频率不同的原因不在语言差异，而在于翻译观、文学观、价值观的差异，因此也就是文化的差异。西方的翻译观是比较多样化的，所以各种策略都有人采用过，而在中国，起码自鲁迅以来，占支配地位的翻译观一向是倾向于充分性。因此，双关语

的零翻译以及非双关语和零译为双关语这两种补偿翻译,在中国极其罕见。① 就连赵元任、金隄等比较着重译出双关语的翻译家,常用的策略也只是双关语译为不同的双关语。② 赵元任虽然用过两种补偿翻译法,但也只是偶一为之,不曾有系统地采用。

最后,还有一个深层的文化因素,就是东西方幽默感的不同。西方的文化传统,很重视幽默感,如果批评一个人没有幽默感,等于暗示他不大是正常人,会被视为很大的冒犯(Powell,1988:102;Chiaro,1992:15 - 16);所以,西方的幽默翻译,在实践和理论两方面自然都有比较丰富的积累。反观中国,"在礼教意识与宗法政治的一体化结构的禁锢之下,'笑君者罪当死'[……]。'不苟言笑'成了规范的行为模式,长此以往,幽默感当然难以蓬勃生长起来"。(胡范铸,1991:32)这种传统,自然不利于幽默翻译的实践和理论的发展。③

由此看来,Delabastita 的理论,无论用于指导中国的翻译研究还是实践,都可能会遇到一定的文化阻力。

八、结束语

从以上的讨论看来,有几个问题值得我们注意:

第一,不单是纯理论可能有跨语言的适用性,就连一些涉及微观操作的应用理论也可能有,因为纯理论与应用理论之间本来就没有分明的界线,而只是一个连续体的两端,而且很多理论同时具备两种性质。

第二,翻译理论不单可能有语言特殊性,而且可能有文化特殊性。因为翻译理论往往与整体文化要么有直接关系,要么通过翻译观、意识形态、幽默感等范畴而有间接关系,而文化特殊性可能是决定适用性的最重要因素。

第三,中国与西方在翻译研究方面的交流还非常不足。国内发表的探讨双关语翻译或幽默翻译的专文,只有欧阳利锋引述了西方一些相关论文,但也没有引述 Delabastita。明摆着的事实是,西方(尤其是 Delabastita)在这方面的研究领先于中国,而中国的学者则继续埋头苦干,从头做起。④ 这种现象的成因,不在于个别的学者,而在于翻译学界甚至整体文化。

---

① 在西方译论中早已流行的"零翻译"这个概念,在中国译论中还不存在。到 2001 年,才有邱懋如撰文"引进"这个概念(2001:26 - 27);但有趣的是,邱所说的"零翻译",与西方译论中约定俗成的概念大不相同。邱所说的第一类零翻译,例如省略冠词、代词等,只在词的层次上是零翻译,而在句子、语篇的层次上就不是了。在西方译论中,只有在语篇的层次上省略某些部分而导致信息损失的,才算是零翻译。而邱所说的第二类,即音译和移译(transference),与西方译论的概念相去更远。邱文完全没有提到西方译论中的那种零翻译,原因可能是他认为那不算是翻译,连零翻译也不算。这种概念上的不同,正反映了东西方主流翻译观的差异。

② 就连"双关语译为相同的双关语(不同类型)"和"双关语译为不同的双关语"这两种策略算不算翻译,在华人地区也颇有争议。香港中文大学出版社的《好的,首相》评审报告以例 2 为例,说"双关语……通常无法翻译,而必须自创替代物"(The puns ... cannot normally be translated, substitutes have to be invented),但同时又对译者的处理方法表示肯定;这显然反映了一种矛盾的态度。韩迪厚更说,赵元任把 porpoise (purpose)译为"鲤鱼(理由)"这样的手段,是"把'翻译工作'变成'编造'"(1969:134 - 137)。

③ 有些译者其实并不欣赏原文的一些双关语。例如萧乾就在《译本序》里说:"对于《尤利西斯》中一些纯文字游戏,我至今仍持保留态度。"(萧乾、文洁若,1994:26)译者的这种幽默观和文学观,看来在很大程度上决定了其翻译策略。

④ 同样,西方的零翻译概念也有参考价值,我们如果不接受,可以提出批评,但不应无视其存在。

选文三　The Translation of Metaphors

Peter Newmark

导　言

本文选自 Peter Newmark，*A Textbook of Translation*，Shanghai：Shanghai Foreign Language Education Press，2001.

本选文中，纽马克基于对"隐喻"的定义，将其划分为六种类型：死喻、陈辞性隐喻、库存式隐喻、新式隐喻、个性化原创隐喻和改装隐喻。在他看来，"隐喻翻译是一切语言翻译的缩影，因为隐喻翻译给译者呈现出多种选择方式：要么传递其意义，要么重塑其形象，要么对其进行修改，要么对其意义和形象进行完美的结合，林林总总，而这一切又与语境因素、文化因素如此密不可分，与隐喻在文内重要性的联系就更不用说了"。在高度概括隐喻翻译复杂多变的特性基础之上，纽马克提出了七种隐喻翻译方法：① 在目的语中重视相同的喻体；② 用目的语中合适的喻体代替源语中的喻体；③ 用明喻来代替隐喻；④ 用明喻和喻底相结合翻译隐喻；⑤ 将隐喻转化为喻底；⑥ 省略；⑦ 隐喻和喻底相结合。

Definitions

Whilst the central problem of translation is the overall choice of a translation method for a text, the most important particular problem is the translation of metaphor. By metaphor, I mean any figurative expression: the transferred sense of a physical word (*naître* as "to originate", its most common meaning); the personification of an abstraction ("modesty forbids me"—*en toute modestie je ne peux pas*); the application of a word or collocation to what it does not literally denote, i. e. to describe one thing in terms of another. All polysemous words (a "heavy" heart) and most English phrasal verbs ("put off", *dissuader*, *troubler*, etc.) are potentially metaphorical. Metaphors may be "single"—viz. one-word or "extended" (a collocation, an idiom, a sentence, a proverb, an allegory, a complete imaginative text).

So much for the substance. The purpose of metaphor is basically twofold: its referential purpose is to describe a mental process or state, a concept, a person, an object, a quality or an action more comprehensively and concisely than is possible in literal or physical language; its pragmatic purpose, which is simultaneous, is to appeal to the senses, to interest, to clarify "graphically", to please, to delight, to surprise. The first purpose is cognitive, the second aesthetic. In a good metaphor, the two purposes fuse like (and are parallel with) content and form; the referential purpose is likely to dominate in a textbook, the aesthetic often reinforced by sound-effect in an advertisement, popular journalism, an art-for-art's sake work or a pop song: "Those stars make towers on vowels" ("Saxophone Song", Kate Bush)—*tours sur foules? Turm auf Spur?* —you have to bear this in mind, when opting for sense or image. Metaphor, both purposes, always involves illusion; like a lie where you are pretending to be someone you are not, a metaphor is a kind of deception, often used to conceal an intention ("Cruise trundling amicably in the English lanes"—*The Economist*).

Note also that metaphor incidentally demonstrates a resemblance, a common semantic area between two or more or less similar things—the image and the object. This I see first as a process not, as is often stated, as a function. The consequence of a surprising metaphor (a "papery" cheek? —thin, white, flimsy, frail, feeble, cowardly?) may be the recognition of a resemblance, but that is not its purpose.

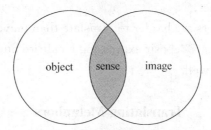

Figure 1. The translation of metaphor

Note that one of the problems in understanding and translating an original or an adapted and, to a lesser extent, a stock metaphor is to decide how much space to allot to the criss-crossed area of sense, and further to determine whether this area is: (a) positive *or* negative; (b) connotative *or* denotative. Thus in the sentence: "Kissinger: A TV *portrait* featuring a Metternich of today", it is not clear whether "Metternich" refers to: (a) Metternich's career as a European statesman; (b) his craftiness (negative); (c) his shrewdness (positive); (d) less likely, his autocratic nature. (This may be clarified in the subsequent sentences.) Here, broadly, the translator has the choice of: (a) a literal translation, leaving the onus of comprehension on the (educated) reader; (b) transferring "Metternich" and adding the preferred interpretation, e. g. "a statesman of Metternich's cunning"; (c) for a readership that knows nothing of Metternich, translating simply as "a cunning (world) statesman".

I use the following terminology for discussing metaphors:

Image: the picture conjured up by the metaphor, which may be *universal* (a "glassy" stare), cultural (a "beery" face), or individual (a "papery" cheek); "her continual 'forgive me' was another professional deformation" (of a Catholic).

Object: what is described or qualified by the metaphor, e. g. "P. J.", in "P. J. was binding up his wounds".

Sense: the literal meaning of the metaphor; the resemblance or the semantic area overlapping object and image; usually this consists of more than one sense component—

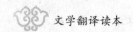

otherwise literal language would do. Thus, "save up for a rainy day"—time of need, financial shortage, gloom, worry, etc.—*une poire pour la soif*, *Notpfennig zurücklegen*. Note that these metaphors are hardly expressive. Usually the more original the metaphor, the richer it is in sense components.

Metaphor: the figurative word used, which may be one-word, or "extended" over any stretch of language from a collocation to the whole text.

Metonym: a one-word image which replaces the "object". It may be a cliché metaphor ("crown" as monarchy), recently standardised ("juggernaut", *mastodome*) or original ("sink" as hold-all receptacle). Metonym includes synecdoche (i. e. part for whole, or whole for part) e. g. "bottom" (boat) or "army" (one solider). Many technical terms such as *arbre*, *tour*, *métier*, *élément*, *pile*, *chien* are metonyms.

Symbol: a type of cultural metonym where a material object represents a concept—thus "grapes" as fertility or sacrifice.

Usually cultural metaphors are harder to translate than universal or personal metaphors. I see language not primarily as a deposit expressing a culture but as a medium for expressing universals and personality as well.

Translating Metaphors

Whenever you meet a sentence that is grammatical but does not appear to make sense, you have to test its apparently nonsensical element for a possible metaphorical meaning, even if the writing is faulty, since it is unlikely that anyone, in an otherwise sensible text, is suddenly going to write deliberate nonsense. Thus, if you are faced with, say, *L'après-midi, la pluie tue toujours les vitres*, you first test for a misprint. If it is an authoritative or expressive text, you translate "In the afternoons, the rain always kills the window-panes", and perhaps leave interpretation for a footnote. But if it is an anonymous text, you must make an attempt: "In the afternoons, the rain darkens/muffles/blocks the light from the window-panes." You cannot avoid this, you have to make sense of everything. Usually, only the more common words have connotations but, at a pinch, any word can be a metaphor, and its sense has to be teased out by matching its primary meaning against its linguistic, situational and cultural contexts.

Types of Metaphor

I distinguish six types of metaphor: dead, cliché, stock, adapted, recent and original, and discuss them in relation to their contextual factors and translation procedures.

Dead Metaphors

Dead metaphors, viz. metaphors where one is hardly conscious of the image, frequently relate to universal terms of space and time, the main part of the body, general ecological features and the main human activities: for English, words such as: "space", "field", "line", "top", "bottom", "foot", "mouth", "arm", "circle", "drop", "fall", "rise". They are particularly used graphically for concepts and for the language of science to clarify or define. Normally dead metaphors are not difficult to translate, but they often defy literal translation, and therefore offer choices. Thus, for "(in the) field" of human knowledge, French has *domaine* or *sphère*, German *Bereich* or *Gebiet*, Russian *oblast*. For "at the bottom of the hill", French has *au fond de la colline* but German only *am Fuß des Bergs*. Some simple artefacts such as "bridge", "chain", "link", also act as dead metaphors in some contexts, and these are often translated literally. Lastly, common words may attain a narrow technical sense in certain contexts: e. g. "dog", "fin", "element", "jack", *arbre* ("shaft"), *plage* ("bracket"), *métier* ("loom"), *Mutter* ("thread"). These are just as surprising in all foreign languages, and are particularly insidious and irritating if they make half-sense when used in their primary sense. Remember Belloc's advice, which one cannot take seriously even though it has a certain truth: look up every word, particularly the words you think you know—and now I will add to Belloc: first in a monolingual, then in a bilingual encyclopaedic dictionary, bearing in mind the rather general tendency in many languages to "decapitalise" (remove the capital letters from) institutional terms.

Note that in English, at least, dead metaphors can be livened up, sometimes into metonyms, by conversion to phrasal words ("drop out", "weigh up") and this must be accounted for in the translation (*marginal*, *mettre en balance*).

Cliché Metaphors

I define cliché metaphors as metaphors that have perhaps temporarily outlived their usefulness, that are used as a substitute for clear thought, often emotively, but without corresponding to the facts of the matter. Take the passage: "The County School will in effect become not *a backwater* but *a breakthrough* in educational development which will *set trends* for the future. In this its *traditions* will help and it may *well* become *a jewel* in the crown of the county's education." This is an extract from a specious editorial, therefore a vocative text, and in translation (say for a private client), the series of clichés have to be retained (*mare stagnante*, *percée*, *donnera le ton*, *joyau de la couronne*, *traditions*, not to mention the tell-tale *en effect* for "well") in all their hideousness; if this were part of a political speech or any authoritative statement, the same translation procedures would be appropriate.

However, a translator should get rid of clichés of any kind (collocations as well as metaphors), when they are used in an "anonymous" text, viz. an informative text where only facts or theories are sacred and, by agreement with the SL author, in public notices, instructions, propaganda or publicity, where the translator is trying to obtain an optimum reaction from readership. Here there is a choice between reducing the cliché metaphor to sense or replacing it with a less tarnished metaphor: "a politician *who has made his mark*"— *ein profilierter* (vogue-word) *Politiker*; *politicien qui s'est fait un nom*, *qui s'est imposé*. For an expression such as "use up every ounce of energy", "at the end of the day", "not in a month of Sundays", there are many possible solutions, not excluding the reduction of the metaphors to simple and more effective sense: *tendre ses demières énergies*, *définitivememt*, *en nulle occasion* and you have to consider economy as well as the nature of the text. Bear in mind that a cultural equivalent, if it is well understood (say "every *ounce* of energy"), is likely to have a stronger emotional impact than a functional (culture-free, third term) equivalent (*grain d'énergie*). If in doubt, I always reduce a cliché metaphor or simile to sense or at least to dead metaphor: "rapier-like wit"—*espriu mordant*, *acerbe*.

Cliché and stock metaphors overlap, and it is up to you to distinguish them, since for informative (i. e. the majority of) texts, the distinction may be important. Note that the many translation decisions which are made at the margin of a translation principle such as this one are likely to be intuitive. The distinction between "cliché" and "stock" may even lie in the linguistic context of the same metaphor.

Stock or Standard Metaphors

I define a stock metaphor as an established metaphor which in an informal context is an efficient and concise method of covering a physical and/or mental situation both referentially and pragmatically—a stock metaphor has a certain emotional warmth—and which is not deadened by overuse. (You may have noticed that I personally dislike stock metaphors, stock collocations and phaticisms, but I have to admit that they keep the world and society going—they "oil the wheels" [*mettre de l'huile dans les rouages*, *schmieren den Karren*, *die Dinge erleichtern*].)

Stock metaphors are sometimes tricky to translate, since their apparent equivalents may be out of date or affected or used by a different social class or age group. You should not use a stock metaphor that does not come naturally to you. Personally I would not use: "he's in a giving humour" (*il est en veine de générosité*); "he's a man of good appearance" (*il présente bien*); "he's on the eve of getting married" (*il est à la veille de se marier*). All these are in the Harrap dictionary but they have not "the implications of utterance" (J. R. Firth) for me; but if they have to you, use them.

The first and most satisfying procedure for translating a stock metaphor is to reproduce the same image in the TL, provided it has comparable frequency and currency in the appropriate TL register, e. g. "keep the pot boiling", *faire bouillir la marmite* ("earn a living", "keep something going"); *jeter un jour nouveau sur*, "throw a new light on". This is rare for extended metaphors (but probably more common for English-German than English-French), more common for single "universal" metaphors, such as "wooden face", *visage de bois*, *holzernes Gesicht*; "rise", "drop in prices": *la montée*, *la baisse des prix*, *die Preissteigerung*, *rückgang*. Note, for instance, that the metaphor "in store" can be translated as *en réserve* in many but not all collocations, and in even fewer as *auf Lager haben* (*eine Überraschung auf Lager haben*).

Symbols or metonyms can be transferred provided there is culture overlap: "hawks and doves", *faucons et colombes*, *Falken und Tauben*; this applies to many other animals, although the correspondence is not perfect: a dragon is maleficent in the West, beneficent in the Far East. The main senses are symbolised by their organs, plus the palate (*le palais*, *der Gaumen*), for taste; non-cultural proverbs may transfer their images; "all that glitters isn't gold"; *alles ist nicht Gold wasglänzt*; *tout ce qui brille n'est pas or*.

But a more common procedure for translating stock metaphors is to replace the SL image with another established TL image, if one exists that is equally frequent within the register. Such one-word metaphors are rare: "a drain on resources", *saignée de ressources*, *unsere Mittel belasten* (all these are rather inaccurate); "spice", *sel*. Extended stock metaphors, however, often change their images, particularly when they are embedded in proverbs, which are often cultural, e. g. "that upset the applecart"; *ça a tout fichu par terre*; *das hat alles über den Haufen geworfen*. These examples are characteristic of translated stock metaphors, in that the equivalence is far from accurate: the English denotes an upset balance or harmony and is between informal and colloquial; the French stresses general disorder and, being more colloquial, has the stronger emotional impact; the German has the same sense as the French, but is casual and cool in comparison.

When the metaphors derive from the same topic, equivalence is closer; "hold all the cards"; *alle Trümpfe in der Hand halten* (cf. *avoir tous les atouts dans son jeu*). Note that the French and German are stronger than the English, which can keep the same image: "hold all the trumps."

English's typical cultural source of metaphor may be cricket—"keep a straight bat", "draw stumps", "knock for six", "bowl out", "bowl over", "on a good/ sticky wicket", "that's not cricket" (cf. "fair play"; "fair"); I'm stumped; "field a question". Note that all these metaphors are rather mild and educated middle-class, and you normally have to resist the temptation to translate them too colloquially and strongly. "Fair play" has gone into many European languages, which represents a weakness of foreign translators (in principle, non-cultural terms such as qualities of character should not be transferred)—but "fair" is only transferred to German, Czech and Dutch.

A stock metaphor can only be translated exactly if the image is transferred within a correspondingly acceptable and established collocation (e. g. "widen the gulf between them", *élargir le gouffre entre eux*, *die Kluft erweitern*). As soon as you produce a new image, however acceptable the TL metaphor, there is a degree of change of meaning and usually of tone. Thus, *des tas de nourriture* may be a precise equivalent of "heaps of food"; "tons of food" or "loads of food" may be adequately rendered by *des tas de nourriture*, *un tas de nourriture*, but "loads" is heavier than "heaps", as is "tons" than "loads". (Much depends on the imagined tone of voice.) These additional components cannot be economically rendered within the collocation (*grand tas* would not help, as there is no reference criterion for grand), so there is a choice between compensation elsewhere in the linguistic context and intermitting or under-translating. When you translate there is always the danger of pursuing a particular too far, accreting superfluous meaning, and so the whole thing gets out of balance. Everything is possible, even the reproduction of the sound-effects, but at the cost of economy.

The same caveat applies to the third and obvious translation procedure for stock metaphors, reducing to sense or literal language: not only will components of sense be missing or added, but the emotive or pragmatic impact will be impaired or lost. Thus the metaphor: "I can read him like a book" has an immediacy which is lacking even in *ich kann ihn wie in einem Buch lesen* ("I can read him as in a book"), which weakens half the metaphor into a simile; *je sais, je devine tout ce qu'il pense* merely generalises the meaning—it should be preceded by *à son aspect, à son air*—and the emphasis is transferred from the completeness of the reading to the comprehensiveness of the knowledge. Even though the English metaphor is standard, it still has the surprising element of a good metaphor, and the French version is prosaic in comparison. Again, "a sunny smile" could be translated as *un sourire radieux* which is itself almost a metaphor, or *un sourire épanoui*, but neither translation has the warmth, brightness, attractiveness of the English metaphor. The "delicacy" or degree and depth of detail entered into in the componential analysis of a stock metaphor will depend on the importance you give it in the context. Maybe a synonym will do: *Notre but n'est pas defaire de la Pologne un foyer de conflits*: "It isn't our purpose to make Poland into a centre (source, focus) of conflict." For a metaphor such as *visiblement englué dans la toile d'araignée des compromis et des accommodements*, you may wish to keep the vividness of "visibly ensnared in the spider's web of compromises and accommodation", but, if in an informative text this is too flowery and obtrusive, it could be modified or reduced to "clearly hampered by the tangle of compromise he is exposed to". Or again, *il a claqué les portes du PCE* may just be a familiar alternative to "he left the Spanish Communist Party" or "he slammed the door on", "he refused to listen to", "he rebuffed". The meaning of a word such as *claquer* can be explicated referentially ("left abruptly, finally, decisively") or pragmatically ("with a bang, vehemently, with a snap"), extra-contextually or contextually, again depending on considerations of referential accuracy or pragamatic economy.

Further, you have to bear in mind that reducing a stock metaphor to sense may clarify, demystify, make honest a somewhat tendentious statement. Sometimes it is possible to do this naturally, where the TL has no metaphorical equivalent for a SL political euphemism: "In spite of many redundancies, the industry continues to flourish"—*Malgré les licenciements (Entlassungen), la mise en chômage de nombreux employés, cette industrie n'en est pas moins en plein essor*. Stock metaphors are the reverse of plain speaking about any controversial subject or whatever is taboo in a particular culture. They cluster around death, sex, excretion, war, unemployment. They are the handiest means of disguising the truth of physical fact. Inevitably, a stock metaphor such as *disparaître* (*si je venais a disparaître*, "if I were to die") becomes harsher when reduced to sense.

Stock cultural metaphors can sometimes be translated by retaining the metaphor (or converting it to simile), and adding the sense. This is a compromise procedure, which keeps some of the metaphor's emotive (and cultural) effect for the "expert", whilst other readers who would not understand the metaphor are given an explanation. Thus *il a une mémoire d'éléphant*—"He never forgets—like an elephant." *Il marche à pas de tortue*—"He's as slow as a tortoise." *Il a l'esprit rabelaisien*—"He has a ribald, Rabelaisian wit." The procedure (sometimes referred to as the "Mozart method", since it is intended to satisfy both the connoisseur and the less learned), is particularly appropriate for eponymous stock or original metaphor, e. g. *un adjecrif hugolesque*—a "resounding" ("lugubrious" etc. depending on context) "adjective, such as Victor Hugo might have used". When an eponymous metaphor becomes too recherché, or the image is classical and likely to be unfamiliar to a younger educated generation, the metaphor may be reduced to sense (*victoire à la Pyrrhus*, "ruinous victory"; *c'est un Crésus*, "a wealthy man", *le benjamin*, "the youngest son") but this depends on the importance of the image in the SL and correspondingly the TL context.

Stock metaphors in "anonymous" texts may be omitted if they are redundant. I see no point in his "sharp, razor-edge wit"(*esprit mordant*).

Translation of sense by stock metaphor is more common in literary texts, where it is not justified, than in non-literary texts, where it may be so, particularly in the transfer from a rather formal to a less formal variety of language, or in an attempt to enliven the style of an informative text. Expressions like *das ist hier einschlügig* can be translated as "that's the point here"; *er verschob es*, *das zu tun*, "he puts off doing that"—here the metaphors are dead rather than stock; *man muß betonen daß*—"one must highlight the fact that …"

This procedure may be better applied to verbs than to nouns or adjectives since these metaphorical variants ("tackle", "deal with", "see", "go into", "take up", "look into" [a subject]) are often less obtrusive than other types of metaphors.

Adapted Metaphors

In translation, an adapted stock metaphor should, where possible, be translated by an equivalent adapted metaphor, particularly in a text as "sacred" as one by Reagan (if it were translated literally, it might be incomprehensible). Thus, "the ball is a little in their court"—*c'est peut-être à eux de jouer*; "sow division"—*semer la division* (which is in fact normal and natural). In other cases, one has to reduce to sense: "get them in the door"—*les introduire* (*faire le premier pas?*); "outsell the pants off our competitors"—*épuiser nos produits et nos concurrents* (?). The special difficulty with these "sacred" texts is that one knows they are not written by their author so one is tempted to translate more smartly than

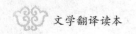

the original.

There are various degrees of adapted stock metaphors ("almost carrying coals to Newcastle"—*presque porter de l'eau à la rivière*; "pouring Goldwater on the missiles"—*Goldwater se montre peu enthousiaste pour les engins*) but since their sense is normally clear the translation should "err" on the side of caution and comprehension.

Recent Metaphors

By recent metaphor, I mean a metaphorical neologism, often "anonymously" coined, which has spread rapidly in the SL. When this designates a recently current object or process, it is a metonym. Otherwise it may be a new metaphor designating one of a number of "prototypical" qualities that continually "renew" themselves in language, e. g. fashionable ("in", "with it", *dans le vent*); good ("groovy", *sensass*; *fab*); drunk ("pissed", *cuit*); without money ("skint", *sans le rond*); stupid ("spastic", "spasmoid"); having sex ("doing a line"); having an orgasm ("making it", "coming"); woman chaser ("womaniser"); policeman ("fuzz", *flic*).

Recent metaphors designating new objects or processes are treated like other neologisms, with particular reference to the "exportability" of the referent and the level of language of the metaphor. A recent neologism, "head-hunting", being "transparent", can be through-translated (*chasse aux têtes*), provided its sense (recruiting managers, sometimes covertly, from various companies) is clear to the readership. Again "greenback", a familiar alternative for a US currency note, has probably only recently come into British English, and is translated "straight". "Walkman", a trade name, should be decommercialised, if possible (*transistor portatif*).

Original Metaphors

We must now consider original metaphors, created or quoted by the SL writer. In principle, in authoritative and expressive texts, these should be translated literally, whether they are universal, cultural or obscurely subjective. I set this up as a principle, since original metaphors (in the widest sense): (a) contain the core of an important writer's message, his personality, his comment on life, and though they may have a more or a less cultural element, these have to be transferred neat; (b) such metaphors are a source of enrichment for the target language. Tieck and Schlegel's translations of Shakespeare's great plays have given German many original expressions, but many more metaphors could have been transferred. Take Wilfred Owen's "We wise who with a thought besmirch Blood over all our soul" ("Insensibility") and Gunter Böhnke's translation: *Wit weisen, die mit einem Gedanken Blutbesudeln unsere Seele*, whatever this means, the translator can only follow the original lexically since the metre will not quite let the grammar be reproduced—the metaphor is virtually a literal rendering, and the readers of each version are faced with virtually the same difficulties of interpretation. However, if an original cultural metaphor appears to you to be a little obscure and not very important, you can sometimes replace it with a descriptive metaphor or reduce it to sense. Evelyn Waugh's "Oxford, a place in Lyonnesse" could be "Oxford, lost in the mythology of a remote, vanished region" (or even, "in Atlantis").

Finally, I consider the problem of original or bizarre metaphors in "anonymous" non-literary texts. The argument in favour of literal translation is that the metaphor will retain the interest of the readership; the argument against is that the metaphor may jar with the style of the text. Thus in an economics text, *Quelque séduisante que puisse étre une méthode, c'est à la façon dònt elle mord sur le réel qu'il la faut juger* (Lecerf)—"However attractive a working method may be, it must be judged by its bite in real life" is not far from the manner of *The Economist* (or *Spiegel*). The metaphor could be modified by "its impact on reality" or reduced to sense by "its practical effect". It seems to me that one has to make some kind of general decision here, depending on the number and variety of such metaphors in the whole text. Again, a typical *Guardian* editorial starts, under the title "Good Faith amid the Frothings", "and on the second day, the squealing (sic) of brakes was loud in the land... The National Coal Board had gone about as far as it could go". Such metaphorical exuberance would hardly be possible in another European language, and, unless the purpose of a translation were to demonstrate this exuberance ("a ton of enforced silence was dumped on Mr. Eaton ... window of opportunity ... dribbling offers, and trickling talks ... Kinnock scrambles out from under"—all in the first paragraph), the metaphors should be modified or eliminated: "The NCB suddenly issued no more statements... Mr. Eaton made no more statements... An opportunity... Insignificant offers... Slow talks... Mr. Kinnock emerges"— but a great deal of the sense as well as all the picturesqueness, flavour and sound-effect of the original would be lost. (The connection between metaphor and sound-effects, more often than not sacrificed in translation, is close; metaphor can summon the other three senses only visually.)

Original or odd metaphors in most informative texts are open to a variety of translation procedures, depending, usually, on whether the translator wants to emphasize the sense or the image. The choice of procedures in expressive or authoritative texts is much narrower, as is usual in semantic translation.

Nevertheless, in principle, unless a literal translation "works" or is mandatory, the translation of any metaphor is the epitome of all translation, in that it always offers choices in the direction either of sense or of an image, or a modification of one, or a combination of both, as I have shown, and depending, as always, on the contextual factors, not least on the importance of the metaphor within the text.

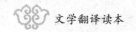
选文四 Metaphor, Translation, and Autoekphrasis in FitzGerald's *Rubáiyát*

Herbert F. Tucker

导 言

本文选自 *Victorian Poetry*,2008 年第 1 期。

《鲁拜集》(*Rubáiyát*)是波斯大诗人莪默·伽亚谟(Omar Khayyam,又译奥马开俨,或奥马·海亚姆等)的四行诗集。《鲁拜集》也称做"柔巴依",该古典抒情诗的基本特征是:每首四行,独立成篇,第一、二、四行押韵,第三行大抵不押韵,与我国的绝句相类似。内容多感慨人生如寄、盛衰无常,以及时行乐、纵酒放歌为宽解。几个世纪之中,莪默·伽亚谟默默无闻,几乎被人们遗忘了。直到 1859 年英国学者兼诗人爱德华·菲茨杰拉德(Edward Fitzgerald)不署名地整理发表了《莪默·伽亚谟之柔巴依集》,共 101 首,404 行。把这本诗集译介到英语世界,他的翻译属于意译,保持了原诗的韵律形式,遂使莪默·伽亚谟名声大振。本选文以大量例证论述菲茨杰拉德在诗集翻译中对于原诗中无处不在的隐喻修辞的成功处理,诚如大文豪、文艺批评家博尔赫斯在《爱德华·菲茨杰拉尔德之谜》一文中评价说:"……或许欧玛尔的灵魂于 1857 年在菲茨杰拉尔德的灵魂中落了户……使两人合成一个诗人。"

Among the many virtues of Christopher Decker's edition of the FitzGerald *Rubáiyát* is its patient elucidation, not only of the various circumstances surrounding the text's multiple versions, but of what we can infer about the translator's equally various attitude toward his work. [①]Enthusiastic, torpid, apologetic, cavalier, across two decades and more between the first edition of 1859 and the final one of 1879 the anonymous agent who once signed himself in correspondence "Fitz-Omar" remains hard to read with assurance—by reason partly of a diffidence that was specific to the man's character, partly of ambivalences that haunt the

---

① Edward FitzGerald, *Rubáiyat of Omar Khayyám: A Critical Edition*, ed. Christopher Decker (Charlottesville: Univ. of Virginia Press, 1997). Subsequent citations of the poem are to this edition, parenthetically indicated by edition year (arabic) and quatrain number (roman).

translator's art generally. [①] But amid this history of many shifts and much effacement, across the variorum *Rubáiyát* there emerges an unswerving commitment that goes far toward explaining the work's extraordinary appeal. I mean FitzGerald's commitment to interpreting Omar Khayyám's quatrains not mystically but—in a term of FitzGerald's that becomes intriguingly complex—literally. The apparatus to each version he authorized sets at defiance all "Pretence at divine Allegory" (1859, p. 6), all trafficking "in Allegory and Abstraction" (1868, p. 35), all "Spiritual" decoction of what "is simply the Juice of the Grape" (1872, p. 67). Keeping faith with his Persian original meant, for FitzGerald, scouting any and all "Mysticism" that might distract from Omar's manifest aim, which his Victorian translator deeply embraced too. That aim was "to soothe the Soul through the Senses into Acquiescence with Things as he saw them" (1868, p. 31).

"No doubt," averred the preface of 1868, "many of these Quatrains seem unaccountable unless mystically interpreted; but many more as unaccountable unless literally." (p. 35) FitzGerald's literalist affirmation so often took a feisty form because it was embroiled from the start in a polemic against Omar Khayyám's allegorizers. They were a tribe who had been around a long time—medieval Christianity had nothing on medieval Islam when it came to wresting heretic texts into hermeneutic line—and had voluble representatives still during the 19th century, and even in Europe. Well before 1859 FitzGerald was politely differing with his young tutor in Persian studies, Edward Cowell, about how to take some of Omar's bitter pills, and then in 1868 he stepped into the public ring to square off against J. B. Nicolas, a French exponent to whom the poems were dark Sufi conceits disclosing an orthodox message after all. FitzGerald survived this challenge handily, but the question that lay behind it has gone on to survive him. It flared up again just a generation ago, when no less an antagonist than the poet Robert Graves placed before the public a defense and illustration of Omar's hidden and mystical meaning. *The Original Rubaiyyat of Omar Khayaam: A New Translation with Critical Commentaries* is a title whose every adjective bristles with polemic—and whose aggressively repossessive orthography prepares us to learn that counterattacks were soon mounted in polemical turn by harder-headed sons of Fitz. The latter have long since carried the day against the allegorically credulous Graves and his

---

① Letter of September 15, 1876 to Anna Biddell, in *The Letters of Edward FitzGerald*, ed. Alfred McKinley Terhune and Annabelle Burdick Terhune (Princeton: Princeton Univ. Press, 1980), 3:704. This author's literary profile-in-camouflage is too well suited by the portmanteau name "Fitz-Omar" to let Graves' heckling usage (see next note) spoil it for the rest of us. See Erik Gray, "Forgetting FitzGerald's Rubáiyát", SEL 41, no. 4 (2001), on "FitzGerald's Menardian knack for writing someone else's poem. Borges is not alone in refusing to ascribe it either to FitzGerald or to Omar: librarians have had the same dilemma, and anyone looking for editions or references is almost invariably required to look under both names" (p. 772).

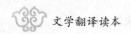

ignorant or unscrupulous informant, the Sufi mystagogue votary Omar Ali-Shah. [1]

I am spectacularly ill equipped to pronounce on the merits of this or any other matter pertaining to the astronomer algebrist with a 900-year-old name. But I can propose that his Victorian popularizer's firm commitment to taking old Omar at his word—taking him "literally", which is to say, in part, linguistically—had, as its cardinal literary consequence, a mode of poetic presentation to which the *Rubáiyát* has owed the breadth and longevity of its circulation among an anglophone public as "the most popular verse translation into English ever made" (Decker, p. xiv). For in FitzGerald's freely translating hands the this-worldly, bodily thematics of the poem found consistent correlates in its poetics. Without the rhetorical and prosodic vehicles that FitzGerald contrived for it, his translation would long ago have exhausted its capacity to shock readers or delight them either. These poetic devices are as textually materialist, performative, and signifier-focused as the poem's themes are philosophically materialist, hedonist, and bound to the orbit of physical experience. I shall pursue here this mutually reinforcing relation between theme and method with respect to three topics: FitzGerald's handling of metaphor, his stance toward translation, and his habitual practice of a reflexive self-reference that annuls, within the performative poetic moment, those binary distinctions which ordinarily ground our thinking about metaphor and translation alike.

1

Start with metaphor, and the trouble it portends for even a fairly relaxed interpretive literalism. By definition as by etymology, metaphor is a rhetorical figure that finds meaning in transit from what is overtly said to what is covertly meant; and to this extent it participates in the letter/spirit dualism of allegory, enshrined now in general usage as the distinction between vehicle and tenor. [2] Yet Khayyám's fondness for metaphor—compounded by Romanticism's

---

① *The Original Rubaiyyat of Omar Khayaam: A New Translation with Critical Commentaries*, trans. Robert Graves and Omar Ali-Shah (Garden City: Doubleday, 1968). Various papers discrediting the alleged twelfth-century "original" (allegedly secreted with the Ali-Shah family in the Hindu Kush) are collected in *Translation or Travesty? An Enquiry into Robert Graves's Version of Some Rubaiyat of Omar Khayyam* (Abingdon: Abbey Press, 1973) by John Bowen, who traveled expressly to Kabul for purposes of verification. That Bowen's "final letter" in the controversy (*The Listener*, August 3, 1972) was regarded as indeed final appears from the silence on the matter observed thereafter by an interested party, the Cambridge scholar Peter Avery. Having endorsed the 1973 exposé in an introductory note, Avery when publishing his own new translation *The Rubaiyat of Omar Khayyam* with John Heath-Stubbs a few years later made no mention of Graves (London: Allen Lane, 1979). Avery does, however, underscore what the extinguished controversy highlights for us here: FitzGerald was "an exception among nineteenth-century explorers of Persian poetry, because he was not looking for a spiritual solace which, in any event, his profound scepticism would have precluded. He was clear in his grasp of the often very austere and unconsoling message" (p. 18).

② The term descends to us via classical and neoclassical rhetoricians from the Greek *metapherein* ([greek], to carry over), which has also, to the surprise of literary travelers but aptly, yielded *metaphor* as the modern Greek word for a truck or lorry.

heavy metaphorical investments, which the Spasmodist craze of the 1850s had lately inflated to the bursting point—obliged FitzGerald despite his proclaimed hostility to metaphor to use the trope prominently. His first gambit was defensively offensive: he worked that prominence for all it was worth and then some. Within both the structural sequence of the text and its evolution across the decades from edition to edition, Fitz metaphorized like gangbusters, so as to bankrupt the allegorical tendencies of metaphor by overindulgence:

> Awake! for Morning in the Bowl of Night
> Has flung the Stone that puts the Stars to Flight:
> And Lo! the Hunter of the East has caught
> The Sultán's Turret in a Noose of Light.
>
> (1859, I)

Coming as it does from an 1850s poem, this quatrain might not unfairly be described as spasmodic. Philip James Bailey, Alexander Smith, Sydney Dobell, and their numerous admirers (including Tennyson, Clough, even their later assailant Matthew Arnold in salad days) would have known how to ooh and ahh at the exclamatory fireworks of such an opening salvo. [1] And we can easily imagine the still-youthful Pre-Raphaelite Brothers, who adored the first *Rubáiyát*, dubbing these lines stunners.

Headstrong, with a nice brain-candy buzz, each conceit in the quatrain goes its own way. True, there is a lot of centripetal prosodic force at play here, a sheerly phonemic noosing that reins in the outward splashiness of the plunging imagery: in line 2, the chiasmus of "flung"—"Stone"—"Stars"—"Flight", and thereupon the flickering identity of this last word with the cinching rhyme "of Light" at stanza's end. Likewise, as visual figures the "Bowl" and the "Noose" both sweep horizontally around a focal point; but the circle they present to the mind is anything but hermeneutic, since the metaphors don't add up, or really have anything in common but (the spasmodist's constant friend) the element of surprise. While they share the binary, othering riddle structure of allegory—declaration: implication; question: answer—the puzzles they pose are of a kind to be readily solved by the mind's eye and then discarded in favor of the next puzzle in line, which in this case is the equally prepossessing yet quickly exhausted trope of "Dawn's Left Hand" from stanza number two. The very extravagance of these early metaphors, with their rapid-fire delivery and ready solubility, militates against the mystic contemplation of hidden truths. One reason why, in decoding them, we pass so swiftly from the signifier to the signified is that in each case the signified is such a common phenomenon: the most everyday thing in the world, the definitively quotidian rising of the sun. If this be allegory, it is allegory on the shortest and most trivial of terms: visionary rather than mystic writing, it neither invites nor rewards the

---

① See the recent special issue of *VP* (42, no. 4 [2004]), guest-edited by Charles LaPorte and Jason Rudy, devoted to "Spasmodic Poetry and Poetics". FitzGerald's diary letter to Cowell of June 23 – July 2, 1857 shows him free-associating as he puzzles over these tropes in the original (*Letters*, 2:280).

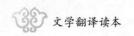 文学翻译读本

gaze of second sight.

FitzGerald backed off from this kind of hyperkinetic riddling in 1868—when the "Stone" and "Bowl" both vanished and the "Noose of Light" paled to a more conventionally Apollonian "Shaft"—and further off again in 1872. In making these changes he acted consistently with the tessellated poetic plot that had unfolded even in the version of 1859. For that first version had found a different way of converting metaphor to purposes that an allegory-aversive literalist might endorse, a way that drew on metaphor's counter-trope metonymy. Metaphor, as classically analyzed, effects a kind of conversion: an instantaneous transformation of the vehicle into its tenor, of the thing declared into its undeclared but understood meaning. This transubstantial mystery is ultimately eucharistic in its significance for a Western audience—something that FitzGerald's wine-dark import of a poem never forgets. But in this work the metaphysics of a metaphorical poetics of conversion are expressly countered by the physics of a metonymical poetics of reversion. Here the paradigmatic transformation is what the poem names, with quite different resonance for the Anglican reader, a zero-sum transformation of "Dust into Dust" (1859, XXⅢ): the recycling of identity, the return of the inevitable same with no claim of value-added. ① The phase of operation for this long-drawn relapse is not the metaphorical magical instant, but the fullness of time within which every instant is absorbed, where all instants are created equal, and every form must dissolve back into its original elements on the level.

This is preeminently the realist logic of mortality; and metonymy, as Jakobson long ago remarked, is its master trope, the figure that asserts the matter-of-fact contingencies of material existence in linear time, linking causes to effects, and processes to ends. En route, however, FitzGerald takes a special glee in tricking this master metonymy out as metaphor, only to demystify it:

> I sometimes think that never blows so
> red The Rose as where some buried Cæsar bled;
> That every Hyacinth the Garden wears
> Dropt in her Lap from some once lovely Head.
>
> And this reviving Herb whose tender Green
> Fledges the River-Lip on which we lean—
> Ah, lean upon it lightly! for who knows
> From what once lovely Lip it springs unseen!
>
> (1872, XIX-XX)

That blood-red roses and hyacinthine locks participate alike in a lethal ecology is a hard

---

① See Gray, especially pp. 775 - 777, on the "recycling" relation among the poem's vaguely amnesiac stanzas in their rhyme-words, sequencing, and strangely pleasurable traffic in body parts.

biochemical fact, which our sips of Omar's metonymic draught can nerve us not to forget. As for the second of these quatrains, it all but springs a metonymic trap on a metaphoric bait: the riverbank we fancied lip-like on account of an accidental downy resemblance discloses a more essential connection; the metamorphic pleasures of the surface yield to a physiological unity based deeper than allegory and its arbitrary, flimsy shape-shifting. ① Distributed throughout the poem, such moments constitute a metonymic network articulating the lips of the poet with those of earthen urns and drinking cups (1859, XXXIV); articulating the exhalation of his grape-embalmed cognacky corpse with the "Air" that will influence his survivors in song (1859, LXVIII); and above all, or below it, articulating the human form with the clay it arose from and relapses to, as dust to dust. An anecdote newly footnoted in 1872 corroborates this last articulation of body with clay: there a thirsty traveler learns that "the Clay from which the Bowl is made was once Man; and, into whatever shape renew'd, can never lose the bitter flavour of Mortality". ② What's the matter, then, with metaphor? Matter's the matter, replies FitzGerald. "Into whatever shape renew'd", the metaphoric transform meets its match, indeed its enabling condition, in the intransubstantiability, the counter-eucharistic declension, that underlies substance as such.

This bedrock realist vision of fatal continuity lets metonymy sponsor the most extended passage of allegorical writing in the *Rubáiyát*, the so-called "Kúza-Náma" section (1859, LIX-LXVI: the name, omitted in later editions, means "writing about jugs"). Here colloquizing pots stand in for the mortal sons of Adam (whose name in its Semitic root means "earth" or "clay"), inconclusively speculating as they will about the power that made, or should we say threw them. The basis for lumping human stuff with ceramic has by this late point in the poem become well enough established to make this comic section an ironic allegory of allegoresis. Shooting the theological breeze, FitzGerald's pot-heads are allegorical figures for those who, since they literally cannot know what they are talking about, are unwitting allegorists trading in potted thought, the idle postulation of received ideas that are ungrounded, untestable, equivalently nil—and soon exposed, once the Ramadan fast is over, as a pretext for killing time until the pubs open and a good fellow can tank up. ③ At roughly

---

① David Sonstroem, "Abandon the Day: FitzGerald's *Rubáiyát of Omar Khayyám*", VN 36 (1969): 11, explores (and deplores) the poem's subversive metaphorics.

② Decker, p. 84n14. The materialist consequence of FitzGerald's metonymic regard for the more typically metaphorized human body is registered at maximum strength by Daniel Schenker, "Fugitive Articulation: An Introduction to *The Rubáiyát of Omar Khayyám*", VP 19 (1981): 49 – 64. His description of the poem as "a veritable butcher shop of dismembered flesh" needs seasoning that Gray's remarks can provide (see note 7 above).

③ The monist or uniform reduction of the soul to "a body built of clay in a clay-built house"—expressly introduced as a "metaphor" and swiftly dismissed as a "bad" one—had already occurred to FitzGerald's collegians as they conversed about metaphor in *Euphranor: A Dialogue of Youth* (London, 1851), p. 29: repr. in *The Variorum and Definitive Edition of the Poetical and Prose Writings of Edward FitzGerald*, ed. George Bentham (1902; repr. New York: Phaeton, 1967), 1: 169. See also FitzGerald's compound note on the potter-and-clay topos, which by 1879 included an anecdote about a bake-faced old man known as "the 'ALLEGORY'" and reckoned by all in the village a half-wit (Decker, p. 114).

the level of allegory that breathes a short life into most editorial cartoons, FitzGerald assembles here from Omar's rubai shards a reductive performance of the all-too-human tendency to entertain questions beyond human wielding. The pot's absurd (and unanswered) interrogation of its potter is what FitzGerald derided as a "Pretence at divine Allegory", no different in kind from the Sufic or idealizing flight out of circumstance into "Abstraction" against which he launched his preface to each edition. It is a nice touch, then, that Khayyám's "loquacious Vessels" (1872, LXXXⅢ) should be vessels indeed. Metaphorical vehicles, their tenor is the flatulent jalopy of metaphor itself: a contraption to think with, but not very well, and at all events of no more use in Fitz-Omar's book than mere thinking ever proves to be.

The subversion of metaphor from within bespeaks FitzGerald's impatience with metaphor's impatience, its hunger to make change in a hurry. This needy rhetorical ardor forms the target of the ironic if hypogrammatical stanza XLⅢ:

> The Grape that can with Logic absolute
> The Two-and-Seventy jarring Sects confute:
> The subtle Alchemist that in a Trice
> Life's leaden Metal into Gold transmute.
>
> (1859, XLⅢ)[1]

The history of controversy over Omar Khayyám's worldview shows how indifferently the parties of Sufi and of scoffer have invoked irony to explain away unfriendly evidence. [2] Still, there is good cause to believe that, in context, the absolute instantaneousness of alchemy in this quatrain can only be a joke. The hope must be drunk that in 1859, the very year of Darwin and heyday of Victorian liberal gradualism, puts much stock in anything that happens "in a Trice". To credit the magic of transmutation is to be swept away by the Bacchic alchemy of alcohol or—same difference—the viewless wings of that metaphoric poesy which FitzGerald here sends up. A more sober assessment of the prospect for fool's gold has been furnished thirty stanzas before:

> And those who husbanded the Golden Grain,
> And those who flung it to the Winds like Rain,
> Alike to no such aureate Earth are turn'd
> As, buried once, Men want dug up again.
>
> (1859, XV)

---

[1] Has interpretive ingenuity resolved the grammar of the last two lines? Presumably from exigency of rhyming, the final verb "transmute" lacks a proper subject, as e. g. my nonce variant "Can leaden Metal into Gold transmute" does not. The sense is plain enough, but the technical error found in every edition remains anomalous.

[2] Thus Graves explains away Omar's apparent heresy and blasphemy as instances of *reductio ad absurdum* that "imitate and follow up a false line of thought in order to demonstrate its shallowness" ("The Fitz-Omar Cult", in *Original Rubaiyyat*, p. 21).

The place of humanity lies not with the philosopher's stone, but within the cyclical economy whereby "Golden Grain" and "aureate Earth" produce and consume one other. In this process a man is but a middleman, "turn'd" to earth whether his hand harvests or scatters seed, directs the swerving plow (that old metaphor for verse-writing itself) or rots in the grave. In each case the "turn" bespeaks reversion not conversion, metonymy not metaphor. Nothing is transmuted after all but what is transmitted in a slow, piecemeal, stepwise rhythm which the annual turning of the soil represents, which the enjambed turning of the last two verses enacts, and which an ear attuned by Garrett Stewart's fine book *Reading Voices* will hear as the phonotextual identity of the stanza's first rhyme: "like Rain" in the second line sounds enough like "Grain" above it to make FitzGerald's point: *Plus ça change, plus c'est la même chose.* [1] Which is also a point that the poem's aaxa rhyme scheme reinforces: "absolute"—"confute"—"Trice"—"transmute"; "Grain"—"Rain"—"turned"—"again". A reader habituated to couplets expects the x rhyme, the sound that terminates each third-line pentameter, to come back in line four and sew the stanza up, conveying in the process a sense that we are going somewhere in our stride from couplet to couplet. But not so: we get instead a third a rhyme that remands us to square one and reproves our illusion of progress as just that, a metrical illusion. [2]

The translator's tempered effect here is a far cry from the splashy spasmody of his opening quatrain, but its more enduring voice is one that a perusal of Decker's long first appendix ("Comparative Texts") shows the translator striving again and again to secure. Thus one juicy line of 1868, "But still a Ruby gushes from the Vine" (V), eventually mellowed to the more subtle and gradual 1879 reading, "But still a Ruby kindles in the Vine". (O for a draught—revised—of vintage!) Where the former reading is in your face, the latter dwells in your mind. Less nose, we might say, but a stronger finish, a more lasting because a more literal truth. The "Ruby" of 1868 is a raw metonymy that can only trope red grapes, and properly not even the wine they may become. But the "Ruby" of 1879 is a quality organic to the plant from seedling to maturity, spring to fall, and root to branch to fruit to beverage. Those with an earthy eye to viniculture will farsightedly discern wine's red essence in the fullness of the processional, endlessly cycling rehearsal of change which it expresses, and from which it is expressed. So it is with poetic composition in this very quatrain: over maturing time, a *rubai* kindles too.

---

① Garrett Stewart, *Reading Voices: Literature and the Phonotext* (Berkeley: Univ. of California Press, 1990). Although Stewart's argument makes no use of the *Rubáiyát*, his attention to Victorian poets on pp. 173-184, including FitzGerald's adored Tennyson, offers a context hospitable to what we are attempting here.

② Sonstroem disconsolately finds in the rhyme scheme a "metric metaphor for the poem's overall movement" (p. 12). As Gray puts it, "The return of the initial rhyme is like a resignation, a refusal to try to struggle with the new terms that have been introduced" (p. 774). We might draw out here, what Gray implies, that the rhyme's return is a re-signing or contractual confirmation, in the arbitrary materiality of the word, of the arbitrary materiality of the world.

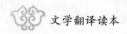

2

That last, illegitimate pun precipitates our second topic, translation, where we shall again find Fitz-Omar nailing his colors to the mast of form. In one obvious sense, translation is a rock on which any thesis about literalism must split, since to the literally literalist eye translation, especially of poetry, is impossible. *Interdit. Verboten. Tabu.* Don't even think about it. And yet we can't help thinking about it. Like allegory and metaphor—the latter, remember, was taken over from Greek into Latin as *translatio*—translation entails conveyance from one system of meanings into another. As the literally given stands to the allegorically figured and the vehicle to the tenor, so stands more or less the translator's target language to the source language of the author: within each of these pairings, we ordinarily suppose, a reader transacts with the former so as to get at the latter. Furthermore, translation is called for only where cultural or historical distance has made systems of meaning so mutually unintelligible as to disqualify in advance even the modified literalism of a transcriptive decoding. So the translator has no choice but to go figure.

This objection is immovable, but FitzGerald implied a detour around it in a letter of 1859 to his collaborator Cowell: "I suppose very few People have ever taken such Pains in Translation as I have: though certainly not to be literal. But at all Cost, a Thing must *live.*"[1] This sails close enough to the wind of St. Paul's mischievous if indispensable plea, about the letter that killeth while the spirit giveth life, that we should try to be clear where FitzGerald expected the life of a translation to transpire. He helped us out by what comes next in his letter: the thing needful was "a transfusion of one's own worse Life if one can't retain the Original's better. Better a live Sparrow than a stuffed Eagle" (*Letters*, 2:335). Translation had to make its living in the work's new linguistic and cultural habitat, where it must breathe the spirit of the age yet where, in order to do that without risk of total assimilation, it must also cleave to a certain core of identity, something unassimilably its own. For the most celebrated of translations into English from Middle-Eastern sources, the King James Bible, such a residuum of unalienated identity was preserved through a stubborn semantic fidelity ultimately rooted in pious veneration.[2] For the *Rubáiyát*, however, FitzGerald had no such veneration nor anything like the degree of competence in Persian studies that would have been required in order to practice such veneration had it existed.

---

[1] Letter of April 27, 1859, to E. B. Cowell, in *Letters*, 2:335.

[2] While FitzGerald could not share the faith of King James' biblical translators, he more than once admired their fidelity to the strangeness of the text and affirmed his wish to imitate it, "keeping so close to almost unintelligible idioms both of Country and Era" as did the King James, and "only using the most idiomatic Saxon words to convey the Eastern Metaphor" (*Letters*, 2: 164, 119). See Stephen Prickett, *Words and The Word: Language, Poetics and Biblical Inspiration* (Cambridge: Cambridge Univ. Press, 1986), for appreciation, against a nineteenth-century intellectual context, of the virtuous literality of the King James Bible.

"But at all Cost, a Thing must *live*." FitzGerald's translation found its *modus vivendi* in a stubborn allegiance, not to meanings, but to certain more or less arbitrary importations of form. A most conspicuous example of this formal allegiance is one that we were just considering: Omar Khayyám's highly effective, conspicuously un-English *aaxa* quatrain. FitzGerald made no secret of the way he "mashed", stretched, cut and reshuffled the contents of Khayyám's quatrains ad libitum. [1] Nevertheless, by sticking like a limpet to the proportions of the *rubai* form itself, he embraced as a principle of unity the functional equivalent of a persistent foreign accent. [2] In the process, he implicitly entered the lists in a robust mid-Victorian debate about how poetry written in other languages ought to be translated into English. This debate possesses great inherent interest, has lately attracted scholarly attention, and deserves still more. [3] It matters especially because so much was at stake, at more or less the time the Victoria and Albert Museum was going up down in South Kensington, in the question of the rights and duties—import duties, for such they were— attendant on the manner in which the world's fast-imperializing superpower went about looting, or was it after all rescuing, the ages and the climes. The most durable entrant in this debate was Matthew Arnold, who in the polemics he would gather as "On Translating Homer" constrained the translator to make proper Englishmen of all the world. [4] Although FitzGerald threw no punches in this mid-century fracas, his quiet and persistent implication in the *Rubáiyát* lay on the other side with Arnold's antagonists. Like D. G. Rossetti in translating Dante—Rossetti who adored the *Rubáiyát* early, and played a part in its dissemination once his friend Whitley Stokes had discovered it languishing unsold on the bookstall—FitzGerald respected the strangeness of his original, its resistance to Englishing. [5] He agreed, that is, with the aim articulated by Arnold's chief opponent in the Homer controversy, F. W. Newman, who had sought in his eccentric 1856 translation of the Iliad "to retain every peculiarity of the original... with the greater care, the more foreign it may be". [6]

---

[1] "Many quatrains are mashed together: and something lost, I doubt, of Omar's simplicity": letter to Cowell of September 3, 1858 (*Letters*, 2:318).

[2] The Persian rubai consists of two lines subdivided into hemistichs and thus four parts—the Arabic root of the term means "foursome"—in which parts one, two, and four must rhyme. Thus FitzGerald's quatrain stanza while not technically a *rubai* is manifestly a faithful equivalent in form. See Avery's analysis, together with discussion of the cultural mobility the form enjoyed in Khayyám's day, in his 1979 *Ruba'iyat*, pp. 7 – 10.

[3] Lawrence Venuti, *The Translator's Invisibility: A History of Translation* (New York: Routledge, 1995), pp. 118 – 135. What Venuti calls "foreignizing" translation evidently applies to FitzGerald, of whom he is not however fond (pp. 188 – 189). See also, even though FitzGerald does not enter the discussion, Simon Dentith's *Epic and Empire in Nineteenth-Century Britain* (Cambridge: Cambridge Univ. Press, 2006), pp. 48 – 63.

[4] Matthew Arnold, *On Translating Homer: Three Lectures Given at Oxford* (London, 1861).

[5] On Rossetti's approach to translation, see Jerome J. McGann, *Dante Gabriel Rossetti and the Game That Must Be Lost* (New Haven: Yale Univ. Press, 2000), pp. 33 – 38, 46 – 65.

[6] Francis W. Newman, *Homeric Translation in Theory and Practice: A Reply to Matthew Arnold, Esq., Professor of Poetry, Oxford* (London, 1861), p. xvi.

At a related level of interlinguistic commerce, to which the Decker edition again offers sumptuously well-appointed guidance, the translator of the *Rubáiyát* sprinkled his English text with a double handful of Persian terms. These unassimilated linguistic forms the canny Fitz-Omar did not translate, but merely transliterated—not always consistently from edition to edition either, and often with pretty capricious support in his supposedly elucidatory footnotes. The twofold effect of this peekaboo assistance was, first, to throw the dependent reader back for pronunciation help on the authority of the metrical quatrain, which in practice never does betray the tongue that trusts it; and, second, to keep the reader indeterminately suspended between two languages, two cultures, two histories. In all likelihood the sometimes threadbare quality of FitzGerald's annotation evinced lacunae in his learning, at least circa 1859. But, if he came to know his scholar's business better by 1879, he also knew his translator's business better than to disturb the delicate balance of managed anxiety in which a little learning, but only a little, had happily left his reader: in English, in fashionable synch with a modern temper of urbane disillusion, yet also in a limbo removed, as FitzGerald said, "from Europe and European Prejudices and Associations". [1]

Somewhere between source and target, cut off alike from the security of a European home and from the authority of a Persian origin, the reader of the *Rubáiyát* learns to live not lost in translation but, so to say, found in transmission. The felt pulse and ratio of an antique verse form, and the visual saliency of FitzGerald's odd, improbable transliterations, help explain what Charles Eliot Norton meant from America when hailing the poem as "not a copy, but a reproduction, not a translation, but the redelivery of a poetic inspiration". [2] Never mind that promissory note of "inspiration": better take the cash and let the credit go, stressing the descriptive rightness of Norton's "reproduction" and "redelivery" as names for the performative presence of the FitzGerald version. Somewhat as we have seen metonymy supervene on metaphor within the rhetorical tactics of the poem, so the transmission of the text conditions its translation, in such a way as to keep it from ever fully arriving, ever seeming fully accommodated at all. (Such resistance to Western naturalization surely ranked among the effects of this Victorian bestseller to which Ezra Pound paid homage half a century later when transmitting in radiant shards, with a poet's kind of faith in language's literal power, the farther Eastern matter of *Cathay*. [3])

One sign of an intention consistent with this betwixt-and-betweenness is FitzGerald's

---

[1] In the quoted letter to Cowell of January 10, 1856, FitzGerald illustrates the principle "in Translation to retain the original Persian Names as much as possible—'Shah' for 'king' for instance—'Yúsuf and Suleymán' for 'Joseph and Solomon', etc". (*Letters*, 2:194).

[2] *North American Review* 109, no. 225 (1869): 575. Schenker's characterization of Norton's review is both discerning and provocative: "the exoticism of the work impressed him with the homeliness of its sentiments" (p. 52).

[3] See Christine Froula, *To Write Paradise: Style and Error in Pound's Cantos* (New Haven: Yale Univ. Press, 1984), pp. 154–155, on the embedded Chinese characters in Pound's text and "the unassimilable difference" betokened by "their alien mode of representation". See also Venuti's caveat against Modernist translators' effacement of "the process of domestication by which the foreign text is rewritten to serve modernist cultural agendas" (p. 189).

own redescription of the work on successive title pages. In 1859 it was "Translated into English Verse", but in 1868 and thereafter "Rendered into English Verse"—a more processive, performative verb, and one that, while still Frenchy, feels more native than the fully Latinate "Translated". Another such sign is the perverse-seeming use, consistent across all FitzGerald's versions, of roman rather than arabic numerals to designate each quatrain: *translatio imperii* indeed! Yet another sign is the poem's last word, "TAMÁM", which means "the end" but is nowhere glossed as that or anything else in any of FitzGerald's editions. That a Persian term should signify the reader's arrival at the English terminus keeps the transit of translation permanently incomplete.

> A Muezzín from the Tower of Darkness cries
> "Fools! your Reward is neither Here nor There!"
> (1859, XXIV)

And that is just where we want our reward to be: neither out here in the modern West nor over there in the medieval East, but in the midst of things, where a translated "Thing must live", without dwindling into the dead letter of total comprehension or evaporating into mute, inscrutable intentionality. ①

3

This transmissive utopia of interpreted semiosis, if it really lay nowhere but in the conceptual vacuum of the double negative, would be worse news poetically speaking than the "Allegory and Abstraction" that FitzGerald always derided. So let us now look again and see that it indeed does lie somewhere, and that this somewhere is the space of the poem made livable—inviting to visit and hard to leave—by an habitual practice of textual self-referentiality. I have argued elsewhere that the social pressure nineteenth-century poets faced, under new conditions of anonymously brokered publication and expanding literacy, put extraordinary stress on their handling of the formal resources of verse and trope in print;

---

① Not that Fitz-Omar's recalcitrant intermediacy escaped complicity with the lighter-fingered, cosmopolitan side of Victorian empire-building, or even meant to. The aesthetic exoticism that savored experience at one or two removes arguably facilitated, not only respite from the conqueror's toils, but the rough business of conquest as well. Unbelief such as the *Rubáiyát* expresses may well have made it easier now and then, during the last century and a half, for imperial functionaries to cultivate lethal detachment from those they had power to hurt; and a searching postcolonialist analysis of the poem, when we get one, should look into the matter—perhaps by way of a global reception-history. Still, the noncommittal ideological levitation that the FitzGerald translation performed remains a remarkable feat of cultural *askesis*. The difficulty of thinking through issues of translation to the contingencies of nation and ethnicity finds illustration in William Cadbury's "FitzGerald's *Rubáiyát* as a Poem", ELH 34, no. 4 (1967): 541 – 563. This essay, an exceptionally thoughtful contribution at a time when the poem was attracting bland notice if any, manages on the same page to praise the poet's fidelity "to things as they are ... and not to transcending man", and then to identify this difficult position with a "full and nonethnic humanity" (p. 563). Clearly in his day Cadbury's critical frame of reference was religious-existential. Just as clearly for us in literary studies today, if the "nonethnic" is not a "transcendental" concept, then we don't know what is.

and that this stress sometimes imploded into modes of what I call "autoekphrasis". [①] In autoekphrasis a poem's description of structures in the referential world doubles as description of its own structures. These are thereby reinforced as ad hoc imaginative common places, where readers however diverse and faceless may convene and, at least for the spacetime of a reading, dwell. In the extremity of such autoekphrastic adaptations, probably no nineteenth-century work outdoes the anonymously published *Rubáiyát of Omar Khayyám*. FitzGerald seems to have let no occasion slip for making a line, a stanza, a brace of rubáiyát its own subject, performing within the space of the page or the interval of recitation an allegory of reading whose content and form coalesce and whose meaning is, literally, itself.

For example—and in such a matter examples are everything—the poem repeatedly figures its frustration with allegorical mysticism in tropes of impasse: "There was a Door to which I found no Key" (1859, XXXII), the poet gazes in vain "up to Heav'n's unopening Door" (1868, LIV), and so on. Passages about blocked passages have a prima facie Wordsworthian appeal, which FitzGerald heightens and customizes by attaching the trope of the door to that of the dwelling, the room, or (suitable to Omar Khayyám's artisanal calling as tentmaker) the tent. To recall that *stanza* means room, while reading in stanza XXII (1859) about the dead that "we ... now make merry in the Room/ They left", is to reflect at once on Omar's theme of life's brevity and on the vivid durability of a form like the foursquare *rubai* he "left" (quit in bequest) to heirs like FitzGerald. Such a form is no less durable for being portable. On the contrary, "a Tent wherein may rest/ A Sultan" has the better chance of traveling across centuries and continents, when "The Sultan rises, and the dark Ferrásh/ Strikes, and prepares it for another guest" (1868, LXX). (Curious about that Ferrásh? A servant of some kind, by reliable inference; but, as the text gives no gloss, he remains a dark conceit, an undocumented worker, the servant of two master languages and thus, in a sense, fully commanded by neither.)

By such means autoekphrasis finds the tented text a local habitation resilient and transient in equal measure. If we bear in mind the clinching effect of the *rubai* quatrain's delayed but sure-returning *aaxa* rhyme, to read a stanza like the following is to feel how a skeptic's bitter draft may hold in solution the artificial sweetener of form:

> Myself when young did eagerly frequent
> Doctor and Saint, and heard great Argument
> About it and about: but evermore
> Came out by the same Door as in I went.
>
> (1859, XXVII)

---

① Herbert F. Tucker, "Of Monuments and Moments: Spacetime in Nineteenth-Century Poetry", *MLQ* 58, no. 3 (1997): 269 – 297; for further applications see Tucker, "Literal Illustration in Victorian Print", in *The Victorian Illustrated Book*, ed. Richard Maxwell (Charlottesville: Univ. of Virginia Press, 2002), pp. 163 – 208.

Even as the last line snaps off the light of wisdom, its rhyme—coming out by the same "ent" ending it went in by in line one—wittily spotlights the stanza itself as the chamber of a different enlightenment, with other and wiser claims of its own. This I suspect is what the poet means in contrasting his wisdom to the Sufi's: "Of my Base Metal may be filed a Key, / That shall unlock the Door he howls without. " (1859, LV) The joke, again, is at alchemical allegory's expense: the elusive key to the *Rubáiyát* lies not in some distant-drumming golden wisdom at which the form gestures, but rather in the poet's craft that files verbal matter into form. Right here, in the first place, which is the place of the text, rings the true metal, with what the final quatrain of 1868 called the "silver Foot" of its passing iambic (CX).

Where rhymes are doors and stanzas rooms, we can see the sequence of joined and readjusted quatrains as a type of what FitzGerald called at one point "this batter'd Caravanserai/ Whose Doorways are alternate Night and Day" (1859, XVI). And I do mean *type*; for the poem's most sustained autoekphrases depict and envoice printed textuality. Jet ink and white paper are the "alternate Night and Day" that mark time to measured lineation; and "this Chequer-board of Nights and Days" (1868, LXXIV) that is the Rubáiyát fairly declares itself to be patterned squares of text, "Play'd in a Box" (1859, XLVI) that figures, in inlaid replication, a whole set of nested structures: the ruled line that measures beats, the neat quatrain that orders lines, the "pretty Page" (p. xxxvii) that arranges quatrains, and the fine art-press book that binds pages. No wonder FitzGerald described his work in terms of mosaic craft, "most ingeniously tesselated into a sort of Epicurean Eclogue in a Persian Garden". [1][27] When autoekphrastic conditions are right, the very characters of typography can become characters in a textual drama, choral players declaiming their alphabetic and prosodic condition:

> We are no other than a moving row
> Of visionary Shapes that come and go
> Round with this Sun-illumin'd Lantern held
> In Midnight by the Master of the Show.
>
> (1868, LXXIII)

With the astonishing opening couplet FitzGerald's anti-allegoresis goes sky-high, or rather hits absolute zero. Its assertion is, literally, literal. What you get is what you see, and what you see is what you read, as the act of the eye sets into motion a row of type shapes whose coming and going—entering and exiting focus, forever eligible to return re-combined in the next alphabetic string—is what the activity of reading primally activates. (A circumstance brought under higher magnification, no doubt, when you are Englishing left-to-right an alphabetic original whose characters run, as Persian does, from right to left.) This

---

① Letter to Cowell of November 2, 1858, in *Letters*, 2:323. The same figure of tessellation occurs in a letter from the previous year (August 6, 1857; Letters, 2:294).

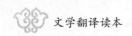

kinetoscopic space of the text, which is "neither Here nor There" yet before our very eyes, is where all the meanings start. And to stray too far from this space—say, to mistake its expressly "visionary" character for a mystic veil—is to forfeit the pleasures that make the text worth reading over.

"We are no other than a moving row/ Of visionary Shapes that come and go". I am not so dazzled by the autoekphrastic aspect of the *Rubáiyát* as to deny that this couplet and others like it operate as metaphors for that disenchanted passivity which Fitz-Omar's keen sense of human transiency famously evokes. Of course they do; and on the reader who doesn't get that cool epicurean point the poem has been wasted beyond my powers of critical revival. My purpose here is to reaffirm that the passage of metaphor is a two-way street, and so to keep clear the route back to the material literality of a poem that has won so many lovers by offering to make them happy there, and by repeatedly making that offer good. To the readerly pleasures of the familiar text Decker's exhibit of "Comparative Texts" adds scholarly pleasures similar in kind if different in degree, such as the quatrains CVI and CVII that FitzGerald freshly introduced into the version of 1868. The first of these quatrains petitions for a rewrite of the page in the "Book of Fate" that has our name on it; and, as fate would have it, the quatrain was rewritten, completely—three times, in fact, as the poet struggled over various proof passes four years later. Quatrain CVII prefers, in blacker mood, to "cancel from the Scroll" our name altogether; and it was, sure enough, canceled at once and is missing from every subsequent edition. Now that we talk of canceling, enough time has elapsed since the event to warrant here a reminder about the last American President but one, as of this writing. A quondam Rhodes Scholar enmeshed in certain amatory difficulties, William Jefferson Clinton quoted for the press corps during his hour of need, in the firm expectation that they would get it—it's the metonymy, stupid—the following lines:

> The Moving Finger writes; and, having writ,
> Moves on: nor all your Piety nor Wit
> Shall lure it back to cancel half a Line,
> Nor all your Tears wash out a Word of it.
>
> (1868, LXXVI)

Well, maybe a word: the 1859 edition of these memorable lines (LI) reads *thy for your*; the 1868 edition in effect enlarges the address from confessional advice into oratorical rhetoric that, invoking the piety, wit, and tears not of an individual but of you-all, seems suited to publishers and presidents alike. ①

These last instances are scholarly arcana, admittedly, but the pedantic fun they offer is not different in kind from the textual pleasure for which FitzGerald took "such Pains" on the

---

① As reported in the *Washington Post* for December 12, 1998, presumably from text furnished by the White House, the quatrain for reasons best known to the Oval Office prints "moving finger" in discreet lower case. The President's recitation was delivered, as seems right, in the Rose Garden.

common reader's behalf. Through closed-circuit feedback loops of theme and form, he made his prosody a subliminal plug for his message, even as the epicurean discipline of that message constituted a virtual manual for the student of his technique with eyes to see and ears to hear. The result is a poetic translation that comes close after all to meeting the impossible criterion of translational literality from which we began. However broad its departures from the letter of what Omar Khayyám wrote, the poem reads like a literal rendition of itself, message and form concurrently glossing each other. FitzGerald's Rubáiyát remains "a Thing"—a textual object—that "must live". To be sure, "The Leaves of Life keep falling one by one" (1868, VⅢ); yet the poem abides, "shrouded in the living Leaf" (1868, XCVⅢ), which is the "fairer leaf" (1868, CVI) of "Youth's sweet-scented Manuscript" (1859, LXXII) or of (oh why not?) "A Book of Verses underneath the Bough" (1872, XII). As everybody knows who knows even one rhyme of FitzGerald's—jug of wine, loaf of bread, and "Thou/ Beside me singing in the Wilderness"—the sweet-leaved, long-lived space beside Omar and underneath the bough is "Paradise enow"! That space is the semantically labile spot of time where you can no longer tell whether textuality tropes life or life textuality, where art comes to you proposing frankly to give nothing but the highest quality to your moments as they pass, and where poetry becomes, by virtue precisely of its absorptive momentaneousness, "the Pastime of Eternity" (1868, LⅢ). At least for the time being it does; and that, in Victorian Paradise, will just have to do.

【翻译鉴赏】

英语修辞表述汉译

[1] At last, a **candid candidate**!

译文:终于找到了一个厚道的候选人!

评析:黑体部分的单词词形、读音都相近,属于英语修辞中的 Alliteration,如果译成:"到底找到了一个老实的候选人!"那就只传达了原文的意美,没有表达原文的音美。如果改成:"忠厚的"或"脸皮不太厚的候选人",那么,"厚"字和"候"字声音相同,多少传达了一点原文的音美和讽刺的意美。

[2] **Able was I ere I saw Elba**!

译文一:我在看到厄尔巴之前曾是强有力的。(钱歌川译)

译文二:不到俄岛我不倒。(许渊冲译)

译文三:落败孤岛孤败落。(马红军译)

评析:据说这是 1814 年各国联军攻陷巴黎后,拿破仑皇帝被放逐于地中海的厄尔巴(Elba)荒岛时所写。该句的妙处在于它的形貌特征,因为无论从左看到右,还是反向看,英文字母的排列顺序都完全相同,是一个典型的回文句(Palindrome)。这种形美,很不容易甚至是不可能翻译的。钱歌川只译出了原文的意思,但原文的"妙味"则无法传递。许渊冲根据汉语"不见棺材不落泪",把这句译成:"不到俄岛我不倒。""岛"和"倒"同韵,"到"和"倒"、"我"和"俄"音似、形似,加上"不"字重复,可以说是用音美来译形美了。但更佳的译文当为译文三。译文和原文碰巧都是七个字。译文没有出现"厄尔巴"三字,而以"孤岛"代替,事实上厄尔巴岛也是孤岛,这个"孤"字更能体现出拿破仑的处境。而且,这个"孤"还和后面的"孤"相呼应,过去的皇帝称自己为"孤"。句首的"落败"二字表示拿破仑兵败滑铁卢后被囚于该岛之意,而句末的"败落"也是表示拿破仑的穷途末路。此译文的妙处是,顺念、倒念意思完全相同,字也完全一样,是一个地道的汉语回文句,且具有一定的寓意。我们不能不佩服译者的精巧构思。

[3] It was a **s**plendid population—for all the **s**low, **s**leepy, **s**luggish-brained **s**loths **s**tayed at home.

译文一:这是一批卓越能干的人民——因为所有这些行动迟缓、瞌睡兮兮、呆如树獭的人都留在家乡了。(余立三译)

译文二:那是一批卓越的人——因为那些慢慢吞吞、昏昏沉沉、反应迟钝、形如树獭的人留在了家乡。(杨莉藜译)

译文三:这是一批卓越能干的人民——因为那些行动迟缓、头脑迟钝、睡眼惺忪、呆如树獭的人留在了家乡。(章和升译)

译文四:(出来的)这帮人个个出类拔萃——因为凡是呆板、呆滞、呆头呆脑的呆子都呆在了家里。(马红军译)

评析:在这个句子里,作者用了五个头韵词(Alliteration)与前面的 splendid 呼应,词义色彩则正好相反,造成了强烈的诙谐和幽默的效果。一般说来,谐音押韵,如头韵、尾韵等的修辞效果是"不可译"的,因为翻译时不得不照顾词义,而破坏了韵律与声调,虽然汉语有双声和叠韵,但把这句中的 slow, sleepy, sluggish-brained, sloths, stayed 五个词的头韵翻译出来,几乎是不可能的。前三个译文虽然有不少可取之处,但作为一句名言,在音、形、意、神方面还有很大差距,总觉得有令人不满意的地方,马红军则比较精彩地传递了这点。译者用五个"呆"字,翻译出了五个押 s 字母的头韵词,真可谓巧夺天工,拍案称妙。

[4] If we don't **hang** together, we shall most assuredly **hang** separately. (Franklin)

译文一:咱们要不摽到一块儿,保准会吊到一块儿。

译文二:我们不紧紧抱在一起,准保会吊在一起。

译文三:如果我们不能紧密地团结在一起,那就必然分散地走上绞刑台。

译文四:我们不紧紧团结一致,必然一个个被人绞死。

译文五:我们必须共同上战场,否则就得分别上刑场。

译文六:我们必须共赴沙场,否则就得分赴法场。

译文七:如果我们不抱成一团,就会被吊成一串。

评析:这是富兰克林在《独立宣言》上签名时说的话,英文句子妙用两个 hang。我们把译文和原文作一比较就会感到,原文掷地有声、意味深长,使人过目不忘,玩笑的口吻中透着严肃,具有名言警句的特征。译文一至四过于口语化,上下句联系不够自然、紧凑,在力度上与原文也有很大的差距。译文五至七则注意到用中文双关语重构,效果才能真正体现。译文五和六用两个"场"体现出原句的两个 hang,就其修辞效果、语言风格都和原文比较接近,但无论是"共同上战场",还是"共赴沙场",和原文语义还有距离,译文七用"抱成一团"对应 hang together,而"抱成一团"在中文里有团结在一起的含义,用"吊成一串"对应 hang separately,同时"一团"和"一串"谐音。

[5] I am **never at a loss for a word**; Pitt is **never at a loss for the word**.

译文一：我总是能凑合找个词儿说说,可是皮特什么时候都能找到恰如其分的词儿。

译文二：我总能找到一个词,而皮特总能找到那个绝妙好词。

译文三：我总能找到一个觉得妙的词,而皮特总能找到那个绝妙的词。

译文四：我总能找到一个意思相当的词,而皮特总能找到那个意思恰当的词。

译文五：我和皮特都能出口成章,但我用的词大都不可言妙,而他用的总是妙不可言。

译文六：我总是滔滔不绝,而皮特则是字字珠玑。(马红军译)

评析：a word 和 the word 系原句的精华所在,体现出英语的简约之美,不着一个修饰词,但意味深长。译文各个费尽九牛二虎之力。译文一略嫌啰唆;译文二比较简洁明快,也最合原意,但略显平白;译文三用"觉得妙"对"绝妙",但与原文前半句含义出入较大;译文四不如原文简明有力;译文五含文字游戏,"不可言妙"对"妙不可言";译文六最为精炼,前后对比鲜明,但还是不如原文简约。

[6] A little more than kin, and less than kind.

译文一：超乎寻常的亲族,漠不相干的路人。(朱生豪译)

译文二：亲上加亲,越亲越不相亲。(卞之琳译)

译文三：比亲戚亲一点,说亲人却说不上。(曹未风译)

译文四：比侄子是亲些,可是还算不得儿子。(梁实秋译)

译文五：说不亲亲上亲,说亲又不亲。(张今译)

评析：比较起来,卞之琳译得最好,其他三家都着力不够,略逊一筹,译文五是对卞译的进一步改进。

[7] I love my love with an **E**, because she's **e**nticing; I hate her with an **E**, because she's **e**ngaged; I took her to the sign of the exquisite, and treated her with an **e**lopement; her name's **E**mily, and she lives in the **e**ast (Dickens: *David Copperfield*)

译文一：我爱我的爱人为了一个 E,因为她是 Enticing(迷人的);我恨我的爱人为了一个 E,因为她是 Engaged(订了婚了)。我用我的爱人象征 Exquisite(美妙),我劝我的爱人从事 Elopement(私奔),她的名字是 Emily(爱弥丽),她的住处在 East(东方)。(董秋斯译)

译文二：我爱我的爱,因为她长得实在招人爱。我恨我的爱,因为她不回报我的爱。我带着她到挂着浮荡子招牌的一家,和她谈情说爱。我请她看一出潜逃私奔,为的是我和她能长久你亲我爱。她的名字叫爱弥丽,她的家住在爱仁里。(张谷若译)

译文三：我爱我的那个"丽",可爱迷人有魅力;我恨我的那个"丽",和他人结伉俪;她文雅大方又美丽,和我出逃去游历;她芳名就叫爱米丽,家住东方人俏丽。(马红军译)

评析：原文是狄更斯小说《大卫·科波菲尔》第 22 章中的一首英文打油诗,全部运用嵌入句,即每一小句最后一个单词都是以同一字母 E 开头。译文一翻译出了原诗的命题意义,却没有处理好原文里的文字游戏,中英文混杂,是个半成品,让不懂英文的人费解。译文二读起来一气呵成,朗朗上口;译者把原文中重复出现的成分——字母 E,统一归化成汉语的双元音 ai(爱),非常巧妙地同时传达出原文的指称意义和言内意义。遗憾的是,译文内容与原诗稍有偏离,如"不回报我的爱"、"挂着浮荡子招牌"、"住在爱仁里"都是原文所没有的。译文三以汉语之"丽"对应英文之"E"(同样出现 5 次)。

[8] Without the sound of drums, Cuba would not exist.

译文：没有**鼓声**,就没有**古巴**。

评析:鼓乐数百年前由非洲奴隶传到古巴,成为古巴音乐的支柱。一些古巴音乐家认为古巴应以鼓乐为国乐。上述这句话是一位音乐家说的。原文没有文字机关,但译文却在"鼓"和"古"上造出了谐音,应该属于张南峰先生推荐的原文零修辞,译文增添修辞,实现译文对原文的超越。

[9] A fool and his words are soon parted; a man of genius and his money. (William Shenstone)

译文:蠢才轻其言,天才轻其钱。

评析:原文后半部有省略,a man of genius and his money = a man of genius and his money are soon parted。其意为:傻瓜记不住说过的话,天才存不住手里的钱。译文将 fool 译成"蠢才",正好和"天才"对仗。"言"与"钱"也押韵。这些修辞都是原文所没有的,可以说艺术性更高。

[10] BETTER **LATE** THAN **THE LATE.**

译文一:迟到总比丧命好。

译文二:晚了总比完了好。

译文三:迟了总比死了好。

译文四:慢行回家,快行回老家。

评析:这是美国高速公路上的一则安全警示语,叫人不要超速行驶。趣味就在这则公示语连用了两个 late。late 一词含"迟到"和"已故"的双义。原文极其幽默诙谐。应该说,上面五种译文都非常精彩。译文一幽默略显不足;译文二、三在音韵上更佳,尤其是译文二,更加意味深长;译文四传达出了形韵("回家"对"回老家")。

[11] Change is part of life and the making of character, hon. When things happen that you do not like, you have two choices: You get **bitter** or **better.**

译文:变化是生活的一部分,而且也塑造了人的意志品德,亲爱的。当你不喜欢的事情发生了,你有两种选择:要么痛苦不堪;要么痛快达观。

评析:英语头韵(Alliteration)得以在译文中完美体现。

[12] "Mine is a long and a sad **tale**!" said the Mouse, turning to Alice, and sighing.

"It is a long **tail**, certainly," said Alice, looking down with wonder at the Mouse's tail, "but why do you call it sad?"

译文:那老鼠对爱丽丝叹了口气道:"唉,说来话长! 真叫我委屈!"

"尾曲?!"爱丽丝听了,瞧着老鼠那光滑的尾巴说:"你这尾巴明明又长又直,为什么说它曲呢?!"(马红军译)

评析:英文中 tail 与 tale 属于谐音双关,译文中"委屈"和"尾曲"同音异形,修辞手法及幽默风趣基本相当。

[13] What flower does everybody have? —**Tulips.** (Tulips = two lips)

译文:人人都有的花是什么花? ——泪花。

评析:可以看出,译文"泪花"已经不同于原文里的答案"郁金香"。译文的前半部是直译原文的,关键在后半部起了变化。它根据译文前半部重造,忠实于原文的修辞意图。

[14] The professor tapped on his desk and shouted: "Young men, **Order!**"—The entire class yelled: "Beer!"

译文一：教授敲击桌子喊道：年轻人，请安静！——学生：啤酒。〔注：英语的 order 含歧义：请安静；点菜，要饮料〕

译文二：教授敲击桌子喊道：你们这些年轻人吃喝（要喝）什么？——学生：啤酒。

评析：译文一完全无法传递原文的妙处，只能做些解释，读者也许能懂，但译文本身是不成功的。译文二则机智地找到汉语谐音词来再现原文的语义双关（order，订单，菜单；秩序），方能妙趣横生。

[15] You reckon your **Dodge** would help you up to all these **dodge**s again?

译文一：你以为坐上你的道奇车就可以再次逃之夭夭？

译文二：你以为坐上你的道奇跑车就可以再次跑掉么？（马红军译）

评析：这是一个警官对他抓到的作案者说的一句话。句中 Dodge 是美国"道奇"牌小汽车，它与普通词 dodge（逃跑）语义相关。原文透出该警官对作案者的讥讽，译文一无法体现这层含义，译文二则巧妙地加了"跑"字，这就使前后两个"跑"字发生了联系，原句的形韵和幽默味道多少有所体现。

[16] The **output** of the United Nations has not been commensurate with the **input**.

译文一：联合国的贡献与其花费已经不相称了。（英汉翻译概要）

译文二：联合国的作用已难抵其费用。（马红军译）

评析：译文一未尝不可，意思也对，但译文的分量与趣味明显不如原文。英文中的 input 和 output 由于"形状"相近而形成明显的反差。译文一未能译出原文的形韵。译文二则简洁有力，非常成功。

[17] The **ballot** is stronger than the **bullet**.

译文一：选举权比子弹更具威力。

译文二：选票比大炮更具威力。

译文三：选票胜于枪炮。（马红军译）

评析：这是一句林肯的名言。林肯所以用 bullet 和 ballot 相比，是由于两者既音似且形似，译文一里"选举权"和"子弹"之间缺乏音韵及字形上的对称关系，因此译文不理想。译文二较好地传达了原文的音韵特征，但译文三在音韵和字形上和原文更加贴近。

[18] "Why is the river rich?"

"Because it has **two banks.** "

"为什么说河水富有？"

译文一："因为它有两条堤岸。"

译文二："因为它总**向前（钱）**流。"

译文三："因为它**年年有余（鱼）**呀。"

评析：原文 bank 是双关语，一指河岸，二指银行。译文一完全忠实于原文的语义，但原文的幽默效果丧失殆尽；译文二、三的谐音双关，和原文的一词多义表面上格格不入，但在修辞效果上是一致的。

——参考：杨士焯，《英汉翻译教程》，北京大学出版社，2007

汉语修辞表述英译

[1] 思君**如满月**，夜夜减清辉。（张九龄，《赋得自君之出矣》）

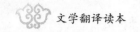

译文：For thinking of you,

    I am like the moon at the full,

    That nightly wanes and loses its bright splendor. (Robert Kotewell 译)

评析：这首诗写的是一位日渐消瘦的思妇形象，诗人用形象的比喻来描绘思妇内心深处的活动。她日日夜夜思念，容颜憔悴，宛如团团圆月在逐渐减弱清辉，变成了缺月。"夜夜减清辉"，比喻含蓄美妙，想象新颖独特，饶富新意，给人以鲜明的美的感受。在中国古代诗词中，月亮常常被作为诗人思亲怀乡、寄托感情的物象。此处，诗人用月亮的形象来烘托思妇对月怀人的愁思，虽然英语文化中月亮并没有这层涵义，但是月亮是思妇形象的喻体，因此在翻译时不能轻易改变。译文将"思君如满月"译为 I am like the moon at the full（我就像圆月一样），虽略作改动，但是没有因文化的隔阂而改变原来的喻体；that nightly wanes（夜夜亏缺）和原文一样，明说月亮日渐亏蚀，实指思妇的脸庞日渐消瘦。译文对诗中的比喻采取直译的方法，忠实地再现了原诗中的人物形象美，使译文读者体味到了异国诗歌形象的风姿，进而获得美的享受。

[2] 东城渐觉风光好，皱壳波纹**迎**客棹。

绿杨烟外晓云轻，红杏枝头**春意闹**。

浮生长恨欢娱少，有爱千金轻一笑。

为君持酒劝斜阳，且向花间留晚照。（宋祁，《玉春楼》）

译文：The scenery is getting fine east of the town;

    The rippling water greets boats rowing up and down.

    Beyond green willows morning chill is growing mild;

    On pink apricot branches spring is running wild.

    In our floating life scarce are pleasures we seek after.

    How can we value gold above a hearty laughter?

    I raise wine cup to ask the slanting sun to stay

    And I leave among the flowers its departing ray. （许渊冲译）

评析：此词通篇运用拟人的手法，将景物赋予生命，写得形象生动，上篇描绘春天的绚丽景色极有韵致，开头一个"迎"字将微波荡漾的湖面、来往如织的客船形象展现在我们面前，我们仿佛看到湖中泛起纱绉般的水波，将游春的船儿迎来送往，分外热情。而后面的"红杏枝头春意闹"更是使得全诗的景物描写达到高潮，生机勃勃的一幅春景形象跃然纸上。其中"闹"字就是采用了拟人的手法，使得本就红艳诱人的红杏变得具有活力。浮现在我们眼前的是这样一幅图画：一枝枝怒放的红杏上头，蜂飞蝶舞、春鸟和鸣，好不热闹，将繁丽的春色点染得十分生动，形象鲜明，意境突出。译文可将这两处拟人手法直接译出，既保持意义传达的忠实性，又不失语言表达上的形象性。译者将"迎"译为 greets 极为生动传神，能立即引起读者的丰富联想，将读者带入原诗的美妙意境之中；而"春意闹"被意译为 Spring is running wild（春天就像散发着活力的孩童一般），充满勃勃生机。两处拟人都得以保留，完美地再现原诗中的生动活泼的形象。

[3] 朝辞白帝彩云间，千里江陵一日还。

两岸猿声啼不住，轻舟已过万重山。（李白，《早发白帝城》）

译文：Leaving at dawn the White Emperor crowned with cloud,

I've sailed a thousand *li* through Canyons in a day.

With the monkey's adieus the river banks are loud,

My skiff has left ten thousand mountains far away. （许渊冲译）

评析："千里江陵一日还"写诗人的意愿,形容船行之速,千里江陵只要一天即可到达。诗人用夸张的手法,写了长江一泻千里之势,同时也抒发了诗人"归心似箭"的心情。第三、四句同样运用夸张的手法,形象地描绘轻舟快驶的情形。两岸猿猴的叫声还没停止,可那轻快的小船已经驶过了千山万岭,诗人急欲东归的心情,洋溢于诗的明快节奏之中。整首诗,诗人极尽夸张之能事,表现行船之快,借不间断的猿声,衬托轻舟的快捷;借万山重叠,衬托长江的一泻千里。呈现出一幅两岸悬崖峭壁,猿猴啼叫,一叶扁舟在湍急的江水中飞流直下的壮丽画面,形象鲜活、精妙无比、令人百读不厌。两处夸张的成功运用使诗歌具有了形象的美感,由于英语中也有大量夸张修辞手法,译文读者不会因这些夸张而有理解的障碍。原文中的夸张"千里"、"万重山"分别被直译为 a thousand *li* 和 ten thousand mountains,原诗中的修辞手法得以保留,艺术形象得到完美的再现,并能在读者心中唤起丰富的联想。

[4] **杳杳**寒山道,**落落**冷涧滨。

　　啾啾常有鸟,**寂寂**更无人。

　　淅淅风吹面,**纷纷**雪积身。

　　朝朝不见日,**岁岁**不知春。（寒山,《杳杳寒山道》）

译文：Long, long the pathway to Cold Hill;

　　　　Drear, drear the waterside so chill.

　　　　Chirp, chirp, I often hear the bird;

　　　　Mute, mute, nobody says a word.

　　　　Gust by gust winds caress my face;

　　　　Flake on flake snow covers all trace.

　　　　From day to day the sun won't swing;

　　　　From year to year I know no spring. （许渊冲译）

评析：这首诗除了用景物渲染气氛、以气氛烘托心情这种传统的表现手法之外,使用叠词是它的特点。通篇句首都用叠词是不多见的。寒山这首诗使用叠词,就很富于变化。"杳杳"具有幽暗的色彩感;"落落"具有空旷的空间感;"啾啾"言有声;"寂寂"言无声;"淅淅"写风的动态感;"纷纷"写雪的飞舞状;"朝朝"、"岁岁"虽同指时间,又有长短的区别。八组叠词,各具情状。就词性看,这些叠词有形容词、副词、象声词、名词,也各不相同。就描绘对象看,或山或水,或鸟或人,或风或雪,或景或情。这就显得变化多姿,字虽重复而不会使人厌烦。许先生在翻译这首诗时,采用了富于变化的手法,通过叠词的运用,在韵律上力求保持原诗的风格,形式上又保持了音节匀称、形式整齐的特点,意象上更体现了原诗的意境。

[5] 春蚕到死丝方尽,蜡炬成灰泪始干。（李商隐,《无题》）

译文：The silkworm till its death spins silk from love-sick heart.

　　　　The candle burned to ashes has no tears to shed.

评析：该句选自李商隐《无题》诗,原诗为:"相见时难别亦难,东风无力百花残。春蚕到死丝方尽,蜡炬成灰泪始干。晓镜但愁云鬓改,夜吟应觉月光寒。蓬山此去无多路,青鸟殷勤为探看。"许渊冲先生在《翻译的艺术》一书中说:"第三句'春蚕到死丝方尽'是传诵千古的名句,'丝'同'思'是谐音,表示诗人的思念悠悠无尽,只有到死了才能够完结。这种刻骨铭心的柔情,通过春蚕的形象,让人看得更加真切,感人的力量也更加深厚。怎样才能传达原句的'丝'和'思'双关的意美呢? 我看只好把'丝'和'思'都译出来。"将"丝"译成silk,又把"思"创造性地译成 love-sick,其中,sick 和 silk 不但音近,而且形近,可以说再现了原文的音美和形美。也有译界同仁认为此双关非彼双关,而是一种阐释说明,但正如福斯特(Leonard Forster)在《翻译:一种介绍》一文中所说:"翻译出来的双关语,尽管译笔巧妙,但不可能是原来的那个双关语。原语中的那个双关语可能是无法翻译的,可译的是原作使用了双关语这一事实。"

[6] 鲁大海:(挣扎)放开我,你们这些强盗!

周　萍:(向仆人)把他拉下去!

鲁侍萍:(大哭)这真是一群强盗!(走到周萍面前)你是**萍……凭……凭**什么打我的儿子?

(曹禺:《雷雨》)

译文:Hai:(struggling) Let go of me, you hooligans!

Ping:(to the servants) Hustle him outside!

Ma:(breaking down) You are hooligans, too! (going across to Zhou Ping) You're **my... mighty** free with your fists! What right have you to hit my son?

——(trans. by Wang Zuoliang & Barns)

评析:这组充满戏剧性的台词出自曹禺《雷雨》:侍萍想认分离多年的儿子周萍,但要信守不相认的承诺而使她欲言又止,加上周萍打了亲弟弟大海,面对如此令人痛心的场面,使得侍萍的感情由"想念"一下子变成了"愤慨"。一道森严的阶级壁垒已横在她面前,她的"**萍……凭**——凭什么打我的儿子"反映了她内心的矛盾与痛苦。如果译文译为 You are Ping, why do you hit my son? 则无法逼真地在译文中再现鲁侍萍内心的苦痛和挣扎,然则易词而译,利用 my 与 mighty 的第一个音节的谐音来译"萍"、"凭"这对谐音,做到形式和内容的高度统一,却使译文顿生光彩,有效再现了原文作者的意图。

[7] **月光如流水一般**,静静地泻在这一片叶子和花上。**薄薄的青雾浮起在荷塘里。叶子和花仿佛在牛乳中洗过一样;又像笼着轻纱的梦。**虽然是满月,天上却有一层淡淡的云,所以不能朗照;但我以为这恰是到了好处——酣眠固不可少,小睡也别有风味。月光是隔了树照过来的,高处丛生的灌木,落上参差的斑驳的黑影,峭楞楞如鬼一般;**弯弯的杨柳的稀疏的倩影,像是画在荷叶上。**塘中的月色并不均匀;但**光与影有着和谐的旋律,如梵婀玲上奏着的名曲。**(朱自清《荷塘月色》)

译文:The moon sheds her liquid light silently over the leaves and flowers, which, in the floating transparency of a bluish haze from the pond, look as if they had just been bathed in milk, or like a dream wrapped in a gauzy hood. Although it is a full moon, shining through a film of clouds, the light is not at its brightest; it is, however, just right for me—a profound sleep is indispensable, yet a snatched doze also has a savour of its own. The moon light is streaming down through the foliage, casting bushy shadows on the ground from high above, dark and checkered, like an army of ghosts; whereas the benign figures of the drooping willows, here and there, look like paintings on the lotus leaves. The moonlight is not spread evenly over the pond, but rather in a harmonious rhythm of light and shade, like a famous melody played on a violin.

(trans. by Zhu Chunshen)

评析:《荷塘月色》是朱自清先生 1927 年 7 月创作于北京清华园的一篇精美散文,堪称中国现代散文的名篇,以其清新淡雅的优美意境赢得了广泛的读者。此外,作品中那种超越时空的美及其所暗示的作者内心的矛盾和对超脱尘世的向往,更是深深地打动着每一位读者的心扉。选文中,作者以静写动,采用通感修辞手法,把月光下静静的荷塘活化了。朱自清早期散文的特色在于描绘渲染、精雕细琢,抒发"淡淡的喜悦,淡淡的哀愁"之情,作者描绘了小路、荷塘、荷叶、荷花、荷香、荷动、月光、树、雾、山等,色彩多样。朱纯深先生的译文不仅从遣词造句上着力传递原文的意境,尤为注重文本的前后照应,极力实现整篇文章风格与气韵的协调一致,比喻、拟人等修辞手法的灵活再现无不围绕再现原文的"淡"展开。对于"光与影有着和谐的旋律,如梵婀玲上奏着的名曲",译者用两个介词短语 in a harmonious rhythm of light and shade, like a famous melody played on a violin 来传递,既没有违背原文的意思,自然转换了原文的句式,而且把原文的修辞格通感也体现出来,前一个短语体现了原文的静态美,后面的短语体现了原文的动态美,动静结合,成功地再现了原文的姿致和风韵。

[8] 思想……

　　是炉火,

　　炉火是墙上的树影,

　　是冬夜的声音。

(冯文炳,《十二月十九夜》)

译文: Thoughts...

　　Are the fire in a stove,

　　The fire in a stove is the tree's shadow on the wall.

　　And the sound in the winter night.

(trans. by Li Dingkun)

评析:本段选自当代诗人语丝派成员冯文炳诗作《十二月十九夜》,全文如下:深夜一枝灯,/若高山流水,/有身外之海。/星之室是鸟林,/是花,是鱼,是天上的梦,/海是夜的镜子。/思想是一个美人,/是家,/是日,是月,/是灯,/是炉火,/炉火是墙上的树影,/是冬夜的声音。这首诗的艺术表现颇有特点:一是它不作架空抒情,而致力于意象的呈现,运用暗示和隐喻展现诗人的心境。它的篇幅短小,然而意象繁复。诗人通过一连串跳动着的意象来表现自己飘忽不定的思绪。诗人不说自己的思想如何美好,而是通过隐喻,将自己的思想比做美人、日、月、灯、炉火。美人、日、月、炉火等都是美好的事物,它们都有助于将情绪客观化,从而使诗篇生动形象,增加感人的艺术魅力。二是观念联络的奇特。晨星与鸟林、花、鱼、梦,思想与美人、家、日、月、灯、炉火,这些不同的事物之间似乎没有共同点,然而诗人却通过想象,发现了它们之间的共同点,在艺术表现时又省掉了联络的字句,从而反映诗人思路的飘忽与意识的流动。三是运用通感手法。这首诗的末两句"炉火是墙上的树影,是冬夜的声音"。诗人以听觉来写视觉,突出了诗人冬夜的强烈感受,抒写了诗人冲破冬夜的寂寞的主观愿望;在艺术上,这一通感手法的运用,使诗的语言富于弹性与

新鲜感,译文采取直译的方式,给英语世界读者熟悉意识流创作和后现代实验诗歌的读者以熟悉的感觉。

【翻译试笔】

【英译汉】

I Have a Dream

Martin Luther King, Jr.

I am happy to join with you today in what will go down in history as the greatest demonstration for freedom in the history of our nation.

Five score years ago, a great American, in whose symbolic shadow we stand today, signed the *Emancipation Proclamation*. This momentous decree came as a great beacon light of hope to millions of Negro slaves who had been seared in the flames of withering injustice. **It came as a joyous daybreak to end the long night of their captivity.**

But one hundred years later, the Negro still is not free. **One hundred years later, the life of the Negro is still sadly crippled by the manacles of segregation and the chains of discrimination. One hundred years later, the Negro lives on a lonely island of poverty in the midst of a vast ocean of material prosperity. One hundred years later, the Negro is still languished in the corners of American society and finds himself an exile in his own land.** And so we've come here today to dramatize a shameful condition.

In a sense we've come to our nation's capital to cash a check. When the architects of our republic wrote the magnificent words of the *Constitution* and the *Declaration of Independence*, they were signing a promissory note to which every American was to fall heir. This note was a promise that all men, yes, black men as well as white men, would be guaranteed the "unalienable Rights" of "Life, Liberty and the pursuit of Happiness". It is obvious today that America has defaulted on this promissory note, insofar as her **citizens of color** are concerned. Instead of honoring this sacred obligation, **America has given the Negro people a bad check, a check which has come back marked "insufficient funds".**

But we refuse to believe that **the bank of justice is bankrupt.** We refuse to believe that there are insufficient funds in the great vaults of opportunity of this nation. And so, we've come to cash this check, a check that will give us upon demand the riches of freedom and the security of justice.

We have also come to this hallowed spot to remind America of the fierce urgency of Now. This is no time to engage in the luxury of cooling off or to take the tranquilizing drug of gradualism. **Now is the time to make real the promises of democracy. Now is the time to rise from the dark and desolate valley of segregation to the sunlit path of racial justice. Now is the time to lift our nation from the quicksands of racial injustice to the solid rock of brotherhood. Now is the time to make justice a reality for all of God's children.**

It would be fatal for the nation to overlook the urgency of the moment. **This sweltering summer of the Negros legitimate discontent will not pass until there is an invigorating autumn of**

freedom and equality. Nineteen sixty-three is not an end, but a beginning. And those who hope that the Negro needed to blow off steam and will now be content will have a rude awakening if the nation returns to business as usual. And there will be neither rest nor tranquility in America until the Negro is granted his citizenship rights. **The whirlwinds of revolt will continue to shake the foundations of our nation until the bright day of justice emerges.**

But there is something that I must say to my people, who stand on the **warm threshold** which leads into **the palace of justice**: In the process of gaining our rightful place, we must not be guilty of wrongful deeds. **Let us not seek to satisfy our thirst for freedom by drinking from the cup of bitterness and hatred.** We must forever conduct our struggle on the high plane of dignity and discipline. We must not allow our creative protest to degenerate into physical violence. Again and again, we must rise to the majestic heights of meeting physical force with soul force.

The marvelous new militancy which has engulfed the Negro community must not lead us to a distrust of all white people, for many of our white brothers, as evidenced by their presence here today, have come to realize that their destiny is tied up with our destiny. And they have come to realize that their freedom is inextricably bound to our freedom.

We cannot walk alone.

And as we walk, we must make the pledge that we shall always march ahead.

We cannot turn back.

There are those who are asking the devotees of civil rights, "When will you be satisfied?" We can never be satisfied as long as the Negro is the victim of the unspeakable horrors of police brutality. We can never be satisfied as long as our bodies, heavy with the fatigue of travel, cannot gain lodging in the motels of the highways and the hotels of the cities. We cannot be satisfied as long as a Negro in Mississippi cannot vote and a Negro in New York believes he has nothing for which to vote. No, no, we are not satisfied, and we will not be satisfied until **"justice rolls down like waters, and righteousness like a mighty stream".**

I am not unmindful that some of you have come here out of great **trials and tribulations.** Some of you have come fresh from narrow jail cells. And some of you have come from areas where your quest—quest for freedom left you battered by **the storms of persecution** and staggered by **the winds of police brutality.** You have been the veterans of creative suffering. Continue to work with the faith that unearned suffering is redemptive. Go back to Mississippi, go back to Alabama, go back to South Carolina, go back to Georgia, go back to Louisiana, go back to the slums and ghettos of our northern cities, knowing that somehow this situation can and will be changed.

Let us not wallow in the valley of despair, I say to you today, my friends.

And so even though we face the difficulties of today and tomorrow, I still have a dream. **It is a dream deeply rooted in the American dream.**

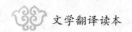

I have a dream that one day this nation will rise up and live out the true meaning of its creed: "We hold these truths to be self-evident, that all men are created equal."

I have a dream that one day on the red hills of Georgia, the sons of former slaves and the sons of former slave owners will be able to sit down together at the table of brotherhood.

I have a dream that one day even the state of Mississippi, **a state sweltering with the heat of injustice, sweltering with the heat of oppression, will be transformed into an oasis of freedom and justice.**

I have a dream that my four little children will one day live in a nation where **they will not be judged by the color of their skin but by the content of their character.**

I have a dream today!

I have a dream that one day, down in Alabama, with its vicious racists, with its governor having his lips dripping with the words of **"interposition" and "nullification"**——one day right there in Alabama little black boys and black girls will be able to join hands with little white boys and white girls as sisters and brothers.

I have a dream today!

I have a dream that one day every valley shall be exalted, and every hill and mountain shall be made low, the rough places will be made plain, and the crooked places will be made straight; "and the glory of the Lord shall be revealed and all flesh shall see it together".

This is our hope, and this is the faith that I go back to the South with.

With this faith, we will be able to hew out of the mountain of despair a stone of hope. With this faith, we will be able to transform the jangling discords of our nation into a beautiful symphony of brotherhood. With this faith, we will be able to work together, to pray together, to struggle together, to go to jail together, to stand up for freedom together, knowing that we will be free one day.

And this will be the day——this will be the day when all of God's children will be able to sing with new meaning:

My country'tis of thee, sweet land of liberty, of thee I sing.

Land where my fathers died, land of the Pilgrim's pride,

From every mountainside, let freedom ring!

And if America is to be a great nation, this must become true.

And so let freedom ring from the prodigious hilltops of New Hampshire.

Let freedom ring from the mighty mountains of New York.

Let freedom ring from the heightening Alleghenies of Pennsylvania.

Let freedom ring from the snow-capped Rockies of Colorado.

Let freedom ring from the curvaceous slopes of California.

But not only that:

Let freedom ring from Stone Mountain of Georgia.

Let freedom ring from Lookout Mountain of Tennessee.

Let freedom ring from every hill and molehill of Mississippi.

From every mountainside, let freedom ring.

And when this happens, when we allow freedom ring, when we let it ring from every village and every hamlet, from every state and every city, we will be able to speed up that day when all of God's children, black men and white men, Jews and Gentiles, Protestants and Catholics, will be able to join hands and sing in the words of the old Negro spiritual:

> Free at last! free at last!
> Thank God Almighty, we are free at last!

【汉译英】

之一　　　　　梦里又飞花（程黛眉）

那一夜，满天的**繁星在梦中流连**，唯有两颗是同伴，彼此情依万千，彼此长久相守。

历经了近十年的爱情印证，我们所理解的爱不再是海誓山盟和大喜大悲，而**是生活中的高山流水，是轻风细雨，是每日每日你归来的脚步，是我手下烫洗干净的衣裤和在外面采撷的一把野草**，是平淡又平淡的日日月月。

如果我们能够体会到这种平淡之中的幸福，能够在一粒沙中见世界，能够在**锅碗瓢盆**中品味出坦然，那么这就是生命中的一个大境界了。我们所期待的，不正是这样的一种德行？

爱情如是，人生亦如是，我们常常所自勉的**淡泊明志，宁静致远**，便在此罢了。

之二　　　　　十八岁出门远行（余华）

我躺在**汽车的心窝里**，想起了那么一个晴朗温和的中午，那时的阳光非常美丽。我记得自己在外面高高兴兴地玩了半天，然后我回家了，在窗外看到父亲正在屋内整理一个红色的背包，我扑在窗口问："爸爸，你要出门？"

父亲转过身来温和地说："不，是让你出门。"

"让我出门？"

"是的，你已经十八了，你应该去认识一下外面的世界了。"

后来我就背起了那个漂亮的红背包，父亲在我脑后拍了一下，**就像在马屁股上拍了一下**。于是我欢快地冲出了家门，**像一匹兴高采烈的马一样**欢快地奔跑了起来。

参考译文

我有一个梦想

马丁·路德·金

今天，我高兴地同大家一起，参加这次将成为我国历史上为了争取自由而举行的最伟大的示威集会。

100年前，一位伟大的美国人签署了《解放宣言》，今天我们就站在他的雕像前集会。这一庄严的宣言，犹如灯塔的光芒，给千百万在那摧残生命的不义之火中受煎熬的黑奴带来希望。它之到来犹如欢乐的黎明，结束了束缚黑人的漫长黑夜。

然而，100年后，黑人依然没有获得自由。100年后，黑人依然悲惨地蹒跚于种族隔离和种族歧视的枷锁之下。100年后，黑人依然生活在物质繁荣瀚海的贫困孤岛上。100年后，黑人依然在美国社会中向隅而泣，依然感到自己在国土家园中流离漂泊。所以，我们今天来到这里，要把这骇人听闻的情况公之于众。

从某种意义上说，我们来到国家的首都是为了兑现一张支票。我们共和国的缔造者在拟写宪法和独立宣言的辉煌篇章时，就签署了一张每一个美国人都能继承的期票。这张期票向所有人承诺——不论白人还是黑人——都享有不可让渡的生存权、自由权和追求幸福权。

然而，今天美国显然对她的有色公民拖欠着这张期票。美国没有承兑这笔神圣的债务，而是开始给黑人一张空头支票——一张盖着"资金不足"的印戳被退回的支票。但是，我们决不相信正义的银行会破产。我们决不相信这个国家巨大的机会宝库会资金不足。

因此，我们来兑现这张支票。这张支票将给我们以宝贵的自由和正义的保障。

我们来到这块圣地还为了提醒美国：现在正是万分紧急的时刻。现在不是从容不迫悠然行事或服用渐进主义镇静剂的时候。现在是实现民主诺言的时候。现在是走出幽暗荒凉的种族隔离深谷，踏上种族平等的阳关大道的时候。现在是使我们国家走出种族不平等的流沙，踏上充满手足之情的磐石的时候。现在是使上帝所有孩子真正享有公正的时候。

忽视这一时刻的紧迫性，对于国家将会是致命的。自由平等的朗朗秋日不到来，黑人顺情合理哀怨的酷暑就不会过去。1963 年不是一个结束，而是一个开端。

如果国家依然我行我素，那些希望黑人只需出出气就会心满意足的人将大失所望。在黑人得到公民权之前，美国既不会安宁，也不会平静。反抗的旋风将继续震撼我们国家的基石，直至光辉灿烂的正义之日来临。

但是，对于站在通向正义之宫艰险门槛上的人们，有一些话我必须要说。在我们争取合法地位的过程中，切不要错误行事导致犯罪。我们切不要吞饮仇恨辛酸的苦酒，来解除对于自由的饥渴。

我们应该永远得体地、纪律严明地进行斗争。我们不能容许我们富有创造性的抗议沦为暴力行动。我们应该不断升华到用灵魂力量对付肉体力量的崇高境界。

席卷黑人社会的新的奇迹般的战斗精神，不应导致我们对所有白人的不信任——因为许多白人兄弟已经认识到：他们的命运同我们的命运紧密相连，他们的自由同我们的自由休戚相关。他们今天来到这里参加集会就是明证。

我们不能单独行动。当我们行动时，我们必须保证勇往直前。我们不能后退。有人问热心民权运动的人："你们什么时候会感到满意?"只要黑人依然是不堪形容的警察暴行恐怖的牺牲品，我们就决不会满意。只要我们在旅途劳顿后，却被公路旁汽车游客旅社和城市旅馆拒之门外，我们就决不会满意。只要黑人的基本活动范围只限于从狭小的黑人居住区到较大的黑人居住区，我们就决不会满意。只要我们的孩子被"仅供白人"的牌子剥夺个性，损毁尊严，我们就决不会满意。只要密西西比州的黑人不能参加选举，纽约州的黑人认为他们与选举毫不相干，我们就决不会满意。不，不，我们不会满意，直至公正似水奔流，正义如泉喷涌。

我并非没有注意到你们有些人历尽艰难困苦来到这里。你们有些人刚刚走出狭小的牢房。有些人来自因追求自由而遭受迫害风暴袭击和警察暴虐狂飙摧残的地区。你们饱经风霜，历尽苦难。继续努力吧，要相信：无辜受苦终得拯救。

回到密西西比去吧；回到亚拉巴马去吧；回到南卡罗来纳去吧；回到佐治亚去吧；回到路易斯安那去吧；回到我们北方城市中的贫民窟和黑人居住区去吧。要知道，这种情况能够而且将会改变。我们切不要在绝望的深渊里沉沦。

朋友们，今天我要对你们说，尽管眼下困难重重，但我依然怀有一个梦。这个梦深深植根于美国梦之中。

我梦想有一天，这个国家将会奋起，实现其立国信条的真谛："我们认为这些真理不言而喻:人人生而平等。"

我梦想有一天,在佐治亚州的红色山岗上,昔日奴隶的儿子能够同昔日奴隶主的儿子同席而坐,亲如手足。

我梦想有一天,甚至连密西西比州——一个非正义和压迫的热浪逼人的荒漠之州,也会改造成为自由和公正的青青绿洲。

我梦想有一天,我的四个儿女将生活在一个不是以皮肤的颜色,而是以品格的优劣作为评判标准的国家里。

我今天怀有一个梦。

我梦想有一天,亚拉巴马州会有所改变——尽管该州州长现在仍滔滔不绝地说什么要对联邦法令提出异议和拒绝执行——在那里,黑人儿童能够和白人儿童兄弟姐妹般地携手并行。

我今天怀有一个梦。

我梦想有一天,深谷弥合,高山夷平,歧路化坦途,曲径成通衢,上帝的光华再现,普天下生灵共谒。

这是我们的希望。这是我将带回南方去的信念。有了这个信念,我们就能从绝望之山开采出希望之石。有了这个信念,我们就能把这个国家的嘈杂刺耳的争吵声,变为充满手足之情的悦耳交响曲。有了这个信念,我们就能一同工作,一同祈祷,一同斗争,一同入狱,一同维护自由,因为我们知道,我们终有一天会获得自由。

到了这一天,上帝的所有孩子都能以新的含义高唱这首歌:

> 我的祖国,
> 可爱的自由之邦,我为您歌唱。
> 这是我祖先终老的地方,
> 这是早期移民自豪的地方,
> 让自由之声,响彻每一座山岗。

如果美国要成为伟大的国家,这一点必须实现。因此,让自由之声响彻新罕布什尔州的巍峨高峰!

让自由之声响彻纽约州的崇山峻岭!

让自由之声响彻宾夕法尼亚州的阿勒格尼高峰!

让自由之声响彻科罗拉多州冰雪皑皑的洛基山!

让自由之声响彻加利福尼亚州的婀娜群峰!

不,不仅如此;让自由之声响彻佐治亚州的石山!

让自由之声响彻田纳西州的望山!

让自由之声响彻密西西比州的一座座山峰,一个个土丘!

让自由之声响彻每一个山岗!

当我们让自由之声轰响,当我们让自由之声响彻每一个大村小庄,每一个州府城镇,我们就能加速这一天的到来。那时,上帝的所有孩子,黑人和白人,犹太教徒和非犹太教徒,耶稣教徒和天主教徒,将能携手同唱那首古老的黑人灵歌:"终于自由了!终于自由了!感谢全能的上帝,我们终于自由了!"

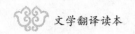

汉译英之一：

On that night, numerous stars were splashing across the sky in my dream, but only two of them being of companion to each other, gently loving, tenderly caressing and constantly caring.

After almost ten years of truly romantic experience, love is no longer an unbreakable vow or the emotional fluctuation of bliss and despair. Love is like a high bourn of life, a gentle breeze and light drizzly rain. Love is the echoes of your footsteps coming up from downstairs, the well-washed and neatly-ironed clothes I leave on the ironing board, and a bunch of wild grass I pick up from outside. After all, love is the days piling up on us with undisturbed regularity.

If we feel a sense of happiness in a simple and peaceful life, if we see a whole world in a grain of sand, and if we develop a taste of calmness in our daily household chores, we must have reached an ideal state of our own being. Isn't it true that we are just pursuing that kind of virtue?

Such an ideal state is all love about and all life about. We often encourage ourselves by quoting a saying: "A genuine vision is derived from simplicity of life, and a real success is conceived in serenity of mind." There is indeed some truth in it.

汉译英之二：

I lie inside the heart of the truck, remembering that clear, warm afternoon. The sunlight was so pretty. I remember that I was outside enjoying myself in the sunshine for a long time, and when I got home I saw my dad through the window packing a red backpack. I leaned against the window frame and asked, "Dad, are you going on a trip?"

He turned and very gently said, "No, I'm letting you go on a trip."

"Letting me go on a trip?"

"That's right. You're eighteen now, and it's time you saw a little of the outside world."

Later I slipped that pretty red backpack onto my back. Dad patted my head from behind, just like you would pat a horse's rump. Then I happily made for the door, and excitedly galloped out of the house, as happy as a horse.

【延伸阅读】

[1] Dagut, M. B. Can "Metaphor" Be Translated? [J]. *Babel*, 1976 22,(1).

[2] Fung, M. Y. Translation of Metaphor[A]. In Chan Sin-wai & D E. Pollard (Eds.), *Encyclopedia of Translation: Academic Press*. Hong Kong: The Chinese University Press, 1995.

[3] Kiu, K. L. Metaphor Across Language and Culture[J]. *Babel*, 1987,33(2).

[4] Lakoff, G. *Metaphors We Live By*[M]. Chicago & London: The University of Chicago Press, 1980.

[5] Newmark, P. *Approaches to Translation*[M]. London: Prentice Hall International (UK) Ltd., 1988.

［6］Shuttleworth，M. *Dictionary of Translation Studies*［Z］. Manchester：St Jerome Publishing，1997.

［7］Snell-Hornby，M. *Translation Studies*：*An Integrated Approach*［M］. Amsterdam/ Philadelphia：John Benjamins Publishing Company，1988.

［8］Venuti，L. *The Translator's Invisibility*－*A History of Translation*［M］. London & New York：Routledge，2008.

［9］Richards，I. A. *The Philosophy of Rhetoric*［M］. New York：OUP，1965.

［10］陈定安. 英汉修辞与翻译［M］. 北京：中国青年出版社，2004.

［11］陈望道. 修辞学发凡［M］. 上海：上海教育出版社，2002.

［12］胡谷明. 篇章修辞与小说翻译［M］. 上海：上海译文出版社，2004.

［13］李亚丹，李定坤. 汉英辞格对比研究简编［C］. 武汉：华中师范大学出版社，2005.

［14］束定芳. 隐喻学研究［M］. 上海：上海外语教育出版社，2003.

［15］谭学纯. 人与人的对话［M］. 合肥：安徽教育出版社，2000.

［16］谭学纯，唐跃，朱玲. 接受修辞学［M］. 合肥：安徽大学出版社，2000.

［17］谭学纯，朱玲. 广义修辞学［M］. 合肥：安徽教育出版社，2002.

［18］王德春，杨素英，黄月圆. 汉英谚语与文化［M］. 上海：上海外语教育出版社，2003.

［19］王伟. 英汉借代修辞方式比较［J］. 解放军外国语学院学报，1994(2).

［20］王希杰. 修辞学通论［M］. 南京：南京大学出版社，1996.

［21］张光明. 英汉修辞思维比较与翻译［M］. 北京：军事谊文出版社，2002.

［22］郑雅丽. 英汉辞格互译导引［M］. 广州：暨南大学出版社，2004.

【问题与思考】

1. 常见的英语修辞格种类有哪些？

2. 汉语的修辞传统源自何时？有哪些历史变化？

3. 对于英汉语中都有的双关辞格，它们的共性与特性何在？

4. 请通过暗喻辞格的跨语言转化，思考中西方文化意象翻译的具体操作方法。

5. 广义修辞学与狭义修辞学的定义区别是什么？

6. 根据 Delabastita 研究发现，有多少种双关语翻译方法？具体是什么？

7. 什么是活隐喻？什么是死隐喻？

8. 隐喻如何成为人类赖以存在的基础？

9. 思维与修辞表述的关系是什么？

10. 为什么说修辞翻译常常构成文学翻译中的"陷阱"？请举例说明。

第四章 诗歌翻译篇

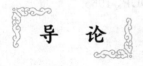

导 论

　　诗歌是一种语言高度精练浓缩,意境丰富,形式工整,富含节奏感和韵律感,极具音乐性的文学体裁,是美的产物和载体,高度集中地概括、反应社会生活,语句一般分行排列,注重结构形式的美。人们普遍认为诗即是歌,歌即是诗。诗歌以灵动的语言表达着人们的喜怒哀乐,用特有的节奏与方式影响着人们的精神世界。诗歌讲究联想,运用象征、比喻、拟人等各种修辞手法,形成了独特的语言艺术。基于诗歌的诸多特性,诗歌是否可以被翻译成其他文字的语言,并保持其诗的特性,在翻译界一直争论不休。

　　最早对诗歌的可译性提出质疑的是文艺复兴时期的但丁,他认为,"任何富于音乐和谐感的作品都不可能译成另一种语言而不破坏其全部优美和谐感"。雪莱在《诗辩》里则断言,"译诗是徒劳无益的,把一个诗人的创作从一种语言译成另一种语言,犹如把一朵紫罗兰投入坩埚"。[①] 美国诗人罗伯特·弗罗斯特干脆把诗定义为"翻译中所丧失的东西"。[②] 王以铸认为"诗这种东西是不能译的……诗歌的神韵、意境或说得通俗些,它的味道(flavor)即诗之所以为诗的东西,在很大程度上有机地融入在诗人写诗时使用的语言之中了,这是无法通过另一种语言或方言来表达的"。如此不绝于耳的论断,使得诗歌翻译似乎被打入万劫不复的宿命绝境。

　　但是,纵观东西方翻译实践历史,虽然诗歌不可译论的呼声一直没有停歇,诗歌却也从没有中断过民族、文化、文明间的翻译和传播。《诗经》和《荷马史诗》早已被其他文化广泛接受,成为人类共享的文化遗产;英国的爱德华·菲茨杰拉德(Edward Fitzgerald)正是因为成功地翻译了欧玛尔·海亚姆(Omar Khayyam)的《鲁拜集》,才得以跻身英国文学史上的诗人行列。在诗歌翻译的历史洪流中,更有无数著名的诗人以自身的翻译实践证明,诗歌不仅可译,而且从根本上具有普遍的审美效果,能超越时代、国度而不变。T. S. 艾略特在他诺贝尔文学奖《受奖辞》中说,诗歌具有某种"超民族价值",他说:"我认为不同国度、不同语种的人们——尽管在任何一个国家都显然只是为数不多的人——可以在诗中彼此理解,这种理解无论何等片面。但依然很重要。"艾略特还说:"虽然语言是一种障碍,但诗本身为我们提供了克服语言障碍的理由。品味别种语言的诗歌,就是对操那种语言的人民的理解,这种理解只能从对诗歌的欣赏中才能得到。我们也不妨回顾一下欧洲的诗歌历史,回顾一下一种语言的诗歌对其他语言诗歌所产生的巨大影响;千万不要忘记每个举足轻重的诗人是如何大大地受益于其他语种

---

　　① 罗新璋编:《翻译论集》,商务印书馆 1984 年版,第 674 页。
　　② 傅浩编译:《二十世纪英语诗选》,河北教育出版社 2003 年版,第 1045 页。

的诗人;我们不妨考虑一下每个国家、每种语言的诗歌如果不从外国诗歌中汲取养分,便会衰竭、灭亡。"英国当代诗人唐纳德·戴维则颠覆性地认为,"最伟大的诗是最能够从翻译中幸存下来的",因为诗更应当是"对普遍真理的探索,而不仅仅是对全部人类语言中某一种语言的独特性质的利用"[①]。

针对诗歌翻译的困难,逃避者多会以抱着罗伯特·弗罗斯特的"救命宣言",其实不然,弗罗斯特本人并无意"非难"诗歌翻译,而是出于对诗歌翻译的艰难和诗歌翻译者所处困境的体认。与弗罗斯特的极端相对的是,美国当代著名解构学者哈罗德·布鲁姆(Harold Bloom)不仅乐观地认为诗歌可以被翻译出来,而且坚信翻译而成的诗作一定会成为另一种作品。我国诗歌翻译家江枫也说:"诗,恰恰应该是翻译过后除了表面信息还留下了美和言外之意的那种东西。留下得越多越是好诗;经不起翻译的就连散文都不是,怎么会是诗,更不会是好诗。"真正经得起翻译的诗才是好诗,原诗所表现的具有人类共通性的美妙的感觉、感受、意象和哲思,即便是经过了翻译的损失也不能完全抹去魅力。

不同语言的特质、文化的差异和审美功能决定了诗歌翻译确实非常困难,具有一定程度的不可译性。但人类文化的共通性,人类经验的相似性,语言认识新事物和新环境的功能,使得诗歌翻译在某种程度上又是可行的。如中文成语"海枯石烂",在苏格兰诗人罗伯特·彭斯的代表作诗歌"A Red, Red Rose"中就有类似的表述:seas gone dry, rock smelt。从辩证主义的观点来看,不可译性和可译性是二元对立的,在一定的条件下可以相互转化。诗歌作为一种独特的文学体裁而具有一些特质,如音乐性、外在表现形式、鲜明的风格等。翻译过程中,这些因素的难以把握使其韵味不易被保留,从而加大翻译难度,造成诗歌似乎不可译的表象。但是,通过译者的主观能动,以其深厚的母语文化功底、高超的文学造诣,以及对译入语语言及文化的深刻了解、掌握与运用,在翻译中进行再创造,以传达诗歌的精髓与精妙,译者能够成功"播散异邦的种子"(苏珊·巴斯奈特语)。

本章选文围绕诗歌翻译的困难和对策、诗歌译作与原作的关系、诗歌翻译的追求和规范等话题,跳出传统关于诗歌可译与不可译的二元争论,从丰富的人类诗歌翻译实践史实出发,分析导致东西方诗歌翻译困难的具体因素,引导读者从文化对话和文明传承的宏观高度看待诗歌翻译问题。

---

① 傅浩编译:《二十世纪英语诗选》,河北教育出版社 2003 年版,第 1045 页。

选 文

选文一 论译诗

林语堂

导 言

本文选自刘靖之编著,《翻译论集》,生活·读书·新知三联书店(香港),1981年版。

林语堂是享誉中外的文学家和翻译家,其国学根底与翻译水准堪称双绝。林语堂翻译生涯中最伟大的贡献,便是以通俗化的策略,把深奥难懂的中国儒道经典文化,生动地传播到西方世界。他认为,文化只有亲和才能更好地凝聚人类的灵魂。正是出于此,他的通俗译本以自然清新的风格,小到品茶烧饭,大至儒道美学,在他的笔下都是娓娓道来,亲切自然,拉近了文本与读者的距离,展示给读者的是一幅幅轻松自如、亲切备至、平等互爱的生活世界。本选文系林语堂读《翻译大难惟意境》之后的感发,他结合自己翻译柳宗元、李清照和苏轼等人的诗作经验和 Arthur Waley,Witter Bynner,Helen Waddell 等西方学者对中国古诗词的翻译与介绍,提出诗歌翻译的见解,诸如用韵的问题、意境传达的问题和练字的问题。

读刘荫续先生《翻译大难惟意境》一文,不觉手痒,想略抒己见。

刘先生举许多例,指出中文的诗句,妙在意境,而意境最难,这自然是识得其中甘苦的人的话。中国诗人,善造意境,表出景物,如"小桥流水人家"短短一句,都不必分出什么主词副词。这话也对。但是诗之所以为诗,而非散文,中文英文道理相同。英文诗主要,一为练词精到,二为意境传神,与中文诗无别。所以译诗的人,尤其应明此点。要知道什么是诗,什么不是诗,而仅是儿童歌曲,或是初中女学生的押韵玩意儿,这才可以译诗。译出来念下去,仍觉得是诗,而不是押韵文而已。

我想在此地谈谈。译事虽难,却有基本条件。中文译英,则中文要看通,而英文要非常好;英文华译,要英文精通,而中文亦应非常好。不然,虽知其原文本意,而笔力不到,达不出来。两样条件都有了,须有闲情逸致,才可译诗。所谓好不好,都是比较的话。凡看见译文不好的,或者是未真懂原文,所以以直译为借口,生吞活剥;或者虽然原文深解了,而找不到恰当的字以译之,又麻烦了。所以说要用字精练恰当。我译柳宗元《愚溪诗序》(见 *The Importance of Understanding*),其中愚溪、愚山、愚亭、愚池很多。怎么想,用 foolish, crazy, stupid 都不妥,后来心血来潮,想到 follies 一字,问题遂解决了。Foolish River, Stupid River 决定不可,而 Follies River 却觉很顺口而雅驯。何以 foolish 与 folly 二字之间,有这么区别呢? 就是英文同中文一样,各字都有弦外之音,懂得这点,始可尝试。

在翻译中文作者当中，成功的是英人韦烈 Arthur Waley。其原因很平常，就是他的英文非常好。所以我译《道德经》（*Modern Library*），有的句子认为韦烈翻得极好，真是英文佳句，我就声明采用了。他译唐诗、乐府古诗十九首及诗经等都不用韵，反而自由，而能信达雅兼到。韦烈偶然也会译错，如西游记赤脚大仙，真真把赤脚译为红脚，这都不必苛求。他们译典故，常有笺注可靠，到了"赤脚"这种字面，字典找不出，就没有办法了。又 Witter Bynner 将《道德经》译成现代美国口语，实在好，因为他是个诗人。

凡译诗，可用韵，而普遍说来，还是不用韵妥当。只要文字好，仍有抑扬顿挫，仍可保存风味。因为要叶韵，常常加一层周折，而致失真。今日白话诗之所以失败，就是又自由随便，不知推敲用字，又不知含蓄寄意，间接传神，而兼又好用韵。随便什么长短句，末字加一个韵，就自称为诗。这是题外不说。在译中文诗时，宁可无韵，而不可无字句中的自然节奏。以前我看蔡廷干译唐诗为英文，但以看得见的音节及叶韵自满，所以不行，幼稚得很。

意境第一，自不必说。瓦德尔女士（Helen Waddell）所译《诗经》二三十首便是好例。这是美国已故文豪卡尔·范多伦（Carl Van Doren）老前辈对我介绍的，称为所译极佳。瓦德尔女士一个中文字不懂。她全靠雷格（James Legge）的译文。雷格在一百年前译中国经书（诗、书、易、礼）是专做学者工夫，有苏州名士王韬帮忙（时王韬因事逃在香港）。雷氏所译，根据马、郑的笺注，及孔颖达的义疏，所以是正经工作。瓦德尔女士根据雷格的译文，专取意境，及天下人同此心的题目，脱胎重写，有时六七段的诗，只并成两段。但是像"毋也天只，不谅人只"译出来真是一字一泪。或寡妇的哀啼，或男人之薄幸，都是亲切动人。所以在我所编的 *Wisdom of China and India* 书中，收入十五首。瓦德尔女士是用韵的，但所用的韵，天生自然，毫无勉强。我译李易安的《声声慢》，那"寻寻觅觅，冷冷清清，凄凄惨惨戚戚"十四字，真费思量。须知全阕意思，就在"梧桐更兼细雨"那种"怎生得黑"的意境。这意境表达，真不容易。所以我用双声方法，译成 so dim, so dark, so dense, so dull, so damp, so dank, so dead 十四字（七字俱用定母）译出，确是黄昏细雨无可奈何孤单的境地，而最后 dead 一字最重，这是译诗的人苦处及乐处，煞费苦心，才可译出。

意境的译法，专在用字传神。我所译最得意的，也就是我所最爱的，是东坡在惠州咏朝云的两首，《赠朝云》的《殢人娇》及所谓《咏梅》的《西江月》。《西江月》名为咏梅，实在是绍圣三年七月朝云病亡葬在栖禅寺时悼朝云所作。

> 玉骨那愁瘴雾。冰姿自有仙风。海仙时遣探芳丛，倒挂绿毛公凤。素面常嫌粉
> 涴。洗妆不褪唇红。高情已逐晓云空，不与梨花同梦。

译文曾入所作东坡传记（*The Gay Genius*）及古文小品英译（*The Importance of Understanding*）。兹录出，以公同好。末两句"高情已逐晓云空，不与梨花同梦"，意境最难，我所译用字与原文不同，而寄意则同。

> Bones of Jade, flesh of snow,
>
> May thy ethereal spirit stand unafraid,
>
> Though the dark mist and the swamp wind blow.
>
> May the sea sprites attend thee,
>
> The para Quets and cockatoos be friend thee,
>
> Thy white face doth powder spurn,

Vermilion must yet from thy lips learn,

Flesh of snow, bones of Jade,

Dream thy dreams, peerless one,

Not for this world thou art made.

　　朝云之玉骨冰姿及东坡之细腻缠绵之意，我想已表达出来。《赠朝云》、《殢人娇》一首，又是另一番维摩境界。

选文二　《中诗英译比录》序

吕叔湘

导　言

　　本文选自吕叔湘，《中诗英译比录》，中华书局（北京），2002 年版。

　　译文不易，译诗更难。本文系已故著名语言学家吕叔湘先生于 20 世纪 40 年代所编著《中诗英译比录》一书的序言部分。鉴于英诗中译远远多于中诗英译这一研究状况，吕叔湘在书中广选外国学者英译中国古典诗歌，以供读者研究比较。《序》文开篇即从语言特性角度展开对汉语语言的分析，指出中国文字艰深、诗词铸语凝练，致使译人误会难免。选文针对中文常不举主语，中文诗句多省略代词、动词无词形变化，诗体译诗之弊端等问题展开详尽个案分析。在广选例证的基础上，吕叔湘指出，译诗并无直译、意译之分，唯有平实与工巧之别。结合"译人究有何种限度之自由？变通为应限于词语，为何兼及意义？何者为必须变通？何者为无害变通？变通逾限之流弊又如何？"等一系列问题，对中诗英译展开了精辟论述。

　　海通以还，西人渐窥中国文学之盛，多有转译，诗歌尤甚；以英文言，其著者亦十有余家。居蜀数载，教授翻译，颇取为检讨论说之资，辄于一诗而重译者择优比而录之，上起风雅，下及唐季，得诗五十九首，英译二百有七首。[①] 客中得书不易，取资既隘，挂漏实多，然即此区区，中土名篇，彼邦佳译，大抵已在。研究译事者足资比较；欣赏艺文者亦得玩索而吟咏焉。将以付之剞劂，辄取昔日讲说之言弁之卷首；所引诸例，杂出各家，不尽在所录之内也。[②]

一

　　以原则言，从事翻译者于原文不容有一词一语之误解。然而谈何容易？以中国文字之艰

深;诗词铸语之凝炼,译人之误会在所难免。前期诸家多尚"达旨",有所不解,易为闪避;后期译人渐崇信实,诠解讹误,昭然易晓。如韩愈山石诗,"僧言古壁佛画好,以火来照所见稀",Bynner(p. 29)译为

> And he brought a light and showed me, and I called them *wonderful*.

以"稀少"为"希奇",此为最简单的误解字义之例。

又如古诗为焦仲卿妻作,"妾不堪驱使,徒留无所施",Waley (*Temple*, p. 114)译为

> I said to myself, "I will not be driven away."
> Yet if I stay, what use will it be?

以"驱使"为"驱逐",因而语意不接,遂误以上句为自思自语,则又因字义之误而滋生句读之误。

其次,词性之误解,亦为致误之因。如杜诗闻官军收河南河北,"却看妻子愁何在?漫卷诗书喜欲狂"句,Bynner(p. 154)误以"愁"为动词,译为

> Where is my wife? Where are my sons?
> Yet crazily sure of finding them, I pack my books and Poems.

读之解颐。杜公虽"欲狂",何至愁及妻子之下落?且"却看"之谓何?

中文动词之特殊意蕴,往往非西人所能识别,如杜诗"感时花溅泪,恨别鸟惊心",泪为诗人之泪,心亦诗人之心,"溅"与"惊"皆致动词也,而 Bynner (p. 141)译为

> ... Where petals have been shed like tears
> And lonely birds have sung their grief.

顿成肤浅。

然一种文字之最足以困惑外人者,往往不在其单个之实字,而在其虚字与熟语,盖虚字多歧义,而熟语不易于表面索解也。此亦可于诸家译诗见之。Waley 在诸译人中最为翔实,然如所译《焦仲卿妻》中,以"四角龙子幡"为

> At its four corners a dragon-*child* flag (*Temple*, p. 121),"子"字实解;又译"著我绣夹裙,事事四五通"为

> ... Takes what she needs, four or five *things* (ibid, p. 116),

以"通"为"件",皆因虚字而误。

余人译诗中亦多此例。如 Fletcher (*More Gems*, p. 12)译太白月下独酌"月既不解饮"作

> The moon then drinks *without a pause*,

由于不明"解"字作"能"讲;译"行乐须及春"作

> Rejoice *until* the Spring comes in,

由于不明"及"字作"乘"讲。又如 Giles (*Verse*, p. 99)译杜诗"今春看又过,何日是归年?"作

> Alas! I *see* another spring *has died*...

因不明"看"字之等于后世之"看看"或"眼见得",遂误以"将过"为"已过",虽小小出入,殊失原诗低回往复之意也。

以言熟语,有极浅显,不应误而误者。如年月序次只以基数为之,不加"第"字,凡稍习中文者不应不解,而 Fletcher (*Gems*, p. 8)译太白长干行"五月不可触"句为

For *five months* with you I cannot meet.

亦有较为生僻,其误可原者。如同篇"早晚下三巴"句不独 Fletcher (ibid. p. 9)误为

Early and late I to gorges go.

Lowell(p. 29)亦误为

From early morning until late in the evening, you descend the three Serpent River,

惟小畑(p. 152)作

Some day when you return down the river,

为得其真象。

熟语之极致为"典故",此则不仅不得其解者无从下手,即得其真解亦不易达其义蕴。如小杜金谷园结句"落花犹似坠楼人",Giles (*Verse*, p. 175)译作

Petals, like nymphs from balconies, come tumbling to the ground,

诚为不当,即 Bynner (p. 178)译为

Petals are falling like a girl's robe long ago.

若非加注(p. 292)亦不明也。又如权德舆玉台体一绝之"昨夜裙带解,今朝蟢子飞",Giles (*Verse*, p. 135)译为

> Last eve thou wert a bride,
> This morn thy dream is o'er...

固是荒谬;而 Bynner(p. 25)译为

> Last night my girdle came undone,
> And this morning a luck beetle flew over my bed.

仍不得不乞灵于附注(p. 244),且亦仅注出一"蟢子",于"裙带"仍不得其解也。(王建宫词"忽地下阶裙带解,非时应得见君王。")

Bynner 所译诗中亦时有类此之错误,如译孟浩然秦中寄远上人诗,"黄金燃桂尽,壮志逐年衰"作

> Like ashes of gold in a cinnamon-flame
> My youthful desires have been burnt with the years (p. 111).

亦复不知所云也。

若干历史的或地理的词语亦具有熟语之性质,常为译家之陷阱。如香山赠梦得诗(长庆集卷六六),"寻花借马烦川守,弄水偷船恼令公",Waley (*More Translations*, p. 90)译为

> When, seeking flowers, we borrowed his horse, the river-keeper was vexed;
> When, to play on the water, we stole his boat the Duke Ling was sore.

以"川守"为 river-keeper 固以己意为之,以"令公"为 Duke Ling 尤可见其疏于考索。时裴度以中书令晋国公为东都留守,史称其与刘白过从甚密,长庆集同卷颇多题咏赠和之作,只应曰 Duke P'ei 或 Duke of Chin,不得以"令"为专名也。

又如"山东"一名,古今异指,而 Fletcher (*Gems*, p. 70)译杜诗兵车行,"君不闻汉家山东二百州,千村万落生荆杞",作 Shantung;"河汉"指天河,而 Waley (*Poems*, p. 44)译古诗十九

首之十，"迢迢牵牛星，皎皎河汉女"，作 Han River。皆易滋误会，显为违失。

至如 Giles（*History*, p. 170）译长恨歌"渔阳鼙鼓动地来"作

But suddenly comes the roll of the *fish-skin* war-drums,

误以地名为非地名；Lowell（p. 98）译太白闻王昌龄左迁龙标遥寄，"杨花落尽子规啼"作

In *Yang-chou*, the blossoms are dropping,

又误以非地名为地名：与"山东"、"河汉"相较，虽事类相同，而难易有别。"渔阳"安得谓为"鱼皮"，"杨"、"扬"更字形悬异，其为谬误尤难宥恕也。

二

中文常不举主语，韵语尤甚，西文则标举分明，诗作亦然。译中诗者遇此等处，不得不一一为之补出。如司空曙贼平后送人北归，云："世乱同南去，时清独北还。他乡生白发，旧国见青山"，Bynner（p. 133）译为

> In dangerous times *we* two came south;
> Now *you* go north in safety, without me.
> But remember *my* head growing white among strangers,
> When *you* look on the blue of the mountains of home.

四句皆补出主语，除第三句容有可商外（亦可指友或兼指二人），余均无误。

然亦往往缘此致误，如上引诗更下一联云"晓月过残垒，繁星宿故关"，"过"与"宿"之主语仍为 you，而 Bynner 译为

> The moon goes down behind a ruined fort,
> Leaving star-clusters above an old gate.

误以"晓月"与"繁星"当之，不知此二语之作用如副词也。

又如古诗十九首之十二，"燕赵多佳人……当户理清曲"继之以"驰情整巾带，沈吟聊踯躅"，乃诗人自谓闻曲而有感也，Waley（*Poems*, p. 45）误以蒙上佳人，译为

> To ease their minds they arrange their shawls and belts;
> Lowering their song, a little while they pause,

索然寡味矣。

又如 Fletcher（*More Gems*, p. 9）译李白长干行，"早晚下三巴，预将书报家"，作

> Early and late, I to gorges go.
> Waiting for news that of thy coming told.

不明"早晚"之为询问，遂以"下"为"我下"，不知自长干至三巴不得云"下"，两地之相去亦非朝暮可往来者。

又如刘长卿逢雪宿芙蓉山，"柴门闻犬吠，风雪夜归人"，闻者诗人自闻也，Fletcher（*Gems*, p. 184）译为

> The house dog's sudden barking, which hears the wicket go,

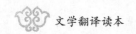

Greets us at night returning through driving gale and snow.

误为犬闻门响而吠,不知中文不容有"宾—动—主"之词序,杜诗"香稻啄余鹦鹉粒"之得失至今犹聚讼纷纭也。

此等错误往往因涉上下文主语而来,如上举"驰情整冠带"误承"当户理清曲","早晚下三巴"则其上既有"坐愁红颜老",其下复有"相迎不道远",不谙中文之常常更易主语而又从略者自易致误。如杜诗兵车行,"况复秦兵耐苦战,被驱不异犬与鸡",即此土不学之人亦难免误解,Bynner(p. 169)译为

> Men of China are able to face the stiffest battle,
> But their officers drive them like chickens and dogs.

其情可原。然"役夫"来自"山东",与"秦兵"正为敌对,上下文足以确定被驱者非秦兵,B. 氏有江亢虎氏为助,不容并此而不达。

又因主语之省略而误解动词之意义者。如 Waley 译焦仲卿妻"谓言无罪过,供养卒大恩"(*Temple*,p. 116)作

> Never in spoken word did I transgress or fail...

又"十七遣汝嫁,谓言无誓违"(p. 118)作

> ... and hears you promise forever to be true,

此两"谓言"同于后世之"只道"、"只说是",宜作 I thought 解,Waley 不了此义,殆由未举主语。

又如古诗十九首之十九,"客行虽云乐,不如早旋归",Waley(*Poems*,p. 48)译作

> My absent love says that he is happy,
> But I would rather he said he was coming back,

又古诗上山采蘼芜,"新人虽言好,不及古人姝"(p. 35)译作

> Although her *talk* is clever...

其实此处"云"、"言"皆无主动词,it is said 之义,仍实字之近于虚字者,缀于"虽"字之后,作用类似衬字,今语亦有"虽说是",可为比较;Waley 视为寻常动词,遂有"言谈"之解。

与主语省略相似者又有宾语之省略,亦为译家致误之由。如元稹遣悲怀,"尚想旧情怜婢仆,也曾因梦送钱财",Bynner(p. 216)译为

> ... Sometimes, in a dream, I bring *you* gifts.

谓梦中送钱财于亡妻,无乃费解? 此则远不及 Fletcher(*More Gems*,p. 191)所译

> The slaves' and servants' love moves me to love,
> And presents I gave them, when I dreamed of you.

之信达而兼雅也。

又有因连词之省略而致误者。如渊明责子诗,"雍端年十三,不识六与七",Budd(p. 150)误于前,

> Yong-tuan is thirteen now.

Waley (*Poems*，p. 76)误于后，

> Yung-tuan is thirteen.

皆昧于中文平联词语常不用连词之惯例，遂以"雍"与"端"为一人也。

三

译诗者往往改变原诗之观点，或易叙写为告语，因中文诗句多省略代词，动词复无词形变化，译者所受限制不严也。其中有因而转更亲切或生动者。试引二三例，则如李商隐嫦娥诗，"嫦娥应悔偷灵药，碧海青天夜夜心"，Bynner (p. 75)译为

> Are *you* sorry for having stolen the potion that has set *you*
> Over purple seas and blue skies, to brood through the long nights?

此由第三身之叙写改为对第二身之告语者，视原来为亲切。如卢纶塞下曲之"野幕敞琼筵，羌戎贺劳旋；醉和金甲舞，雷鼓动山川"，Bynner (p. 104)译为

> *Let* feasting begin in the wild camp!
> *Let* bugles cry our victory!
> *Let us* drink，*let us* dance in our golden armour!
> *Let us* thunder on rivers and hills with our drums!

此由第三身之叙写改为一二身之告语者，视原来为生动。

如王维班婕妤诗，"怪来妆阁里，朝下不相迎；总向春园里，花间笑语声"，Fletcher (*Gems*，p. 120)译为

> Dost wonder if my toilet room be shut?
> If in the regal halls we meet no more?
> I ever haunt the garden of the spring；
> From smiling flowers to learn their whispered lore.

原来为汉帝告婕妤，译诗改为婕妤告汉帝，观点适相反，而译诗似较胜。

但如王建新嫁娘诗，"三日入厨下，洗手作羹汤"，Fletcher (*More Gems*，p. 208)译为

> Now married three days，to the kitchen I go，
> And washing my hands a fine broth I prepare.

杜牧秋夕诗，"银烛秋光冷画屏，轻罗小扇扑流萤"，Bynner (p. 177)译为

> Her candle-light is silvery on her chill bright screen.
> Her little silk fan is for fireflies...

原诗之为一身抑三身，未可遽定：前一诗似是三身，今作一身，后一诗似是一身，今作三身，其间得失，正自难言。然中诗可无主语，无人称，译为英文，即非有主语有人称不可，此亦译中诗者所常遇之困难也。

四

不同之语言有不同之音律,欧洲语言同出一系,尚且各有独特之诗体,以英语与汉语相去之远,其诗体自不能苟且相同。初期译人好以诗体翻译,即令达意,风格已殊,稍一不慎,流弊丛生。故后期译人 Waley,小畑,Bynner 诸氏率用散体为之,原诗情趣,转易保存。此中得失,可发深省。

以诗体译诗之弊,约有三端:一曰趁韵。如 Fletcher (*Gems*, p. 211)译王绩过酒家,"眼看人尽醉,何忍独为醒"作

> With wine o'ercome when all our fellows be,
> Can I alone sit in sobriety?

二曰颠倒词语以求协律。如 Fletcher (*More Gems*, p. 62)译杜诗秋兴,"几回青琐点朝班"作

> Just in dream by the gate when to number I sate
> The courtiers' attendants who throng at its side.

三曰增删及更易原诗意义。如陈子昂登幽州台诗,"前不见古人,后不见来者,念天地之悠悠,独怆然而涕下",Giles (p. 58)译为

> My eyes saw not the men of old;
> And now their age away has rolled
> I weep—to think that I shall not see
> The heroes of posterity!

其第二行为与原诗第三句相当乎,则甚不切合,为不与相当乎,则原句甚重要,不容删省;又如杜诗"露从今夜白,月是故乡明",Giles (p. 101)译为

> The crystal dew is glittering at my feet,
> The moon sheds, as of old, her silvery light.

"今夜"与"故乡"为此联诗眼,而横遭刊落。

与此相反者,如张泌寄人诗,"别梦依依到谢家,小廊回合曲阑斜",Giles (p. 209)译为

> After parting, dreams possessed me and I wandered you know where,
> And we sat in the verandah and you sang the sweet old air.

第二行之下半完全为足成音段而增加。

其全部意义加以更易者,如 Giles (p. 65)译张九龄诗"思君如明月,夜夜减清辉"作

> My heart is like the full moon, full of pains,
> Save that 'tis always full and never wanes.

汉译便是"思君异明月,终岁无盈亏"。

前两种病,中外恶诗所同有,初无问于创作与翻译。第三种病,则以诗体译诗尤易犯之,虽高手如 Giles 亦所不免。Fletcher 尤甚于 Giles;Budd,Martin 诸人更甚于 Fletcher,有依稀仿

佛，面目全非者，其例难于列举。

五

自一方面言，以诗体译诗，常不免于削足适履，自另一方面言，逐字转译，亦有类乎胶柱鼓瑟。硬性的直译，在散文容有可能，在诗殆绝不可能。Waley 在 *More Translations* 序言中云，所译白居易诗不止此数，有若干未能赋以"诗形"，不得不终于弃去。Waley 所谓"诗形"（poetic form），非寻常所谓"诗体"，因所刊布者皆散体也。Waley 举其初稿两首为例，试录其一：早春独登天宫阁（长庆集卷六十八），"天宫日暖阁门开，独上迎春饮一杯。无限游人遥怪我，缘何最老最先来？"

> Tien-kung Sun warm, pagoda door open;
>
> Alone climbing, greet Spring, drink one cup.
>
> Without limit excursion-people afar-off wonder at me;
>
> What cause most old most first arrived!

此 Waley 认为诗的原料，未经琢磨不得为诗者。而 Ayscough 译杜诗，顾以此为已足。如垂老别首四句："四郊未宁静，垂老不得安。子孙阵亡尽，焉用身独完？"（*Tu Fu*，I.，p. 336），译为

> On all four sides, in open spaces beyond the city, no unity, no rest;
>
> Men fallen into old age have not attained peace.
>
> Their sons, grandsons, every one has died in battle：
>
> Why should a lone body finish its course?

Lowell 与 Ayscough 合译《松花笺》集，以不识中文故，不得不惟 Ayscough 之初稿是赖，因之多有不必要之拘泥处，如译太白山中答俗人问（p. 69），"问余何事栖碧山"作

He asks why I *perch* in the *green jade* hills.

然其佳者如刘禹锡石头城（p. 120），"山围故国周遭在，潮打空城寂寞回"，译为

> Hills surround the ancient kingdom; they never change.
>
> The tide beats against the empty city, and silently, silently returns.

亦自具有 Waley 所谓"诗形"，非 Ayscough 自译杜诗可比也。

故严格言之，译诗无直译意译之分，惟有平实与工巧之别。散体诸译家中，Lowell，Waley，小畑，皆以平实胜，而除 Lowell 外，亦未尝无工巧；至于 Bynner，则颇逞工巧，而亦未尝无平实处。

所谓平实，非一语不增，一字不减之谓也。小畑之译太白诗，常不为貌似，而语气转折，多能曲肖。如"两岸猿声啼不住，轻舟已过万重山"（p. 76）译为

> The screams of monkeys on either bank
>
> Had scarcely ceased echoing in my ear
>
> When my skiff had left behind it
>
> Ten thousand ranges of hills.

"已"字,"过"字,"啼不住"三字,皆扣合甚紧,可谓译中上选。又如独坐敬亭山绝句(p. 57)"众鸟高飞尽,孤云独去闲。相看两不厌,只有敬亭山"之译为

> Flocks of birds have flown high and away;
> A solitary drift of cloud, too, has gone, wandering on.
> And I sit alone with the Ching-ting Peak, towering beyond.
> We never grow tired of each other, the mountain and I.

苏台览古(p. 74)"旧苑荒台杨柳新,菱歌清唱不胜春。只今惟有西江月,曾照吴王宫里人"之译为

> In the deserted garden among the crumbling walls,
> The willows show green again,
> While the sweet notes of the water-nut song
> Seem to lament the spring.
> Nothing remains but the moon above the river—
> The moon that once shone on the fair faces
> That smiled in the king's palace of Wu.

皆未尝炫奇求胜,而自然切合,情致具足者。

译人虽以平稳为要义,亦不得自安于苟简或晦塞,遇原来异常凝炼之诗句,固不得不婉转以求曲达。Waley 译古诗有颇擅此胜者,如十九首之九(*Poems*, p. 43),"此物何足贵,但感别经时",后句译为

> But it may remind him of the time that has past since he left.

十九首之十一(p. 44),"立身苦不早"译为

> Success is bitter when it is slow in coming.

十九首之十三(p. 46),"万岁更相送"译为

> For ever it has been that mourners in their turn were mourned.

又如焦仲卿妻(*Temple*, p. 122),"自君别我后,人事不可量;果不如先愿,又非君所详",末句言约而意深,译作

> You would understand if only you knew.

此皆善为婉达,具见匠心者也。

至 Bynner 译唐诗三百首乃好出奇以制胜,虽尽可依循原来词语,亦往往不甘墨守。如孟浩然留别王维(p. 112),"欲寻芳草去,惜与故人违",译为

> How sweet the road-side flowers might be
> If they did not mean good-bye, old friend.

韦应物滁州西涧(p. 206),"春潮带雨晚来急,野渡无人舟自横",译为

> On the spring flood of last night's rain
> The ferry-boat moves as though someone were poling.

同人夕次盱眙县(p. 211),"独应忆秦关,听钟未眠客",译为

At midnight I think of northern city-gate,

And I hear a bell tolling between me and sleep.

皆撇开原文,另作说法,颇见工巧。然措词虽已迥异,意义却无增减,虽非译事之正宗,亦不得谓为已犯译人之戒律也。

六

上举 Bynner 诸例引起译事上一大问题,即译人究有何种限度之自由? 变通为应限于词语,为何兼及意义? 何者为必须变通? 何者为无害变通? 变通逾限之流弊又如何?

译事之不能不有变通,最显明之例为典故。如元稹遣悲怀诗,"邓攸无子寻知命,潘岳悼亡犹费词",Bynner (p. 216)译为

There have been better men than I to whom heaven denied a son,

There was a poet better than I whose dead wife could not hear him.

孟郊古别离诗,"不恨归来迟,莫向临邛去",Fletcher (*Gems*, p. 175)译为

Your late returning does not anger me,

But that another steal your heart away.

皆可谓善于变通,允臻上乘。若将"潘","邓","临邛"照样译出,即非加注不可,读诗而非注不明,则焚琴煮鹤,大杀风景矣。(第一例尤佳,因"知命"与"费词"亦暗中扣紧也。)

亦有不变通而无妨变通者。试举二三简单之例:如太白江上吟之结句云,"功名富贵若长在,汉水亦应西北流",Lowell (p. 43)与小畑 (p. 25)均直译"西北流",小畑加注云汉水东南流入江,实则循上句语气,无注亦明。然若如 Fletcher (*Gems*, p. 44)之译为

But sooner could flow backward to its fountains

This stream, than wealth and honour can remain.

直截了当,亦未尝不可。又如 Fletcher (*Gems*, p. 214)译贾至春思诗,"桃花历乱李花香",作

The peach and pear blossoms in massed fragrance grow.

李花未必不历乱,桃花亦未必不香,正不必拘于原文字面。又如 Giles (*Verse*, p. 164)译白居易后宫词"红颜未老恩先断,斜倚薰笼坐到明",作

Alas, although his love has gone, her beauty lingers yet;

Sadly she sits till early dawn but never can forget.

原云"红颜未老恩先断",今云"君恩已去红颜在",先者后之,后者先之,在译者自为凑次二行之韵脚,而意思似转深入,此亦变通之可取者。又如 Bynner (p. 127)译白居易琵琶行,"暮去朝来颜色故"作

And evenings went and evenings came, and her beauty faded.

中文"暮去朝来"本兼"朝去暮来"言,英文 evenings went and mornings came 则无此涵义,若译为 evenings and mornings went and came,又未免过于絮烦,自惟有如上译法,言简而意赅。

又如杜审言和晋陵陆丞早春游望诗,"忍闻歌古调,归思欲沾襟","归思"下本隐有"使我"

意，为五言所限，不得不尔。照字面译出，虽不至于费解，终觉勉强。Bynner（p. 179）译为

> Suddenly an old song fills
> My heart with home, my eyes with tears.

便较显豁。此种变通实已近于必要矣。

如斯之例，诸家多有，上节所引 Waley 与 Bynner 诸译咸属此类，皆未尝以辞害意，为译人应有之自由。然而词语之变通与意义之更易，其间界限，亦自难言。变通而及于意义，则如履薄冰，如行悬緪，时时有陨越之虞，不得不审慎以将事。试以二例明之。Waley（*Poems*, p. 35）译古诗上山采蘼芜，"新人工织缣，故人工织素。织缣日一匹，织素五丈余"，作

> My new wife is clever at embroidering silk;
> My old wife was good at plain sewing.
> Of silk embroidery one can do an inch a day;
> Of plain sewing, more than five feet.

缣素之别，以及一匹与五丈之分，译出均欠显豁，故改为绣与缝，一寸与五尺，于原文意义颇有更张，而主旨则无出入。此变通之可取者。反之，如 Bynner（p. 4）译张继枫桥夜泊诗，"江枫渔火对愁眠"，作

> Under the shadows of maple-trees a fisherman moves with the torch.

一静一动，与原诗意境迥异。虽或见仁见智，难为轩轾，而谓鹿为马，终非转译所宜。二例之间，界限渐而非顿，然不得谓为无界限。得失寸心，疏漏与穿凿固惟有付之译人之感觉与判断矣。

意义之变通有三，或相异，或省减，或增加。相异之例已如上举。意义之省减，时亦不免，若不关宏旨，亦即不足为病。如 Bynner（p. 148）译杜诗"白头搔更短，浑欲不胜簪"，作

> I stroke my white hair. It has grown too thin
> To hold the hairpins any more.

"更"字"欲"字皆未能传出，而大体不谬。

不可省而省，则失之疏漏。如 Waley（*Temple*, p. 117）译焦仲卿妻诗，"今日还家去，念母劳家里"，作

> Today I am going back to my father's home,
> And this house I leave in Madam's hands.

"念"字"劳"字皆不可省而省者。又如 Bynner（p. 174）译杜荀鹤春宫怨，"承恩不在貌，教妾若为容？"作

> To please a fastidious emperor,
> How shall I array myself?

"不在貌"三字以一 fastidious 当之，全然未达。（若改为 capricious，则庶几近之。）又如所译阙名杂诗"等是有家归未得，杜鹃休向耳边啼"（p. 3），

> We are thinking of our kinsfolk, far away from us.

O cuckoo，why do you follow us，why do you call us home?

"等是"二字何等重要，岂容漏去？类此之例，不尽由于有意之变通，亦有识解不周，或为才力所限，遂至陷于浅薄疲弱，虽其情可原，其病不可不知。以诗体译诗者，为凑韵脚与节拍，尤易触犯此戒，前节已申论之矣。

增饰原诗之意义，亦有无伤大雅者。如 Giles（*Verse*，p. 96）译太白诗"白发三千丈，缘愁似个长"，作

> My whitening hair would make a long long rope，
> Yet could not fathom all my depth of woe.

比原来意义略进一步，而不足为病。

过此则往往流于穿凿。如 Giles（*Verse*，p. 53）译薛道衡诗"入春才七日，离家已二年"，作

> A week in the spring to the exile appears
> Like an absence from home of a couple of years.

即犯"read in"之病，殆以为二句不相连属，未免平淡，遂为"一日三秋"之解。不知此二句本平淡，故陈人有"底言"之诮，及"人归落雁后，思发在花前"二句出，始知名下无虚耳。（见隋唐嘉话）

又如 Waley（*Poems*，p. 35）译古诗上山采蘼芜，"新人从门入，故人从阁去"，作

> My new wife comes in from the road to meet me；
> My old wife always came down from her tower.

原诗只状其得新弃故耳，译文乃言新人好游乐，故人勤女红。（或缘误"去"为"出"？）

更有甚于此者，如 Fletcher（*Gems*，p. 209）译贺知章题袁氏别业诗，"主人不相识，偶坐为林泉。莫谩愁沽酒，囊中自有钱"，作

> The Lord of All to us is all unknown.
> And yet these Woods and Springs must Some One own.
> Let us not murmur if our Wine we Buy；
> In our own Purse have we Sufficiency.

即事之诗，解为论道，刻意求深，翻失真象。又 Giles 译司空图诗品（*History*，p. 179－188），全作道家玄语，与诗文了无关涉。如斯穿凿，宜为厉禁。

至如 Martin（p. 55）之译太白长干行，"郎骑竹马来，绕床弄青梅"，作

> You rode a bamboo horse，
> And deemed yourself a knight，
> With paper helm and shield
> And wooden sword bedight.

则缘根本误会诗中主体，以商人妇为军士妻，因而任意枝蔓，全无依据，无以名之，荒谬而已。

七

中诗大率每句自为段落，两句连贯如"旧时王谢堂前燕，飞入寻常百姓家"者，其例已鲜。西诗则常一句连跨数行，有多至十数行者。译中诗者嫌其呆板，亦往往用此手法，Bynner 书中最饶此例。如译太白诗"但见泪痕湿，不知心恨谁"（p. 53），作

> You may see the tears now, bright on her cheek,
>
> But not the man she so bitterly loves.

利用关系子句，便见连贯。又如译王维九月九日忆山东兄弟（p. 190），"独在异乡为异客，每逢佳节倍思亲，遥知兄弟登高处，遍插茱萸少一人"，作

> All alone in a foreign land,
>
> I am twice as homesick on this day,
>
> When brothers carry dogwood up the mountain,
>
> Each of them a branch—and my branch missing.

虽四行与原诗四句分别相当，而原诗只三四连贯，此则一气呵成矣。

然此二例犹可在逐行之末小作停顿，若如所译王维秋夜曲（p. 191），"桂魄初生秋露微，轻罗已薄未更衣"，作

> Under the crescent moon a light autumn dew
>
> Has chilled the robe she will not change.

即不复有停顿之理。又如 Cranmer-Byng（*A Feast of Lanterns*，p. 43）译王维送春辞，"相欢在樽酒，不用惜花飞"，作

> Then fill the wine-cup of to-day and let
>
> Night and the rose fall, while we forget.

停顿不在上行之末，而在下行之中，纯用西诗节律，与中诗相去更远矣。

此类译作，虽音调不侔，其佳者亦至有情致。然若一味求连贯，有时即不免流于牵强附会。如 Bynner（p. 192）译王维归嵩山作，"清川带长薄，车马去闲闲。流水如有意；暮禽相与还"，作

> The limpid river, past its rushes
>
> Running slowly as my chariot,
>
> Becomes a fellow voyager
>
> Returning home with the evening birds.

即与原诗颇有出入。

至如译李颀听安万善吹觱篥歌（p. 51），"……变调如闻杨柳春，上林繁花照眼新。岁夜高堂列明烛，美酒一杯声一曲"，作

> ... They are changing still again to Spring in the Willow-Trees.

Like Imperial Garden Flowers，brightening the eye with beauty，

Are the high-hall candles we have lighted this cold night...

"上林繁花"句显然属上，今以属下，其为不妥，无任何理由可为藉口也。

中诗尚骈偶，不独近体为然。古体诗中亦时见偶句；英诗则以散行为常，对偶为罕见之例外。译中诗者对于偶句之处理，有时逐句转译，形式上较为整齐，有时融为一片，改作散行。试以 Bynner 所译为例：如王维汉江临眺(p. 195)，"江流天地外，山色有无中。郡邑浮前浦，波澜动远空"，译为

This river runs beyond heaven and earth，

Where the colour of mountains both is and is not.

The dwellings of men seem floating along

On ripples of the distant sky.

前一联较为整齐，后一联便一气呵成，不分两截(意义之切合与否为另一问题)。

诗中偶句亦有上下相承，本非并立者，译来自以连贯为宜。如韦应物淮上喜会梁川故人诗，"浮云一别后，流水十年间"，Bynner（p. 207)译为

Since we left one another，floating apart like clouds，

Ten years have run like Water—till at last we join again.

自是顺其自然，非故事更张。

然亦有本甚整齐，而有意破坏之，以求得参差错落之效者，如 Bynner（p. 87)译李益夜上受降城闻笛诗，"回乐峰前沙似雪，受降城外月如霜"，作

The sand below the border-mountain lies like snow，

And the moon like frost beyond the city-wall.

甚可觇中西风尚之殊异。

与此相反，有原诗散行，译者假一二相同之字以为线索，化散以为整者。如王昌龄诗"秦时明月汉时关，万里长征人未还"，Bynner（p. 181)译为

The moon goes back to the time of Chin，the wall to the time of Han，

And the road our troops are travelling goes back three hundred（thousand?)

miles.

王维诗"深林人不知，明月来相照"，Giles(*Verse*，p. 70)译为

No ear to hear me，save my own；

No eye to see me，save the moon.

然类此之例，不数数觌。一般言之，中诗尚整，西诗尚散，译诗者固末由自外也。

选文三　Guido's Relations

Ezra Pound

导　言

本文选自 Lawrence Venuti, *The Translation Studies Reader*，New York：Routledge，2000.

埃兹拉·庞德是 20 世纪西方现代文学的主要奠基者之一，意象派诗歌运动的发起人，他一生成功地翻译了许多中国古典诗歌、南欧普罗旺斯的抒情歌谣及盎格鲁萨克逊时期的古英语诗歌。他出版的中国诗歌的译本《华夏集》，是他翻译实践的一大突出贡献。Guido Cavilacanti（古依多·卡瓦肯提，1255—1300）是 13 世纪意大利诗人。庞德第一个译本就是翻译了他的诗歌"The Sonnets and Ballads of Guido Cavalcanti"。而"Guido's Relations"这篇文章就是庞德在翻译完这首诗歌，根据自己的翻译感想所写的一篇文章，集庞德的诗歌创作思想及诗歌翻译思想于一体。面对维多利亚式的语言，庞德认为，译者用词要精练准确，译文要有自己的特色，诗歌译文应在节奏上做文章，使译文的节奏与原文节奏对等，以达到忠实原文的效果。在"Guido's Relations"结尾部分，庞德作为总结提出了自主性翻译理论，强调译者在翻译过程中的能动作用。

The critic, normally a bore and a nuisance, can justify his existence in one or more minor and subordinate ways: he may dig out and focus attention upon matter of interest that would otherwise have passed without notice; he may, in the rare cases when he has any really general knowledge or "perception of relations" (swift or other), locate his finds with regard to other literary inventions; he may, thirdly, or as you might say, conversely and as part and supplement of his activity, construct cloacae to carry off the waste matter, which stagnates about the real work, and which is continuously being heaped up and caused to stagnate by academic bodies, obese publishing houses, and combinations of both, such as the Oxford Press. (We note their particular infamy in a recent reissue of Palgrave.)

Since Dante's unfinished brochure on the common tongue, Italy may have had no general literary criticism, the brochure is somewhat "special" and of interest mainly to practitioners of the art of writing. Lorenzo Valla somewhat altered the course of history by his close inspection of Latin usage. His prefaces have here and there a burst of magnificence, and the spirit of the Elegantiae should benefit any writer's lungs. As he wrote about an ancient idiom, Italian and English writers alike have, when they have heard his name at all, supposed that he had no "message" and, in the case of the Britons, they returned, we may suppose, to Pater's remarks on Pico. (Based on what the weary peruser of some few other parts of Pico's output, might pettishly denounce as Pico's one remarkable paragraph.)

The study called "comparative literature" was invented in Germany but has seldom if ever aspired to the study of "comparative values in letters".

The literature of the Mediterranean races continued in a steady descending curve of renaissance-ism. There are minor upward fluctuations. The best period of Italian poetry ends in the year 1321. So far as I know one excellent Italian tennis-player and no known Italian writer has thought of considering the local literature in relation to the rest of the world.

Leopardi read, and imitated Shakespeare. The Prince of Monte Nevoso has been able to build his unique contemporary position because of barbarian contacts, whether consciously, and *via* visual stimulus from any printed pages, or simply because he was aware of, let us say, the existence of Wagner and Browning. If Nostro Gabriele started something new in Italian. Hating Barbarism, teutonism, never mentioning the existence of the ultimate Britons, unsurrounded by any sort of society or milieu, he ends as a solitary, superficially eccentric, but with a surprisingly sound standard of values, values, that is, as to the relative worth of a few perfect lines of writing, as contrasted to a great deal of flub-dub and "action".

The only living author who has ever taken a city or held up the diplomatic crapule at the point of machine-guns, he is in a position to speak with more authority than a batch of neurasthenic incompetents or of writers who never having swerved from their jobs, might be, or are, supposed by the scientists and the populace to be incapable of action. Like other serious characters who have taken 70 years to live and to learn to live, he has passed through periods wherein he lived (or wrote) we should not quite say "less ably", but with less immediately demonstrable result.

This period "nel mezzo", this passage of the "selva oscura" takes men in different ways, so different indeed that comparison is more likely to bring ridicule on the comparer than to focus attention on the analogy—often admittedly far-fetched.

In many cases the complete man makes a "very promising start", and then flounders or appears to flounder for 10 years, or for 20 or 30 (cf. Henry James's middle period) to end, if he survive, with some sort of demonstration, discovery, or other justification of his having gone by the route he has (apparently) stumbled on.

When I "translated" Guido 18 years ago I did not see Guido at all. I saw that Rossetti had made a remarkable translation of the *Vita Nuova*, in some places improving (or at least enriching) the original; that he was undubitably the man "sent", or "chosen" for that particular job, and that there was something in Guido that escaped him or that was, at any rate, absent from his translations. A *robustezza*, a masculinity. I had a great enthusiasm (perfectly justified), but I did not clearly see exterior demarcations—Euclid inside his cube, with no premonition of Cartesian axes.

My perception was not obfuscated by Guido's Italian, difficult as it then was for me to

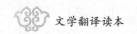

read. I was obfuscated by the Victorian language.

If I hadn't been, I very possibly couldn't have done the job at all. I should have seen the too great multiplicity of problems contained in the one problem before me.

I don't mean that I didn't see dull spots in the sonnets. I saw that Rossetti had taken most of the best sonnets, that one couldn't make a complete edition of Guido simply by taking Rossetti's translations and filling in the gaps, it would have been too dreary a job. Even though I saw that Rossetti had made better English poems that I was likely to make by (in intention) sticking closer to the direction of the original. I began by meaning merely to give prose translation so that the reader ignorant of Italian could see what the melodic original meant. It is, however, an illusion to suppose that more than one person in every 300,000 has the patience or the intelligence to read a foreign tongue for its sound, or even to read what are known to be the masterworks of foreign melody, in order to learn the qualities of that melody, or to see where one's own falls short.

What obfuscated me was not the Italian but the crust of dead English, the sediment present in my own available vocabulary—which I, let us hope, got rid of a few years later. You can't go round this sort of thing. It takes 6 or 8 years to get educated in one's art, and another 10 to get rid of that education.

Neither can anyone learn English, one can only learn a series of Englishes. Rossetti made his own language. I hadn't in 1910 made a language, I don't mean a language to use, but even a language to think in.

It is stupid to overlook the lingual inventions of precurrent authors, even when they are fools or flapdoodles or Tennysons. It is sometimes advisable to sort out these languages and inventions, and to know what and why they are.

Keats, out of Elizabethans, Swinburne out of a larger set of Elizabethans and a mixed bag (Greeks, *und* so *weiter*), Rossetti out of Sheets, Kelly, and Co. plus early Italians (written and painted); and so forth, including *King Wenceslas*, ballads and carols.

Let me not discourage a possible reader, or spoil anyone's naïve enjoyment, by saying that my early versions of Guido are bogged in Dante Gabriel and in Algernon. It is true, but let us pass by it in silence. Where both Rossetti and I went off the rails was in taking an English sonnet as the equivalent for a sonnet in Italian. I don't mean in overlooking the mild difference in the rhyme scheme. The mistake is "quite natural", very few mistakes are "unnatural". Rime looks very important. Take the rimes off a good sonnet, and there is a vacuum. And besides the movement of some Italian sonnets is very like that in some sonnets in English. The feminine rhyme goes by the board... again for obvious reasons. It had gone by the board, quite often, in Provençal. The French made an ecclesiastical law about using it 50/50.

As a bad analogy, imagine a Giotto or Simone Martini fresco, "translated" into oils by "Sir Joshua", or Sir Frederick Leighton. Something is lost, something is somewhat denatured.

Suppose, however, we have a Cimabue done in oil, not by Holbein, but by some contemporary of Holbein who can't paint as well as Cimabue.

There are about 7 reasons why the analogy is incorrect, and 6 more to suppose it inverted, but it may serve to free the reader's mind from preconceived notions about the English of "Elizabeth" and her British garden of song-birds. —And to consider language as a medium of expression.

(Breton forgives Flaubert on hearing that Father Gustave was trying only to give "l'impression de la couleur jaune" [*Nadja*, p. 12]).

Dr. Schelling has lectured about the Italianate Englishman of Shakespeare's day. I find two Shakespeare plots within 10 pages of each other in a forgotten history of Bologna, printed in 1596. We have heard of the effects of the travelling Italian theatre companies, *commedia dell' arte*, etc. What happens when you idly attempt to translate early Italian into English, unclogged by the Victorian era, freed from sonnet obsession, but trying merely to sing and to leave out the dull bits in the Italian, or the bits you don't understand?

I offer you a poem that "don't matter", it is attributed to Guido in Codex Barberiniano Lat. 3953. Alacci prints it as Guide's; Simone Occhi in 1740 says that Alacci is a fool or words to that effect and a careless man without principles, and proceeds to print the poem with those of Cino Pistoia. Whoever wrote it, it is, indubitably, not a *capo lavoro*.

> Madonna la vostra belta enfolio
> Si li mei ochi che menan lo core   MS. oghi
> A la bataglia ove l' ancise amore
> Che del vostro placer armato uscio;   usio
>
> Si che nel primo asalto che asalio
> Passo dentro la mente e fa signore,
> E prese l' alma che fuzia di fore
> Planzendo di dolor che vi sentio.
>
> Però vedete che vostra beltate
> Mosse la folia und e il cor morto
> Et a me ne convien clamar pietate,
>
> Non per campar, ma per aver conforto
> Ne la morte crudel che far min fate
> Et o rason sel non vinzesse il torto.

Is it worth an editor's while to include it among dubious attributions? It is not very attractive: until one starts playing with the simplest English equivalent.

> Lady thy beauty doth so mad mine eyes,

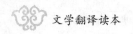

> Driving my heart to strife wherein he dies.

Sing it of course, don't try to speak it. It thoroughly falsifies the movement of the Italian, it is an opening quite good enough for Herrick or Campion. It will help you to understand just why Herrick, and Campion, and possibly Donne are still with us.

The next line is rather a cliché; the line after more or less lacking in interest. We pull up on:

> Whereby thou seest how fair thy beauty is
> To compass doom.

That would be very nice, but it is hardly translation.

Take these scraps, and the almost impossible conclusion, a tag of Provençal rhythm, and make them into a plenum. It will help you to understand some of M. de Schloezer's remarks about Stravinsky's trend toward melody. And you will also see what the best Elizabethan lyricists did, as well as what they didn't.

My two lines take the opening and two and a half of the Italian, English more concise; and the octave gets too light for the sestet. Lighten the sestet.

> So unto Pity must I cry
> Not for safety, but to die.
> Cruel Death is now mine ease
> If that he thine envoy is.

We are preserving one value of early Italian work, the cantabile; and we are losing another, that is the specific weight. And if we notice it we fall on a root difference between early Italian, "The philosophic school coming out of Bologna", and the Elizabethan lyric. For in these two couplets, and in attacking this sonnet, I have let go the fervour and the intensity, which were all I, rather blindly, had to carry through my attempt of twenty years gone.

And I think that if anyone now lay, or if we assume that they mostly then (in the expansive days) laid, aside care for specific statement of emotion, a dogmatic statement, made with the seriousness of someone to whom it mattered whether he had three souls, one in the head, one in the heart, one possibly in his abdomen, or lungs, or wherever Plato, or Galen, had located it; if the anima is still breath, if the stopped heart is a dead heart, and if it is all serious, much more serious than it would have been to Herrick, the imaginary investigator will see more or less how the Elizabethan modes came into being.

Let him try it for himself, on any Tuscan author of that time, taking the words, not thinking greatly of their significance, not baulking at clichés, but being greatly intent on the melody, on the single uninterrupted flow of syllables—as open as possible, that can be sung prettily, that are not very interesting if spoken, that don't even work into a period or an even metre if spoken.

And the mastery, a minor mastery, will lie in keeping this line unbroken, as unbroken in sound as a line in one of Miro's latest drawings is on paper; and giving it perfect balance, with no breaks, no bits sticking ineptly out, and no losses to the force of individual phrases.

> Whereby thou seest how fair thy beauty is
> To compass doom.

Very possible too regularly "iambic" to fit in the finished poem.

There is opposition, not only between what M. de Schloezer distinguishes as musical and poetic lyricism, but in the writing itself there is a distinction between poetic lyricism, the emotional force of the verbal movement, and the melopœic lyricism, the letting the words flow on a melodic current, realized or not, realizable or not, if the line is supposed to be sung on a sequence of notes of different pitch.

But by taking these Italian sonnets, which are not metrically the equivalent of the English sonnet, by sacrificing, or losing, or simply not feeling and understanding their cogency, their sobriety, and by seeking simply that far from quickly or so-easily-as-it-looks attainable thing, the perfect melody, careless of exactitude of idea, or careless as to which profound and fundamental idea you, at that moment, utter, perhaps in precise enough phrases, by cutting away the apparently non-functioning phrases (whose appearance deceives) you find yourself in the English *seicento* song-books.

Death has become melodious; sorrow is as serious as the nightingale's, tombstones are shelves for the reception of rose-leaves. And there is, quite often, a Mozartian perfection of melody, a wisdom, almost perhaps an ultimate wisdom, deplorably lacking in guts. My phrase is, shall we say, vulgar. Exactly, because it fails in precision. Guts in surgery refers to a very limited range of internal furnishings. A 13th-century exactitude in search for the exact organ best illustrating the lack, would have saved me that plunge. We must turn again to the Latins. When the late T. Roosevelt was interviewed in France on his return from the jungle, he used a phrase which was translated (the publication of the interview rather annoyed him). The French at the point I mention ran: "Ils ont voulu me briser les reins mais je les ai solides."

And now the reader may, if he likes, return to the problem of the "eyes that lead the heart to battle where him love kills". This was not felt as an inversion. It was 1280. Italian was still in the state that German is to-day. How can you have "PROSE" in a country where the chambermaid comes into your room and exclaims: "Schön ist das Hemd!"

Continue: who is armed with thy delight, is come forth so that at the first assault he assails, he passes inward to the mind, and lords it there, and catches the breath (soul) that was fleeing, lamenting the grief I feel.

"Whereby thou seest how thy beauty moves the madness, whence is the heart dead (stopped) and I must cry on Pity, not to be saved but to have ease of the cruel death thou puttest on me. And I am right (?) save the wrong him conquereth."

When the reader will accept this little problem in melopœia as substitute for the cross-

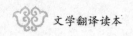

word puzzle I am unable to predict. I leave it on the supposition that the philosopher should try almost everything once.

As second exercise, we may try the sonnet by Guido Orlando which is supposed to have invited Cavalcanti's *Donna mi Prega*.

> Say what is Love, whence doth he start
> Through what be his courses bent
> Memory, substance, accident
> A chance of eye or will of heart
>
> Whence he state or madness leadeth
> Burns he with consuming pain
> Tell me, friend, on what he feedeth
> How, where, and o'er whom doth he reign
>
> Say what is Love, hath he a face
> True form or vain similitude
> Is the Love life, or is he death
>
> Thou shouldst know for rumour saith:
> Servant should know his master's mood—
> Oft art thou ta'en in his dwelling-place.

I give the Italian to show that there is no deception, I have invented nothing, I have given a verbal weight about equal to that of the original, and arrived at this equality by dropping a couple of syllables per line. The great past-master of pastiche has, it would seem, passed this way before me. A line or two of this, a few more from Lorenzo Medici, and he has concocted one of the finest gems in our language.

> Onde si move e donde nasce Amore
> qual è suo proprio luogo, ov' ei dimora
> Sustanza, o accidente, o ei memora?
> E cagion d' occhi, o è voler di cuore?
>
> Da che procède suo stato o furore?
> Come fuoco si sente che divora?
> Di che si nutre domand' io ancora,
> Come, e quando, e di cui si fa signore?
>
> Che cosa è, dico, amor? ae figura?
> A per se forma o pur somiglia altrui?

E vita questo am ore ovvero e morte?

Ch'l serve dee saver di sua natura:
Io ne domando voi, Guido, di lui:
Odo che molto usate in la sua corte.

We are not in a realm of proofs, I suggest, simply, the way in which early Italian poetry has been utilized in England. The Italian of Petrarch and his successors are of no interest to the practising writer or to the student of comparative dynamics in language, the collectors of bric-à-brac are outside our domain.

There is no question of giving Guido in an English contemporary to himself, the ultimate Britons were at that date unbreeched, painted in woad, and grunting in an idiom far more difficult for us to master than the Langue d'Oc of the Plantagenets or the Lingua di Si.

If, however, we reach back to pre-Elizabethan English, or a period when the writers were still intent on clarity and explicitness, still preferring them to magniloquence and the thundering phrase, our trial, or mine at least, results in:

Who is she that comes, makying turn every man's eye
And makying the air to tremble with a bright clearenesse
That leadeth with her Love, in such nearness
No man may proffer of speech more than a sigh?

Ah God, what she is like when her owne eye turneth, is
Fit for Amor to speake, for I cannot at all;
Such is her modesty, I would call
Every woman else but an useless uneasiness.

No one could ever tell all of her pleasauntness
In that every high noble vertu leaneth to herward,
So Beauty sheweth her forth as her Godhede;

Never before so high was our mind led,
Nor have we so much of heal as will afford
That our mind may take her immediate in its embrace.

The objections to such a method are: the doubt as to whether one has the right to take a serious poem and turn it into a mere exercise in quaintness; the "misrepresentation" not of the poem's antiquity, but of the proportionate feel of that antiquity, by which I mean that Guido's 13th-century language is to 20th-century Italian sense much less archaic than any 14th-, 15th-, or early 16th-century English is for us. It is even doubtful whether my bungling version of 20 years back isn't more "faithful", in the sense at least that it tried to

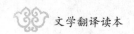

preserve the fervour of the original. And as this fervour simply does not occur in English poetry in those centuries there is no ready-made verbal pigment for its objectification.

In the long run the translator is in all probability impotent to do all of the work for the linguistically lazy reader. He can show where the treasure lies, he can guide the reader in choice of what tongue is to be studied, and he can very materially assist the hurried student who has a smattering of a language and the energy to read the original text alongside the metrical gloze.

This refers to "interpretative translation". The "other sort", I mean in cases where the "translator" is definitely making a new poem, falls simply in the domain of original writing, or if it does not it must be censured according to equal standards, and praised with some sort of just deduction, assessable only in the particular case.

选文四　Transplanting the Seed: Poetry and Translation

Susan Bassnett

导　言

本文选自 Susan Bassnett & André Lefevere, *Constructing Cultures*, Shanghai: Shanghai Foreign Language Education Press, 2001.

在巴斯奈特《种子移植:诗歌与翻译》一文的开头,她批判了诗歌不可译的观点,认为:尽管诗歌不能从一种语言输入到另一种语言,但是却可以移植,就仿佛将种子放在新的土壤里,让一种新的植物长出来,译者的任务就是去决定在什么地方放入那颗种子并着手移植。接着,她指出了怎样移植诗歌的问题,认为诗歌的移植关系到文化的移植,并且依赖于大量其他方面的知识,这些问题都是对同时作为读者和作者的译者的严峻考验。同时,她也赞成一首诗歌是其内容和形式的有机结合体,认为诗歌的内容和形式密不可分。尽管她认为诗歌是可译的,并且也承认诗歌翻译过程中可能会损失某些方面,如玩味性、形式和基调等,但巴斯奈特在文章最后坚信:"诗者,译之非所失也;诗者,恰为译之所得也。"也就是说,诗歌不是在翻译过程中丧失的东西,而是通过译者和翻译所获得的东西。

There are countless book-shelves, probably enough to fill entire libraries, of self-indulgent nonsense on poetry. In comparison with the quantity of poetry actually produced, the amount of redundant commentary must be at least double. A great deal of this literature claims that poetry is something apart, that the poet is possessed of some special essential quality that enables the creation of a superior type of text, the poem. And there is a great deal of non-sense written about poetry and translation too, of which probably the best known is Robert Frost's immensely silly remark that "poetry is what gets lost in translation", which implies that poetry is some intangible, ineffable thing (a presence? a spirit?) which, although constructed *in* language cannot be transposed *across* languages.

A good deal of the fault lies with post-Romanticism, with its vague ideas about poets as beings set apart from other people, divinely inspired and often motivated by a death wish. A comedian on stage has only to fling a black cloak around himself for an audience to cry: Poet! and laugh. This image of the poet as an effete young man (women do not feature in this myth!) of delicate sensibility has further been encouraged in the Anglo-Saxon world by questions of class consciousness, for as English literature established itself in the universities in the early years of this century, so poetry rose up the social scale, away from the masses and towards an intellectual and social elite who took it over and claimed it as their own.

This sorry state of affairs, happily, is by no means universal. Poets have very different functions in different societies, and this is a factor that translators need to bear in mind. In certain countries in Europe, for example, poetry sold in big print-runs (now replaced by western soft-porn and blockbuster crime novels); poets were significant figures, who often spoke out against injustice and oppression. Likewise in Latin America, and in Chile, after Pablo Neruda's death in 1973 people took to the streets, and even illiterate peasants and workers in the barrios could quote from his vast poetic output.

Neruda saw the role of the poet as speaking for those who had no power to speak. The poet, for him, gave a voice to the voiceless. Elsewhere the poet has taken on the role of the conscience of a society, or as its historian. In some cultures, the poet is a shaman, a creator of magic, a healer. In others the poet is a singer of tales, an entertainer and a focal point in the community. If we consider how many times poets have been imprisoned, tortured, even killed, then we have some sense of the power that poets can hold. Queen Elizabeth I, herself a poet and translator, presided over the passing of laws that condemned to death those Irish bards whose role was seen as subversive and treasonable. This brief sketch of the diverse roles of the poet underlines the fact of the different function of poetry in different cultural contexts. This is of great significance for the translator, for such cultural differences may well affect the actual process of translating. Poetry as cultural capital cannot be consistently measured across all cultures equally.

Many writers have struggled to define the difficulties of translating poetry. Shelley famously declared that

> it were as wise to cast a violet into a crucible that you might discover the formal principle of its colour and odour, as to seek to transfuse from one language into another the creations of a poet. The plant must spring again from its seed, or it will bear no flower—and this is the burthen of the curse of Babel. (Shelley, 1820)

This passage is sometimes taken as an example of the impossibility of translation. It is as absurd to consider subjecting a flower to scientific analysis to determine the basis of its scent and colour as it is to try and render a poem written in one language into another. But there is another way to read Shelley's very graphic description of the difficulties of the translation process. The imagery that he uses refers to change and new growth. It is not an imagery of loss and decay. He argues that though a poem cannot be transfused from one language to another, it can nevertheless be transplanted. The seed can be placed in new soil, for a new plant to develop. The task of the translator must then be to determine and locate that seed and to set about its transplantation.

The Brazilian poet and translator, Augusto de Campos, one of the leading proponents of a post-colonial translation practice, rejects the notion that poetry belongs to a particular language or culture. "A poesia, por definição, não tem patria. Ou melhor, tem una patria maior." (Poetry by definition does not have a homeland. Or rather, it has a greater homeland) (De Campos, 1978). And if a text is not the property of any individual culture, then the translator has every right to help in its transfer across linguistic frontiers.

The history of translating and literary transfer would appear to bear out De Campos' proposition. How could we argue, for example, that Homer "belongs" to Greece, since even contemporary Greeks have to learn the Greek in which he wrote as a foreign language. Equally, we might ask whether Shakespeare "belongs" to England? Tolstoy, after all, declared that Shakespeare was primarily German:

> Until the end of the 18th century Shakespeare not only failed to gain any special fame in England, but was valued less than his contemporary dramatists: Ben Jonson, Fletcher, Beaumont and others. His fame originated in Germany, and thence was transferred to England. (Tolstoy, 1906)

The English, Tolstoy argues, failed to recognise the genius of one of their native writers and only learned about him in a roundabout way through the Germans. This is a disconcerting perspective if you are English, but serves to highlight the important role that is played so often by translation. For, as Walter Benjamin points out, translation secures the survival of a text, and it often continues to exist only because it has been translated (Benjamin, 1923).

The translation of Shakespeare across Europe in the late 18th and 19th centuries is a fascinating example of the intricacies of intercultural transfer and reinforces De Campos' point about textual homelands. For the writer who was so extensively translated into so many languages, at a point in time when great revolutionary ideals were sweeping across the continent, and concepts of national identity were being raised more forcefully than ever before was certainly not translated because of his specifically English origins. Shakespeare was not perceived as an emblem of Englishness, but was celebrated for his radical stagecraft, which challenged norms and expectations of good taste, and also for his politically charged subject matter. The Shakespeare who found his way into German, Russian, Polish, Italian, French or Czech was essentially seen as a political writer, whose texts raised crucial issues concerning power structures, the rights of the common people, definitions of good and bad government and the relationship of the individual to the state. A significant writer in the age of revolutions, we might say, though not everyone was of the same opinion. Voltaire, for example, was extremely critical:

> What is frightful is that this monster has support in France; and, at the height of calamity and horror, it was I who in the past first spoke of this Shakespeare; it was I who was the first to point out to Frenchmen the few pearls which were to be found in this enormous dunghill. It never entered my mind that by doing so I would one day assist the effort to trample on the crowns of Racine and Corneille in order to wreathe the brow of this barbaric mountebank. (Voltaire, 1776)

Voltaire was complaining about the revolution in taste and effectively in dramatic poetics that writers such as Shakespeare provoked. And here, of course, we touch on a fundamental question in translation history which has special relevance to the translation of poetry: the impact upon a literary system that translation can have and the power of translated texts to change and innovate. But if poetry is indeed that which is lost in translation, how can such power be possible? The answer must surely lie in the ways in which translated texts have been received by the target system, and that in turn is inextricably linked to time, place and technique. For a translation to have an impact upon the target system, there has to be a gap in that system which reflects a particular need, and the skills of the translator have to be such that the end product is more than merely acceptable.

Frederic Will, a translator who has reflected at length upon the problems of translation, urges us to reconsider the relationship between the translation and the idea of an adamantine original:

> Original texts are not icons. They are symbolically coded patterns of movement: intention, argument, and the expression of both, theme. They are neither hard nor soft, but are basically process. I like to think of them as participial, rather than nounlike or verblike. Works of literature, there to translate, have a character, a nature which is like their substance, their mark of personality; but they can make this substance clear, only by enacting it. That action is their verblike side, needed to reveal the nouns in them. In this sense they, literary originals, are participles. They enact the nouns they are by becoming verbs. They become verbs by enacting the nouns they are. (Will, 1993)

What is trying here to define is the special nature of a text, what he calls its "mark of personality". But he also reminds us helpfully that texts consist of language, they are composed of nouns and verbs and all kinds of lexical and grammatical patterns, and this is the dimension with which a translator needs to be primarily concerned. In order to translate poetry, the first stage is intelligent reading of the source text, a detailed process of decoding that takes into account both textual features and extratextual factors. If, instead of looking closely at a poem and reading it with care, we start to worry about translating the "spirit" of something without any sense of how to define that spirit, we reach an impasse.

It is also often the case that the reading of a poem depends on the dialectic between the constituent elements of that poem on the page and extra-textual knowledge that we bring to it. One of my favourite contemporary poets is the Pakistani-British writer, Moniza Alvi. Her work derives from her experience as a woman belonging to more than one culture, and that hybridity is an essential part of her creativity. She writes from her own experience as a being in-between, a woman with a place in two cultures and consequently perhaps not entirely located in either. Her writing is therefore emblematic of the position occupied by millions in today's world. A theme to which she returns in many poems is that of belonging and not-belonging. One such poem is an eight line unrhymed work, "Arrival 1946" (Alvi, 1993).

The protagonist of the poem is a figure named only as Tariq who reflects on what he sees after he arrives at Liverpool and takes a train down to London. He looks out on "an unbroken line of washing" and tries to square this with what he knows of the British:

> These are strange people, he thought—
> an Empire, and all this washing,
> the underwear, the Englishman's garden.

What Tariq does not know is that it is Monday, the traditional English washing-day. The fact of his not knowing this elementary fact about English life serves to accentuate his foreignness, and hints at difficulties to come. Moreover, the image of washing serves also to emphasize the contrast between what he sees in England and what he has seen of the superior British rulers in India, where presumably their washing was always kept out of sight and done by Indian servants. In this way, the contrast between the imperial ideal and the banal reality of daily life is underlined.

But it is not enough to know that Monday is washing day in order to understand what is going on in this poem. The image of washing reminds us of the old proverb about not washing dirty linen in public. Dirty linen, in this case is both actual and symbolic: the dirty linen of imperialism is symbolised by the linen that English people are hanging out to dry. And in Tariq's naive remark about the Englishman's garden, another set of references emerges. For the great poem of the imperial age, Kipling's *"The Glory of the Garden"*, presents all England as a garden, a magnificent garden surrounding a stately home, and kept in order by ranks of massed and willing gardeners. Concealed in the strata that make up this poem is the idealised English garden of the nineteenth century.

Any translator tackling this poem has a complex task indeed. The semantic items are straightforward, though the tight eight line format enables Alvi to foreground words at the start and end of lines. The last word of the poem is the adjective "sharp" that has a large field of meaning. It is used here to describe a Monday, and presumably refers to the state of the weather, even as it hints at prospects of future pain. The principal problem, though, is not lexical or grammatical or formal: it is the problem of the knowledge required for a reader to be able to grasp the implications of the text, most of which are only hinted at. The geographical data are precise. If the reader does not know that Euston is a station in London, Tariq's journey does not make much sense. The joke about washing provides the basic structure of the narrative. Even the title is significant. Tariq has arrived in England at a moment of in-betweenness. The Second World War ended in 1945; and the independence of India and creation of the state of Pakistan was not to happen until 1947. Tariq is one of the first wave of immigrants in the post-war period. He may be too early, or he may be too late. The problems of how to transplant a poem like this, which has as its basis the idea of cultural displacement and relies upon so much additional knowledge, test the translator both as reader and as writer.

James Holmes, a great translator of poetry across several languages and distinguished scholar of translation, attempted to produce a basic set of categories for verse translation. He lists a series of basic strategies used by translators to render the formal properties of a poem. The first such strategy he calls "mimetic form", for in this case the translator reproduces the form of the original in the target language. This can obviously only happen where there are similar formal conventions already in existence, so that the translator can use a form with which readers are already familiar. However, Holmes points out that since a verse form cannot exist outside language, "it follows that no form can be 'retained' by the translator" and no verse form can ever be completely identical across literary systems (Holmes, 1970). This means, therefore, that an illusion of formal sameness is maintained, while in actuality the target language readers are being simultaneously confronted with something that is both the same and different, i. e. that has a quality of "strangeness". Holmes suggests that this is the case with blank-verse translations of Shakespeare into German, and he argues that

It follows that the mimetic form tends to come to the fore among translators in a period when genre concepts are weak, literary norms are being called into question and the target culture as a whole stands open to outside impulses. (Holmes, 1970)

The second strategy outlined by Holmes involves a formal shift. Employing what he calls "analogical form", he suggests that the translator determines what the function of the original form is and then seeks an equivalent in the target language. The most obvious example of this technique would be the translation of the French alexandrine into English blank verse and vice versa. Both these forms are employed in the classical drama of each of the two languages. Similarly, when E. V. Rieu produced his translation of Homer for Penguin in 1946, he argued in his preface that *The Iliad* should be seen as a tragedy and *The*

Odyssey as a novel. Transforming his argument into practice, he then proceeded to render *The Odyssey* as a novel, in prose rather than in verse.

The third strategy is defined as "content-derivative", or "organic form". In this process, the translator starts with the semantic material of the source text and allows it to shape itself. This is basically Ezra Pound's strategy when translating Chinese poetry, and has come to be a dominant strategy in the 20th century, fuelled also by the development of free verse—In this kind of translation, the form is seen as distinct from the content, rather than as an integral whole.

Holmes' fourth category is described as "deviant or extraneous form". In this type of translation, the translator utilises a new form that is not signalled in any way in the source text, either in form or content. It might be possible to argue that Pound does this in parts of his Cantos, but on the whole it is more helpful to conflate Holmes' idea of the "organic" and the "extraneous" into a single strategy and use the term "organic" for both, De Campos' translation of William Blake's *"The Sick Rose"* into a concrete poem, with the words in Portuguese shaped across a page to form petals of a flower, into the heart of which the text eventually disappears could be arguably "organic" or "extraneous" if we continue to use Holmes' terms. But such a distinction is pointless: what we can say is that De Campos' translation reflects a reading of Blake that demonstrates his sensitivity to the text and his desire to experiment in terms that would not have been accessible to Blake two centuries earlier.

Holmes suggests that the organic strategy has been most favoured in the 20th century. However, it traces its ancestry clearly back to Shelley, whose use of organic imagery to describe the translation process has been referred to above. The idea of translation as an organic process is also clearly present in the thinking of Ezra Pound, who, like so many poets and translation theorists before and after, was concerned to try and categorise what happens when a poem is rendered from one language into another.

Pound stresses the importance of the target language for translators. Discussing medieval poetry, for example, he remarks

> The devil of translating medieval poetry into English is that it is very hard to decide HOW you are to render work done with one set of criteria into a language NOW subject to different criteria. Translate the church of St. Hilaire of Poitiers into barocco? You can't, as anyone knows, translate it into English of the period. The Plantagenet Kings' Provençal was Langue d'Oc. (Pound, 1934)

Pound is being ironic here, for as he and everyone knew, a great deal of medieval poetry had indeed been translated in the 19th century into a mock medieval English, a kind of translation that was intended to signal a quality of antiquity about the source text. Pound's point is that this is absurd: the end product is unreadable, because it is written in a language that has no vitality, because it is completely fictitious.

Pound was concerned primarily with the translation of texts from earlier periods or from non-Western cultures, hence his emphasis is less on the problems of translating formal properties of verse, for he recognised that forms are by no means equivalent across literatures. What he insists upon, though, is that the translator should first and foremost be a reader. Through his many notes and comments on translation, there is a consistent line of thought, which attributes to the translator a dual responsibility. The translator needs to read well, to be aware of what the source text is, to understand both its formal properties and its literary dynamic as well as its status in the source system, and then has to take into account the role that text may have in the target system. Time and again Pound reminds us that a translation should be a work of art in its own right, for anything less is pointless.

He also makes another kind of distinction in his thinking about the translation of poetry and endeavours to define elements that are more or less translatable. There are, he suggests, three kinds of poetry that may be found in any literature. The first of these, is *melopoeia* where words are surcharged with musical property that directs the shape of the meaning. This musical quality can be appreciated by "the foreigner with the sensitive ear", but cannot be translated, "except perhaps by divine accident or even half a line at a time" (Pound, 1928).

The second, *phanopoeia*, he regards as the easiest to translate, for this involves the creation of images in language. The image was, of course, central to Pound's poetics, as his deliberate choice of the highly imagistic Japanese and Chinese verse forms as models demonstrates.

His third category, *logopoeia*, "the dance of the intellect among words" is deemed to be untranslatable, though it may be paraphrased. However, Pound suggests that the way to proceed is to determine the author's state of mind and start from there. We have come back again to Shelley and to the notion of transplanting the seed.

Time and again, translation scholars struggle with the problem of the inter-relationship between the formal structure of the poem, its function in the source language context and the possibilities offered by the target language, Robert Bly talks about eight stages of translation (Bly, 1984). André Lefevere in his book on translating the poetry of Catullus talks about seven strategies and a blueprint (Lefevere, 1975). The missing element in so much writing about poetry and translation is the idea of the ludic, of *jouissance*, or playfulness. For the pleasure of poetry is that it can be seen as both an intellectual and an emotional exercise for writer and reader alike. The poem, like the sacred text, is open to a great range of interpretative readings that involve a sense of play. If a translator treats a text as a fixed, solid object that has to be systematically decoded in the "correct" manner, that sense of play is lost.

A sign that informs us to "Keep off the grass" is issuing an instruction. It is a four-word text with a precise function, and if we were to translate it, we would be translating its functionality, not necessarily its semantic components. But what do we do with a four-word

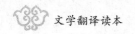

text that is included in the works of the great Italian poet, Giuseppe Ungaretti:

> M'illumino
>
> D'immenso

We could start by taking a dictionary, and discovering that the first line consists of a reflexive verb, *illuminarsi*, that can be rendered in English as to illuminate oneself/to light up oneself/to enlighten oneself. The second line consists of the preposition "*di*" meaning "of/with/from" and an adjective, "immenso", meaning "immense/huge/boundless", which is curious because we might expect the noun *immensita* here instead. So a rough version might be "I am illuminated with the immense". Or, "I am immensely illuminated", or "I am enlightened by immensity". We should pause here, because it is becoming obvious that this four line poem, hailed as a great work in Italian, is dreadful in English. The translations veer between the banal and the pretentious. This would seem to be a classic case of Pound's logopoeia, of a text that is so embedded in the literary and philosophical traditions of its writer that it is not accessible to readers from another culture, despite apparent lack of semantic difficulties. To an Italian reader, the idea of *illuminare* and of *l'immensita* trigger whole fields of referents. These words are embedded into the cultural system. They cannot be translated literally, even though literal meanings exist. The only way for a translator to approach a text like this is to follow Shelley's organic principles, and endeavour to understand and absorb the text to such a degree within one's own system that a new plant can begin to grow. Yves Bonnefoy echoes this, when he says that we should try to see what motivates the poem in the first place, "to relive the act which both gave rise to it and remains enmeshed in it" (Bonnefoy, 1989).

In his lucid essay on translating poetry, Octavio Paz makes a vital distinction between the task of the poet and the task of the translator:

> The poet, immersed in the movement of language, in constant verbal preoccupation, chooses a few words—or is chosen by them. As he combines them, he constructs his poem: a verbal object made of irreplaceable and immovable characters. The translator's starting point is not the language in movement that provides the poet's raw material, but the fixed language of the poem. A language congealed, yet living. His procedure is the inverse of the poet's: he is not constructing an unalterable text from mobile characters; instead he is dismantling the elements of the text, freeing the signs into circulation, then returning them to language. (Paz, 1971)

The poet plays with language and comes to create a poem by fixing language in such a way that it cannot be altered. But the translator has a completely different task, that involves a different kind of play. The translator starts with the language that the poet has fixed, and then has to set about dismantling it and reassembling the parts in another language altogether. Paz argues that this process of freeing the signs into circulation parallels the original creative process invertedly. The task of the translator is to compose an analogous text in another language, and the translator is therefore not firstly a writer and then a reader, but firstly a reader who becomes a writer. What happens, says Paz, is that the original poem comes to exist inside another poem: "less a copy than a transmutation."

This is a very helpful way of looking at the translation process, a very liberating way. It is, in terms of theory, related to Walter Benjamin's idea of the translation providing the life-hereafter of a text, enabling it to survive and sometimes even resurrecting it. It is a liberationist view of translating, because it never enters into the vexed question of whether a translation is or is not an inferior copy of an original. The task of the translator is simply a different kind of writerly task, and it follows on from the primary task of reading.

A translator to whom I have returned frequently over the years is Sir Thomas Wyatt, one of the poets credited with introducing the sonnet into English in the early sixteenth century. I keep coming back to *Wyatt*, because although he never formulated any views on translation, or at least if he did none have come down to us, his translation practice stands out even in an age of extensive translation activity. R. A. Rebholtz, who edited the complete edition of Wyatt's poetry in 1978, was uncomfortable with Wyatt's translations, describing them variously as translations of Petrarch, free imitations and even very free imitations (Rebholz, 1978). His discomfort probably arises from the fact that if we set Wyatt's translations of Petrarch alongside the originals, we come face to face with an example of Paz' liberationist translation practice. Wyatt takes Petrarch as his starting point and frees the signs into circulation for a completely different readership, in another language and another age.

Petrarch's *"Una Candida cerva sopra l'erba"* (Rime, 190) in Wyatt's version becomes a completely new poem, with a different focus and altered tone. The Italian text reads as follows:

> Una Candida cerva sopra l'erba
> verde m'apparve, con duo coma d'oro,
> fra due riviere, all'ombra d'un *alloro*,
> levando'l sole, a la stagione acerba.
> Era sua vista si dolce superba,
> Ch'i lasciai per seguirla ogni lavoro,
> come l'avaro, ch'n cercar tesoro,
> con diletto l'affanno disacerba,
> "Nessun mi tocchi—al bel collo d'intomo
> scritto avea di diamanti e di topazi—
> libera farmi al mio cesare parve",
> Et era'l sol gia volto al mezzo giomo;
> gli occhi miei stanchi di mirar non sazi,
> quand'io caddi ne l'acqua, et ella sparve.

This is a poem full of classic Petrarchan imagery. It is structured in terms of two basic units, eight lines with an ABBA rhyme pattern that repeats, and six lines with a repeating ODE pattern. There is a reference to his beloved Laura, through the image of the laurel tree (*alloro*) and the setting of the poem is the landscape of the courtly love-lyric: green meadows in springtime, running water, early morning that gradually moves into mid-day, a metaphor for the passing of a life time. The lover is represented as passive—the white deer appears to him, he leaves everything he has been doing to gaze upon her, he is still gazing enraptured when he falls into the water and she vanishes.

Two elements are distinctive to this poem, however, the image in lines 7 – 8 of the miser, who enjoys collecting treasure so much that he ceases to be aware of the effort it costs him, and the details in lines 9 – 11 of the collar round the deer's neck. "Let no one touch me," reads the message in diamonds and topaz, "it is for my Caesar to set me free."

Wyatt's version is a transplanting of Petrarch's:

> Who so list to hounte I know where is an hynde;
> But as for me, helas, I may no more:
> The vayne travaill hath weried me so sore,
> I am of them that farthest cometh behinde;
> Yet may I by no meanes my weried mynde
> Drawe from the Diere: but as she fleeth afore
> Faynting I folowe; I leve of therefore,
> Sithens in a nett I seke to hold the wynde.
> Who list her hount I put him out of dowte,
> As well as 1 may spend his tyme in vain:
> And graven with Diamonds in letters plain
> There is written her faier neck rounde abowte:
> "Noli me tangere for Caesar's I ame,
> And wylde for to hold though I seme tame."

There are several striking differences between the two poems. Firstly and most obviously, Wyatt has altered the form of the sonnet to a rhyme scheme that runs ABBA ABBA, CDDC, EE. This has the effect of breaking the sonnet into three parts rather than two: there is an eight line unit, followed by a distinctive four line unit and then the poem culminates in the final couplet. This is the form that would later be taken up by Sidney, Spenser and Shakespeare, because what the final couplet offers a writer is a tremendous potential for ironic reversal. Whereas the Petrarchan sonnet is a more graceful, more integrated form in which the component parts of the rhyme scheme hold together more concisely, the English version foregrounds the last two lines and gives them infinite possibility. The sonnet, once a vehicle for courtly pronouncements of love or mystical expressions of the poet's relationship with the divine, has had its function extended, by the simple device of altering the pattern of foregrounding constructed by the rhyme scheme.

Wyatt makes other changes too. English, unlike Italian, demands the use of a pronoun with a verb, but even allowing for this grammatical factor, Wyatt's poem is full of self-referential "I"s and "me"s. The capitalising of the "I" in English, as Southey famously noted, tends to stress the importance of the speaking subject. In a short poem such as this, the "I" is foregrounded almost to excess. Where Petrarch's sonnet opens with a vision of the white deer that appears to the speaker, Wyatt's opens with a blunt piece of man to man advice to fellow huntsmen. Petrarch's deer may or may not be visionary; Wyatt's is made of flesh and blood. His pursuit of the deer has exhausted him, and the speaker complains about the effort that he has wasted in the attempt. The tone of the Petrarch sonnet is one of tranquillity, but the tone of the Wyatt poem is one of agitation and even anger.

The image of the miser cherishing his hoard is not present in the English, but significantly there is an image in exactly the same position, in lines 9 – 10. Wyatt's image continues the motif of tiredness and frustration, through the idea of a man trying to catch the wind in a net.

The most significant shifts occur in the last six lines. Wyatt's deer is wearing a jewelled collar too, but its message is different. Petrarch's deer is said to belong to Caesar who has the power to grant her freedom. There is no reference to freedom in Wyatt's poem, and his deer wears a collar with a Latin inscription and a warning about her savagery despite her apparent docility.

We can begin to understand what has happened in the translation process when we consider the contexts within which these two writers created their very similar, yet very different texts. Petrarch's poem was part of his sequence of poems that deals with his unrequited love for Laura and his endeavours, through that love, to become closer to God. His use of the term Caesar recalls the Biblical reference to the division of the earthly and heavenly kingdoms. But Wyatt lived in another age, the age of Renaissance Humanism, of Machiavelli and the new courts, the age when men began to challenge not so much the existence of God but the idea of their abjectness before God. The speaker in Wyatt's poem is not having a mystical vision of any kind, he is engaged in the fruitless pursuit of a woman who belongs to someone else and who appears to have been leading him on. His is the voice of a cynical, disconsolate lover, who is giving up the chase in despair. That this poem is *a clef*, and actually refers to Wyatt's love for Queen Ann Boleyn, wife of Henry VIII in whose service Wyatt was employed, adds an additional dimension to the reading.

Is Wyatt's poem a translation of Petrarch? Of course it is. It is a translation that enables us to see how cleverly the translator has read and reworked the source text to create something new and vital. He has kept the form of the original, thereby introducing a new poetic form into the target system, which bears out James Holmes' contention that mimetic form can indeed have an innovatory function at key moments in literary history. However, he has subtly altered that form, creating new possibilities for it in the target language. He has maintained the image of the beloved as a white deer, but has changed the relationship between the lady and the lover. The perspective is different, and as a result the tone is different, though in keeping with the age in which he lived and wrote. Paraphrasing Bonnefoy, we can say that the energy generated by the source text has been sufficiently great for the translator to follow it and in consequence create something great of his own.

We may, at this juncture, make two assertions: firstly, that the translation of poetry requires skill in reading every bit as much as skill in writing. Secondly, that a poem is a text in which content and form are inseparable. Because they are inseparable, it ill behoves any translator to try and argue that one or other is less significant. What a translator has to do is recognise his or her limitations and to work within those constraints. James Holmes suggests, helpfully, that every translator establishes a hierarchy of constituent elements during the reading process and then re-encodes those elements in a different ranking in the target language. If we compare translation and source, then the ranking of elements becomes visible. Holmes describes this process as a "hierarchy of correspondences" (Holmes, 1978).

One of the most useful critical methods for approaching translation is the tried and trusted comparative one. When we compare different translations of the same poem, we can see the diversity of translation strategies used by translators, and locate those strategies in a cultural context, by examining the relationship between aesthetic norms in the target system and the texts produced. Crucially, the comparative method should not be used to place the translations in some kind of league table, rating x higher than y, but rather to understand what went on in the actual translation process.

Probably the most famous canto in Dante's *Inferno* is Canto V, when Dante meets the doomed lovers, Paolo and Francesca da Rimini in the second circle of hell, where the lustful are punished. The story of their illicit passion and of their murder by Francesca's husband, Paolo's brother, is related by Francesca herself, as she and Paolo are dragged past the horrified poet by an infernal black wind. The story of their love and brutal death so moves the poet, that he faints, an action that will have significance throughout his journey, since the fainting always coincides with moments when his own emotions overflow.

The high moment of Francesca's narrative is virtually a poem-within-a-poem:

> Amor, ch'al cor gentil ratto s'apprende,
> prese costui de la bella persona
> che mi fu tolta, e'l modo ancor m'offende.
> Amor, ch'a nullo amato amar perdona,
> mi prese del costui piacer si forte
> che, come vedi, ancor non m'abbandona.
> Amor condusse noi ad una morte.
> Caina attende chi a vita ci spense'.
> Queste parole da lor ci fuor porte. (11. 100 – 108)

Here Francesca summarizes their story: she was overcome by love for "la bella persona", whom she never names, and is still resentful of the manner of their death. The power of their love was so great that they are bound together in death for eternity, and their murderer will be allocated a place in the depths of hell after his death, that is yet to come.

For a 13th-century reader, one of the most obvious features of these lines is the direct reference to the famous poem by Guido Guinizelli, one of the founding members of the *dolce stil nuovo*, "Al cor gentil rempara sempre amore", Dante greatly admired Guinizelli, but here the implications are clear: illicit love leads downwards to hell, and Paolo and Francesca admit that their passion was kindled by reading a book of love poetry together. Through the deliberate references to the love poetry that he so admired and sought to produce himself, Dante is making a serious point about the need to put morality above aesthetics. Not only do readers have a moral responsibility, so also do writers. Dante as writer is therefore implicated in the downfall of these two lovers, and his pain on hearing their story is exacerbated by this awareness. A 13th-century reader would have had no problem understanding the point that is being made through the conscious references to the *dolce stil nuovo*. The anaphora of amor at the start of each three line unit signals the importance of the formal structure of this passage, making it stand out from the rest of the canto.

Translators have wrestled in various ways with these lines. Of the dozens of English translations, I have selected a sample, starting with Cary, author of the first complete translation of the *Divine Comedy*, through to Robert Durling (1996) whose new version of the *Inferno* has recently appeared. Cary (1814), who does not use rhyme, adopts a pseudo-medieval English, in keeping with early 19th century convention. Longfellow's 1867 version does likewise. Interestingly, Byron chose to translate Francesca's narrative, taking it out of the context of the rest of the canto, Charles Eliot Morton, in 1941, turns the whole work into prose, but keeps the medievalised language. Dorothy Sayers' Penguin translation of 1949 is also written in mock medieval English, but she does use rhyme throughout. More recently, Sisson (1980) and Durling (1996) have produced unrhymed versions in modern English.

Let us consider these different versions of the first six lines of this passage:

> Love, that in gentle heart is quickly learnt
> Entangled him by that fair form, from me
> Ta'en in such cruel sort, as grieves me still:
> Love, that denial takes from none beloved,
> Caught me with pleasing him so passing well,
> That, as thou seest, he yet deserts me not. (Cary: 1816)

> Love, which the gentle heart soon apprehends,
> Seized him for the fair person which was ta'en
> From me, and even yet the mode offends.

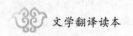

Love, who to none beloved to love again
Remits, seized me with wish to please so strong.
That, as thou seest, yet, yet it doth remain. (Byron: 1820)

Love, that on gentle heart doth swiftly seize,
Seized this man for the person beautiful
That was ta'en from me, and still the mode offends me.
Love, that exempts no one beloved from loving,
Seized me with pleasure of this man so strongly,
That, as thou seest, it doth not yet desert me. (Longfellow: 1867)

Love, which quickly lays hold on gentle heart, seized
this one for the fair person that was taken from me, and the
mode still hurts me. Love, which absolves no loved one
from loving, seized me for the pleasing of him so strongly
that, as thou seest, it does not even now abandon me. (Norton, 1941)

Love, that so soon takes hold in the gentle breast,
Took this lad with the lovely body they tore
From me; the way of it leaves me stil distrest.
Love, that to no loved heart remits love's score,
Took me with such great joy of him, that see!
It holds me yet and never shall leave me more. (Sayers, 1949)

Love, which quickly fastens on gentle hearts,
Seized that wretch, and it was for the personal beauty
Which was taken from me; how it happened still offends me.
Love, which allows no one who is loved to escape,
Seized me so strongly with my pleasure in him.
That, as you see, it does not leave me now. (Sisson, 1980)

Love, which is swiftly kindled in the noble heart,
seized this one for the lovely person that was taken
from me; and the manner still injures me.
Love, which pardons no one loved from loving in
return, seized me for his beauty so strongly that, as
you see, it still does not abandon me. (Durling, 1996)

All the translators, regardless of the form they have employed, maintain the anaphora.
But beyond this, what is most apparent are the differences between the versions, and the

incomprehensibility of parts of most of them. What happens in the Italian is that Francesca's narrative changes focus several times: she begins with a statement about love and the "cor gentil", moves to describe how love overcame Paolo, then immediately shifts back to her own feelings, in the here and now. She is, she tells Dante, unable to forget the circumstances of her death, and this signals to the reader that she has not repented and is therefore justifiably condemned to hell. The foregrounding of "m'offende" at the end of line 3, contrasts with "perdona" at the end of line 4. Francesca is here, not because her husband did not pardon her, but because she has not been able to pardon him. The second three line unit opens again with a statement about love, though this time the negative emphasizes love's cruel tyranny, then moves to describe the unending power of love over her. Her desire for Paolo endures even after death, though Cary offers a version of the line that makes Paolo, rather than "piacer" the subject.

Space does not permit detailed examination of these translations, but if we return to Paz' image of the translator liberating the fixed signs set down by the original writer, and connect that to Shelley and Pound insisting upon the importance of the reading process that precedes the rewriting, then it becomes apparent that all the translators are in their different ways unable to break free of their source and appear uncertain about their readers. The prose versions are, if anything, the most obscure. Norton, Sisson and Durling all endeavour to simplify Dante and clarify the ambiguities in his writing, but their syntax, which reflects an attempt to follow the Italian, renders the meaning unclear. Longfellow is obsessed with the verb "to seize", Byron appears to have put all his energy into lines 1 and 4 and left the rest to chance, Sayers uses colloquial language, turning the idealised medieval lover into "the lad with the lovely body". The translators appear caught between producing a close rendering of the source text and explicating that source for their readers. There is no sense of playfulness in any of them.

The problem they share here, of course, is that these lines are deliberately written in a particular style and are consciously ambiguous in their structure. It is not only the character of Francesca that emerges from these lines, it is also an autobiographically framed moral statement about the role of the writer. This aspect of the text has disappeared. In the 19th and 20th centuries, the courtly love ideal and the medieval notion of sin and repentance have ceased to have meaning, except as intellectual curiosities. Dante's poem has become just such an intellectual curiosity itself. Editors and translators supply readers with detailed footnotes to enable them to access the text. The status of the work demands that it should be read and translated; Pound would argue that somewhere along the way, the idea of the *Divine Comedy* as a poem has evaporated.

Bonnefoy suggests that a work has to be compelling, or it is not translatable. Pound would certainly have agreed with this. For if translation is, as Lefevere others claim, rewriting, then the relationship between writer and rewriter has to be established as productive. Translations of poems are part of a process of reading continuity. Writers create for readers, and the power of the reader to remake the text is fundamental. Different readers will produce different readings, different translators will always produce different translations. What matters in the translation of poetry is that the translator should be so drawn into the poem that he or she then seeks to transpose it creatively through the pleasure generated by the reading. If we follow Bonnefoy's view, he would point out that none of the translators of Dante appear to have relived the act that gave rise to it and remains enmeshed in it; rather, they appear to have taken the source as a monolithic whole and chipped away at it. Justifying his own approach to translation, Bonnefoy talks about releasing a creative energy that can then be utilised by the translator.

The positive imagery of translation as energy-releasing, as freeing the linguistic sign into circulation, as transplanting, as reflowering in an enabling language is a long way removed from the negativity of Frost and the pundits of untranslatability. A great deal of this imagery has been around a long time, but it is only recently, as post-modernists reject the idea of the monolithic text that a discourse of translation as liberating has come to the fore. The boundaries between source and target texts, never clearly determined in any genre, cannot be sustained if a poem is to have an existence as a poem in another language. Perhaps the most succinct comment on the symbiosis between writer and translator/rewriter of a poem are these lines by the Earl of Roscommon, Dillon Wentworth, composed more than three hundred years ago:

> Then seek a Poet who your way does bend,
> And choose an Author as you choose a Friend:
> United by this sympathetic Bond,
> You grow familiar, intimate and fond;
> Your Thoughts, your Words, your Styles, your Souls agree
> No Longer his Interpreter, but he.

When the rewriter is perfectly fused with the source, a poem is translated. That this happens so frequently is a cause for celebration. Poetry is not what is lost in translation, it is rather what we gain through translation and translators.

【翻译鉴赏】

以英国诗人罗塞蒂的《闪光》为例探讨英诗汉译技巧

探讨诗歌翻译技巧最好的办法就是从一首诗的具体翻译过程来讨论具体的技巧。翻译标准多元互补论意味着一般翻译技巧的多样性,也意味着诗歌翻译技巧的多样性。下面我以英国著名诗人罗塞蒂的《闪光》一诗为例来具体探讨英诗汉译的若干技巧。

罗塞蒂原诗:

Sudden Light[1]

Dante Gabriel Rossetti (1828—1882)

I have been here before,

But when or how I cannot tell：[2]

I know the grass beyond the door，

The sweet keen smell．

The sighing sound，[3] the lights around the shore.

You have been mine before——

How long ago I may not know：[4]

But just when at that swallow's soar

Your neck turned so，[5]

Some veil did fall，I knew it all of yore. [6]

Has this been thus before?

And shall not thus time's eddying flight[7]

Still with our lives our loves restore[8]

In death despite，[9]

And day and night yield one delight once more?[10]

[1] sudden light：突发的光。此处应结合第 10 行 Some veil did fall 来理解。"某种纱巾"表面上指诗人爱人所戴的纱巾，但也可以理解为是指掩蔽事物真相的纱巾。一旦纱巾脱落，真相大白，诗人便获得一种刹那间的电光火石般的感悟，或者叫做顿悟。sudden light 寓意在此。罗塞蒂的诗歌充满神秘性，因此，这种突发的感悟虽然和禅宗的顿悟不是一回事，却有相通处：一个极小的或平常的行为、言词等可以如导火线般触发人心灵深处的东西，使人的灵魂升华到一种具有震撼效应的感悟状态。

[2] But when or how I cannot tell：倒装句。应为：But I cannot tell when and how (I have been here). 诗人使用倒装形式，有时是为了强化某种特殊的语势或艺术效果，有时则只是为了谐韵或取得更好的节奏效果等。

[3] the sighing sound：叹息声，此处指隐约的海涛声。

[4] How long ago I may not know：倒装句，作用类似注 2。

[5] But just when at that swallow's soar / Your neck turned so：But just when your neck turned at the swallow's soar：但是，正当燕子凌空飞翔而你扭头观望的时候。

[6] Some veil did fall，I knew it all of yore：some veil 指某种纱巾，某种遮蔽性的帷幕，某种假象。yore：(书面语)往昔，很久以前。此句可联系上一行末尾的 so 来理解：so... I knew it all of yore. 所以从前的这些事我原本都知道。

[7] And shall not thus time's eddying flight：shall not 的用法有"禁止"的意思，此处用做反意疑问句，使语势大大增强；time's eddying flight，指时间的飞旋，转意为"时间的轮回"，与 the wheel of fortune（命运的转轮）有异曲同工之处，eddying 意为"旋转的，有旋涡的"。

[8] with our lives our loves restore：restore our loves with our lives. 恢复我们的爱与生活。

[9] in death's despite：in spite of death. 不顾、不怕死亡或死神。

[10] yield one delight once more? （时间的飞轮何以不能）再度（让我们）感到一场欢欣呢？注

意此句的主语还是 time's eddying flight。

参考译文：

闪 光

(英)但丁·迦百利·罗塞蒂

辜正坤译

译文一：词曲风味体(步原诗多元韵式)

曾留遗踪于此，

但忘了何年何月何因。

还记得门前芳草如旧时，

无言暗送香轻。

潮卷吹息,岸畔灯火低迷。

曾赢得你芳心属意，

悠悠岁月,何处淹留。

猛可里见飞燕惊起，

你流盼回眸,

纱巾飘落,——唉,当年旧事堪提!

莫非前事直如此?

莫非荏苒光阴不再轮回

令我们恩爱如往昔，

休道无常相催，

只不分昼夜,再度鱼水乐如斯?

译文二：词曲风味体(用中诗一元韵式)

似曾浪迹此邦，

何故何年费思量，

但记得门前芳草，

犹吐旧时香。

涛声,惆怅,岸畔灯火迷茫。

似曾长驻你心上，

苦忘却日久天长。

蓦然,有飞燕凌空，

你顾盼回望，

纱巾落,——唉,往事翻然在心房!

当时情景非真相?

凭谁问:轮回,流光，

唤不醒离魂,鸳梦难温旧时帐?

管它生死，

分啥昼夜，或再度春情喜欲狂？

译文三：文白相间体（步原诗多元韵式）

　　我曾在这里留停，

　　却忘了何时、何故留踪：

　　还记得门前草儿青青，

　　乱把微香吹送，

　　沿岸的灯火，叹息的涛声。

　　你曾长属于我——

　　只忘了是什么时候：

　　但随着燕子掠空飞过，

　　你惊起回头，

　　纱巾旁落！——往事翩然又回到心窝。

　　难道这一切就是如此？

　　难道时光的飞轮

　　不会让你我的爱与生活重新比翼，

　　穿过死亡之门，

　　引我们不分昼夜，再享欢乐无羁？

译文四：全白话文体（自由韵式）

　　我从前曾来过这里，——

　　但却忘了是什么时候，是什么情形，

　　我熟悉这门外的草儿青青，

　　有香气四溢，

　　岸边叹息伴着灯火微明。

　　你曾是属于我的——

　　虽然究竟是多少年前，我已记不清，

　　但当燕子飞掠长空，

　　你回首盼顾，

　　抖落了纱巾！——忽记起这一切我原本知情。

　　难道这一切本就只能如此？

　　难道这时光的飞旋之轮，

　　不能使你我的爱情与生活枯木逢春，

　　逃避了死亡，

　　让我们白天黑夜地重享一次欢欣？

【背景介绍】

英国诗人但丁·迦百利·罗塞蒂(1828—1882),先以画名,后以诗名影响了19世纪末的艺坛与诗坛。在艺术上,他是英国前拉菲尔派的创始人,曾以崇拜爱和美著称于世。其代表作有《妹妹的睡眠》、《升天少女》、《修女海伦》、《生命之宫》以及《罗塞蒂诗集》等。

罗塞蒂的诗歌创作具有三大特色。其一,极度地崇尚美和爱,因此,他的诗往往标榜唯美主义,在微妙的肉欲体验方面,招致了传统英国评论家的批评;其二,具有宗教神秘色彩,这使他的诗免于过分的直露,往往有一点迷幻朦胧的官能美象征,同时也有一种哲理性暗示;其三,他的诗画意特别浓,这可能与他本来就是画家有关。他习惯于以画意入诗。故他的诗颇强调声、色、光、影的梦幻性叠加效果。他甚至认为,诗的表现应该高于诗的思想。就一个19世纪的诗人而言,他的这种观念已经大大地超前了,实际上20世纪的许多西方文学理论家们都宣扬过这一思想。

这里所选的《闪光》一诗,是他的爱情和悼亡诗集《生命之宫》中的一首。要读懂这首诗,须得稍稍了解一下罗塞蒂个人情感生活方面的一些遭遇。

1850年,22岁的罗塞蒂爱上了能诗善画的姑娘伊丽莎白·西德尔。西德尔刚好属于那种神秘而又带梦幻气质的姑娘,具有一种和罗塞蒂追求的诗画效果相契合的特质。可以想见,这样一位画家兼诗人和这样一位理想女神般的恋人之间的结合无疑当得珠联璧合之称。然而他们的婚姻却因为经济拮据等原因而耽延了10年。这10年内,西德尔无疑是罗塞蒂艺术创作最理想的灵感与模特儿。然而结婚后的罗塞蒂却遇到了更大的不幸。一年之后,西德尔溘然去世。罗塞蒂悲愤欲狂,决意以自己的全部诗稿为妻子殉葬。又过了7年,由于友人的极力劝说,罗塞蒂才同意从坟墓中掘出诗稿,以《罗塞蒂诗集》为名出版。诗集一出版就震动了英国文坛,但同时招致猛烈的批评。

《闪光》是作者晚期诗集《生命之宫》中的一首。深深地弥漫着诗人早期爱情生活不幸的气氛。从中我们仍可感悟到诗人那种如痴如醉的对爱的执著精神。诗篇一开始就以一种梦幻式的不确定感,对青草、门廊、涛声、灯火进行了叙述,使人感到一种梦幻效果,产生瞻之在前,忽焉在后的感觉。在第二节诗中,通过"惊燕"、"回首"、"纱巾落"三个相对明晰的意象,给了读者一个焦点镜头。正如在朦胧中忽然闪进一道灼眼的光芒(sudden light),使诗歌进入高潮,一种电流般的如梦初醒的感觉攫住了诗人。然而这种感觉又很快消失。一种沉思的、忧郁的思索重新笼罩了诗篇。但现在诗人的思考已经不同于诗篇开首处的困惑般的叙述,而是苏醒的欲望要求重新获得尊严与感情满足的呼声,这是爱神试图挑战死神的号角。可以想象,假如说这样的诗由莎士比亚来写,他一定会把爱情和自己的不朽诗篇当做起死回生的法宝,然而罗塞蒂不同,他把希望寄托于哲理性探索,相信时间的轮回可能会给予他哪怕一次曾失去过的快乐。从另一个角度看,这无疑透露出诗人深沉的绝望情绪,也透露出罗塞蒂对挚爱的忠诚与追求。闪光是诗人灵魂深处的一种回光返照,一种神秘的感触与顿悟。昼夜与轮回这些意象都容易在敏感的中国读者心中唤起一种黑白分明的阴阳太极图式的玄想。在宗教性的直观领悟层面上,东西方人心灵的触角是可以如灵犀一点通的——这也是一种闪光。

翻译罗塞蒂此诗的理论准备

诗歌翻译是文学翻译中最难的。文学翻译的一般原理当然适用于解释诗歌翻译现象。但诗歌翻译还有自己的独特的理论要点需要译者在进行诗歌翻译实践之前有所了解。做一次两次翻译练习并不是最主要的,最主要的是要通过练习加深对诗歌翻译原理的把握与理解。要实现这一点,至少有下面这几点需要作为诗歌翻译实践进行之前的理论准备。

第一,如何理解欣赏欲翻译的原诗。这一点实际上我已在"作者与作品简介"中简略讨论过,这里不赘言。我想要强调指出的是:翻译诗歌,不仅需要中外文知识,更需要诗歌鉴赏能力。诗歌翻译既然是所有翻译中层次最高的一种翻译,如果译者无法较好地领略原诗的美妙,那么他进行翻译的时候就只能是在机械地译文字,而不是在译诗。诗的语言如此精妙,哪怕挪动一个字或词的位置,其诗味立刻要受到明显的影响。这一点,凡稍具诗歌鉴赏能力的人都能体会个中奥妙。简而言之,诗歌具有五象美:音象美、视象美、义象美、事象美和味象美。前三美不言而喻,事象美指的是一种叙事因素构成的美。味象美指的是诗歌给予读者印象的整体风格美。相应于五象美,产生了诗歌翻译的五大类标准。(当然,这些原理也适用于其他文体翻译,只是程度不同。而正是这一程度区别构成了关键性区别。)一个译者要欣赏诗歌,首先得学会至少能从这五个方面欣赏原作,对原作的五象美大体有一个基本的把握,然后才可能来谈如何着手翻译诗歌的问题。

第二,确定此诗的可译度。依据翻译标准多元互补论的原理,我们不宜笼统地说诗可译还是不可译,而应该说,诗歌翻译大致具有四种情形:① 全可译;② 大半可译;③ 小半可译;④ 不可译。

首先从音象美来看,《闪光》这首诗是严谨的格律体,韵式为 ababa,取抑扬格长短句,用的是 3-4-4-2-5 音步。即第一行 3 个音步,第二行和第三行 4 个音步,第四行只有 2 个音步,第五行 5 个音步,其余两节诗情况与此相同。从这一点,可以看出前拉菲尔派在诗歌创作上的美学追求是很严肃的,宜加以重视。虽然具体的声音效果通常都是不可译的,但是 ababa 这种二元韵式,还是属于大半可译因素。就音步格律而言,3-4-4-2 的模式大半可以套用。它很像中国传统的词或者曲的长短句,参差不齐,可以非常方便地表达诗人变幻多端的情绪。与英语诗歌格律相比,一个汉语双字词或三字词可以大体对应于英语诗歌中的一个音步。例如:I have been here before,共三音步,可以译作:似曾—浪迹—此邦。也是三个音节,基本能套上。所以,格律方面,也可以说此诗是大半可译的(确切点说,叫大半可仿译)。但要注意,对音步的追求不要太死板,因为英汉两种文字毕竟具有根本的差别,如机械套用,往往会削足适履,使原本生动的汉语失掉活力。因此,在一般情况下,音步大体相当也就可以了,多一个或少一个音节,甚至有时多两三个音节也可容忍,只要念起来顺口就行。

从视象美来看,视象美分为内视象美和外视象美。外视象指诗歌的外部排列形式,如诗行的长短等。其实,只要音象美的问题解决了,视象美的外部视象美的问题也差不多基本解决,所以这里主要谈内视象美问题。内视象美指的是诗歌的意象美(包括种种比喻之类),例如诗中的 sighing sound, time's eddying flight, swallow soar 之类。本诗的音象美引起的歧义不多,所以也可以算是大半可仿译。

从义象美来看,本诗义象有明显的朦胧性。义象朦胧并不意味着语言文字本身必须朦胧,文字可以是清楚明白的,而若干用语连缀描绘出的诗的整体义象却可以是相当朦胧的。这就造成在诗歌鉴赏上产生行行都懂,整首诗却不懂的现象。除非有其他必要,诗中的象征性含义通常亦无须故意揭示出来,那样有点强作解人(虽然有时不得不如此)。一般说来,只要尽可能近似地模仿表达了原诗的音象、视象等,则义象的朦胧效果也就可以基本传输,所以这一条也可以算是大半可译。

从事象美来看,事象美指诗中的叙事因素。本诗叙事因素不多,与义象朦胧相表里。要注意本诗叙事上故意采用的排比重复性质：have been here before, have been mine before, have been thus before。这种安排产生一种循环往复、相关呼应的沉思性叙述效果，应加以注意。但这种句式并不难处理。所以总体来说，此诗的事象美也是大半可译。

最后，从味象美来看，味象美是诗歌给予读者的整体感受，尤其是风格上的感受。它是前四种美的综合效果，所以只要前面四个方面的把握有分寸，通常味象美也就能表现出来。但这一诗美是最不容易捉摸、却又至关重要，万不可小视的。译者要将原诗的作品反复吟诵，直至获得一种较为准确的审美印象，然后才在这种总体印象的观照下，细心处理前面的四象美。所以味象美既是判断译作整体风格效果的标准，也是指导、规约译者进行翻译实践、采取适当的翻译对策的标准。

味象美因为牵涉颇难加以定量分析的风格问题，所以这里拟多谈几句。首先要解决的问题依然是：我们应该采用什么样的文体风格来译？仿词曲体？还是文白相间体？还是全白话体？要解决这些问题，又须首先要解决下面这些问题：

第一，原作与译作的时空对应关系问题。第二，针对什么读者群的问题。第三，翻译的目的问题。第四，原作审美特点及义象的复杂特点问题。

关于原作与译作的时空对应关系问题及原作审美特点与译作的复杂特点问题是我在2000年第3期的《中国翻译》上刊登的英译汉练习讨论中提出的。这个原理当然照样适用于解释诗歌翻译。从时空对应关系来看，原作大约写于19世纪80年代，那时清王朝还有20多年才寿终正寝，所以当时中国的诗坛上盛行的仍然是古体诗，如黄遵宪、林纾、严复、康有为、谭嗣同、章太炎等人都还在写古诗。罗塞蒂如身处中国，自不能例外。即便罗不处于中国，当时如有人译他的诗，也肯定是译成古体诗，如苏曼殊之译拜伦诗，辜鸿铭之译辜律勒己（即柯勒律治）诗一样。因此，将罗塞蒂的诗译成古体诗，是对应时空关系的一种作法，可以作为风格之一加以尝试。

从读者角度而言，满足当代读者，尤其要满足较年轻的当代读者，似乎译成白话体为佳。原因我在上面提到的那篇文章中已讲过，不赘。

再从翻译目的来看，本文主要是为了作英译汉练习，探讨英诗汉译的种种可能性，以便为读者提供较多的选择。因此，在文体风格种类上自然就可以宽泛一些，不妨多取几种，以资对照，增进理解。

最后，从原作本身所含的审美特点来看，一部诗歌作品往往涵盖多方面的审美特质和意蕴，也往往仁者见仁，智者见智，所谓诗无达诂。若只有一种风格的译诗，很难表现原作特质的若干方面。如果多几种译文，就可以几种译文互相参照，互补生辉。虽然笔者不主张所有的诗都应该采用多译本形式，但重要的、有影响的诗多几种译文肯定是有益的。

为此，我使用了四种译风来印证上面的讨论。具体阐述，则在下面的翻译对策举隅中加以引申。

综上所述，《闪光》这首诗没有太多的典故或很难处理的意象之类，格律方面也能够以换类模拟的方式进行一定程度的仿译。因此，它属于可译性较大的原诗。我们从可译度方面对这首诗进行了粗略的评估之后，在译诗的时候就有一定的信心了。

（辜正坤评析）

七律·登高[1]

[唐]杜 甫

风急天高猿啸哀,渚清沙白鸟飞回。[2]

无边落木萧萧下,不尽长江滚滚来。[3]

万里悲秋常作客,百年多病独登台。[4]

艰难苦恨繁霜鬓,潦倒新停浊酒杯。[5]

【注释】

[1] 此诗所写的登高,应是代宗大历二年九月九日,诗人"重阳少饮杯中酒,抱病独等江上台"。

[2] 猿啸:巫峡多猿啼,声哀。渚:水中小岛。

[3] 落木:树木落叶称落木。萧萧:风吹落叶声。不尽:言江波浩淼。

[4] 万里:既指秋天高阔的空间,也指离家遥远的距离。悲秋:秋天为悲,秋气萧瑟。一作"悲愁",也通。百年:尤言一生,百岁。

[5] 艰难苦恨:既感叹个人身世多舛,老病缠身,孤苦伶仃,也忧虑国家内忧外患,当时吐蕃侵扰,州郡兵乱。鬓:做动词用,多白发(霜鬓)。潦倒:人生失意。新停浊酒杯:新近因肺病而戒酒。

【译文】

The Heights[1]

By Du Fu

trans. W. J. B. Fletcher

The wind so fresh, the sky so high

Awake the gibbons' wailing cry. [2]

The isles clear-cut, the sand so white,

Arrest the wheeling sea-gulls' flight. [3]

Through endless space with rustling sound

The falling leaves are whirled around. [4]

Beyond my ken a yeasty sea

The Yangtze's waves are rolling free. [5]

From far away, in autumn drear,

I find myself a stranger here. [6]

With dragging years and illness wage

Lone war upon this lofty stage.

With troubles vexed and trials sore

My locks are daily growing hoar: [7]

Till Time, before whose steps I pine,

Set down this failing cup of wine! [8]

【译文评析】

[1] 标题《登高》,直接译成"高处"(The Heights),意思已足够。另有侧重攀登动作的,例如吴钧陶的 Mounting;也有夸张攀登过程的,如 Witter Bynner 的 A Long Climb。

[2] 汉语诗歌包含了一个一个的小句,尤其是这首诗,基本上是两三个字构成的主谓或动宾关

系词组,缓慢而吃力地推进,似乎在模仿登台的艰难和呼吸的困难。译者深明此理,借助英语的词组进行缓慢地推进,一句译为两行,第一行多吃力而顿挫 The wind so fresh, the sky so high,第二行则比较连贯而舒缓 Awake the gibbons' wailing cry. 这样造成一张一弛的节奏。这是难能可贵的。

[3] 这种情况,到第二个联句,即可看出和第一个联句的对应关系,而且对应得十分工整:The isles clear-cut, the sand so white, / Arrest the wheeling sea-gulls' flight. 其连接部分,则在于第二行的 awake 和第四行的 arrest,而且有头韵关系。至此,两行一韵的格式也基本显示出来了。

[4] "无边落木萧萧下",在译文中既有声音的模仿,也有落木在风中回旋飘舞(whirled around),可谓得个中三昧。Through endless space with rusting sound / The falling leaves are whirled around. 此外,从结构来看,译句呈状语在前,构成描述在先,信息中心靠后的奇特效果。这种效果一直保持到下一句。

[5] 如果说在此之前一直是客观的写景,那么,在"不尽长江滚滚来"一句,译者利用文字的空隙,增加了第一人称主语和诗人的主观感受,这样就大大地扩大了诗人的视野,扩充了诗歌的容量:

> Beyond my ken a yeasty sea
> The Yangtze's waves are rolling free.
>
> 我的视野之外,一片苍茫而骚动的海,
> 扬子江的巨浪在滚滚向前排排推开。

[6] 于是,从眼前景色转入心理的描写,在译文中就是水到渠成的了:From far away, in autumn drear, / I find myself a stranger here. "从遥远的地方来,在秋天的萧瑟中,/我发现我原来是一个陌生的客人。"但是这样一来,"万里悲秋常作客"和"百年多病独登台"的上下句关系的连接就中断了,造成了一个单独的、有力而拖长的韵味,仍耐人回味。

[7] 译者并没有对此束手无策,而是将"百年多病独登台"和下一句"艰难苦恨繁霜鬓"运用相同的 with 结构,连为一体,构成一组关系:

> With dragging years and illness wage
> Lone war upon this lofty stage.
> With troubles vexed and trials sore
> My locks are daily growing hoar:
> 艰难的岁月,病弱的身体,
> 我独自挣扎着登上高台。
> 恼人的麻烦,痛苦的折磨,
> 我的鬓发在日见发白。

[8] 这样,最后"潦倒新停浊酒杯"就获得了单独成句的特权,有一种特殊的、终极的强调效果(尽管如此,虽然有节奏的变换,整首诗那艰苦的、顿挫的行进,并没有轻易改变):

> Till Time, before whose steps I pine,
> Set down this failing cup of wine!

我随着时光的脚步苦痛悲叹，
直到有一天放下这未尽的酒杯！

（王宏印评析）

【翻译试笔】

【英译汉】

The Soul Selects Her Own Society

Emily Dickinson

The soul selects her own society—
Then—shuts the door—
To her divine Majority—
Present no more—

Unmoved—she notes the Chariots—pausing—
At her low Gate—
Unmoved—an emperor be kneeling
Upon her Mat—

I've known her—from an ample nation—
Choose one—
Then—close the Valves of her attention—
Like Stone—

【汉译英】

水调歌头

苏 轼

明月几时有？把酒问青天。不知天上宫阙、今夕是何年？我欲乘风归去，惟恐琼楼玉宇，高处不胜寒。起舞弄清影，何似在人间？

转朱阁，低绮户，照无眠。不应有恨、何事长向别时圆？人有悲欢离合，月有阴晴圆缺，此事古难全。但愿人长久，千里共婵娟。

【参考译文】

The Soul Selects Her Own Society 汉译
灵魂选择自己的朋友

余光中 译

灵魂选择她自己的朋友，
然后将房门关死；
请莫再闯进她那神圣的
济济多士的圈子。

她漠然静听着高轩驷马
停在她矮小的门前；

她漠然让一个帝王跪倒
在她的草垫上面。

我曾见她自泱泱的大国，
单单选中了一人；
然后闭上她留意的花瓣，
象石头一般顽硬。

灵魂选择自己的伴侣

江　枫　译

灵魂选择自己的伴侣，
然后，把门紧闭——
她神圣的多数——
再不容介入——

无动于衷——
发现车辇，停在，她低矮的门前——
无动于衷——
一位皇帝，跪倒，在她的席垫——

我知道她，从人口众多的整个民族——
选中了一个——
从此，封闭关心的阀门——
像块石头——

《水调歌头》英译

To the Tune of Shuidiaoketou

trans. Lin Yutang

How rare the moon, so round and clear!
With cup in hand, I ask of the blue sky,
"I do not know in the celestial sphere
What name this festive night goes by?"
I want to fly home, riding the air,
But fear the ethereal cold up there,
The jade and crystal mansions are so high!
Dancing to my shadow,
I feel no longer the mortal tie.
She rounds the vermilion tower,
Stoops to silk-pad doors,

Shines on those who sleepless lie.

Why does she, bearing us no grudge,

Shine upon our parting, reunion deny?

But rare is perfect happiness—

The moon does wax, the moon does wane,

And so men meet and say goodbye.

I only pray our life be long,

And our souls together heavenward fly!

Prelude to Water Melody

trans. Xu Yuanchong

How long will the full moon appear?

Wine cup in hand, I ask the sky.

I do not know what time of the year

T would be tonight in the palace on high.

Riding the wind, there I would fly,

Yet I'm afraid the crystalline palace would be

Too high and cold for me.

I rise and dance, with my shadow I play.

On high as on earth, would it be as gay?

The moon goes round the mansions red

Through gauze-draped window soft to shed

Her light upon the sleepless bed.

Why then when people part, is the oft full and bright?

Men have sorrow and joy; they part or meet again;

The moon is bright or dim and she may wax or wane.

There has been nothing perfect since the olden days.

So let us wish that man

Will live long as he can!

Though miles apart, we'll share the beauty she displays.

【延伸阅读】

[1] Bloom, H. *Emily Dickinson*[M]. Broomall, PA: Chelsea House Publishers, 1999.

[2] Bloom, H. *Robert Frost*[M]. Broomall, PA: Chelsea House Publishers, 1999.

[3] Bowie, A. *Aesthetics and Subjectivity: From Kant to Nietzsche* [M]. Manchester, GBR: Manchester University Press, 2003.

[4] Brodzki, B. *Can These Bones Live? —Translation, Survival, and Cultural Memory* [M]. Stanford, CA: Stanford University Press, 2007.

[5] Cai，Zongqi. *Chinese Literary Mind：Culture，Creativity，and Rhetoric in Wenxin Diaolong*[M]. Palo Alto, CA, USA：Stanford University Press，2001.

[6] Ellis, S. *Chaucer at Large：The Poet in the Modern Imagination*[M]. Minneapolis, MN，USA：University of Minnesota Press，2000.

[7] Eoyang, E. C. *"Borrowed Plumage"：Polemical Essays on Translation*[M]. Amsterdam，New York：Rodopi，2003.

[8] Gass, W. H. *Reading Rilke：Reflections on the Problems of Translation*[M]. Westminster, MD, USA：Alfred A. Knopf Incorporated，1999.

[9] Iser，W. *The Act of Reading：a Theory of Aesthetic Response*[M]. Baltimore and London：The John Hopkins University Press，1978.

[10] Jauss, H. R. *Toward an Aesthetic of Reception*[M]. Minneapolis，MN，USA：University of Minnesota Press，1982.

[11] Sawyer, J. F. *Sacred Languages and Sacred Texts*[M]. London, GBR：Routledge，1999.

[12] Schäffner, C. *The Role of Discourse Analysis for Translation and in Translator Training*[C]. Clevedon, Buffalo, Toronto, Sydney：Multilingual Matters Ltd.，2002.

[13] Wardy, R. *Aristotle in China：Language，Categories and Translation*[M]. West Nyack，NY，USA：Cambridge University Press，2000.

[14] 蔡华. 译逝水而任幽兰——汪榕培诗歌翻译纵横谈[M]. 北京:北京师范大学出版集团,2011.

[15] 狄金森,江枫. 暴风雨夜　暴风雨夜[C]. 北京:机械工业出版社,2010.

[16] 傅浩. 窃火传薪——英语诗歌与翻译教学实录[M]. 上海:上海外语教育出版社,2011.

[17] 辜正坤. 中西诗比较鉴赏与翻译理论[M]. 北京:清华大学出版社,2004.

[18] 顾正阳. 古诗词曲英译美学研究[M]. 上海:上海大学出版社,2006.

[19] 海岸. 中西诗歌翻译百年论集[C]. 上海:上海外语教育出版社,2007.

[20] 胡安江. 寒山诗:文本旅行与经典建构[M]. 北京:清华大学出版社,2011.

[21] 廖七一. 胡适诗歌翻译研究[M]. 北京:清华大学出版社,2006.

[22] 刘华文. 汉诗英译的主体审美论[M]. 上海:上海译文出版社,2005.

[23] 吕叔湘. 英译唐人绝句百首[M]. 长沙:湖南人民出版社,1980.

[24] 思果. 功夫在诗外:翻译偶谈[M]. 香港:牛津大学出版社,1996.

[25] 许渊冲. 翻译的艺术(第二版)[M]. 北京:五洲传播出版社,2006.

[26] 许渊冲. 唐诗三百首(中英文对照)[M]. 北京:中国出版集团,2007.

[27] 张炳星. 中国古典诗词名篇百首[M]. 北京:中华书局,2002.

[28] 朱徽. 中国诗歌在英语世界[M]. 上海:上海外语教育出版社,2009.

【问题与思考】

1. 诗歌抗拒翻译的特质有哪些?

2. 中西诗歌传统分别是什么?

3. 爱德华·菲茨杰拉德作为诗歌翻译家,成功之处何在?

4. 诗歌翻译中,内容与形式的传递,孰轻孰重?

5. 如何评价埃兹拉·庞德对于中国诗歌的翻译与介绍?

6. 中国现代新诗创作与翻译的关系如何?

7. 诗歌翻译的单位是什么?

8. 诗歌翻译会影响一个国家的文学形象吗?

9. 如何评价诗歌翻译与文学经典建构的关系?

10. 诗歌的音乐美与意象美,在翻译过程中如何取舍?

第五章 散文翻译篇

导 论

　　散文是一个内涵和外延都相当模糊的范畴。"散文"之名起源于南宋罗大经《鹤林玉露》，用来指称一切句法不整齐的文章。我国古代曾将不押韵、不重对偶的散体文章均称为散文，包括传史书在内，与韵文、骈文对举；又将散文与诗歌对举，泛指不讲究韵律的小说及其他抒情记事之作。随着文学概念的演变和文学体裁的发展，散文的概念也时有变化，在某些历史时期又将小说与其他抒情、记事的文学作品统称为散文，以区别于讲求韵律的诗歌。现代散文是指除小说、诗歌、戏剧等文学体裁之外的其他文学作品。其本身按其内容和形式的不同，又可分为杂文、小品、随笔等。

　　散文是最方便、最实际，也是运用最广泛的文体，体裁灵活多样，风格不拘一律。郁达夫说，"散文清淡易为，并且包括很广，人间天上，草木虫鱼，无不可谈"。鲁迅说，散文的"题材应听其十分自由选择，风景静物，虫鱼，即一花一叶均可"。周立波说，"举凡国际国内大事，社会家庭的细故，掀天之浪，一物之微，自己的一段历史，一丝感触，一撮悲欢，一星冥想。往日的凄惶，今朝的欢快，都可以移于纸上，贡献读者"。散文的内容涉及自然万物、各色人等、古今中外、政事私情……可以说是无所不包、无所不有。可以写国内外和社会上的矛盾、斗争，写经济建设，写文艺论争，写伦理道德，也可以写文艺随笔，读书笔记，日记书简；既可以是风土人物志、游记和偶感录，也可以是知识小品、文坛轶事；它能够谈天说地，更可以抒情写趣。凡是能给人以思想启迪、美的感受、情操的陶冶，使人开阔视野，丰富知识，心旷神怡的，都可选作散文的题材。

　　散文取材广泛，内容丰富，为其服务的形式也灵活多样，不拘一格。散文的结构中心多样，结构形式不拘一格，表达方式自由灵活。散文可以自由地使用叙述、描写等五种最基本的表达方式，也可使用暗示、象征、比兴、联想等手法。记叙散文以叙述、描写和议论为主；议论散文以议论为主，间用叙述、描写和抒情。散文不像小说、戏剧靠虚构的故事情节、矛盾冲突和塑造的人物形象吸引读者，而是靠浓郁的诗意和理趣来感染读者。在抒情、叙事类散文中要追求诗意。有的散文家说，真正的散文是充满诗意的，就像苹果饱含果汁一样。毫无诗意的散文是没有生命力的。因此，散文作者努力在生活中寻求诗意，并使自己的作品富有诗意。

　　散文第一大特点是"文"。古人要求散文像花纹一样美丽，线条清晰，色彩斑斓，即文章美——有节奏感，读起来朗朗上口；语言简洁，表达力强，生动活泼，富有感染力；文章结构严谨，层次分明，逻辑性强。散文作者通过写景、叙事、抒情、论证或创造形象来传达其意图，而作品的审美价值往往是通过语言的声响和节奏表现出来的，这在所有的语言中普遍存在。因此，要在译文中再现原文的声响和节奏之妙。一篇好的译文应该读起来琅琅上口,听上去声声入耳。散文都有一种意境和氛围,这往往通过作者在作品中所表达的精神气质、思想情操、审美志趣以及作品所创造的情景或意象表达出来。每个作者都以其独特的方式表达自己,或明快,或高雅,或简洁,或热情奔放,或充满哲理,因此要研究作者的语言风格,通过语言风格再现作者气质。翻译是语言转化过程,也是文化移植过程。语言转换需要遵循语言规律,文化移植则需要适应读者需求。

五四以后,我国白话散文成就突出,其主要原因之一就是引进、吸收了外国散文(特别是英国散文/论说文——Essay)的长处,借鉴了外国散文的形式和文风。英国 Essay 究竟是什么?Essay 是在欧洲文艺复兴运动中诞生的,开山鼻祖是法国的蒙田。1603 年,蒙田的小品文被译成英文正式介绍到英国。从此,这株从国外移植来的树在英国土壤里生根、发芽、开花。最初的硕果是 1625 年培根的 58 篇文章。他的文章闪烁着理性的光芒,但不动声色,不苟言笑,俨然摆出一本正经的架势,缺乏一点人情的温暖,与富于个人风趣的亲切笔调的蒙田迥然不同。由于培根的领路,Essay 逐渐在 17 世纪的英国流行起来。

日本著名文艺理论家厨川白村在《说 Essay》中作过这样的解释:"和小说戏曲诗歌一起,也算是文艺作品之一体的这 Essay(散文),并不是议论呀论说似的麻烦类的东西……如果是冬天,便坐在暖炉旁边的安乐椅子上,倘在夏天,则披浴衣,汲苦茗,随随便便,和好友任心闲话,将这些话照样地移在纸上的东西,就是 Essay。兴之所至,也说些以不至于头痛为度的道理罢,也有冷嘲,也有警句罢,既有 humour(滑稽),也有 pathos(感愤)。所谈的题目,天下国家的大事不待言,还有市井的琐事,书籍的批评,相识者的消息,以及自己的过去的追怀。想到什么就纵谈什么,而托于即兴之笔者,是这一类的文章。"可见,Essay 是一种独特的文体,它属于散文范畴,但要准确地把它译成汉语并非易事。

当代著名散文翻译家刘炳善教授在谈到散文翻译和文学翻译时说:"散文之所以能够吸引读者,关键在于作者通过自己的文章风格透露出自己独特的个性。"因此,风格问题是决定散文翻译的核心问题,能否掌握并体现作者风格是决定散文译作成败的关键。风格是一位作家的个性经过个人独特社会环境的塑造,经过一定思想文化的陶冶,再通过某种语言艺术的手段自然表现出来的精神和物质两个方面的辩证统一。风格并非虚无缥缈的行文气质,具有典型的物质性,可以见诸于"形",表现在原文的语言形式上,就是可被译者辨识的风格标记。

本单元所选文章围绕中国散文英译、英语 Essay 汉译的技巧与风格、散文翻译中观点与风格的关系、如何做好散文翻译等方面展开,通过对翻译家译述的宏观点评进入具体翻译方法的讲述,通过对文学规律的阐发进入对散文特点的归纳和散文翻译的论述,翻译史与翻译主体兼顾,希冀使用者通过阅读能够关注翻译与文学体裁变迁、文学翻译与文学创作等的关系。

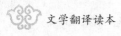

选文一　从翻译的角度看英国随笔

——1992 年 10 月 20 日在香港中文大学翻译研究中心的讲演

刘炳善

导　言

本文选自刘炳善著,《译事随笔》,中国电影出版社(北京),2000 年版。

选文简要梳理英国随笔(散文)在中国的译介历史,指出英国随笔引进中国对于中国白话散文的发展起过的作用,并归纳出英国随笔文学在中国的译介特点。该文是刘炳善教授《英国散文与兰姆随笔翻译琐谈》论作的有效补充,集中体现了刘炳善教授翻译 18 世纪到 20 世纪英国散文、兰姆随笔(《伊利亚随笔选》)和维吉尼亚·吴尔夫书评基础之上的理论升华。对他而言,"英国散文都不大好译——读起来行云流水,译起来句句沉重——而兰姆的文章特别难译。难译首先在于他的语言外壳——文白杂糅、迂回曲折的'拟古'文体把他的'文心'紧紧裹住,必须像吃胡桃似地先把一层硬壳咬碎,才能尝到他文章里那种略带苦涩的香味儿"。刘先生充分体认随笔翻译中三个特别难以捉摸的问题——个性、风格、幽默,并结合自己翻译毛姆、吴尔夫随笔的典型例证,逐一加以说明。结论指出,译者必须调动自己全部的方法和手段,以确保全文精妙的传递。

一

1597 年,培根出版了他的 58 篇《随笔》,到现在将近 400 年了。培根这个书名,是从法国蒙田的《随笔》(1595)那里借来的,所以严格说来,英国的随笔是以蒙田为鼻祖。1603 年,弗洛里奥翻译的《蒙田随笔》英文本出版,这才是后世英国随笔作家学习的榜样。17 世纪,在蒙田的影响下,英国出现一批以优美多姿的文笔写出作者微妙复杂的精神世界的散文名著,像伯顿的《忧郁的剖析》等。虽不是短篇随笔,但内容情调和后来的随笔相通——这是英国随笔发展的酝酿阶段。18 世纪,作家大办期刊,运用随笔散文形式向中产阶级进行启蒙工作,促使随笔大大发展起来。阿狄生和斯梯尔在《闲话报》和《旁观者报》上发表的一大批文章,就成为英国随笔的典范作品。19 世纪初,英国随笔作为浪漫主义文学的一部分,又形成一个高潮,出了兰姆、赫兹利特等著名随笔作家。19 世纪末叶,斯蒂文生承上启下,使得随笔在世纪之交又振兴一个时期。直到 20 世纪前半,还出现过维吉尼亚·吴尔夫这样以意识流手法写的散文——实际上是英国随笔的新发展。此后,由于"二次大战"对人思想感情的影响,以及现代生活的急剧变化,随笔在英国再没有什么重要的作家。这就像一条河流,滥觞于一泓清泉,慢慢流成一道山涧,然后进入平原,由小河增成为一条大河,波澜壮阔流了很久,大河又变细小,流入地下,仍然滋润着地面上的庄稼和林木花草。

二

英国文学分四大类:诗歌、戏剧、小说、随笔。英国随笔介绍到中国比小说、诗歌、戏剧稍晚一些。1907 年(光绪三十年),林纾翻译美国欧文的《拊掌录》,作者是以 18 世纪英国的阿狄生为师的;而 1911 年上海商务印书馆出版的《阿狄生文报捃华》(*Sir Roger De Coverley Papers*)则是目前我所能找到的英国随笔介绍到中国的最早物证。不过,只有到 1919 年五四运动以后,由于新文学运动的需要,对英国随笔的介绍、翻译、编选、评论才进入一个大发展的时期。1921 年,周作人在北京《晨报副刊》发表短评《美文》,提到了阿狄生、兰姆、吉辛和契斯透顿等英国随笔作家。鲁迅在 1925 年也翻译了日本厨川白村关于英国随笔的两篇文章。周氏兄弟这三篇文章引起了中国文学界对于随笔的重视。此后,从 20 年代末到 30 年代,做这方面工作的人很多,但最突出的是梁遇春。他在二三十年代之交,接连出版了三种英国小品文(即随笔)的选译本,向中国读者介绍了斯梯尔、阿狄生、高尔斯密、兰姆、赫兹利特、利·亨特、契斯透顿、贝洛克、鲁卡斯、林德、洛根·斯密、加丁纳等一大批英国随笔作家的文章。他还写了一篇洋洋万言、才气横溢的《兰姆评传》。因此,梁遇春是本世纪前期在这一领域中最有贡献的人。

英国随笔引进中国,对于五四以后中国白话散文的发展起过有益的作用。除了形式和文风的借鉴,对于作者和读者的个性解放,也是有帮助的。关于这一点,拙文《英国随笔简论》略有涉及,此处不赘。

从抗日战争爆发到 60 年代中期这 30 年间,由于战争和社会大变动,对于英国随笔的翻译比较稀少,只出了《培根论说文集》(水天同译)和吉辛《四季随笔》(李霁野译)两种译本。不过在大学英语教材当中,英国随笔作品一直没有断绝。当然,在"文化大革命"当中,一切都不说了。但"文化大革命"一结束,从 1979 年北京《世界文学》上发表李赋宁教授翻译的德·昆西《论麦克佩斯剧中的敲门声》,似乎敲开了长期关闭的英国随笔翻译的大门。从此,北京的《世界文学》、《外国文学》,上海的《外国文艺》,还有一些专门的散文刊物,像北京的《散文世界》、天津的《散文》、广州的《随笔》,都发表过英国随笔译文。此外,全国各地出版的外国散文选本,必选英国随笔,还出了一些英国随笔散文的选集和英国随笔名家专集。改革开放十几年来,虽然并没有人振臂一呼、大力提倡,英国随笔散文的翻译介绍工作却在不声不响之中得到了四五十年来空前的发展,而且看来这一势头还会发展下去。

从七八十年来我国对英国随笔文学的翻译介绍,可以看出这么一些特点:

一、英国随笔是一种非常适合具有较高文化素养的知识分子口味的文学作品。郁达夫在1935 年所写的《中国新文学大系·散文二集导言》中说得好:"英国散文的影响,在我们的知识分子中间,是再过十年二十年也绝不会消灭的一种根深底固的潜势力。"他这句话说过去,已经50 多年了。从现在的情况来看,在可以预见的未来,至少在爱好文学的知识分子当中,英国随笔还是会有人喜欢读的。

二、但是,英国随笔的翻译介绍工作,需要有一个国家社会相当安定、文化氛围比较宽松的环境。否则,它就很容易被挤掉。这也就是说,它需要一个国泰民安的时代背景。只要知识分子能静下来,坐在自己屋子里安安生生看书、思考、欣赏文学、艺术、学术,总会有那么一些人想起英国随笔,把它们翻译出来,也会有那么一些读者高兴看,因此也就有刊物愿发表、有出版社愿出版,虽然它们不可能成为"畅销书",也不可能赚大钱。

三、只有在一个文学相当繁荣的时代,而且是在一个散文创作比较发达的时代,作家、读者、译者才对英国随笔特别有兴趣。道理很简单:只有散文创作发达,才会感觉到需要翻译介绍外国散文,作为参考借鉴。

看来,对客观条件的要求还相当高的。当然,随笔散文的译者并没有权利要求时代,而是相反:只要时代条件具备,散文创作自然就会繁荣,读者自然爱看散文,散文翻译也自然会相应发展起来。

我认为,为了吸收外国的优秀文化,为了开拓作家和读者的视野,我国对于英国随笔和其他散文作品的翻译介绍,还应该发展。在这方面,还有很多工作可做。

三

在 80 年代当中,我曾用八九个年头从事英国随笔散文的翻译。其中甘苦,写过《英国散文与兰姆随笔翻译琐谈》一文。现在再举几个例子,补充说明那篇短文里的看法。

我认为,应该用艺术再创作的态度来对待文学翻译工作。翻译工作,特别在准备阶段,自然要牵扯许多技术性的问题,譬如说查字典和其他参考书、工具书,这都是不可避免的。但是要让艺术来指导技术。一篇好随笔本身是件小小的杰作,译出来后也应该成为一篇令人爱读的好文章。所以,每一篇散文名篇的翻译应该是一种在精研原文基础上的文学再创作活动,而不应是死抠着一个个单词的硬译。字典自然要查,但查完字典,就得摆脱字典释义的束缚,"以全句为单位",活泼泼地思考,不能受一个一个单词的支配。举例来说,威廉·赫兹利特文风汪洋恣肆、用词繁富,素称难译。当我译他的《论青年不朽之感》时,译到以下这句:"... as we grow old, we become more feeble and querulous, every object 'reverts its own hollowness', and both worlds are not enough to satisfy the peevish importunity and extravagant presumption of our desires!"开始,我照原文逐字直译,但译出一看,简直不知所云,为之搁笔。在疲劳困乏之中,偶然翻开手边《红楼梦》的一页,描写一群小丫头在打水时互相打闹笑谑的场面,深为那种活灵活现的语言所打动,从中得到启发。于是把原来逐字硬译的初稿推翻,从原文的语词丛莽中摆脱出来,细察文意,另铸新词,译成这样:"人到老年,性情变得脆弱,又爱埋三怨四,但见'世事转烛,无非空虚二字';而且,这时欲望又高又多,脾气又怪又躁,似乎天堂、人间加在一起也无法叫他满意!"定稿再读,虽然还不能完全满意,但觉得这才像一句中国话,文章才活了起来。

在随笔翻译中,还有三个特别难以捉摸的问题,即个性、风格、幽默。

个性是随笔的灵魂。蒙田的名言"我描画我自己"(It is myself I paint.)乃是每位随笔作家的座右铭。随笔的魅力即在字里行间所流露出作者的鲜明个性。"他谈自己七零七杂的事情所以能够这么娓娓动听,那是靠着他能够在说闲话时节,将他的全性格透露出来。"(梁遇春语)为了在翻译中传达出作者的一定性格特色,就需要在动手之前对作者的生平和个性尽量多了解些。譬如说,兰姆随笔中自传的成分非常浓厚,但他又在"伊利亚"这个假名掩护之下,对真人真事加以改写。因此,在翻译之前,就要通过阅读传记材料,了解哪些是真人真事,哪些属于兰姆的"艺增",以便找出兰姆的真面目、真性情。

作家的个性通过自己的风格表现出来。每位作家个性不同,风格也不同。风格是一位作家的个性经过个人独特生活环境的塑造,经过一定思想文化的陶冶,再通过某些语言艺术的手段自然表现出来的。翻译某位随笔作家,就得酌磨和传达他的文风。当然,这很难。领会作家的风格已经不易,在译文中再现他的风格就更难。但应该也可以尝试。因为把风格不同的作家的文章都翻得一模一样,是文学翻译者的大忌。

兰姆在他的随笔中(与他的书信不同)采用了一种很特殊的、文白杂糅、迂回曲折的文体,把他的"文心"包藏起来。这是一种很难对付的语言风格。译者必须先把这一层语言硬壳"嚼碎",尝出文章中的略带苦涩的香味儿,并且看出在这种文风中躲藏着一个脆弱的灵魂。对于这么一种特殊的风格,自然不能采用规规矩矩、四平八稳的语言来翻译。我尝试着在白话文当中点缀一些"之乎者也"之类的文言词语(特别是用文言文来译原文中的拉丁语),以此传达出兰姆的那种稍带滑稽意味的拟古文风:

"据说,当年在我们慈幼学校的黄金时代,学生们每顿晚餐都能吃上冒热气儿的大块烤肉。可是,后来某位笃信宗教的恩公认为这些小孩子的仪表比他们的嘴巴更值得可怜,因此把肉菜换成了校服;于是——至今思之,犹有余悸焉——就取消了羊肉,只发给我们长裤。"(《饭前的祷告》)

"我的身分已经不是某公司的职员某某。我成了退休的大闲人。如今,我的出入之地乃是那些林木错落有致的公园。别人开始注意我那无牵无挂的脸色,悠闲自在的举止,以及步履徜徉、漫无目的、游游荡荡的样儿。我信步而行,不管何所而来,亦不问何所而去。人们告诉我说:某种雍容华贵的神态,原来和我种种其他方面的禀赋一同被埋没不彰,如今都脱颖而出,在我身上流露出来了。我渐渐有了绅士派头。拿起一张报纸,我只看歌剧消息。人生劳役,斯已尽矣。我活在世上应做之事业已做完。昨日之我,是为他人做嫁;从今往后,我的余年将属于我自己了。"(《退休者》)

维吉尼亚·吴尔夫别有一种风格。那是一种女性的、细腻而灵活的文风,娓娓而谈,飘逸飞动,能放能收,舒卷自如。对此,翻译时不可鲁莽从事,必须追随原文,亦步亦趋,把她这种意识流的、仿佛印象派画法似的文风多多少少描摹下来:

"对英国文学稍有涉猎的人,一定会感觉出来,它有时候处于一个萧条的季节,好像乡下的早春似的,树木光秃秃的,山上一点儿绿意也没有;茫茫大地,稀疏枝条,统统无遮无掩,一览无余。我们不禁思念那众生躁动、万籁并作的六月,那时候,哪怕一片小小的树林里也是生机益然;你静静地站着,就会听见矮树棵子里有些身体灵巧的小动物在那里探头探脑、哼哼唧唧、走来走去,忙着它们的什么活动。在英国文学当中也是这样:我们必须等到十六世纪结束、十七世纪过了很久,那一派萧条景象才能有所改变,变得充满生机和颤动,我们才能在伟大作品产生的间歇,听到人们说长道短的声音。"(《多萝西·奥斯本的〈书信集〉》,收入《普通读者二集》)

风格不容易体会,要在译文中传达出来更难。翻译一篇文章,对于第一段要特别多下点工夫,必要时得反复推敲修改,为的是捕捉住作者的语气和调子。一旦基调抓住,全文的笔调也就"顺流而下"。

英国随笔的另一要素是幽默。幽默是英吉利民族的一种特性,而每一位随笔作家又各有自己不同的个性特征。因此,要给幽默下一个笼统而无所不包的定义是不可能的,但读英国随笔又往往随时感到它的存在。据说兰姆的幽默是无从模仿的。为了猜一猜兰姆的幽默这个谜,我查阅过一些关于幽默的解释。最后,我认同了《剑桥英国文学史》中认为兰姆的幽默属于"含泪的微笑"(laughter in tears)。批评家佩特也谈到过兰姆幽默中的悲剧因素。对此饱经忧患的中国知识分子是能够理解的。基于这种理解,我译出了 30 多篇兰姆随笔。自然,其他随笔作家,像阿狄生、斯梯尔、高尔斯密、赫兹利特、斯蒂文生、鲁卡斯、林德、吴尔夫等,个人生平遭际和性格特征各自不同,他(她)们的幽默并不属于"含泪的微笑",对每个人需要单独进行"定性分析"。总的来说,我感到幽默似乎是善良宽厚的人性处在种种遭遇当中仍然能够发出和保持的一种微笑。这只是我个人妄加揣测。不过,前面说过,要给幽默下一个定义实在很难,几乎是不可能。

(1999 年 4 月 25 日整理)

选文二　介绍一部中国散文经典译作

——兼谈 David Pollard 的汉英翻译艺术

刘士聪

导　言

本文选自《中国翻译》,2005 年第 2 期。

选文首先介绍了 David Pollard 先生在香港中文大学任职期间完成的一部译作《古今散文英译集》,高度肯定 Pollard 肩负着文化交流的使命,做了一件非常"值得"的事情。选文从《古今散文英译集》的插图、致谢、参考书目等副文本入手,介绍了该书独特的体例,认为该书不仅是一部翻译作品,同时也具有研究的性质,系统分析了中国散文的发展脉络及其演变过程,以及这一演变过程与时代、与主流思想的关系。书中的序和引言、对相关作家的评论与译者说明和译者后记,不仅体现了其研究的深度,也解决了译文里需要解释的具体词义和文化内涵。选文结合具体的翻译实例,从译文集对于文化内容的处理、词义结构的处理和语言风格的处理等方面进行具体阐发,指出,译者准确而地道的英语译文,他对作者和文章背景的介绍和对文化问题的解读,以及他在翻译过程中对一些细节的思考,均可令翻译学人得到很多启示,值得学习和研究。

这里介绍的是 *The Chinese Essay*(《古今散文英译集》),香港中文大学出版社 1999 年出版。

作者兼译者 David Pollard 先生,英国汉学家,对中国语言、文学和文化有很深的研究。1958—1961 年间在英国剑桥大学学习中文,曾在伦敦亚非研究学院(School of Oriental & African Studies)任职,讲授汉语。1970 年获博士学位,其博士论文于 1973 年以 *A Chinese Look at Literature:The Literary Values of Chou Tso jen*(周作人)为题发表。1979 年晋升为教授,此后直至 1989 年 10 年间,在伦敦大学从事汉语教学。1989 年开始在香港中文大学教授翻译,并任该校翻译研究中心主办的翻译杂志 *Renditions* 的编辑,1997 年退休。

在香港中文大学任职期间,与 Chan Sinwai 合作编辑了 *An Encyclopaedia of Translation*,出版了研究晚清翻译的论文集 *Translation and Creation* 和 *The True Story of Lu Xun*。现正为该大学出版社翻译周作人散文。这里介绍的《古今散文英译集》,也是 David Pollard 先生在香港中文大学任职期间完成的一部译作。

一、概　述

《古今散文英译集》,就其所涉内容及其性质看,不仅是一部中国散文的英译作品,也是一部研究中国散文发展的著作,再加上书中所收入的现当代知名作家的照相和手迹,以及古代文人学者的书法墨迹,足以使其成为一部翻译、学术和艺术三者合而为一的书。其严谨的学术规范使我们看到作者承继着优良的治学传统,其独特的内容和形式使我们看到作者在学术上的创新精神。不论是看其翻译还是看其研究,此书皆堪称典范。

阅读此书,常常被它的装帧、版式和内容安排上的新颖与考究所吸引,随之便不由得产生一种怡然舒适之感,因而深深感受到作者对学术的执著和对读者的真诚。

Pollard 在谈及他所做的这番工作是否值得的时候说,自英国汉学家翟理斯(Herbert A. Giles)于 1884 年出版 *Gems of Chinese Literature:Prose*(《中国文学精华·散文》)100 多年来,西方汉学界还没有一部系统介绍中国散文的选集,主要有两个原因:

第一,讨论别国语言的散文创作本来就是一件很困难的事情,何况散文的个人风格又是一个非常重要的问题,因此,向不懂汉语或对汉语只有些许知识的西方人介绍中国散文自然很困难;

第二,在西方,散文的声誉在下降。有一种观点认为,与其说散文属于文学,不如说它更像新闻报道。但正如罗伯特·林德(Robert Lynd)所说:"新闻报导和文学之间的唯一重要区别在于文学能流传。能流传的新闻报导是文学。"因此,Pollard 认为,散文是能够流传的。而且,现在已有迹象表明,人们对散文的兴趣正在复苏,1997 年由菲茨罗伊·迪尔伯恩(Fitzroy Dearborn)主编的《散文百科全书》(*The Encyclopedia of the Essay*)就是一个有力的证明。Pollard 翻译这部《古今散文英译集》的目的就是向那些对中国了解甚少、对中国语言知之不多的西方读者介绍中国散文,并希望以此提高人们对散文的兴趣,使散文正在开始复苏的趋势继续下去。Pollard 是肩负着文化交流的使命,做了一件非常"值得"的事情。

二、本书的特色

"鉴其所长,赏其独至",本书有很多引人入胜的新颖之处。还没有打开书,封面上张大千的一幅泼墨画,已经将你带进秋山黄昏万千斑斓的景象之中。打开书之后,一应俱全的目录展示了详尽的内容,依次为:Illustrations, Acknowledgement, Preface, Skeleton Chronology, Introduction,然后便一一列出 36 位作家的名字和 74 篇文章的标题。作家的名字是以汉语拼音与中文名字同时出现,作家的生卒年代附在括号里,文章标题也是译名与原名并列;最后是References,凡与本书相关的信息应有尽有。

下面分别简略说明,Preface 和 Introduction 部分留待后叙。

Illustrations(插图)

此部分包括 28 幅精致的插图,其中有难得一见的古代文人韩愈、欧阳修、苏轼、方孝儒、归有光、袁宏道、袁枚等的书法墨宝,李渔的书法扇面,以及鲁迅、郁达夫、梁实秋、余光中、杨绛等现当代作家的照相及书信手迹。这在一般学术著作和翻译作品里不多见。

Acknowledgement(致谢)

作者在对各方表示谢意时,没有说一句那些常见的陈词套话,我们从他简明的言辞里所感受到的尽是发自肺腑的真诚。比如,一开始他说:

> Thanks should go first to Christopher Hurst, who has been prodding me to write another book for him ever since he published my first one, *A Chinese Look at Literature*, in 1973, despite the fact that it set a record for slow sales. In our present old age there are better things to look forward to than slow sales, so I hope his constancy will be more suitably rewarded with this anthology.

笔者不由得想起美国散文作家怀特(E. B. White)讲写作风格时就特别强调作者的"真诚"(sincere)。

References(参考书目)

参考书目分两个部分,一是 Source(原始资料),一是 Translations and Studies(翻译与研究)。

1) 原始资料:历来学者在附录"参考书目"时多是按英文字母或汉语拼音字母顺序将作者名和书目名逐一开列出来。Pollard 没有采取这种形式,而是用说明的方式介绍几部主要参考书,并说明为什么他参考这几部书的理由。此外,因大部分文章(少数几位作者的作品除外)可在常见的选集、全集里找到,便没有在此一一列出。

2) 翻译与研究:Pollard 在翻译和研究中国散文过程中对英美汉学家和翻译家的英译和研究资料做了详细调查,也是采取说明的方式将其列出。所列资料对从事中国散文翻译和研究的人很有用。

独特的体例

《古今散文英译集》是第一部集中国古代散文和现当代散文于一体的英译本。书中选取古今 36 位作家的 74 篇作品——15 位古代作家的 29 篇,21 位现当代作家(包括一部分台湾作家)的 45 篇。除将每篇文章译成英语,并为每位作者写了详细的评论(Commentary),有的评论篇幅很长,写得很详细,讲述作者的身世经历、思想倾向和写作特色等,还为 14 篇译文加了"译者说明"(Translator's Note),有一篇附了"译者后记"(Translator's Afterword)。这虽然是 Pollard 根据翻译此书的目的和译文读者的实际需要而自然想到需要这样做,但和常见的翻译作品相比较这确实是值得效仿的创造。

前面提到的 19 世纪末 20 世纪初英国汉学家、剑桥大学汉语教授翟理斯(Herbert A.

Giles)翻译的 *Gems of Chinese Literature：Prose* 于 1884 年出版,后经修订于 1923 年再版,篇幅比初版增加了一倍,时间跨度也从周公、老子、孔子延续到 20 世纪初的梁启超,涵盖其间近90 个人物的作品,但基本上仍属于古代散文范畴。

翟理斯是向英语世界介绍中国古代散文的先驱。他在浩瀚的中国古典文献中寻珍觅宝,选取精华,逐篇译成英语。*Gems of Chinese Literature：Prose* 应是第一部向西方介绍中国古代散文的书。

但在翟理斯的时代,汉学作为一个专门的学问,还没有在国际上形成。译者在介绍中国古代散文时,也多偏重于作品本身的翻译,研究的成分不多。对所节选的文章作者做了简单的介绍,对其思想倾向和创作特征以及时代的思潮等涉猎很少。

Pollard 的《古今散文英译集》产生于世纪之交,随着国际间政治、经济和文化的互动越来越紧密,中国与世界的交往日益深入广泛,文化方面的交流更是其中一个重要内容。Pollard通过这本英译集,向不懂汉语和对中国了解甚少的西方读者介绍中国散文,以期使他们进而了解不同时期中国人的生活、思想、情趣等。作为译者兼作者的 Pollard 先生更觉有必要的是,通观中国散文的发展脉络理出其演变过程,以及这一演变过程与时代、与主流思想的关系。这就使得本书不仅是一部翻译作品,同时也具有研究的性质。

三、研究的主要内容

这里所说的研究,主要不是对于翻译本身的研究,而是关于中西散文的对比和中国古今散文演变过程的研究,这一研究的性质主要从三方面的内容体现出来:一是序(Preface)和引言(Introduction),二是关于作家的评论(Commentary),三是关于文章的译者说明(Translator's Note)和译者后记(Translator's Afterword)。

序和引言

在序和引言里,作者简要论述了古希腊和古罗马传统奠定了欧洲文明的基础,同时也发展了雅俗并存的散文文学。但在中国,经过历朝历代的分裂而又终归统一的反反复复的历史,其文化传统从未中断,以文言文为媒介的书面语言一直延续了 2 000 年之久。

作者还论述了西方散文概念和中国古代散文概念的不同,以及中国现当代散文因受西方散文影响而演变的情况。20 世纪初期,特别是五四以后,欧洲文学作品——法国蒙田、英国培根式的散文被译介到中国。当时的文学界对如何称呼散文这种文体没有形成共识,比较倾向于称其为小品文(minor works)或随笔(occasional jottings)。现在是通称"散文",其性质和英语的 essay 类似。因此,中国现当代散文的概念和西方 essay 的概念是一致的。

但传统上,中国古代散文选集之类所包含的范围比现当代散文的概念要广泛——凡不属于韵文的文体(也不包括小说)都归于散文范畴。如官方的史记(official memorials),法令、文告(rescripts),序言(prefaces),书信(letters),讣告(obituaries),散文诗(prose poems),传记(biographies),历史著作和哲学著作的节选(excerpts from historical and philosophical works),等等。古代散文的语言皆为文言文,一直延续到清朝末年。

在讨论西方散文和中国古代散文的不同时,作者主要涉及语言和思想倾向(mindset)。

就语言而言,作者说,欧洲国家于十六十七世纪开始用本国语言代替拉丁语作为教育的媒介语言(medium for educated discourse)。蒙田(Montaigne)于 1580 年开始用法语发表

Essais,培根(Bacon)于 1597—1625 年间用英语发表 *Essays*。作者特别指出,语言媒介的选择不仅影响到怎么写,也影响到写什么。在欧洲,民族语言的使用一方面带来了民族意识的觉醒,另一方面扩大了写作的主题范围。欧洲的散文家,以及后来美国的散文家,自觉不自觉地在影响思潮的走向上、在创建新的国家政体上发挥着作用。自 18 世纪早期,英美散文家们便在杂志上宣传他们的思想和主张,他们的文章在文化阶层里享有广泛读者。

中国的情况则不同。中国自汉代确立儒家思想的统治地位,虽然朝代频繁更迭,但思想和政体没有根本变化。直到 19 世纪末期,才开始有了比较自由的新闻。因此,古代中国没有赋予它的作家和知识分子以新的视角和方式去观察世界的使命和动力。中国古代知识分子关于外界的知识是很局限的。

同时,作者也谈到文章的娱乐性。英语散文很重视娱乐性,散文里机智、幽默的内容很突出,因为登载文章的杂志都希望畅销。在中国古代散文作家里,李渔是唯一注重文章娱乐性的作家。

在引言里,作者还讨论了中国古代和现当代散文各个时期所表现出来的特征及其发展变化的历史因缘。比如,关于五四时期,作者认为,19 世纪 40 年代以来,中国遭受一系列军事挫折,特别是五四以后,一些知识分子开始思考向西方学习。在文化方面开始介绍西方文学,散文作为一种独立的文学样式,是受西方散文的启示提出和建立起来的。随着五四以来新文学的兴起,也实现了中国散文从文言文到白话文的过渡。关于"文化大革命"以后改革开放以来的情况,作者谈到人们开始关注个人生活和文化问题,散文的本质特征——真实性和客观性又开始发挥作用。人们通过媒体或国外旅行获得更多的知识,从而扩大了视野,表现在散文里的理智和人性得到恢复。

作者在介绍散文在台湾的发展情况时说,总体上,台湾的文学体现了传统的与现代的相融合,本土的与外国的相融合的特征。自上世纪 50 年代以来,由于台湾文学受世界现代主义文学潮流的影响,散文的形式也在革新。但作品多为速写之类,发人深省的作品比较少。在介绍台湾的具体作家和作品时,作者讲得更具体些。

作家评论

在作家评论里,作者对所选的每一位作家都做了详略不同的评论。从这一部分我们可以看出作者对作家所做的深入的研究。比如,书里选了李渔于 1671 年出版的《闲情偶记》(《闲情偶寄》)中的四篇文章,分别为:《闲情偶记·选姿》("Pleasant Diversions:Judging Beauty"),《闲情偶记·习技》("Pleasant Diversions:Accomplishments"),《闲情偶记·文艺》("Pleasant Diversions:Literacy"),《闲情偶记·衣衫》("Pleasant Diversions:Clothes")。

作者选取李渔的文章是因为,他认为所有称得上是文化的东西都有其娱乐性,而在中国古代作家里,李渔是唯一追求文章娱乐性的作家,他的文章很有风趣。作者在评论里简要叙述了李渔的生平和文学活动之后说,李渔写文章是为了卖,他的作品是为一般读者而写的,不是为受过很高教育的上层人士而写的。因为他的作品的缘故,他在上层人士当中的名声不好。假如很多人都知道他是色情小说《肉蒲团》(*The Prayer Mat of Flesh*)的作者,他的名声会更加狼藉。但是,他以他写作的商业目的背叛了他自己的社会阶层,他就以他的机智和幽默重塑了当时已变得十分刻板的短篇小说,他以他那独具见解的思维把索然无味的作品注释之类变成读来使人感到愉悦的文章。

笔者读到余怀为李渔《闲情偶寄》写的《序言》里也有与作者相类似的评论,余说:"悲者读之愉,拙者读之巧,愁者读之作且舞,病者读之霍然兴。"

再如,作者选了鲁迅的四篇杂文,分别为《夏三虫》("Three Summer Pests")、《男人的进化》("The Evolution of the Male Sex")、《阿金》("Ah Jin")和《在现代中国的孔夫子》("Confucius in Modern China")。作者深感鲁迅的文史知识之广、国学修养之深。他说,鲁迅的两部短篇小说集足以奠定他持久的文学声誉。对鲁迅的《野草》和《朝花夕拾》评价也很高,特别推崇鲁迅的杂文以及他在杂文里所表现出来的机智与幽默。他认为鲁迅是 20 世纪中国最有成效的散文家,也是世界级的辩论文作家。

译者对鲁迅的评价是很中肯的。最近,天津师范大学文学院王国绶教授在他的《百年中国文学第一人》一文中提到,2000 年香港《亚洲周刊》组织来自全球的 14 位文学名家,评选"20 世纪中文小说 100 强",鲁迅的《呐喊》荣登榜首。同年,日本读书界公推《呐喊》为世界百年百部优秀创作第一名。

译者说明和译者后记

关于作品的选材,译者曾讲过他的两个原则:一方面要全面展现中国古代和现当代散文的面貌;一方面也有个人的喜好和倾向。因为,他说,译者不喜欢的东西是译不好的,无论这些文章名声有多高。比如,诸葛亮的《出师表》("To Lead Out the Army"),表面上看,不过是诸葛丞相呈请给皇帝的一篇奏章,但他认为,这篇奏章比中国文学的任何一篇作品都更能体现曹丕所说的"气"(曹丕曾在其《典论·论文》中讲过"文以气为主,气之清浊有体,不可力强而致……")。因此,译者选择翻译《出师表》是有明确用意的。

译者对所选文章中的 14 篇做了说明,介绍写作背景及文章特点,引导读者阅读和欣赏;对我们更有吸引力的是,译者时而结合文章里的语言现象谈翻译问题。如韩愈的《祭鳄鱼文》("Address to the Crocodiles of Chaozhou"),译者介绍说,韩愈于公元 819 年被贬至远离京城的潮州做刺史,在任期间,曾代表天子向鳄鱼宣战,限令它们离开潮州,远徙海上。译者看到其中的滑稽与幽默。在涉及翻译问题时,译者说,韩愈的长句子错综复杂如同迷宫,但当他跟踪作者的思路找到句子的归宿时,也着实令译者感到愉快,甚至是感到荣幸。我们作为读者是可以想象得到的,一个母语为英语的汉学家阅读中国古文中比较难懂的文章时,当他克服了语言的挑战,进而理解文章的奥妙,他的感觉一定是很好的。

再如,译者对周作人的《苦雨》("Relentless Rain")也做了简短的说明。他说这是周作人早期的一篇作品,采取给孙伏园写信的形式,具有那个时代散文创作的几个特点:一、书信体散文在当时被认为是最真实的一种文学形式。二、人生的兴趣,即使是个人生活中的小事,也足以构成文学创作的素材。三、文章故作随意之状,以此来表现作者的性情,同时也为了幽默而夸大了脱俗的文人的性情,但译者说,如果作者没有幽默感,作品也就谈不上幽默了。

《苦雨》结尾时说,"我本等着看你的秦游记,现在却由我先写给你看,这也可以算是'意表之外'的事吧"。译者说,他将"意表之外"译作 outside of expectation,这样译也许有些费解,这是因为现在对这个词的正确含义有争议,他这样译意在暗示这个短语的意义的不确定性。

译者说明和译者后记既体现了本书的研究性质,也解决了译文里需要解释的具体词义和文化内涵,是一个可借鉴的经验。

四、关于翻译的问题

《古今散文英译集》不是专门讨论翻译问题的书,但在译者准确而地道的英语译文里,在他对作者和文章背景的介绍和对文化问题的解读里,以及他在翻译过程中对一些细节的思考里,我们得到很多启示,其中有很多问题值得我们学习和研究。

关于文化内容的处理

翻译中国古代散文往往涉及很多历史、典故和逸闻逸事,有时一个典故、一段逸闻就是一个故事,在原文里顺便提及是很自然的事,但如照直译出来,则难以把事情说清楚,会给西方读者带来阅读的困难。况且,很多文章的写作又是有背景的,比如,苏轼的散文《方山子传》,有些与文章相关的事情没有在文内出现,也需向读者介绍,便于理解。比如,文中的方山子是谁,他与文章作者是什么关系等,译者在"译者说明"里都做了交代:方山子真名陈慥,字季常,其父陈希亮,宋仁宗天圣年间(公元 1023—1032 年)进士,官至太常少卿,早年苏轼曾任他的下属,与陈慥是至交。苏轼谪居黄州期间,于元丰三年(公元 1080 年)正月与陈慥偶然相遇。第二年,苏轼便写了《方山子传》。这个"译者说明"对读者理解文章是很需要的。

接着译者又说:"The extent of their intimacy is not revealed in this essay; Chen is, rather, treated as the seat of an enigma."这句话则是对文章结尾的一个暗示。文章的结尾处有这样一段文字:"而其(指陈慥)家在洛阳,园宅壮丽,与公侯等。河北有田,岁地帛千匹,亦足以富乐。皆弃不取,独来穷山中,此岂无得而然哉?"

针对这个问题,译者又在译者说明的最后处做了如下说明:

> He pictures Chen Jichang as another man of ability, who could have served the state either as a military man or as a civil official. In pondering why he chose not to do either, or indeed to enjoy his inherited wealth, Su is asking the general question of what a man should do with his life. Untypically, however, Su does not volunteer an answer: Chen becomes an empty space between contradictions.

这就为读者理解这篇文章的宗旨提供了一把钥匙。

译者在翻译类似的文章时,着意交代文章的写作背景、作者与被描写人物的关系和文章的内涵等,这是一种更加彻底的文化翻译的策略。这同时对我们也是一个深刻的启示,即翻译必须与研究相结合,而 Pollard 在这方面做得非常之好。

文章中也常有一些含有文化内容的字词,译成英语时需要解释,但译文本身又容不得这样的解释。凡遇到这种情况,译者也都在译者说明里做了补充。如,《方山子传》的第一句,"方山子,光、黄间隐人也",译文:Master Table Mountain is a recluse who is to be found in the Guangzhou-Huangzhou area. 这里将"隐人"译作 recluse。实际上,"隐人"是中国古代文化的一种特殊现象,跟英语的 recluse 不完全一样,《新牛津英语词典》这样解释 recluse:a person who lives a solitary life and tends to avoid other people,而汉语的"隐人"则有更深一层的意思。有学者在解释《方山子传》时说,陈慥"晚年'乃遁于光、黄间',隐然有不平之意"。这里的"不平之意"比 lives a solitary life 所含内容就多了。因此,为了让西方读者了解汉语"隐人"的确切含义,译者在"译者说明"里做了如下的解释:

Su describes him as a "recluse" (*yinren*), but as we see that term does not signify extreme solitariness; it means only that he lives a simple life as a commoner. In the modern vernacular he might be said to have dropped out of the rat race.

这一解释就把汉语"隐人"的含义说得很清楚了。

也有一些属于修辞或具有文化背景的词汇，译文难以准确传达原文含义。遇到这种情况，译者便也在译者说明或译者后记里加以解释。

比如，朱自清的《背影》里的"背影"一词，译者认为在汉语里它能引起诗意的联想（poetical associations）。在英语里则没有相应的词，只好将其译作 a view of him from the rear，但译者说，这样译，其"诗意的联想"就不复存在。

在叶圣陶写于 1944 年的《知识分子》一文里，"伙计"一词出现了近 20 次之多，如何翻译这个词，译者在"译者后记"里说，他反复斟酌，想到了 flunky，也想到了 assistants，但觉得都不甚合适，并说明了为什么不合适；最终将其译作 hired help，并说，对 hired help 仍然有保留等。

关于语义结构

笔者认为，从语言层面看，翻译的过程，本质上是两种语义结构转换的过程。在英汉翻译中，目前有"归化"与"异化"两种不同的处理方法。"归化"翻译一般是尽量符合汉语语义结构。"异化"翻译则保留一些英语句式的特点。但传统上"归化"的翻译居多，现在采取"异化"方法翻译的作品也逐渐增多，将来的英汉翻译也可能出现"归化"与"异化"并荣的局面。

但在汉英翻译中，就语言的表达方式而言，更多的是求"归化"，即要求译文符合英语的语义结构，从词汇、句子到篇章都是如此。所以，汉英翻译实际上也就是从汉语的语义结构到英语的语义结构的转换过程。从翻译实践看，在好的汉英翻译作品里，都有这样的倾向。从中国古典小说的翻译（如，David Hawkes 和 John Minford 翻译的《红楼梦》*The Story of the Stone*，1973—1986；W. J. F. Jenner 翻译的《西游记》*Journey to the West*，1982；Sidney Shapiro 翻译的《水浒传》*Outlaws of the Marsh*，1988；Moss Roberts 翻译的《三国演义》*Three Kingdoms*，1994；以及 Denis C. & Victor H. Mair 翻译的《聊斋志异选》*Strange Tales from Make-Do Studio*，2001）中可以看出来，从葛浩文（Howard Goldblatt）的译文（如《萧红短篇小说选》*Selected Stories of Xiao Hong*，1982），David Pollard 的译文（如《古今散文英译集》*The Chinese Essay*，1999），以及施晓菁的译文（如《骆驼祥子》*Camel Xiangzi*，2001）里也表现得很突出。

目前从事汉英翻译的群体里，一部分是以汉语为母语者，一部分是以英语为母语者。一般来讲，前者在语言的翻译上注意忠实原文，但在语言的处理上，因受潜意识里汉语语义结构的影响，译文往往有汉语词汇意义和句子结构的影子。而以英语为母语的译者（如前面所列举的几位）在忠实原文的同时（理解有误的情况除外），在语言的处理上表现灵活，往往能够摆脱原文词汇表层意义和汉语语义结构的束缚，在词汇、句子和篇章各个层面上能够运用自如。他们翻译出来的英语韵味浓厚，耐人寻味。这是值得研究的。

关于语义结构问题，复旦大学陆国强教授在他的《英汉和汉英语义结构对比》里有过如下的论述："就中国的学者而言，有的擅长于英译汉，有的擅长于汉译英。就成功率来看，前者占压倒多数，而后者却是凤毛麟角；就成果而言，英译汉在数量和质量上也大大超过汉译英。究其原因不外乎是语义能力的问题。"他在解释"语义能力"时说："语义能力实指说话人的内在语义知识,即每个人脑中内在地掌握了本族语的语义结构,从而能正确地生成(generate)和解释语言信息。这种语义能力实际上是一种语感(a sense of language),或者说是一种语言直觉(linguistic intuition)。要把一种语言卓有成效地转换成另一种语言,培养和提高语义能力是成败的关键。"

他所说的"掌握本族语的语义结构"与"培养和提高语义能力"是翻译"成败的关键",是有见地的。我们从 Pollard 的译文里可以得到证实。Pollard 是以英语为母语的译者,他的英语语义结构意识和语义能力是特别的强。当然,他的汉英翻译的成功还有别的因素,如他在汉语言文学方面的修养和在翻译理论上的博学,都在他汉英翻译成功的道路上起了作用。让我们从他的译文中摘取一些例子共同欣赏。

例 1. 诸葛亮的《出师表》有一句话:"今天下三分,益州疲敝,此诚危急存亡之秋也。"译文:The world is still divided into three, and our base in Shu is beleaguered. At this time our very survival hangs in the balance.

用 survival 表示汉语的"危急存亡"这一概念,一下子就抓住了它的实质,再和成语 hangs in the balance 连用,不但意思准确,且行文节奏也与原文非常符合。

例 2. 陆龟蒙的《野庙碑》开始这样说:"碑者,悲也。古者悬而窆,用木。后人书之以表其功德,固留之不忍去,碑之名由是而得。"译文:

The word for "monument" (*bei*) comes from "mourning (*bei*)". In olden days a wooden post was used in winching the coffin down into the grave pit; later on, inscriptions were written on these posts to make known the deeds and virtues of the deceased, so they came to be preserved for their sentimental value. This is the origin of the name *bei*.

原文里的"碑"是指古代下葬时在墓穴旁边树立的木柱,上面记述死者的事迹功业,然后埋进墓穴。后来改为留在墓穴旁。这里要说的是关于"固留之不忍去"的翻译,译者将其译作 so they came to be preserved for their sentimental value。"固留之不忍去"意义上多少有点重复,在汉语里这种现象并不少见,也很自然。但英语译文避免了这种现象。且用 for their sentimental value 来翻译"不忍"之意,说明译者体悟出"不忍"所包含的感情因素。这是一个绝好的短语译文,因而也孕育出一个绝好的英语句子。值得以汉语为母语的译者借鉴研究。

例 3. 杨绛《隐身衣》里说,"要炼成刀枪不入,水火不伤的功夫,谈何容易! 如果没有这份功夫……"译文:It is idle to talk of making yourself invulnerable to cuts and burns. Yet if you do not have that invulnerability...

译文里的 invulnerable 是译文的灵魂,它完全超越了"功夫"的表层意思,而是更深入了一步,即有这样的"功夫"就会有 invulnerable 的本领。而且,invulnerable to 和 cuts and burns 又极具语义的相容性。这样,用 invulnerable to cuts and burns 来翻译"刀枪不入,水火不伤的功夫"就是理想的搭配了。后面的"这份功夫"译作 that invulnerability,照应了前面的 invulnerable,产生极好的连贯效果。

以上是语义结构在词汇和短语层面上变通的例子。

例 4. 鲁迅的杂文《在现代中国的孔夫子》里有一句,"总而言之,孔夫子之在中国,是权势者们捧起来的……"译文:To sum up, Confucius owes his exalted position in China to the wielders of power...

译文不受原文句式和词性的约束,用了一个常见而又能够统领全句的英语句式 owe...

to... 意即 be indebted to。句式的变化和词汇的变化是同步的,这就有了以英语的形容词短语 exalted position 译汉语的被动句式"是······捧起来的",以英语的介词短语 the wielders of power 译汉语的名词短语"权势者们"等一系列变通。更重要的是译文的文字简洁——而文字的力量来源于简洁。

书中还选了梁遇春的《途中》一文,译者对梁遇春十分推崇,称他是中国的"世界公民",因为梁遇春的兴趣不仅在"同胞",而且在"全人类"。

例 5.《途中》有一句近乎谚语的话,"人生难得秋前雨"。汉英之间对应的谚语是有的,但多数汉语谚语译成英语时则考验译者的智慧。下面是 Pollard 的译文:One of the best things in life is the rain that heralds autumn.

译文用 one of the best things 译"难得",以 the rain that heralds autumn 译"秋前雨"。原文是很有诗意的,译文同样富有诗意。译文不说 the rain before autumn,而是 the rain that heralds autumn。这让我们领悟到文学语言和一般语言的区别。假设英语读者对"秋前雨"也有类似的感受,这句充满诗意的英语译文也可能会变成一个英语谚语。

以上是语义结构在句子层面上变通的两个例子。这样的例子随处都是。关于篇章变通的好例子也多,因为篇幅的关系不在此处细谈。

关于语言风格

本书选了朱自清的《背影》,关于这篇散文的风格及其翻译问题,译者在"译者说明"里说,20 年代新文学提倡用字简单,朱自清注重语言的明白易懂,译文也应努力保持在基本英语的水平。我们从几个例句的译文可以看出译者为了在行文风格上与原文保持一致所做的努力。

例 1. 我与父亲不相见已二年余了,我最不能忘记的是他的背影。

It has been two years and more since I saw my father. My most vivid memory of him is a view of him from the rear.

例 2. 事已如此,不必难过,好在天无绝人之路。

What has happened has happened, you shouldn't upset yourself. Heaven helps those who help themselves.

例 3. 这些日子,家中光景很是惨淡,一半为了丧事,一半为了父亲赋闲。

Those days at home were very gloomy, partly because of the funeral, partly because of father being out of work.

Pollard 的英语和 *Good News New Testament* 里的英语风格十分相似。

书里也选了一些抒情和写景的散文,它们特别能体现文章的"情韵"。正如郁达夫所说,"在散文里似以情韵或情调两字来说,较为妥当。这一种要素,尤其是写抒情或写景的散文时,包含得特别的多"。译者翻译了郁达夫的著名散文《江南的冬景》,其中关于抒情和写景的文字很多,比如:

到得冬天,不时也会下着微雨,而这微雨寒村里的冬霖景象,又是一种说不出的悠闲境界。

作者将雨中江南小村朦胧的景色描写得特别真切,使读者有身临其境之感。译者也以朦胧的笔触再现了这一如画的景致,成功地传达了郁达夫所说的情韵:

In winter you often get drizzling rain, and the winter scene of an out of the way village shrouded in drizzle conveys an inexpressible sense of pastoral peace.

这本《古今散文英译集》不但是汉英翻译的范本,也为翻译研究提供了难得的好材料。总之,这本书以其考究的译文和新颖的研究范式,为英语读者和学者提供了一本难得的经典译作。

选文三　Principles of Literature

Charles Batteux

导　言

本文选自 André Lefevere, *Translation/History/Culture*. London & New York: Routledge,1992.

夏尔·巴托(Charles Batteux)系卢梭同时代人,古典主义美学的代表之一,广为翻译学界所知的就是其关于作者与译者关系的论断:认为原作者是主人,译者是仆人,译者只能紧跟原作者忠实地再现和反映原作的思想及风格,不能僭越仆人的身份进行创作。选文起篇便颠覆性地指出:如同绘画一样,描摹难于创作,翻译文本的生产远远难于文学创作和文本理解。作者面对客观世界的呈现,总可以调动自己的才思,付诸文字,对于言所不逮的地方,可以采取,可以回避;而译者却身无长物,只能亦步亦趋跟在原作者之后,殚精竭虑再现原作的语气、题旨与语势。论者接着分析了可能造成作者情思、风格迥异的诸多因素,因此,合格译者的第一条件便是熟谙两种语言的精妙,这一素养的具备不仅可以通过长期研习获得,也可以通过跟翻译经验丰富的人交流取得。论者提出成功翻译的第一即终极准则——再现原作的全部文体特色,并提出可资参考的11条具体操作方法。

Only those who have never translated classical authors would doubt the difficulty of the enterprise. Those who have had the experience know that you often need more time, more effort, and more diligence to copy a beautiful painting than to create one.

When you translate the big problem is not to understand the author's thoughts. You can usually do so with the help of good editions and commentaries, and certainly if you examine the link between the thoughts. But the problem is to render things, thoughts, expressions, stylistic features, the general tone of the work and the particular tones of the particular styles of poets, orators, historians, and to render things as they are, without adding anything, moving anything, or taking anything away. The thoughts must be rendered with their colors, degrees, nuances. You must render the stylistic features that give fire, spirit, life to the discourse, as well as the expressions, natural or figurative, strong, rich, gracious, delicate. And you must do all this while trying to follow a model that commands without pity and wants to be obeyed with ease. It is obvious, therefore, that you need at least as much taste, if not as much genius, to translate well as you need to write well—or maybe more.

The author, guided by his genius that is always free and by his subject matter that presents him with ideas he may accept or reject as he pleases, is the absolute master of his thoughts and expressions. He is allowed to dismiss what he cannot express. The translator is master of nothing, he must bend with infinite suppleness to all the variations he finds in his author. Just consider the variety of tones that can be found within the same subject matter and, *a fortiori*, within the same genre. If the parts that make up the subject matter have been attuned and brought into proper harmony you can observe the rising and falling of the style and see how it grows softer and stronger, more or less constricted, without overreaching the unity of its fundamental character. Terence has a style that is suited to comedy all the way through. It is always simple and delicate, but it is so to different degrees whether spoken by Simon or Daves, by Sostrates, Mysis, or Pamphilus. The degrees vary with the actors' emotions, whether they are moved or not, or caught up in one passion or another.

Let us take matters even further: the epistolary style must be a simple one. It is said that you have to write a letter the way you speak (as long as you speak well, of course). Imagine a scale that runs from baker to king. There are so many social conditions differentiated by education, talent, birth, fortune, and there are so many simple styles that correspond to them. You must not use one where the other is appropriate. You cannot do so without offending taste and decorum. But the writer must also be true to himself, his personality, his age, his position, what he has been, what he has done, what he hopes, and what he fears. All these factors map out stylistic possibilities for him which he is able to implement if he has excellent taste. You cannot render all these possibilities in translation unless you have experienced them first and then you must master at your discretion the language you want to enrich with foreign loot. Strong languages break elegance when they try to transfer it. Weak languages dilute power. Try to imagine what a successful translation must be like!

The first requirement the translator has to meet is that he should master in depth the genius of the two languages he wants to deal with. He may have done so by means of some confused sentiment resulting from the habit with which you speak a language. But would it be useless to shed some light on the road of feeling and to give the translator a few hints to make sure he does not lose his way?

Sometimes you cannot find the words that correspond to the words you want to translate. This does by no means happen only to beginners or to those who do not know their languages well. When they are unable to find the simple words that are in existence they go looking for flaccid circumlocutions that cannot possibly take their place. We must tell them to study first and to learn their own language well. Once they have done so they will have problems only with syntactic constructions. They can then share those problems with people who have more experience because they have been using the language for a longer period of time. They will be able to solve those problems, at least in part, if they take to heart the concepts we are about to develop.

The first principle of translation is that you must use all stylistic features present in the original when both languages are amenable to this.

(1) You must never tamper with the order of things, whether facts or arguments, since that order is the same in all languages and since it is tied to human nature, not the particular genius of different nations.

(2) You must also preserve the order of ideas, or at least their parts. There must have been a reason, no matter how hard to detect, that made the author use one order rather than another. It may have been harmony, but sometimes it is also energy.

(3) You must also preserve periods, no matter how long, because a period is nothing but a thought that consists of a number of other thoughts linked by an inner necessity, and those links are the life of those thoughts and they represent the speaker's main intention.

On the other hand, there are cases in which you can cut up periods that are too long. But then the parts you cut off are linked by an external logic and in an artificial manner. They are no longer parts of periods proper.

(4) You must preserve all conjunctions. They are like joints that keep the parts together. Their position and their meaning should not be changed. They can be omitted only when the mind can easily supply them, that is when the mind propels itself from one part of a period to another and when the conjunction, if expressed, would merely hold it back and not help at all.

(5) All adverbs must be placed next to the verb, in front of it or behind it according to the demands of harmony or energy. The Romans always gave them their place based on those two principles.

(6) Symmetrical periods must be rendered symmetrically or in some equivalent manner. Their symmetry in the discourse lies in the relationship between a number of ideas or a number of expressions. The symmetry of expressions may be found in the sounds, the number of syllables, the length of the words or their endings, or the ways in which the parts of the period are arranged.

(7) Brilliant thoughts should be rendered by approximately the same number of words to make sure their brilliance is preserved in the translation. Otherwise you will either brighten their splendor or darken it, and you are

not allowed to do either.

(8) You must preserve the figures of thought because they are the same in all minds. They can arrange themselves in the same order everywhere. This is the way to render interrogations, conjunctions, expectorations, etc. Figures of speech such as metaphors, repetitions, combinations of words and phrases can usually be replaced by equivalents in the other language.

(9) Proverbs, which are popular maxims, and which can almost be considered one word, must be rendered by means of other proverbs. Since they only deal with things that are common in a society all nations have many proverbs in common, at least as far as the sense goes, even though they may be expressed in different ways.

(10) All circumlocutions are evil: they are commentary, not translation. Yet necessity may serve as the translator's excuse if there is no other way to make the sense known.

(11) Finally, we must totally abandon the style of the text we translate when meaning demands that we do so for the sake of clarity, when feeling demands it for the sake of vividness, or when harmony demands it for the sake of pleasure. This becomes a second principle, which is the reverse of the first one.

Ideas may present themselves under different guises and yet remain the same and they may combine themselves or fall apart in the words we use to express them. They may appear as verbs, adjectives, adverbs, or nouns. The translator has four ways to chose from. Let him take his scales, let him weigh expressions on either side, let him bring them into equilibrium in various ways. He will be forgiven all metaphors as long as he makes sure the thought keeps the same body and the same life. He will do as the traveler who gives a gold coin in exchange for various pieces of silver, or vice versa, as he pleases.

These are a few very simple procedures. I venture to say they will always achieve the desired effect. They will show the translator in need a way out of his predicament—the very way he has been trying to discover for a long time if he has allowed himself to be guided by instinct alone.

选文四　Translating Prose

Susan Bassnett

导　言

本文选自 Susan Bassnett，*Translation Studies*（3rd Edition）．London & New York：Routledge，2002．

鉴于目前翻译理论界诗歌翻译研究在数量上远远超过其他文体的翻译研究，尤其是包括小说在内的散文翻译研究（本文论者选取一个较为宽泛的散文定义），苏珊·巴斯奈特通过在学生中开展调查实验，发现一个奇怪的现象：大多数的同学都会选择他们从未读过或很久以前读过的小说的开首章节进行翻译，鲜有顾及开篇段落与全文结构关系的，大多数同学认为散文翻译可以不像诗歌翻译那般注重形式与内容的统一。接着，论文以若干经典著作的卷首段落翻译为例，阐释说明开篇语句之与鸿篇巨制全文的重要性。选文引用英国作家希莱尔·贝洛克关于翻译的六条指导性原则，逐一结合广义散文的翻译加以说明，指出散文翻译的若干具体困难：翻译单位的定制、文本功能界定、专有名词翻译、对等问题等。全文以翻译理论家列维的一系列问题作结，颇具启发和引导性。

Although there is a large body of work debating the issues that surround the translation of poetry, far less time has been spent studying the specific problems of translating literary prose. One explanation for this could be the higher status that poetry holds, but it is more probably due to the widespread erroneous notion that a novel is somehow a simpler structure than a poem and is consequently easier to translate. Moreover, whilst we have a number of detailed statements by poet-translators regarding their methodology, we have fewer statements from prose translators. Yet there is a lot to be learned from determining the criteria for undertaking a translation, as has been demonstrated above.

For a number of years I have used an exercise designed to discover how the translation of a novel is approached. Students are asked to translate the opening paragraph(s) of any novel and the translations are then examined in group discussion. What has emerged from this exercise, time and again, is that students will frequently start to translate a text that they have not previously read or that they have read only once some time earlier. In short, they simply open the SL text and *begin at the beginning*, without considering how that opening section relates to the structure of the work as a whole. Yet it would be quite unacceptable to approach the translation of a poem in this way. This is significant because it shows that a different concept of the imaginary distinction between form and content prevails when the text to be considered is a novel. It seems to be easier for the (careless) prose translator to consider content as *separable* from form.

As an example of what can happen when the translator stresses content at the expense of the total structure, let us take the following extract, the opening of *The Magic Mountain*:

> An unassuming young man was travelling in midsummer, from his native city of Hamburg to Davos-Platz in the Canton of Grisons, on a three weeks' visit.
>
> From Hamburg to Davos is a long journey—too long, indeed, for so brief a stay. It crosses all sorts of country; goes up hill and down dale, descends from the plateaus of Southern Germany to the shores of Lake Constance, over its bounding waves and on across marshes once thought to be bottomless.
>
> (trans. H. T. Lowe-Porter)*

This fast-moving, energetic passage, consisting of three sentences with four verbs of action and movement pulls the reader straight into the narrative. The no-nonsense details of the journey and the time of the young man's proposed stay combine with the authorial value judgement on the brevity of the visit. In short, what we have here is a strong descriptive opening, with a powerful authorial presence, and the world picture painted here has close affinities with what the reader perceives as his own rational world.

The problem with this translation comes when it is set against the original German text, and the extent of the distance between the SL and the TL versions is compared. Mann's novel opens as follows:

> Ein einfacher junger Mensch reiste im Hochsommer von Hamburg, seiner Vaterstadt, nach Davos-Platz im Graubündischen. Er fuhr auf Besuch für drei Wochen.
>
> Von Hamburg bis dorthinauf, das ist aber eine weite Reise; zu weit eigentlich im Verhältnis zu einem so kurzen Aufenthalt. Es geht durch mehrerer Herren Länder, bergauf and bergab, von der süddeutschen Hochebene hinunter zum Gestade des Schwäbischen Meeres und zu Schiff über seine springende Wellen hin, dahin über Schlünde, die früher für unergründlich galten.

In this opening passage, the reader is given a series of clues that key him in to some of the codes operating through the novel. It is, of course, not restricted within the boundaries imposed by the realist world and depicts the ideological struggle between such dramatic opposites as health and sickness, life and death, democracy and reaction, and is set in a sanatorium where the characters are "on holiday", removed from the struggle for existence. The journey depicted in the first few sentences is therefore functioning on more than one level: there is the young man's actual journey; the symbolic journey across a nation; the

---

* I am grateful to my colleague, Tony Phelan, for bringing this example to my attention.

journey as a metaphor for the quest on which the reader is about to embark. Moreover, in Mann's description of the journey there are deliberate devices (e. g. the use of the classical term *Gestade for shore*) recalling eighteenth-century modes, for another major line through the novel is an attempt to bring together two stylistic modes, the lyrical and the prosaic. The English translator's compression of Mann's sentence structures reduces the number of levels on which the reader can approach the text, for clearly the translator's prime concern has been to create a sense of rapid movement. So the second sentence has been integrated with the first to form a single unit and the fourth sentence has been shortened by deliberate omissions (e. g. *zu Schiff*—by boat). The stylized terms describing places have been replaced by straight-forward, geographical names and the stately language of Mann's text has been replaced with a series of clichés in a conversational account of an overly long journey.

There are also other variations. The introduction of the protagonist in Mann's first sentence in such deliberately decharacterized terms is yet another key to the reader, but by translating *einfacher* (ordinary) as *unassuming*, the English translator introduces a powerful element of characterization and alters the reader's perspective. And it is difficult not to conclude that the English translator has inadequately grasped the significance of the novel when there is even a case of mistranslation, *Schlünde* (abysses) rendered as *marshes*.

An example of a different kind of deviation through translation can be found by considering the following passages:

> Il primo di giugno dell'anno scorso Fontamara rimase per la prima volta senza illuminazione elettrica. Il due di giugno, il tre di giugno, il quattro di giugno. Fontamara continuò a rimanere senza illuminazione elettrica. Così nei giorni seguenti e nei mesi seguenti, finché Fontamara si riabituò al regime del chiaro di luna. Per arrivare dal chiaro di luna alla luce elettrica, Fontamara aveva messo un centinaio di anni, attraverso l'olio di oliva e il petrolio. Per tornare dalla luce elettrica al chiaro di luna bastò una sera.
>
> (*Fontanara*, I. Silone)
>
> On the first of June last year Fontamara went without electric light for the first time. Fontamara remained without electric light on the second, the third and the fourth of June.
>
> So it continued for days and months. In the end Fontamara got used to moonlight again. A century had elapsed between the moon-light era and the electric era, a century which included the age of oil and that of petrol, but one evening was sufficient to plunge us back from electric light to the light of the moon.
>
> (*Fontamara*, G. David and E. Mossbacher)

The opening passage of *Fontamara* introduces the reader immediately to the tone of the work, a *tone* that will remain through the device of the series of fictitious narrators whose accounts Silone is supposedly recording. And it is the tone, always downbeat and gently ironic even when the most moving and painful experiences are being described, that gives this novel its special quality. In the opening paragraph the narrator describes the transitoriness of progress, the way in which the long, slow development of technology that led to the arrival of electric light in a small mountain village can be overturned in a single night, and the faintly mocking, almost resigned tone is immediately established.

The Italian text consists of five sentences. The first two open with time phrases—*il primo di giugno* locates the start of the narrative on a definite date; *il primo di giugno* opens the sentence that expands on that initial blunt statement and moves the reader on in time. The third sentence again opens with a time phrase, now qualified by the conversational first word *così*, and moves still further into time future, through weeks and months. The final two sentences both open with a verbal phrase of movement: *per arrivare and per tornare*, that sum up the point being made in the opening paragraph about the slow movement of technological advancement compared to the speed with which that technology can be abandoned. The language of this paragraph is therefore misleadingly simple, and the almost conversational tone camouflages a heavily rhetorical passage, carefully structured to build to a point of climax and utilizing a series of patterns of repetition (e. g. the various time phrases; phrases such as *illuminazione elettrica*, *luce elettrica*, *chiaro di luna*, etc.).

The English translation has not made any attempt to retain the pattern of five sentences, beginning with either a time phrase or a verb of movement. Instead the second sentence inverts the time phrases, and puts them at the end—which could be defended in terms of English stylistic modes—and the remaining three sentences are formed by splitting one SL sentence into two and then by joining two other SL sentences together. This device works well in the first instance, creating the two short, conversational statements beginning "*So it continued*" and "*In the end*". But by joining the two SL sentences into a single, long TL sentence, the sense of movement of the original is lost in the clumsy structure. The infinitives *arrivare* and *tornare* have become *elapsed* and *to plunge back*, the phrase *attraverso l'olio di oliva e il petrolio* has been expanded (but not made clearer) into *a century which included the age of oil and that of petrol*. The use of era strikes a jarring note, the inversion of the final part of the sentence means that all the impact of the last words of the SL text is lost, and the introduction of the personal pronoun us makes the shift in register between the first four sentences and the final one all the more incongruous. Yet there has clearly been an attempt to set up patterns of repetition in the English text (e. g. the repetition of *era*, *century*) even though phrases such as *chiaro di luna and luce elettrica* are not translated consistently. In short, it is difficult to see what the criteria behind the English translation were, for there are so many inconsistencies. What does seem apparent, however, is that the English translators have not given adequate consideration to the function of the stylistic devices used by Silone.

Wolfgang Iser, developing Roman Ingarden's discussion of the "intentional sentence

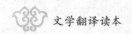
correlatives" that make up the world presented in the literary text, [①] points out that

> the intentional correlatives disclose subtle connections which individually are less concrete than the statements, claims and observations, even though these only take on their real meaningfulness through the interaction of their correlatives. [②]

Iser goes on to state that the sentence does not consist solely of a statement "but aims at something beyond what it actually says", since sentences within a literary text "are always an indication of something that is to come, the structure of which is foreshadowed by their specific content". If the translator, then, handles sentences for their specific content alone, the outcome will involve a loss of dimension. In the case of the English translation of the texts above, the sentences appear to have been translated at face value, rather than as component units in a complex overall structure. Using Popovič's terminology, the English versions show several types of *negative shift* involving:

> (1) mistranslation of information;
> (2) "subinterpretation" of the original text;
> (3) superficial interpretation of connections between intentional correlatives.

Having begun by stating that I intended to avoid value judgements of individual translations, it might now seem that I have deviated from my original plan. Moreover, it might seem unfair to lay so much emphasis on cases of negative shift that emerge from the first few sentences of a vast work. But the point that needs to be made is that although analysis of narrative has had enormous influence since Shlovsky's early theory of prose, there are obviously many readers who still adhere to the principle that a novel consists primarily of *paraphrasable material content* that can be translated straight-forwardly. And whereas there seems to be a common consensus that a prose paraphrase of a poem is judged to be inadequate, there is no such consensus regarding the prose text. Again and again translators of novels take pains to create *readable* TL texts, avoiding the stilted effect that can follow from adhering too closely to SL syntactical structures, but fail to consider the way in which individual sentences form part of the total structure. And in pointing out this failure, which is first and foremost a deficiency in reading, I believe that I am not so much passing judgement on the work of individuals as pointing towards a whole area of translation that needs to be looked at more closely.

Hilaire Belloc [③] laid down six general rules for the translator of prose texts:

> (1) The translator should not "plod on", word by word or sentence by sentence, but should "always 'block out' his work". By "block out", Belloc means that the translator should consider the work as an integral

---

① Roman Ingarden, *The Literary Work of Art* (Evanston: The Northwestern University Press, 1973).

② Wolfgang Iser, *The Implied Reader* (Baltimore and London: The Johns Hopkins Press, 1974), 277.

③ Hilaire Belloc, *On Translation* (Oxford: The Clarendon Press, 1931).

unit and translate in sections, asking himself "before each what the whole sense is he has to render".

(2) The translator should render *idiom by idiom* and idioms of their nature demand translation into another form from that of the original. Belloc cites the case of the Greek exclamation "By the Dog!" which, if rendered literally, becomes merely comic in English, and suggests that the phrase "By God!" is a much closer translation. Likewise, he points out that the French historic present must be translated into the English narrative tense, which is past, and the French system of defining a proposition by putting it into the form of a rhetorical question cannot be transposed into English where the same system does not apply.

(3) The translator must render "intention by intention", bearing in mind that "the intention of a phrase in one language may be less emphatic than the form of the phrase, or it may be more emphatic". By "intention", Belloc seems to be talking about the weight a given expression may have in a particular context in the SL that would be disproportionate if translated literally into the TL. He quotes several examples where the weighting of the phrase in the SL is clearly much stronger or much weaker than the literal TL translation, and points out that in the translation of "intention", it is often necessary to *add* words not in the original "to conform to the idiom of one's own tongue".

(4) Belloc warns against *les faux amis*, those words or structures that may appear to correspond in both SL and TL but actually do not, e. g. *demander*—to ask translated wrongly as *to demand*.

(5) The translator is advised to "transmute boldly" and Belloc suggests that the essence of translating is "the resurrection of an alien thing in a native body".

(6) The translator should never embellish.

Belloc's six rules cover both points of technique and points of principle. His order of priorities is a little curious, but nevertheless he does stress the need for the translator to consider the prose text as a structured whole whilst bearing in mind the stylistic and syntactical exigencies of the TL. He accepts that there is a moral responsibility to the original, but feels that the translator has the right to significantly alter the text in the translation process in order to provide the TL reader with a text that conforms to TL stylistic and idiomatic norms.

Belloc's first point, in which he discusses the need for the translator to "block out" his work, raises what is perhaps the central problem for the prose translator: the difficulty of determining *translation units*. It must be clear at the outset that the text, understood to be in a dialectical relationship with other texts (see *intertextuality* p. 82) and located within a

specific historical context, is the prime unit. But whereas the poet translator can more easily break the prime text down into translatable units, e. g. lines, verses, stanzas, the prose translator has a more complex task. Certainly, many novels are broken down into chapters or sections, but as Barthes has shown with his methodology of five reading codes (see S/Z, discussed by T. Hawkes, *Structuralism and Semiotics*, London, 1977) the structuring of a prose text is by no means as linear as the chapter divisions might indicate. Yet if the translator takes each sentence or paragraph as a minimum unit and translates it without relating it to the overall work, he runs the risk of ending up with a TL text like those quoted above, where the paraphrasable content of the passages has been translated at the cost of everything else.

The way round this dilemma must once again be sought through considering the *function* both of the text and of the devices within the text itself. If the translators of Silone had considered the function of the tone they would have understood why the careful rhetorical patterning of the opening paragraph needed closer examination. Likewise, if the translator of Mann had considered the function of the description of both the young man and the journey, she would have understood the reasons for Mann's choice of language. Every prime text is made up of a series of interlocking systems, each of which has a determinable function in relation to the whole, and it is the task of the translator to apprehend these functions.

Let us consider as an example the problem of translating proper names in Russian prose texts, a problem that has bedeviled generations of translators. Cathy Porter's translation of Alexandra Kollontai's *Love of Worker Bees* contains the following note:

> Russians have a first ("Christian") name, a patronymic and a surname. The customary mode of address is first name plus patronymic, thus, Vasilisa Dementevna, Maria Semenovna. There are more intimate abbreviations of first names which have subtly affectionate, patronizing or friendly overtones. So for instance Vasilisa becomes Vasya, Vasyuk, and Vladimir becomes Volodya, Volodka, Volodechka, Volya. ①

So the translator explains, quite properly, the Russian naming system, but this note is of little help during the actual reading process, for Cathy Porter retains the variations of name in the TL version and the English reader is at times confronted with the bewildering profusion of names on a single page all referring to the same character. In short, the SL system has been transported into the TL system, where it can only cause confusion and obstruct the process of reading. Moreover, as Boris Uspensky has shown in his valuable book *A Poetics of Composition*②, the use of names in Russian can denote shifts in point of

---

① Alexandra Kollontai, *Love of Worker Bees*, tr. Cathy Porter (London: Virago, 1977), 226.

② Boris Uspensky, *A Poetics of Composition* (Los Angeles: University of California Press, 1973).

view. So in discussing *The Brothers Karamazov* Uspensky shows how the naming system can indicate multiple points of view, as a character is perceived both by other characters in the novel and from within the narrative. In the translation process, therefore, it is essential for the translator to consider the function of the naming system, rather than the system itself. It is of little use for the English reader to be given multiple variants of a name if he is not made aware of the function of those variants, and since the English naming system is completely different the translator must take this into account and follow Belloc's dictum to render "idiom by idiom".

The case of Russian proper names is only one example of the problem of trying to render a SL system into a TL that does not have a comparable system. Other examples might be found in the use by an author of dialect forms, or of regional linguistic devices particular to a specific region or class in the SL. As Robert Adams puts it, rather flippantly:

> Paris cannot be London or New York, it must be Paris; our hero must be Pierre, not Peter; he must drink an aperitif, not a cocktail; smoke Gauloises, not Kents; and walk down the rue du Bac, not Back Street. On the other hand, when he is introduced to a lady, he'll sound silly if he says, "I am enchanted, Madame. "①

In the discussion of equivalence (see pp. 30 – 6) it was shown that any notion of *sameness* between SL and TL must be discounted. What the translator must do, therefore, is to first determine the *function* of the SL system and then to find a TL system that will adequately render that function. Levy posed the central questions that face the translator of literary prose texts when he asked:

> What degree of utility is ascribed to various stylistic devices and to their preservation in different types of literature...? What is the relative importance of linguistic standards and of style in different types of literature...? What must have been the assumed quantitative composition of the audiences to whom translators of different times and of different types of texts addressed their translations?②

【翻译鉴赏】

Of Delays

Francis Bacon

Fortune is like the market; where many times if you can stay a little, the price will fall. Again, it is sometimes like Sibylla's offer[1]; which at first, offers the commodity at full, then consumes part and part, and still holds up the price. For occasion (as it is in the

---

① Robert M. Adams, *Proteus, His Lies, His Truth* (New York: W. W. Norton, 1973), 12.

② Jiři Levý, Translation as a Decision Process, *To Honour Roman Jakobson III* (The Hague: Mouton, 1967), 1171 – 1182.

common verse) turns a bald noddle, after she has presented her locks in front, and no hold taken;[2] or at least turns the handle of the bottle, first to be received, and after the belly, which is hard to clasp. There is surely no greater wisdom, than well to time the beginnings, and onsets, of things. [3] Dangers are no more lighter, if they once seem light; and more dangers have deceived men, than forced them. Nay, it were better, to meet some dangers halfway, though they come nothing near, than to keep too long a watch upon their approaches; for if a man watch too long, it is odds he will fall asleep. On the other side, to be deceived with too long shadows (as some have been, when the moon was low, and shone on their enemies' back), and so to shoot off before the time; or to teach dangers to come on, by over early buckling towards them; is another extreme.

The ripeness, or unripeness, of the occasion (as we said) must ever be well weighed; and generally it is good, to commit the beginnings of a great actions to Argus[4], with his hundred eyes, and the ends to Briareus[5], with his hundred hands; first to watch, and then to speed. [6] For the helmet of Pluto[7], which makes the politic man go invisible, is secrecy in the counsel, and celerity in the execution. For when things are once come to the execution, there is no secrecy, comparable to celerity; like the motion of a bullet in the air, which flies so swift, as it outruns the eye.

【背景介绍】

弗兰西斯·培根(Francis Bacon,1561—1626)英国政治家、散文家,著名的唯物主义哲学家与科学家。他竭力倡导"读史使人明智,读诗使人灵秀,数学使人周密,科学使人深刻,伦理学使人庄重,逻辑修辞之学使人善辩"。他推崇科学、发展科学的进步思想和崇尚知识的进步口号,一直推动着社会的进步,被马克思称为"英国唯物主义和整个现代实验科学的真正始祖"。著有《新工具》、《论说随笔文集》等。后者收入58篇随笔,从各个角度论述广泛的人生问题,精妙、有哲理,拥有广泛的读者。

【注释】

[1] Sibylla's offer:西拉比,古代西方善于预卜的女巫,曾作书九卷献给罗马王,索重金。罗马王拒绝。西比拉烧掉三册,仍索原价。罗马王感到奇怪,读其书发现所预言之事极为重要,因而买其书,但已不全。

[2] For occasion (as it is in the common verse) turns a bald noddle, after she has presented her locks in front, and no hold taken 是中世纪学者格里纳厄斯的《谚语集》中的话,在西方几乎是家喻户晓的关于经济方面的格言。

[3] There is surely no greater wisdom than well to time the beginnings and onsets of things. 所以,善于在做一件事的开端识别时机,这实在是一种极难得的智慧。亦可译为:抓住机遇,不误时机——这肯定是最大的智慧。

[4] Argus:阿加斯,希腊神话中巨人,据说有一百只眼睛,可意译为"千眼神"。

[5] Briareus:阿瑞欧斯,希腊神话中的百手巨人,可意译为"千手神"。

[6] The ripeness, or unripeness, of the occasion (as we said) must ever be well weighed; and generally it is good, to commit the beginnings of a great actions to Argus, with his hundred eyes, and the ends to Briareus, with his hundred hands; first to watch, and

then to speed. 该句是全文最集中体现作者修辞风格的表述，文化意蕴丰富，如何进行文化信息传达和修辞风格对等，是采取直译移植文化信息还是意译传递文章修辞之妙，取决于译者针对的读者群和译者的翻译策略。有译者将其直译为：最好让巨人阿尔格斯用他的一百只眼注视一切伟大行动的开始，让巨人布里亚勒斯用他的一百只手保卫行动的成功。

[7] Pluto：普鲁特，希腊神话中的冥王，有人将其意译为中国民间传说中的"阎王"。

【译文】

论时机

弗兰西斯·培根

幸运之机好比市场，稍一耽搁，价格就变。它又像那位西比拉的预言书，如果当能买时不及时买，那么等你发现了它的价值再想买时，书却找不见。所以古谚说得好，机会老人先给你送上它的头发，如果你一下没抓住，再抓就只能碰到它的秃头了。或者说它先给你一个可以抓的瓶颈，你没有及时抓住，再摸到的就是抓不住的圆瓶肚了。所以，善于在做一件事的开端识别时机，这实在是一种极难得的智慧。例如在一些危险关头，总是看来吓人的危险比真正压倒人的危险要多许多。只要能挺过最难熬的时机，再来的危险就不那么可怕了。因此，当危险逼近时，善于抓住时机迎头邀击它要比犹豫躲闪更有利。因为犹豫的结果恰恰是错过了克服它的机会。但也要注意警惕那种幻觉，不要以为敌人真像它在月光下的阴影那样高大，因而在时机不到时过早出击，结果反而失掉了获胜的机会。

总而言之，善于识别与把握时机是极为重要的。在一切大事业上，人在开始做事前要像千眼神那样察视时机，而在进行时要像千手神那样抓住时机。特别对于政治家来说，秘密的策划与果断的实行就是地神普鲁托的隐身盔甲。果断与迅速是最好的保密方法——就像疾掠空中的子弹一样，当秘密传开的时候，事情已经成功了。

窗

钱钟书

又是春天，窗子可以常开了。春天从窗外进来，人在屋子里坐不住，就从门里出去。不过屋子外的春天太贱了！到处是阳光，不像射破屋里阴深的那样明亮；到处是给太阳晒得懒洋洋的风，不像搅动屋里沉闷的那样有生气。就是鸟语，也似乎琐碎而单薄，需要屋里的寂静来做衬托。我们因此明白，春天是该镶嵌在窗子里看的，好比画配了框子。

同时，我们悟到，门和窗有不同的意义。当然，门是造了让人出进的。但是，窗子有时也可作为进出口用，譬如小偷或小说里私约的情人就喜欢爬窗子。所以窗子和门的根本分别，决不仅是有没有人进来出去。若据赏春一事来看，我们不妨这样说：有了门，我们可以出去；有了窗，我们可以不必出去。窗子打通了大自然和人的隔膜，把风和太阳逗引进来，使屋子里也关着一部分春天，让我们安坐了享受，无需再到外面去找。

【背景介绍】

钱钟书先生的这篇散文说的是窗子，但是其用意绝不仅仅是说说窗子而已，而是要以窗子来比喻生活、比喻人生。从语言上看，《窗》延续了一贯的钱派手法，用词平实、普通，没有长句，没有什么复杂结构，非常从容地叙述、说理，却又紧紧地扣住了主题。这样的特点对翻译构成的难度不言而喻，翻译中应当时时充分考虑上述特点，尽量在译文中体现出来。

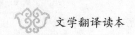

【译文】

Random Thoughts on the Window

Qian Zhongshu

It is spring again and the window can be left open as often as one would like. As spring comes in through the windows, so people—unable to bear staying inside any longer—go outdoors. The spring outside, however, is much too cheap, for the sun shines on everything, and so does not seem as bright as that which shoots into the darkness of the house. Outside the sun-slothed breeze blows everywhere, but it is not so lively as that which stirs the gloominess inside the house. Even the chirping of the birds sounds so thin and broken that the quietness of the house is needed to set it off. It seems that spring was always meant to be put behind a windowpane for show, just like a picture in a frame.

At the same time it also becomes clear that the door has a different significance from the window. Of course, doors were made for people to pass through; but a window can also sometimes serve as an entrance or as an exit, and is used as such by thieves and by lovers in novels. In fact the fundamental difference between a door and a window has nothing to do with them being either entrances or exits. When it comes to the admiration of spring, it could be put this way: a door makes it possible for one to go out, whereas a window makes it possible for one not to have to. A window helps to pull down the partition between man and nature. It leads breezes and sunlight in, and keeps part of the spring in the house. It allows one to sit and enjoy the spring in peace, and makes it unnecessary to go looking for it outside.

【译文评析】

[1] 窗:random thoughts on the window。

题目中的这个窗字,包含的意思较为丰富,使人有多种联想,因此译成 random thoughts on the window。

[2] 又是春天:It is spring again.

中文是无主句,英文没有这样的句子结构,因此用 It is... 句型。原文里"又"用在句首,但是英文如果也把 again 放在句首,这个词就太突出,分量太重了。所以 again 一词在译文中放在句末和原文"又"放在句首分量相当。

[3] 窗子可以常开了:And the window can be left open as often as one would like.

用定冠词 the 加单数名词 window 来代表所有的窗子。英语里表示"全部"可以有几种方法:① 复数名词,② 不定冠词 a/an+名词,③ 定冠词+名词。这里就是用的第三种,更侧重其一致性。"常开"不能译成 can open often 或 can be opened often。因为原文是从人的角度说的,人们什么时候想开窗都行,所以用了 one would like 这样的说法。

[4] 春天从窗外进来:As spring comes in through the windows.

这句把春天拟人化了,英文也用同样的结构就行。窗外:out of the window。但是,如果把"从窗外进来"理解成一个过程,用 through 表示更好些。

[5] 人在屋子里坐不住,就从门里出去:So people—unable to bear staying inside any longer—go outdoors.

破折号之间的形容词短语说明人们在屋里坐不住的原因。bear:忍受,后面既可跟-ing 动词,也可跟不定式动词。

[6] 不过屋子外的春天太贱了:The spring outside, however, is much too cheap.

这里的"贱",是说春天多阳光,以多为贱,中外同理,用 cheap 也就顺理成章了。

[7] 到处是阳光:For the sun shines on everything.

这里和上一句是连接在一起的,所以用了连接词 for 来说明原因。最好不要译成 The sunshine is everywhere. 因为阳光并不是一种存在,而是说照耀在所有的一切上面,因此说 shine。

[8] 不像射破屋里阴深的那样明亮:And so does not seem as bright as that which shoots into the darkness of the house.

用 seem 是指屋里屋外阳光是一样的,只是环境的反差使阳光显得不同罢了。as... as 是表示屋里屋外阳光的比较。that 指 the sun。

[9] 到处是给太阳晒得懒洋洋的风:Outside the sun-slothed breeze blows everywhere.

这里加了一个词 outside,因为后面马上要说到的"屋里"并不包括在"到处"一词里;"晒"字英文里与之相当的词就是 shine,但是 shine 并没有带复合宾语的用法,所以换了一个角度来说这句话。sun-slothed 是一个复合词。

[10] 不像搅动屋里沉闷的那样有生气:But it is not so lively as that which stirs the gloominess inside the house.

沉闷这个词在这里不是形容词,而是名词,所以用 gloomy 加上词尾-ness 构成了表示状态的名词。

[11] 就是鸟语,也似乎琐碎而单薄,需要屋里的寂静来做衬托:Even the chirping of the birds sounds so thin and broken that the quietness of the house is needed to set it off.

说 thin and broken 而不说 broken and thin 只是因为语音的关系,音节少的词放在前面,多的放在后面,结构上显得平稳,不至于头重脚轻。只要把这几个词连在一起朗读一下就可体会出来。

[12] 我们因此明白,春天是该镶嵌在窗子里看的,好比画配了框子:It seems that spring was always meant to be put behind a windowpane for show, just like a picture in a frame.

"我们因此明白"译成 It seems... 因为这是一种比喻的说法,直译成英文会给人以突兀的感觉,所以用"似乎如此"的说法。be meant to be 的意思是"原本为……",加了 always 等于从语气上与原文更相符合,并没有特别具体的含义。中文说"窗子里",而英文却不能说 in a windowpane,windowpane 指的是窗子上的玻璃,这就是用 behind 的原因。

[13] 同时,我们悟到,门和窗有不同的意义:At the same time it also becomes clear that the door has a different significance from the window.

悟到和上一句中的"明白"是相同的意思,it becomes clear that 这一说法比 it seems that 要肯定一些。

[14] 当然,门是造了让人出进的:Of course, doors were made for people to pass through.

出进可以译成 to come out and go in,但译成 to pass through 就显得句子紧凑、精炼。

[15] 但是,窗子有时也可作为进出口用:But a window can also sometimes serve as an entrance or as an exit.

entrance 和 exit 这两个词比 door 和 window 抽象化了，充分表明了"进出口"的字面意思和含义。

[16] 譬如小偷或小说里私约的情人就喜欢爬窗子：and is used as such by thieves and by lovers in novels.

译文用了 by thieves and by lovers，而不说 by thieves and lovers，因为这本来就是两类人，不能放在一起混为一谈。

[17] 所以窗子和门的根本分别，决不仅是有没有人进来出去：In fact the fundamental difference between a door and a window has nothing to do with them being either entrances or exits.

比较一下 different between 和前文的 different（from）：说两者之间的区别，用 different between A and B；而说 A 怎样不同于 B 则说 A is different from B。

[18] 若据赏春一事来看，我们不妨这样说：When it comes to the admiration of spring, it could be put this way.

when it comes to 是比较中庸的说法，不那么正式，但也不那么随意，意思是"说起赏春……"，让人们对下文有一个期待。

[19] 有了门，我们可以出去：A door makes it possible for one to go out.

"有了门"不能译成 with a/the door，因为这里不是说有还是没有，而是有门存在，人们就可以进出房屋。

[20] 有了窗，我们可以不必出去：whereas a window makes it possible for one not to have to.

whereas 意为"而……"。这是一个连接词，表示一种前后的比较或对照。这里的句型和上面是一样的，但是后面的 not to have to 是不定式的否定形式，后面省略了 go out。

[21] 窗子打通了大自然和人的隔膜：A window helps to pull down the partition between man and nature.

"由于有了窗子，人和大自然之间的隔膜才得以打破"，窗子起的是一种促进作用，其本身并不能去"打破"什么，因此用了 helps to pull down。partition 意为"隔离墙"。"隔膜"是解剖学词汇，这里用的是其引申意义，不能按字面译成 diaphragm，那样意思就不对了。man and nature：man 是指整个人类，所以不用任何冠词；nature 则是不可数名词。

[22] 把风和太阳逗引进来，使屋子里也关着一部分春天：It leads breezes and sunlight in, and keeps part of the spring in the house.

lead：引导，引领。keep... in the house：使停留在屋里不能外出。

[23] 让我们安坐了享受，无需再到外面去找：It allows one to sit and enjoy the spring in peace, and makes it unnecessary to go looking for it outside.

原文是说"安坐"，而实际上"安"的意思也应当能涵盖"享受"，只是从词的节奏上感觉"安坐"和"享受"都是两个字的词，似乎是并列的。译文里译成了 sit... in peace，等于将状语移了一个位。注意这句中几个 it 的含义，第一个 it 指代 window，第二个 it 是形式宾语，引出后面的 to go，第三个 it 是指代 the spring。

——北京外国语大学申雨平教授讲解

【翻译试笔】

【英译汉】

Of Beauty

Francis Bacon

Virtue is like a rich stone, best plain set; and surely virtue is best in a body that is comely, though not of delicate features; and that has rather dignity of presence than beauty of aspect. Neither is it almost seen, that very beautiful persons are otherwise of great virtue; as if nature were rather busy not to err, than in labor to produce excellency. And therefore they prove accomplished, but not of Great Spirit; and study rather behavior than virtue. But this holds not always: for Augustus Caesar, Titus Vespasianus, Philip le Belle of France, Edward the Fourth of England, Alcibiades of Athens, Ismael the Sophy of Persia, were all high and great spirits; and yet the most beautiful men of their times.

In beauty, that of favor is more than that of color; and that of decent and gracious motion, more than that of favor. That is the best part of beauty, which a picture cannot express; no, nor the first sight of the life. There is no excellent beauty that has not some strangeness in the proportion. A man cannot tell whether Apelles or Albert Durer were the more trifler; whereof the one would make a personage by geometrical proportions; the other, by taking the best parts out of divers faces, to make one excellent. Such personages, I think, would please nobody, but the painter that made them. Not but I think a painter may make a better face than ever was; but he must do it by a kind of felicity (as a musician that makes an excellent air in music), and not by rule. A man shall see faces, that if you examine them part by part, you shall find never a good; and yet altogether do well.

If it be true that the principal part of beauty is in decent motion, certainly it is no marvel, though persons in years seem many times more amiable; pulchrorum autummus pulcher. Beauty is as summer fruits, which are easy to corrupt, and cannot last; and for the most part it makes a dissolute youth, and an age a little out of countenance; but yet certainly again, if it light well, it makes virtue shine, and vices blush.

【汉译英】

差不多先生传

胡 适

你知道中国最有名的人是谁?

提起此人,人人皆晓,处处闻名。他姓差,名不多,是各省各县各村人氏。你一定见过他,一定听说过别人谈起他。差不多先生的名字天天挂在大家的口头,因为他是中国全国人的代表。

差不多先生的相貌和你和我都差不多。他有一双眼睛,但看的不很清楚;他有两只耳朵,但听的不很分明;有鼻子和嘴,但他对于气味和口味都不很讲究。他的脑子也不小,但他的记性却不很精明,他的思想也不很细密。

他常常说:"凡事只要差不多,就好了。何必太精明呢?"

他小的时候,他妈叫他去买红糖,他买了白糖回来。他妈骂他,摇摇头说:"红糖白糖不是差不多吗?"

他在学堂的时候,先生问他:"直隶省的西边是哪一省?"他说是陕西。先生说:"错了。是山西,不是陕西。"他说:"陕西同山西,不是差不多吗?"

后来他在一个钱铺里做伙计,他也会写,也会算,只是总不会精细。十字常常写成千字,千字常常写成十字。掌柜的生气了,常常骂他。他只是笑嘻嘻地赔小心道:"千字比十字只多一小撇,不是差不多吗?"

有一天他为了一件要紧的事,要搭火车到上海去。他从从容容地走到火车站,迟了两分钟,火车已经开走了。他白瞪着眼,望着远远的火车上煤烟,摇摇头道:"只好明天再走了,今天走同明天走,也差不多。可是火车公司未免太认真了。8点30分开,同8点32分开,不是差不多吗?"他一面说,一面慢慢地走回家,心里总不明白为什么火车不肯等他两分钟。

有一天,他忽然得了急病,赶快叫家人去请东街的汪医生。那家人急急忙忙地跑去,一时寻不着东街的汪大夫,却把西街牛医王大夫请来了。差不多先生病在床上,知道寻错了人;但病急了,身上痛苦,心里焦急,等不得了,心里想道:"好在王大夫同汪大夫也差不多,让他试试看罢。"于是这位牛医王大夫走近床前,用医牛的法子给差不多先生治病。不上一点钟,差不多先生就一命呜呼了。

差不多先生差不多要死的时候,一口气断断续续地说道:"活人同死人也……差……差不多……凡事只要……差……差……不多……就……好了……何……何……必……太……太认真呢?"他说完了这句格言,方才绝气了。

他死后,大家都很称赞差不多先生样样事情看得破,想得通;大家都说他一生不肯认真,不肯算账,不肯计较,真是一位有德行的人。于是大家给他取个死后的法号,叫他做圆通大师。

他的名誉越传越远,越久越大。无数无数的人都学他的榜样。于是人人都成了一个差不多先生。——然而中国从此就成为一个懒人国了。

【参考译文】

论 美
弗兰西斯·培根

美德好比宝石,最好用朴素的材料来加以衬托。毫无疑问,如一个形体端庄、气度严肃,但面容并不清秀的人具有美德,那将是很好的。美貌的人通常并不见得在其他才能上也出众。就仿佛是造物主在他的工作中但求不出差错,而并不刻意去追求尽善尽美似的。因此,许多容颜俊秀的人却胸无大志,他们孜孜不倦所追求的只不过是外在美而不是品德。但这话也不全对,因为罗马的奥古斯都·恺撒、菲斯帕斯、法国"英俊的"腓力普、英王爱德华四世、雅典的阿尔西巴底斯、波斯王伊斯梅尔等,都是精神高尚的人,然而他们又是他们那个时代著名的美男子。

就美而言,形态之美要胜于容貌之美,而得体且优雅的行为又胜于形态之美。最高境界的美是图画所无法表现的,也无法在生活中初睹。每种绝伦之美在其轮廓结构上都有其不同的奇特之处。我们不好说在阿皮雷斯和阿伯特·杜勒二人之中究竟谁更会开玩笑一些,他们一个是按照几何比例绘画人像,而另一个则通过摄取不同人身上最美的特点来合成一张最完美的人像。像这样画出来的美人,我想恐怕只有画家本人会喜欢他们,而其他人是不会喜欢的。我并不是认为一个画家不能画出一幅比以前任何容貌都要美的面容,而是认为他应当以一种

"神来之笔"做到此点（就如同音乐家谱成优美的歌曲一样），不能凭借公式。我们能看到有些脸型，如果一部分一部分地加以观察，是找不到什么优点的，但作为一个整体却非常动人。

如果美的主体确实存在于端庄的举止中的话，那么有些老人反而显得更为可爱，就不足为奇了。"美人的秋天也是美的"。美犹如盛夏的果实，容易腐烂难以保持。在大多数的情况下，美往往促使人在青年时放荡无度，在老年时代愧悔不已。然而毫无疑问的是，如果美恰如其分地附在一个人身上，它可以使有美德者光辉倍增，使有恶行者羞愧和汗颜。

Mr. About-the-Same
Hu Shih

Do you know who is the most well-known person in China?

The name of this person is a household word all over the country. His name is *Cha* and his given name, *Buduo*, which altogether mean "About the Same". He is a native of every province, every county and every village in this country. You must have seen or heard about this person. His name is always on the lips of everybody because he is representative of the whole Chinese nation.

Mr. *Cha Buduo* has the same physiognomy as you and I. He has a pair of eyes, but doesn't see clearly. He has a pair of ears, but doesn't hear well. He has a nose and a mouth, but lacks a keen sense of smell and taste. His brain is none too small, but he is weak in memory and sloppy in thinking.

He often says, "Whatever we do, it's OK to be just about right. What's the use of being precise and accurate?"

One day, when he was a child, his mother sent him out to buy her some brown sugar, but he returned with some white sugar instead. As his mother scolded him about it, he shook his head and said, "Brown sugar or white sugar, aren't they about the same?"

One day in school, the teacher asked him, "Which province borders Hebei on the west?" He answered, "Shaanxi." The teacher corrected him, "You are wrong. It's Shanxi, not Shaanxi." He retorted, "Shaanxi or Shanxi, aren't they about the same?"

Later Mr. *Cha Buduo* served as an assistant at a money shop. He could write and calculate all right, but his mathematics were often faulty. He would mistake the Chinese character 十 (meaning 10) for 千 (meaning 1,000) or vice versa. The shop owner was infuriated and often took him to task. But he would only explain apologetically with a grin, "The character 千 differs from 十 in merely having one additional short stroke. Aren't they about the same?"

One day, he wanted to go to Shanghai by train on urgent business. But he arrived at the railway station unhurriedly only to find the train already gone, because he was two minutes late. He stood staring helplessly at the smoke belching from the diminishing train, and shook his head, "Well, all I can do is to leave tomorrow. After all, today and tomorrow are about the same. But isn't the railway company taking it too seriously? What's the difference between departing at 8:30 and 8:32?" He walked home slowly while talking to himself and kept puzzling over why the train hadn't waited for him for two minutes more.

One day he suddenly fell ill and immediately told one of his family to fetch Dr. Wang of East Street. The latter went in hurry, but couldn't find the physician on East Street. So he fetched instead Veterinarian Wang of West Street. Mr. *Cha Buduo*, lying on his sickbed, knew that a wrong person had been brought home. But, what with pain and worry, he could not afford to wait any longer. So he said to himself, "Luckily, Vet Wang is about the same as Dr. Wang. Why not let Vet Wang have a try?" There-upon, the veterinarian walked up to his bed to work on him as if he were a cow. Consequently, Mr. *Cha Buduo* kicked the bucket before an hour was out.

When Mr. *Cha Buduo* was about to breathe his last, he uttered intermittently in one breath, "Live or die, it's about... about... the same... Whatever we do... it's OK... to be... just... just about right... Why... why... take it... so seriously?" As soon as he finished this pet phrase of his, he stopped breathing.

After Mr. *Cha Buduo*'s death, people all praised him for his way of seeing through things and his philosophical approach to life. They say that he refused to take things seriously all his life and that he was never calculating or particular about personal gains or losses. So they called him a virtuous man and honored him with the posthumous reverent title Master of Easy-Going.

His name has spread far and wide and become more and more celebrated with the passing of time. Innumerable people have come to follow his example, so that everybody has become a Mr. *Cha Buduo*. However, China will hence be a nation of lazybones!

【延伸阅读】

[1] Anderman, G. M. *Translation Today: Trends and Perspectives* [M]. Clevedon, Buffalo, Toronto, Sydney: Multilingual Matters Limited, 2003.

[2] Bowie, A. *Aesthetics and Subjectivity: from Kant to Nietzsche* [M]. Manchester: Manchester University Press, 1990.

[3] Cronin, M. *Across the Lines: Travel-Language-Translation* [M]. Cork, Ireland: Cork University Press, 2000.

[4] Eoyang, E. & Lin Yaofu. *Translating Chinese Literature* [M]. Bloomington and Indianapolis: Indiana University Press, 1995.

[5] Gentzler, E. *Contemporary Translation Theories* [M]. Shanghai: Shanghai Foreign Language Education Press, 2004.

[6] Gutt, Ernst-August. *Translation and Relevance: Cognition and Context* [M]. Shanghai: Shanghai Foreign Language Education Press, 2001.

[7] Hatim, B. & Mason, I. *Discourse and the Translator* [M]. Shanghai: Shanghai Foreign Language Education Press, 2001.

[8] Landers, C. E. *Literary Translation: A Practical Guide* [M]. Clevedon, Buffalo, Toronto, Sydney: Multilingual Matters Limited, 2001.

[9] Munday, J. *Introducing Translation Studies* [M]. London: Routledge, 2001.

［10］Newmark，P. *A Textbook of Translation*［M］. Shanghai：Shanghai Foreign Language Education Press，2001.

［11］Raffel，B. *The Art of Translating Prose*［M］. Philadelphia：Pennsylvania State University Press，2004.

［12］Rose，M. G. *Translation and Literary Criticism*：*Translation as Analysis*［M］. Manchester：St. Jerome Publishing，1997.

［13］Real，H. J. *Reception of Jonathan Swift in Europe*［M］. London，GBR：Continuum International Publishing，2005.

［14］Wang, Zuoliang. *Articles of Affinity*：*Studies in Comparative Literature*［M］. Beijing：Foreign Language Teaching and Research Press，1987.

［15］阿狄生等. 刘炳善译. 伦敦的叫卖声——英国随笔选译［C］. 上海：上海译文出版社，2008.

［16］陈铭. 意与境：中国古典诗词美学三昧［M］. 杭州：浙江大学出版社，2001.

［17］韩林德. 境生象外［M］. 北京：三联书店，1996.

［18］赫列兹. 潘文国. 赫列兹散文精选［M］. 上海：上海外语教育出版社，2011.

［19］纪伯伦. 李唯中. 纪伯伦散文诗经典［M］. 北京：中国城市出版社，2010.

［20］吉辛. 李霁野. 四季随笔［M］. 台北：台湾省编译馆，1947.

［21］兰姆. 刘炳善. 伊利亚随笔选［M］. 上海：上海译文出版社，2006.

［22］梁实秋. 陈达遵.《雅舍小品》英译［M］. 香港中文大学出版社，2005.

［23］梁遇春. 春醪集·泪与笑［M］. 南京：江苏文艺出版社，2009.

［24］林奇. 梁遇春与英国 Essay［J］. 福建师范大学学报，1989(2).

［25］刘炳善. 译事随笔［M］. 北京：中国电影出版社，2000.

［26］培根. 何新. 培根人生随笔［M］. 北京：人民日报出版社，2007.

［27］钱灵杰，操萍. 刘炳善散文翻译思想研究［J］. 广东外语外贸大学学报，2011(2).

［28］乔萍等. 散文佳作108篇（英汉·汉英对照）［C］. 南京：译林出版社，2002.

［29］王佐良. 英语文体学论文集［M］. 北京：外语教学与研究出版社，1986.

［30］王佐良. 英国散文的流变［M］. 北京：商务印书馆，1998/2011.

［31］杨自伍. 英国散文名篇欣赏［C］. 上海：上海外语教育出版社，2010.

［32］于中先. 散文中的散文—《世界文学》散文精选［C］. 南京：译林出版社，2010.

［33］张培基. 英译中国现代散文选［C］. 上海：上海外语教育出版社，2007.

［34］赵秀明，赵张进. 英美散文研究与翻译［M］. 吉林：吉林大学出版社，2010.

【问题与思考】

1. 中国散文与英语世界引入的 Essay 文体，区别何在？
2. 请从散文文体的历史流变角度谈一谈翻译对于文学发展的作用。
3. 如何处理散文翻译中"传神"与"达意"的辩证关系？
4. Essay 译为"散文"是术语学中的概念对等吗？
5. 请结合梁遇春的翻译实践，谈一谈散文翻译与创作的关系如何？
6. 如何处理中国古代散文翻译中的文化专有名词？
7. 散文翻译宜以直译为主还是意译为主？为什么？

8. 散文翻译是否牵涉意识形态问题,如何处理?

9. 散文翻译中的作者个性如何凸显?

10. 散文翻译中,修辞和风格是压倒一切的关键问题吗? 为什么?

第六章 小说翻译篇

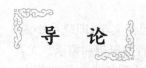

导 论

　　在文学翻译理论与实践的圈子里,似乎有个不争的事实:多数人认为,译诗最难,译小说比较容易。此说似乎不无事实依据,至少译小说的比译诗的多。可是,如果译小说比译诗容易,那么写小说是不是比写诗容易呢? 文学翻译大师翁显良先生据此认为,写是创作,译是再创作,说难都难,说易都易。难易不在于是诗歌还是小说,而在于作品艺术价值的高低。原作艺术价值越高就越难;以为容易,随便译出,恐怕难免在艺术上对原作不忠实。

　　小说是指以叙述事物为创作手法,营造典型性为审美特征的一种文学创作体裁。小说以塑造人物形象为中心,通过完整故事情节的叙述和深刻的环境描写反映社会生活,是以完整的布局、合理的发展及贯穿主题的美学原理为表现的文学艺术作品。小说的价值本质是以时间为序列、以某一人物或几个人物为主线的,非常详细地、全面地反映社会生活中各种角色的价值关系(政治关系、经济关系和文化关系)的产生、发展与消亡过程;非常细致地、综合地展示各种价值关系的相互作用。与其他文学样式相比,小说的容量较大,可以细致地展现人物性格和人物命运,可以表现错综复杂的矛盾冲突,同时还可以描述人物所处的社会生活环境,其优势是可以提供整体的、广阔的社会生活。

　　我国古代小说萌芽于先秦,发展于两汉魏晋南北朝,当时被称为笔记小说,主要有志人小说和志怪小说两种。唐代是小说的成熟期,当时的小说被称做传奇,宋金时期流行话本小说。元末与明清时期小说发展至高峰,出现了长篇白话小说。但中国古代小说长期并且一直归属于社会的边缘,为文人士大夫不齿。原有的小说虽然历经魏晋南北朝到清千余年的发展,出现过《三国演义》、《水浒传》、《西游记》、《红楼梦》四大名著,但是至清末,已有的小说模本再也不能激发新作品和新作家,长篇小说不外"海淫海盗"两类,短篇小说虽然曾经出现过唐传奇、明代"三言二拍"白话短篇小说等优秀作品,但"到了乾隆后期,白话短篇小说基本绝迹,文言短篇小说则再也跳不出'聊斋'框套,短篇小说没有多少发展潜力了"。(陈平原语)在这样的情况下,中国小说只有借助外国小说新元素来革新。

　　在中国翻译历史上,清末民初的翻译小说隶属于翻译文学的初期阶段,在这一阶段的各类文学体裁翻译中,小说翻译最为活跃,数量最多,类型最全,影响最广,在整个翻译文学中占据绝对的优势,翻译小说在数量上甚至远远超过创作小说。日本学者樽本照雄近年编订的目录里,明确指出,1840 至 1911 年间,至少有 1 016 种翻译小说,狄更斯、大小仲马、雨果、托尔斯泰等读者耳熟能详的名字纷纷被译入中国;至于畅销作家,则有福尔摩斯的创造者柯南道尔、感伤奇情作家哈葛德,以及科幻小说之父凡尔纳名列前茅。1902 年,梁启超提出"小说界革命"

口号,更是掀起了翻译小说和创作小说在中国的空前高潮。在这股强大的洪流中,翻译小说是中流砥柱,在组织样式、诗学语言和创作技巧等方面为创作小说提供了模本和方向。梁启超的文学革命,其实多是从作为学术知识之载体的角度入手的,比如他由《饮冰室诗话》所推出的新派诗,就是在强调以旧诗格律去表现新的知识。而小说作为叙事、说理功能强大的文类,在这方面则更胜过诗歌,因而说部之西学成为此后一个更受瞩目的阅读对象。如此,中国读者对于陌生新鲜的异域世界,才逐渐产生兴趣;抽象生硬的学理,也因此借助生动亲切的典雅语言,为中国的读书人所消化。

从当时的社会环境来看,这些翻译小说中占主要地位的是所谓的通俗文学,即政治小说、科学小说和侦探小说等。这些小说盛行的原因是它们能够满足当时读者的愿望和需求。尤其是在当时的封建制度、虚伪的共和制度及列强的压迫下,中国人深切地感到科学力量的伟大,人们迫切地想从所翻译的政治小说中领悟到新的民主制度、在科学小说中领略到科技的力量、在侦探小说中获得公正的法制。当时的译者带有的这种翻译动机,迎合了当时政治改良、文化改良和启迪民智的需求,给民众带来了民主思想、自由平等观念和竞争进取的精神。

从创作角度来讲,这个时期的翻译小说在价值观念、人物塑造和小说的写作技巧则比之中国古代小说发生了巨大的变化。清末民初,翻译小说的大量输入促使创作小说的叙事模式和艺术技巧发生变化。西方小说的翻译者多为当时的作家,或者后来成为作家,他们一边翻译,一边创作,致使创作小说明显留有翻译小说的痕迹,有的原创小说甚至与翻译作品之间界限模糊。严格说来,清末民初翻译小说的大量输入提升了小说作为一个门类在中国文学界的地位。

相较于其他文学体裁,小说能够更大规模、更深层次地影响人们对于社会价值、生活世界的思考,西方小说中以反映社会问题的写实、平民倾向也更容易为处于社会变革震荡之中的知识分子接受,进而引发中国文学领域、乃至思想领域的巨变。清末民初经由小说翻译而引入的新思想、新思潮,并非是当时处于风雨飘摇中的旧中国的特例。在其他一些东方古国,如土耳其、以色列等国,也大致经历了一个类似的情况,甚至在具体的小说类属选择上都有着异曲同工之妙。

本单元所选文章围绕小说翻译的文本类属、主旨内容,以及小说翻译的政治功能等宏观方面展开,希望在语言文字的双语转化之外,能够引导读者关注宏大的文化交互系统,更多关注小说体裁的社会教化功用。

选文一　林纾的翻译

钱钟书

导　言

本文节选自钱钟书,《林纾的翻译》,商务印书馆(北京),1981 年版。

林纾是近代文学翻译的开创者,但林纾不懂外语,又用文言文进行翻译,翻译作品却得到广泛接受,是一个值得深入探讨的文化现象。《林纾的翻译》是钱钟书先生在 20 世纪 60 年代写就的著名论作,是体现钱钟书先生翻译理论的代表性作品。钱钟书通篇围绕"诱"、"媒"、"讹"、"化"展开对林纾译作的分析和评价。在文中,钱先生对翻译的作用,使用了"诱"、"媒"两字,非常生动形象:一是具体地说明读者可能会因为翻译的原因而对原作品产生更浓厚的兴趣,从而勾起想读原著的冲动;另外这个"诱"和"媒"字就是从广义上翻译对于文化交流所起到的巨大作用。钱先生列举了林译作品中存在的"讹",并做出标定,如某些"讹"是译者的不细心造成,如"排印之误不会没有,但有时一定由于原稿的字迹潦草"。某些"讹"则是译者主观为之,其原因有对原作的理解不彻底而产生误解,也有的是为了能理顺译文,使之更顺应译语文化和阅读习惯强而改之的。此文中,钱钟书提出了著名的"化境"翻译标准。

汉代文字学者许慎有一节关于翻译的训诂,义蕴颇为丰富。《说文解字》卷十二《口》部第 26 字:"囮,译也。从'口','化'声。率鸟者系生鸟以来之,名曰'囮',读若'譌'。"南唐以来,"小学"家都申说"译"就是"传四夷及鸟兽之语",好比"鸟媒"对"禽鸟"所施的引"诱","譌"、"讹"、"化"和"囮"是同一个字。"译"、"诱"、"媒"、"讹"、"化"这些一脉通连、彼此呼应的意义,组成了研究诗歌语言的人所谓"虚涵数意"(manifold meaning),把翻译能起的作用、难于避免的毛病、所向往的最高境界,仿佛一一透示出来了。文学翻译的最高标准是"化"。把作品从一国文字转变成另一国文字,既能不因语文习惯的差异而露出生硬牵强的痕迹,又能完全保存原有的风味,那就算得入于"化境"。17 世纪有人赞美这种造诣的翻译,比为原作的"投胎转世"(the transmigration of souls),躯壳换了一个,而精神姿致依然故我。换句话说,译本对原作应该忠实得以至于读起来不象译本,因为作品在原文里决不会读起来象经过翻译似的。但是,一国文字和另一国文字之间必然有距离,译者的理解和文风跟原作品的内容和形式之间也不会没有距离,而且译者的体会和他自己的表达能力之间还时常有距离。从一种文字出发,积寸累尺地度越那许多距离,安稳到达另一种文字里,这是很艰辛的历程。一路上颠顿风尘,遭遇风险,不免有所遗失或受些损伤。因此,译文总有失真和走样的地方,在意义或口吻上违背或不尽贴合原文。那就是"讹",西洋谚语所谓"翻译者即反逆者"（Traduttore traditore）。中国古人也说翻译的"翻"等于把绣花纺织品的正面翻过去的"翻"，展开了它的反面。释赞宁《高僧传三集》卷三《译经篇·论》："翻也者，如翻锦绮，背面俱花，但其花有左右不同耳"，这个比喻使我们想起堂·吉河德说阅读译本就象从反面来看花毯（es como quien mira los tapices flamencos por el reves）。"媒"和"诱"当然说明了翻译在文化交流里所起的作用。它是个居间者或联络员，介绍大家去认识外国作品，引诱大家去爱好外国作品，仿佛做媒似的，使国与国之间缔结了"文学因缘"。

彻底和全部的"化"是不可实现的理想，某些方面、某种程度的"讹"又是不能避免的毛病，于是"媒"或"诱"产生了新的意义。翻译本来是要省人家的事，免得他们去学外文、读原作的，却一变而为导诱一些人去学外文、读原作。它挑动了有些人的好奇心，惹得他们对原作无限向往，仿佛让他们尝到一点儿味道，引起了胃口，可是没有解馋过瘾。他们总觉得读翻译象隔雾赏花，不比读原作那么情景真切。歌德就有过这种看法，他很不礼貌地比翻译家为下流的职业媒人（Uebelsetzer sind als geschaftige Kuppler anzusehen）——中国旧名"牵马"，因为他们把原作半露半遮，使读者想象它不知多少美丽，抬高了它的声价。要证实那个想象，要揭去那层遮遮掩掩的面纱，以求看得仔细、看个着实，就得设法去读原作。这样说来，好译本的作用是消灭自己；它把我们向原作过渡，而我们读到了原作，马上掷开了译本。勇于自信的翻译家也许认为读了他的译本就无需再读原作，但是一般人能够欣赏货真价实的原作以后，常常薄情地抛弃了翻译家辛勤制造的代用品。倒是坏翻译会发生一种消灭原作的效力。拙劣晦涩的译文无形中替作品拒绝读者；他对译本看不下去，就连原作也不想看了。这类翻译不是居间，而是离间，摧灭了读者进一步和原作直接联系的可能性，扫尽读者的兴趣，同时也破坏原作的名誉。法国 17 世纪德·马露尔神父（Abbé de Marolles）的翻译就是一个经典的例证，他所译古罗马诗人《马夏尔的讽刺小诗集》（*Epigrams of Martial*）被时人称为《讽刺马夏尔的小诗集》（*Epigrams Against Martial*）。许多人都能从自己的阅读经验里找出补充的例子。

林纾的翻译所起的"媒"的作用，已经是文学史上公认的事实。他对若干读者也一定有过歌德所说的"媒"的影响，引导他们去跟原作发生直接关系。我自己就是读了他的翻译而增加学习外国语文的兴趣的。商务印书馆发行的那两小箱《林译小说丛书》是我十一二岁时的大发现，带领我进了一个新天地、一个在《水浒》、《西游记》、《聊斋志异》以外另辟的世界。我事先也看过梁启超译的《十五小豪杰》、周桂笙译的侦探小说等，都觉得沉闷乏味。接触了林译，我才知道西洋小说会那么迷人。我把林译里哈葛德、欧文、司各特、迭更司的作品津津不厌地阅览。假如我当时学习英文有什么自己意识到的动机，其中之一就是有一天能够痛痛快快地读遍哈葛德以及旁人的探险小说。40 年前，在我故乡那个县城里，小孩子既无野兽电影可看，又无动物园可逛，只能见到"走江湖"的人耍猴儿把戏或者牵一头疥骆驼卖药。后来孩子们看野兽片、逛动物园所获得的娱乐，我只能向冒险小说里去追寻。因为翻来覆去地阅读，我也渐渐对林译发生疑问。我清楚记得这个例子。哈葛德《三千年艳尸记》第五章结尾刻意描写鳄鱼和狮子的搏斗，对小孩子来说，这是一个惊心动魄的场面，紧张得使他眼瞪口开、气也不敢透的。林纾译文的下半段是这样：

> 然狮之后爪已及鳄鱼之颈，如人之脱手套，力拔而出之。少须，狮首俯鳄鱼之身作异声，而鳄鱼亦侧其齿，尚陷入狮股，狮腹为鳄所咬亦几裂。如是战斗，为余生平所未睹者。

狮子抓住鳄鱼的脖子，决不会整个爪子象陷在烂泥里似的，为什么"如人之脱手套"？鳄鱼的牙齿既然"陷入狮股"，物理和生理上都不可能去"咬狮腹"。我无论如何想不明白，家里的大人也解答不来。而且这场恶狠狠的打架怎样了局？谁输谁赢，还是同归于尽？鳄鱼和狮子的死活，比起男女主角的悲欢，是我更关怀的问题。书里并未明白交代，我真觉得心痒难搔，恨不能知道原文是否照样糊涂了事。我开始能读原文，总先找林纾译过的小说来读。后来，我的阅读能力增进了，我也听到舆论指摘林译的误漏百出，就不再而也不屑再看它。它只成为我生命里累积的前尘旧蜕的一部分了。

最近，偶尔翻开一本林译小说，出于意外，它居然还没有丧失吸引力。我不但把它看完，并且接二连三，重温了大部分的林译，发现许多都值得重读，尽管漏译误译随处都是。我试找同一作品后出的——无疑也是比较"忠实"的——译本来读，譬如孟德斯鸠和迭更司的小说，就觉得宁可读原文。这是一个颇耐玩味的事实。当然，能读原文以后，再来看错误的译本，有时也不失为一种消遣。有人说，译本愈糟糕愈有趣。我们对照着原本，看翻译者如何异想天开，把胡猜乱测来填补理解上的空白，无中生有，指鹿为马，简直象一位"超现实主义"的诗人。但是，我对林译的兴味绝非想找些岔子，以资笑柄谈助，而林纾译本里不忠实或"讹"的地方也并不完全由于他的助手们语文程度低浅、不够理解原文。举一两个例来说明。

《滑稽外史》第一七章写时装店里女店员的领班那格女士听见顾客说她是"老妪"，险些气破肚子，回到缝纫室里，披头散发，大吵大闹，把满腔妒愤都发泄在年轻貌美的加德身上，她手下的许多女孩子也附和着。林纾译文里有下面的一节：

> 那格……始笑而终哭，哭声似带讴歌。曰："嗟乎！吾来十五年，楼中咸谓我如名花之鲜妍。"——歌时，顿其左足，曰："嗟夫天！"又顿其右足，曰："嗟夫天！十五年中未被人轻贱。竟有骚狐奔我前，辱我令我肝肠颤！"

这真是带唱带做的小丑戏，逗得读者都会发笑。我们忙翻开迭更司原书（第一八章）来看，颇为失望。略仿林纾的笔调译出来，大致不过是这样：

> 那格女士先狂笑而后嘤然以泣，为状至辛楚动人。疾呼曰："十五年来，吾为此楼上下增光匪少。邀天之佑。"——言及此，力顿其左足，复力顿其右足，顿且言曰："吾未尝一日遭辱。胡意今日为此婢所卖！其用心诡鄙极矣！其行事实玷吾侪，知礼义者无勿耻之。吾憎之贱之，然而吾心伤矣！吾心滋伤矣！"

那段"似带讴歌"的顺口溜是林纾对原文的加工改造，绝不会由于助手的误解或曲解。他一定觉得迭更司的描写还不够淋漓尽致，所以浓浓地渲染一下，增添了人物和情景的可笑。批评家和文学史家承认林纾颇能表达迭更司的风趣，但从这个例子看来，他不仅如此，而往往是捐助自己的"谐谑"，为迭更司的幽默加油加酱。不妨从《滑稽外史》里再举一例，见于第三三章（迭更司原书第三四章）：

> 司圭尔先生……顾老而夫曰："此为吾子小瓦克福……君但观其肥硕，至于莫能容其衣。其肥乃日甚，至于衣缝裂而铜钮断。"乃按其子之首，处处以指戟其身，曰："此肉也。"又戟之曰："此亦肉，肉韧而坚。今吾试引其皮，乃附肉不能起。"方司圭尔引皮时，而小瓦克福已大哭，摩其肌曰："翁乃苦我！"司圭尔先生曰："彼尚未饱。若饱食者，则力聚而气张，虽有瓦屋，乃不能阂其身……君试观其泪中乃有牛羊之脂，由

食足也。"

　　这一节的译笔也很生动。不过迭更司只写司圭尔"处处戟其身",只写他说那胖小子若吃了午饭,屋子就关不上门,只写他说儿子眼泪是油脂(oiliness),什么"按其子之首"、"力聚而气张"、"牛羊之脂,由食足也"等都出于林纾的锦上添花。更值得注意的是,迭更司笔下的小瓦克福只"大哭摩肌",没有讲话。"翁乃苦我"这句怨言是林纾凭空穿插进去的,添个波折,使场面平衡;否则司圭尔一个人滔滔独白,他儿子那方面便显得呆板冷落了。换句话说,林纾认为原文美中不足,这里补充一下,那里润饰一下,因而语言更具体、情景更活泼,整个描述笔酣墨饱。不由我们不联想起他崇拜的司马迁在《史记》里对过去记传的润色或增饰。林纾写过不少小说,并且要采用"西人哈葛德"和"迭更先生"的笔法来写小说。他在翻译时,碰见他心目中认为是原作的弱笔或败笔,不免手痒难熬,抢过作者的笔代他去写。从翻译的角度判断,这当然也是"讹"。尽管添改得很好,终变换了本来面目,何况添改处不会一一都妥当。方才引的一节算是改得好的,上面那格女士带哭带唱的一节就有问题。那格确是一个丑角,这场哭吵也确有做作矫饰的成分。但是,假如她有腔无调地"讴歌"起来,那显然是在做戏,表示她的哭泣压根儿是假装的,她就制造不成紧张局面了,她的同伙和她的对头不会把她的发脾气当真了,不仅我们读着要笑,那些人当场也忍不住要笑了。李贽评论《琵琶记》里写考试那一出说:"太戏!不象!"又说:"戏则戏矣,倒须似真,若真反不妨似戏也。"林纾的改笔夸张过火,也许不失为插科打诨的游戏文章,可是损害了入情入理的写实,正所谓"太戏!不象!"了。

　　大家一向都知道林译删节原作,似乎没注意它也象上面所说的那样增补原作。这类增补,在比较用心的前期林译里,尤其在迭更司和欧文的译本里,出现得很多。或则加一个比喻,使描叙愈有风趣,例如《拊掌录》里《睡洞》:

　　　　……而笨者读不上口,先生则以夏楚助之,使力跃字沟而过。

原文只仿佛杜甫《漫成》诗所说"读书难字过",并无"力跃字沟"这个新奇的形象。又或则引申几句议论,使含意更能显豁,例如《贼史》第二章:

　　　　凡遇无名而死之儿,医生则曰:"吾剖腹视之,其中殊无物。"外史氏曰:"儿之死,正以腹中无物耳!有物又焉能死?"

"外史氏曰"云云在原文是括弧里的附属短句,译成文言只等于:"此语殆非妄"。作为翻译,这种增补是不足为训的,但从修辞学或文章作法的观点来说,它常常可以启发心思。林纾反复说外国小说"处处均得古文义法","天下文人之脑力,虽欧亚之隔,亦未有不同者",又把《左传》、《史记》等和迭更司、森彼得的叙事来比拟,并不是在讲空话。他确按照他的了解,在译文里有节制地掺进评点家所谓"顿荡"、"波澜"、"画龙点睛"、"颊上添毫"之笔,使作品更符合"古文义法"。一个能写作或自信能写作的人从事文学翻译,难保不象林纾那样的手痒,他根据自己的写作标准,要充当原作者的"净友",自以为有点铁成金或以石攻玉的义务和权利,把翻译变成借体寄生的、东鳞西爪的写作。在各国翻译史里,尤其在早期,都找得着可和林纾作伴的人。正确认识翻译的性质,严肃执行翻译的任务,能写作的翻译者就会有克己工夫,抑止不适当的写作冲动,也许还会鄙视林纾的经不起引诱。但是,正象背着家庭负担和社会责任的成年人偶而羡慕小孩子的放肆率真,某些翻译家有时会暗恨自己不能象林纾那样大胆放手的,我猜想。

上面所引司圭尔的话:"君但观其肥硕,至于莫能容其衣",应该是"至于其衣莫能容"或"至莫能容于其衣"。这类颠倒讹脱在林译里相当普遍,看来不能一概归咎于排印的疏忽。林纾"译书"的速度是他引以自豪的,也实在是惊人的。不过,下笔如飞、文不加点有它的代价。除掉造句松懈、用字冗赘以外,字句的脱漏错误无疑是代价的一部分。就象前引《三千年艳尸记》那一节里:"而鳄鱼亦侧其齿,尚陷入狮股"(照原来的断句),也很费解,根据原作推断,大约漏了一个"身"字:"鳄鱼亦侧其身,齿尚陷入狮股。"又象《巴黎茶花女遗事》。"余转觉忿怒马克揶揄之心,逐渐为欢爱之心渐推渐远","逐渐"两字显然是衍文,似乎本来想写"逐渐为欢爱之心愈推愈远",中途变计,而忘掉把全句调整。至于那种常见的不很利落的句型,例如:"然马克家日间谈宴,非十余人马克不适"(《巴黎茶花女遗事》),"我所求于兄者,不过求兄加礼此老"(《迦茵小传》第四章),"吾自思宜作何者,讵即久候于此,因思不如窃马而逃"(《大食故宫余载·记帅府之缚游兵》),它已经不能算是衍文,而属于刘知几所谓"省字"和"点烦"的范围了(《史通:内篇·叙事》、外篇·点烦)。排印之误不会没有,但有时一定由于原稿的字迹潦草。最特出的例是《洪罕女郎传》的男主角Quaritch,名字在全部译本里出现几百次,都作"爪立支","爪"字准是"瓜"字,草书形近致误。这里不妨摘录民国元年至六年主编《小说月报》的恽树珏先生给我父亲的一封信,信是民国三年10月29日写的,末了讲到林纾说:"近此公有《哀吹录》四篇,售与敝报。弟以其名足震俗,漫为登录。就中杜撰字不少:"翻筋斗"曰"翻滚斗","炊烟"曰"丝烟"。弟不自量,妄为窜易。以我见侯官文字,此为劣矣!"这几句话不仅写出林纾匆忙草率,连稿子上显著的"杜撰字"或别字都没改正,而且无意中流露出刊物编者对投稿的名作家常抱的典型的两面态度。

　　在"讹"字这个问题上,大家一向对林纾从宽发落,而严厉责备他的助手。林纾自己也早把责任推得干净:"鄙人不审西文,但能笔达,即有讹错,均出不知"(《西利亚郡主别传·序》)。这不等于开脱自己是"不知者无罪"么?假如我前面没有讲错,那么林译的"讹"决不能完全怪助手,而"讹"里最具特色的成分正出于林纾本人的明知故犯。也恰恰是这部分的"讹"起了一些抗腐作用,林译多少因此而免于全被淘汰。试看林纾的主要助手魏易单独翻译的迭更司《二城故事》(《庸言》第一卷13号起连载),它就只有林、魏合作时那种删改的"讹",却没有合作时那种增改的"讹"。林译有些地方,看来助手们不至于"讹错",倒是"笔达"者"信笔行之",不加思索,没体味出原话里的机锋。《滑稽外史》一四章(原书一五章)里番尼那封信是历来传诵的。林纾把第一句笔达如下,没有加上他惯用的密圈来表示欣赏和领会:

　　　　先生足下:吾父命我以书与君。医生言吾父股必中断,腕不能书,故命我书之。

无端添进一个"腕"字,真是画蛇添足!对能读原文的人说来,迭更司这里的句法(... the doctors considering it doubtful whether he will ever recover the use of his legs which prevents his holding a pen)差不多防止了添进"腕"或"手"字的任何可能性。迭更司赏识的盖司吉尔夫人(Mrs. Gaskell)在她的小说里有相类的笑话,一位老先生代他的妻子写信,说"她的脚脖子扭了筋,拿不起笔"(she being indisposed with sprained ankle, which quite incapacitated her from holding pen)。唐代一个有名的话柄是:"李安期……看判曰:'书稍弱。'选人对曰:'昨坠马伤足。'安期曰:'损足何废好书!'"(《太平广记》卷二五〇引《朝野金载》)林纾从容一些,准会想起它来,也许就改译为"股必中断,不能作书"或"足胫难复原,不复能执笔",不但加圈,并且加注了。当然,助手们的外文程度都很平常,事先准备也不一定充分,临时对本口述,又碰上这位应声直书的"笔达"者,不给予迟疑和考虑的间隙。忙中有错,口述者会看错说错,笔达者难保不听错写错,助手们事后显然也没有校核过林纾的写稿。在那些情况下,不犯"讹错"才真是奇迹。不过,苛责林纾助手们的人很容易忽视或忘记翻译这门艺业的特点。我们研究一部文学作品,事实上往往不能够而且不需要一字一句都透彻了解的。有些字、词、句以至无关重要的章节都可以不求甚解,我们一样写得出头头是道的论文,完全不必声明对某字、某句和某节缺乏了解,以表示自己特别诚实。翻译可就不同。原作里没有一个字可以滑溜过去,没有一处困难躲闪得了。一部作品读起来很顺畅容易,到翻译就会出现疑难,而这种疑难常常并非翻翻字典所能解决。不能解决而回避,那就是任意删节的"讹",不肯躲避而强解,那又是胡猜乱测的"讹"。翻译者蒙了"反逆者"的恶名,却最不会制造烟幕来掩饰自己的无知和误解。譬如《滑稽外史》原书第三五章说赤利伯尔弟兄是"German-merchants",林译第三四章译为"德国巨商"。我们一般也是那样理解的,除非仔细再想一想。迭更司决不把德国人作为英国社会的救星;同时,在 19 世纪描述本国生活的英国小说里,异言异服的外国角色只是笑柄,而赤利伯尔的姓氏和举止是道地的英国人。那个平常的称谓此地有一个现代不常用的意义:不指"德国巨商",而指和德国做生意的进出口商人。写文章谈论《滑稽外史》时,只要不根据误解来证明迭更司是个德国迷,我们的无知很可能免于暴露;翻译《滑稽外史》时,就不那么安全了。

所以,林纾助手的许多"讹错",都还可以原谅。使我诧异的只是他们教林纾加添的注解和申说,那一定经过一番调查研究的。举两个我认为最离奇的例。《黑太子南征录》第五章:"彼马上呼我为'乌弗黎'(注:法兰西语,犹言'工人'),且作势,令我辟此双扉。我为之启关,彼则曰:'懋尔西'(注:系不规则之英语)。"《孝女耐儿传》第五一章:"白拉司曰:'汝大能作雅谑,而又精于动物学,何也?汝殆为第一等之小丑!'英文 Buffoon 滑稽也,Bufon 癞蟆也;白拉司本称圭而伯为'滑稽',音吐模糊,遂成'癞蟆'。"把"开门"(ouvre)和"工人"(ouvrier)混为一字,不去说它,为什么把也是"法兰西语"的"谢谢"(merci)解释为"不规则之英语"呢?法国一位"动物学"家的姓和"小丑"那个字声音相近,雨果的诗里就也把它们押韵打趣,不知道布封这个人,不足为奇,为什么硬改了他的本姓(Buffon)去牵合拉丁文和意大利文的"癞蟆"(bufo,bufone),以致法国的动物学大家化为罗马的两栖小动物呢?莎士比亚《仲夏夜之梦》第三幕第一景写一个角色遭了魔术的禁咒,变成驴首人身,他的伙伴大为惊讶说:"天呀!你是经过了翻译了"(Thou art transtated)。那句话可以应用在这个例子上。

林纾四十四五岁,在逛石鼓山的船上,开始翻译,他不断译书,直到逝世,共译 170 余种作品,几乎全是小说。传说他也可能翻译基督教《圣经》。据我这次不很完备的浏览,他接近 30 年的翻译生涯显明地分为两个时期。"癸丑三月"(民国二年)译完的《离恨天》算前后两期之间的界标。在它以前,林译十之七八都很醒目,在它以后,译笔逐渐退步,色彩枯暗,劲头松懈,使读者厌倦。这并非因为后期林译里缺乏出色的原作。分明也有塞万提斯的《魔侠传》,有孟德斯鸠的《鱼雁抉微》等书。不幸经过林纾 60 岁后没精打采的译笔,它们恰象《鱼雁抉微》里所嘲笑的神学著作,仿佛能和安眠药比赛功效。塞万提斯的生气勃勃、浩瀚流走的原文和林纾的死气沉沉、支离纠绕的译文,孟德斯鸠的"神笔"(《鱼雁抉微·序》,《东方杂志》第一二卷九号)和林译的钝笔,成为残酷的对照。说也奇怪,同一个哈葛德的作品,后期译的《铁盒头颅》之类,也比前期所译他的任何一部书读起来沉闷。袁枚论诗所说"老手颓唐"那四个字(《小仓山房诗集》卷二〇《续诗品·辨微》又《随园诗话》卷一),完全可以借评后期林译:一个老手或能手不肯或不能再费心卖力,只依仗积累的一点儿熟练来搪塞敷衍。前期的翻译使我们想象出一个精神饱满而又集中的林纾,兴高采烈，随时随地准备表演一下他的写作技巧。后期翻译所产生的印象是，一个困倦的老人机械地以疲乏的手指驱使着退了锋的秃笔，要达到"一时千言"的指标。他对所译的作品不再欣赏，也不甚感觉兴趣，除非是博取稿费的兴趣。换句话说，这种翻译只是林纾的"造币厂"承应的一项买卖，形式上是把外文作品转变为中文作品，而实质上等于把外国货色转变为中国货币。林纾前后期翻译在态度上的不同，从这一点看得出来。他前期的译本绝大多数有自序或旁人序，有跋，有《小引》，有《达旨》，有《例言》，有《译余剩语》，有《短评数则》，有自己和旁人所题的诗、词，在译文里还时常附加按语和评语。这种种都对原作的意义或艺术作了阐明或赏析。尽管讲的话不免迂腐和幼稚，流露的态度是郑重的、热情的。他和他翻译的东西关系亲密，甚至感情冲动得暂停那支落纸如飞的笔，腾出工夫来擦眼泪。在后期译本里，这些点缀品或附属品大大地减削。题诗和题词完全绝迹，卷头语例如《孝友镜》的《译余小识》，评语例如《烟火马》第二章里一连串的"可笑！""可笑极矣！""令人绝倒！"等，也极少出现，甚至象《金台春梦录》，以北京为背景，涉及中国风土和掌故，也不能刺激他发表感想。他不象以前那样亲热、隆重地对待他所译的作品。他的整个态度显得随便，竟可以说是冷淡、漠不关心。假如翻译工作是"文学因缘"，那末林纾后期的翻译就颇象他自己的书名"冰雪因缘"了。

林纾是古文家，他的朋友们称他能用"古文"来译外国小说，就象赵熙《怀畏庐叟》："列国虞初铸马、班"（陈衍《近代诗钞》第一八册）。后来的评论者也都那样说。这个问题似乎需要澄清。"古文"是中国文学史上的术语，自唐以来，尤其在明、清两代，有特殊而狭隘的涵义。并非一切文言都算"古文"，同时，在某种条件下，"古文"也不一定跟白话对立。

"古文"有两方面。一方面就是林纾在《黑奴吁天录·例言》、《撒克逊劫后英雄略·序》、《块肉余生述·序》里所谓"义法"，指"开场"、"伏脉"、"接笋"、"结穴"、"开阖"等——一句话，叙述和描写的技巧。从这一点说，白话作品完全可能具备"古文家义法"。明代李开先《词谑》早记载古文家象唐顺之、王慎中之流把《水浒传》来匹配《史记》。林纾同时人李葆恂《义州李氏丛刊》里《旧学盦笔记》记载"阳湖派"最好的古文家恽敬的曾孙告诉他："其曾孙子居先生有手写《红楼梦论文》一书，用黄、朱、墨绿笔，仿震川评点《史记》之法。"《笔记》里还有很少被人征引的一条："阮文达极赏《儒林外史》，谓：'作者系安徽望族，所记乃其乡里来商于扬而起家者，与土著无干。作者一肚皮愤激，借此发泄，与太史公作谤书，情事相等，故笔力亦十得六七。'倾倒极矣！予谓此书，不惟小说中无此奇文，恐欧、苏后具此笔力者亦少；明之归、唐，国朝之方、姚，皆不及远甚。只看他笔外有笔，无字句处皆文章，褒贬讽刺，俱从太史公《封禅书》得来"。简直就把白话小说和八家"古文"看成同类的东西，较量高下。林纾自己在《块肉余生述·序》、《孝女耐儿传·序》里也把《石头记》、《水浒》和"史、班"相提并论。不仅如此，上文已经说过，他还发现外国小说"处处均得古文义法"。那末，在"义法"方面，外国小说原来就符合"古文"，无需林纾来转化它为"古文"。不过，"古文"还有一个方面——语言。只要看林纾渊源所自的桐城派祖师方苞的教诫，我们就知道"古文"运用语言时受多少清规戒律的束缚。它不但排除白话，并且勾销了大部分的文言："古文中忌语录中语、魏晋六朝人藻丽俳语、汉赋中板重字法、诗歌中隽语、南北史佻巧语。"后来的桐城派作者更扩大范围，陆续把"注疏"、"尺牍"、"诗话"等的腔吻和语言都添列为违禁品。受了这种步步逼进的限制，古文家战战兢兢地循规守矩，以求保持语言的纯洁性，一种消极的、象雪花那样而不象火焰那样的纯洁。从这方面看，林纾译书的文体不是"古文"，至少就不是他自己所谓"古文"。他的译笔违背和破坏了他亲手制定的"古文"规律。譬如袁宏道《记孤山》有这样一句话:"孤山处士妻梅子鹤,是世间第一种便宜人!"林纾《畏庐论文·十六忌》之八《忌轻儇》指摘说:"'便宜人'三字亦可入文耶?"然而我随手一翻,看见《滑稽外史》第二九章明明写着:"惟此三十磅亦非巨,乃令彼人占其便宜,至于极地。"又譬如《畏庐论文·拼字法》说:"古文之拼字,与填词之拼字,法同而字异;词眼纤艳,古文则雅炼而庄严耳";举"愁罗恨绮"为"填词拼字"的例子。然而林译柯南达利的一部小说,恰恰以《恨绮愁罗记》为名称。更明显表示态度的是《畏庐论文·十六忌》之一四《忌糅杂》:"糅杂者,杂佛氏之言也……适译《洪罕女郎传》,遂以《楞严》之旨,掇拾为序言,颇自悔其杂。幸为游戏之作,不留稿。"这充分证明林纾认为翻译小说和"古文"是截然两回事。"古文"的清规戒律对译书没有任何裁判权或约束力。其实方苞早批评明末遗老的"古文"有"杂小说"的毛病,其他古文家也都摆出"忌小说"的警告。试想,翻译"写生逼肖"的小说而文笔不许"杂小说",那不等于讲话而咬紧自己的舌头吗?所以,林纾并没有用"古文"译小说,而且也不可能用"古文"译小说。

林纾译书所用文体是他心目中认为较通俗、较随便、富于弹性的文言。它虽然保留若干"古文"成分,但比"古文"自由得多,在词汇和句法上,规矩不严密,收容量很宽大。因此,"古文"里绝不容许的文言"隽语"、"佻巧语"象"梁上君子"、"五朵云"、"土馒头"、"夜度娘"等形形色色地出现了。口语象"小宝贝"、"爸爸"、"天杀之伯林伯"等也经常掺进去了。流行的外来新名词——林纾自己所谓"一见之字里行间便觉不韵"的"东人新名词"——象"普通"、"程度"、"热度"、"幸福"、"社会"、"个人"、"团体"、"脑筋"、"脑球"、"脑气"、"反动之力"、"梦境甜蜜"、"活泼之精神"等应有尽有了。还沾染当时的译音习气,"马丹"、"密司脱"、"安琪儿"、"苦力"、"俱乐部"之类不用说,甚至毫不必要地来一个"列底(尊闺门之称也)",或者"此所谓'德武忙'耳(犹华言为朋友尽力也)"。意想不到的是,译文里包含很大的"欧化"成分。好些字法、句法简直不象不懂外文的古文家的"笔达",却象懂外文而不甚通中文的人的硬译。那种生硬的——毋宁说死硬的——翻译是双重的"反逆",既损坏原作的表达效果,又违背了祖国的语文习惯。林纾笔下居然会有下面的例句!第一类象

　　　　侍者叩扉曰:"先生密而华德至"(《迦茵小传》5 章)。

把称词"密司脱"译意为"先生",而又死扣住原文的次序,位置在姓氏之前。第二类象

　　　　自念有一丝自主之权,亦断不收伯爵(《巴黎茶花女遗事》,原书 5 章);
　　　　人之识我,恒多谀辞,直敝我耳。(《块肉余生述》19 章)

译 spoils me 为"敝我",译 reçu le comte 为"收伯爵",字面上好象比"使我骄恣"、"接待伯爵"忠实。可惜是懒汉、懦夫或笨伯的忠实,结果产生了两句外国中文,和"他热烈地摇摆(shake)我的手"、"箱子里没有多余的房间(room)了"、"这东西太亲爱(dear),我买不起"等属于同一范畴。第三类象

　　　　今此谦退之画师,如是居独立之国度,近已数年矣(《滑稽外史》19 章)。

按照文言的惯例,至少得把"如是"两字移后:"……居独立之国度,如是者已数年矣。"再举一个较长的例:

　　　　我……思上帝之心,必知我此一副眼泪实由中出,诵经本诸实心,布施由于诚意。且此妇人之死,均余搓其目,着其衣冠,扶之入柩,均我一人之力也。(《巴黎茶花女遗事》)。

"均我"、"均余"的冗赘，"着其衣冠"的语与意反（当云："为着衣冠"，原文亦无此句），都撇开不讲。整个句子完全遵照原文秩序，浩浩荡荡，一路顺次而下，不重新安排组织。在文言语法里，孤零零一个"思"字无论如何带动不了后面那一大串词句，显得尾大不掉，"知"字虽然地位不那么疏远，也拖拉的东西太长，欠缺一气贯注的劲头。译文只好缩短拖累，省去原文里"亦必怜彼妇美貌短命"那个意思。但是，整句里的各个子句，总是松散不够团结；假如我们不对照原文而加新式标点，就要把"且此妇人之死"另起一句。尽管这样截去后半句，前半句还嫌接筍不严、包扎欠紧，在文言里不很过得去。也许该把"上帝之心必知"那个意思移到后面去："自思此一副眼泪实由中出，诵经本诸实心，布施出于诚意，当皆蒙上帝鉴照，且伊人美貌短命，非我则更无料理其丧葬者，亦当邀上帝悲悯。"这些例子足以表示林纾翻译时，不仅不理会"古文"的限止，而且往往忽视了中国语文的习尚。他这种态度使我们想起《撒克逊劫后英雄略》那个勇猛善战的"道人"，一换上盔甲，就什么清规都不守了。

　　在林译第一部小说《巴黎茶花女遗事》里，我们看得出林纾在尝试，在摸索，在摇摆。他认识到，"古文"关于语言的戒律要是不放松（姑且不说放弃），小说就翻译不成。为翻译起见，他得借助于文言小说以及笔记的传统文体和当时流行的报章杂志文体。但是，不知道是良心不安，还是积习难除，他一会儿放下、一会儿又摆出"古文"的架子。"古文"惯手的林纾和翻译新手的林纾之间仿佛有拉锯战或跷板游戏；这种此起彼伏的情况清楚地表现在《巴黎茶花女遗事》里。那可以解释为什么它的译笔比其他林译晦涩、生涩、"举止羞涩"；紧跟着的《黑奴吁天录》就比较晓畅明白。古奥的字法、句法在这部译本里随处碰得着。"我为君洁，故愿勿度，非我自为也"，就是一例。"女接所欢，嬲，而其母下之，遂病"——这个常被引错而传作笑谈的句子也正是"古文"里叙事简敛肃括之笔。司马迁还肯用浅显的"有身"或"孕"（例如《外戚世家》、《五宗世家》、《吕不韦列传》、《春申君列传》、《淮南·衡山列传》、《张丞相列传》），林纾却从《说文》所引《尚书·梓材》挑选了一个斑驳陆离的古字"嬲"，班固还肯说"饮药伤堕"（《外戚传》下），林纾却仿《史记·扁鹊仓公列传》，只用了一个"下"字。这就是《畏庐论文》里所谓"换字法"。另举一个易被忽略的例。小说里报导角色对话，少不得"甲说"、"乙回答说"、"丙也说"那些引冒语。外国小说家常常用些新鲜花样，以免连行接句的"你说"、"我说"、"他说"，读来单调；结果可能很纤巧做作，以致受到修辞教科书的指摘。中国文言里报导对话也可以来些变化，只写"曰"、"对曰"、"问"、"答"而不写明是谁。更古雅的方式是连"曰"、"问"等都干脆省掉，《史通》内篇《模拟》所谓，"连续而脱去其'对曰'、'问曰'等字"，象

　　　　"……邦无道，谷，耻也。""克伐怨欲不行焉，可以为仁矣。"曰"可以为难矣，仁则
　　　　吾不知也。"（《论语·宪问》）；

　　　　"……则具体而微。""敢问所安？"曰："姑舍是。"（《孟子·公孙丑》）。

佛经翻译里往往接连地省掉两次，象

　　　　"……是诸国土，若算师、若算弟子能得边际，知其数不？""不也，世尊。""诸比丘，
　　　　是人所经国土，若点不点，尽抹为尘……"（《妙法莲华经·化城喻品第七》）；

　　　　"……汝见是学、无学二千人不？""唯然，已见。""阿难，是诸人等……"（同书《授
　　　　学·无学人记品第九》）。

这种方式在中国文言小说里并不常见。传奇里象

曰："金也……""青衣者谁也?"曰："钱也……""白衣者谁也?"曰："银也……""汝谁也?"(《列异传·张奋》);

女曰："非羊也,雨工也。""何为雨工?"曰："雷霆之类也。"

……君曰："所杀几何?"曰："六十万。""伤稼乎?"曰："八百里。"(《柳毅传》);

或者《聊斋志异》里象

道士问众:"饮足乎?"曰："足矣。""足宜早寝,勿误樵苏。"(《崂山道士》);

都不是常规,而是偶例。《巴黎茶花女遗事》却反复应用这个"古文"里认为最高简的方式。

配曰："若愿见之乎? 吾与尔就之。"余不可。"然则招之来乎?";

曰："然。""然则马克之归谁送之?"

曰："然。""然则我送君。";

马克曰："客何名?"配唐曰："一家实瞠。"马克曰："识之。""一亚猛著彭。"马克曰："未之识也。";

突问曰："马克车马安在?"配唐曰："市之矣。""肩衣安在?"又曰："市之矣。""金钻安在?"曰："典之矣。";

余于是拭泪向翁曰："翁能信我爱公子乎?"翁曰："信之。""翁能信吾情爱,不为利生乎?"翁曰："信之。""翁能许我有此善念,足以赦吾罪戾乎?"翁曰："既信且许之。""然则请翁亲吾额……"。

值得注意的是,在以后的林译里,似乎再碰不到这个方式。第二部林译是《黑奴吁天录》,书里就不省去"曰"和"对曰"了(例如九章马利亚等问意里赛、二十章亚妃立问托弗收)。

　　林译除迭更司、欧文以外,前期的那几种哈葛德的小说也颇有它们的特色。我这一次发现自己宁可读林纾的译文,不乐意读哈葛德的原文。理由很简单:林纾的中文文笔比哈葛德的英文文笔高明得多。哈葛德的原文很笨重,对话更呆蠢板滞,尤其是冒险小说里的对话,把古代英语和近代语言杂拌一起。随便举一个短例,《斐洲烟水愁城录》第五章:"乃以恶声斥洛巴革曰:'汝何为恶作剧? 尔非痫当不如是。'"这是很明快的文言,也是很能表达原文意义的翻译。它只有一个缺点:没有让读者看出那句话在原文里的说法。在原文里,那句话(What meanest thou by such mad tricks? Surely thou art mad)就仿佛中文里这样说,"汝干这种疯狂的把戏,是诚何心? 汝一定发了疯矣"。对语文稍有感性的人看到这些不伦不类的词句,第一次觉得可笑,第二、三次觉得可厌了。林纾的译笔说不上工致,但大体上比哈葛德的轻快明爽。翻译者运用"归宿语言"的本领超过原作者运用"出发语言'的本领,那是翻译史上每每发生的事情。讲究散文风格的裴德(Walter Pater)就嫌爱伦·坡的短篇小说文笔太粗糙,只肯看波德莱亚翻译的法文本,一个年轻的唯美主义者(un jeune esthète)告诉法朗士(A. France)说《冰雪因缘》只有在译本里尚堪一读。传说歌德认为纳梵尔(Gerard de Nerval)所译《浮士德》法文本比自己的德文原作来得清楚,惠特曼也不否认弗拉爱里格拉德(F. Freiligrath)用德文翻译的《草叶集》里的诗有可能胜过英文原作。林纾译的哈葛德小说颇可列入这类事例里——当然,只是很微末的例子。近年来,哈葛德在西方文坛的地位渐渐上升,主要是由于一位有世界影响的心理学家对《三千年艳尸记》的称道;一九六〇年英国还出版了一本哈葛德评传。水涨船高,也许林译可以沾点儿光,至少我们在评论林译时,不必礼节性地把"哈葛德在外国是个毫不足道的作家"那句老话重说一遍了。

传记里说林纾"译书虽对客不辍,惟作文则辍";上面所讲也证实他"译书"不象"作文"那样慎重。也许可以在这里回忆一下有关的文坛旧事。

不是一九三一年、就是一九三二年,我有一次和陈衍先生谈话。陈先生知道我懂外文,但不知道我学的专科是外国文学,以为总不外乎理工科或政法科之类。那一天,他查问明白了,就慨叹说:"文学又何必向外国去学呢!咱们中国文学不就很好么?"我不敢跟他理论,只抬出他的朋友来挡一下,就说读了林纾的翻译小说,因此对外国文学发生兴趣。陈先生说:"这事做颠倒了。琴南如果知道,未必高兴。你读了他的翻译,应该进而学他的古文,怎么反而向往外国了?琴南岂不是'为渊驱鱼'么?"他顿一顿,又说:"琴南最恼人家恭维他的翻译和画。我送他一副寿联,称赞他的画,碰了他一个钉子。康长素送他一首诗,捧他的翻译,也惹他发脾气。"我记得见过康有为"译才并世数严、林"那首诗,当时也没追问下去。事隔七八年,李宣龚先生给我看他保存的师友来信,里面两大本是《林畏庐先生手札》,有一封信说:

> ……前年我七十贱辰,石遗送联云:"讲席推前辈;画师得大年。"于吾之品行文章
> 不涉一字。来书云:"尔不用吾寿文……故吾亦不言尔之好处。"

这就是陈先生讲的那一回事了。另一封信提到严复:

> ……然几道生时,亦至轻我,至当面诋毁。

我想起康有为的诗,就请问李先生。李先生说,康有为一句话得罪两个人。严复一向瞧不起林纾,看见那首诗,就说康有为胡闹,天下哪有一个外国字也不认识的"译才",自己真羞与为伍。至于林纾呢,他不快意的有两点。诗里既然不紧扣图画,都是题外的衬托,那末第一该讲自己的"古文",为什么倒去讲翻译小说?舍本逐末,这是一。在这首诗里,严复只是个陪客,难道非用"十二侵"韵不可,不能用"十四盐"韵,来一句"译才并世数林、严"么?"史思明懂得的道理,安绍山竟不懂!"喧宾夺主,这是二。文人好名争名,历来是个笑话;只要不发展成为无情无耻的倾轧和陷害,它终还算得"人间喜剧"里一个情景轻松的场面。

林纾不乐意人家称他为"译才",我们可以理解。刘禹锡《刘梦得文集》卷七《送僧方及南谒柳员外》说过:"勿谓翻译徒,不为文雅雄";就表示一般人的成见以为翻译家是说不上"文雅"的。一个小例也许可以表示翻译的不受重视。远在刘禹锡前,有一位公认的"文雅雄",搞过翻译——谢灵运。他对"殊俗之音,多所通解",流传很广的《大般涅盘经》卷首标明:"谢灵运再治",抚州宝应寺曾保留"谢灵运翻经台"的古迹。但是评论谢灵运的文史家对他是中国古代唯一的大诗人而兼翻译家这一点,都置之不理。这种偏见也并不限于中国。林纾原自负为"文雅雄",没料到康有为在唱和应酬的诗里还只品定他是个翻译家;"译才"和"翻译徒"虽非同等,总是同类。他重视"古文"而轻视翻译,那也并不奇怪,因为"古文"是他的一种创作,一个人总认为创作比翻译更亲切地是"自家物事"。要知道两者相差多少,就得看林纾对自己的"古文"评价有多高。他早年自认不会作诗,晚年要刻诗集,给李先生的信里说:

> 吾诗七律专学东坡、简斋;七绝学白石、石田,参以荆公;五古学韩;其论事之古诗
> 则学杜。惟不长于七古及排律耳。

可见他对于自己的诗也颇得意,还表示门路很正,来头很大。但是,跟着就是下面这一节:

> 石遗已到京,相见握手。流言之人吾耳者——化为云烟。遂同往便宜坊食鸭,

畅谈至三小时。石遗言吾诗将与吾文并肩,吾又不服,痛争一小时。石遗门外汉,安

知文之奥妙!……六百年中,震川外无一人敢当我者;持吾诗相较,特狗吠驴鸣。

杜甫、韩愈、王安石、苏轼等真可怜,原来都不过是"狗吠驴鸣"的榜样!为了抬高自己某一门造诣,不惜把自己另一门造诣那样贬损甚至糟蹋,我一时上记不起第二个例。虽然林纾在《震川集选》里说翻译《贼史》时"窃效"《书张贞女死事》,料想他给翻译的地位决不会比诗高,而可能更低一些。假如有人做一个试验,向他说,"不错!比起先生的古文来,先生的诗的确只是'狗吠驴鸣',先生的翻译象更卑微的动物"——譬如"癞蟆"?——"的叫声",他将怎样反应呢?是欣然引为知己?还是怫然"痛争",反过来替自己的诗和翻译辩护?这个试验似乎没人做过,也许是无需做的。

选文二　论西方现代文学文体学在小说翻译中的作用

申　丹

导　言

本文选自《外语与翻译》,1998 年第 4 期。

选文从回顾西方文体学历史入手,切入文学文体学的定义——20 世纪初在现代语言学的影响与渗透下逐渐形成的一个具有一定独立地位的新的理论学科。论者指出,文学文体学对于小说翻译批评与实践具有三方面重要意义:其一,通常的(非文学性的)翻译理论不适用于文学语篇的翻译。其二,就文学翻译研究本身来说,往往只注重诗歌翻译而不注重小说翻译,尤其不重视传统现实主义小说翻译所特有的问题。其三,小说翻译中的很多问题只有通过文体分析才能得到有效的解决。选文借用文学文体学的理论和方法,通过对《红楼梦》、《骆驼祥子》和《傲慢与偏见》翻译片断中三个典型译例的分析,探讨这一新兴的边缘学科在小说翻译中的意义和价值。论者在结论中肯定指出,小说翻译应更注重形式与内容的不可分离性,注重形式本身所蕴涵的意义,小说翻译中的很多问题能够通过文体分析得以有效地解决,呼吁小说翻译理论和实践工作者更为注意文学文体学的作用,更多的文体学家参与小说翻译批评。

一

西方现代文学文体学采用语言学模式来研究文学作品,属于生命力较强的交叉或边缘学科。西方对文体的研究可谓渊远流长,可追溯到古希腊、罗马的修辞学研究,早在公元 100 年,就出现了德米特里厄斯(Demetrius)的《论文体》这样集中探讨文体问题的论著。但在 20 世纪之前,对文体的讨论一般不外乎主观印象式的评论,而且通常出现在修辞学研究、文学研究或语法分析之中,没有自己相对独立的地位。20 世纪初以来,随着现代语言学的发展,文体学才逐渐成为一个具有一定独立地位的交叉学科。50 年代末以前,文体学的发展势头较为弱小,而且主要是在欧洲大陆展开(在英美盛行的为新批评)。俄国形式主义、布拉格学派和法国结构主义等均对文体学的发展做出了贡献。在英美,随着新批评的逐渐衰落,越来越多的学者意识到了语言学理论对文学研究的重要性。1958 年在美国印地安那大学召开了一个重要的国际会议——“文体学研讨会”,这是文体学发展史上的一个里程碑。在这次会议上,雅克布森(R. Jakobson)宣称:“……倘若一位语言学家对语言的诗学功能不闻不问,或一位文学研究者对语言学问题不予关心,对语言学方法也一窍不通,他们就显然过时落伍了。”就英美来说,这个研讨会标志着文体学作为一门交叉学科的诞生;就西方来说,它标志着文体学研究的全面展开并即将进入兴盛时期。60 年代初以来,转换生成语法、功能语言学、社会语言学、话语分析、言语行为理论等各种语言学研究的新成果被逐渐引入文体学,增加了文体学研究的广度和深度。就小说翻译批评和实践来说,文学文体学尤为值得重视(参见申,1998a 和 1998b)。

文学文体学特指以阐释文学文本的主题意义和美学价值为目的的文体学派。文学文体学是连接语言学与文学批评的桥梁,注重探讨作者如何通过对语言的选择来表达和加强主题意义和美学效果。这一文体学派将语言学仅仅视为帮助进行分析的工具,他们不限于采用某种特定的语言学理论,而是根据分析的实际需要,选用一种或数种适用的语言学模式或方法。文学文体学的阐释路子基本上同于传统批评,借助于阐释经验、直觉和洞察力。但文学文体学家反对一味凭藉主观印象,主张对文本进行细读,要求言必有据。同时,他们认为只有采用现代语言学的理论和方法才能较好地掌握语言结构,较深入地理解语言的作用,对语言特征做出较为精确、系统的描写。这是他们与新批评或“细读”派最根本的区别之一。

文学文体学对于小说翻译批评和实践的重要性可以从三方面来看。其一,通常的(非文学性的)翻译理论不适用于文学语篇的翻译。60 年代以来,西方翻译研究界吸取语言学理论、信息理论、人类学、符号学、心理学等各领域的新成果,取得了长足进展。但总的来说,普通翻译研究一般停留在所指对等这个层面上,所以无法解释文学语篇所特有的问题。在探讨诗歌翻译中的对等问题时,Robert de Beaugrande(1978:101)区分了两个不同的对等层次:一为通常的 A 层次,该层次的问题属于语言系统之内或之间的问题,这些问题可通过语言学和比较语言学来解决。另一为比较特殊的 B 层次,它包含使用诗学语言的特殊问题,这些问题则需通过诗学研究和文学分析来解决(参见 Broeck,1978;Prochazka,1964;Popovic,1970;Brislin,1976;Holmes,1978;Bassnett-McGuire,1993)。通常的(非文学性的)翻译研究往往停留在 A 层次上,故难以解决 B 层次所特有的问题。其二,就文学翻译研究本身来说,往往只注重诗歌翻译而不注重小说翻译,尤其不重视传统现实主义小说翻译所特有的问题。其三,小说翻译中的很多问题只有通过文体分析才能得到有效的解决。笔者认为,小说翻译中的一个突出问题堪称为“假象等值”,即译文与原文所指相同但文学价值或文学意义不同。在翻译诗歌时,译者通常会考虑语言形式的美学效果,但在翻译小说时,译者却往往将对等建立在“可意译的物质内容”(paraphrasable material content)这一层次上(Bassnett-McGuire,1993)。在诗歌翻译中,倘若译者仅注重传递原诗的内容,而不注重传递原诗的美学效果,人们不会将译文视为与原文等值。但在翻译小说,尤其是现实主义小说时,人们往往忽略语言形式本身的文学意义,将是否传递了同样的内容作为判断等值的标准。这样的“等值”往往是假象等值,这在下面分析的例子中可看得很清楚。

当然,在传统的小说翻译研究中,批评家不仅关注所指相同这一层次,而且也关注译文的美学效果。但这种关注容易停留在印象性的文字优雅这一层次上,不注重从语言形式与主题意义的关系入手来探讨问题,而这种关系正是文学文体学所关注的焦点。我们不妨借用文体学的理论与方法,通过对三个译例的分析,来看一看文学文体学对小说翻译批评与实践所具有的理论指导价值。

二

首先,让我们探讨一下《红楼梦》中一段的不同译法:

原文:(……不想[黛玉]刚走进来,正听见湘云说"经济"一事,宝玉又说:"林妹妹不说这些混帐话,要说这话,我也和他生分了。")黛玉听了这话,不觉又喜又惊,又悲又叹。所喜者:果然自己眼力不错,素日认他是个知己,果然是个知己。所惊者:他在人前一片私心称扬于我,其亲热厚密竟不避嫌疑。所叹者:你既为我的知己,自然我也可为你的知己,又何必有"金玉"之论呢?既有"金玉"之论,也该你我有之,又何必来一宝钗?……

(《红楼梦》第 32 回)

译文甲:This surprised and delighted Tai-yu but also distressed and grieved her. She was delighted to know she had not misjudged him, for he had now proved just as understanding as she has always thought. Surprised that he had been so indiscreet as to acknowledge his preference for her openly. Distressed because their mutual understanding ought to preclude all talk about gold matching jade, or she instead of Pao-chai should have the gold locket to match his jade amulet...

(trans. Hsien-yi Yang and Gladys Yang, Vol. Ⅰ: 469 - 470)

译文乙:Mingled emotions of happiness, alarm, sorrow and regret assailed her.

Happiness:

Because after all (she thought) I wasn't mistaken in my judgement of you. I always thought of you as a true friend, and I was right.

Alarm:

Because if you praise me so unreservedly in front of other people, your warmth and affection are sure, sooner or later, to excite suspicion and be misunderstood.

Regret:

Because if you are my true friend, then I am yours and the two of us are a perfect match. But in that case why did there have to be all this talk of "the gold and the jade"? Alternatively, if there had to be all this talk of gold and jade, why weren't we the two to have them? Why did there have to be a Bao-chai with her golden locket? ...

(trans. David Hawkes, Vol. 2:131 - 132)

原文中的"所喜者"、"所惊者"、"所叹者"为叙述者的评论,冒号后面出现的则是用自由直接引语表达的黛玉的内心想法。也就是说,有三个平行的由叙述者的话语向人物内心想法的突然转换。这三个平行的突转在《红楼梦》这一语境中看起来较为自然,但直接译入英语则会显得很不协调。

也许是为了使译文能较好地被当代英文读者接受,译文甲通过叙述者来间接表达黛玉的想法,这样译文显得言简意赅、平顺自然。从表面上看,译文与原文大致表达了同样的内容,是等值的。但通过对译文进行细致的文体分析,则不难发现,这种等值只是表面上的假象等值。我们可以从以下三方面来看这一问题:

(一)将人物的想法客观化或事实化

在像《红楼梦》这样的传统第三人称小说中,故事外的叙述者较为客观可靠,而故事内的人物则主观性较强。译文甲将黛玉的内心想法纳入客观叙述层之后,无意中将黛玉的想法在一定的程度上事实化了:

She was delighted to know [**the fact that**] she had not misjudged him, for he had now proved just as understanding as she has always thought. Surprised [**at the fact**] that he had been so indiscreet as to acknowledge his preference for her openly.

这样一来,叙述的焦点就从内心透视转为外部描述,黛玉也就从想法的产生者变成了事实的被动接受者。值得注意的是,在原文中,黛玉的想法与"喜"、"惊"、"叹"等情感活动密不可分,想法的开始标志着情感活动的开始;黛玉的复杂心情主要是通过直接揭示她的想法来表达的。在译文甲中,由于原文中的内心想法以外在事实的面目出现,因此成为先于情感活动而存在的因素,仅仅构成情感活动的外在原因,不再与情感活动合为一体。不难看出,与原文中的内心想法相比,译文中的外在"事实"在表达黛玉的情感方面起的作用较为间接,而且较为弱小。

此外,将黛玉的内心想法纳入叙述层也不利于反映黛玉特有的性格特征。原文中,黛玉对宝玉评价道:"他在人前一片私心称扬于我,其亲热厚密竟不避嫌疑。"实际上,宝玉仅仅在史湘云说经济一事时,说了句,"林妹妹不说这些混帐话,若说这话,我也和他生分了"。宝玉的话并无过于亲密之处,黛玉将之视为"亲热厚密竟不避嫌疑"主要有两方面的原因。一是她极其循规蹈矩,对于言行得体极度重视;二是她性格的极度敏感和对宝玉的一片痴情,多少带有一点自作多情的成分。可以说,黛玉对宝玉的评论带有较强的主观性和感情色彩,这一不可靠的人物评论有助于直接生动地揭示黛玉特有的性格特征。在译文甲中,he had been so indiscreet as to ... 成了由叙述者叙述出来的客观事实,基本上失去了反映黛玉性格特征的作用。

(二)人称上无可避免的变化

在原文中,"他"和"你"这两个人称代词所指为宝玉一人。开始时,黛玉以第三人称"他"指称宝玉。随着内心活动的发展,黛玉改用第二人称"你"指称宝玉,情不自禁地直接向不在场的宝玉倾吐衷肠,这显然缩短了两人之间的距离。黛玉接下去说,"既有'金玉'之论,也该你我有之",至此两人已被视为一体。这个从第三人称到第二人称的动态变化发生在一个静态的语境之中,对于反映黛玉的性格有一定作用。黛玉十分敏感多疑,对于宝玉的爱和理解总是感到疑虑,因此在得知"他"的理解和偏爱时,不禁感到又喜又惊。可黛玉多情,对宝玉已爱之至深,因此情不自禁地以"你"代"他",合"你我"为一体。这个在静态小语境中出现的动态代词变化,在某种意义上也可以说象征着黛玉和宝玉之间的感情发展过程,与情节发展暗暗呼应,对表达小说的主题意义有一定作用。

从理论上说,无论是在叙述层还是在人物话语层,均可以采用各种人称。但倘若人物话语通过叙述者表达出来,第一、二人称就必然会转换成第三人称。因此,译文甲在将黛玉的想法纳入叙述层之后,就不可避免地失去了再现原文中人称转换的机会,无法再现原文中通过人称变化所取得的文体和主题价值。

令人感到遗憾的是,译文乙虽然有机会保留原文中的人称转换,却没有这么做,而是持续性地采用第二人称来指称宝玉。这可能有两方面的原因:一是译者忽略了原文中人称转换的文体价值和主题意义。二是由于译者偏爱这种在心里与不在场者展开对话的形式,这种形式具有很强的直接性、生动性和情感效果。但值得注意的是,在原文中,这一偏离常规的形式正是在与前面符合常规的形式的对照下方取得了较为强烈的效果,而且这一对照本身对于反映人物性格和表达主题意义不无作用。由于译文乙持续性地采用第二人称来指称宝玉,原文中在人称上的对照被完全埋没。

(三) 在情态表达形式上的变化

译文甲在将黛玉的想法纳入叙述层之后,无法再现原文中由陈述句向疑问句的转换,这跟以上论及的其他因素交互作用,大大地影响了对人物的主观性和感情色彩的再现。请比较:

原文:你既为我的知己,自然我也可为你的知己,既你我为知己,又何必有"金玉"之论呢?既有"金玉"之论,也该你我有之,又何必来一宝钗?

译文甲:… their mutual understanding ought to preclude all talk about gold matching jade, or she instead of Pao-chai should have the gold locket to match his jade amulet.

原文中黛玉的推理、发问体现出了她的疑惑不安。译文中直截了当的定论 their mutual understanding 则大大减弱了这种疑惑不安的心情。原文中的推理发问呈一种向高潮发展的走向,译文甲的平铺直叙相比之下显得过于平淡。不难看出,译文甲采用的并列陈述句式难以起到同样的反映人物心情和塑造人物性格的作用。总而言之,译文甲与原文只是在表面上看起来基本等值,其实两者在文体功能上相去较远。

译文乙相比之下较好地保留了原文中人物想法的文体价值。为了使译文能较好地被译入语读者接受,译文乙也有意采取了一些措施来减少译文中由叙述话语向人物想法的突然转换所造成的不协调。首先,译文乙采用了一个特殊的版面安排,将(用斜体标示的)叙述者的评论和(用 she thought 引导的)黛玉的想法摆到两个不同的层次上,为两种话语之间的突然转换做了铺垫。为了进一步减少不协调感,译文乙还在黛玉想法前面加上了 because 这一连接词。从语境分析,这个词实际上只能出自叙述者之口:

Happiness (she was happy) *because*:after all (she thought) I wasn't mistaken…

译文乙将 because 悄悄移入黛玉的话语,目的是让黛玉暗暗地与叙述者进行合作,以减少不协调感:

Happiness (she was happy): **Because** after all (she thought) I wasn't mistaken...

我们甚至可以说译文乙暗暗地将第三人称叙述转换成了第一人称叙述：

Happiness (I was happy): **Because** after all I wasn't mistaken...

不难看出，译文乙采用 happiness，alarm，regret 等抽象名词，为减少三个平行突转造成的不协调感起了一定作用。诚然，译文乙采用的这些措施也许走得太远，有不忠实于原文之嫌。但有一点是值得肯定的，即译文乙较好地保留了原文中三个平行突转所具有的主题意义和美学效果。

我们不妨再看看老舍的《骆驼祥子》中一段的不同译法：

原文：这么大的人，拉上那么美的车，他自己的车，弓子软得颤悠颤悠的，连车把都微微的动弹；车厢是那么亮，垫子是那么白，喇叭是那么响；跑得不快怎能对得起自己呢，怎能对得起那辆车呢？（1978:11）

译文甲：How could a man so tall, pulling such a gorgeous rickshaw, his own rickshaw too, with such gently rebounding springs and shafts that barely wavered, such a gleaming body, such a white cushion, such a sonorous horn, face himself if he did not run hard? How could he face his rickshaw?

（trans. James, 1979:11）

译文乙：(Every time he had to duck through a low street gate or door, his heart would swell with silent satisfaction at the knowledge that he was still growing. It tickled him to feel already an adult and yet still a child.) With his brawn and his beautiful rickshaw springs so flexible that the shafts seemed to vibrate; bright chassis, clean, white cushion and loud horn he owed it to them both to run really fast. (This was not out of vanity but a sense of duty. For after six months this lovable rickshaw of his seemed alive to what he was doing...)

（trans. Shi, 1981: 18）

原文中出现的是用"自由间接引语"表达出来的祥子的内心想法。"自由间接引语"这一表达形式兼间接引语与直接引语之长，既能较好地与叙述流相融合（也用第三人称和过去时），又能保留体现人物主体意识的语言成分（如疑问句）。就译文来说，甲版本较好地保留了原文中的表达形式，乙版本却改用了叙述陈述这一表达形式。在译文乙中，标示祥子内心想法的语言特征可谓荡然无存。从表面上看，译文乙与原文表达了大致相同的内容，是等值的。但这种等值恐怕只能称之为"假象等值"。

前文中提到，在第三人称叙述中，故事外的叙述者和故事中的人物分别具有客观性/可靠性和主观性/不可靠性。原文中的"这么大的人，拉上那么美的车"与译文乙中的 with his brawn and his beautiful rickshaw 之间的对照，是充满情感的内心想法与冷静的叙述话语之间的对照，也是人物的主观评价与叙述者的客观描述之间的对照。也许正因为这种由主观方式向客观方式的转换，译文乙将原文中"车厢是那么亮，垫子是那么白，喇叭是那么响"这一串夸张强调的排比句译成了冷静平淡的 bright chassis, clean, white cushion and loud horn。

译文乙的客观化译法在一定程度上影响了对祥子这一人物的性格塑造。在小说中，人物的特定看法和眼光常常通过其对事物的不可靠评价反映出来。祥子对自己的人力车有着极其特殊的感情。他拼死拼活地干了至少三四年方挣来了这辆车。可以说,这辆人力车是他的全部财产,也是他未来的全部希望。他对这辆车爱之至深,可谓到了一种"情人眼里出西施"的地步。不难看出,原文采用的自由间接引语是表达祥子主观性评价的理想形式,它在与叙述话语自然融为一体的情况下,很好地体现了人物的眼光和情感。实际上,在译文乙选择了叙述陈述这一表达形式之后,很难表达出祥子眼光的主观性和不可靠性。倘若"车厢是那么亮,垫子是那么白,喇叭是那么响"这一串夸张强调的排比句被译成 very bright chassis, extremely clean, white cushion and very loud horn,恐怕也会被译文读者误认为是被叙述者认同的事实,反映出来的是叙述者和人物共同具有的客观眼光。译文乙的译者很可能意识到这一连串"那么"的过于强调夸张,因此有意将其略去不译,以使译文更为客观可靠。令人感到遗憾的是,译者显然未意识到原文中的主观性和不可靠性有助于体现人物特有的情感,对于人物塑造有重要意义。

在这里,我们应该充分认识到自由间接引语所起的作用。倘若译文乙未采用叙述陈述而是采用了自由间接引语这一表达形式(譬如中间插入了 he thought 以标示人物的想法),即便保留现有的措辞,效果也会大不相同。且以 with his brawn and his beautiful rickshaw 为例,倘若它在自由间接引语中以祥子内心想法的面目出现,马上就会失去其客观性,因为自由间接引语的内容只不过是"一个不可靠的自我的断言或假定"(Banfield, 1983:218; Pascal, 1977:50)。读者也许会在 with his brawn and his beautiful rickshaw 这一不可靠的断言中觉察到人物的自信和洋洋自得,甚至虚荣心。在原文和译文甲中,不仅表达形式为自由间接引语,而且词汇和句法也具有明显的人物主观性特征,这样有利于塑造一个鲜明的人物自我,读者可以强烈地感受到人物的自信和洋洋自得。这些人物情感与小说的主题紧密关联。在这部小说中,祥子对自己力量的盲目自信与将他的所有努力完全击败的残酷社会现实之间形成了强烈的对照。小说的主题意义主要通过这一悲剧性的对照体现出来。毋庸置疑,译文乙的客观化译法既不利于反映人物情感和塑造人物性格,也不利于表达小说的悲剧性主题意义。

在上文中,我们探讨了在汉译英中出现的问题。现在我们不妨看看下面这例英译中的情况:

原文:Mrs. Bennet was in fact too much overpowered to say a great deal while Sir William remained; but no sooner had he left them than her feelings found a rapid vent. In the first place, she persisted in disbelieving the whole of the matter; secondly, she was very sure that Mr. Collins had been taken in; thirdly, she trusted that they would never be happy together; and fourthly, that the match might be broken off. Two inferences, however, were plainly deduced from the whole; one, that Elizabeth was the real cause of all the mischief, and the other, that she herself had been barbarously used by them all; and on these two points she principally dwelt during the rest of the day. Nothing could console and nothing appease her. (Jane Austen, *Pride and Prejudice*, vol. 1, chapter 23)

译文甲:在威廉爵士没有告辞之前,贝纳太太竭力压制自己的情绪,可是,当他走了后,她立即大发雷霆,起先,她坚说这消息完全是捏造的,跟着她又说高林先生上了他们的当,她赌咒他们永远不会快乐,最后她又说他们的婚事必将破裂无疑。她非常愤恼,一方面她责备伊丽莎白,另一方面她懊悔自己被人利用了。于是,她整天絮絮不休地损骂,无论如何也不能使她平静下来。

(东流译,107－108)

译文乙:班纳特太太在威廉爵士面前,实在气得说不出话;可是他一走,她那一肚子牢骚便马上发泄出来。第一,她坚决不相信这回事;第二,她断定柯林斯先生受了骗;第三,她相信这一对夫妇决不会幸福;第四,这门亲事可能会破裂。不过,她却从整个事件上简单地得出了两个结论——一个是:这场笑话全都是伊丽莎白一手造成的;另一个是,她自己受尽了大家的欺侮虐待;在那一整天里,她所谈的大都是这两点。随便怎么也安慰不了她,随便怎么也平不了她的气。

(王科一译,1957:153)

在《傲慢与偏见》这一小说中,因为家产的关系,贝内特太太一心想要远房侄子柯林斯先生娶女儿伊丽莎白为妻,但伊丽莎白却断然拒绝了柯林斯的求婚。柯林斯转而与夏洛特订了婚,贝内特太太则完全被蒙在鼓里。因此,当威廉爵士登门通报女儿与柯林斯订婚的消息时,就出现了上面这一幕。在读这一段时,我们可以明显地感受到一种反讽的效果。这一效果主要来自于 in the first place, secondly, thirdly 等顺序词所带来的表面上的逻辑性与实际上的逻辑混乱(she persisted in disbelieving the whole of the matter 然而她却 was very sure that Mr. Collins had been taken in)之间形成的强烈反差。从表达方式来说,这一段属于总结性叙述,对于贝内特太太滔滔不绝的唠叨,叙述者仅进行了简要描述。这些制造逻辑性假象的顺序词很有可能是叙述者在编辑总结贝内特太太的话时添加的。从表面上看,叙述者是想将贝内特太太的话组织得更有条理。实际上,这些顺序词通过对照反差只是讽刺性地突出了贝内特太太话语的自相矛盾之处。

值得注意的是,尽管所描述的是贝内特太太说出来的话,叙述者却选用了 persisted in disbelieving,was very sure 等通常用于表达内心想法的词语。叙述者还用了 dwell on 一词来描述贝内特太太的言语行为,而这个词语也可指涉"老是想着"这一内心活动。

此外,通常用于描述逻辑推理的 Two inferences, however, were plainly deduced from the whole 也加深了"内心想法"这一印象。我们知道,口头话语只能按前后顺序逐字表达出来,而不同的想法却可同时并存于头脑中;"第一"、"第二"等顺序词通常指涉的也是同时存在的理由等因素。这些都使人觉得贝内特太太并不是在随着时间的推移改变她的想法(这属于较为正常的情况),而是在"坚持不相信"柯林斯与夏洛特订了婚的同时又"十分确信"柯与夏订了婚,这无疑令人感到十分荒唐可笑。值得注意的是,原文中的 Two inferences, however, were plainly deduced from the whole... 这一表达方式具有较强的学术味,它与推论本身的庸俗气形成了鲜明对照,使人更感到贝内特太太俗不可耐,这是叙述者暗地嘲讽人物的绝妙手法。

在译文甲中,"第一"、"第二"、"第三"、"第四"等顺序词被"起先"、"跟着"、"最后"等表示时间的状语替代。此外,"坚持不相信"、"十分确信"、"相信"等词语也分别被"坚说"、"又说"、"又说"等明确表达口头行为的词语替代。这样一来,表面上的逻辑性与实际上的逻辑混乱之间形成的具有强烈反讽效果的鲜明对照就不复存在了;叙述者通过遣词造句制造出来的贝内特太太同时具有相互矛盾的想法这一印象在译文中也荡然无存。此外,一句直来直去的"她非常愤恼"取代了原文中的"她从整件事简明地推导出了两个结论",将原文中的学术外表与平庸内容之间的对比也冲得无影无踪。也就是说,这一译文中不存在表达方式与所描述的内容之间的对照和张力。原文中这一对照的形成在于全知叙述者在叙事手法上做了文章,含蓄地表达出自己对人物的嘲讽。在某种意义上,叙述者是在与读者暗暗地进行交流,读者需要对表达形式和所表达的内容进行双重阐释,在两者的对照中领会作者的态度和主题意义。我们在认真对比了原文和译文甲之后,也许能得出这样的结论:译文甲的表达方式出自常人之手,而原文中的表达方式出自一位艺术大师之手;原文中的艺术性主要在于其表达方式,而不在于所表达的内容。译文甲在保持原文的艺术性方面无疑是失败的。造成这一失败的原因并不是语言不同所形成的障碍(这在译文乙中可以看得很清楚),而是译者未能很好地把握原文的艺术性所在。值得注意的是,小说翻译中最易被改动的成分之一是原文中带有美学价值和主题意义但表面上不合逻辑的表达形式。这样的语言成分因与译者认识、解释和表达事物的常规方式发生冲突而被改为更合乎常规逻辑的方式,从而造成对原文的某种歪曲。就上面分析的前两例来说,虽然没有不合逻辑的成分,但原文中表达形式的突然转换或遣词造句上的夸张强调也是造成译者误译的原因之一。

小说翻译中的"假象等值"有一个颇为发人深省的特点:译者的水平一般较高,在理解原文的内容上不存在任何问题,之所以会出现"假象等值",是因为译者均有意识地对原文进行改动或"改进",以求使文本或变得更合乎逻辑,或变得更流畅自然,或变得更客观可靠,如此等等。由于对原文中的语言形式与主题意义的关系缺乏认识,这一"改进"的结果则是在不同程度上造成文体价值的缺损。要避免这样的假象等值,就需要对原文进行深入细致的文体分析,以把握原文中语言形式与主题意义的有机关联。

因篇幅所限,在本文中我们仅举了三个例子来说明文体分析对于小说翻译的重要性。笔者在《文学文体学与小说翻译》(英文版,1998 重印)一书中,通过大量的例证,系统讨论了文学文体分析对于小说翻译的作用。文体学分析的主要作用就是使译者对小说中语言形式的美学功能更为敏感,促使译者使用功能等值的语言形式,避免指称对等带来的文体损差。在小说翻译中,我们应更为注重形式与内容的不可分离性,注重形式本身所蕴涵的意义。应该说,小说翻译中的很多问题能够通过文体分析得以有效地解决。笔者希望小说翻译理论和实践工作者更为注意文学文体学的作用,也希望更多的文体学家参与小说翻译批评。

选文三　Sherlock Holmes in the Interculture

—Pseudotranslation and Anonymity in Turkish Literature

Şehnaz Tahir-Gürçağlar

导　言

本文选自 Anthony Pym, Miriam Shlesinger & Daniel Simeoni, *Beyond Descriptive Translation Studies*. Amsterdam / Philadelphia: John Benjamins Publishing Company, 2008.

福尔摩斯故事在英美推出后,马上成为一个热潮,刊登这些故事的 *Strand* 杂志销量激增至每期 50 万本,而且持续多年不变。这类小说不仅在西方广受欢迎,这一独特小说品种在世界各地也普遍受欢迎,19 世纪末 20 世纪初达到高峰期。与中国清朝末年的译介情况相似,土耳其奥特曼帝国后期对于英语世界侦探小说的翻译和介绍也带有浓重的文化、文学交流初期特质——大量的伪译作模糊了翻译与创作的边缘。本选文分析了 19 世纪末至 20 世纪中叶土耳其文学界的两种不同类型诗学形式:知识分子与精英阶层希冀通过新文类的引入创建新的文学范式;而另一方面,通俗文学翻译领域生产出大量模糊边界的伪翻译作品,在创作手法上依然沿袭奥特曼帝国时期的民间传说体裁。选文以福尔摩斯侦探小说翻译为个案群体,展开对于文化接触地带的文学形式的深度分析。

Studying the emergence of new literary forms in a given culture provides insight not only into processes of change within the literary field, but also into possible social and cultural transformation. One can thus study the emergence of the Turkish novel in the 19th century both as a culmination of Western influence and as a cursor of the changing social and cultural life, particularly in the urban centers. Translations, especially from French, played a significant role in introducing new literary genres such as the drama and the novel. Translations were done from canonical works, which in turn became a shaping force in terms of "high literature". At the same time, however, translations and adaptations of more popular works were active on a lower level, and their interaction led to many literary innovations in the home system (Paker, 1991: 18). Detective fiction was a part of the non-canonical field, yet was instrumental in the development of a new prose style especially through the translated and original works by the famous author Ahmed Midhat Efendi (Özön, 1985: 230 – 231). It was a genre denounced by some and welcomed by many, including a major figure like Sultan Abdulhamid II. Nevertheless, it was little discussed as a literary form in terms of its function or reception.

This paper will not attempt to trace the development of detective fiction in Turkey. Rather, it will look at how detective fiction in one of its forms, namely the dime format, aligned with and drew inspiration from traditional Turkish folk literature. This provides an interesting example of how literary forms and definitions change over time, and how this change is invariably accompanied by some kind of resistance manifested in individual or collective literary practices. The topic of the present study is neither original nor translated detective fiction; it is instead an excursion into what Anthony Pym refers to as "borderline cases" (Pym, 1998: 65). This borderline area will be explored through pseudotranslations of Sherlock Holmes stories alongside original Turkish fiction that had Sherlock Holmes as an imported character.

Gideon Toury has done much to introduce pseudotranslations as an important topic within Translation Studies. Acknowledging the rich information pseudotranslations have to offer to researchers, Toury has called for an approach that incorporates pseudotranslations as legitimate objects of study (1995: 46). For him, pseudotranslations are "texts which have been presented as translations with no corresponding source texts in other languages ever having existed—hence no factual 'transfer operations' and translation relationships". (Toury, 1995:40) Although pseudotranslations are not translations in the strict sense of the word, Toury's concept of "assumed translation" enables them to be regarded and treated as such. When we talk about "assumed translations", we deem all utterances presented, regarded or revealed as translations to be legitimate objects of Descriptive Translation Studies (Toury, 1995: 32). So regardless of whether a target text has a corresponding source text in another language, we can study it in relation to the way the readership receives it as a translation. In many instances, the decision to present an indigenous text as a translation is a deliberate act, with social and ideological implications. The pseudotranslator offers new options for a culture or presents material that would be unaccepted or censored in indigenous texts (Toury, 1995: 41 - 42). The Turkish system of translated literature is rich in pseudotranslations, however, there is evidence that pseudotranslators did not always have a sociopolitical agenda. Many pseudotranslations aimed to capitalize on the commercial success of popular authors and characters. The way the readership read and liked these pseudotranslations points to the complex reception and production patterns of a culture in transition.

Despite the absence of translation relationships, pseudotranslations reveal interesting information about the concept of translation in a given time. All we have to do is to study the features that distinguish them from originals. Yet for certain traditions and periods there are no clear borders between the two. Douglas Robinson calls a clear distinction between translation and original a recent "social fiction" and writes that "the concept of psuedotranslations is interesting in large part because it calls into question some of our most cherished beliefs, especially the belief in the absolute difference between a translation and an original work" (1998: 185).

The Sherlock Holmes pseudotranslations in Turkish reveal a grey area at the intersection of translation and original. I will argue that they inherited this area from the anonymous Turkish folk story. While originality was an important issue in translated canonical literature in the 20th century, the authors of the pseudotranslations displayed a certain indifference towards this issue and continued to produce their work in an interculture, at the crossroads of the old and the new. I will argue that this interculture is indicative of two different literary habituses (Bourdieu, 1993: 5) present among Turkish writers, translators and readers until the middle of the 20th century. The ruling elite and the intellectuals propagated and even imposed a new set of dispositions that would be established through the imports of Western literary sources and a Western poetics into Turkey. This poetics had special focus on authorial originality and canonicity. On the other hand, the poetics dominant in popular literature helped an older literary habitus to endure. Unlike the newer one, this habitus could be associated with an approach that emphasized popular characters over authors, generic features over canonicity, and anonymity over originality.

A Brief History of Early Detective Fiction in Turkey

The first translation of a detective novel appeared in Turkey in 1881, 22 years after the translation of the first Western novel into Turkish and 40 years after Edgar Allen Poe published his *The Murders in the Rue Morgue*, acknowledged as the forerunner of the detective genre. Erol Üyepazarcı, suggests that the three factors behind a potential interest in the detective novel were the establishment of an organized police force in the 1840s, the increasingly cosmopolitan structure of the major Ottoman cities, and the development of the novel as a literary genre (1997: 64 – 65). This potential materialized with the translation of Ponson du Terrail's *Les Tragédies de Paris* by Ahmet Münif in 1881. This was followed in 1884 by Ahmed Midhat Efendi's translation of Emile Gaboriau's *Le Crime d'Orcival*. Ahmed Midhat Efendi proved to be not only a revolutionary and popular figure in Turkish literature, with an ability to combine entertainment with education, but also one of the pioneers in translated and original detective fiction. Following his Gaboriau translation, he wrote an original detective novel called *Esrar-ıCinayat* (*The Mystery of Murders*), highly influenced by Gaboriau's style (Üyepazarcı, 1997: 73). This was followed by translations of works by Gaboriau, du Terrail, Pierre Delcourt, Edmond Tarbé, and Fortuné de Boisgobey, among others, between 1884 and 1902. In the meantime, two seminal works—Eugène Sue's *Les Mystères de Paris* and Edgar Allen Poe's *The Murders in the Rue Morgue*—were also translated and published, in 1889 and 1902 respectively. The works translated in this period were mainly by French authors and were often a mixture of crime and melodrama.

Translation of detective fiction came to a halt in 1903. This situation was not unique to detective fiction and was mainly due to the deteriorating political atmosphere in the country and the heavy censorship that affected both authors and translators. Publishing activity was revived in 1908 within the relatively liberal environment created by the proclamation of the Second Constitution (İskit, 1939: 130). Translated detective fiction took on a new turn after this date and expanded to cover American and English works in addition to French ones. While the founding fathers of detective fiction such as Sir Arthur Conan Doyle, Maurice Leblanc, Gaston Leroux, and Allain-Souvestre started to be translated, there also appeared series of "dime novels (cheap fiction booklets, so called because they originally cost 10 cents, a "dime", in the United States)". These covered adventures of dime heroes such as Nick Carter, Nat Pinkerton, Nick Winter and even Sherlock Holmes and Arsène Lupin stories, some of which were pseudotranslations. In the meantime, domestic novels and adaptations grew in number. By 1928, when the Latin alphabet was adopted to replace the Arabic-based Ottoman script, detective fiction had become a popular and well-established genre. The pattern changed little after 1928; there were new translations and new originals produced. Many well-known authors translated and wrote detective fiction under assumed names well into the 1960s. The detective novel as an imported form became a successful instance of transfer and found itself a place alongside other forms, challenging some of them in terms of popularity.

Ever since its emergence in Turkey in the 19th century, detective fiction has constituted an interesting field where translations, originals, pseudotranslations, pseudooriginals, and adaptations co-existed, opening up a rich literary sphere (about whose literary value there was much doubt and little debate). A review of these works also reveals that this field was a haven for an older mode of literary production, namely rewriting.

Criticized and marginalized in favor of more canonized genres, rewriting as a literary mode lived on in re-editions of traditional folk stories, in a group of works termed "people's books". These targeted a rural readership and offered reading material to a largely illiterate population. On the other hand, as the urban population increased along with the literacy rate, there emerged a need for more diverse forms of reading material. The traditional experience of collective reading gave way to individual reading. In this process, detective fiction, especially the dime novel, addressed the newly literate, male, lower urban classes that had little formal education. To understand this process, it may be useful to consider the political and cultural changes Turkey underwent in the first half of the 20th century.

A Nation in the Making: Early Republican Turkey

The Republic of Turkey was proclaimed on October 29, 1923, a date considered a milestone in Turkish history in terms not only of politics or economics but also of culture and social life. In 1923, Turkey had just gone through a war of liberation against occupying powers and was opening a new page in its history. It was a country with a new name and a new political system that placed Westernization at its crux. The Ottoman Empire had been occupied with the question of modernization and Westernization since the 18th century, but it was the Republican era, under the leadership of Mustafa Kemal Atatürk, that finally institutionalized this trend. The first 20 years of the Republic were marked by intensive planning activity aimed to Westernize Turkey while building a nation equipped with a unique Turkish identity. The young Republic was trying to establish a new and secular Turkish identity that would ideally rise up from a common culture, language and history instead of the older order of religion (Güvenç, 1997: 225, 245). This new national identity was constructed through a series of essentially secular reforms that have had strong implications not only on how the Turkish state was run but also on how people went about living their daily lives. The reforms included unity in education (1924), adoption of Western time and calendar (1925), universal suffrage (1928), adoption of the international numeric system (1928), and alphabet reform (1928). These reforms may also be considered elements of an emerging repertoire in Turkey composed of a largely Western inventory. One of the most important steps was the alphabet reform, which re-shaped the cultural configuration of the newly founded Republic and symbolized a major cultural and social transformation. The proponents of the reform suggested that the Arabic-based Ottoman script was difficult to learn and therefore impeded the cultural development of the nation. Yet the intention was not only to increase the rate of literacy, which was around 10 per cent in the first few years of the Republic; the adoption of the Latin alphabet would also serve as a signifcant break with the Islamic past symbolized by the Arabic letters and contribute to the new secular cultural policies (Katoğlu, 1997: 413; Lewis, 1961: 273). Immediately after the alphabet reform was announced, Millet Okulları (Nation Schools) were established with the aim of teaching the Latin alphabet to the people. Within the first ten years of the reform, over two and a half million people attended these schools (İskit, 1939: 188).

For the first time in the history of the country, Turkey could not just adopt only selected items of the Western repertoire, as had been the case in the 19th century (Arıkan, 1998: 4). The aim was to absorb Western civilization and consequently to produce a unique version that some referred to as "Turkish humanism (Sinanoğlu, 1980: 8)". This ambitious project could not be realized overnight. Ottoman traditions rooted in several centuries would not be so easily overthrown. While many intellectuals gave explicit support to Westernization, it is difficult to know the opinion of the more silent groups such as ordinary people or agents active in the production of peripheral literary works. Were they willing and/or able to replace their reading or writing habits with the ones propagated by the new regime? Or alternatively, did they experience a transition and adjustment process whereby they combined elements of both worlds, the traditional and the new? This paper accepts the second alternative as a hypothesis and looks at how that period of adjustment may have reflected on literary practices on a popular scale. The term "interculture" will be used to refer to popular literature at this specific transition period, adopting Anthony Pym's definition of the term as "beliefs and practices found in intersections or overlaps of cultures, where people combine something of two or more cultures at once (1998: 177)".

The state and the intellectuals attached great importance to translation within the Westernization project. The mission attributed to translation was to import Western ideas to prepare a background for the creation of a new form of literature and thought. However, not all translations were desirable. Translations of Western classics were called for with a sense of urgency. This idea was not unique to the Republican period. Already in 1874, only 15 years after the appearance of the first translated novel, the newspaper *Hayal* printed an article about the kinds of books that should and should not be translated from Western languages. The authors advised against translations of "immoral" narratives that would threaten Muslim principles, while they recommended the translation of historical and educational narratives (reprinted in Akbayar, 1985: 450). The discrimination continued, although in later periods the works were judged not so much on their moral vices but on their

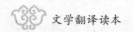

literary value and position vis-à-vis the canon in their home systems. Translation of seminal works of Western literature into Turkish was considered vital for the development of a new Turkish culture, severing its ties with the Ottoman heritage (Nayır, 1937: 162; various authors in Özdenoğlu, 1949).

The Position of Detective Fiction Within the Turkish Literary System

Translation activity was often criticized throughout the pre-Republican and early Republican periods. Translations were found to be unsystematic, arbitrary and hasty (Ülken, 1997: 347). Lack of revision, control and criticism was stressed (Vala Nureddin in *Birinci Türk Neşriyat Kongresi* 1939: 149). Translations were said to be full of mistakes, and some translated titles were judged ill-chosen (Sevük, 1940b: 607). The publication of non-canonical popular novels was considered to be a commercial pursuit lacking in dignity (İskit, 1939: 287, 298).

In fact, literary critics mostly ignored popular fiction altogether, let alone detective fiction. Even negative comments were rather rare. Although hundreds of original and translated detective novels had been published, in 1940 the literary historian İsmail Habib Sevük included only twelve translated detective novels among the 1,210 pages of his two-volume anthology of translated European literature in Turkey. He wrote in his preface that he offered nearly a complete list of translated European literature in Turkey. Yet he also added that he had neither the urge nor the opportunity to include an exhaustive list of "detective and adventure" novels (Sevük, 1940a: Ⅶ-Ⅷ). In the second volume he declared that "detective and adventure novels", which made up a significant proportion of publishing activity, lacked literary value (Sevük, 1940b: 603). In his memoirs, author Suut Kemal Yetkin recalled having read Sherlock Holmes and Nat Pinkerton novels as a child, and added that many adults read such novels in secret, as if they were committing a misdemeanor (Yetkin in *Milliyet Sanat*, 1985: 9).

Small wonder that publishers felt the need to defend themselves. Semih Lutfi, a major publisher of popular novels in the 1930s and 1940s with a series called "cheap novels", said in an interview that his sole criterion was the people and all he did was to give people what they wanted (İskit 1939: 295). Another case is Türkiye Publishing House, which noted in the first book of a detective series they launched in 1949:

> Detective novels are not simple novels that have a negative effect on people, as some suggest. A well-chosen selection of such books can help develop the intellect and provide opportunities for taming one's will and nerves. This is a fact acknowledged by the greatest psychologists and educators of the West (Editor's note in Christie 1946; our translation here and throughout)

Panned or praised, popular novels, with detective fiction to the fore, provided reading material to a section of a society changing worlds. The few rural readers continued with their previous habit of reading traditional folk stories. Even after the adoption of the Latin alphabet and the literacy campaign, people who could read were still overwhelmingly urban. Literacy figures remained low. While in 1927 around 10 percent of the population was literate, this rate increased to about 20 percent in 1933 ("Onuncu Yılında Maarifmiz Rehberinden", 1933), growing every year thereafter but at a slower pace.

Reading Material for an Emerging Readership

In 1936 the literary historian Mustafa Nihat Özön divided Turkish readers into three groups: first class (readers of canonized literature), second class (readers of popular novels consisting mainly of detective and adventure fiction) and third class (readers of folk stories) (Özön, 1985: 110). Özön based this analysis on especially the pre-Republican readership but suggested that the categories were still valid in his day. The shortcomings of such a broad categorization are clear. Yet for the sake of argument, we may propose that the changing life styles and the rising literacy created a new group of readers between the second and the third classes.

If we go beyond Özön's classification and look at the division based on the types of texts read, we can come up with a fourth group of texts. These were dime novels, both those written originally in Turkish and the ones that were translated. Although it is difficult to reconstruct the kind of readership these texts addressed, I would like to argue that they mainly targeted groups of readers who were familiar with the folk tradition but were attracted to different themes such as detective plots. These readers were either unable or unwilling to move on to popular novels and enjoyed the less voluminous format and less sophisticated plots of the dime novels. There exist kinship ties between these short novels and the larger and more prestigious examples of the detective genre. However, the dime novels appear closer to the folk story in terms of their production and marketing strategies. It was not uncommon to see the same authors (such as Selami Münir Yurdatap and Vedat Örf) behind the rewrites of folk stories and the translated dime novels. Likewise, the ads for folk stories published in detective dime novels (see for example the "Sherlock Holmes' in Arsène Lupin ile Sergüzeştleri" series by Selami Münir Yurdatap—a Sherlock Holmes pseudotranslation series from 1926) suggest that these books addressed a similar readership. Furthermore, the same publishers would be involved in the publishing and distribution of both types of books (Cemiyet Printing House in the 1920s and Güven Printing House in the 1940s).

The intellectuals of the early Republican period referred to folk stories as "people's books" (see the Proceedings of the First Turkish National Publishing Congress, *Birinci Türk Neşriyat Kongresi*, or *Türkiye Bibliyografyası 1938—1948*, the official bibliography of books published in Turkey). Faruk Rıza Güloğul, who published a book titled *Halk*

Kitaplarına Dair (On People's Books) in 1937, included as "people's books" religious books, religion-inspired battle stories, romances, folk poetry, national battle stories as well as recent imitations of these (1937: 3). Some of these books, especially the earlier examples, were looked down upon to a large extent and were regarded as having a bad effect on people. This mainly had to do with the fact that they were based on religious legends and they reinforced superstitions. For instance, in a letter to the First Turkish Publishing Congress in 1939 publisher Halit Yaşaroğlu wrote:

> Unfortunately, the semi-literates in our society, that is to say those belonging to the older generation, only read those meaningless and harmful books called folk literature. It would be a wise step to pass a law to ban the publication of these books that are rather detrimental with their grammar, illustrations, style and ideas. However, we also need to prepare a body of works to replace these. (Birinci Türk Neşriyat Kongresi 1939: 368 – 369)

In his book Güloğul was pleased to announce that the lithograph-printed versions written in Ottoman script, which were the products of a "backward mind", had disappeared after the alphabet reform. Yet he also added that some publishers "unfortunately" printed transliterations of the Ottoman texts in the new script, while some published "improved" copies (1937: 4). The improvements consisted of omitting religious and superstitious elements, while some retained those but added the following note in the preface or epilogue: "Read these books not to believe them but to have a good time. Because none of them are based on history or real stories (Muharrem Zeki in Güloğul, 1937: 5)."

Folk stories were read in manuscript format as early as the 18th century. There is evidence indicating that they were read out in public places like coffee houses. We also know that these books were sometimes rented out, since they were expensive and only the lucky few could afford them (Özön, 1985: 73). The availability of these books expanded after 1835 following the establishment of the first lithograph press in Turkey. The first printed "people's books" were published in the 1840s and became immensely popular. Only a few of them were attributed to a specific author, and even those with a known author had the style of anonymous stories (Özön, 1985: 72). Most of these books had their roots in the oral story-telling tradition. The first publishers recorded some of the known stories, bought manuscripts or commissioned authors to rewrite oral stories they had discovered (Boratav, 1988: 160). The early Turkish novels were influenced by the language and style of these folk stories (Boratav, 1939: 139). However, as they developed a language and style of their own, they started having an effect on the new rewrites of folk stories. Some publishers and authors modified the language and style of the folk stories, correcting linguistic errors and omitting some elements while retaining the basic features. They put these books in their own names, even though everyone knew the stories were from anonymous tradition. There was no debate about authorship or the extent to which the rewriters could claim the stories were their own. The official bibliography gave their names as the authors. Some authors acted much more radically and wrote original stories under the heading "folk story". They used patriotism, heroism and the newly emerging Turkish identity as their themes. However, these works never became as popular as the older anonymous stories (Boratav, 1988: 162).

The Directorate General of Press approved and even encouraged the rewrites. Seeing the popularity of folk stories, the Directorate General launched a campaign to modernize the stories as an educational and ideological instrument. Their reasoning was simple, as expressed in a note sent to known literary personalities:

> People like the protagonists of people's books. These characters should be kept
> as they are, but they should be depicted in new plots that agree with the spirit of
> the regime and carry a higher meaning. So the people will be instructed through the
> books they like. For instance, the character Mickey Mouse stays the same, yet
> becomes the protagonist of a different plot, a different setting in each film.
> Likewise we want to use the popular characters within new themes and let them live
> on in adventures that propagate the aims of the Turkish revolution and civilization.
> (cited in Güloğul 1937: 56 – 57)

In the meantime, rewriting had become common practice in an adjacent field of popular literature, namely detective fiction. The rewriters of detective fiction probably did not share the aims of the Directorate General. Nevertheless, they seem to have capitalized on the same assumption that people would like to see their favorite characters involved in different plots. The characters they chose for their rewriting activity had already been created for the series format. They were Sherlock Holmes, Arsène Lupin, Nick Carter and Nat Pinkerton, i. e. characters that had already traveled from plot to plot, creating a dedicated readership. Their adventures were sometimes translated from the source language they were originally written in. Some of the stories were marketed as translations but their originals cannot be traced, making them instances of pseudotranslation. Still others claimed to be original stories but had international heroes of detective fiction as their characters. The last two cases are especially interesting, since they tell of the tendency of Turkish authors to appropriate the foreign. The authors of the pseudotranslations and of the originals with imported characters felt equally free to adopt existing material as their own and treated it as if it were anonymous, without an original creator. Among these characters, Sherlock Holmes appears to be one of the most popular, building himself a successful career in Turkey and appearing in over 200 dime-format pseudotranslations and originals in four decades.

Enter Sherlock Holmes

The first Sherlock Holmes story to be translated into Turkish was "The Man with the Twisted Lip", under the title "Dilenci (The Beggar)". This 54-page translation by Faik

Sabri Duran was published in 1909 and was followed by translations of "The Hound of the Baskervilles", "The Read Headed League" and "The Engineer's Tumb" in the same year. Why was Sherlock Holmes translated into Turkish at that specific point in time? As it happens, Conan Doyle and his wife had been to Istanbul in 1907, two years before the first translations appeared. They were guests of Sultan Abdulhamid II, known for his fondness for detective fiction. While the couple was in Istanbul, the Sultan received them in the palace and decorated Conan Doyle with a royal medal (memoirs of Sir Henry Woods in Üyepazarcı, 1999: 4). However, this visit does not seem to have created much excitement in the country, as popular interest in Sherlock Holmes exploded only after Pierre de Coursel's play *Sherlock Holmes*, inspired by Conan Doyle's stories, was staged in Istanbul in 1909 (A. Enver in Üyepazarcı, 1997: 93; Sevengil, 1968: 89). In 1912 there was a translation of *The Adventures of Sherlock Holmes* and a series consisting of four volumes, including some of the stories from *The Return of Sherlock Holmes*. The year 1912 indeed represented a milestone in terms of Turkish versions of Sherlock Holmes. This year saw the publication of the first pseudotranslations and the first original novel hosting Sherlock Holmes as one of its characters. The original novel was written by Yertvard Odyan, an author of Armenian origin, and was called *Abdulhamid ve Sherlock Holmes*. Odyan told the story of the "real" Sherlock Holmes, or rather the character Conan Doyle presumably based his Sherlock Holmes stories on: a retired Scotland Yard detective called McLane who lived in Scotland with his wife and four children. Odyan used McLane as an instrument of political criticism. His book was not a detective story but a political piece criticizing Abdulhamid II's politics (Üyepazarcı, 2007). This novel comprised 832 pages and in 1913 its sequel appeared under the title *Saliha Hanım* (Birkiye, 2006).

Pseudotranslations

The original Sherlock Holmes stories had by no means all been translated when the first series of pseudotranslations appeared in 1912. Only one novel and 15 stories had been rendered, which means that many were still not available in Turkish. The first series of pseudotranslations was titled *The Secret Files of the King of Policemen Sherlock Holmes*. It comprised 16 books of between 100 and 150 pages each (Üyepazarcı, 1997: 97). Üyepazarcı suggests that this prototype of pseudotranslations bore certain resemblances to some of the stories in *The Case Book of Sherlock Holmes*. However, this does not seem very likely, since *The Case Book of Sherlock Holmes* was published in English for the first time in 1927. The Turkish series nevertheless set the tone for the later Sherlock Holmes pseudotranslations and proved to be an archetype. It was the first series that presented Sherlock Holmes as a member of the official police force, a feature imitated by many of the following pseudotranslations. The adventures are not narrated by Dr. Watson, who is completely absent from the stories except for one where he pays Sherlock Holmes a medical visit. Watson is replaced by a Harry Taxon, who acts as Sherlock Holmes' assistant. (Harry Taxon appears off and on in many pseudotranslations well into the 1950s.) The stories do not have a named narrator and are told in the third person, another feature inherited by later pseudotranslations (Üyepazarcı, 1997: 98). The major difference between this series and the later pseudotranslations is perhaps their length, since all series of Sherlock Holmes pseudotranslations published after 1912 were in the dime format, comprising between 10 and 35 pages.

There is little doubt that this form of writing became quite popular, and lay readership received the products well. Between 1912 and 1927, 33 Sherlock Holmes pseudotranslations appeared in various series. The second pseudotranslation series was much more short-lived than its forerunner and featured only two books. Yet these books, or rather booklets, are interesting, since they completely altered Sherlock Holmes' character and made him subordinate to a woman. The series, published in 1914, had the title *Sherlock Holmes'in Metresi* (*Sherlock Holmes' Mistress*). This title is remarkable in itself, given Sherlock Holmes' traditional celibacy and standoffish approach towards women. The first book of the series, *Esrarengiz Bir Cinayet* (*A Mysterious Murder*), caricatures Holmes as an inept detective, much akin to the Scotland Yard detectives in the authentic stories. Faced with an impossible case of murder, Sherlock Holmes seeks advice from his mistress Miss Barclay, who not only takes over the case but also mocks Sherlock Holmes for his lack of skill and calls him a fool in more than one instance. To solve the mystery, she changes guise twice, makes plans (rather than a detective working on deductive premises, she seems to be a cunning planner) and traps the murderer using her feminine charms. The story appears to be inspired by "The Adventure of the Dying Detective" in *His Last Bow*. Similar to the original story there is a highly contagious disease (the tropical disease replaced by typhoid fever, certainly much more familiar to the Turkish readership) and the method of contraction is the same: the pricking of a sharp object.

The next Sherlock Holmes translation was published in 1920. This was a seven-page story with the title "Karanlıklar Padişahı ("The King of Darkness")". It appeared as number 14 in a series of "famous stories". On the front page the translator is indicated as Vedat Örfi, with no author mentioned. There is also a one-sentence introduction telling the readers that this is a "highly exciting story from the extraordinary adventures of the famous police inspector Sherlock Holmes(Örfi 1920, cover page)". Sherlock Holmes has an office in Bridge Street and Harry Taxon is his assistant. Throughout the story Sherlock Holmes appears to know a lot about the case but the reader is not told his sources and there no trace of the famous deductive method. Unlike original Sherlock Holmes stories, there is more weight on action than reasoning, a feature that characterizes the pseudotranslations especially before the alphabet reform.

The same publishing company (Cemiyet Kitabhanesi) published another pseudotranslation series between 1925 and 1927. The stories were in the dime format and comprised 16 pages. The ads on the books suggest they were weekly publications. The first series consisted of 6 stories and bore the title *Meşhur Polis Hafyesi Şerlock Holmes* (*Famous Police Inspector Sherlock Holmes*). The stories are longer and more sophisticated than the previous series, with more characters involved. The first title, "Esrarengiz Parola" (*The Mysterious Password*), is a collage of two Sherlock Holmes stories rather than a pure pseudotranslation. M. Kemaleddin put together "The Adventure of the Empty House" and "The Adventure of the Dancing Men", both from *The Return of Sherlock Holmes*. The sum of these two stories produced quite a different plot. The other stories in the series are pseudotranslations. In these texts Sherlock Holmes makes some use of his deduction skills, but the weight is more on the detective's adventures in disguise. This time his assistant is called Harry Watson, who carries no other resemblance to Dr. Watson and is an apprentice to the detective, whom he calls "Master".

Another pseudotranslation series was published by the same company in 1926. The author, Selami Münir, wrote about adventures involving Sherlock Holmes and Arsène Lupin ("Sherlock Holmes in Arsène Lupin ile Sergüzeştleri"). These stories do not bear any similarity to those written by Maurice Leblanc where the two characters are also brought together. Seven stories were published weekly in dime format. They depict Sherlock Holmes as an official police inspector helping the Paris police to catch Arsène Lupin. He is aided by his assistant Harry and is much more passive, putting Harry in charge of much of his detective work. The focus is totally on action. Sherlock Holmes is presented as inferior to Arsène Lupin since the thief always devises a cunning trick to escape at the last moment. In 1927 a series of three books came out (Üyepazarcı, 1997: 110). They were credited to Selami Münir and another translator called Remzi. Although we have not been able to locate copies of these titles, the names of the two of the books (*Fahişeler—Prostitutes* and *Zevk Çılgınlıkları—Crazy with Bliss*) suggest that they were a combination of detective and erotic fiction.

This was the last pseudotranslation series to appear before the alphabet reform. However, another series with Sherlock Holmes as one of its leading characters needs to be mentioned as an example of borderline cases. This series, *Cingöz Recai Şerlok Holmes'e Karşı* (*Cingöz Recai Against Sherlock Holmes*), was written by the famous Turkish author Peyami Safa under the penname Server Bedi. Cingöz Recai was inspired by Arsène Lupin. He had the same characteristics: a thief but also a gentleman, well-educated, a lady's man and never a murderer. In 1926, Server Bedi brought Cingöz Recai and Sherlock Holmes together. In these stories Sherlock Holmes and Dr. Watson come to Istanbul upon the invitation of the Turkish police to help them catch Cingöz Recai. Although they come very close to catching him in each story, Cingöz Recai is able to escape at the last moment and proves to be superior to Sherlock Holmes in terms of intellectual capability. This series was very popular and went through many reprints in the Latin alphabet.

Sherlock Holmes pseudotranslations continued to be published after the adoption of the

Latin alphabet. The major change distinguishing these from earlier pseudotranslations is a shift of emphasis from action to deduction. There were two major series published in 1944—1945 and 1955 respectively. The former was published by Güven Yayınevi, a publishing company active mainly in the field of popular literature. This series was called *Meşhur İngiliz Polis Hafyesi Şerlok Holmes Serisi* (*The Famous English Police Inspector Sherlock Holmes Series*) and consisted of 83 dime novels offering a mixture of translations and pseudotranslations, although pseudotranslations make up the overwhelming majority. The translations display systematic omissions: the main plot is kept while secondary issues and dialogues not essential for the progression of the plot have been deleted. The resulting text is a rough retelling of the story, without reference to relationships and tensions between the characters, reducing their complexities and simplifying the language. There is no attempt to recreate Conan Doyle's style. This series shared many features with the 1955 series called *Şerlok Holmes Harikulade Maceralar* (*Sherlock Holmes' Wonderful Adventures*). Both comprised 16-page booklets appearing weekly. The latter series appears to be the last of its kind. It ran to over 85 stories. Both series had the same paratextual properties: their cover design, the illustrations on the cover and the type-set are the same. They were also marketed through the same channel, i. e. as dime novels to be sold at newspaper stands. Even their price (10 kuruş) agreed with their dime format. The plots of these stories distinguish themselves from earlier examples, as they foreground Sherlock Holmes' brainpower over his physical capabilities. Sherlock Holmes is still referred to as a police inspector, indicating that the readership had a difficult time imagining a private detective working outside of the police force. In terms of their style, the texts are made up of short sentences and have several sections divided by sub-headings. There is extreme use of paragraph breaks. In short, they display a style that would be considered typical of children's books today. One feature common to both series is that they claimed to be anonymous and did not print the translator/author's name on the text. This was common practice even in the translations of original Sherlock Holmes stories.

Contextualizing Pseudotranslations

Pseudotranslations are an interesting mode of literary production. In the case of the Turkish versions of Sherlock Holmes, they provide insight into several points. First of all, they suggest the fuidity of literary categories of "original" and "translation". The early pseudotranslations, i. e. those written in the Ottoman script, seem to have developed a variety of strategies in order to keep their status as pseudotranslations veiled. Some of the books mentioned neither an author's nor a translator's name (i. e. *Sherlock Holmes' Mistress* or the series in the 1940s and 1950s). Some called the author of the same series "author" on some weeks, and "translator" on others, although all of the books were pseudotranslations. Some used the term *nâkil* (renderer) (e. g. stories by Selami Münir Yurdatap). This term

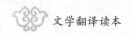

was operational in the Ottoman and early Republican periods and could refer to creators of both originals and translations.

Even when these books made no claim to be translations, catalogues and bibliographies did not include them among original literature. The comprehensive bibliography of works written in Ottoman script prepared by Seyfi Özege classified these stories as translations. The Republican bibliographies were not that clear about their status and placed these books in mixed sections such as Children's Literature (Türkiye Bibliyografyası, 1955) and Serialized Publications (Türkiye Bibliyografyası, 1938—1948), where no distinction was made between translations and originals.

The anonymity of the last two series is especially interesting. They were published at a time of much discussion about translation and its capacity to reshape Turkish culture and literature. The official Translation Bureau established in 1940 published over a thousand translations of mainly Western classics until 1966. These books were sold at low prices and were designed to reach the masses through the network of the Ministry of Education. The Bureau also published a journal called *Tercüme* (Translation), offering articles on translation history, theory and criticism. The efforts of the Bureau gave new impetus to translation activity in the private sector, especially in terms of the translation of canonized works from the West. In the sphere of canonized works the issue of source and authorship was well-defined. "Fidelity to the original", "creating the same effect of the original", and "mentality of the author" were some of the phrases that characterized the discourse on translations (Yücel, 1940: 1 - 2; Nüzhet Haşim Sinanoğlu in Birinci Türk Neşriyat Kongresi, 1939: 390 - 395). It is interesting that certain fields of popular literature (as exemplified by the Sherlock Holmes pseudotranslations) remained so immune to these discussions and trends. The popularity of these series indicates that some parts of the readership remained unaware of and/or indifferent to the intellectual debates. Their expectations did not include a clear division between original and translation. This may be because these readers had been exposed to the folk tradition, where the idea of anonymity prevailed and source mattered little.

The pseudotranslations of the 1940s and 1950s were part of a private marketplace, existing alongside a state-regulated publishing market. Working from Bourdieu, Jean-Marc Gouanvic writes,

> Published translations enter into the logic of the cultural marketplace. In Western liberal economies [...] what regulates the production, distribution and consumption of cultural goods everywhere is the law of the market place, free enterprise, and "laissez-faire". (Gouanvic 1997: 127)

That was not so much the case in Turkey, especially in the 1940s. The state, with considerable support from the intelligentsia, was trying to create a market for Western classics through its own production and distribution mechanism. The pseudotranslation series stand in contrast to that attempt as an example of commercial publishing without an underlying social or political agenda. Although intellectuals criticized the series harshly, these publications met a real demand for reading material in a section of the public not catered for by the state or private publishers of canonical literature.

However, if we should call this form of publishing a merely commercial endeavor, severed from what we might refer to as publishing with a socio-political agenda, this does not mean it was an isolated form without any cultural role to play. The pseudotranslations of the 1940s and 1950s were very much a part of the book market. They were thus among the factors determining the success of the culture planning partly carried out through publications of canonized Western literature. As Even-Zohar writes,

> Since, by definition, the implementation of culture planning entails the introduction of change into a current state of affairs, the prospects of success also depend on an effective exploitation of market conditions. The chance for the planning to be frustrated may therefore be expected constantly. (Even-Zohar 1994: 12)

The popularity of the series does show at least one instance where the planning reinforcing the translation of canonized works was frustrated. The publishers and authors of pseudotranslations may have been commercially driven, but the cultural and literary implications of their works mean that a solely commercial explanation would be reductionist.

Conclusion

The Sherlock Holmes pseudotranslations published in Turkey over the course of several decades created a Sherlock Holmes different from that in Conan Doyle's stories. Sherlock Holmes' detective pursuit, his pipe, his assistant (baptized with several different names) and his talent to disguise himself are perhaps the only things the Turkish Sherlock Holmes holds in common with Conan Doyle's hero. In fact, Sherlock Holmes changes his character throughout the Turkish series, some of which foreground his talent for deduction while some present him as an action hero. In some pseudotranslations he is the cool and cynical man Conan Doyle created him as, while other pseudotranslations make him a passionate and avenging hero. All in all, simplicity of plot and reasoning, lack of humor and the lack of a marked literary style are the properties that unite the Sherlock Holmes pseudotranslations across several decades and distinguish them from the original stories. These are very similar to the features of the American detective fiction translated in France after World War II, as revealed by Clem Robyns (1990). Robyns suggests that this translation model may partly be due to the persistence of the *belles infidèles* tradition.

In the case of the Turkish Sherlock Holmes, a similar claim can be made. The model of these pseudotranslations can be traced back to another tradition, namely the rewrites of folk stories. As the social fabric in the country changed, the anonymous folk story was marginalized as part of an older and undesirable culture. Its realm gradually shrank, but its rewriting tradition caught on in a certain section of the field of detective fiction. There the agents of production (publishers and translators) resorted to rewriting not only as a commercial strategy but also as a creative tool. They were sparked by their position in the interculture of the traditional and the new, and by a field of literary production that fostered two distinct yet co-existing literary habituses.

No other Turkish pseudotranslations of Sherlock Holmes appeared after the series of 1955. Since the translations of original Sherlock Holmes stories started to appear less frequently from that date, we can speculate that the readership lost interest in Sherlock Holmes to the benefit of more modern and action-oriented characters such as Mike Hammer by Mickey Spillane. It might also be assumed that the readership for these dime pseudotranslations started disappearing and blending in with other categories. It is little coincidence that rewrites of folk stories also started to decline around the same period (Kabacalı, 1976: 1; Kabacalı, 1994: 90). Rapid urbanization and social transformation may be considered significant factors in this.

The unproblematic approach towards the question of authorship, exemplified by appropriation of characters and stories, no longer exists in the Turkish literary system. This is indicative that somewhere along the way, the concepts of translation and original were redefined in the field of popular literature, which in turn put an end to the relaxed attitude of the translators, authors, publishers and readers towards literary categories. This is no doubt closely connected with the gradual disappearance of the older literary habitus and its replacement by a more uniform Western-inspired one.

选文四 Enhancing Cultural Changes by Means of Fictitious Translations

Gideon Toury

导 言

本文选自 Eva Hung, *Translation and Cultural Change*, Amsterdam / Philadelphia: John Benjamins Publishing Company, 2005.

选文从"变化是文化的特质"与"文化系统对变化具有一定程度的抵抗"这一对立命题切入,探讨伪翻译对于加速文化变化所起的巨大推动作用。以色列学者吉登·图里将"伪翻译"

(fictitious translation/pseudotranslation)界定为"名为翻译而实际上根本无原文可依的译作",这些"译作"并没有发生语际转换,也不存在任何翻译关系,是用来向本土文化推出一种新的文学类型或文学新风的捷径,由此可以在墨守成规的传统文学实践中不引起非议。按照图里的解释,伪译有的是因为作家想改变路数,但又不希望读者把新的作品与代表自己原有特色的人名联系在一起,于是就打着翻译的幌子推出自己的新作品;也有的是为了躲避查禁,把一个假设的作者当做替身。伪翻译与所谓的真翻译(genuine translation)就其文化地位来看有着紧密联系,从另一个角度显示了"翻译"这块招牌在目的语文化中的"通行证"功能,能够大大提高翻译作为一种文学类型的地位,加速文化变化的实现。

I

At this point in the evolution of culture theory, very few would contest the claim that **change is a built-in feature of culture.** Implied is not only that cultures are changeable in principle, so to speak, but also that, given the time, every single cultural system would indeed undergo some change. In fact, a culture which would have failed to show change over a considerable period of time is bound to get marginalized and become obsolete, if not stop functioning as a living culture altogether. At the same time, cultural systems are also prone to manifest **a certain resistance to changes**, especially if they are deemed too drastic. When renewal seems to involve such changes, they may well be rejected in an attempt to maintain what has already been achieved; in other words, retain whatever equilibrium the culture has reached. Innovation and conservation thus appear as two major contending forces in cultural dynamics.

One "big" hypothesis which has been put forward in an attempt to reconcile these two extremes claims that new models do manage to make their way into an extant cultural repertoire in spite of the system's inherent resistance to changes if and when those novelties are introduced under disguise; that is, as if they still represented an established option within the culture in question. Inasmuch as the cover is effective, it is only when penetration of products and production processes pertaining to the new model has been completed that the receiving culture would appear to have undergone change, often bringing it to the verge of a new (and different) state of equilibrium. Needless to say, the process as such may take a while. Also, it tends to involve a series of smaller, more intricate changes, which may not be recognized as changes as they are occurring. Even something which appears to represent a cultural "revolution" would thus normally be found to have followed an *evolutionary* process (Shavit, 1989: 593 - 600).

A lot of this tends to go unnoticed by the average person-in-the-culture, precisely because many of the potentially new products she/he may encounter in daily life have been disguised as standing for something else, much more established, much less alien, and hence much less of a threat to the culture's stability. By contrast, those who act in accordance with the new model, and produce the behaviour which will be paving the way for its ultimate reception, often do realize its explosive potentials. It is precisely out of such a realization that they may decide to conceal the true nature of their behaviour, namely, in an attempt to introduce whatever innovations they may entail in a controlled way, and in smaller doses, so that they may go unnoticed by the masses, or those who dominate the culture while all this is happening, until the innovations have been [partly] incorporated into the culture and are no longer felt as a potential threat.

My intention in this paper is far from claiming that this is the only way a new model may make its way into a cultural repertoire (because I don't believe it is). On the other hand, I have no wish to devote too many efforts to modifying—and necessarily complexifying—the "disguise" hypothesis either (for instance, by specifying the conditions under which it is more or less likely to gain/or lose validity). What I'll be doing instead would amount to adding some weight to the very feasibility of such a "big", overarching hypothesis as a possible explanation of cultural dynamics; and I will do so on the basis of one kind of evidence: the creation and utilization of fictitious translations (also known as pseudo-translations); a recurring type of cultural behaviour which I have been preoccupied with for almost twenty years, and from changing points of view.

II

As has been demonstrated so many times, translations which deviate from sanctioned patterns—which many of them certainly do—are often tolerated by a culture to a much higher extent than equally deviant original compositions. Given this fact, the possibility is always there to try and put the cultural gate-keepers to sleep by **presenting a text as if it were translated**, thus lowering the threshold of resistance to the novelties it may hold in store and enhancing their acceptability, along with that of the text incorporating them as a whole. In its extreme forms, pseudo-translating amounts to no less than **an act of culture planning**—a notion which, as I have been claiming lately, deserves to be given much higher prominence in Translation Studies than has normally been the case; at least while trying to account for translation behaviour under specific circumstances, that is, as a descriptive-explanatory tool.

Be that as it may, it is clear that recourse to fictitious translations entails **a disguise mechanism** whereby advantage is taken of a culture-internal conception of translation: not an essentialistic "definition" (that is, a list of [more or less] fixed features, allegedly specifying what translation inherently "is"), but a functional conception thereof which takes heed of the immanent *variability* of the notion of translation: difference across cultures, variation within a culture and changes over time.

The underlying assumption here is that a text's systemic position (and ensuing function), including the position and function which go with a text's being regarded as a translation, are determined first and foremost by considerations originating in the culture which actually hosts it. Thus, when a text is offered as a translation, it is quite readily accepted *bona fide* as one, no further questions asked. By contrast, when a text is presented as having been originally composed in a language, reasons will often manifest themselves— for example, certain features of textual make-up and verbal formulation, which persons-in-the-culture have come to associate with translations and translating—to at least suspect, correctly or not, that the text has in fact been translated into that language.

Within such a so-called "target culture", any text which is regarded as a translation, on no matter what grounds, can be accounted for as a cluster of (at least three) interconnected postulates:

>   (1) The Source-Text Postulate;
>   (2) The Transfer Postulate;
>   (3) The Relationship Postulate.

Regarded as postulates, all three are *posited* rather than factual; at least not of necessity. It is precisely this nature of theirs which makes it so possible for producers of texts, or various agents of cultural dissemination, to offer original compositions as if they were translations: neither the source text nor the transfer operations (and the features that the assumed "target" and "source" texts are regarded as sharing, by virtue of that transfer), nor any translational relationships (where the transferred—and shared—features are taken as an invariant core), have to be exposed and made available to the consumers; not even in the case of genuine translations. Very often it is really the other way around: a "positive" reason has to be supplied if a text assumed to be a translation is to be deprived of its culture-internal identity as one.

Thus, it is only when a text presented (or regarded) as a translation has been shown to have *never* had a corresponding source text in any other language, hence no text-induced "transfer operations", shared (transferred) features and accountable relationships, that it is found to be "what it really is": an original composition disguised as a translation. To be sure, this is a far cry from saying that a translation proved to be fictitious has "no basis" in any other culture, which is not necessarily true either: like genuine translations, fictitious ones may also serve as a vehicle of imported novelties. However, to the extent that such a basis can be pointed to, it would normally amount to a whole *group* of foreign texts, even the [abstractable] *model* underlying that group, rather than any individual text.

From the point of view of any retrospective attempt to study pseudo-translating and its implications, a significant paradox is precisely that a text can only be identified as a fictitious translation after the veil has been lifted, i. e. when the function it was intended to have, and initially had in the culture into which it was introduced, has already changed; whether the fact that it used to function as a translation still has some reality left or whether it has been completely erased from the culture's "collective memory". Only then can questions be asked as to why a disguised mode of presentation was selected in the first place, and why it was this particular language, or cultural tradition, that was picked as a "source", as well as what it was that made the public fall for it for a longer or a shorter period of time. At the same time, if any historically valid accounts are to be attempted, the text will have to be properly contextualized. In other words, it will have to be reinstated in the position it had occupied *before* it was found out to be fictitious. (Of course, there may exist myriad fictitious translations, with respect to which the mystification has not been dispelled, and maybe never will be. These texts can only be tackled as translations whose sources have remained unknown; but then, so many *genuine* translations are in that same position, especially if one goes back in time. Moreover, there is no real way of distinguishing between the two, which—in terms of their cultural position (that is, from the internal point of view of the culture which hosts them)—tend to be the same anyway.

By contrast, the lifting of the veil itself, and the circumstances under which it occurred, form an integral part of the story we are after. Thus, when an under-cover mission has been accomplished, there is little need for that cover any more. On the contrary, sometimes a wish may arise precisely to *publicize* the way by which the new dominating group (or individual) has managed to "outsmart the establishment" and smuggle in its own goods. All this does not rule out the possibility that the veil could also be lifted prior to a successful fulfillment of the task: this may certainly happen. After all, a strategy's success is never guaranteed. In cases like this, fulfillment may well be stopped, or even reverted, which constitutes another important aspect of any attempt to study cultural dynamics.

III

To be sure, a fictitious translation is not necessarily just *presented* to the public as if it were a genuine one (which—based as it is on make-believe alone—would still represent a disguise, but a rather superficial one indeed). In many cases, the text is *produced* "as a translation" right from the start. Entailing as it does the possibility of putting the claim that the text "is" indeed a translation to some kind of test, this would certainly count as a far more elaborate form of disguise.

Thus, features are often embedded in a fictitious translation which have come to be habitually associated with genuine translations in the culture which would host it, and which the pseudo-translator is part of, on occasion so much as a privileged part; whether the association is with translations into the hosting culture in general, or translations into it of texts of a particular type, or, more often, translations from a particular source language/culture. By enhancing their resemblance to genuine translations, pseudo-translators simply make it easier for their textual creations to pass as translations without arousing too much suspicion.

Interestingly enough, due to the practice of embedding features in fictitious translations which have come to be associated with genuine translations, it is sometimes possible to "reconstruct" from a fictitious translation bits and pieces of a text in another language as a kind of an "possible source text"—one that never enjoyed any textual reality, to be sure—as is the case with so many genuine translations whose sources have not (or not yet) been identified. In fact, as is the case with parodies (which are akin to them in more than one respect), fictitious translations often represent their fictitious sources in a rather exaggerated manner, which may render the said reconstruction quite easy as well as highly univocal. It is simply that the possibility, if not the need, to actually activate an "original" in the background of a text is often an integral part of its proper realization as an "intended translation", and hence of the very disguise involved in pseudo-translating.

No wonder, then, that fictitious translations are often in a position to give a fairly good idea as to the notions shared by the members of a community, not only concerning the *position* of translated texts in the culture they entertain, but concerning the most conspicuous *characteristics* of such texts as well; in terms of both textual-linguistic traits as well as putative target-source relationships. "The point is that it is only when humans recognize the existence of an entity and become aware of its characteristics that they can begin to imitate it" (James, 1989: 35), and overdoing-in-imitation is a clear, if extreme, sign of such a recognition.

One final remark of a general nature: there is no doubt that putting forward, even producing a text as if it were a translation always involves an *individual* decision. However, such a decision will inevitably have been made within a particular cultural set-up which is either conducive to pseudo-translating or else may hinder recourse to it. No wonder, then, that there seems to be circumstances which give rise to a *multitude* of fictitious translations, often from the same "source" tradition, and/or executed in a similar way, thus introducing into the culture in question a true model whose cultural significance is of course much greater than that of the sum-total of its individual (i. e. textual) realizations. Such a proliferation always attests to the internal organization of the culture involved and very little else. In particular, it bears out the position and role of [genuine] translations, or of a certain sub-group thereof, within that culture, which the pseudo-translators seem to be putting to use, trying to deliberately capitalize on it.

For instance, Russian literature of the beginning of the 19th century was crying out for what became known as "Gothic novels". In order not to be rejected, however, the texts put forward as novels of this type had to draw their authority from an external tradition, and a very particular one at that: the English Gothic novel. As Iurij Masanov has shown, in response to this requirement—a reflection of the internal interests of Russian literature itself which had very little to do with the concerns of the English culture—a great number of books were indeed produced in Russia itself—and in the Russian language—which were presented, and accepted, as translations from the English. Many of those were of "novels by Ann Radcliffe", who was at that time regarded in Russia as the epitome of the genre (Masanov,

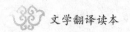

1963: 99 – 106).

In a similar vein, a former Tel Aviv student, Shelly Yahalom, has argued convincingly that one of the most effective means of bringing about changes in French writing of almost the same period was to lean heavily on translations from English, genuine and fictitious alike, with no real systemic difference between the two (Yahalom, 1978: 42 – 52, 74 – 75). As a third example of an over-riding tendency towards pseudo-translating I would cite the work of another former student at Tel Aviv University, Rachel Weissbrod, who demonstrated the decisive role fictitious translations, mainly "from the English" again, have played in establishing particular sectors of non-canonized Hebrew literature of the 1960s, most notably westerns, novels of espionage, romances and pornographic novels, where—as previous attempts had shown—*un*disguised texts of domestic origin would almost certainly have been considered inappropriate and relegated to the culture's extreme periphery, if not totally ejected from it (Weissbrod, 1989: 94 – 99, 354 – 356).

IV

If by "culture planning" we understand any attempt made by an individual, or a small group, to incur changes in the cultural repertoire, and the ensuing behaviour, of a much larger group, pseudo-translating would surely count as a case of cultural planning, especially in its most radical forms. Let me conclude by outlining three instances of pseudo-translating exhibiting growing extents of planning along various dimensions.

(a) *Papa Hamlet*

In January, 1889, a small book was published in the German town of Leipzig, whose title-page read:

Bjarne p. Holmsen

PAPA HAMLET

Uebersetzt

und mit einer Einleitung versehen

von

Dr. Bruno Franzius

The book opened with the translator's preface—the *Einleitung* announced on the cover—a rather common habit at that time, especially in translations which made a claim of importance. The preface itself was typical, too. In the main, it consisted of an extensive biography of the author, Bjarne Peter Holmsen, claimed to be a young Norwegian, but one of the central passages of the preface discussed the difficulties encountered by the translator while dealing with the original text and the translational strategies he chose to adopt. It even expressed some (implicit) concern that a number of deviant forms may have crept into the

German text in spite of the translator's prudence, forms which would easily be traceable to Norwegian formulations.

During the first few months after its publication, *Papa Hamlet* enjoyed relatively wide journalistic coverage. It was reviewed in many German newspapers and periodicals, where it was invariably treated as a translation. The claim was thus taken at face value, precisely as could have been expected. At the same time, none of the reviewers, mostly typical representatives of the German cultural milieu of the turn of the 20th century, had any idea about Bjarne Peter Holmsen and his literary (or any other) career. In fact, all of the information they supplied—which current norms of reviewing encouraged them to do—was drawn directly from the preface supplied by the translator, whose doctoral degree must have enhanced the trust they placed in it, as did the fact that the author's biography seemed to correspond so very closely to what would have been expected from a contemporary Scandinavian writer. Comical as it may sound, at least one reviewer went so far as to draw conclusions from the author's portrait, which appeared on the book's jacket. Quite a number of reviewers also referred to the translation work and its quality, in spite of the fact that none of them detected—or, for that matter, made any serious attempt to detect—a copy of the original; all on the clear assumption that a book presented as a translation actually is one. Unless, of course, there is strong evidence to the contrary.

And, indeed, a few months later, counter-evidence began to pile up, until it became known that *Papa Hamlet* was not a translation at all. Rather, the three stories comprising the small book were original German texts, the first results of the joint literary efforts of Arno Holz (1863—1929) and Johannes Schlaf (1862—1941). (The portrait on the jacket—a visual aspect of the overall disguise—belonged to a cousin of Holz's, one Gustav Uhse.)

Thus, towards the end of 1889, it was the *uncovered* disguise which became a literary fact (in the sense assigned to this notion by the Russian Formalist Jurij Tynjanov [1967]) for the German culture. However, an essential factor for any historically valid account of the case is that, for several months, Papa Hamlet did serve as a translation. Although factually wrong, this identity had been functionally effective; among other things, in enhancing the acceptance of what the two authors wished to achieve, and for whose achievement they decided to pseudo-translate in the first place.

Thus, Holz's and Schlaf's main objective was to experiment in freeing themselves—as German authors—from what they regarded as the narrow confines of French naturalism and getting away with this breach of sanctioned conventions. And they chose to do so by adopting a series of models of contemporary Scandinavian literature as guidelines for their writing, which were considered "naturalistic" too, only in a different way.

At that time, Scandinavian literature was indeed rapidly gaining in popularity and esteem in Germany. As such, it was in a good position to contribute novelties to German literature, and ultimately even reshape its very centre. However, when Holz and Schlaf were writing *Papa Hamlet*, German original writing was still firmly hooked to the French-like models. This made it highly resistant to the new trends, so that Scandinavian-like models were still acceptable only inasmuch as they were tied up with actual texts of Scandinavian origin; in other words, translations.

Disguising a German literary work which took after Scandinavian models as a translation was thus a most convenient way out of a genuine dilemma, where both horns—giving up the very wish to innovate as well as presenting the unconventional text as a German original—were sure to yield very little. Nor was this the only case of fictitious translation in modernizing German literature at the end of the 19th century, notably in the circles where Holz and Schlaf then moved, which may well have reinforced their decision to pseudo-translate.

The two authors were quite successful in attaining their goal too: Papa Hamlet indeed introduced "Scandinavian-like" novelties into German literature, many of them disguised—at least by implication—as instances of interference of the Norwegian original. A non-existent original, to be sure. In fact, the book came to be regarded as one of the most important forerunners of so-called *konsequenter Naturalismus*, a German brand of naturalism which owes quite a bit to Scandinavian prototypes. A successful instance of transplantation by any standard, due to an ingenious act of planning!

(b) *Book of Mormon*

A more extreme case of planning is represented by the *Book of Mormon* (1830): here, the innovations which were introduced by means of a text presented (and composed) as a translation gave birth to an altogether new Church, which brought in its wake a redeployment of much more than just the religious sector of American culture. One cannot but wonder what history would have looked like, had Joseph Smith Jr. claimed he had been given golden plates originally written in English, or had everybody taken the claim he did make as a mere hoax! (According to one Mormon tradition, the golden plates looked very much like a piece of 19th century office equipment, a kind of a ring binder.)

To be sure, it is only those who bought the claim that the *Book of Mormon* was a genuine translation from an old, obsolete (or, better still, obscure) language nicknamed "reformed Egyptian"—in spite of the enormous difficulties in accepting such a claim—who were also willing to accept its contents as well as the sacredness associated with it. As a result, it was not the entire American culture which absorbed the innovation. Rather, a relatively small group partly detached itself from mainstream culture and formed what became known as "the Church of Jesus Christ of Latter-day Saints". Moreover, the new Church developed not only due to a marked refusal to lift the veil connected with the *Book of Mormon*, but actually due to an ongoing struggle to improve the disguise and fortify it; in other words, to make the Book look more and more like a genuine religious book, which—according to previous traditions in the Anglo-American cultural space—had to be a translation.

Another aspect of the novelty of the *Book of Mormon* could well be literary. Thus, it has been claimed that

> the book is one of the earliest examples of frontier fiction, the first long Yankee narrative that owes nothing to English literary fashions ... its sources are absolutely American. (Brodie, 1963: 67)

In fact, in the 19th century there have been persistent allegations that use had been made of a lost manuscript of a novel by one Solomon Spaulding, which was supposed to have been stolen and passed on to Joseph Smith (Brodie, 1963: 419 - 433).

The possible literary intentions notwithstanding, it is clear that the producers of the *Book of Mormon*, struggling to establish a third *Testament*, took advantage first and foremost of large portions of the tradition of Bible translation into English. Regard the way the Book as a whole was divided into lower-level "Books", and especially the names that were given to the latter; for instance,

> first (and Second) Book of Nephi
> Book of Jacob
> Book of Mosiah.

Obviously, there is nothing "natural" about that division or the book names, nor can there be a doubt that both conventions were taken over from the *biblical* tradition.

As to the subdivision of each individual "Book" to "Chapters" and "Verses", it too was modelled on the Bible (more correctly, on its English translations, because Smith didn't even claim to know either Hebrew or Greek). However, this subdivision didn't even exist when the *Book of Mormon* first came into being. Rather, it was imposed on the English text some 50 years later, not even by the original pseudo-translator himself. There can be little doubt that this was done in a (rather successful) attempt to further reduce the difference between the *Book of Mormon* and the other two Testaments, thus enhancing its "authenticity" and adding to its religious authority—within the group which had already formed around the *Book*, that is. Can there be any doubt that what we are facing here is a whole series of gradual planning moves connected with a particular conception of translation?

To be sure, it is not all that clear what Smith had in mind when the Church was not yet in existence; not even whether he initially planned a religious work with a historical narrative at its base or just a historically-oriented narrative with some religious overtones. Moreover, in spite of the detailed story about how he received the golden plates and translated them, on the title-page of the first edition of the *Book of Mormon* he chose to refer to himself as "author and proprietor". Only in later editions was the reference changed to "translator". By contrast, it is very clear what happened to the *Book* in future times; namely, in a secondary, much more focused act of planning. In the same vein, references were later added to "prophecies" mentioned in the *Book*, which "had come true", as so many missionary groups have been doing in their versions of the New Testament (and "the Church of Jesus Christ of

Latter-day Saints" has indeed adopted a strong missionary orientation).

The names used in the Book constitute another feature which reveals a biblical model:

> Of the 350 names in the book he [Smith] took more than a hundred directly
> from the Bible. Over a hundred others were biblical names with slight changes in
> spelling or additions of syllables. But since in the Old Testament no names began
> with the letters F, Q, V, W, X, or Y, he was careful not to include any in his
> manuscript. (Brodie 1963: 73)

To which one could add those names (such as *Mosiah*) that end with the syllable *ah*, imitating a common ending in Hebrew whose retention has become part of standard transliteration of truly biblical names even in cases where the Hebrew closing *h* is silent, and hence phonetically superfluous.

Finally, in terms of its linguistic formulation, the *Book of Mormon* is an extreme case of what I have called "overdoing it *vis-à-vis* the source it is modelled on", which is so typical of fictitious translations. Take, for example, the way quotations from the Bible were used in the *Book*. As is well known, occasional quotation from the Old Testament has already been one of the literary devices of the New Testament, but it was used quite sparsely. By contrast, about 25,000 words of the *Book of Mormon* consist of passages from the Old Testament, and about 2,000 more words were taken from the New Testament. As Fawn Brodie, Smith's biographer, put it, it is almost as if, whenever "his literary reservoir... ran dry... he simply arranged for his Nephite prophets to quote from the Bible (1963: 58)". To be sure, Smith often "made minor changes in these Biblical extracts, for it seems to have occurred to him that readers would wonder how an ancient American prophet could use the exact text of the King James Bible". However, "he was careful to modify chiefly the italicized interpolations inserted for euphony and clarity by the scholars of King James; the unitalicized holy text he usually left intact". In the same vein, the phrase "and it came to pass" [=it so happened], which is typical to the book's style, appears at least 2,000 times (1963: 63), which is really a lot!

(c) The "Kazakh Poet" Dzhambul Dzhabayev

In the most extreme of cases, planning may be so much as imposed on a society from above, by agents endowed with the power to do so; most notably political institutions in a totalitarian society. This is precisely the way pseudo-translating was used, misused and abused in Stalin's Soviet Union, a famous case in point being the patriotic poetry of Dzhambul Dzhabayev.

During the first decades after the Soviet Revolution, an old Kazakh folk singer named Dzhambul Dzhabayev (1846—1945) became famous throughout the Empire. Yet, nobody has ever encountered that man's poems in praise of the regime in anything but Russian, a language he himself didn't speak. Several of those poems were translated into other languages too, most notably in East Germany, always from the Russian version.

Now, at least since the memoirs of the composer Dmitri Shostakovitch "as related to and edited by Solomon Volkov" (Shostakovitch, 1979: 161 ff.), it has become common knowledge that the Russian "translations" of Dzhambul's poems were in fact written "by an entire brigade of Russian poetasters" (derogatory noun—Shostakovitch's), who, in turn, didn't know any Kazakh. Some of the real authors were actually rather well-known figures in Soviet letters, which is why they were assigned the job in the first place: they knew only too well what the authorities expected of them and of their poems. The team "wrote fast and prolifically", Shostakovitch goes on, "and when one of the 'translators' dried up, he was replaced by a new, fresh one". "The factory was closed down only on Dzhambul's death", which was made known throughout the world; that is, when he could no longer be taken advantage of in person. Luckily enough (for the planners), he lived to be ninety-nine.

Evidently, the Soviet authorities resorted to this practice in a highly calculated attempt to meet two needs at once, each drawing on a different source: the poems had to praise "the great leader" and his deeds in a way deemed appropriate. People of the Russian *intelligentsia* were in the best position to do that. On the other hand, the new norms which were then being adopted in the Soviet Union demanded that "the new slaves... demonstrate their cultural accomplishments to the residents of the capital", in Shostakovitch's harsh formulation (1979: 164). Consequently, an author for the concoction had to be found in the *national republics* such as Kazakhstan, and not in the Russian centre; and in case a suitable one couldn't be found, one had to be invented.

In this case, as in many others, the invention was not *biographical*: a forgery of such magnitude—the invention of a person that has had no form of existence whatsoever—would have been too easy to detect, with all the ensuing detrimental consequences. However, it most certainly was a *functional* kind of invention: the required figure was thus not made up as a person, but rather as a persona; namely, the "author" in the Kazakh language of a growing corpus of poems which, in point of fact, came into being in Russian. The invented persona was superimposed on an existing person, among other things, in order that someone could be present in the flesh on selected occasions, thus enhancing the "authenticity" of the poems as well as that of their [fictitious] author.

Significantly, comparable methods were used in music, [folk] dance, and several other arts too, which renders the use of fictitious translations in Stalin's Soviet Union part of a major culture-planning operation, and a very successful one, at that (from the point of view of those who thought it out): mere disguise systematically turned into flat forgery.

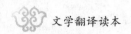

【翻译鉴赏】

Noethanger Abbey[1]

(An Excerpt from Chapter 5)

Jane Austen

The progress of the friendship between Catherine [Morland] and Isabella was quick as its beginning had been warm; and they passed so rapidly through every graduation of increasing tenderness, that there was shortly no fresh proof of it to be given to their friends or themselves. They called each other by their Christian name, were always arm-in-arm when they walked, pinned to each other's train for the dance, and were not to be divided in the set[2]; and if a rainy morning deprived them of other enjoyments, they were still resolute in meeting in defiance of wet and dirt[3], and shut themselves up to read novels together. Yes, novels; for I will not adopt that ungenerous and impolitic custom, so common with novel writers, of degrading, by their contemptuous censure, the very performances to the number of which they are themselves adding: joining with their greatest enemies in bestowing the harshest epithets on such works, and scarcely ever permitting them to be read by their own heroine, who, if she accidentally take up a novel, is sure to turn over its insipid pages with disgust. Alas! if the heroine of one novel be not patronized by the heroine of another, from whom can she expect protection and regard? I cannot approve of it. Let us leave it to the Reviewers to abuse such effusions of fancy at their leisure, and over every new novel to talk in threadbare strains of the trash with which the press now groans. Let us not desert one another; we are an injured body. Although our productions have afforded more extensive and unaffected pleasure than those of any other literary corporation in the world, no species of composition has been so much decried. From pride, ignorance, or fashion, our foes are almost as many as our readers; and while the abilities of the nine-hundredth abridger of the History of England[4], or of the man who collects and publishes in a volume some dozen lines of Milton, Pope[5], and Prior[6], with a paper from the Spectator[7], and a chapter from Sterne[8], are eulogized by a thousand pens[9], there seems almost a general wish of decrying the capacity and undervaluing the labour of the novelist, and of slighting the performances which have only genius, wit, and taste to recommend them. "I am no novel reader; I seldom look into novels; do not imagine that I often read novels; it is really very well for a novel." Such is the common cant. "And what are you reading, Miss—?" "Oh! it is only a novel!" replies the young lady, while she lays down her book with affected indifference, or momentary shame. "It is only *Cecilia*, or *Camilla*[10], or *Belinda*[11]"; or, in short, only some work in which the greatest powers of the mind are displayed, in which the most thorough knowledge of human nature, the happiest delineation of its varieties[12], the liveliest effusions of wit and humour, are conveyed to the world in the best chosen language. Now, had the same young lady been engaged with a volume of the Spectator, instead of such a work, how proudly would she have produced the book, and told its name;

though the chances must be against her being occupied by any part of that voluminous publication，of which either the matter or manner would not disgust a young person of taste；the substance of its papers so often consisting in the statement of improbable circumstances，unnatural characters，and topic of conversation which no longer concern anyone living；and their language，too，frequently so coarse as to give no very favourable idea of the age that could endure it.

【译文】

诺桑觉寺
（第五章节选）
简·奥斯汀

　　凯瑟琳与伊莎贝拉之间的友谊，一开始就很热烈，因而进展得也很迅速。两人一步步地越来越亲密，没过多久，无论她们的朋友还是她们自己，再也见不到还有什么进一步发展的余地了。她们相互以教名相称，同行时总是臂挽着臂，跳舞时相互帮着别好拖裙，就是在舞列里也不肯分离，非要挨在一起不可。如果逢上早晨下雨，不能享受别的乐趣，那她们也要不顾雨水与泥泞，坚决聚到一起，关在屋里一道看小说。是的，看小说，因为我不想采取小说家通常采取的那种卑劣而愚拙的行径，明明自己也在写小说，却以轻蔑的态度去诋毁小说。他们同自己不共戴天的敌人串通一气，对这些作品进行恶语中伤，从不允许自己作品中的女主角看小说。如果有位女主角偶尔拾起一本书，这本书一定乏味至极，女主角一定怀着憎恶的心情在翻阅着。天哪！如果一部小说的女主角不从另一部小说的女主角那里得到庇护，那她又能指望从何处得到保护和尊重呢？我可不赞成这样做。让那些评论家穷极无聊地去咒骂那些洋溢着丰富想象力的作品吧，让他们使用那些目今充斥在报刊上的种种陈词滥调去谈论每本新小说吧。我们可不要互相背弃，我们是个受到残害的整体。虽然跟其他形式的文学作品相比，我们的作品给人们提供了更广泛、更实在的乐趣，但是还没有任何一种作品遭到如此多的诋毁。由于傲慢、无知或赶时髦的缘故，我们的敌人几乎和我们的读者一样多。有人抛出《英国史》的不知是第几百个节本，有人把弥尔顿、蒲柏和普赖尔的几十行诗，《旁观者》的一篇杂文，以及斯特恩作品里的某一章，拼凑成一个集子加以出版，诸如此般的才干受到了上千文人墨客的赞颂；然而人们几乎总是愿意诋毁小说家的才能，贬损小说家的劳动，蔑视那些只以天才、智慧和情趣见长的作品。"我不是小说读者，很少浏览小说。别以为我常看小说。这对一本小说来说还真够不错的了。"这是人们常用的口头禅。"你在读什么，小姐！""哦！只不过是本小说！"小姐答道，一面装着不感兴趣的样子，或是露出一时羞愧难言的神情，赶忙将书摞下。"这只不过是本《西西丽亚》、《卡米拉》，或《贝林达》。"总而言之，只是这样一些作品，在这些作品中，智慧的伟力得到了最充分的施展，因而，对人性的最透彻的理解，对其千姿百态的恰如其分的描述，四处洋溢的机智幽默，所有这一切都用最精湛的语言展现出来。假如那位小姐是在看一本《旁观者》杂志，而不是在看这类作品，她一定会十分骄傲地把杂志拿出来，而且说出它的名字！不过，别看那厚厚的一本，这位小姐无论在读哪一篇，其内容和文体都不可能不使一位情趣高雅的青年人为之作呕。这些作品的要害，往往在于描写一些不可能发生的事件，矫揉造作的人物，以及与活人无关的话题；而且语言常常如此粗劣，使人对于能够容忍这种语言的时代产生了不良印象。

【译文评析】

[1] 在英国小说的历史上,简·奥斯汀发挥了极其重要的作用。18 世纪末,由于福音派信徒不断诋毁的缘故,小说在英国被视为一种无聊甚至有害的消遣,一时陷入遭人唾弃的境地。面对这股邪风,奥斯汀义无反顾,在《诺桑觉寺》第五章,特意离开故事的发展线索,气势昂昂地捍卫小说的神圣地位,写出了一段堪称"小说独立宣言"的文字。

[2] set 在此是指一种男女对舞的方舞队形。

[3] wet and dirt 是奥斯汀小说语言的特色之一,充满音乐美的押韵方法,在此不可理解为"潮湿和肮脏",而应为"雨水和泥泞"。

[4] the nine-hundredth abridger of the History of England(《英国史》的第九百个删节者),系夸张说法,意即概述的删节本多如牛毛。翻译时,考虑到汉语的习惯,似乎写成"有人抛出《英国史》的不知第几百个节本"为好,更容易被中国读者接受。

[5] 亚历山大·蒲柏(1688—1744),英国著名诗人兼翻译家。

[6] 马修·普赖尔(1664—1721),英格兰诗人和随笔作家。

[7] 《旁观者》,英国 1711 年 3 月 1 日至 1712 年 12 月 6 日出版的一种杂志,主要撰稿人有著名随笔作家乔瑟夫·艾迪生和理查德·斯蒂尔等人。

[8] 劳伦斯·斯特恩(1713—1768),英国小说家。

[9] pen 是转喻修辞法,意思是指"笔杆子",即作家或者评论家。

[10] *Cecilia* 和 *Camilla*(《西西丽亚》和《卡米拉》),系英国女作家范妮·勃尼(1752—1840)所写的两部感伤小说,出版后曾经风靡一时。

[11] *Belinda*(《贝林达》)系英国女作家玛丽亚·埃奇沃思(1767—1840)所作的一部描写上流社会生活的小说。

[12] happy 在此译为"恰当的、合适的、巧妙的",而与单词本意"幸福的"稍有距离。

——参考孙致礼译文及评析

西式幽默
冯骥才

学院请来一位洋教师,长得挺怪,红脸,金发,连鬓大胡须,有几根胡子一直逾过面颊,挨近鼻子,他个子足有二米,每进屋门必须低头,才能躲过门框子的拦击,叫人误以为他进门先鞠躬,这不太讲究礼貌了吗?顶怪的是,他每每与中国学生聊天,聊到可笑之处时,他不笑,脸上也没表情,好象他不喜欢玩笑;可是有时毫不可笑的事,他会冷不防放声大笑,笑得翻江倒海,仰面朝天,几乎连人带椅子要翻过去,喉结在脖子上乱跳,满脸胡子直抖。常使中国学生面面相觑,不知这位洋教师的神经是不是有点问题?

一天,洋教师出题,考察学生们用洋文作文的水准,题目极简单,随便议论议论校园内的一事一物,褒贬皆可。中国学生很灵,一挥而就,洋教师阅后。评出了最佳作文一篇,学生们听后大为不解,这种通篇说谎的文章怎么能被评为"最佳"?原来这篇作文是写学校食堂。写作文的学生来自郊区农村,人很老实,胆子又小,生怕得罪校方,妨碍将来毕业时的分数、评语、分配工作等等,便不顾真假,胡编乱造,竭力美化,唱赞歌。使得一些学生看后愤愤然。可是……洋教师明知学校食堂糟糕透顶的状况,为什么偏要选这篇作文?有人直问洋教师。

洋教师说:"这文章写得当然好,而且绝妙无比,你们听——"他拿起作文念起来,"我们学校最美的地方,不是教室,不是操场,也不是校门口那个带喷水的小花坛,而是食堂。瞧,玻璃干净得几乎叫你看不到它的存在——。"洋教师念到这儿,眼睛调皮地一亮,眉毛一挑,"听听,多么幽默!"

幽默? 怎么会是幽默大家还没弄明白。

洋教师接着念道:"如果你不小心在学校食堂跌了一跤,你会惊奇地发现你并没跌跤,因为你身上半点尘土也没留下;如果你长期在学校食堂里工作,恐怕你会把苍蝇是什么样子都忘了……"洋教师又停住,舌头"得"地弹一声,做一个怪脸说,"听呀,还要多幽默,我简直笑得念不下去了。"

学生们忽然明白了什么。

洋教师一边笑,一边继续往下念:"食堂天天的饭菜有多么精美、多么丰富、多么解馋! 只有在学校食堂里,你才会感到吃饭是一种地道的享受……"

忽然,学生们爆发起大笑来!

依照这种思维,我们会从身边发现多少聪明、机智、绝妙、令人捧腹的好文章啊!

【译文】

Western Humour[1]

Feng Jicai

Our institute employed an English teacher. He looked very strange—red-faced, golden-haired and with a thick growth of whiskers, a few hairs of which traveling all the way to the nose. He was really tall—sufficiently six feet five inches. When he came in through the door, he had to lower his head to avoid banging against the doorframe. It looked as though he always bowed to you at the door and that was much too polite. What was most strange about him that when he chatted with the Chinese students on amusing topics, he did not laugh, nor did his face show any expression as if he had no sense of humour at all. However, when it came to topics of the most unamusing nature, he would burst out laughing, roaring while rocking in his chair, almost tipping off and falling flat on his back, his Adam's apple dancing up and down in his throat and his whiskers fluttering all over his face. The students would look at each other, wondering if this guy was in his right mind. [2]

One day he set the students an essay to see how well they could write in English, the topic being "A Comment on Campus Life"—either complimentary or critical. That was simple. The Chinese students, quick at writing, finished it off at one go and turned it in no time. Having gone through the students' essays the teacher picked one that he thought was the best. When he read it out to the students, they were perplexed. Of all the essays, why did he like this one better? Not a single word of it was true. The article was about the institute cafeteria and the author was a peaceable and timid student from a village in the outskirts. Taking care not to offend the institute authorities—the decisive factor concerning his final grading, evaluation and, most important of all, where he was to go after graduation—he had made up a high-sounding story in praise of the cafeteria, regardless of the realities, and that made his classmates very angry. [3] The teacher, however, not unaware of the cafeteria's terrible conditions, but why did he have his eye on this one in particular? Someone asked.

"This is certainly a good essay," he explained. "Absolutely matchless! Just listen... " He picked up the composition and began to read. "The most beautiful spot on campus is not the classroom-building, nor the sports-ground, nor the lawn with the fountain at the gate; the most beautiful spot on campus is our cafeteria. Look! The window-panes are so clean that you scarcely notice there is glass in them... " He paused, his eyes flashing with a glint of wits and his brows shooting upward. "Listen! Isn't it humorous?"

Humorous? But what was humorous about it? The students were puzzled.

"If you were not careful enough," he continued, "and had a fall on the floor, you would be amazed to find that you had not fallen at all because you did not get a single particle of dust on your clothes. If you had been working in the cafeteria long enough, you would have forgotten what a fly looks like... " He stopped, his tongue clicking rapidly to show admiration. Working up a funny expression on his face, he went on, "Listen, please! Do you think anyone else could've made it more humorous? " He laughed so heartily that he could hardly continue.

By now the students seemed to be cottoning on.

The teacher went on, his reading punctuated by fits of laughter. [4] "How wonderfully is the food cooked here! What a great variety of dishes you have on the menu and how well your appetite is satisfied! In fact it is only at the cafeteria of the institute that you find eating an enjoyable business... "

Suddenly the students laughed, rocking the classroom with their laughter.

Following this logic, God knows how many articles we would be able to produce, articles that are just as well-worded, quick-witted, artfully-conceived and set you rolling with laughter![5]

【译文评析】

[1]《西式幽默》是讽刺小说，围绕某校食堂展开故事，颇具针砭时弊的功效。篇幅虽小，人物形象刻画得细致入微，故事情节声情并茂。行文自然畅达，收放自如，体现浓郁的"汉语味"。小说组织松散、疏放，呈流泄式铺排，句子无主从之分，只有先后之序；句子、词组不辨，主语、谓语难分，作者信手拈来，笔随意转，浑然天成。

[2] 首段写人记事流水句多，短句多，语段中句断并不明显，形断意属，整个语段以"洋教师"为起点呈流散型扩展。但英语译文长句多，句子多包孕环扣，语段中断句明显，语段先总起，后分述，层次清楚；各句主从分明，主语、谓语易辨，整个语段围绕"洋教师"（an English teacher/he）呈聚集型扩散。

[3] 原句多动态描写，动词频频出现，这是汉语的特点；在译句中，介词词组多，贴合英语表述的特点。

[4] punctuate 一词选择巧妙而独到，既传递了原句的句义与情景，又与前文的 He laughed so heartily that he could hardly continue. 相呼应。

[5] 原句多定语前置，符合汉语句首开放性和句尾收缩性的特点；译句多定语后置，符合英语句首封闭性和句尾开放性的特点。

【翻译试笔】

【英译汉】

Old Man and the Sea (excerpt)

Ernest Hemingway

For eighty four days old Santiago had not caught a single fish. At first a young boy, Manolin, had shared his bad fortune, but after the fortieth luckless day the boy's father told his son to go in another boat. From that time on Santiago worked alone. Each morning he rowed his skiff out into the Gulf Stream where the big fish were. Each evening he came in empty-handed.

The boy loved the old fisherman and pitied him. If Manolin had no money of his own, he begged or stole to make sure that Santiago had enough to eat and fresh baits for his lines. The old man accepted his kindness with humility that was like a quiet kind of pride. Over their evening meals of rice or black beans they would talk about the fish they had taken in luckier times or about American baseball and the great DiMaggio. At night, alone in his shack, Santiago dreamed of lions on the beaches of Africa, where he had gone on a sailing ship years before. He no longer dreamed of his dead wife.

On the eighty-fifth day Santiago rowed out of the harbor in the cool dark before dawn. After leaving the smell of land behind him, he set his lines. Two of his baits were fresh tunas the boy had given him, as well as sardines to cover his hooks. The lines went straight down into deep dark water.

As the sun rose he saw other boats in toward shore, which was only a low green line on the sea. A hovering man-of-war bird showed him where dolphins were chasing some flying fish, but the school was moving too fast and too far away. The bird circled again. This time Santiago saw tuna leaping in the sunlight. A small one took the hook on his stern line. Hauling the quivering fish aboard, the old man thought it a good omen.

Toward noon a marlin started nibbling at the bait which was one hundred fathoms down. Gently the old man played the fish, a big one, as he knew from the weight on the line. At last he struck to settle the hook. The fish did not surface. Instead, it began to tow the skiff to the northwest. The old man braced himself, the line taut across his shoulders. Although he was alone and no longer strong, he had his skill and knew many tricks. He waited patiently for the fish to tire.

The old man shivered in the cold that came after sunset. When something took one of his remaining baits, he cut the line with his sheath knife. Once the fish lurched suddenly, pulling Santiago forward on his face and cutting his cheek. By dawn his left hand was stiff and cramped. The fish had headed northward; there was no land in sight. Another strong tug on the line sliced Santiago's right hand. Hungry, he cut strips from the tuna and chewed them slowly while he waited for the sun to warm him and ease his cramped fingers.

That morning the fish jumped. Seeing it leap, Santiago knew he had hooked the biggest marlin he had even seen. Then the fish went under and turned toward the east. Santiago drank sparingly from his water bottle during the hot afternoon. Trying to forget his cut hand and aching back, he remembered the days when men had called him Campeon and he had wrestled with a giant Negro in the tavern at Cienfuegos. Once an airplane droned overhead on its way to Miami.

Close to nightfall a dolphin took the small hook he had rebaited. He lifted the fish aboard, careful not to jerk the line over his shoulder. After he had rested, he cut fillets from the dolphin and kept also the two flying fish he found in its maw. That night he slept. He awoke to feel the line running through his fingers as the fish jumped. Feeding line slowly, he tried to tire the marlin. After the fish slowed its run. he washed his cut hands in sea water and ate one of the flying fish. At sunrise the marlin began to circle. Faint and dizzy, he worked to bring the big fish nearer with each turn. Almost exhausted, he finally drew his catch alongside and drove in the harpoon. He drank a little water before he lashed the marlin to bow and stern of his skiff. The fish was two feet longer than the boat. No catch like it had ever been seen in Havana harbor. It would make his fortune, he thought, as he hoisted his patched sails and set his course toward the southwest.

An hour later he sighted the first shark. It was a fierce Mako, and it came in fast to slash with raking teeth at the dead marlin. With failing might the old man struck the shark with his harpoon. The Mako rolled and sank, carrying the harpoon with it and leaving the marlin mutilated and bloody. Santiago knew the scent would spread. Watching, he saw two shovel nosed sharks closing in. He struck at one with his knife lashed to the end of an oar and watched the scavenger sliding down into deep water. The other he killed while it tore at the flesh of the marlin. When the third appeared, he thrust at it with the knife, only to feel the blade snap as the fish rolled. The other sharks came at sunset. At first he tried to club them with the tiller from the skiff, but his hands were raw and bleeding and there were too many in the pack. In the darkness, as he steered toward the faint glow of Havana against the sky, he heard them hitting the carcass again and again. But the old man thought only of his steering and his great tiredness. He had gone out too far and the sharks had beaten him. He knew they would leave him nothing but the stripped skeleton of his great catch.

All lights were out when he sailed into the little harbor and beached his skiff. In the gloom he could just make out the white backbone and the upstanding tail of the fish. He started up the shore with the mast and furled sail of his boat. Once he fell under their weight and lay patiently until he could gather his strength. In his shack he fell on his bed and went to sleep.

There the boy found him later that morning. Meanwhile other fishermen, gathered about the skiff, marveled at the giant marlin, eighteen feet long from nose to tail. When Manolin returned to Santiago's shack with hot coffee, the old man awoke. The boy, he said, could have the spear of his fish. Manolin told him to rest, to make himself fit for the days of fishing they would have together. All that afternoon the old man slept, the boy sitting by his bed. Santiago was dreaming of lions.

【汉译英】

《围城》（节选）
钱钟书

　　红海早过了。船在印度洋面上开驶着。但是太阳依然不饶人地迟落早起，侵占去大部分的夜。夜仿佛纸浸了油，变成半透明体；它给太阳拥抱住了，分不出身来，也许是给太阳陶醉了，所以夕照晚霞隐褪后的夜色也带着酡红。到红消醉醒，船舱里的睡人也一身腻汗地醒来，洗了澡赶到甲板上吹海风，又是一天开始。这是七月下旬，合中国旧历的三伏，一年最热的时候。在中国热得更比常年利害，事后大家都说是兵戈之象，因为这就是民国二十六年〔一九三七年〕。

　　这条法国邮船白拉日隆子爵号（Vicomte de Bragelonne）正向中国开来。早晨八点多钟，冲洗过的三等舱甲板湿意未干，但已坐立满了人，法国人、德国流亡出来的犹太人、印度人、安南人，不用说还有中国人。海风里早含着燥热，胖人身体给炎风吹干了，蒙上一层汗结的盐霜，仿佛刚在巴勒斯坦的死海里洗过澡。毕竟是清晨，人的兴致还不没给太阳晒萎，烘懒，说话做事都很起劲。那几个新派到安南或中国租界当警察的法国人，正围了那年轻善撒娇的犹太女人在调情。俾斯麦曾说过，法国公使大使的特点，就是一句外国话不会讲；这几位警察并不懂德文，居然传情达意，引得犹太女人格格地笑，比他们的外交官强多了。这女人的漂亮丈夫，在旁顾而乐之，因为他几天来，香烟、啤酒、柠檬水沾光了不少。红海已过，不怕热极引火，所以等一会甲板上零星果皮、纸片、瓶塞之外，香烟头定又遍处皆是。法国人的思想是有名的清楚，他们的文章也明白干净，但是他们的做事，无不混乱、肮脏、喧哗，但看这船上的乱糟糟。这船，倚仗人的机巧，载满人的扰攘，寄满人的希望，热闹地行着，每分钟把沾污了人气的一小方水面，还给那无情、无尽、无际的大海。

　　照例每年夏天有一批中国留学生学成回国。这船上也有十来个人。大多数是职业尚无着落的青年，赶在暑假初回中国，可以从容找事。那些不愁没事的学生，要到秋凉才慢慢地肯动身回国。船上这几位，有在法国留学的，有在英国、德国、比国等读书，到巴黎去增长夜生活经验，因此也坐法国船的。他们天涯相遇，一见如故，谈起外患内乱的祖国，都恨不得立刻就回去为它服务。船走得这样慢，大家一片乡心，正愁无处寄托，不知哪里忽来了两副麻将牌。麻将当然是国技，又听说在美国风行；打牌不但有故乡风味，并且适合世界潮流。妙得很，人数可凑成两桌而有余，所以除掉吃饭睡觉以外，他们成天赌钱消遣。早餐刚过，下面餐室里已忙着打第一圈牌，甲板上只看得见两个中国女人，一个算不得人的小孩子——至少船公司没当他是人，没要他父母为他补买船票。那个戴太阳眼镜、身上摊本小说的女人，衣服极斯文讲究。皮肤在东方人里，要算得白，可惜这白色不顶新鲜，带些干滞。她去掉了黑眼镜，眉清目秀，只是嘴唇嫌薄，擦了口红还不够丰厚。假使她从帆布躺椅上站起来，会见得身段瘦削，也许轮廓的线条太硬，像方头钢笔划成的。年龄看上去有二十五六，不过新派女人的年龄好比旧式女人合婚帖上的年庚，需要考订学家所谓外证据来断定真确性，本身是看不出的。那男孩子的母亲已有三十开外，穿件半旧的黑纱旗袍，满面劳碌困倦，加上天生的倒挂眉毛，愈觉愁苦可怜。孩子不足两岁，塌鼻子，眼睛两条斜缝，眉毛高高在上，跟眼睛远隔得彼此要害相思病，活像报上讽刺画里中国人的脸。

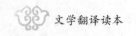

【参考译文】

老人与海

（节选）

海明威 著 杨枕旦 译

桑提亚哥老人已经八十四天没有捕到一条鱼了。最初，一个年轻的孩子曼诺林和他一起分担恶运，但在过了四十天倒霉日子之后，孩子的爸爸让孩子到另一条船上干活去了。从那个时候起，桑提亚哥只是一个人干活。每天早晨他划着小船到有大鱼出没的墨西哥湾流去，每天晚上他总是两手空空地回来。

孩子喜欢并且可怜这个老渔人。曼诺林要是自己没有挣到钱，就会乞讨或偷窃以保证桑提亚哥有足够的食物和新鲜的鱼饵。老人谦卑地接受孩子的好意，谦卑中带有某种隐而不露的自豪感。晚餐时（吃的是大米饭和黑蚕豆）他们总会谈论在运气好的日子里一起捕获的大鱼，或是谈论美国的棒球赛和伟大的狄马吉奥。夜间桑提亚哥一个人躺在自己的小棚屋里，梦见非洲海滩上的狮子，几年前他航海去过那个地方。他不再梦见自己死去的老婆了。

在第八十五天，桑提亚哥在寒冷的黎明前的黑暗中，把小船划出了港口。在把陆地的气息抛在身后之后，他放下了钓丝。他的两个鱼饵是孩子给他的鲜金枪鱼，还有把鱼钩遮盖起来的沙丁鱼。钓丝垂直地下到暗黑的深水里。

太阳升起时，他看到别的一些船只都头朝着海岸，在海上看来海岸象是一条接近地平线的绿带子。一只盘旋的军舰鸟给老人指明了海豚追逐飞鱼的地方。但是鱼群游得太快、也太远了。这只猛禽又在盘旋了，这次桑提亚哥瞧见金枪鱼在太阳光下跃起。一条小金枪鱼咬住了他艉缆上的鱼钩。老人在把颤动的金枪鱼拉上船板以后，心想这可是一个好兆头。

快到中午时，一条马林鱼开始啃起一百米深处的那块鱼饵来了。老人轻轻地摆布那条上了钩的鱼，根据钓丝的份量他知道那准是一条大鱼。最后他猛拉钓丝把鱼钩给稳住了。但是，那条鱼并没有浮出水面，反而开始把小船拖着往西北方向跑。老人打起精神，斜挎在肩膀上的钓丝绷得紧紧的。他虽然孤身一人，体力也不如从前，但是他有技术，他懂得许多诀窍。他耐心地等待鱼累乏下来。

日落之后，寒意袭人，老人冷得发抖。当他剩下的鱼饵中有一块被咬住时，他就用自己那把带鞘的刀把钓丝给割断了。有一次那条鱼突然一个侧身，把桑提亚哥拉得脸朝下地跌了一跤，老人的颊部也给划破了。黎明时分，他的左手变得僵硬并抽起筋来了。那条鱼还是一直往北游，一点陆地的影子都瞧不见了。钓丝又一次猛的一拉，把老人的右手给勒伤了。老人肚子饿得发慌，就从金枪鱼身上割下几片肉，放在嘴里慢慢嚼着，等着太阳出来晒暖他的身子和减轻手指抽筋的痛苦。

第二天早上，这条鱼蹦出了水面。桑提亚哥瞧见鱼的跃起，知道自己钓到了一条未见过的最大的马林鱼。一会儿鱼又往下沉去，转向了东方。在炽热的下午，桑提亚哥节省地喝起水壶里的水。为了忘掉划破的手和疼痛的背，他回想起过去人们如何称他为"优胜者"和他如何在西恩富戈斯地方一家酒馆里和一个大个子黑人比手劲。有一次一架飞机嗡嗡地从头上掠过，向迈阿密飞去。

黄昏之际，一条海豚吞食了他重新放上鱼饵的小钩子。他把这条"鱼"提到了船板上，小心不去拉动他肩上的钓丝。休息一会之后，他切下几片海豚肉并且把在海豚胃中发现的两条飞鱼留了下来。那天夜里他睡着了。他醒来时觉得当这条鱼跳起时钓丝就滑过他的手指。他缓慢地把钓丝放松,尽力想把这条马林鱼拖乏。在这条大鱼放慢跳跃时,他把划破的双手放在海里洗,并且吃了一条飞鱼。日出时,这条马林鱼开始打起转来了。老人感到头晕目眩,但他尽力把大鱼在每转一圈时拉得更近一些。他虽然几乎筋疲力尽,终于还是把自己的捕获物拉得和小船并排在一起并用鱼叉猛击这条马林鱼。他喝了一点水,然后把马林鱼捆绑在他那条小船的头部和尾部。这条马林鱼比船还长两英尺。哈瓦那港从来没有见过捕到这么大的鱼,他扯起有补丁的船帆开始向西南方向驶去,心想这下要发财了。

一个小时以后,他瞧见了第一条鲨鱼。这是一条凶猛的尖吻鲭鲨。它飞快地游了过来,用耙一样的牙齿撕这条死马林鱼。老人用尽余力把鱼叉往鲨鱼身上扎去。尖吻鲭鲨打着滚沉下去了,带走了鱼叉,而且已经把马林鱼咬得残缺不全,鲜血直流。桑提亚哥知道血腥味会散开来。他望着海面,看到两条犁头鲨游近来了。他用绑在桨的一头的刀子击中了其中的一条,并看着这条食腐动物滑到深海里去了。他杀死了正在撕食马林鱼的另一条鲨鱼。当第三条鲨鱼出现时,他把刀子向鲨鱼戳去。鲨鱼打了一个滚,结果把刀给折断了。日落时又有一些鲨鱼游过来了。起初他设法用舵把朝它们劈过去,但是他双手磨破了皮在流着血,而游来的鲨鱼多得成了群。在暮色中,他望着地平线上的哈瓦那的微弱的灯光,听着鲨鱼一次一次在啃咬马林鱼的尸体。老人此时想到的只是掌舵,和他自己极度的疲乏。他出海太远了,那些鲨鱼把他打败了。他知道那些鲨鱼除了大马林鱼的空骨架之外,是什么也不会给他留下的。

当他划进小港,让小船冲上沙滩时,岸上的灯火都已灭了。在朦胧之中,他只能分辨出那条马林鱼白色的脊背和竖着的尾巴。他拿着桅竿和卷起的船帆,往岸上爬去。有一次他在重压下跌倒了,他耐心地躺在地上,积蓄力气。等他进了自己的棚屋时,他一头倒在床上就睡。

那天早上晚些时候,孩子发现他时他还躺着。这个时候,一些渔民聚在那只小船的周围,对这条从头到尾长有十八英尺的大马林鱼啧啧称奇。当曼诺林拿着热咖啡回到桑提亚哥的棚屋时,老人醒了。他告诉孩子可以把他那条鱼的长吻拿走。曼诺林要老人休息,把身体养好,以便日后再一起出去捕鱼。整个下午老人都在睡觉,那孩子就坐在他的床旁边。桑提亚哥正在梦见那些狮子呢。

Fortress Besieged(excerpt)
By Ch'ien Chung-shu
trans. by Jeanne Kelly and Nathan K. Mao

The red sea had long since been crossed, and the ship was now on its way over the Indian Ocean; but as always the sun mercilessly rose early and set late, encroaching upon the better part of the night. The night, like paper soaked in oil, had become translucent. Locked in the embrace of the sun, the night's own form was indiscernible. Perhaps it had become intoxicated by the sun, which would explain why the night sky remained flushed long after the gradual fading of the rosy sunset. By the time the ruddiness dissipated and the night itself awoke from its stupor, the passengers in their cabins had awakened, glistening with sweat; after bathing, they hurried out on deck to catch the ocean breeze. Another day had begun.

It was toward the end of July, equivalent to the "san-fu" period of the lunar calendar—the hottest days of the year. In China the heat was even more oppressive than usual. Later everyone agreed the unusual heat was a portent of troops and arms, for it was the twenty-

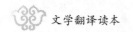

sixth year of the Republic (1937).

The French liner, the *Vicomte de Bragelonne*, was on its way to China. Some time after eight in the morning, the third-class deck, still damp from swabbing, was already filled with passengers standing and sitting about—the French, Jewish refugees from Germany, the Indians, the Vietnamese, and needless to say, the Chinese. The ocean breeze carried with it an arid heat; the scorching wind blew dry the bodies of fat people and covered them with a frosty layer of salt congealed with sweat, as though fresh from a bath in the Dead Sea in Palestine. Still, it was early morning, and people's high spirits had not yet withered or turned limp under the glare of the sun. They talked and bustled about with great zest. The Frenchmen, newly commissioned to serve as policemen in Vietnam or in the French Concession in China, had gathered around and were flirting with a coquettish young Jewish woman. Bismarck once remarked that what distinguished French ambassadors and ministers was that they couldn't speak a word of any foreign language, but these policemen, although they did not understand any German, managed to get their meaning across well enough to provoke giggles from the Jewish woman, thus proving themselves far superior to their diplomats. The woman's handsome husband, who was standing nearby, watched with pleasure, since for the last few days he had been enjoying the large quantities of cigarettes, beer, and lemonade that had been coming his way.

Once the Red Sea was passed, no longer was there fear of the intense heat igniting a fire, so, besides the usual fruit peelings, scraps of paper, bottle caps, and cigarette butts were everywhere. The French are famous for the clarity of their thought and the lucidness of their prose, yet in whatever they do, they never fail to bring chaos, filth, and hubbub, as witness the mess on board the ship. Relying on man's ingenuity and entrusted with his hopes, but loaded with his clutter, the ship sailed along amidst the noise and bustle; each minute it returned one small stretch of water, polluted with the smell of man, back to the indifferent, boundless, and never-ending ocean.

Each summer as usual a batch of Chinese students were returning home after completing their studies abroad, and about a dozen of them were aboard. Most were young people who had not as yet found employment; they were hastening back to China at the start of the summer vacation to have more time to look for jobs. Those who had no worries about jobs would wait until the cool autumn before sailing leisurely toward home. Although some of those on board had been students in France, the others, who had been studying in England, Germany, and Belgium, had gone to Paris to gain more experience of night life before taking a French ship home. Meeting at a far corner of the earth, they became good friends at once, discussing the foreign threats and internal turmoil of their motherland, wishing they could return immediately to serve her. The ship moved ever so slowly, while homesickness welled up in everyone's heart and yearned for release. Then suddenly from heaven knows where appeared two sets of mahjong, the Chinese national pastime, said to be popular in America as well. Thus, playing mahjong not only had a down-home flavor to it but was also in tune with world trends. As luck would have it, there were more than enough people to set up two tables of mahjong. So, except for eating and sleeping, they spent their entire time gambling. Breakfast was no sooner over than down in the dining room the first round of mahjong was to begin.

Up on deck were two Chinese women and one toddler, who didn't count as a full person—at least the ship's company did not consider him as one and had not made his parents buy a ticket for him. The younger woman, wearing sunglasses and with a novel spread on her lap, was elegantly dressed. Her skin would be considered fair among Orientals, but unfortunately it looked stale and dry; and even though she wore a light lipstick, her lips were a little too thin. When she removed her sunglasses, she exposed delicate eyes and eye brows, and when she rose from the canvas lounge chair, one could see how slight she was. Moreover, the outline of her figure was perhaps too sharp, as if it had been drawn with a square-nibbed pen. She could be twenty-five or twenty-six, but then the age of modern women is like the birth dates traditional women used to list on their marriage cards, whose authentication required what the experts call external evidence, since they meant nothing in and by themselves. The toddler's mother, already in her thirties, was wearing an old black chiffon Chinese dress; a face marked by toil and weariness, her slanting downward eyebrows made her look even more miserable. Her son, not yet two years old, had a snub nose, two slanted slits for eyes, and eyebrows so high up and removed from the eyes that the eyebrows and the eyes must have pined for each other—a living replica of the Chinese face in newspaper caricatures.

【延伸阅读】

[1] Bassnett, S. & Lefevere, A. *Constructing Cultures: Essays on Literary Translation* [C]. Shanghai: Shanghai Foreign Language Education Press, 2001.

[2] Borovaia, O. The Role of Translation in Shaping the Ladino Novel at the Time of Westernization in the Ottoman Empire [J]. *Jewish History*, 2002, (16):263–282.

[3] Even-Zohar, I. The Position of Translated Literature within the Literary System [J]. *Poetic Today* 11:1 (1990) p. 46.

[4] Gentzler, E. *Contemporary translation Theories* [M]. Shanghai: Shanghai Foreign Language Education Press, 2004.

[5] Hanan, P. *Chinese Fiction of the Nineteenth and Early Twentieth Centuries* [M]. New York, NY, USA: Columbia University Press, 2004.

[6] Hsia, Chih-Tsing. *Chinese Literature* [M]. New York: Columbia University Press, 2004.

[7] Hung, E. *Translation and Cultural Change* [C]. Amsterdam/Philadelphia: John Benjamins Publishing Company, 2005.

[8] Kearney, R. *Poetics of Imagining: Modern to Post-modern* [M]. New York: Fordham University Press, 1998.

[9] Pym，A. *et al*. *Beyond Descriptive Translation Studies*[C]. Amsterdam/Philadelphia：John Benjamins Publishing Company，2008.

[10] Schaffner，C. ＆ Helen K. H. *Cultural Functions of Translation*[M]. Clevedon/Philadelphia · Adelaide：Multilingual Matters Ltd. ，1995.

[11] Whited，L. A. *Ivory Tower and Harry Potter：Perspectives on a Literary Phenomenon*[M]. Columbia，MO，USA：University of Missouri Press，2002.

[12] Wong，Sau-Ling C. *Reading Asian American Literature：From Necessity to Extravagance*[M]. Ewing，NJ，USA：Princeton University Press，1993.

[13] 阿英. 晚清小说史[M]. 北京：东方出版社，1996.

[14] 包天笑. 钏影楼回忆录[M]. 北京：中国大百科全书出版社，2009.

[15] 陈平原. 二十世纪中国小说史（第一卷，1897—1916）[M]. 北京：北京大学出版社，1989.

[16] 胡翠娥. 文学翻译与文化参与——晚清小说翻译的文化研究[M]. 上海：上海外语教育出版社，2007.

[17] 谷梁. “小说界革命”与文化上海的崛起[N]. 文汇报，2002-07-01.

[18] 郭建中. 当代美国翻译理论[M]. 武汉：湖北教育出版社，2000.

[19] 郭建中，李亚舒，黄忠廉. 科普与科幻翻译：理论、技巧与实践[M]. 北京：中国对外翻译出版公司，2004.

[20] 郭延礼. 中国近代翻译文学概论[M]. 武汉：湖北教育出版社，1998.

[21] 郭延礼. 文学经典的翻译与解读——西方先哲的文化之旅[M]. 济南：山东教育出版社，2007.

[22] 胡谷明. 篇章修辞与小说翻译[M]. 上海：上海译文出版社，2004.

[23] 胡缨著. 翻译的传说[M]. 龙瑜宬，彭姗姗译. 南京：江苏人民出版社，2009.

[24] 鲁迅. 中国小说史略[M]. 北京：东方出版社，1996.

[25] 申丹. 文学文体学与小说翻译[M]. 北京：北京大学出版社，2001.

[26] 翁显良. 见全牛又不见全牛——谈小说翻译[A]. 意态由来画不成——文学翻译丛谈. 北京：中国对外翻译出版公司，1983.

[27] 严家炎. 中国现代小说流派史[M]. 北京：人民文学出版社，1995.

[28] 于中先. 我译法国新小说. http：//www. chinawriter. com. cn，2011-06-10.

[29] 樽本照雄. （新编增补）清末民初小说目录[C]. 济南：齐鲁书社，2002.

【问题与思考】

1. 翻译对于中国近现代小说的形成起到的作用有哪些？

2. 请结合清末民初小说翻译的历史事实，谈一谈你对 Itamar Even-Zohar“多元系统理论”的理解。

3. 在何种条件下翻译小说积极促进了目的语文学的改革？

4. 翻译小说的主要功绩和地位在哪里？

5. 如何看待“林译小说”的风行及传播？

6. 为什么东方国家在政治风云变化的关头，大多选择翻译西方社会的侦探小说、科幻小说等具体文类？

7. 西方小说汉译和中国小说英译各自的特色是什么?

8. 葛浩文是中国现当代文学"首席且唯一的'接生婆'"吗?

9. 请选读杨宪益、戴乃迭夫妇与霍克思所译《红楼梦》章节,并结合相关理论知识,展开分析。

10. 请阅读傅雷翻译的某一作品,结合具体文本阐释"傅雷体华文语言"说明小说翻译中的什么问题?

第七章　戏剧翻译篇

导　论

　　戏剧是由演员扮演角色,在舞台上当众表演故事情节的一种艺术,是一种综合的舞台艺术,借助文学、音乐、舞蹈、美术等艺术手段塑造舞台艺术形象,揭示社会矛盾,反映现实生活。狭义专指以古希腊悲剧和喜剧为开端,首先在欧洲各国发展起来继而在世界广泛流行的舞台演出形式,英文为 drama,中国称之为话剧。广义还包括东方一些国家、民族的传统舞台演出形式,如中国的戏曲、日本的歌舞伎、印度的古典戏剧、朝鲜的唱剧。(参见《中国大百科全书》)

　　戏剧作品是各国文学艺术一个不可或缺的重要组成部分,其在各国之间译介、流传的历史源远流长。公元前三世纪中叶开始,被誉为罗马文学三大鼻祖的安德罗尼柯、涅维乌斯和恩尼乌斯,以及后来的普劳图斯、泰伦斯等大文学家用拉丁语翻译或改编荷马史诗和埃斯库罗斯、索福克勒斯、欧里庇得斯、米南德等人的希腊戏剧作品,从而掀起欧洲乃至整个西方历史上第一次大规模的翻译高潮,开创了翻译的局面,把古希腊文学特别是戏剧介绍到罗马,促进了罗马文学的诞生和发展,对罗马以至日后西方继承古希腊文学起到了重要的桥梁作用。因此,严格说来,西方历史上的第一次翻译高潮就是戏剧作品翻译。古罗马戏剧在翻译古希腊戏剧的基础上得以形成,英国早期戏剧也是在吸取古希腊、古罗马戏剧的翻译精华中发展和繁荣起来的,而在世界戏剧翻译的基础上中国话剧逐渐成为一种新的文学创作体裁,获得极大发展。

　　从艺术表现形式看,戏剧可分为话剧、歌剧、舞剧、戏曲等,按篇幅长短可分为独幕剧、多幕剧,从内容、性质及美学范畴则可以分为悲剧、喜剧、正剧等,而从题材的时代性来分,又可以分成历史剧和现代剧。但不管哪一种形式的戏剧,其作为一种高度综合的文学艺术区别于小说、散文等其他文学形式的特点在于:戏剧艺术受演出时间和空间的限制,要求在有限的时间内,在人物有限的语言里,完美地展现广阔的斗争画面,深刻地表现丰富的思想内容,生动地刻画人物性格,因此戏剧语言比起其他文学语言呈现出一种动作化的语言特质。戏剧的语言传递不仅是“由口到耳”的过程,更是一种“从耳到眼”的过程,要使人能够“看”出其相应的特定动作、行为意图、心理意图、心理状态和情感流动,并与人物语言的个性化因素协调统一,形成有机的暗示信息,以便创造出生动突出的舞台艺术景象。

　　学术界公认文学翻译难,而诗歌、戏剧翻译尤甚,主要的原因在于戏剧文本具有双重性,一部戏剧作品既可以被视为文学作品,同时戏剧的本质又决定了它是舞台艺术的一个有机组成部分,一部戏剧的书面文本和演出文本是彼此依存、无法分割的。戏剧文本的翻译不仅涉及一个特定文本从原语到目的语的转移,还涉及很多语言学以外的因素。比如,用法语写作的比利时剧作家克罗麦林克作品 20 世纪二三十年代誉满欧洲与拉美,但是在英语国家却不受欢迎,除了文化上的差异之外,最大的困难在于话语系统不同,他的华美、抒情的文体几乎无法译成英文。

剧本台词重诗意、口语化、讲修辞、含蓄性、个性化、动作性,这六个方面的特质是构成戏剧语言舞台魅力的基本元素,却也正是译者在进行翻译操作时可能遭遇到的最大的"抗拒"翻译的因素。从语言审美接受角度来看,戏剧翻译者应该首要地考虑剧本的使用目标群。苏珊·巴斯奈特在《依旧身陷迷宫:对戏剧与翻译的进一步思考》("Still Trapped in the Labyrinth: Further Reflections on Translation and Theatre")一文中,将剧本的阅读方式分为七类:

1. 将剧本纯粹作为文学作品来阅读,此种方式多用于教学;

2. 观众对剧本的阅读,此举完全出于个人的爱好与兴趣;

3. 导演对剧本的阅读,其目的在于决定剧本是否适合上演;

4. 演员对剧本的阅读,主要为了加深对特定角色的理解;

5. 舞美对剧本的阅读,旨在从剧本的指示中设计出舞台的可视空间和布景;

6. 其他任何参与演出的人员对剧本的阅读;

7. 用于排练的剧本阅读,其中采用了很多辅助语言学的符号,例如:语气(tone)、曲折(inflexion)、音调(pitch)、音域(register)等,对演出进行准备。

译者可能与上述七种阅读方式都发生联系,这七种阅读方式实际上不仅反映了剧本的两大功能:文学作品和演出蓝本;同时,也表明了剧本翻译的两大途径:单纯作为文学作品的剧本翻译和以舞台演出为目的的剧本翻译。鉴于戏剧兼具文学性和舞台性的双重特点,苏珊·巴斯奈特明确指出,"译者除了考虑戏剧文本中动作性的翻译之外,还必须考虑可表演性与目的语观众的接受程度的兼容性"。戏剧写作和戏剧翻译的直接目的是戏剧表演,而戏剧表演的目标群体是人。因此从演出的角度看,戏剧翻译原封不动地照搬原文是不行的,而应将目的语观众的期待考虑进去。在处理译文时,仅像翻译文学作品,只注重如何把原文中丰富的词汇、联想、俗语一点不漏地介绍过去,这种只考虑是否能为读者所接受而不考虑舞台"直接效果"的做法,不仅违背戏剧创作的目的,而且会影响戏剧的传播与发展。为了使译作适合表演,满足目的语观众对戏剧译作的期待,译者可采取多种方式:如补充人物角色指示语言,关注舞台气氛和意境的烘托,同时增加剧中人物的表情动作及性格的描述,以便更好地帮助读者和演员把握角色。

本单元所选文章,既有从具体可感的语言转换角度谈论戏剧翻译具体情境的言说和从译者主体方面展开的论述,也包括从形而上的宏观文化传承、意识形态、诗学等范畴展开对戏剧翻译与文学接受的深度思考。

选文一 说说朱生豪的翻译

苏福忠

导　言

本文选自《读书》，2004 年第 5 期。

选文简要介绍莎士比亚戏剧作品的渊源，以及朱生豪选择翻译莎翁戏剧的因由，高度评价朱生豪先生所译《莎士比亚戏剧集》在中国近代英译汉历史上的划时代意义及其给中国读者带来的学术福泽。选文明确指出朱生豪在莎翁戏剧中奉行的“诗体译诗”实践，并以《威尼斯商人》第三幕第二场中的 Song 为例，具体分析朱生豪如何成功地以旧体诗对之进行翻译，既照顾到每句原文的意思，又兼顾原文的形式与用韵，一韵到底。译文朗朗上口，且翻译出了喜剧色彩。莎士比亚既博大精深，也庞杂通俗，朱生豪的翻译是在深刻体认莎翁剧作精髓基础上对其展开的汉语传递。论者结合自己从事编辑工作的深刻体会，博引朱生豪本人的翻译感悟，指出朱生豪选择极其口语化的白话文作为翻译莎士比亚戏剧极其重要的一个载体，是传统的、典雅的文言文根本无法承载的，完全译出了莎剧的风格。

　　朱生豪翻译的《莎士比亚戏剧集》（以下简称《莎剧集》）在中国近代英译汉的历史上，堪称划时代的翻译文献。他在 20 岁之前就选择了莎士比亚，会写诗放弃了写诗，会写文章放弃了写文章，潜心研读莎士比亚的作品，用他的话说：“余笃嗜莎剧，尝首尾研诵全集至十余遍，于原作精神，自觉颇有会心。”想当初，莎士比亚在伦敦戏剧舞台上功成名就，带着钱财和名誉荣归故里，享度晚年，几十个剧本是生是灭根本没往心里去。在莎士比亚死后七年（1623 年），他的两位演员朋友约翰·赫明斯和亨利·康德尔，把他的 36 个剧本收集成册，加上颂辞补充完整，付梓出版，称为“第一对折本”。人们一点没有意识到，赫明斯和康德尔仅仅出于对朋友的敬意而采取的这一行动，是启动了一个多么巨大的文化工程。这个工程进入中国，认真准备接下来进行另一种文字施工的，直到 21 世纪伊始的今天，也仍只能算朱生豪一个人。除了他，别说把莎剧全部研诵十几遍，就是一个剧本读够十遍，恐怕也很少有几个人做得到，包括《哈姆雷特》诸多译本的译家们。

　　说是运气也好，巧合也罢，重大的文学事件往往令人难以捉摸却必然会发生。朱生豪在他血气方刚时选择了莎士比亚，是莎翁的运气，是中国读者的福气。朱生豪在世界书局出版的他的大译《莎士比亚全集》（以下简称《全集》）“译者自序”里说：“中国读者耳莎翁大名已久，文坛知名之士，亦尝将其作品，译出多种，然历观坊间各译本，失之于粗疏草率者尚少，失之于拘泥生硬者实繁有徒。拘泥字句之结果,不仅原作神味,荡焉无存,甚且艰深晦涩,有若天书,令人不能卒读,此则译者之过,莎翁不能任其咎者也。"这番话有两层意思:其一,这是他调动了全部智慧与心血尝试翻译诗体莎剧后的严肃结论。读过朱译本《莎剧集》的人都知道,朱生豪在每个剧本中都尽量试着用诗体翻译莎剧里的诗;有些译作相当精彩,例如,《哈姆雷特》中的"戏中戏",《罗密欧与朱丽叶》中的大量诗篇等。其二,对莎剧在中国的翻译经过了解一些情况的人应该知道,大约在上世纪 30 年代,中英某些好事机构内定了包括徐志摩、梁实秋等人来翻译莎剧。这种行为恐怕深深刺激了默默无闻的朱生豪。朱生豪在 32 岁就译出了莎剧 31 种,莎翁地下有灵知道后都会惊愕万分的。莎翁写出他的第一个剧本《亨利六世》时 26 岁(1590 年),而最后一个剧本《亨利八世》则是在他年近 50 岁时(1612 年)写出来的,创作时间跨度为 22 年。仅以这 22 年的人生体验计,要尽可能贴近真实地理解并翻译成另一种美丽的文字,只能说是朱生豪的悟性,或者就是他与莎翁的一种默契。

朱生豪英年早逝是不幸的。但从人生能有几多运道的角度看,他可算应运而生——应中国汉语发展的运道。中国白话文冠冕堂皇地登堂入室,始于五四新文化运动。生于 1912 年的朱生豪赶上汉语白话文从不成熟走向成熟的整个过程。他的家庭出身让他打下了扎实的古文功底,新文化运动又使他的白话文得到充分的发展。他写过诗,写过杂文,白话文的使用远远高出一般人。他翻译莎剧与其说选择了散文,不如说选择了极其口语化的白话文风格。这对翻译莎士比亚戏剧是极其重要的一个载体,是传统的典雅的文言文根本无法承载的。现在我们提及朱生豪的《莎剧集》译本,笼统地称之为"散文"译本,而实际上其中有大量非常经典的诗歌翻译。选其一首欣赏一下:

Song

Tell me where is fancy bred,

Or in the heart, or in the head?

How begot, how nourished?

Reply, reply,

It is engender'd in the eyes,

With gazing fed; and Fancy dies

In the cradle where it lies:

Let us all ring Fancy's knell;

I'll begin it, —Ding, dong, bell.

—Ding, dong, bell.

这首诗从音步到音韵以及形式,都非常有特色。我们看看朱生豪如何翻译这样的诗歌。

歌

告诉我爱情生长在何方?

还是在脑海? 还是在心房?

它怎样发生? 它怎样成长?

回答我,回答我。

爱情的火在眼睛里点亮,

凝视是爱情生活的滋养,

　　　　　　　　它的摇篮便是它的坟堂。
　　　　　　　　让我们把爱的丧钟鸣响。
　　　　　　　　叮！叮！
　　　　　　　　叮！叮！

　　本诗摘自《威尼斯商人》第三幕第二场，是剧中角色唱的，最后一句"叮，叮"为合唱。以旧体诗翻译，本诗译得基本上照顾到了每句原文的 meaning（意思），形式基本相同，尾韵也基本相同，而且一韵到底，上口，还翻译出了喜剧色彩。译者不仅中英文底子厚，对民间小曲也极熟，否则很难译出这样传神的小唱小吟。如前所述，这样的译诗在朱译莎剧里数量很大，由此我们看得出朱生豪对英诗汉译所持的原则：译诗应该有译诗的形式和规则，不可机械照搬原诗的形式。

　　莎士比亚的写作究竟是怎样的形式，不妨听听英国学者的声音。比如，英国当代著名莎学家罗勃·格拉汉姆在他的《莎士比亚》的《前言》里谈到莎士比亚的写作时，这样写道：

　　　　这种写作前无古人，后无来者。他应有尽有：诗句，形象，情节，诗歌，幽默，韵律，深入细致的心理和哲学见解，所创造的隐喻，极尽思想和感情的优美和力量。然而，莎士比亚并非为后世写作；他不得不为取悦观众而写。正因如此，他的写作既有独白、洋洋洒洒的演说，又有插科打诨、出口伤人甚至不折不扣的胡说八道。他借用故事不分地点，不论国界（有些故事显然不值一借）。他笔下的人物可以俗不可耐，也可以口无遮拦，夸夸其谈，或者呼天抢地，狂泻怒斥。然而，他用心写，用才智写，用理智写，写得雄辩，写出风格。

　　这段文字道出了莎士比亚既博大与精深，也庞杂与通俗。目前不少人把莎剧当做典雅的译事来做，把莎士比亚的语言当做优美的文体，以为只有用诗体译才能接近莎士比亚，这显然是一种片面的看法。莎士比亚的戏剧写作用了近三万个单词的词汇量（一般作家充其量五六千），而且为了更富于表达力，他独创了一种属于自己的英语表达形式。用英国当代文艺批评家科里·贝尔的话说："介乎马洛与琼生两者之间，莎士比亚创造了英语的想象力，把这种语言发挥到了表达力的极致……他写出了无韵诗（亦称素体诗）——不加韵的短长格五音步诗行——一种具有无限潜力的媒质。"

　　面对这样一位富有创造精神的莎士比亚，任何所谓亦步亦趋的翻译实践，都会让他的剧作大打折扣，既存不了形，又求不了神。莎士比亚一生都在寻求突破，有些剧本全用散文体写作（如《温莎的风流娘儿们》），而有的剧本几乎全用无韵诗写就（如《朱利乌斯·恺撒》），而有的剧本段落又会使用古老的经典韵律诗，我们没有任何理由再用一个什么刻板的尺寸来翻译他的作品。这是违反莎士比亚精神的。朱生豪显然领悟到了这些，因此他在《全集》的《译者自序》里写了一段类似宣言的文字：

　　　　余译此书之宗旨，第一在求于最大可能之范围内，保持原作之神韵；必不得已而求其次，亦必以明白晓畅之字句，忠实传达原文之意趣；而于逐字逐句对照式之硬译，则未敢赞同。凡遇原文中与中国语法不合之处，往往再四咀嚼，不惜全部更易原文之结构，务使作者之命意豁然呈露，不为晦涩之字句所掩蔽。每译一段竟，必先自拟为读者，察阅译文中有无暧昧不明之处。又必自拟为舞台上之演员，审辨语调之是否顺口，音节之是否调和。一字一句之未惬，往往苦思累日。

显然,朱生豪在探寻一种最大程度上翻译出莎剧的汉语文体。中国的戏剧是唱,而外国戏剧是说。既然是说,那就万万不可脱离口语。因此,他译出了汉语版莎剧的风格,那便是口语化的文体。这是一种很了不起的文体,剧中角色不管身份如何,都能让他们声如其人;人物在喜怒哀乐的情绪支配下说出的十分极端的话,同样能表达得淋漓尽致。例如《哈姆莱特》第四幕第五场中,雷欧提斯因为父亲在宫中突然被哈姆莱特误杀,怒气冲冲地来找国王算账。他破门而入,对左右说:

> Laer：　I thank you；keep the door. O thou vile king,
> 　　　　Give me my father!
> Queen：Calmly, good laertes.
> Laer：　That drop of blood that's calm proclaims bastard,
> 　　　　Cries cuckold to my father, brands the harlot
> 　　　　Even here, between the chaste unsmireched brows
> 　　　　Of my true mother,
> King：　What is the cause, Laertes,
> 　　　　That thy rebellion looks so giant-like?

　　请留心这几句引文,读者会看出雷欧提斯的开场话是两行,但第二行只有半句,王后说的话虽低了一行,却是与上面半行接着的。后边两个人对话,同样是雷欧提斯说了半句,国王接着说下去。这种看似怪怪的排行法,实质上都是为了服务于莎翁的五音步无韵诗。甲角色说了若干音步,乙角色还可以接着说完。这在汉语诗歌来说实在不可思议,但在英语诗歌里却是理所当然。这好比中国任何戏种,唱腔和道白总是分开的,而在西方歌剧里却是张口必唱曲子的。不管你对莎剧有多么不熟悉,但只要你学过英语,一看这种英语形式,一定会感觉到莎翁的无韵诗达到了多么高的口语化程度。朱生豪对此认识得显然更为深刻,于是为了让人物角色活起来,让人物角色的语言活起来,这样译道:

> 雷欧提斯:谢谢你们;把门看好了。啊,你这万恶的奸王!还我的父亲来!
> 王后:安静一点,好雷欧提斯。
> 雷欧提斯:我身上要是有一点血安静下来,我就是个野生的杂种,我的父亲是个
> 王八,我的母亲的贞洁的额角上,也要雕上娼妓的恶名。
> 国王:雷欧提斯,你这样大张声势,兴兵犯上,究竟为了什么原因?

　　雷欧提斯的年轻气盛和怒火中烧、王后的息事宁人、国王的居心叵测和以退为进,从这些不长的对话中看得清清楚楚,甚至超出了原文表达的内涵。在继续进行的对话中,当国王问雷欧提斯是否不分敌友,见人就要报仇时,又出现了这样的对话:

> Laer：None but his enemies.

　　这半句话的意思是:只跟他的敌人报仇申冤,但朱译道:

> 雷欧提斯:冤有头,债有主,我只要找我父亲的敌人算账。

　　译文看似多出"冤有头,债有主",但绝无半点发挥,只是把英语 none 充分调动到了极致,却又是百分之百的口语化。翻译莎士比亚的作品既要死扣 meaning(意思),又必须注意

information（信息），message（启示）和 image（形象）的综合传达，否则别说翻译莎士比亚的作品，就是一般作家的作品，也很难说把翻译做到了位。

由于工作关系，我比较仔细、系统地接触莎剧是在上世纪 90 年代中。我知道许多赞赏朱译莎剧的人都认为他的译文典雅优美、才气横溢，而我在研读他的译文时却每每被他译文的口语化程度深深折服。我至今想象不出那是 50 多年前的译文。要知道，能够熟练地富于创造性地驾驭口语，是运用语言的最高境界。朱译莎剧在解放后没有被淘汰，在很大程度上是顺应了白话文更加大众化（即口语化）的趋势。

　　我到文学出版社的时候，出版社已经印出一本洋洋大观的五年出书计划，差不多把英语文学作品所有有名气的都列在上面。莎士比亚当然是一个重点。当时编辑部已经决定抛弃朱生豪的译本，另外组织人翻译莎士比亚。我把朱生豪的本子仔细看看，觉得译得很不错，现在要赶上他可不是一件容易的事。编辑部抛弃朱译的一个很重要的理由是，朱译是散文体，想搞成一个诗体的新版本莎士比亚。那时候已经有两个所谓"自由诗体"的版本印行了。我对比着一看，所谓的诗体也不过是将散文拆成许多行写出来而已，根本说不上有什么诗的味道，而且文字本来就不高明，加上要凑成诗体，就更显得别扭。我觉得总的讲来，新译本远远赶不上朱生豪的旧译。朱生豪的中文很有修养，文字十分生动，而且掌握了原剧中不同人的不同口气。我为了说服编辑部的同志，曾经不止一次在办公室里朗诵朱生豪的翻译和新译中的相同段落，我问他们到底哪个听起来舒服得多。最后终于让编辑部的同志同意我的意见，仍保留朱生豪的旧译，可以分别找人校订一下，补入文学出版社出版的莎士比亚全集。

　　这件事我做得很痛快，觉得做了一件有意义的事。实在说，我认为用自由诗体翻译莎士比亚是一件十分困难的事。因为所谓的 blank verse 有它的一套规律，对中国读者完全陌生。如果非要翻成诗体，不用说是十分困难的；如果当时没有这一改变，莎士比亚全集恐怕到今天也出不来，而且朱生豪的翻译从此埋没下去，实在是一件很可惜的事。

我在这里不惜篇幅引用这样两段文字，当然是因为它们十分珍贵。这是我的前辈编辑黄雨石先生的录音整理稿。黄雨石先生本打算写一本自传，说说这些历史陈迹，但可惜上世纪 90 年代初突然患了帕金森病，且病情每况愈下。后来，我力劝他用录音形式口述一些自己特别想说的话。他做了，虽片片断断，难成文章，但近两万字的自述材料仍是十分珍贵的。

我们差一点与朱生豪的汉译莎剧失之交臂！但是我们没有，除了应该感谢黄雨石以及其他有见地的编辑之外，自然还是因为朱生豪的译文是金子，货真价实，没有因为改朝换代而被淘汰。上世纪 50 年代出版社甄别了一大批新中国成立前的译本，被淘汰的绝大部分是因文字不文不白，佶屈聱牙。能保证译文明白晓畅的最好保障是口语化：生动、活泼、诙谐、幽默和文采。口语本身就有高低之分。这全取决于译者对语言、生活和环境的领悟。朱生豪，据他的夫人宋如清在《全集》的《译者介绍》里所写："在学校时代，笃爱诗歌，对于新旧体，都有相当的成就，清丽，自然，别具作风。"又说："他在高中时期，就已经读过不少英国诸大诗人的作品，感到莫大的兴趣，所以他与他们的因缘，实在不浅。"

　　每读朱译莎剧，我都会想到朱生豪与莎士比亚的因缘"实在不浅"。他能把莎剧翻译得通俗易懂而文采四溢，实在是因为他完全理解、吃透并消化了莎剧的缘故。借工作之便，这些年比较系统地阅读朱译莎剧，我认为主要成就有以下几点特别之处：朱生豪提炼出来的口语化译文，是其最大特色，也与莎剧的文字风格最合拍，因为有口语化做基础，译文的表达力极强，剧中各类人物的语言都能体现出他们的身份；朱译本中大量的诗体译文，十分珍贵，是译者用改革的旧体诗翻译莎剧中的散诗的可贵尝试；译本对剧中部分人物用有含义的汉语名字，例如"试金石"、"快嘴桂嫂"等，颇具文学味道；据我对其他译本的粗略统计，较之所有别的译本，朱译莎剧的词汇量是最大的，这与莎剧中独一无二的大词汇量十分吻合。最重要的是，他告诉后来者如何翻译莎士比亚的作品。

　　诚然，翻译作品历来总有遗憾之处，朱译莎剧也不能例外。朱译莎剧"谬误之处，自知不免"，益因"乡居僻陋，既无参考之书籍，又鲜质疑之师友"造成的。今天，我们所拥有的条件十分优越，应该珍惜朱译莎剧，纠正错误和不妥之处，使之更上一层楼。

　　朱译莎剧的划时代意义在于英汉两种文字互相"移植"中的空前吻合。尽管到目前为止出了几种不同译法的莎剧版本，但是仍然没有任何一种译本超过朱生豪的译本，这是不争的事实。至于理由，前面已经谈到很多，而我始终看重的另一个原因是：朱生豪在翻译莎士比亚戏剧的时候，消耗的是他22岁到32岁这样充满才情、诗意、热情、血气方刚而义无反顾的精华年龄段！这是任何译家比不了的。很难想象七老八十的头脑会把莎剧中的激情和厚重转达多少！诚如朱在完成莎剧大部分翻译时写给他弟弟朱文振的信中所说："不管几日可以出书，总之已替中国近百年来翻译界完成了一件最艰巨的工程。"

　　（《莎士比亚戏剧集》，朱生豪译，人民文学出版社，1958年版，九卷）

选文二　与王尔德拔河记
——《不可儿戏》译后
余光中

导　言

　　本文选自余光中著，《余光中谈翻译》，中国对外翻译出版公司（北京），2002年版。

　　选文首先介绍王尔德在世界文坛的重要性，以及"五四"以来中国文艺界对其作品的翻译、介绍和接受情况。然而，出于种种原因，王尔德剧本中译情况却不尽如人意。长期的翻译教学需要，余光中先生立意将《不可儿戏》译成中文，与更多的中国读者分享。动笔之前，论者对王尔德作品中抗拒翻译的因素了然于胸，并定下"要译原意，不要译原文"的准则。选文结合翻译《不可儿戏》的具体过程，分析了剧本中对话翻译的表演性、译文语言的口语化、四字结构在剧本翻译中的优势、长句的顺（逆）译选择等形形色色的问题和困难。对于彰显王尔德机锋犀利、妙语逼人特色的双声、文字游戏等语言"趣克"，余光中先生则用实例说明创造性翻译的有效性。

　　《不可儿戏》（*The Importance of Being Earnest*）不但是王尔德最流行最出色的剧本，也是他一生的代表杰作。批评家对他的其他作品，包括诗与小说，都见仁见智，唯独对本剧近乎一致推崇，认为完美无陷，是现代英国戏剧的奠基之作。王尔德自己也很得意，叫它做"给正人看的闲戏"（a trivial comedy for serious people），又对人说："不喜欢我的五个戏，有两种不喜欢法。一种是都不喜欢，另一种是只挑剩《不可儿戏》。"

然而"五四"以来，他的五部戏里，中国人最耳熟的一部却是《少奶奶的扇子》（*Lady Windermere's Fan*）。这是 1925 年洪深用来导演的改译本，由上海大通图书社出版。此剧尚有潘家洵的译本，名为《王德米尔夫人的扇子》。两种译本我都未看过，不知谁先谁后。其他的几部，据说曾经中译者尚有《莎乐美》和《理想丈夫》；《莎乐美》译者是田汉，《理想丈夫》的译者不详。至于《不可儿戏》，则承宋淇见告，他的父亲春舫先生曾有中译，附在《宋春舫论剧》五册之中，却连他自己也所藏不全了。剩下最后的一部《无足轻重的女人》，未闻有无译本。

60 年来，王尔德在中国的文坛上几乎无人不晓。早在 1917 年 2 月，陈独秀的《文学革命论》里，就已把他和歌德、狄更斯、雨果、左拉等并列，当做取法西洋文学的对象了。然而迄今他的剧本中译寥落，究其原因或有三端。一是唯美主义的名义久已成为贬词，尤为写实的风尚所轻。二是王尔德的作品说古典不够古，说现代呢又不够新。但是最大的原因，还是王尔德的对话机锋犀利，妙语逼人，许多好处只能留在原文里欣赏，不能带到译文里去。

我读《不可儿戏》，先后已有十多年；在翻译班上，也屡用此书做口译练习的教材，深受同学欢迎。其实不但学生喜欢，做老师的也愈来愈入迷。终于有一天，我认为长任这么一本绝妙好书锁在原文里面，中文的读者将永无分享的机会，真的是"悠然心会，妙处难与君说"。要说与君听，只有动手翻译。

当然，王尔德岂是易译之辈？《不可儿戏》里的警句隽言，真是五步一楼，十步一阁，不，简直是五步一关，十步一寨，取经途中，岂止八十一劫？梁实秋说得好：英文本来就不是为翻译而设。何况王尔德当年写得眉飞色舞，兴会淋漓，怎么还会为未来的译者留一条退路呢？身为译者，只有自求多福，才能绝处逢生了。

我做译者一向守一个原则：要译原意，不要译原文。只顾表面的原文，不顾后面的原意，就会流于直译、硬译、死译。最理想的翻译当然是既达原意，又存原文。退而求其次，如果难存原文，只好就径达原意，不顾原文表面的说法了。试举二例说明：

> Algernon：How are you, my dear Earnest? What brings you up to town?
>
> Jack：　　Oh, pleasure, pleasure! What else should bring one anywhere?

这是第一幕开始不久的对话。杰克的答话，如果只译原文，就成了"哦，乐趣，乐趣！什么别的事该带一个人去任何地方吗？"这样，表面是忠于原文了，其实并未照顾到原意，等于不忠。这种直译，真是"阳奉阴违"。我的译文是"哦，寻欢作乐呀！一个人出门，还为了别的吗？"

> Lady Bracknell：Where is that baby?
>
> Miss Prism：　　Lady Bracknell, I admit with shame that I do not know. I only wish I could.

这是第三幕接近剧终的一段，为全剧情节所系，当然十分重要。答话的第二句如果译成"我但愿我能够知道"，错是不错，也听得懂，可是不传神，所以无力。我把它译成"要是我知道就好了"。这虽然不是原文，却是原意。要是王尔德懂中文，也会这么说的。

以前我译过诗、小说、散文、论文，译剧本这却是第一次。当然小说里也有对话，可说和剧本相通。不过小说人物的对话不必针锋相对,更少妙语如珠。戏剧的灵魂全在对话,对话的灵魂全在简明紧凑,入耳动心。讽世浪漫喜剧如这本《不可儿戏》,尤其如此。小说的对话是给人看的,看不懂可以再看一遍。戏剧的对话却是给人听的,听不懂就过去了,没有第二次的机会。我译此书,不但是为中国的读者,也为中国的观众和演员。所以这一次我的翻译原则是:读者顺眼,观众入耳,演员上口。(其实观众该是听众,或者该叫观听众。这一点,英文的说法是方便多了。)希望我的译本 是活生生的舞台剧,不是死板板的书斋剧。

因此,本书的译笔和我译其他文体时大异其趣。读我译诗的人,本身可能就是诗人,或者是个小小学者。将来在台下看这戏的,却是大众,至少是小众了。我的译文必须调整到适度的口语化,听起来才像话。同样的字眼,尤其是名词,更尤其是抽象名词,就必须译得响亮易懂,否则台下人听了无趣,台上人说来无光。例如下面这一段:

> Gwendolen: Earnest has a strong upright nature. He is the very soul of truth and honour. Disloyalty would be as impossible to him as deception.

抽象名词这么多,中文最难消化。末句如果译成"不忠对于他将如欺骗一样不可能",台上和台下势必都显得有点愚蠢。我的译文是"他绝对不会见异思迁,也不会做假骗人"。千万不要小看中文里四字词组或四字成语的用处。在新诗和散文里,它也许不宜多用,但在一般人的口头或演员的台词里,却听来响亮而稳当,入耳便化。

> Lady Bracknell: Sit down immediately. Hesitation of any kind is a sign of mental decay in the young, of physical weakness in the old.

第二句的抽象名词也不少。尤其句首的一词,如果只译成二字词组"犹豫"或"迟疑",都会显得突兀不稳。我是这样译的:"犹豫不决,无论是什么姿态,都显示青年人的智力衰退,老年人的体力虚弱。"

遇见长句时,译者要解决的难题,往往首在句法,而后才是词语。对付繁复长句之道,不一而足,有时需要拆开重拼,有时需要首尾易位。一般译者只知顺译(即依照原文次序),而不知逆译才像中文,才有力。

> Lady Bracknell: I should be much obliged if you would ask Mr. Bunbury, from me, to be kind enough not to have a relapse on Saturday, for I rely on you to arrange my music for me.

这种句法顺译不得。我便拆而复装,成为"要是你能替我求梁勉仁先生做做好事,别尽挑礼拜六来发病,我就感激不尽了,因为我还指望你为我安排音乐节目呢"。

> Miss Prism: I do not think that even I could produce any effect on a character that according to his own brother's admission is irretrievably weak and vacillating. I am not in favor of this modern mania for turning bad people into good people at a moment's notice.

两个长句,或因附属子句尾大难掉,或因介系词片语一层层相套,都不宜顺译。我的译文是:"他自己的哥哥都承认他性格懦弱,意志动摇,到了不可救药的地步;对这种人,我看连我也起不了什么作用。一声通知，就要把坏蛋变成好人，现代人的这种狂热我也不赞成。"看得出，两句都是逆译了。还请注意，两句译文都以动词结尾，正说明了在不少情况下，英文句子可拖一条受词的长尾巴，中文就拖不动。所以我往往先解决复杂迤长的受词，再施以回马一枪。

其他的难题形形色色，有的可以克服，有的可以半悬半决，有的只好放弃。例如典故，此剧用典不多，我一律把它通俗化了，免得中国观众莫名其妙。像 Gorgon 就译成"母夜叉"；It is rather Quixotic of you 就译成"你真是天真烂漫"。如果译诗，我大概会保留原文的专有名词。最好笑的一句是电铃忽响，亚吉能说："啊！这一定是欧姨妈。只有亲戚或者债主上门，才会把电铃按得这么惊天动地。"后面一句本来是 Only relatives, or creditors, ever ring in that Wagnerian manner. 我个人是觉得好笑极了。因为这时华格纳刚死不久，又是萧伯纳一再鼓吹的歌剧大师，以气魄见长。可惜这典故懂的人固然一听到就好笑，不懂的人一定更多。

双声是另一个问题。拜伦《哀希腊》之 the hero's harp, the lover's lute，胡适译为"英雄瑟与美人琴"，音调很畅，但不能保留双声。双声与双关，是译者的一双绝望。有时或可乞援于代用品。例如 I hear her hair has turned quite gold from grief. 最后三字是从 grey from grief 变来的，妙在双声之格未破。我译成"听说她的头发因为伤心变色像黄金"。双声变做叠韵，算是妥协。

最难缠的当然是文字游戏，尤其是一语双关，偏偏王尔德又最擅此道。从本书中，有不少这样的"趣克"(trick)都给我应付了过去。有时候实在走不通，只好变通绕道，当然那"趣克"也变质了。例如下面的对话：

Jack： Well, that is no business of yours.
Algernon： If it was my business, I wouldn't talk about it. It is very vulgar to
talk about one's business. Only people like stockbrokers do that,
and then merely at dinner parties.

这不能算是王尔德最精彩的台词，可是其中 business 一字造成的双关"趣克"却成了译者的克星。我只好绕道躲它，把 stockbroker 改成"政客"，成了"要是跟我有关系，我才不讲呢。讲关系最俗气了。只有政客那种人才讲关系，而且只在饭桌上讲"。

有时候变通变出来的新"趣克"，另有一番胜境，想王尔德看了也不免一笑。例如，劳小姐劝蔡牧师结婚，有这样的妙语：

Miss Prism： You should get married. A misanthrope I can understand—a
womanthrope, never!

劳小姐咬文嚼字，把 misogynist（憎恨女人者）误成 womanthrope，但妙在和前文的 misanthrope 押同一格式，虽然不通，却很难缠。如果我不接受挑战，只译成"一个厌世者我可以了解——一个厌女者，决不！"当然没有大错，可是听众不懂之外，还漏掉了那半通不通的怪字。最后我是这样变通的："一个人恨人类而要独善其身，我可以了解——一个人恨女人而要独抱其身，就完全莫名其妙！"

王尔德用人名也有深意。主角杰克原名 Earnest，当然是和 earnest 双关，我也用谐音的"任真"。"梁勉仁"当然是影射"两面人"。劳小姐原文为 Miss Prism，取其音近 prim（古板）。我改为"劳"，暗寓"牢守西西丽"之意，因为它音近 prison，何况她也真是"老小姐"呀。

最后要交代的是：《不可儿戏》写成于 1894 年，首演于 1895 年，出版于 1899 年；1952 年曾拍电影。王尔德的初稿把背景设在 18 世纪，不但情节更为复杂，而且还比今日的版本多出整整一幕来。终于他听从了演出人兼演员乔治·亚历山大的劝告,把初稿删节成今日的三幕,整曲戏才畅活起来。可见即使才高八斗,也需要精益求精,才能修成正果。

不过王尔德毕竟是天才。当日他写此剧,是利用与家人去华兴(书中提到的海边小镇)度假的空暇,只花了三星期就完成的。我从今年2月初译到3月中,花了一倍的时间。王尔德的妙语警句终于捧到中国读者和观众的面前,了却了我十几年来的一桩心愿。

俏皮如王尔德,读了我的译本,一定忍不住会说:So you have presented me in a new version of Sinicism? It never occurred to me I could be made so Sinical.

萧条异代不同时。只可惜,他再也听不到自己从没讲过的这句妙语了。

1983年清明节黄昏
王尔德的幽灵若在左右

选文三　Theatre and Opera Translation

Mary Snell-Hornby

导　言

本文选自 Piotr Kuhiwczak & Karin Littau, *A Companion to Translation Studies*. Clevedon & Buffalo & Toronto: Multilingual Matters Ltd., 2006.

1848年,德国著名作家路德维希·蒂克(Ludwig Tieck)在致歌剧《埃莱克特拉》译者的一封信中对于译文语言的戏剧性、自然流畅和地道给予高度肯定。选文基于此段引文的基础之上,提出戏剧翻译的忠实原则与戏剧翻译的可表演性之间的张力——文字翻译还是舞台翻译?选文接着描述了翻译研究视域中的舞台剧翻译演变过程,依次介绍了20世纪70年代的新方法、新观念,80、90年代的独立理论构架——符号学方法和整体性方法。选文从社会文化学角度分析戏剧文本与听众的关系,进而具体分析歌剧翻译、歌剧唱词字幕翻译、舞台剧译者与演员阵容之间的关系等问题。经过一番具体细致的分析和描画,选文提出“翻译还是改编”这一刻不容缓的对立命题,并有针对地描画歌剧文本的翻译前景。

Introduction: Page or Stage?

Up until the 1980s the theatre was a neglected field in translation studies. In the world of academe the stage play was traditionally viewed as a work of literature, and in translating the dramatic text the same scholarly criteria (such as equivalence or faithfulness) were applied as to other types of literary translation. There were of course notable exceptions: in

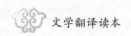

1848 Ludwig Tieck, in his famous "Letter to the Translator of Elektra", wrote as follows:

> *Denn das scheint mir ein Hauptvorzug Ihrer Übersetzung, dass die Sprache so ganz dramatisch, so ungeschwächt und ungezwungen ist, dass sie jedes Mal Leidenschaft richtig ausdrückt, ohne die oft etwas linkischen und erzwungenen Wendungen zu gebrauchen, in welche der Gelehrte, der Philologe oft verfällt, der sich nicht die wirkliche Rede, den natürlichen wahren Dialog des Theaters deutlich machen kann. (Tieck, 1848: 420f.)*

(For to me it seems to be one of the chief merits of your translation that the language is so entirely dramatic, so natural and undiluted that it is always a genuine vehicle of passion, without resorting to the often rather awkward and strained expressions frequently adopted by the scholar, the man of letters, who is unable to produce real spoken language, the true and natural dialogue of the theatre. *My translation.*)

Among literary scholars and the theatre world, the question of the faithful scholarly translation of dramatic dialogue on the one hand and the "actable", "performable" stage text on the other has been a common bone of contention. In the late 1950s, there was a furore created among German academics—and fought out in the national weekly *Die Zeit*—by the Shakespeare translator Hans Rothe. His explicit aim was to produce, not a faithful reproduction of the printed English version with its wealth of imagery and meanwhile barely comprehensible allusions, but a text to be performed and understood on the mid-20th century German stage (Schröder *et al.*, 1959).

The Stage Play in Translation Studies

The 1970s: New Approaches and New Concepts

At this time translation studies had not yet established itself as a modern academic discipline, and the topic of translating for the stage was broached by only a few individual literary scholars (e. g. Levý, 1969; Mounin, 1967; Bednarz, 1969) and translators (e. g. Corrigan, 1961; Brenner-Rademacher, 1965; Hamberg, 1966; Hartung, 1965; Sahl, 1965). Once again, the debate centred round the question of the "actable", "performable" stage text on the one hand and the faithful scholarly translation on the other. Theatre practitioners also objected that translated theatre texts often had to be changed during rehearsals to make them suitable for a stage performance (cf. Snell-Hornby, 1984). Early impulses from the emerging interdisciplinary perspectives of translation studies, though still within the framework of literary studies, came in the 1970s, in particular from the international colloquium "Literature and translation" held in Leuven in April, 1976. In her contribution, "Translating spatial poetry: An examination of theatre texts in performance",

Susan Bassnett described a play as "much more than a literary text, it is a combination of language and gesture brought together in a harmonious frame of timing" (Bassnett-McGuire, 1978: 161), and she presents "patterns of tempo-rhythm" and "basic undertextual rhythms" as new key concepts. In the French-speaking scientific community a semiotic approach was adopted: Anne Übersfeld (1978: 153) describes the theatre text as one that merges into a dense pattern of synchronic signs, and Patrice Pavis (1976) equates the staging of a written text, the *mis en scène*, with a *mis en signe*.

The 1980s and 1990s: Developing Independent Theoretical Approaches

The early contributions on stage translation unanimously point out that at the time this was an area previously ignored by translation theory, and it was during the course of the 1980s that the deficit was corrected. The first major step was to describe the specific characteristics of the dramatic text and what makes it so different from other kinds of literary text. One striking feature is that the stage text as such consists of two clearly separate components: the stage directions on the one hand and the spoken dialogue on the other. It is above all this latter component that is meant when the term "stage translation" is used. In her text typology of 1971 the German translation scholar Katharina Reiß had already identified "audiomedial" (later "multimedial") texts as those written, not to be read silently, but to be spoken or sung, and that are hence dependent on a non-verbal medium or on other non-verbal forms of expression, both acoustic and visual, to reach their intended audience. Unlike the case of the novel, short story or lyric poem, in multimedial texts the verbal text is only one part of a larger and complex whole—and this poses particular problems for translation. Examples of multimedial texts in this definition are film scripts, radio plays, opera libretti and drama texts. The latter two share the characteristic that they are written specifically for live performance on the stage, and they have been compared with a musical score which only realises its full potential in the theatrical performance (Snell-Hornby, 1984; Totzeva, 1995).

The Semiotic Approach

The theatrical sign as icon, index and symbol

In the early 1980s semiotics, as the study of signs, was systematically applied as a basis for the theoretical discussion of drama (Fischer-Lichte, 1983). The concept of the sign is indeed helpful in explaining the basic workings of theatre, particularly in the famous trichotomy established by Charles S. Peirce, according to which a sign can be an *icon*, an *index* or a *symbol*:

> A sign can refer to an Object by virtue of an inherent similarity ("likeness") between them (*icon*), by virtue of an existential contextual connection of spatiotemporal (physical) contiguity between sign and object (*index*), or by virtue of a general law or cultural convention that permits sign and object to be interpreted as connected (*symbol*). (cf. Gorlée, 1994: 51)

The system of signs belonging to the world of the theatre presents a kaleidoscope of these three types, and the differentiation between them is essential for the spectator's interpretation of what he/she is seeing and hearing on stage. An iconic sign (such as a Tudor costume in a naturalistic production or a table set for dinner) can be taken as it stands, and it is fully interpretable as long as the spectator can situate it in context. An indexical sign is interpretable as long as the spectator can understand the point of connection (e. g. that smoke can stand for fire). A symbolic sign is only understandable if the spectator is familiar with its meaning in the culture concerned (e. g. that in Western cultures black is the colour of mourning). The theatrical experience varies with the spectator's previous experience and knowledge, and hence with his/her ability to arrange and interpret the abundance of sensory perceptions conveyed to him/her by the performance. The problem for stage translation is that the interpretation of the signs can also vary radically from one culture to another (particularly so with symbolic signs: the colour of mourning in Asiatic cultures for example is white), and much even depends on the acting styles and stage conventions of the country or cultural community concerned.

The above observations referred only to non-verbal signs. What is important for verbal language, and is therefore of special significance for translation, is the insight that the linguistic sign is essentially arbitrary and symbolic. In other words it is interpretable only if the recipient (or spectator) is familiar with its position or meaning within the language system and culture concerned. And this is where the stage text assumes its significance as dramatic potential.

Paralanguage, kinesics, proxemics and the stage text

As well as their potential for interpretation as signs, the naked words of the printed stage text provide a basis for action and co-ordination with the immediate environment of the dramatic world in which they are to be embedded. The means for such co-ordination are *paralinguistic*, *kinesic* and *proxemic*. The basic paralinguistic features concern vocal elements such as intonation, pitch, rhythm, tempo, resonance, loudness and voice timbre leading to expressions of emotion such as shouting, sighing or laughter. Kinesic features are related to body movements, postures and gestures and include smiling, winking, shrugging or waving (Poyatos, 1993). Proxemic features involve the relationship of a figure to the stage environment, and describe its movement within that environment and its varying distance or physical closeness to the other characters on stage.

The performability of a stage text as a dramatic "score" is closely connected with the possibilities it offers for generating such vocal elements, gestures and movements within the framework of its interpretability as a system of theatrical signs. An outstanding example of the performable stage text—not unsurprisingly taken from Shakespeare—with paralinguistic, kinesic and proxemic potential is Macbeth's famous monologue before the murder of Duncan, "Is this a dagger which I see before me?" What is generated by the text is a kind of optical illusion, described by Nicholas Brooke in his edition of *The Tragedy of Macbeth* as follows:

Words play a great part here, but not words alone: the invisible dagger is necessarily created also by his body, gesture, and above all by his eyes, which focus on a point in space whose emptiness becomes, in a sense, visible to the audience. (Brooke, 1990: 4)

The focusing of the eyes on a point in space is the natural consequence of various verbal elements in the text—including the reiterated phrase "I see (thee)". It is also a consequence of the personification of the object throughout the passage, whereby its presence is established in a quasi-dialogue as a kind of partner with whom the speaker naturally maintains eye contact. In this case the dramatic effect arises from the interaction of word, gesture and motion needed to create the ominous vision of the poised dagger. Usually, however, in dramatic discourse such interaction takes place within the framework of real dialogue involving two or more partners. Here, too, the same principle applies: the performability of the verbal text depends on its capacity for generating non-verbal action and effects within its scope of interpretation as a system of theatrical signs (ef. Snell-Hornby, 1997). Sometimes the methods used by the dramatist are amazingly simple: misunderstandings arising from puns, for example, differing social conventions, irony or multiple associations have for centuries been the essence of stage dialogue.

The Holistic Approach

For the concert-goer the musical score is usually an abstract entity rationally analyzed only by the musicologist or critic: what counts is the global sensory effect of the music itself. A similar relationship exists between the stage text and the dramatic performance. But it is quite possible to analyse the dramatic score and identify the basic factors that make up its theatrical potential. The key words, much discussed over the last 20 years but still only vaguely defined, are *performability/actability* (*jouabilité/Spielbarkeit*) as discussed above, *speakability* (*Sprechbarkeit*), and in the case of the opera or musical *singability* (*Sangbarkeit*). What is considered performable, speakable or singable depends to a great extent on the theatrical tradition and on the acting styles of the language community involved. Back in 1985 Susan Bassnett aptly described the difference between British, German and Italian acting styles:

British classical acting requires the actor to physicalise the text, to reinforce possible textual obscurities with kinesic signs, to push forward through the language of the text, even at times *against* the text. The German tradition, which is more intensely intellectual, tends to the opposite extreme—the text acquires a weightiness that the spatial context reinforces and it is the text that carries the actor forward rather than the reverse. The Italian tradition of virtuosity on the part of the individual actor creates yet another type of performance style: the text of the play becomes the actor's instrument and the performance of that play is an orchestration of many different instruments playing together. (Bassnett-McGuire,

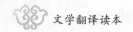

Given such divergences, it seems inevitable that precise and at the same time generally accepted definitions will remain utopian. The term *speakability* (*Sprechbarkeit*) was discussed in detail in the 1960s by Jiří Levý (1969), for whom speakable language depends on the interplay of syntax and rhythm, vowels and consonants. More recently, in 1984, the term was complemented by the concept of *Atembarkeit* ("*breathability*"), which was introduced by the German stage director Ansgar Haag (1984) and means that stress patterns and sentence structures should fit inwith the emotions expressed in the dialogue. All these features contribute towards making a text performable, a phenomenon that I investigated in the 1980s, partly on the basis of interviews with a stage producer and an actor from the Schauspielhaus in Zürich (Snell-Hornby, 1984). The conclusions I then reached, which contain various criteria of performability, can be summarised as follows (ef. Snell-Hornby, 1996):

(1) Theatre dialogue is essentially an *artificial language*, written to be spoken, but never identical with ordinary spoken language. If we compare a stage dialogue with a transcription of normal conversation, we find that the dialogue is characterised by special forms of textual cohesion, by semantic density, highly sophisticated forms of ellipsis, often rapid changes of theme, and special dynamics of deictic interaction offering large scope for interpretation. This is what since Stanislavsky has been known as the sub-text, which, as Harold Pinter put it, is "the language where, under what is said, another thing is being said" (Brown, 1972:18).

(2) It is characterised by an *interplay of multiple perspectives*, resulting from the simultaneous interaction of different factors and their effect on the audience. Eminently effective on the stage are elements of paradox, irony, allusion, wordplay, anachronism, climax, sudden anticlimax and so on (as demonstrated in innumerable examples by Shakespeare or Stoppard).

(3) Theatre language can be seen as *potential action in rhythmical progression*; in this sense rhythm does not only refer to stress patterns within sentences, but also involves the inner rhythm of intensity as the plot or action progresses, the alternation of tension and rest, suspense and calm. This also applies to the structure of the dialogue, whereby rhythm is closely bound up with the tempo, which is faster in an exchange of short, sharp utterances and slows down in long sentences with complicated syntax.

(4) For the actor his/her lines combine to form a kind of individual idiolect, a "*mask of language*". For him or her, language is primarily a means of expressing emotion, through the voice, facial expression, gestures and

movements. The dramatic discourse and the actor's performance should form a coherent and convincing whole, hence the demand for translations which are speakable, breathable and performable.

(5) For the *spectator* in the audience, language and the action on stage are perceived sensuously, as a more or less personal experience; he/she is not just a bystander, looking on curiously but uninvolved. As long as the stage events are convincing, the spectator should feel drawn into them and respond to them—either through empathy or alienation.

Theatre and Audience: The Sociocultural Perspective

A "good" theatre text is invariably described by theatre practitioners as one that "works", and hence it must be interpretable by both actors and audience. To explain these mechanisms in terms of stage translation, Sirkku Aaltonen extended the semiotic approach to include a sociocultural perspective:

> In order to understand what is going on stage, the audience needs to be able to decode, if not all, at least a sufficient minimum of the signs and sign systems within the text. In consequence, adjustments may be made in the translation process in relation to the general cultural conventions covering the language, manners, moral standards, rituals, tastes, ideologies, sense of humour, superstitions, religious beliefs, etc. (Aaltonen, 1997: 93)

In other words, a translated text is closely bound up with the sociocultural circumstances of its conception:

> Although the text will always mean different things to different individuals and a multitude of meanings will always arise from the interaction between the content of the signs it emits and the spectator's competence to decode them, it all still happens in particular social and historical circumstances. When John Millington Synge wrote *The Playboy of the Western World*, it gave rise to riots in Dublin. It could never have the same impact again in another time or culture. The further the text recedes in time, the less relevant become the original meanings, and the more different the "message". The great advantage of stage drama lies in the fact that each translation and performance can take the particular cultural, social, historical and geographical situation of its audience into account and adapt the play to these changing circumstances. (Aaltonen, 1997: 94)

These apt observations focus on yet another special characteristic of stage translation as compared with the "faithfulness" required for "sacred originals" as in Bible translation or narrative prose. The need to adapt the play to changing circumstances applies particularly where, as with *The Playboy of the Western World*, specific historic circumstances or

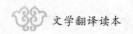

outdated ethical principles are involved. Similar scandals accompanied the first productions of Molière's *Tartuffe*, Oscar Wilde's *Salome* and Arthur Schnitzler's *Reigen*, for example—for reasons that would be completely foreign to a modern audience.

The relationship between stage text and audience has been further investigated by Fabienne Hörmanseder (2001) who, in her list of basic criteria for a successful stage text, has added to those discussed above the features *Hörbarkeit* ("audibility"), *Fasslichkeit* ("comprehensibility") and *Klarheit* ("clarity").

It is, however, important to stress that no concrete, universally applicable rules can be drawn up for applying the terms discussed here. Actors are given intensive training in articulation and breathing techniques, and hence can master language that the layperson might consider "unspeakable", but which the dramatist used deliberately to create tension or special effects, and terms like "speakability" or "comprehensibility" must remain relative to the production and situation concerned.

Opera Translation

With texts written to be sung on stage—as in the case of opera or musicals—the problems only increase. The issue of opera translation has been investigated by Klaus Kaindl (1995), who advocates an approach that is interdisciplinary (combining insights from theatre studies, literary studies and musicology) and holistic—whereby the opera text becomes a synthesis of the libretto, music and performance (both vocal and scenic). The criteria of "performability" and "breathability" are here complemented by that of "singability" (Sangbarkeit). The call for singable opera texts is nothing new in the field—back in 1935 Edward Dent (1935: 83) stated clearly: "It is essential to have words which can be easily sung and pronounced on the particular notes or musical phrases where they occur." One of the basic rules here is that open vowels like /a/ are especially suitable for high notes and /o/ and /u/ for low notes, whereas consonant clusters are problematic. This applies especially with fast tempos that require rapid articulation from the singer.

This means that the translator of musical texts is faced with a challenging task. In her study of the translation of modern musicals, Claudia Lisa (1993) interviewed Herbert Kretzmer, the translator of the English text of *Les Misérables*, who correlated singability with characterisation. In describing his work, Kretzmer made the following remarks:

> I never finish a translation for Aznavour until I hear him sing a song. When I hear him sing the song there is (sic) always half a dozen ideas that come to me or certain words can be mistaken or misconstrued, or I can see that on that particular note of music the word I have given it does not sound right. It is to nasal or whatever and it needs a more open sound. (Lisa, 1993: 66)

Examples of the interplay of music, vocal performance and language are given by Kaindl (1995) in his discussion of Carmen and of various renderings through the centuries of the aria

"*Fin ch'han dal vino*" in *Don Giovanni*, where it becomes clear that in opera, to an even more drastic extent than in spoken drama, the verbal text is only one of a whole complex of elements simultaneously at work. For the translator Edward Dent's words may still be valid:

> An opera libretto is not meant to be read as a poem, but to be heard on the stage as set to music; if the translator feels that his words may appear bald and commonplace he must remember that it is the musician's business to clothe them with beauty. (Dent, 1935: 82)

Surtitling

In recent years opera houses have been adopting the practice of staging a work in its original language version and providing surtitles with the translated content of the verbal text similar to the subtitles of works on screen. Such translations are purely informative texts, of course, and criteria such as performability and singability do not apply. Surtitles are, however, growing increasingly sophisticated: apart from technical innovations such as installing small monitors in the seating so that the individual spectator can decide whether or in which language a text can be used, there have been attempts to integrate the translated text into the production on stage. Christina Hurt (1996) has compared French and English surtitles of Wagner's *Siegfried* based on the two different translation policies at the Royal Opera House Covent Garden and the Théâtre du Châtelet in Paris. While at Covent Garden the surtitles are seen as part of the general service provided by the house, and standard versions are offered that are valid for all productions, at the Théâtre du Châtelet surtitles are considered to be an integral part of the individual production and are created as part of an artistic whole. Hurt (1996) reaches the conclusion that the quality of the surtitles is superior if they form part of the production as in Paris, and if the translator is integrated into the production team—as an artist who uses technological media, but who can by no means be replaced by a machine.

The Stage Translator and the Production Team

Not only for surtitles has the need arisen for the translator to join the production team. In recent years this has been recommended by many scholars who have written on stage translation. Aaltonen describes two categories of translators:

> The first category of translators are those whose only connection with the stage is the translation work. They are fairly powerless and their relationship to the dramatic text is comparable to that of an actor. The text sets the parameters of the work, and both the translator and the actor must bow to the text. Their role is seen as that of mediators rather than of creators. The second category are translators who work within the theatre, such as dramaturges or directors. They exercise more power and retain this power when they work as translators. As

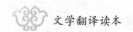

translators they are closer to being creators than mediators. They can, if they so wish, make adjustments or interpret the text according to need. (Aaltonen, 1997: 92)

It is clearly this second category of translator who has the means and the influence to create and then produce the performable text. This does not only mean that stage directors can take over the translator's job, as has frequently been the case, but also that professional translators, as experts in text design, can cooperate with the production team. Working with Justa Holz-Mänttäri's (1984) concept of "*translatorisches Handeln*" (translatorial action), Klaus Kaindl (1995: 164 – 168) has sketched modalities of interaction for opera translation, and Fabienne Hörmanseder (2001: 256 – 309) has made detailed and concrete suggestions for such cooperation in producing translated stage plays. Herbert Kretzmer, as indicated in the above quotation, has shown how such cooperation has already worked for the English production of *Les Misérables*. The German translator of the same musical, the rock-singer Heinz Rudolf Kunze—in an interview with Claudia Lisa (1993)—describes virtually ideal conditions for his work in the Vienna production. Kuntze approached his task holistically (as did Kretzmer for the English version): he first read Victor Hugo's novel, then saw the London and New York musical productions several times. He bought dictionaries of slang (including 19th century expressions) and listened to Claude Michel Schönberg's music, writing down his thoughts and ideas, which were later used in his text. As he was given 18 months to complete his task, he had time for contemplation and revision. During rehearsals and the preparation period, he was completely integrated into the production team, and like Kretzmer, he was able to change the text where necessary to make it more singable. He quotes one of the singers as saying: "*Ich kann das nicht singen. Ich muss dabei tanzen, und da stolpere ich über die Konsonanten. Mach' das ein bisschen einfacher.*" (Lisa, 1993: 77: "I can't sing that. I've got to dance at the same time and I stumble over the consonants. Make it a bit easier", my translation) Kuntze was only too willing to cooperate, and although he was not a dramaturge or director and so does not strictly speaking belong to Aaltonen's second category of translators, he was given the time and scope to work creatively and was given the necessary influence in the production. The result was a high-quality German text—and a resoundingly successful production.

Translation or Adaptation?

A question frequently raised is whether the creative, performable foreign language version of a theatre text is actually a translation at all. It is probably the low prestige and the lack of influence associated with the work of the translator that makes anyone who does more than merely transcode want to see the result as being a creative adaptation. Herbert Kretzmer was quite vehement in his refusal to see his work as a translation:

The work that I did for *Les Misérables* can be described in any terms other than direct translation. It is a term that I absolutely reject. About a third of the piece might be described as translation of a kind, a rough translation following the line of the story, which was of course important to the project. Another third might be described as rough adaptation and the other third might be described as original material because there are at least six or seven songs now in the show that did not exist in the original French production at all. (Lisa, 1993: 62)

These remarks may be partially explained by the fact that Kretzmer—following common practice in stage translation—was provided with an interlinear translation of the French text along with English material from James Fenton, the first translator engaged for the project, and he did indeed add new material of his own. However, on being asked the reasons why he so vehemently rejected the term "translation" for his work, he replied:

I resist and resent the word "translator" because it is an academic function and I bring more to the work than an academic function. It is very unacademic in fact. (...) I like to think that I brought something original to the project, that I was not a secretary to the project or a functionary, that I was as much a writer of *Les Misérables* than (*sic*!) Boublil and Schönberg and anyone else. So that is why I reject the term "translator". It is a soulless function. You do not have to bring intelligence, you do not have to bring passion to the job of translation, you only have to bring a meticulous understanding of at least another language. You have to understand the language and you have to translate it into another language. You do not bring yourself, you just bring knowledge and skill. (Lisa, 1993: 62)

It is interesting that Heinz RudolfKuntze—as well as being a rock singer he is a graduate in German Literature—did not pretend to do anything other than translate. However, he sees this absolutely as a creative and poetic activity ("*Nach-und Neudichten*") that aims at evoking a "similar effect" in the target language, and not at merely reproducing individual linguistic items (Lisa, 1993: 76). Kunze expresses complete disdain for those producers in London and the USA who, in the early stages of the venture, gave him no scope for creativity, but "... *sich nicht nur Zeile für Zeile, sondern Silbe für Silbe alles haben übersetzen lassen*" ("had everything translated, not only line for line, but even syllable for syllable") (Lisa 1993: 75).

As indicated above, interlinear versions such as these are common in theatre practice, reducing the translator's contribution even more to hack work which is then refined and improved by the "creative" expert who produces the final version. This is especially the case when the expert concerned is not familiar with the language of the source version. An outstanding example is Tom Stoppard, who has created English versions of a Polish play (*Tango* by Slawomir Mrozek), a Spanish play (*La casa de Bernarda Alba* by Garcia Lorca), German plays by Arthur Schnitzler (*Liebelei* and *Dasweite Land*), Nestroy's *Einen Juxwill er sichmachen*, and Pirandello's *Henry IV*, without being proficient in any of the source languages involved (cf. Snell-Hornby, 1993). The ensuing translation process was described by Stoppard as follows (he is referring to his version of Schnitzler's *Das weite Land*):

> [...] the National Theatre provided me with a literal transcript which aspired to be *accurate and readable rather than actable*. I was also given the services of a German linguist, John Harrison. Together—he with the German text, I with the English—we went through the play line by line, during which process small corrections were made and large amounts of light were shed on the play I had before me. After several weeks of splitting hairs with Harrison over alternatives for innumerable words and phrases, the shadings of language began to reveal themselves: carving one's way by this method into the living rock is hardly likely to take one around the third dimension, but as the relief becomes bolder so does the translator, until there is nothing to do but begin. (Stoppard, 1986: ix, *emphasis added*)

Stoppard goes on to describe how during rehearsals further changes between source and target texts:

> [...] were often provoked by the sense that in its original time and place the text gave a sharper account of itself than it seemed to do on the page in faithful English in 1979. The temptation to add a flick here and there became irresistible. (Stoppard, 1986: ix)

It is interesting that Stoppard has no inhibitions about describing himself as "the translator"—though definitely of Aaltonen's second category—but he does have reservations about calling the resulting version—*Undiscovered Country*—a translation:

> So the text here published, though largely faithful to Schnitzler's play in word and, I trust, more so in spirit, departs from it sufficiently to make one cautious about offering it as a "translation": it is a record of what was performed at the National Theatre. (Stoppard, 1986: x)

One might well ask if the same remarks could not be made about any foreign language theatre text, and one can only take up Susan Bassnett's words in discussing the issue back in 1985:

> Because of the multiplicity of factors involved in theatre translation, it has become a commonplace to suggest that it is an impossible task. Translators have frequently tried to fudge issues further, by declaring that they have produced a "version" or "adaptation" of a text, or even, as Charles Marovitz described his *Hedda Gabler*, a "collage". None of these terms goes any way towards dealing with the issues, since all imply some kind of ideal SL [source language] text towards which translators have the responsibility of being "faithful". The

distinction between a "version" of an SL text and an "adaptation" of that text seems to me to be a complete red herring. It is time the misleading use of these terms were set aside. (Bassnett-McGuire, 1985: 93)

Conclusion: Future Prospects

After long years of heated debate, it is now accepted in translation studies that translation as it is understood today goes far beyond the mechanical and "soulless" activity described by Herbert Kretzmer, performed by a secretary or functionary and needing only knowledge or skill, but no creativity or passion—although unfortunately outside translation studies such prejudices are still widespread. The conception of translation as mere interlingual transcoding unfortunately still exists in the minds of many who work with language, and it is also still kept alive in theatre practice when a translator is asked to provide raw material that is then "recreated" by someone familiar with the needs of the stage. We have seen that the theatre text, and the task of translating for the theatre, is immensely complicated, and the result might seem most promising if the translator is given the scope of a creative artist working within the production team. From the 19th century "man of letters" and the 20th century "functionary" the theatre translator of the future might develop into an expert working with texts in the theatre, and translation studies should get the message across to a larger audience that the issues involved lie between disciplines and across boundaries.

选文四 Mother Courage's Cucumbers

——Text, System and Refraction in a Theory of Literature

André Lefevere

导 言

本文选自 Lawrence Venuti, *The Translation Studies Reader*. New York: Routledge, 2000.

本文以德国戏剧家布莱希特作品在英美的译介和评论为例,阐述关于折射与改写的理论。文章首先指出英美译者在翻译布莱希特作品时出现的种种"错误",由此引出论者称之为"折射"的观点,并对"折射"的本质进行了深入的分析,指出其实质是文学作品针对不同读者所进行的改编,目的是对读者阅读作品的方式产生影响。接着,论者从系统理论出发对折射的具体规律进行了阐发。在勒弗维尔看来,翻译是两套文学系统边界上产生的文本,而折射如果希望能够将一部文学从一个系统带入另外一个系统,就会表现为两种系统间的妥协,显现出两种系统中的约束机制。勒弗维尔详细描述了布莱希特在英美文学系统中的译介和评论情况,从而得出结论:从不大被接受到被"确切"翻译,布莱希特的翻译已经通过了一个必要的进化过程,由于接受系统的操纵因素在不断变化,新的折射和改写势必还会不断发生。

Translation studies can hardly be said to have occupied a central position in much theoretical thinking about literature. Indeed, the very possibility of their relevance to literary theory has often been denied since the heyday of the first generation of German Romantic theorists and translators. This article will try to show how a certain approach to translation studies can make a significant contribution to literary theory as a whole and how translations or, to use a more general term, refractions, play a very important part in the evolution of literatures.

H. R. Hays, the first American translator of Brecht's *Mutter Courage und ihre Kinder*, translates "Da ist ein ganzes Messbuch dabei, aus Altötting, zum Einschlagen von Gurken" as "There's a whole ledger from Altötting to the storming of Gurken (B26/H5)", in which the prayerbook Mother Courage uses to wrap her cucumbers becomes transformed into a ledger, and the innocent cucumbers themselves grow into an imaginary town, Gurken, supposedly the point at which the last transaction was entered into that particular ledger. Eric Bentley, whose translation of *Mother Courage* has been the most widely read so far, translates: "Jetzt kanns bis morgen abend dauern, bis ich irgendwo was Warmes in Magen krieg" as "May it last until tomorrow evening, so I can get something in my belly (B128/B65)", whereas Brecht means something like "I may have to wait until tomorrow evening before I get something hot to eat". Both Hays and Bentley painfully miss the point when they translate "wenn einer nicht hat frei werden wollen, hat der König keinen Spass gekannt" as "if there had been nobody who needed freeing, the king wouldn't have had any sport" (B58/H25) and "if no one had *wanted* to be free, the king wouldn't have had any fun" (B58/B25) respectively. The German means something bitterly ironical like "the king did not treat lightly any attempts to resist being liberated". Even the Manheim translation nods occasionally, as when "die Weiber reissen sich unidich" (the women fight over you) is translated as "the women tear each other's hair out over you (B37/ M143)". This brief enumeration could easily be supplemented by a number of other howlers, some quite amusing, such as Hays' "if you sell your shot to buy rags" for "Ihr verkaufts die Kugeln, ihr Lumpen" (you are selling your bullets, you fools—in which Lumpen is also listed in the dictionary as rags (B51/H19). I have no desire, however, to write a traditional "Brecht in English" type of translation-studies paper, which would pursue this strategy to the bitter end. Such a strategy would inevitably lead to two stereotyped conclusions: either the writer decides that laughter cannot go on masking tears indefinitely, recoils in horror from so many misrepresentations, damns all translations and translators, and advocates reading literature in the original only, as if that were possible. Or he administers himself a few congratulatory pats on the back (after all, he has been able to spot the mistakes), regrets that even good translators are often caught napping in this way, and suggests that "we" must train "better and better" translators if we want to have "better and better" translations. And there an end.

Or a beginning, for translations can be used in other, more constructive ways. The situation changes dramatically if we stop lamenting the fact that "the Brechtian 'era' in England stood under the aegis not of Brecht himself but of various second-hand ideas and concepts *about* Brecht, an image of Brecht created from misunderstandings and misconceptions"[1] and, quite simply, accept it as a fact of literature—or even life. How many lives, after all, have been deeply affected by translations of the Bible and the *Capital*?

A writer's work gains exposure and achieves influence mainly through "misunderstandings and misconceptions", or, to use a more neutral term, refractions. Writers and their work are always understood and conceived against a certain background or, if you will, are refracted through a certain spectrum, just as their work itself can refract previous works through a certain spectrum.

An approach to literature which has its roots in the poetics of Romanticism, and which is still very much with us, will not be able to admit this rather obvious fact without undermining its own foundations. It rests on a number of assumptions, among them, the assumption of the genius and originality of the author who creates *ex nihilo* as opposed to an author like Brecht, who is described in the 1969 edition of the *Britannica* as "a restless piecer together of ideas not always his own".[2] As if Shakespeare didn't have "sources", and as if there had not been some writing on the Faust theme before Goethe. Also assumed is the sacred character of the text, which is not to be tampered with—hence the horror with which "bad" translations are rejected. Another widespread assumption is the belief in the possibility of recovering the author's true intentions, and the concomitant belief that works of literature should be judged on their intrinsic merit only: "Brecht's ultimate rank will fall to be reconsidered when the true quality of his plays can be assessed independently of political affiliations",[3] as if that were possible.

A systemic approach to literature, on the other hand, tends not to suffer from such assumptions. Translations, texts produced on the borderline between two systems, provide an ideal introduction to a systems approach to literature.

First of all, let us accept that refractions—the adaptation of a work of literature to a

[1] Martin Esslin, *Reflections* (New York, 1969), p. 79.

[2] *Encyclopedia Britannica* (Chicago, 1969), IV, 144a.

[3] A. C. Ward, ed., *The Longman Companion to Twentieth Century Literature* (London, 1970), p. 88a.

different audience, with the intention of influencing the way in which that audience reads the work—have always been with us in literature. Refractions are to be found in the obvious form of translation, or in the less obvious forms of criticism (the wholesale allegorization of the literature of Antiquity by the Church Fathers, e. g.), commentary, historiography (of the plot summary of famous works cum evaluation type, in which the evaluation is unabashedly based on the current concept of what "good" literature should be), teaching, the collection of works in anthologies, the production of plays. These refractions have been extremely influential in establishing the reputation of a writer and his or her work. Brecht, e. g. achieved his breakthrough in England post-humously with the 1965 Berliner Ensemble's London production of *Arturo Ui*, when "the British critics began to rave about the precision, the passion, acrobatic prowess and general excellence of it all. Mercifully, as none of them understands German, they could not be put off by the actual content of this play". [1]

It is a fact that the great majority of readers and theatre-goers in the Anglo-Saxon world do not have access to the "original" Brecht (who has been rather assiduously refracted in both Germanies anyway, and in German). They have to approach him through refractions that run the whole gamut described above, a fact occasionally pointed out within the Romanticism-based approaches to literature, but hardly ever allowed to upset things: "a large measure of credit for the wider recognition of Brecht in the United States is due to the drama critic Eric Bentley, who translated several of Brecht's plays and has written several sound critical appreciations of him. "[2] It is admitted that Brecht has reached Anglo-Saxon audiences vicariously, with all the misunderstandings and misconceptions this implies, and not through some kind of osmosis which ensures that genius always triumphs in the end. But no further questions are asked, such as: "how does refraction really operate? and what implications could it have for a theory of literature, once its existence is admitted?"

Refractions, then, exist, and they are influential, but they have not been much studied. At best their existence has been lamented (after all, they are unfaithful to the original), at worst it has been ignored within the Romanticism-based approaches, on the very obvious grounds that what should not be, cannot be, even though it is. Refractions have certainly not been analysed in any way that does justice to the immense part they play, not just in the dissemination of a certain author's work, but also in the development of a certain literature. My contention is that they have not been studied because there has not been a framework that could make analysis of refractions relevant within the wider context of an alternative theory. That framework exists if refractions are thought of as part of a system, if the spectrum that refracts them is described.

The heuristic model a systems approach to literature makes use of, rests on the following assumptions: (a) literature is a system, embedded in the environment of a culture

① Esslin, *Reflections*, p. 83.
② S. Kunitz, ed. , *Twentieth Century Authors*, *First Supplement* (New York, 1965), p. 116a.

or society. It is a contrived system, i. e. it consists of both objects (texts) and people who write, refract, distribute, read those texts. It is a stochastic system, i. e. one that is relatively indeterminate and only admits of predictions that have a certain degree of probability, without being absolute. It is possible (and General Systems Theory has done this, as have some others who have been trying to apply a systems approach to literature) to present systems in an abstract, formalized way, but very little would be gained by such a strategy in the present state of literary studies, while much unnecessary aversion would be created, since Romanticism-based approaches to literature have always resolutely rejected any kind of notation that leaves natural language too far behind.

The literary system possesses a regulatory body: the person, persons, institutions (Maecenas, the Chinese and Indian Emperors, the Sultan, various prelates, noblemen, provincial governors, mandarins, the Church, the Court, the Fascist or Communist Party) who or which extend(s) patronage to it. Patronage consists of at least three components: an ideological one (literature should not be allowed to get too far out of step with the other systems in a given society), an economic one (the patron assures the writer's livelihood) and a status component (the writer achieves a certain position in society). Patrons rarely influence the literary system directly; critics will do that for them, as writers of essays, teachers, members of academies. Patronage can be undifferentiated—in situations in which it is extended by a single person, group, institution characterized by the same ideology—or differentiated, in a situation in which different patrons represent different, conflicting ideologies. Differentiation of patronage occurs in the type of society in which the ideological and the economic component of patronage are no longer necessarily linked (the Enlightenment State, e. g. as opposed to various absolutist monarchies, where the same institution dispensed "pensions" and kept writers more or less in step). In societies with differentiated patronage, economic factors such as the profit motive are liable to achieve the status of an ideology themselves, dominating all other considerations. Hence, *Variety*, reviewing the 1963 Broadway production of *Mother Courage* (in Bentley's translation), can ask without compunction: "Why should anyone think it might meet the popular requirements of Broadway—that is, be commercial?"[1]

The literary system also possesses a kind of code of behaviour, a poetics. This poetics consists of both an inventory component (genre, certain symbols, characters, prototypical situations) and a "functional" component, an idea of how literature has to, or may be allowed to, function in society. In systems with undifferentiated patronage the critical establishment will be able to enforce the poetics. In systems with differentiated patronage various poetics will compete, each trying to dominate the system as a whole, and each will have its own critical establishment, applauding work that has been produced on the basis of its own poetics and decrying what the competition has to offer, relegating it to the limbo of

---

[1] Quoted in K. H. Schieps, *Bertolt Brecht* (New York, 1977), p. 265.

"low" literature, while claiming the high ground for itself. The gap between "high" and "low" widens as commercialization increases. Literature produced for obviously commercial reasons (the Harlequin series) will tend to be as conservative, in terms of poetics, as literature produced for obviously ideological reasons (propaganda). Yet economic success does not necessarily bring status in its wake: one can be highly successful as a commercial writer (Harold Robbins) and be held in contempt by the highbrows at the same time.

A final constraint operating within the system is that of the natural language in which a work of literature is written, both the formal side of that language (what is in grammars) and its pragmatic side, the way in which language reflects culture. This latter aspect is often most troublesome to translators. Since different languages reflect different cultures, translations will nearly always contain attempts to "naturalize" the different culture, to make it conform more to what the reader of the translation is used to. Bentley, e. g. translates "Käs aufs Weissbrot" as "Cheese on pumpernickel (B23/B3)", rather than the more literal "cheese on white bread", on the assumption that an American audience would expect Germans to eat their cheese on pumpernickel, since Germany is where pumpernickel came from. Similarly "in dem schönen Flandern" becomes the much more familiar "in Flanders fields (B52/B22)", linking the Thirty Years' War of the 17th century with World War I, as does Bentley's use of "Kaiser", which he leaves untranslated throughout. In the same way, Hays changes "Tillys Sieg bei Magdeburg" to "Tilly's Victory at Leipsic (B94/H44)", on the assumption that the Anglo-American audience will be more familiar with Leipzig than with Magdeburg. It is obvious that these changes have nothing at all to do with the translator's knowledge of the language he is translating. The changes definitely point to the existence of another kind of constraint, and they also show that the translators are fully aware of its existence; there would be no earthly reason to change the text otherwise. Translations are produced under constraints that go far beyond those of natural language—in fact, other constraints are often much more influential in the shaping of the translation than are the semantic or linguistic ones.

A refraction (whether it is translation, criticism, historiography) which tries to carry a work of literature over from one system into another, represents a compromise between two systems and is, as such, the perfect indicator of the dominant constraints in both systems. The gap between the two hierarchies of constraints explains why certain works do not "take", or enjoy at best an ambiguous position in the system they are imported into.

The degree of compromise in a refraction will depend on the reputation of the writer being translated within the system from which the translation is made. When Hays translated Brecht in 1941, Brecht was a little-known German immigrant, certainly not among the canonized writers of the Germany of his time (which had burnt his books eight years before). He did not enjoy the canonized status of a Thomas Mann. By the time Bentley translates Brecht, the situation has changed: Brecht is not yet canonized in the West, but at least he is talked about. When Manheim and Willett start bringing out Brecht's collected works in English, they are translating a canonized author, who is now translated more on his own terms (according to his own poetics) than on those of the receiving system. A historiographical refraction in the receiving system appearing in 1976 grants that Brecht "unquestionably can be regarded, with justice, as one of the 'classic authors' of the twentieth century". [1]

The degree to which the foreign writer is accepted into the native system will, on the other hand, be determined by the need that native system has of him in a certain phase of its evolution. The need for Brecht was greater in England than in the US. The enthusiastic reception of the Berliner Ensemble by a large segment of the British audience in 1956, should also be seen in terms of the impact it made on the debate as to whether or not a state subsidized National Theater should be set up in England. The opposition to a National Theater could "at last be effectively silenced by pointing to the Berliner Ensemble, led by a great artist, consisting of young, vigorous and anti-establishment actors and actresses, wholly experimental, overflowing with ideas—and state-subsidized to the hilt". [2] Where the "need" for the foreign writer is felt, the critical establishment will be seen to split more easily. That is, part of the establishment will become receptive to the foreign model, or even positively champion it: "Tynan became drama critic of the London *Observer* in 1954, and very soon made the name of Brecht his trademark, his yardstick of values. "[3] In the US, that role was filled by Eric Bentley, but he did have to tread lightly for a while. His 1951 anthology, *The Play*, does not contain any work by Brecht; he also states in the introduction that "undue preoccupation with content, with theme, has been characteristic of Marxist critics". [4] In 1966, on the other hand, Series Three of *From the Modern Repertoire*, edited by Eric Bentley, is "dedicated to the memory of Bertolt Brecht". [5] All this is not to imply any moral judgment. It just serves to point out the very real existence of ideological constraints in the production and dissemination of refractions.

Refractions of Brecht's work available to the Anglo-Saxon reader who needs them are mainly of three kinds: translation, criticism, and historiography. I have looked at a representative sample of the last two kinds, and restricted translation analysis to *Mother Courage*. Brecht is not represented at all in 13 of the introductory drama anthologies published between 1951 (which is not all that surprising) and 1975 (which is). These anthologies, used to introduce the student to drama, do play an important part in the American literary system. In effect, they determine which authors are to be canonized. The student entering the field, or the educated layman, will tend to accept the selections, offered in these anthologies as "classics", without questioning the ideological, economic, and

---

① A. Nicoll, ed., *World Drama* (New York, 1976), p. 839.
② Esslin, *Reflections*, pp. 75 - 76.
③ Esslin, *Reflections*, p. 76.
④ E. Bentley, ed., *The Play* (Englewood Cliffs, 1951), p. 6.
⑤ E. Bentley, ed., *From the Modern Repertoire*, *Series Three*, (Bloomington, 1966), p. i.

aesthetic constraints which have influenced the selections. As a result, the plays frequently anthologized achieve a position of relative hegemony. The very notion of an alternative listing is no longer an option for the lay reader. Thus, formal education perpetuates the canonization of certain works of literature, and school and college anthologies play an immensely important part in this essentially conservative movement within the literary system.

When Brecht is represented in anthologies of the type just described, the play chosen is more likely to be either *The Good Woman of Sezuan* or the *Caucasian Chalk Circle*. From the prefaces to the anthologies it is obvious that a certain kind of poetics, which cannot be receptive to Brecht, can still command the allegiance of a substantial group of refractors within the American system. Here are a few samples, each of which is diametrically opposed to the poetics Brecht himself tried to elaborate: "The story must come to an inevitable end; it does not just stop, but it comes to a completion."[1] Open-ended plays, such as *Mother Courage*, will obviously not fit in. Soliloquy and aside are admitted to the inventory component of the drama's poetics, but with reservations: "both of these devices can be used very effectively in the theater, but they interrupt the action and must therefore be used sparingly"[2]—which does, of course, rule out the alienation effect. "The amount of story presented is foreshortened in a play: the action is initiated as close as possible to the final issue. The incidents are of high tension to start with, and the tension increases rapidly"[3]—which precludes the very possibility of epic drama. The important point here is that these statements are passed off as describing "the" drama as such, from a position of total authority. This poetics also pervades the 1969 *Britannica* entry on Brecht, which states quite logically and consistently that "he was often bad at creating living characters or at giving his plays tension and scope".[4]

Brecht "did not make refraction any easier", by insisting on his own poetics, which challenged traditional assumptions about drama. Refractors who do have a receptive attitude towards Brecht find themselves in the unenviable position of dealing with a poetics alien to the system they are operating in. There are a number of strategies for dealing with this. One can recognize the value of the plays themselves, while dismissing the poetics out of hand: "The theory of alienation was only so much nonsense, disproved by the sheer theatricality of all his better works."[5] One can also go in for the psychological cop-out, according to which Brecht's poetics can be dismissed as a rationalization of essentially irrational factors: "Theory does not concern me. I am convinced that Brecht writes as he does, not so much from a predetermined calculation based on what he believes to be the correct goals for the present

---

① S. Barnet, M. Berman and W. Burto, eds, *Classic Theatre: The Humanities in Drama* (Boston, 1975), p. v.

② L. Perrine, ed. , *Dimensions of Drama* (New York, 1970), p. 4.

③ L. Altenberg and L. L. Lewis, ed. , *Introduction to Literature: Plays* (New York, 1969), p. 2.

④ *Encyclopedia Britannica*, IV, 144a.

⑤ M. Gottfried, *Opening Nights* (New York, 1969), p. 239.

revolutionary age, as from the dictates of temperament. "[1] A third strategy for adapting a refraction to the native system is to integrate the new poetics into the old one by translating its concepts into the more familiar terminology of the old poetics: "If there is *anagnorisis* (italics mine) in *Mother Courage*, it doesn't take place on stage, as in the Aristotelian tradition, but in the auditorium of Brecht's epic theatre. "[2] The final strategy is to explain the new poetics and to show that the system can, in fact, accommodate it, and can allow it to enter into the inventory and functional components of its poetics, without necessarily going to pieces: "Some critics have interpreted alienation to mean that the audience should be in a constant state of emotional detachment, but in actuality Brecht manipulated esthetic distance to involve the spectator emotionally and then jar him out of his emphatic response so that he may judge critically what he has experienced. "[3]

The same strategies surface again in interpretations of *Mother Courage* itself: (i) *Variety*'s review of the 1963 Broadway production: "Sophomorically obvious, cynical, self-consciously drab and tiresome (ii). "[4] "His imagination and his own love of life created a work that transcends any thesis... He could not take away Mother Courage's humanity; even rigidly Marxist critics still saw her as human (iii). "[5]

The Zürich audience of 1941 may have come away with only sympathy for Courage the Mother who, like Niobe, sees her children destroyed by more powerful forces but struggles on regardless. But to see the play solely in these terms is to turn a blind eye to at least half the text, and involves complete disregard for Brecht's methods of characterization. [6]

"Mother Courage learns nothing and follows the troops. The theme, in lesser hands, might well have led to an idealisation of the poor and the ignorant. Brecht made no concessions, showing Mother Courage for nothing better than she is, cunning, stubborn, bawdy (iv). "[7]

Of the three translations, Manheim's is situated between iii and iv. Both Hays and Bentley weave in and out of ii and iii. The main problem seems to accommodate Brecht's directness of diction to the poetics of the Broadway stage. Hence the tendency in both Hays and Bentley to "make clear" to the spectator or reader what Brecht wanted that reader or spectator to piece together for himself. Brecht's stage direction: "Die stumme Kattrin springt vom Wagen und stösst rauhe Laute aus" is rendered by Hays as "Dumb Kattrin makes a hoarse outcry *because she notices the abduction* (B37/H12—Italics mine)". Mother

[1]　H. Clurman, *"Bertolt Brecht"* in *Essays in Modern Drama*, ed. M. Freedman (Boston, 1974), p. 152.

[2]　K. A. Dickson, *Towards Utopia* (Oxford, 1978), p. 108.

[3]　O. G. Brockett, *Perspectives on Contemporary Theatre* (Baton Rouge, 1971), p. 216.

[4]　*Variety* review of the 1963 Broadway production, quoted in Schieps, *Bertolt Brecht*, p. 265.

[5]　M. Seymour-Smith, *Funk and Wagnall's Guide to World Literature* (New York, 1973), p. 642.

[6]　M. Morley, *Brecht* (London, 1977), p. 58.

[7]　K. Richardson, ed., *Twentieth Century Writings* (London, 1969), p. 89.

Courage's words to Kattrin: "Du bist selber ein Kreuz: du hast ein gutes Herz" are translated by Hays as "You're across yourself. *What sort of a help to me are you? And all the same* what a good heart you have" (B34/H11) and by Manheim as "you're across yourself *because* you have a good heart" (B34/M142)—what is italicized is not in the German. Bentley tries to solve the problem of making Brecht completely "lucid" by means of excessive use of hyphens and italics: "Wer seid ihr?" becomes "Who'd you think *you* are?" instead of plain "Who are you?" (B25/B4). "Aber zu fressen haben wir auch nix" is turned into "A fat lot of difference that makes, *we* haven't got anything to eat either" (B39/B13), instead of "we don't have anything to eat either" and "der Feldhauptmann wird Ihnen den Kopf abreissen, wenn nix aufm Tisch steht" is rendered as "I know your problem: if you don't find something to eat and quick, the Chief will-cut-your-fathead-off" (B40/B14) instead of "the captain will tear your head off if there's nothing on the table".

Hays and Bentley also do their best to integrate the songs fully into the play, approximating the model of the musical. For example, Bentley adds "transitional lines" between the spoken text and the song in "Das Lied vom Weib und dem Soldaten", thus also giving the song more of a musical flavor:

> To a soldier lad comes an old fishwife
> and this old fishwife says she (B45/B18).

In the translation there is a tendency towards the vague, the abstract, the cliché. The need to rhyme, moreover, leads to excessive padding, where the original is jarring and concrete, as in

> Ihr Hauptleut, cure Leut marschieren
> Euch ohne Wurst nicht in den Tod
> Lasst die Courage sie erst kurieren
> Mit Wein von Leib und Geistesnot
>
> (Commanders, your men won't march to their death without sausage
> Let Courage heal them first
> with wine of the pains of body and soul)

which Hays translates as

> Bonebare this land and picked of meat
> The fame is yours but where's the bread?
> So here I bring you food to eat
> And wine to slake and soothe your dread (B25/4)

Bentley also makes the text of the songs themselves conform more to the style and the register of the musical. The lapidary, and therefore final

> In einer trüben Früh

Begann mein Qual und Müh
Das Regiment stand im Geviert
Dann ward getrommelt, wies der Brauch
Dann ist der Feind, mein Liebster auch
Aus unsrer Stadt marschiert

(one drab morning
my pain and sorrow began
the regiment stood in the square
then they beat the drums, as is the custom
Then the enemy, my beloved too
marched out of our town)

is padded out with a string of clichés into

The springtime's soft amour
Through summer may endure
But swiftly comes the fall
And winter ends it all
December came. All of the men
Filed past the trees where once we hid
Then quickly marched away and did
Not come back again (B55/B23).

Little of Brecht is left, but the seasons and the sad reminiscence, so often *de rigueur* for Broadway, are certainly in evidence. The musical takes over completely when Bentley translates

ein Schnaps, Wirt, sei g'scheit
Ein Reiter hat keine Zeit
Muss für sein Kaiser streiten

(A schnapps, mine host, be quick
A soldier on horseback has no time
he has to fight for his emperor)

as

One schnapps, mine host, be quick, make haste!
A soldier's got no time to waste
He must be shooting, shooting, shooting
His Kaiser's enemies uprooting (B101/B49).

Other refrain lines in the song are treated with great consistency: "Er muss gen Mähren

reiten" becomes

> He must be hating, hating, hating
> he cannot keep his Kaiser waiting

instead of the more prosaic "he has to go fight in Moravia", which is in the German text, while "Er muss fürn Kaiser sterben" is turned into

> He must be dying, dying, dying
> His Kaiser's greatness glorifying (B101/B50)

whereas the German merely means "he has to die for his emperor". The least that can charitably be said is that Bentley obviously works to a different poetics than Brecht; he must have believed that this difference would make Brecht more acceptable than a straight translation. These examples again make it clear that the problem lies not with the dictionary, that it is not one of semantic equivalence, but rather one of a compromise between two kinds of poetics, in which the poetics of the receiving system plays the dominant part.

The terse, episodic structure of Brecht's play and the stage directions designed to give some hint as to the way actors should act are two more features of the Brechtian poetics not seen as easily transferable from one system to another. Hays therefore redivides Brecht's text into acts and scenes, in accordance with the norms of receiving poetics. Bentley keeps Brecht's scenes, while giving each of them a title, which turns out to be the first line of Brecht's text. Both turn a lapidary stage direction like "Wenn der Koch kommt, sieht er verdutzt sein Zeug" (when the cook enters, he starts as he sees his things) into something more elaborate, more familiar to a generation of actors brought up on Stanislavsky: "Then the Cook returns, still eating. He stares in astonishment at his belongings" and "A gust of wind. Enter the Cook, still chewing. He sees his things (B192/H72/B72)". Even Manheim does not always trust Brecht on his own: when Kattrin is dead, Mother Courage says: "Vielleicht schlaft sie." The translation reads: "Maybe I can get her to sleep." Mother Courage then sings the lullaby and adds "Now she's asleep" (B153/M209)—the addition is not in the original. Similarly, when Mother Courage decides not to complain to the captain after all, but simply to get up and leave, thereby ending the scene, Bentley adds a stage direction: "The scrivener looks after her, shaking his head (B90/B44)."

Brechtian dialogue is another problem. It must be made to flow more if it is to fit in with the poetics of the receiving system. As a result, lines are redistributed: actors should obviously not be allowed to stand around for too long, without anything to say. Consequently:

> Yvette: Dann Können wir ja suchen gehn, ich geh gern herum und such mir was aus, ich geh gern mit dir herum, Poldi, das ist ein Vergnügen, nicht? Und wenns zwei wochen dauert?

(Then we can go look, I love walking about and looking for things, I love walking about with you, Poldi, it's so nice, isn't it? Even if it takes two weeks?)

Yvette: Yes, we can certainly look around for something. I love going around looking, I love going around with you, Poldy...

The Colonel: Really? Do you?

Yvette: Oh, it's lovely. I could take two weeks of it!

The Colonel: Really? Could you? (B76/B36).

In the same way, a little emotion is added where emotion is too patently lacking, and never mind Brecht's poetics. Yvette's denunciation of the Cook: "das ist der schlimmste, wo an der ganzen flandrischen Küste herumgelaufen ist. An jedem Finger eine, die er ins Unglück gebracht hat" becomes "he's a bad lot. You won't find a worse on the whole coast of Flanders. He got more girls in trouble than... (*concentrating on the cook*) Miserable cur! Damnable whore hunter! Inveterate seducer!" (B125/B63) The stage direction and what follows it have been added.

Brecht's ideology is treated in the same way as his poetics in critical refractions produced in the receiving system. Sometimes it is dismissed in none too subtle ways: "Brecht made changes in the hope of suggesting that things might have been different had Mother Courage acted otherwise." (What could she have done? Established Socialism in seventeenth-century Germany?)[1] Sometimes it is engulfed in psychological speculation: "In a world without God, it was Marx's vision that saved Brecht from nihilistic despair"[2] and "Communist ideology provided Brecht with a rational form of salvation, for it indicated a clearly marked path leading out of social chaos and mass misery. At the same time, Communist discipline provided Brecht's inner life with the moral straitjacket he desperately needed at this time".[3]

Attempts to integrate Brecht into the American value system start by fairly acknowledging the problem: "Brecht's status as a culture hero of Communist East Germany further enhanced his appeal to the left and correspondingly diminished his chances of ever pleasing the artistic and political right wing",[4] and end by stating the influence that the ideology Brecht subscribed to is supposed to have exerted on his artistic productions: "Nevertheless, Brecht maintains a neutral stance. That is, he pretends not to have any specific remedy in mind, although it is generally agreed that he favored a socialistic or communistic society. But he avoids saying so in his plays and instead declares that the

---

[1]　E. Bentley, ed. , *The Great Playwrights* (New York, 1970), p. 2169.

[2]　J. A. Bédé and W. B. Edgerton, eds, *The Columbia Dictionary of Modern European Literature* (New York, 1980), p. 116a.

[3]　Bédé and Edgerton, *Columbia Dictionary*, p. 114b.

[4]　Esslin, *Reflections*, p. 77.

audience must make up its own mind. "[1] The multiplication of statements like this last one in recent years indicates a growing acceptance of Brecht in the receiving system. The Manheim translation, chronologically the latest, is easily the "best" of the three translations examined here, since it translates Brecht more on his own terms. But things are not that simple. It would be easy to say—as traditional translation studies have done time and again—that "Manheim is good; Hays and Bentley are both bad". It would be closer to the truth, however, to say that Manheim can afford to be good because Hays, and especially Bentley, translated Brecht before he did. They focused attention on Brecht and, in so doing, they got the debate going. If they had translated Brecht on his own terms to begin with, disregarding the poetics of the receiving system, chances are that the debate would never have got going in the first place—witness the disastrous performance of Brecht's *The Mother* in 1936. Hays and Bentley established a bridgehead for Brecht in another system; to do so, they had to compromise with the demands of the poetics and the patronage dominant in that system.

This is not to suggest that there is some kind of necessary progression ranging from the less acceptable all the way to the "definitive" translation—that Brecht, in other words, need now no longer be translated. Both the natural language and the politics of the receiving system keep changing; the spectrum through which refractions are made changes in the course of time. It is entirely possible, e. g. that Brecht can be used in the service of a poetics diametrically opposed to his own, as in the Living Theater's production of *Antigone*. To put this briefly in a somewhat wider context, it is good to remember that literary systems are stochastic, not mechanistic. Producers of both refracted and original literature do not operate as automatons under the constraints of their time and location. They devise various strategies to live with these constraints, ranging hypothetically from full acceptance to full defiance. The categories that a systems approach makes use of are formulated in some kind of "inertial frame", similar to the ideal world physicists postulate, in which all experiments take place under optimal conditions, and in which all laws operate unfailingly. Like the laws of physics, the categories of the systems approach have to be applied to individual cases in a flexible manner.

Hays and Bentley treat ideological elements in *Mother Courage* in ways roughly analogous to those used by their fellow refractors, the critics. Translating in 1941, Hays consistently plays down the aggressive pacifism of the play, omitting whole speeches like the bitterly ironical

> Wie alles Gute ist auch der Krieg am Anfang hält schwer zu machen. Wenn er
> dann erst floriert, ist er auch zäh; dann schrecken die Leute zurück vorm Frieden
> wie die Würfler vorn Aufhören, weil dann müssens zahlen, was sie verloren haben.
> Aber zuerst schreckens zurück vorm Krieg. Er ist ihnen was Neues.

---

[1] Brockett, *Perspectives*, p. 125.

(Like all good things, war is not easy in the beginning. But once it gets going, it's hard to get rid of; people become afraid of peace like dice players who don't want to stop, because then they have to pay up. But in the beginning they are afraid of the war. It's new to them.)

Hays also weakens the obvious connection between war and commerce in the person of Mother Courage by omitting lines Brecht gives her, like "Und jetzt fahren wir weiter, es ist nicht alle Tage Krieg, ich muss tummeln" (and now let's drive on; there isn't a war on every day, I have to get cracking). Bentley, translating after the second world war, nevertheless follows partly the same course:

> Man merkts, hier ist zu lang kein Krieg gewesen. Wo soll da Moral herkommen, frag ich? Frieden, das ist nur Schlamperei, erst der Krieg schafft Ordnung. Die Menschheit schiesst ins Kraut im Frieden.

> (You can see there hasn't been a war here for too long. Where do you get your morals from, then, I ask you? Peace is a sloppy business, you need a war to get order. Mankind runs wild in peace.)

simply becomes "what they could do with here is a good war (B22/B3)". In addition, certain war-connected words and phrases are put into a nobler register in translation: "Wir zwei gehn dort ins Feld und tragen die Sach aus unter Männern" (the two of us will go out into that field and settle this business like men) becomes "the two of us will now go and settle the affair on the field of honor" (B30/B8) and "mit Spiessen und Kanonen" (with spears and guns) is rendered as "with fire and sword". (B145/B76) Not surprisingly, Manheim, translating later and in a more Brecht-friendly climate, takes the opposite direction and makes the pacifism more explicit, rendering

> So mancher wollt so manches haben
> Was es für manchen gar nicht gab
> (so many wanted so much
> that was not available for many)

as

> Some people think they'd like to ride out
> The war, leave danger to the brave (B113/M185).

Comprehension of the text in its semantic dimension is not the issue; the changes can be accounted for only in terms of ideology.

Finally, both Hays and Bentley eschew Brecht's profanities in their translations, submitting to the code of the US entertainment industry at the time the translations were written, albeit with sometimes rather droll results: "führt seine Leute in die Scheissgass", e. g. (leads his people up shit creek) becomes "leads his people into the smoke of battle" and "leads his soldiers into a trap" (B45/H17/ B17); and "Du hast mich beschissen" is turned into "A stinking trick!" and "You've fouled me up!" (B33/H9/B9). Even Manheim, years later, goes easy on the swear words: "der gottverdammte Hund von einem Rittmeister" is toned down to "that stinking captain". (B83/M170)

The economic aspect of refraction is touched on in some of the prefaces to the anthologies in which Brecht is not represented, and in some of the reviews of American productions of *Mother Courage*. The economics of inclusion or exclusion obviously have something to do with copyright; it is not all that easy (or cheap) to get permission to reprint Brecht in English, and certain editors just give up—the economic factor in its purest form. Less obvious, but no less powerful, economic considerations are alluded to by Barnet in the introduction to *Classic Theatre*, a collection of plays designed to be the companion volume to PBS' series of the same name, and therefore doubly under economic pressure. First, the order in which the plays are presented

> is nearly chronological: the few exceptions were made to serve the balance of television programming. Thus, because the producers wished the series to begin with a well-known play, Shakespeare's *Macbeth* (written about 1605 – 6) precedes Marlowe's *Edward II* (written in the early 1590's). [①]

It further turns out that two of the "classics" have never been written for the "theatre" at all, but that they were written more or less directly for the series, or certainly for television: "of the thirteen plays in this book, two were written for television, one of these is an adaptation of Voltaire's prose fiction, *Candide*, and the other is a play about the life of the English poet John Milton". [②] It is hard to see what these plays could possibly have to do with either "classic" or "theatre", and there would certainly have been room for Brecht if one or the other of them had been left out. The conclusion must be that Brecht was still, in 1975, considered commercially and poetically too unsafe (and maybe also too expensive) for inclusion in a series on "classic theatre". The same introduction claims that "the most vital theatre in the second half of the twentieth century is a fairly unified body of drama neatly labelled the "Theatre of the Absurd", [③] hailing Artaud as the most pervasive influence on the modern stage.

The *Variety* review of the 1963 Broadway production of *Mother Courage* asks the million dollar question: "why should anyone think it might meet the popular requirements of Broadway—that is, be commercial", thus pointing with brutal honesty to an important element in American patronage Brecht never managed to get on his side. In 1963, Brecht's patrons could not guarantee a more or less complete production of his work under prevailing economic regulations:

---

① Barnet, *Classic Theatre*, p. v.
② Barnet, *Classic Theatre*, p. xvii.
③ Barnet, *Classic Theatre*, p. xviii.

The original text contains nine songs. I have the impression that several of these have been cut—probably because, if they were retained, the time allowed to sing and play them might exceed twenty four minutes and the Musicians' Union would list the production as a "musical". According to regulations, this classification would entail the employment of twenty-four musicians at heavy cost. [①]

And yet, to the Broadway goer with no German, or even to the Broadway goer with German, who prefers to watch plays rather than to read them, that was Brecht's *Mother Courage*. The refraction, in other words, is the original to the great majority of people who are only tangentially exposed to literature. Indeed, it would hardly be an exaggeration to say that this kind of reader is influenced by literature precisely through refractions, and little else. In the US, he or she will tell you that *Moby Dick* is a great novel, one of the masterpieces of American literature. He will tell you so because he has been told so in school, because she has read comic strips and extracts in anthologies, and because captain Ahab will forever look like Gregory Peck as far as he or she is concerned. It is through critical refractions that a text establishes itself inside a given system (from the article in learned magazines to that most avowedly commercial of all criticism, the blurb, which is usually much more effective in selling the book than the former). It is through translations combined with critical refractions (introductions, notes, commentary accompanying the translation, articles on it) that a work of literature produced outside a given system takes its place in that "new" system. It is through refractions in the social system's educational set-up that canonization is achieved and, more importantly, maintained. There is a direct link between college syllabi and paperback publishers' backlists of classics (Mann's *The Magic Mountain* and *Dr. Faustus* rather than *Joseph and His Brothers*).

All this is by no means intended to be moralistic; I am not lamenting an existing state of affairs, I am merely describing it and suggesting that it is eminently worthy of description, since refractions are what keeps a literary system going. They have been ignored by Romanticism-based approaches to literature, but they have been there all along. Their role should not be overestimated, but it should no longer be underestimated either.

Brecht defined his poetics against the dominant poetics of his time in Germany, and he managed to win a certain degree of acceptance for them by the time he died. He had achieved this through a combination of "original work" (the texts of the plays, the theoretical writings) and refractions: productions of his plays, reviews of those productions, translations, the ensuing critical industry. The functional component of his poetics (what the theater is for) was a fairly radical departure from the prevailing poetics of his time (though perhaps not so radical when compared to the poetics of a previous historical

① H. Clurman, *The Naked Image* (New York, 1966), p. 62.

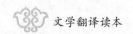

manifestation of the system he worked in, namely medieval morality plays), despite the fact that many of the devices he used existed in non-canonized forms of the theater of his time (e. g. Valentin's cabaret) or in the theater of other cultures (e. g. Chinese opera).

Small wonder, then, that a Romanticism-based approach to literature should ask the wretched question "in how far is all this new"? It is a wretched question because nothing is ever new; the new is a combination of various elements from the old, the non-canonized, imports from other systems (at about the same time Brecht was experimenting with adaptations from Chinese opera, the Chinese poet Feng Chi refracted the European sonnet into Chinese) rearranged to suit alternative functional views of literature. This holds true for both the implicit and the explicit concept of a poetics, *and* for individual works of literature which are, to a certain extent, recombinations of generic elements, plots, motifs, symbols, etc. — in fact, essentially the "piecing together of other people's ideas", but in such a way as to give them a novel impact.

The question of originality is also wretched because it prevents so many adherents of Romanticism-based approaches to literature from seeing so many things. Originality can only exist if texts are consistently isolated from the tradition and the environment in which (against which) they were produced. Their freshness and timelessness, their sacred and oracular status are achieved at a price: the loss of history, the continuum of which they are a part and which they help to (re)shape. Literature in general, and individual works, can, in the final analysis, be contemplated, commented on, identified with, applied to life, in a number of essentially subjective ways; and these activities are all refractions designed to influence the way in which the reader receives the work, concertizes it. Present-day refractions usually operate on underlying principles essentially alien to literature and imported into it, such as psychoanalysis and philosophy. In other words, the "natural" framework of investigation that was lost for literary studies when originality became the overriding demand, has to be replaced by frameworks imported from other disciplines, a state of affairs rendered perhaps most glaringly obvious in the very way in which works of literature are presented to students who are beginning the task of studying literature: syllabi, reading lists, anthologies, more often than not offering disparate texts and pieces of texts, brought together in a more or less arbitrary manner to serve the demands of the imposed framework.

The word, then, can only be said to really create the world, as the Romanticism-based approaches would have it, if it is carefully isolated from the world in which it originates. And that is, in the end, impossible; the word does not create a world *ex nihilo*. Through the grid of tradition it creates a counterworld, one that is fashioned under the constraints of the world the creator lives and works in, and one that can be explained, understood better if these constraints are taken into account. If not, all explanation becomes necessarily reductionistic in character, essentially subservient to the demands of imported frameworks.

A systems approach to literature, emphasizing the role played by refractions, or rather, integrating them, revalidates the concept of literature as something that is made, not in the vacuum of unfettered genius, for genius is never unfettered, but out of the tension between genius and the constraints that genius has to operate under, accepting them or subverting them. A science of literature, a type of activity that tries to devise an "imaginative picture" of the literary phenomenon in all its ramifications, to devise theories that make more sense of more phenomena than their predecessors (that are more or less useful, not more or less true), and that does so on the basis of the methodology that is currently accepted by the consensus of the scientific community, while developing its own specific methods suited to its own specific domain, will also have to study refractions. It will have to study the part they play in the evolution of a literary system, and in the evolution of literary systems as such. It will also have to study the laws governing that evolution: the constraints that help shape the poetics that succeed each other within a given system, and the poetics of different systems as well as individual works produced on the basis of a given poetics, or combination of poetics.

A systems approach does not try to influence the evolution of a given literary system, the way critical refractions and many translations avowedly written in the service of a certain poetics tend to do. It does not try to influence the reader's concretization of a given text in a certain direction. Instead, it aims at giving the reader the most complete set of materials that can help him or her in the concretization of the text, a set of materials he or she is free to accept or reject.

A systems approach to literary studies aims at making literary texts accessible to the reader, by means of description, analysis, historiography, translation, produced not on the basis of a given, transient poetics (which will, of course, take great pains to establish itself as absolute and eternal), but on the basis of that desire to know, which is itself subject to constraints not dissimilar to the ones operating in the literary system, a desire to know not as literature itself knows, but to know the ways in which literature offers its knowledge, which is so important that it should be shared to the greatest possible extent.

Notes

The text of Brecht's *Mutter Courage und ihre Kinder* referred to in this article is that published by Aufbau Verlag, Berlin in 1968. H. R. Hays' translation was published by New Directions, New York, in the anthology for the year 1941. It was obviously based on the first version of *Mother Courage*, and I have taken that into account in my analysis. The Bentley translation I refer to is the one published by Methuen in London in 1967. The Manheim translation is the one published in volume five of the collected plays of Bertolt Brecht, edited by Manheim and John Willet, and published by Vintage Books, New York in 1972.

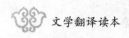 文学翻译读本

【翻译鉴赏】

To Be, or Not to Be
William Shakespeare

To be, or not to be: that is the question:
Whether 'tis nobler in the mind to suffer
The slings and arrows of outrageous fortune,
Or to take arms against a sea of troubles,
And by opposing end them? To die: to sleep—
    No more; and by a sleep to say we end
    The heart-ache and the thousand natural shocks
That flesh is heir to, 'tis a consummation
Devoutly to be wish'd. To die, to sleep;
To sleep: perchance to dream. Ay, there's the rub;
For in that sleep of death what dreams may come,
When we have shuffled off this mortal coil,
Must give us pause. There's the respect
That makes calamity of so long life;
For who would bear the whips and scorns of time,
The oppressor's wrong, the proud man's contumely,
The pangs of despis'd love, the law's delay,
The insolence of office, and the spurns
That patient merit of the unworthy takes,
When he himself might his quietus make
With a bare bodkin? who would fardels bear,
To grunt and sweat under a weary life,
But that the dread of something after death—
The undiscovered country, from whose bourn
No traveller returns—, puzzles the will
And makes us rather bear those ills we have
Than fly to others that we know not of?
Thus conscience does make cowards of us all;
And thus the native hue of resolution
Is sicklied o'er with the pale cast of thought,
And enterprises of great pitch and moment,
With this regard, their currents turn awry,
And lose the name of action. —Soft you now!
The fair Ophelia! —Nymph, in thy orisons
Be all my sins remember'd.

364

—Hamlet

Act Three，Scene One

【译文】(朱生豪译)

生存还是毁灭,这是一个值得考虑的问题[1];

默然忍受命运的暴虐的毒箭[2],或是挺身反抗人世的无涯的苦难[3],

通过斗争把它们扫清,这两种行为,哪一种更高贵?

死了;睡着了;什么都完了;

要是在这一种睡眠之中,我们心头的创痛,

以及其他无数血肉之躯所不能避免的打击,都可以从此消失,

那正是我们求之不得的结局。

死了;睡着了;睡着了也许还会做梦;

嗯,阻碍就在这儿:

因为当我们摆脱了这一具朽腐的皮囊[4]以后,

在那死的睡眠里,究竟将要做些什么梦,那不能不使我们踌躇顾虑。

人们甘心久困于患难之中[5],也就是为了这个缘故;

谁愿意忍受人世的鞭挞和讥嘲、压迫者的凌辱、

傲慢者的冷眼[6]、被轻蔑的爱情的惨痛、法律的迁延、

官吏的横暴和费尽辛勤所换来的小人的鄙视[7];

要是他只要用一柄小小的刀子,就可以清算他自己的一生[8]?

谁愿意负着这样的重担,

在烦劳的生命的压迫下呻吟流汗,倘不是因为惧怕不可知的死后[9],

惧怕那从来不曾有一个旅人回来过的神秘之国[9],

是它迷惑了我们的意志,使我们宁愿忍受目前的磨折,

不敢向我们所不知道的痛苦飞去?

这样,重重的顾虑[10]使我们全变成了懦夫,

决心的赤热的光彩,被审慎的思维[11]盖上了一层灰色,

伟大的事业[12]在这一种考虑之下,也会逆流而退,

失去了行动的意义[13]。

且慢,美丽的奥菲利娅!

——女神,在你的祈祷之中,不要忘记替我忏悔我的罪孽。

——《哈姆雷特》(第三幕第一场)

【译文评析】

[1] "值得考虑"是译者的强调,为照顾后文的思想活动,属翻译规则范围之内。

[2] in mind译为"默然",好! 后文仍延续上文的调子,便有了"命运的暴虐的毒箭"的译文,应译为"暴虐命运的明枪暗箭"更准确。

[3] "挺身"是译者的强调,照顾了前面的"默然",显出文采。

[4] this mortal coil意为"尘世的混乱",译者将之具体化为"腐朽的皮囊",虽然偏离原文的意思,但传递出原文的意涵,显示出译者自身文化的影响。

[5] 这句原文之意为"正因为顾虑重重才让生命受苦受难活得长久";"人们甘心久困于患难之中"的译文更汉语化,更流畅。

[6] contumely 译为"冷眼",显然与下句的"鄙视"呼应起来,足见译者的用心。

[7] 不用"侮辱"这类词,而用视觉方面的"鄙视"一类词,更让人不能忍受。

[8] 前边的主语是"刀子",后句完全可以译为"了结自己的生命",但是译者显然注意到 queitus 这个词的特别所在,所以译为"清算他自己的一生",更准确。

[9] undiscovered country"未发掘国度"之意,译为"神秘之国",更接近"天国"的含义。

[10] thus conscience 译为"重重的顾虑",既灵活又传神。

[11] the pale cast of thought 实为"顾虑重重"之意,"审慎的思维"是对白话文表达的丰富。

[12] enterprises of great pitch and moment 译为"重大的事业"似乎更好些。

[13] the name of action"行动的名分"之意,类似"师出有名"的意思。"行动的意义"译得活泛。

——参考苏福忠《读点莎士比亚》

茶 馆
（第二幕　选段）
老 舍

吴祥子　瞎混呗! 有皇上的时候,我们给皇上效力,有袁大总统的时候,我们给袁大总统效力;现而今,宋恩子,该怎么说啦?

宋恩子　谁给饭吃,咱们给谁效力!

常四爷　要是洋人给饭吃呢?

松二爷　四爷,咱们走吧!

吴祥子　告诉你,常四爷,要我们效力的都仗着洋人撑腰! 没有洋枪洋炮,怎能够打起仗来呢?

松二爷　您说的对! 嗻! 四爷,走吧!

常四爷　再见吧,二位,盼着你们快快升官发财!（同松二爷下）

宋恩子　这小子!

王利发　(倒茶)常四爷老是那么又倔又硬,别计较他!（让茶）二位喝碗吧,刚沏好的。

宋恩子　后面住着的都是什么人?

王利发　多半是大学生,还有几位熟人。我有登记簿子,随时报告给"巡警阁下"。我拿来,二位看看?

吴祥子　我们不看簿子,看人!

王利发　您甭看,准保都是靠得住的人!

宋恩子　你为什么爱租给学生们呢? 学生不是什么老实家伙呀!

王利发　这年月,作官的今天上任,明天撤职,作买卖的今天开市,明天关门,都不可靠! 只有学生有钱,能够按月交房租,没钱的就上不了大学啊! 您看,是这么一笔帐不是?

宋恩子　都叫你咂摸透了! 你想的对! 现在,连我们也欠饷啊!

吴祥子　是呀,所以非天天拿人不可,好得点津贴!

宋恩子　就仗着有错拿,没错放的,拿住人就有津贴! 走吧,到后边看看去!

王利发　二位,二位! 您放心,准保没错儿!

宋恩子　不看,拿不到人,谁给我们津贴呢?

吴祥子　王掌柜不愿意咱们看,王掌柜必会给咱们想办法! 咱们得给王掌柜留个面子! 对吧? 王掌柜!

王利发　我……

宋恩子　我出个不很高明的主意:干脆来个包月,每月一号,按阳历算,你把那点……

吴祥子　那点意思!

宋恩子　对,那点意思送到,你省事,我们也省事!

王利发　那点意思得多少呢?

吴祥子　多年的交情,你看着办! 你聪明,还能把那点意思闹成不好意思吗?

【背景介绍】

1. 老舍(1899—1966)的《茶馆》描写了清末、民初、抗战胜利后三个历史时期的北京社会风貌。全剧共分三幕,作者以独特的艺术手法,截取横跨半个世纪三个旧时代的断面,通过茶馆这个小窗口以及出入于茶馆的北京各阶层及其言谈举止折射出整个社会大背景。其中,《茶馆》第二幕展现了民国初年连年不断的内战给普通老百姓带来的深重苦难。以上段落选自第二幕,描写了侦缉队两位老式特务来裕泰茶馆进行敲诈的过程。

2. 审美鉴赏

本选段对话句子短小,多数句子不到七八个字,十个以上的句子很少;句子结构单纯,口语特点鲜明,随着谈论话题的演进形成自然流畅、不疾不徐的日常会话节奏;对话中所用词句在语境中除表达基本理性意义之外,还附带着诸多感性意义,从而将戏剧语言之“潜台词”彰显得颇为充分;对话中使用的句式特点鲜明,体现出简洁明快、生动活泼的口语色彩。

【译文】

Teahouse

(Act Two Excerpt)

Lao She

trans. Ying Ruocheng

Wu Xiangz：Oh, muddling along! When there was an emperor, we served him. When there was President Yuan Shikai, we served him.[1] Now, Song Enz, how should I put it?

Song Enz：Now we serve anyone who puts rice in our bowls.[2]

Chang：Even foreigners?

Song：Master Chang, let's get going!

Wu Xiangz：Understand this, Master Chang. Everyone we serve is backed by some foreign power. How can anyone make war without foreign arms and guns?

Song：You're so right! Master Chang, let's go.

Chang：Goodbye, gentlemen. I'm sure you'll soon be rewarded and promoted![3]

(*Goes off with Song.*)

Song Enz：Bloody fool!

Wang Lifa：(*pouring out tea*) Master Chang has always been stubborn, won't bow down to anyone![4] Take no notice of him. (*offering them tea*) Have a cup, it's fresh.

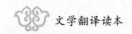

Song Enz： What sort of people do you have as lodgers?

Wang Lifa： Mostly university students，and a couple of acquaintances. I've got a register. Their names are always promptly reported to the local police-station. Shall I fetch it for you?

Wu Xiangz： We don't look at books. We look at people!

Wang Lifa： No need for that. I can vouch for them all.

Song Enz： Why are you so partial to students? They're not generally quiet characters.

Wang Lifa： Officials one day in and out of office the next. It's the same with tradesmen. In business today and broke tomorrow. Can't rely on anyone![5] Only students have money to pay the rent each month，because you need money to get into university in the first place. That's how I figure it. What do you think?

Song Enz： Got it all worked out! You're quite right. Nowadays even we aren't always paid on time.

Wu Xiangz： So that's why we must make arrests every day，to get our bonus.

Song Enz： We nick people at random，but they never get out at random. [6] As long as we make arrests，we get our bonus. Come on，let's take a look back there!

Wang Lifa： Gentlemen，gentlemen! Don't trouble yourselves. Everyone behaves himself properly，I assure you.

Song Enz： But if we don't take a look，we can't nab anyone. How will we get our bonus?

Wu Xiangz： Since the manager's not keen to let us have a look，he must have thought of another way. Ought to try to help him keep up a front. Right，Manager Wang?

Wang Lifa： I...

Song Enz： I have an idea. Not all that brilliant perhaps. [7] Let's do it on a monthly basis. On the first of every month，according to the new solar calendar，you'll hand in a...

Wu Xiangz： A token of friendship!

Song Enz： Right. You'll hand in a token of friendship. That'll save no end of trouble for both sides.

Wang Lifa： How much is this token of friendship worth?

Wu Xiangzi： As old friends，we'll leave that to you. You're a bright fellow. I'm sure you wouldn't want this token of friendship to seem unfriendly，would you?[8]

【译文评析】

[1] 原文中独语句"瞎混呗!"译文也为独语句 Oh, muddling along! 并根据会话情景对语气词进行了语序调整。同样的，原文中后面形式整饬的整句，译文也为整句，并依照英文的特点对"皇上"、"袁世凯"在剧中第二次出现时以代词指代。译文简练得体，传译出了原文的语义与语势。

[2] 该句成功再现侦缉队老牌特务盛气凌人、专横跋扈的语气。

[3] "升官发财"释义精炼准确，音韵铿锵，语境效果尤佳。

[4] 将原文的"又倔又硬"一分为二，便于口头言说，也突出了重点。

[5] 原文为整句,译文也是整句,依实出华,形式简练,表达准确。

[6] 该句口语句式鲜明,既平稳了对话节奏,也突出了谈话的重点,nick 一词典型地烘托出说话人社会文化层次不高的人物形象。

[7] 将原句一分为二,口语节奏平稳,重点突出。

[8] 该句如实转存,口语句式特点鲜明。a token of friendship 与 unfriendly 从形式与内容上转存了"意思"的双关修辞,成功地译出了吴祥子的"意图":表面和善友好,讲情义,实质是敲诈勒索。

——参考张保红《文学翻译》评析内容

【翻译试笔】

【英译汉】

The Importance of Being Earnest

Oscar Wilde

[Enter Lady Bracknell.]

LADY BRACKNELL. Mr. Worthing! Rise, sir, from this semi-recumbent posture. It is most indecorous.

GWENDOLEN. Mamma! [He tries to rise; she restrains him.] I must beg you to retire. This is no place for you. Besides, Mr. Worthing has not quite finished yet.

LADY BRACKNELL. Finished what, may I ask?

GWENDOLEN. I am engaged to Mr. Worthing, mamma. [They rise together.]

LADY BRACKNELL. Pardon me, you are not engaged to anyone. When you do become engaged to someone, I, or your father, should his health permit him, will inform you of the fact. An engagement should come on a young girl as a surprise, pleasant or unpleasant, as the case may be. It is hardly a matter that she could be allowed to arrange for herself—And now I have a few questions to put to you, Mr. Worthing. While I am making these inquiries, you, Gwendolen, will wait for me below in the carriage.

GWENDOLEN. [Reproachfully.] Mamma!

LADY BRACKNELL. In the carriage, Gwendolen! [Gwendolen goes to the door. She and Jack blow kisses to each other behind Lady Bracknell's back. Lady Bracknell looks vaguely about as if she could not understand what the noise was. Finally turns round.] Gwendolen, the carriage!

GWENDOLEN. Yes, mamma. [Goes out, looking back at Jack.]

LADY BRACKNELL. [Sitting down.] You can take a seat, Mr. Worthing.

[Looks in her pocket for note-book and pencil.]

JACK. Thank you, Lady Bracknell, I prefer standing.

LADY BRACKNELL. [Pencil and note-book in hand.] I feel bound to tell you that you are not down on my list of eligible young men, although I have the same list as the dear Duchess of Bolton has. We work together, in fact. However, I am quite ready to enter your name, should your answers be what a really affectionate mother requires. Do you smoke?

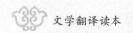

JACK. Well, yes, I must admit I smoke.

LADY BRACKNELL. I am glad to hear it. A man should always have an occupation of some kind. There are far too many idle men in London as it is. How old are you?

JACK. Twenty-nine.

LADY BRACKNELL. A very good age to be married at. I have always been of opinion that a man who desires to get married should know either everything or nothing. Which do you know?

JACK. [After some hesitation.] I know nothing, Lady Bracknell.

LADY BRACKNELL. I am pleased to hear it. I do not approve of anything that tampers with natural ignorance. Ignorance is like a delicate exotic fruit; touch it and the bloom is gone. The whole theory of modern education is radically unsound. Fortunately in England, at any rate, education produces no effect whatsoever. If it did, it would prove a serious danger to the upper classes, and probably lead to acts of violence in Grosvenor Square. What is your income?

JACK. Between seven and eight thousand a year.

LADY BRACKNELL. [Makes a note in her book.] In land, or in investments?

JACK. In investments, chiefly.

LADY BRACKNELL. That is satisfactory. What between the duties expected of one during one's lifetime, and the duties exacted from one after one's death, land has ceased to be either a profit or a pleasure. It gives one position, and prevents one from keeping it up. That's all that can be said about land.

JACK. I have a country house with some land, of course, attached to it, about fifteen hundred acres, I believe; but I don't depend on that for my real income. In fact, as far as I can make out, the poachers are the only people who make anything out of it.

LADY BRACKNELL. A country house! How many bedrooms? Well, that point can be cleared up afterwards. You have a town house, I hope? A girl with a simple, unspoiled nature, like Gwendolen, could hardly be expected to reside in the country.

JACK. Well, I own a house in Belgrave Square, but it is let by the year to Lady Bloxham. Of course, I can get it back whenever I like, at six months' notice.

LADY BRACKNELL. Lady Bloxham? I don't know her.

JACK. Oh, she goes about very little. She is a lady considerably advanced in years.

LADY BRACKNELL. Ah, nowadays that is no guarantee of respectability of character. What number in Belgrave Square?

JACK. 149.

LADY BRACKNELL. [Shaking her head.] The unfashionable side. I thought there was something. However, that could easily be altered.

JACK. Do you mean the fashion, or the side?

LADY BRACKNELL. [Sternly.] Both, if necessary, I presume. What are your politics?

JACK. Well, I am afraid I really have none. I am a Liberal Unionist.

LADY BRACKNELL. Oh, they count as Tories. They dine with us. Or come in the evening, at any rate. Now to minor matters. Are your parents living?

JACK. I have lost both my parents.

LADY BRACKNELL. To lose one parent, Mr. Worthing, may be regarded as a misfortune; to lose both looks like carelessness. Who was your father? He was evidently a man of some wealth. Was he born in what the Radical papers call the purple of commerce, or did he rise from the ranks of the aristocracy?

JACK. I am afraid I really don't know. The fact is, Lady Bracknell, I said I had lost my parents. It would be nearer the truth to say that my parents seem to have lost me … I don't actually know who I am by birth. I was… well, I was found.

LADY BRACKNELL. Found!

JACK. The late Mr. Thomas Cardew, an old gentleman of a very charitable and kindly disposition, found me, and gave me the name of Worthing, because he happened to have a first-class ticket for Worthing in his pocket at the time. Worthing is a place in Sussex. It is a seaside resort.

LADY BRACKNELL. Where did the charitable gentleman who had a first-class ticket for this seaside resort find you?

JACK. [Gravely.] In a handbag.

LADY BRACKNELL. A handbag?

JACK. [Very seriously.] Yes, Lady Bracknell. I was in a handbag—a somewhat large, black leather handbag, with handles to it—an ordinary handbag in fact.

LADY BRACKNELL. In what locality did this Mr. James, or Thomas, Cardew come across this ordinary handbag?

JACK. In the cloakroom at Victoria Station. It was given to him in mistake for his own.

LADY BRACKNELL. The cloakroom at Victoria Station?

JACK. Yes. The Brighton line.

LADY BRACKNELL. The line is immaterial. Mr. Worthing, I confess I feel somewhat bewildered by what you have just told me. To be born, or at any rate bred, in a handbag, whether it had handles or not, seems to me to display a contempt for the ordinary decencies of family life that reminds one of the worst excesses of the French Revolution. And I presume you know what that unfortunate movement led to? As for the particular locality in which the handbag was found, a cloakroom at a railway station might serve to conceal a social indiscretion—has probably, indeed, been used for that purpose before now—but it could hardly be regarded as an assured basis for a recognised position in good society.

JACK. May I ask you then what you would advise me to do? I need hardly say I would do anything in the world to ensure Gwendolen's happiness.

LADY BRACKNELL. I would strongly advise you, Mr. Worthing, to try and acquire some relations as soon as possible, and to make a definite effort to produce at any rate one parent, of either sex, before the season is quite over.

JACK. Well, I don't see how I could possibly manage to do that. I can produce the handbag at any moment. It is in my dressing-room at home. I really think that should satisfy you, Lady Bracknell.

LADY BRACKNELL. Me, sir! What has it to do with me? You can hardly imagine that I and Lord Bracknell would dream of allowing our only daughter—a girl brought up with the utmost care—to marry into a cloakroom, and form an alliance with a parcel? Good morning, Mr. Worthing!

[LADY BRACKNELL sweeps out in majestic indignation.]

【汉译英】

窦娥冤·法场
关汉卿

(监斩官上)

监斩官　下官监斩官是也。今日处决犯人,把住巷口,休放往来人走。

(丑发鼓三通,打锣三下科)(刽子磨刀科)(刽子磨旗科)(定头通锣鼓科)(窦娥带枷上)

刽子　行动些,把住巷口。

窦娥　[正宫端正好]没来由犯王法,葫芦提遭刑宪。叫声屈动地惊天,我将天地合埋怨。天也! 你不与人为方便。[滚绣球]有日月朝暮显,有山河今古监。天也! 却不把清浊分辨,可知道看了盗跖颜渊。有德的受贫穷更命短,造恶的享富贵又寿延。天也! 做得个怕硬欺软,不想天地也顺水推船。地也! 你不分好歹难为地。天也! 我今日负屈衔冤哀天,空教我独语独言。

刽子　窦娥行动些,误了时辰也。

窦娥　[倘秀才]则被这枷的我左侧右偏,人拥的我前合后偃。窦娥向哥哥行有句言。

刽子　你有什么话说?

窦娥　前街里去心怀恨,后街里去死无冤。非是我自专。

刽子　你当刑,如今来赴法场,有甚亲眷?

窦娥　[叨叨令]你道我当刑赴法场何亲眷?

刽子　你前街去是怎生? 后街去是如何?

窦娥　前街里去告您些颜面,我片后街里去呵不把哥哥怨,前街里去只恐怕俺婆婆见。

刽子　你的性命也顾不得,怕他怎的?

窦娥　他见我披枷带锁赴法场餐刀去呵。枉将他气杀也么哥,枉将他气杀也么哥。告哥哥临危好与人行方便。

(蔡婆上)

蔡婆　云天呵,兀的不是我媳妇儿。我儿也,不痛杀我也。

刽子　婆子靠后。

窦娥　叫俺婆婆来,嘱咐他几句话咱。

刽子　那婆子近前来,你媳妇要嘱咐你话里。

蔡婆　孩儿,痛杀我也。

窦娥　婆婆。都只为你身子不快,思量羊肚儿汤吃,我安排了,又道少盐醋。被张驴儿赚的我取盐醋去,他将毒药放在汤里。可着我拿过去与你吃,谁想你让与他老子吃。实指望药死你,要霸占我为妻。不想把他老子药死了。因报前仇,把我拖去官司,我怕连累婆婆,我屈招了。今日赴法场典刑。婆婆澄不了的浆水饭。澄半碗儿与我吃。烧不了的纸钱,与窦娥烧一陌儿。则是看你死的孩儿面上。(唱)[快活三]看窦娥葫芦提当罪愆着窦娥身首不完全,想窦娥从前已往干家缘。婆婆,看窦娥少爷无娘面。[鲍老儿]看窦娥服侍婆婆这几年,看时节将碗凉浆奠。

蔡婆　孩儿放心,兀的不痛杀也。

窦娥　你去那受刑法尸骸上列些纸钱,看你那化去孩儿面。啼啼哭哭,烦烦恼恼,怨气冲天。我不分说,不明不暗负屈衔冤。

刽子　兀那婆子靠后,时辰到了也。

(窦娥跪下科)(刽子开枷科)

窦娥　窦娥告监斩官,要一领净席。我有三件事,肯依窦娥,便死无怨。要太二白练挂在旗枪上。若刀过处头落,一腔热血休落在下,都飞在白练上者,若委实冤枉。如今是三伏天道,下心瑞雪,遮了窦娥尸首。着这楚州亢旱三年。

刽子　打嘴,那得此话。

(刽子磨旗科)

窦娥　(唱)[尾声]当日个哑妇含药反受殃,耕牛为主遭鞭。

刽子　天色阴了,呀下雪了。

(刽子扇雪天发愿科)(磨旗刽子遮住科)

窦娥　霜降始知邹衍说,雪飞方表窦娥冤。

(行刃刽子开刀钋头)(付净撺尸)

刽子　好妙手也!咱吃酒去来。

(众和下。抬尸下)

【参考译文】

不可儿戏

王尔德

余光中译(选自第一幕)

巴夫人上

巴夫人　华先生!站起来,别这么不上不下的怪样子。太不成体统了。

关多琳　妈!(他要站起来,被她阻止)求求您回避一下,这儿没您的事。况且,华先生还没做完呢。

巴夫人　什么东西没做完,请问?

关多琳　我正跟华先生订了婚，妈。（两人一同站起）

巴夫人　对不起，你跟谁都没有订婚。你真跟谁订了婚，告诉你这件事的是我，或者是你爸爸，如果他身体撑得住的话。订婚对一个少女，应该是突如其来，至于是惊喜还是惊骇，就得看情形而定。这种事，由不得女孩子自己做主……华先生，现在我有几个问题要问你。我盘问他的时候，关多琳，你下楼去马车上等我。

关多琳　（怨恨地）妈！

巴夫人　马车上去，关多琳！（关多琳走到门口，跟杰克在巴夫人背后互抛飞吻。巴夫人茫然四顾，似乎不明白声自何来。终于她转过身去）关多琳，马车上去！

关多琳　好啦，妈。（临去回顾杰克）

巴夫人　（坐下）你坐下来吧，华先生。
　　　　探袋寻找小簿子和铅笔。

杰　克　谢谢您，巴夫人，我情愿站着。

巴夫人　（手握铅笔和小簿子）我觉得应该告诉你，你并不在我那张合格青年的名单上：我的那张跟包顿公爵夫人手头的一模一样。老实说，这名单是我们共同拟定的。不过嘛，我很愿意把你的名字加上去，只要你回答我的话能满足一个真正爱女心切的母亲。你抽烟吗？

杰　克　呃，抽的，不瞒您说。

巴夫人　听到你抽烟，我很高兴。男人应该经常有点事作。目前在伦敦，闲着的男人太多了。你几岁啦？

杰　克　二十九。

巴夫人　正是结婚的大好年龄。我一向认为，有意结婚的男人，要嘛应该无所不知，要嘛应该一无所知。你是哪一类呀？

杰　克　（犹豫了一下）巴夫人，我一无所知。

巴夫人　这我很高兴。我最不赞成把天生懵懂的人拿来改造。懵懂无知就像娇嫩的奇瓜异果一样，只要一碰，就失去光彩了。现代教育的整套理论根本就不健全。无论如何，幸好在英国，教育并未产生什么效果。否则，上流社会就会有严重的危机，说不定格罗夫纳广场还会引起暴动呢。你的收入有多少？

杰　克　七八千镑一年。

巴夫人　（记在簿上）是地产还是投资？

杰　克　大半是投资。

巴夫人　很好。一个人身前要缴地产税，死后又要缴遗产税，有块地呀早就是既不能生利又不能享福啰。有了地产就有地位，却又撑不起这地位。除此之外，也没有什么好说的了。

杰　克　我在乡下还有座别墅，当然还连着一块地，大约一千五百亩吧，我想；可是我真正的收入并不靠这个。其实嘛，照我看呀，只有非法闯进来的猎人才有利可图呢。

巴夫人　一座别墅！有多少卧房呀？呃，这一点以后再清算吧。想必你城里也有房子啰？总不能指望像关多琳这样单纯的乖女孩住到乡下吧。

杰　克　嗯，我在贝尔格瑞夫广场是有栋房子，不过是论年租给了布夫人。当然我随时都可以收回来，只要六个月前通知她就行了。

巴夫人　布夫人？我可不认得她。

杰　克　呃,她很少出来走动。这位夫人年纪已经很大了。

巴夫人　哼,这年头呀年高也不一定就德劭。是贝尔格瑞夫广场几号呢?

杰　克　一百四十九号。

巴夫人　(摇摇头)那一头没有派头。我就料到有问题。不过,这一点很容易修正。

杰　克　你是指派头呢,还是地段?

巴夫人　(严厉地)必要的话,我想,两样都有份。你的政治立场呢?

杰　克　这个,只怕我根本没什么立场。我属于自由联合党。

巴夫人　哦,那就算是保守党了。这班人来我们家吃饭的,至少饭后来我们家做客。现在来谈谈细节吧。你的双亲都健在吧?

杰　克　我已经失去了双亲。

巴夫人　失去了父亲或母亲,华先生,还可以说是不幸;双亲都失去了就未免太大意了。令尊是谁呢?他当然有几文钱。到底他是出身于前进报纸所谓的商业世家呢,还是从贵族的行伍里面出人头地的呢?

杰　克　恐怕我根本说不上来。说真的,巴夫人,刚才我说我失去了双亲,但是实在一点儿,不如说是我的双亲失去了我……我其实不知道自己生在谁家。我是……呃,我是拣来的。

巴夫人　拣来的!

杰　克　拣到我的,是已故的贾汤姆先生,一位性情很慈善很温厚的老绅士。他取了"华"做我的姓,因为当时他口袋里正好有一张去"华兴"的头等车票。华兴在塞西克斯县,是海边的名胜。

巴夫人　这位买了头等票去海边名胜的善心绅士,在哪儿拣到你的呢?

杰　克　(严肃地)在一只手提袋里。

巴夫人　一只手提袋里?

杰　克　(极其认真地)是啊,巴夫人。当时我是在一只手提袋里——一只相当大的黑皮手提袋,还有把手——其实嘛就是一只普普通通的手提袋。

巴夫人　这位贾詹姆还是贾汤姆先生,是在什么地方发现这普普通通的手提袋呢?

杰　克　在维多利亚火车站的行李间。

杰　克　是呀。去布莱敦的月台。

巴夫人　什么月台无关紧要。华先生,坦白说吧,你刚才这一番话有点令我不懂。在一只手提袋里出世,或者,至少在一只手提袋里寄养,在我看来,对家庭生活的常规都是不敬的表示:这种态度令人想起了法国革命的放纵无度。我想你也知道那倒霉的运动是怎样的下场吧?至于发现手提袋的地点嘛,火车站的行李间正好用来掩饰社会上的丑事——说不定实际上早派过这种用场了——可是上流社会的正规地位,总不能靠火车站的行李间做根据呀。

杰　克　那么,我该怎么办,是否可以请您指点?不用说,为了保证关多琳的幸福,什么事我都愿做。

巴夫人　那我就要郑重劝告你,华先生,要尽快设法去找几个亲戚来,而且乘社交季节还没结束,要好好努力,不论是父亲还是母亲,至少得提一个出来。

杰　克　这个,我实在想不出有什么办法。那手提袋嘛我随时都提得出来:就在我家的梳妆室里。说真的,巴夫人,我想这样你也该放心了吧。

巴夫人　我放心,华先生! 跟我有什么关系呀? 你只当我跟巴大人真会让我们的独生女——嫁到行李间里去,跟一个包裹成亲吗? 再见了,华先生!

巴夫人气派十足地愤愤然掉头而去。

Snow in Midsummer
Guan Hanqing
trans. Yang Hsien-yi & Gladys Yang

(Enter the officer in charge.)

OFFICER: I am the officer in charge of executions. Today we are putting a criminal to death. We must stand guard at the end of the road, to see that no one comes through.

(Enter the Attendants. They beat the drum and the gong three times; then the executioner enters, sharpens his sword and waves a flag. Dou E is led on in a cangue. The gong and drum are beaten.)

EXECUTIONER: Get a move on! Let no one pass this way.

DOU E: Though no fault of mine I am called a criminal,
　　　　And condemned to be beheaded——
　　　　I cry out to Heaven and Earth of this injustice!
　　　　I reproach both Earth and Heaven
　　　　For they would not save me
　　　　The sun and moon give light by day and by night,
　　　　Mountains and rivers watch over the world of men;
　　　　Yet Heaven cannot tell the innocent from the guilty;
　　　　And confuses the wicked with the good!
　　　　The good are poor, and die before their time;
　　　　The wicked are rich, and live to a great old age.
　　　　The gods are afraid of the mighty and bully the weak;
　　　　They let evil take its course.
　　　　Ah, Earth! You will not distinguish good from bad,
　　　　And, Heaven! You let me suffer this injustice!
　　　　Tears pour down my cheeks in vain!

EXECUTIONER: Get a move on! We are late.

DOU E: The cangue round my neck makes me stagger this way and that,
　　　　And I'm jostled backward and forward by the crowd.
　　　　Will you do me a favor, brother?

EXECUTIONER: What do you want?

DOU E: If you take me the front way, I shall bear you a grudge;

If you take me the back way, I shall die content.

Please do not think me willful!

EXECUTIONER: Now that you're going to the execution ground, are there any relatives you want to see?

DOU E: I am going to die. What relatives do I need?

EXECUTIONER: Why did you ask me just now to take you the back way?

DOU E: Please don't go by the front street, brother,

But take me by the back street.

The other way my mother-in-law might see me.

EXECUTIONER: You can't escape death, so why worry if she sees you?

DOU E: If my mother-in-law were to see me in chains being led to the execution ground—

She would burst with indignation!

She would burst with indignation!

Please grant me this comfort, brother, before I die!

(Enter Mistress Cai.)

MRS. CAI: Ah, Heaven! Isn't that my daughter-in-law? This will be the death of me!

EXECUTIONER: Stand back, old woman!

DOU E: Let her come closer so that I can say a few words to her.

EXECUTIONER: Hey, old woman! Come here. Your daughter-in-law wants to speak to you.

MRS. CAI: Poor child! This will be the death of me!

DOU E: Mother, when you were unwell and asked for mutton tripe soup, I prepared some for you. Donkey Zhang made me fetch more salt and vinegar so that he could poison the soup, and then told me to give it to you. He didn't know his old man would drink it. Donkey Zhang poisoned the soup to kill you, so that he could force me to be his wife. He never thought his father would die instead. To take revenge, he dragged me to court. Because I didn't want you to suffer, I had to confess to murder, and now I am going to be killed. In future, mother, if you have gruel to spare, give me half a bowl; and if you have paper money to spare, burn some for me, for sake of you dead son!

Take pity on one who is dying an unjust death;

Take pity on one whose head will be struck from her body;

Take pity on one who has worked with you in your home;

Take pity on one who has neither mother nor father;

Take pity on one who has served you all these years;

And at festivals offer my spirit a bowl of cold gruel.

MRS. CAI: (weeping): Don't worry. Ah, this will be the death of me!

DOU E: Burn some paper coins to my headless corpse,

For the sake of your dead son

We wail and complain to Heaven；

There is no justice! DOU E is wrongly slain!

EXECUTIONER：Now then, old woman, stand back! The time has come.

(DOU E kneels and Executioner removes the cangue from her neck.)

DOU E：I want to say three things, officer. If you will let me, I shall die content. I want a clean mat and a white silk streamer twelve feet long to hang on the flag-pole. When the sword strikes off my head, not a drop of my warm blood will stain the ground. It will all fly up instead to the white silk streamer. This is the hottest time of summer, sir. If injustice has indeed been DOU E, three feet of snow will cover my dead body. Then this district will suffer from drought for three whole years.

EXECUTIONER：Be quiet! What a thing to say!

(The Executioner waves his flag.)

DOU E：A dumb woman was blamed for poisoning herself；

A buffalo whipped while it toils for its master.

EXECUTIONER：Why is it suddenly so overcast? It is snowing!

(He prays to Heaven.)

DOU E：Once Zou Yan caused frost to appear；

Now snow will show the injustice DOU E to me!

(The Executioner beheads her, and the Attendant sees to her body.)

EXECUTIONER：A fine stroke! Now let us go and have a drink.

(The Attendants assent, and carry the body off.)

【延伸阅读】

[1] Bassnett, S. *Translation Studies* (3rd Edition)[M]. London & New York：Routledge, 2002.

[2] Birch, C. Translating Ming Plays：*Lumudan (The Green Peony)* [A]. In Eoyang, E. & Lin Yaofu, *Translating Chinese Culture*. Bloomington and Indianapolis：Indiana University Press, 1995.

[3] Boyd, D. & Palmer, R. *After Hitchcock：Influence, Imitation, and Intertextuality* [M]. Barton. Austin, TX, USA：University of Texas Press, 2006.

[4] Chesterman, A. *Memes of Translation* [M]. Amsterdam/Philadelphia：Benjamins Publishing Company, 1997.

[5] David, S. *Speech and Performance in Shakespeare's Sonnets and Plays* [M]. Cambridge：Cambridge University Press, 2002.

[6] de Rooy, R. *Divine Comedies for the New Millennium：Recent Dante Translations in America and the Netherlands* [M]. Amsterdam, NLD：Amsterdam University Press, 2003.

[7] Jauss, H. R. *Toward an Aesthetic of Reception* [M]. Minneapolis. MN. USA：

University of Minnesota Press，1982.

[8] Lefevere，A. *Translation/ History/ Culture*[C]. London & New York：Routledge，1992.

[9] Lefevere，A. Translation and Canon Formation：Nine Decades of Drama in the United States[A]. In Román，Álvarez & M. Carmen-África Vidal（Eds.），*Translation，Power，Subversion*. Clevedon & Philadelphia & Adelaide：Multilingual Matters Ltd.，1996.

[10] Levith，M. J. *Shakespeare in China*[M]. London，GBR：Continuum International Publishing，2004.

[11] Mundy，J. *Introducing Translation Studies：Theories and Applications*[M]. London & New York：Routledge，2001.

[12] Newmark，P. *A Textbook of Translation*[M]. Shanghai：Shanghai Foreign Languages Education Press，2001.

[13] Poyatos，F. *Nonverbal Communication across Disciplines. Volume 3：Narrative literature，theater，cinema，translation*[M]. Amsterdam/Philadelphia：John Benjamins Publishing Company，2002.

[14] Zatlin，P. *Theatrical Translation and Film Adaptation：A Practitioner's View*[M]. Clevedon，GBR：Multilingual Matters Limited，2005.

[15] 布鲁克.敞开的门:谈表演和戏剧[M].于东田译.北京:新星出版社,2007.

[16] 曹文涛.英语世界的中国传统戏剧研究与翻译[M].广州:广东高等教育出版社,2011.

[17] 丁涛.戏剧三人行——重读曹禺、田汉、郭沫若[M].厦门:厦门大学出版社,2009.

[18] 冯世则.翻译匠语[M].上海:文汇出版社,2005.

[19] 胡导.戏剧表演学:论斯氏演剧学说在我国的实践与发展[M].北京:中国戏剧出版社,2009.

[20] 黄忠廉.变译理论[M].北京:中国对外翻译出版公司,2002.

[21] 李奭学.得意忘言:翻译、文学与文化评论[M].生活·读书·新知三联书店,2007.

[22] 刘靖之.和谐的乐声[M].//巴别达文丛.武汉:湖北教育出版社,2002.

[23] 马会娟.论英若诚译《茶馆》的动态表演性原则[J].解放军外国语学院学报,2004(5).

[24] 任晓霏.登场的译者——英若诚戏剧翻译系统研究[M].北京:中国社会科学出版社,2007.

[25] 莎士比亚.莎士比亚全集[M].朱生豪.南京:译林出版社,1998.

[26] 莎士比亚.莎士比亚戏剧精选:英汉对照[M].朱生豪译.北京:世界知识出版社,2010.

[27] 王宏印.新译学论稿[M].北京:人民大学出版社,2011.

[28] 文军.杨宪益先生的 Pygmalion 两译本比较——兼论戏剧翻译[J].外国语,1995(4).

[29] 吴朱红.西方现代戏剧译作:吴朱红外国新剧译作集[M].北京:中国传媒大学出版社,2005.

[30] 吴朱红.西方现代戏剧译作(第二辑)[M].北京:中国传媒大学出版社,2008.

[31] 祝朝伟.浅论戏剧的翻译[J].四川外语学院学报,2002(1).

【问题与思考】

1. 东西方戏剧文本有何异同?
2. 为什么说戏剧文本是具有"双重性特质"?
3. 戏剧翻译的可表演性原则是什么?
4. 戏剧文本阅读与其他文学体裁译本阅读相比,读者期待区别何在?
5. 戏剧翻译过程中,如何进行积极补偿?
6. 诗体译莎(莎士比亚戏剧)还是散文体译莎更合理?
7. 如何处理戏剧文本中的文化典故?
8. 你认为,戏剧翻译最大的障碍是什么?
9. 戏剧文本中的语言游戏是否可以忽略不译?
10. 西方戏剧翻译对中国戏剧现代化有何影响和意义?

第八章　影视译制篇

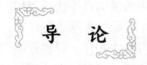

　　所谓影视文学是指通过广播电视声画媒介，以听觉和视觉传达设计为着眼点，运用文学创作的一般规律结构情节、塑造形象、营造氛围、抒发感情，给受众以文学审美情趣的文学类型。从本质属性来看，影视文学首先是文学，它是文学的一种样式，因而它同其他文学样式有着密切的血缘关系和共同规律；同时，由于影视文学借助于影视传播媒介，因而不可避免地带上了影视媒介特点。影视文学可以说是古老的传统文学与新兴影视相结合的产物，融合了文学与电影两种不同类型的艺术门类彼此的优长之势，既有"读"的优长，又有"看"的优长，既可作用于欣赏者的视觉，又可作用于欣赏者的听觉。

　　影视文学的基本特征主要是：视觉性、动作性和蒙太奇结构。视觉性，即影视文学剧本用文学所描写的形象能够鲜明地体现出视觉形象，具有具体、实在的视象性；动作性，即影视文学剧本对人物的描写是具有清晰、丰富的动作的描写；蒙太奇结构方式，即影视文学剧本把许多内容不同、场景各异的画面，按照创作的意图予以组接，使之产生连贯、对比、联想、衬托、悬念和节奏等艺术效果的特殊结构方式。而从影视翻译研究角度讲，影视作品的主要特征可以归纳为本质特征（大众文化娱乐产品）、文学属性（决定影视翻译是一种特殊的文学翻译或者文学翻译的一个特殊分支）以及影视语言的综合性。其中，大众文化娱乐产品属性是影视作品的本质特征。

　　国外影视作品的引进和译制，在我国历来都受到许多国家望尘莫及的重视。其中的原因应该是多方面的，有意识形态领域的，有语言方面的，也有文化方面的。当今社会，各国文化交流日益频繁密切，引进国外影视剧作已经成为中外文化交流的重要途径之一，影视剧作翻译在我国得到空前发展。人类已步入 21 世纪，影视文化对我们的意识形态、文化观念、生活方式以及生存状态均产生着深刻影响。随着科学技术的突飞猛进，影视作品早已跨越印刷品所设置的读者群和文字限制，并以视听语言宣布新的影像阅读时代的到来。在这种大背景下，我国影视翻译呈现出前所未有的特点，传播手段日趋丰富多样，涵盖电影、电视电影、电视、计算机、网络、手机、多媒体等各种现代化媒体，所引进的外国影片和电视剧数量与质量均令人瞩目。

　　影视作品的译制形式主要有两种，即配音和字幕。影视翻译与影视作品的译制形式之间有着密切的联系，配音片和字幕片对影视翻译的要求也有所不同。从翻译角度分析，关乎一部作品能否进入摄制阶段、能否成功被大众接受的关键问题在于影视译制过程中对于作品文学性和大众娱乐属性的把握。这两种属性落实到语言层面——画面语言与人物语言（人物对白，独白，旁白）时，则具体表现为互补性、简洁性、通俗性、个性化、民族性、时代性等彼此之间联系密切的若干特点。熟悉和掌握上述影视语言特点及其规律,是一个称职的影视翻译工作者必备的基本条件。同时,对影视语言特点的科学总结,有助于影视翻译若干基本理论问题的解决和影视翻译策略的归纳。

画面语言是影视作品受众通过视觉解读的部分,而人物语言则是通过听觉理解的部分。二者之间高度互补,使之成为影视文学区别于其他文学样式语言的最典型特点。影视语言的大量叙事与刻画人物任务由画面语言承担,因而在很大程度上减轻了人物语言方面的任务,为影视作品中人物语言的简洁性提供了充分条件。而影视作品创作中使用的蒙太奇手法频繁切换画面中各个镜头,人物语言为了做到"声画同步",在确保简洁的同时,还必须兼顾通俗性原则。从语言运用规律角度讲,简洁性与通俗性往往是一对孪生兄弟,两者相生相伴。影视作品的欣赏需要视听两觉共同参与其中——听话语,看画面;而影视作品的传播方式却决定话语与画面的一瞬而过。人物语言与画面语言的这种瞬间性,要求影视语言一定要通俗易懂,尽量不要给观众制造理解障碍。另外,影视作品的本质属性——大众文化娱乐产品,也决定影视语言的通俗性。

影视语言的有机组成部分——人物语言,是塑造典型人物、刻画人物形象的重要手段之一。众所周知,语言是区分不同民族的第一要素,一个民族有别于其他民族最重要的标志就是它的语言,这种特征表现在语言的各个方面,即语音、词汇、语法等层面。语言本身的这种社会属性、民族属性,使得任何一部影视作品,都毫无例外地打上本民族的印记。语音层面的民族差异,使"口型一致"原则成为影视配音翻译的第一大困难,为实现对等戏剧效果,译者常常不得不添加、减少或进行较大幅度的"变译"。语言本身的鲜活性也给影视作品翻译带来极大的挑战,作为大众娱乐方式的影视语言必须要能够与时俱进。语言的时代特征主要表现在词汇层面,这是由于词汇是语言中最活跃的部分,每当出现新事物、新概念、新现象时,自然会产生大量与之相应的新词汇。社会越是处于变革或者动荡时期,词汇的这种时代特征越是明显,任何语言都有大量时代性鲜明的词汇。

影视翻译是文学翻译的一个特殊分支或者是一种特殊的文学翻译,其目的在于利用通俗、口语化、个性化的语言,将某一时期国外影视作品的内容如实传达给我国的广大观众,并使他们在一定范围内对异域文化充分了解的同时,在教益、审美等方面获得等同于原作品观众的感受。本单元所选文章围绕影视语言的双语特征、影视剧脚本翻译的审美特征、影视翻译的礼貌性原则、影视翻译的基本概念及历史梳理和理论框架探索等方面展开,既有微观的技巧分析,又有宏观的意识形态探索,在大众娱乐时代,当一部部英语大片令人应接不暇之际,力图引导更多的翻译学人关注目前仍鲜有系统探索的影视作品翻译领域。

选 文

选文一　影视翻译——翻译园地中愈来愈重要的领域

钱绍昌

导　言

本文选自《中国翻译》,2000 年第 1 期。

选文简单回顾我国影视译制的历史,结合目前翻译界对这一现象的关注与其社会作用不相称,点明影视翻译的重要性,呼吁翻译界重视影视翻译。作者分析了影视语言与书面语言的不同点,将影视语言的特点归结为以下五条,即聆听性、综合性、瞬间性、通俗性和无注性。结合自己 600 多部(集)影视翻译的实践,论者总结了七条经验,并用大量鲜活电影对白翻译实例,逐一让读者明白人称性别词的凸显、演员台词与口形相吻合、对白中停顿、对白中示意动作、双关语和文字游戏,以及文化负载信息等的翻译处理手段,将明白易懂、通顺流畅作为影视作品翻译的基本条件。最后,作者认为,在影视翻译时,翻译的"信、达、雅"三项原则中以"达"(通顺)最为重要,因为影视对白不是科技论文,不是法律文书,不是商业合同,加之还得受画面的制约,为了译文通顺有时不得不在翻译时略微变通一些。

我国的影视翻译始于新中国成立后。新中国成立前我国尚无电视。电影也没有真正的译制片(即先由翻译将对白译成中文,再由配音演员配成中文对白的片子)。不懂外文的观众只能通过"译意风"(装在座位上的耳机)中粗糙的同声翻译或是银幕上简单的字幕的帮助大致了解剧情。1948 年底东北新中国成立后,长春电影制片厂首先开始了译制片的制作,翻译工作者着手翻译苏联的电影,是为我国影视翻译之滥觞。不久上海和北京很快跟上。但在改革开放前我国译制的电影来源较窄,数量亦不大。更由于电视未普及,故其影响面较小。自 70 年代末改革开放以来,放宽了影视片的进口,加之电视机逐渐进入千家万户,译制片的观众即十倍百倍地增长。

无疑地,如今译制片受众(观众)的数量远远超过翻译文学作品受众(读者)的数量,影视翻译对社会的影响也决不在文学翻译之下。但与之相反,翻译界对影视翻译的重视却远不如文学翻译。反映在大学里有关课程之开设、学术刊物上有关论文之发表、学术团体中有关组织之建设等方面,均与影视翻译的社会作用不相称。这一现象亟应引起翻译界的注意。

笔者自 1984 年起开始为上海科教片厂和上海电视台将一些科教片和专题片译成英语。但这尚不能算是真正的影视翻译,因为其中很少对白,即使有对白也不必由配音演员来对着口形配音,故对翻译的要求较简单。我真正的影视翻译则始于 1988 年的美国长篇电视连续剧《鹰冠庄园》,此后《大饭店》、《成长的烦恼》、《浮华世家》、《迷人的香水》、《冷暖人间》、《根》、《后

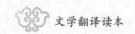

代》、《拿破仑与约瑟芬》、《荆棘鸟》……一部接一部,至今600余部(集)。积多年之经验,深感影视翻译之不易,其中很多困难之处是翻译一般文学作品时遇不到的。故不揣冒昧,愿将其中甘苦得失,供诸同道,冀高明有以教之。

影视翻译为文学翻译之一部分,故与一般文学翻译有共同之处,如要求译者对中文及外文均须有一定根底,在翻译时须对原文意义有全面深刻的了解,对译文字斟句酌反复推敲,掌握"信、达、雅"之原则等。这些普遍性不拟赘述。本文着重探讨两者之异,也就是英汉影视翻译的特殊性。

欲研究影视翻译之特点,则必须首先研究影视语言与书面文学语言不同之处。

影视语言的五个特性

影视语言的特点在于其聆听性、综合性、瞬时性、通俗性和无注性。由于以上五个性的存在,从而产生了影视翻译的特殊要求。

1. 聆听性

欣赏文学作品是通过眼睛阅读的,而影视作品的语言则是通过耳朵聆听的。这在影视翻译中会出现一些令译者头痛的事。例如"he, she, it"三个字,译成汉语分别为"他、她、它"。这三个汉字虽然发音一样,但外形不同。因而对于文学作品的读者,其区分并不成为问题。但是对于影视作品的观众,常会发生麻烦。He beat her 译成中文为"他打了她",读者不会误解。但听众就伤脑筋了。是"他打了她"还是"她打了他"?

2. 综合性

文学作品是书面文字的艺术,而影视作品是综合性艺术,观众在听到演员说话的同时还看到演员的表演。当然还有画面的各种变化以及音乐和音响效果等。对于影视翻译工作者来说,最重要的是认识到演员的对白和表演两者之间的密切关系。这两者是一个完整的统一体,后者对前者不仅起着辅助性的作用,也起着制约性的作用。具体地说,演员的对白受到演员说话时的口形、停顿和示意动作这三点的制约。示意动作(如手势、点头等)实际上是身势语言(body language),是影视语言的一部分。由于这些制约的存在,对影视翻译也提出了特殊的要求。以上三点将在下文中逐点予以讨论。

3. 瞬间性

读者对于小说中人物的语言或情景的描述若看不明白,可以反复地阅读,因为那是印在纸上的文字。影视剧的观众却没有这个条件。影视剧中人物的对白是有声语言,一瞬而过,若听不懂只能放弃,既不能让你再听一遍,也不容你思索,因为一思索便听不清后面的话。当然,如果是录像带或影碟,可以倒过来再放一遍。不过这样做便太乏味了。因此影视对白的译文必须流畅通顺,含意明白,让观众一听就懂,不能让他们伤脑筋地思索。

4. 通俗性

要求影视对白通俗易懂,不仅仅由于其瞬间性,更由于影视观众面之广。读文学作品必须有一定文化程度,但即使文盲也看得懂影视。看电视时往往全家围坐在一起。这就要求影视语言雅俗共赏,老少皆宜。其对白不能过于典雅,太晦涩。

5. 无注性

文学翻译遇到读者难以理解之处可以在该页或该章节之处做注解。但影视翻译工作者却享受不到这种待遇。这就给译者带来很大的困难,也是影视翻译最难之处。影视片中允许在对白之外做文字说明,这就是字幕。如在片头以字幕介绍故事的历史背景,或在片末介绍故事的结尾,或在片中打上地名和年份,如"巴黎 1940 年",等等。在翻译时必须将之译成中文字幕。影视片中有时也用旁白介绍剧情的转折或说明某一人物的心情。这些旁白亦应译出而由配音演员配为旁白。但那全是原片中就有的,绝不允许译者为了注解而在译制片中另外加字幕或旁白。另加的字幕使观众目不暇接,另加的旁白使观众不知所云。

笔者觉得以下两种情况在没有注解的条件下是很难译的:

(1) 因中外观众知识面和文化背景的巨大差异而造成的难点

例如,多数中国人对于基督教和圣经相当生疏。在一部片子中某人说:"他犯了圣经中第七诫。"中国人里有百分之几念过圣经? 更有多少能背出十诫? 反之,中国人对于庙宇、菩萨、和尚之类倒是比较熟悉的。

(2) 双关语和文字游戏

这是最难译的,也往往是无法译的。大家都知道英语中一例很出名的双关语:Seven days without water make one weak. 由于 weak 与 week 同音,此句既可译成"七天没水使人虚弱",亦可译成"七天没水就是一周没水"。但其中诙谐之处不谙英语者无法领会。反之亦如此。记得数年前在报上看到电影界前辈刘琼对一位记者开玩笑地说:"我如今是三等公民。等吃、等睡、等死。"我不知道哪一位翻译家能不加注解而将之译成英语?

双关语也是文字游戏的一种,但文字游戏不限于双关语。文字游戏的翻译也是极不易的。例如在《成长的烦恼》中小捣蛋本有一天放学回家对父亲贾森说的一段话:

Ben:　Mrs. Zenko reamed me for being truculent.
Jason:　Do you know what truculent means?
Ben:　No, but it can't be good.
Jason:　Ben, truculent means angry, ready to fight.

这段对白的关键在于 truculent 这个词。它比较难,本听不懂,因而构成了笑料。但它却并不是双关语,因此这段对白是一种文字游戏。truculent 平时可以译成"凶猛"或"野蛮",可是在这里必须译成比较深奥的汉语,这样本才会听不懂。因此我将之译成:

本:　今天老师批评我"桀骜不驯"。(我未将 Mrs. Zenko 译成"曾可太太",因为中国人无此习惯)
贾森:你知道那是什么意思?
本:　不,反正不是好话。
贾森:本,就是说你很凶,爱打架。

由于影视作品有以上五个特性,便对影视翻译提出特殊的要求。下面作者想介绍一些个人的经验。

七条经验

1. 让观众明白对白中的第三人是指男人还是女人

虽然在汉语中"他、她"同音,但在多数情况下观众根据上下文不致误解。在观众可能混淆时,则应按具体情况灵活改变译文。

例如在《大饭店》(*Hotel*)中,有一天饭店的老板 Mrs. Cabot 在饭店的餐厅里请一位饭店业巨头 Jake 吃饭。Jake 吃了后很满意,称赞厨师手艺高,却想不到这位厨师竟然是女的。原文的一段对话如下:

> Jake: A fine lunch, Victoria. My compliments to your chef.
> Mrs. Cabot: She'll be grateful to know the source of the compliment.
> Jake: She?

Jake 在称赞午餐很好以后请 Mrs. Cabot 向厨师致意。后者的回答中表明厨师是女的,这使前者大吃一惊。在英语的对话中用了两个 she 字,就把意思交代清楚了。可是在翻译时却不能简单地把 she 译成"她",因为观众辨不清那是男的或是女的。所以我就把第二句话译成"厨娘能得到你的称赞一定很感激",这样中国观众就能听懂厨师是女的。我又把 Jake 说的"She?"译成"女的?",这段对话的含义就一清二楚了。

有时观众分不清男女并不是"他、她"引起的。例如:在《大饭店》中,女招待梅甘的好友安琪想请她替自己介绍一位男友。当她看到饭店大堂里有一个男青年走过时觉得此人不错,可是梅甘对她说:"他的情人是理查。"西方人都知道理查是男人的名字,所以一听就知他是同性恋者。但中国人不一定知道,我就将之译成"这男人是同性恋"。

2. 演员台词与其口形必须相吻合

原版片中演员所说的台词是外文,由译者译成中文,再由配音演员配好后播放给中国观众看。这就要求配音演员配出来的中国话跟片中演员的口形相吻合。如果外文长而中文短,则观众看到片中演员还在说话而却听不到他(她)在说什么。反之,如果外文短而中文长,则观众看到演员的嘴巴已不动而却仍能听到说话声。这岂不是很滑稽?

要避免这个现象,译文和原文的长度就必须一样,这就要求译者在翻译时将每一句中文的字数(注意,是字数而不是词数)译得和外文句子的音节数基本相吻合。这是因为我们说中文时,每说一个字嘴巴动一下。而说外文时,则基本上是每一个音节嘴巴动一下。因此,一句含有 10 个音节的外文译成 10 个字左右的中文句子,口形就能基本相吻。

但是做到这点有时并不十分容易。例如:He is a university student 这句有 10 个音节的英语译成中文只有 5 个字:"他是大学生。"在这种情况下只能设法将中文译文尽量拉长而不损其原意,不妨译成"他如今是在大学里念书"。反之,如果外文短而中文长,就得尽量将译文缩短。例如:He came from D. P. R. K. 有 7 个音节,若加以全译则中文长达 14 个字——"他来自朝鲜民主主义人民共和国",就只好将之译成 7 个字的一句——"他是来自朝鲜的"。

3. 对白中有停顿时的译法

一个人说话的时候有抑、扬、顿、挫。影视翻译必须注意的是这个"顿"字,也就是停顿的意思。由于中、外文在语法和结构上的巨大差异,外文中的停顿放在中文里往往并不对位。因此在将外文译成中文后必须让这些停顿仍显得很自然,不然观众就会感到很奇怪。

例如在《冷暖人间》(*Berrenger's*)中有下面一段对话:

> Cammie：How much do you owe?
> Billy：　　One hundred... and eighty thousand.
> Cammie：Dollars?
> Billy：　　Yeah，dollars.

这一段话难在第二句的翻译。若是直译则为"一百千……以及八十千"当然不行,所以我就添上几个字而译为"一共是……一万八千元"。

4. 对白中有示意动作时的译法

一种示意动作是手势,例如:

《天使爱心》(*Heartbeat*)第一集中有一个叫文蒂的姑娘得了乳腺癌。外科医生主张做根治手术,而文蒂的家庭医生库珀为了怕影响姑娘的心理而建议做一个比较小的手术,他在解释时说:"I have been Wendy's family doctor since she was... this high."在句中停顿时库珀做了一个手心向下的手势,说明文蒂才这么高的时候他就已经是她的家庭医生了。这句原文若加以直译就成了"我在文蒂这么高时就是她的家庭……医生"。这样他的手势就落在"医生"前面而不是"这么高"前面。观众看到这个手势就会感到莫名其妙,不可理解。所以我就把这一句译成"我开始做文蒂家庭医生时她才……这么高"。这样,译文既通顺,手势也用得很合理,观众就能充分理解了。

另有一种示意动作是点头或摇头。在英语中对疑问句做肯定或否定的回答跟汉语不一样,翻译时必须注意。例如在《凶杀报警》(*Murder Call*)中有两名侦探的对话如下:

> Tessa：So we shouldn't rule out murder.
> Lance：No.（同时摇头）

前者说不能排除谋杀,后者表示同意的同时摇摇头。而中国人在同意对方时通常是点头。我们若把这个 No 译成"不",则按中国人的说话习惯是不同意对方的意见,而实际上后者是同意前者的意见。但是如果译成"对",则后者在回答 No 时却在摇头。

因此我把这两句对白译成:

> 泰莎:因此不能排除他杀。
> 兰斯:不能。

5. 如何翻译因文化背景和知识面差异造成的难点

由于中外观众文化背景和知识面的巨大差异,英语中许多词语若予以直译中国观众往往无法理解。而电视翻译又不能像小说翻译那样可以做注解,因此译者有责任将对白译得让中

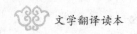

国观众一听就懂。

例如，在《大饭店》的第一集中，饭店经理彼得有一个老朋友兰里先生在饭店里包了一个房间"金屋藏娇"。这件事彼得是知道的，而兰里太太却一直被蒙在鼓里。直到有一天此事终于给兰里太太发现了。彼得为此感到很尴尬。可是兰里太太却安慰他说："你没有责任在饭店里抓第七诫。"西方人大多信基督教，他们都知道第七诫是"不得通奸"，但中国人知道者却极少。我在给上海外国语大学高年级学生上大课时问学生有谁知道第七诫是什么。结果全班100个学生中只有一个知道。外语专业的大学生尚且如此，一般的中国人知道者当然更少了。所以我就将这句话译成"你没有责任在饭店里抓男女问题"。这样观众就能听懂。

再举一个例子。在电影《蒙特卡罗》里，"二战"中德国的一些要人聚集在法国南部的旅游城市蒙特卡罗开会，英国军方得知这消息后打算轰炸这座城市。这时英国的空军司令说："这事我得请示唐宁街。"中国人大概多数知道白宫是美国总统办公地点（我未做过统计），不过不一定知道唐宁街是英国首相办公地点，因此我将这句话译成"这事我得请示首相"，免得有些观众听不懂。

在描述17世纪英国清教徒横渡大西洋前往美洲的电影《五月花号》中，有一名乘客霍普金斯的妻子在船上生了一个儿子。霍普金斯高兴极了。他就说：

His name will be Oceanus—Oceanus Hopkins!

这句话若是直译，则为"他将取名为欧谢纳斯——欧谢纳斯·霍普金斯！"中国观众就无法听懂霍普金斯把儿子取名为"欧谢纳斯"的用意，而西方观众一听就懂，因为oceanus这字是拉丁语中的"海洋"，英文的ocean就源于此字。但是若把这句话译成"给他取名为海洋——海洋·霍普金斯！"也不妥，因为"海洋·霍普金斯"是个不中不西的名字。因此我只能灵活一下，把这句话译成"给他取名为海洋——海洋的孩子！"这样既能让中国观众听懂，又比较通顺。

6. 双关语和文字游戏的翻译

这是影视翻译中最难之处，因为大家都知道一种语言里的双关语和文字游戏译成另一种语言就会索然无味或甚至无法理解。在翻译《成长的烦恼》中这点尤为突出。这是因为该剧充满了笑料，特别是遇到可笑之处时背景中会出现预录笑声（Canned Laughter）。因此中国观众若是听到预录笑声而觉得对白并不可笑时，这翻译就失败了。

例如：在《成长的烦恼》第52集中，专门捣蛋不好好念书的迈克想竞选学生会主席。他的弟弟本对此事极感兴趣，努力帮他哥哥竞选。他做了许多标语牌，他打算在上面写I like Mike.（我喜欢迈克）可是他的拼法很糟糕，竟将like拼成lick(舔)。迈克的语文水平虽然也很差，但毕竟是个中学生，知道本写错了，就当场给本指出。这两个字在英文中很相似，而意义却截然不同，这自然会引起观众哄堂大笑。但是在中文里"喜欢"跟"舔"毫无相似之处，谁也不会把"喜欢"错写成"舔"。因此我就将I lick Mike译成"我受迈克"，接着迈克就给本指出："你把'爱'错写成'受'了。"这两个字很相似，一个小孩子把"爱"写成笔画比较简单的"受"是完全可能的。

再举一个例子。有一天本正在跟他的好朋友臭蛋说话的时候他们的同学维多来了。维多问臭蛋："你参不参加我家里举行的鬼节晚会？"臭蛋回答说："我当然参加。"维多又问："我在请帖上不是明明写着RSVP吗？"RSVP是法语Repondez s'il vous plait的简写，意思是"请赐复"。西方国家的正式请柬上都印着这 4 个字母,就是请收到请柬者立即回复是否参加,让主人可以预先知道参加者的人数以做好准备。可是臭蛋不懂 RSVP 的意思,只好答非所问,混了过去。维多一走,臭蛋就问本 RSVP 是什么意思。本这个活宝也不知道 RSVP 的意思。他脑筋一转,想出一个解释:Refreshments served at Vito's party. 这句中几个字的首字母刚巧是 RSVP,而其意思完全不是"请赐复"而成了"维多的晚会上有茶点供应"。本不懂装懂,竟然给他想出这么一句话来搪塞,真是妙不可言。可是要将这个文字游戏译成中文实在不容易。我就把维多对臭蛋的问句译成"我在请帖上不是明明写着'请赐复'吗?"而把本对臭蛋的回答译为"请吃全家福"。这一句基本上跟"请赐复"谐音。勉强也可以算是笑料,但跟原文比是差远了。

7. 译文必须明白易懂,通顺流畅

由于影视语言的瞬间性以及影视观众面之广,译文必须明白易懂,通顺流畅。要求做到雅俗共赏,老少咸宜。不能太典雅晦涩。当然,不要太典雅并不是说要很粗俗,而是应该根据角色的身份而定,该雅的时候就雅,该俗的时候就俗。例如在《鹰冠庄园》中 Mrs. Charming 的律师 Philip 向她求婚,因而有下面一段对话:

> Mrs. Charming: My father used to call me a hell-cat. Were you meant to marry a hell-cat?
> Philip:　　　We make a hell-of-a-team.

这段对话中值得推敲的是 hell-of-a-team 的译法。若译成"正好一对"或"半斤八两"就俗了一些,不符合律师的文化教养,我就将它译成"旗鼓相当"。因此这段对话的译文如下:

> 钱宁夫人:我的父亲说我是个泼妇。你真的愿意娶个泼妇?
> 菲利普:　咱俩是旗鼓相当。

下面是一个比较粗俗的例子:

在《大饭店》中一名妓女凯乐在饭店里被一伙流氓轮奸了,住在医院里。妓女虽然是以出卖肉体为职业,但遭到轮奸自然是很痛苦的。作为饭店总经理的彼得去慰问她。可是凯乐的态度却十分硬。她说:

> What the hell are you going to do for me? If you want to do something, you can pay the hospital bill. The hooker's union doesn't have a group medical plan! I don't want any favors! I'll pay you back—cash or trade, whatever you want. I have my body. When it is back on working order, you can have your shot at it.

这段话的原文是极为粗俗的,译文相应地也得粗一些。我是这样译的:

> 凯乐:你他妈的想为我做什么? 你真要做一点事,那就替我付医院的帐。婊子工会是不管会员医药费的! 我不要你做好事! 我会还你的——要钱还钱—要玩让你玩。我有个身体,等它能干活的时候,就可以跟你上床。

要而言之,我觉得在影视翻译中,"信、达、雅"三项原则恐怕以"达"最为重要。为了"达"(通顺),有时不得不略微牺牲一点"信"。影视对白不是科技论文,不是法律文书,不是商业合同,不必要求其绝对忠实于原文。何况译文还得受画面的制约,不可能把每一句原文都全译出

来。当然,这里说的"牺牲"绝不是抛开原文,胡译一通,而是为了译文更通顺不得不在翻译时略为变通一些。至于"雅"的标准,若是像严复那样要求为"古雅",那观众根本无法接受。若是像林语堂那样将之解释为"美",则是影视翻译工作者应该争取做到的。

结论

1. 作者呼吁翻译界对影视翻译的重视。

2. 作者指出影视语言不同于书面文学语言的五个特点:聆听性、综合性、瞬间性、通俗性、无注性。

3. 作者基于影视语言的特点介绍了影视翻译的七条个人经验。

4. 作者认为在影视翻译时,翻译的"信、达、雅"三项原则中以"达"最为重要。

选文二　影视剧脚本的翻译及审美特征

麻争旗

导　言

本文选自《北京第二外国语学院学报》,2003 年第 2 期。

选文论证指出,文学翻译的共同特征是情感化和人物性格再造,而文学形态的多样性又赋予了翻译重建形式美的不同艺术品格。这三个方面便构成了文学翻译艺术审美的主要内涵,同时也赋予了翻译作为艺术的特殊品质。影视剧脚本的翻译是文学翻译的一种特殊形式,其典型特征不仅体现了媒介跨文化传播的人文品质,而且反映了文学翻译再创作的审美特征。选文从五个方面说明影视剧脚本的基本翻译方法,并从审美的角度分析这些方法所表现出来的艺术品质,得出如下结论:"口语化"要求译文具有生活气息,使对话像"话";"人物性格化"要求言如其人,使话语带着人物个性;"情感化"要求语出有情,使言语真实感人;"口型化"是对译文在形式、结构等方面的严格规定;而"通俗化"则是在翻译已经承担的多重使命中又赋之予一个为观众着想的新内容。这五个方面可以说是影视剧脚本翻译最主要的特征,也是翻译在创作中所必须遵循的最基本原则。

一、口语会话原则

"信、达、雅"是传统的翻译准则,现在一般理解为"忠实、通顺"。影视剧脚本的翻译自然不能离开这一原则。但是如何实现"忠实、通顺"则值得研究。仅从"通顺"的要求来看就未免过于笼统。影视剧中人物对话的翻译不是供读者去慢慢阅读品味的,而是要转化为配音演员的声音,使观众在观赏的瞬间去理解接受。因此,仅仅达到文字上的"通顺"、"通达"是不够的,还必须使之贴近生活,使之易于上口,便于听懂。这样的译文,经过配音,才能与人物表情(包括口型)相吻合,才能最终求得自然、逼真的艺术效果。

试比较下列对话的两种不同译法(选自美国电视系列剧《亡命追凶》中"天命难违"一集):

(金布尔到兽医马丁家求职)

Kimble:I don't know much about animals.

金布尔:① 我对牲畜知道得并不多。

　　　　② 我对兽医可不大懂。

Doc:You don't have to. Folks around here believe I do. Been fooling them for
　　　forty years...

马丁医生:① 你没必要知道。周围的乡民们相信我知道。40 年了我一直愚弄
　　　　　　他们……

　　　　　② 呃,不用你懂。乡亲们都以为我懂。我蒙了他们 40 年了……

(在汽车上)

Doc:Well,Simmon's beliefs forbid the use of medicines... When his wife took
　　　to bed, I had that hospital send a doctor to her. But Joshua held him off
　　　with a shotgun.

马丁医生:① 呃,西蒙的信条禁止使用药物,他妻子卧病在床时,我让医院给她
　　　　　　派来了个医生,可乔舒亚用枪把他拒之门外。

　　　　　② 呃,乔舒亚这个人不信医疗这一套。他老婆病倒时,我请医院派了
　　　　　　个医生来,他端着枪把医生赶跑了。

对照原文,上述两种译法均可谓"忠实、通顺"。但是笔者认为第二种更与剧中人物、情境等相吻合,更具有生活气息。这样的译文配音时更"带劲儿",听起来更"有味儿"。这就是"口语化"的基本含义。

请比较下列对话的两种不同译法(选自美国影片《居里夫人》中"居里论女人"一段):

P:Well,there's a pupil of Professor Perot's who's going to be doing some
　　work here for a short time.

皮埃尔:① 呃……有个佩罗特教授的学生要……要到这里来进行一项短期的研
　　　　　究工作。

　　　　② 呃……有个佩罗特教授的学生要……要到这里来做一项研究。是短
　　　　　期的。

D:Yes, sir.

戴　维:① 是的,先生。

　　　　② 是这样。

P:Uh—her name is—Marie—uh—uh—funny, I ought to remember it, I was
　　introduced to her twice. Uh—Sklodovska! Uh—she's a girl.

皮埃尔:① 呃……她的名字叫……玛丽……呃呃……真滑稽,我应该记住,我被

向她介绍了两次。呃……呃……斯可罗多夫斯卡！呃…她是个女孩子。

② 呃……她叫呃……玛丽……呃呃……奇怪,我应该记得,人家向我介绍了两遍。呃……呃……斯可罗多夫斯卡！呃……是个姑娘。

D: Oh!

戴　维:噢!

P: Well, I didn't find out in time. Always the continual struggle against woman, David. When we wish to give all our thoughts to some work which estranges us from humanity, we always have to struggle against woman.

皮埃尔:① 我呃……没有及时发现。总是要不断地和女人做斗争。当我们要集中全部精力从事某项跟人性分离的工作时,我们总是要跟女人做斗争。

② 我呃……知道得太晚了。我们总是要不断地抵抗女人,因为我们要集中精力搞研究,这是远离尘世的事业,所以我们总是要跟女人做斗争。

D: Yes, sir. And woman scientists are particularly unattractive, I find, sir.

戴　维:① 是的,先生。而且我发现女科学家尤其不迷人,先生。

② 是的,先生。再说,我发现女科学家没有一个长得好看的。

P: Woman loves life for the living of it. In the world of abstract research she's a danger and a distraction. She's the natural enemy of science.

皮埃尔:① 女人爱生活就是为了生活。在抽象研究的世界里,她是一种危险——她使人分散注意。她是科学的自然的敌人。

② 女人的天性就是爱生活。在抽象研究的领域里,女人是干扰物,是危险品,女人是科学的天敌。

D: There's no doubt of it, sir.

戴　维:① 毫无疑问,先生。

② 完全正确,先生。

P: Women and science are incompatible. Women of genius are rare. No true scientist can have anything to do with women.

皮埃尔:① 女人和科学是互不相容的。女人中的天才是罕见的。真正的科学家不会跟女人有任何关系。

② 女人和科学水火不相容。女人很少有天才。真正的科学家跟女人没什么缘分。

仔细比较可以发现,上述第二种译法比第一种念起来更顺口、听起来更入耳,因而更具有生活气息。

总之,对话语言是口语会话,因此翻译的首要原则就是使译文"好配",使之念起来上口,听起来顺畅。所谓"通顺"就表现为念得很"顺",听得很像"话",使人感觉剧中人物就像平常生活那样真实。这正是影视剧脚本翻译所追求的艺术境界。

二、声画对位原则

重建形式美是文学翻译进行艺术再创作的重要表现。译诗的原则就是再创诗的意境。剧本的翻译要考虑到其中停顿、节奏及动作、人物性格,还要琢磨俏皮话、机智语、幽默、言外意、潜台词。最后还要考虑到戏是上演的,还要"上口"。[①] 正是这些要素赋予了剧本翻译力求重建舞台演剧形式美的品格。

影视剧配音脚本的翻译与戏剧脚本的翻译很相似。剧本要拿去上演,译制脚本供配音用,所以译文都要求"上口"。但是两者之间也有很大的差异。剧本译好了,交给剧团,演员看了译文,然后表演,对白依据译文而行。译制脚本则不然。原作的人物对话、表演已经存在,脚本是依据人物的实际话语译出的,然后拿去让配音演员给剧中人物"对口型"。这与剧本的翻译——上演过程正好相反。

影视译制的结果至少能使观众闻其声、见其人,知道哪句话出自谁的口,这是最起码的要求。为此译文必须尽可能与原话字数相当,长短一致。译文过长过短都会给配音带来困难,甚至影响、破坏人物性格的塑造和情绪的表达。

从翻译方法来看,对于较为简单的语句,求得译语和原语长短一致并不太难。例如(选自美国电视系列剧《亡命天涯》中"目击者"一集):

Marcia：That's me. You're you.
马西娅：你是你,我是我。(对等)
Kimble：Didn't he tell you?
金布尔：① 难道他没有跟你说过吗?(过长)
　　　② 他没告诉你吗?(相当)
Marcia：Good as new.
马西娅：① 和新的一样好。(过长)
　　　② 像新的。(对等)
Marcia：What do you think you're doing?
马西娅：① 你干什么?(过短)
　　　② 你干什么? 你想干什么?(相当)
Kimble：I want to thank you again.
金布尔：① 我想再一次向你表示感谢。(过长)
　　　② 再次向你表示感谢。(对等)
Dawes：Well, I figure he knows only two people here. You and me. Me, he's
　　　running from. You're nice run into. Have you seen him?
道斯：我想他在这里只认识两个人——我和你。我是他想躲的,你是他想见的。
　　　看见他了吗?(相当)

---

① 张君川:《我的文艺翻译》,载于巴金等著《当代文学翻译百家谈》,北京大学出版社 1989 年版,第 443 页。

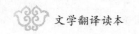

对于较为复杂的段落,有时则需要重新断句。例如:

Marcia:Please! I'm sorry. No good-byes. I mean don't think of me as just
kind—if you ever think of me again. No... don't... don't say anything.
I'll leave first. You wait a few minutes and then go.

马西娅:别谢了! 对不起。不说再见。如果你将来记得我,请你不要……只记得
我很热情。不必……多说了。我先走。过几分钟后,你再走。

另外,可尽量选用发音口型相近的字,尤其是独词句及句首句尾的字。如:

Oh—噢;Hey—嘿;Hello—你好。

试比较下列对话两种译法的差异:

Gaines ... If charges are filed...
盖恩斯:① 如果指控成立……
        ② 万一指控成立……
Dawes:Not if, old friend. When.
道斯:① 不时如果,是到时候。
      ② 不是万一,是一万。

通过比较不难看出,把 if 译成"如果"或"万一"没有本质差别,但是"万"和 when 口型相近,因此②比①显然要高明一些。

这样看来,影视译制有点像演双簧,用剧中人物的口型装配音演员的声音,使所言所语如出其口。翻译的任务是为配音提供蓝本,所以译文要在保证准确、生动、感人的前提下,力图在长短、节奏、换气、停顿乃至口型开合等诸方面求得与剧中人物说话时的表情、口吻相一致,最终使观众闻其声、见其人,知道哪句话出自谁的口。

严格地说,译制一部片子像填一首词,思想内容自然不能更改,每句每行的"平仄音韵"也有了严格的限定。假如译者忽视"口型化"的规律,不管话语的"轻重缓急",译文任长任短,"意思对了就可以了",那么,这样的译文,如果拿去配音,比如,短句译得过长,配音只好加快节奏"赶"——结果平静的心情变得焦急不安,沉稳的性格显出浮躁轻率;反之,长句译得过短,配音只能放慢速度"拖"——结果激动热情变得呆滞冷漠,干练果断成了优柔不决,如此等等。这表明剧本翻译不是简单的解码、编码,也不是根据基本意思进行自由发挥,而是一种切合原著的务使语感得体的再创造。

三、雅俗共赏原则

从理论上讲,"通俗"并不为众家所共识。最早的翻译理论讲"信、达、雅",要求"忠实、古雅"。后来才发展为"忠实、通顺",只要"顺达、流畅",不必拘泥于"古雅"。但"通顺"绝不要求"通俗",因为"通俗"是指大众化,而达到"通顺"并不意味着具有了大众化的特点。可见,"通俗化"的原则是要求在"通顺"的基础上力求语言靠近大众、清楚明白、雅俗共赏。

"通俗"不等于"低俗"或"平淡"。现代汉语里大众化的语言有着极其丰富的表现力,它能反映简朴的思想,也能表达复杂的情感,关键在于能否使之生动活泼、准确自然。

例如(《亡命追凶》中的片头解说词):

> Narrator: *The Fugitive*. A Q. M. production. Starring David Janssen as Doctor Richard Kimble, an innocent victim of blind justice. Falsely convicted for the murder of his wife. Reprieved by faith when a train reck freed him oh route to the death house... freed him to hide in lonely desperation... to change his identity... to toil at many jobs... freed him to search for a one-armed man he saw leave the scene of the crime... freed rim to run before the relentless pursuit of the police lieutenant obsessed with his capture.

> 解说:《亡命追凶》——QM 公司出品。主演:戴维·詹森。理查德·金布尔医生,清白无辜,却蒙冤受屈,被错判为谋杀妻子的凶手。幸好,一起车祸使他在遣送途中死里逃生,从此,他隐姓埋名,东躲西藏,在孤独和绝望中忍辱负重。他要找到那个逃离犯罪现场的独臂人,同时还要躲避穷追不舍的探长为他布下的天罗地网。

上面这段话,语言精练,结构严谨,具有高度的概括性。如果译文过于平白,显得淡而无力;反之,如果译得生涩古雅,恐怕普通听众难以听得明白。所以要把握雅俗共赏的原则,力争既清楚明了,又生动准确。

广义地讲,"通俗化"不仅指语言表达的风格。由于文化差异、专业术语等因素的作用,有的地方翻译并没有"作难",可观众听了,恐怕还是不能马上转过弯儿来。因此,为了便于观众理解,翻译时对某些译法可做适当的"变通"。比如对某些数量单位,可以把英尺换算成米,英里换算成公里,等等。

从以上分析可见,所谓"通俗化"的原则实际上是一个为观众服务、对观众负责的原则,就是要求翻译在下笔时,设身处地,为普通观众想一下,想一想哪种译法较容易理解,哪种表达至少不至于引起误解,如此等等。这就是"通俗化"原则的道理所在。影视片的翻译要遵循通俗化的原则,这是由大众媒体的固有特性所决定的。一部思想性、艺术性很强的影片,译得通俗明白,就能为普通百姓所理解、所接受,从而更好、更广泛地起到教育人,特别是教育青少年的作用。如果译得过"雅",甚至艰深难懂,那就违背了它的初衷。

要做到通俗明白,翻译必须对原文语言现象,尤其是专业性问题充分理解,然后在表达上深入浅出,力争既简单明了,又不失严谨准确,朴实而不乏味,深刻却不莫测,从而求得雅俗共赏的效果。

影片《居里夫人》十分详细地再现了居里夫妇发现并提炼镭元素的研究过程,涉及许多专业性知识和名词术语。为了便于观众看懂,原作的风格就是"通俗化"的典范。翻译理应忠实并发扬这一风格,既保持科学严谨的态度,又考虑普通观众的接受能力,从而努力创作自己的艺术品格。

试比较下列原文与译文在表达上的特点:
例 1(贝克勒尔发现铀沥青矿石具有放射性。)

Pierre: You mean then that there is something about that rock that gives off rays of its own—rays powerful enough to go through black paper and affect this photographic plate.

皮埃尔：你是说这块矿石有某种特性，能够自己发光，而且光线很强，能够穿透黑色的纸，并对底片产生作用。

例2（玛丽萌发深入研究放射性的念头。）

Marie：What are these rays that are given off, and why are they given off? It's an accepted principle in science that nothing can go on forever without running down, isn't it?

玛丽：这种光线是什么光线？为什么会释放出来？没有一种东西可以永远不停地运动下去。这是一条科学公理，对吗？

Marie：I mean a clock will run down if it isn't wound—a fire will burn out if it isn't replenished—life will die if it isn't fed. And yet, in these rocks which have been in the middle of the earth for millions of years, and never seen the sun, rays are constantly being given off, all by themselves. What is this energy? Where does it come from?

玛丽：比如说钟表不上发条就会停止，火不添加燃料会最后熄灭，人不吃饭就会死去。可是，那些铀矿深埋在地底下几百万年，从来没有见过阳光，竟然会不停地自己发出光来。这是什么能量？是从哪儿产生的？

例3（玛丽和皮埃尔分析测量铀和钍能量的结果。）

Marie：When the uranium and thorium are in the pitchblende, the reading is eight, but individually they only total four. Why, then, do they give out twice as much when they're in the pitchblende as they do when they're tested separately? Where are those four missing points?

玛丽：当铀和钍包含在铀矿里的时候，读数是八，而分别测量后加起来只有四，那么为什么存在于铀矿中所产生的能量竟是单独产生能量之和的两倍？这个差数在哪里？

Marie：What if there exists a matter that is not inert, but alive—dynamic？Do we dare think that our four missing points—this strange power—is in that one thousandth of one per cent? Pierre, We've discovered a new element—an active element!

玛丽：假如有一种物质不是惰性，而是活性的，结果会怎么样？敢不敢想相差的那四点——那四点能量——就在剩下的这十万分之一物质里？皮埃尔，我们发现了一种新元素，一种活性元素！

从上面的例子中可以看出，通俗不等于平淡，更不是低俗，而是在朴实之中见哲理。所谓仁者见仁、智者见智，正是通俗明白、雅俗共赏所追求的效果。

然而，提倡译制"通俗化"，恐怕在影视界颇遭非议。中外影视人士皆有否定译制的必要性的。有的主张原文加字幕，有的则认为要看就是看原文的，这样才能绝对"原汁原味"。连"译"

都成为不可能,哪还容得了"通俗"?

笔者则力主"通俗化"。影视作品不仅仅是艺术家的艺术。作为一种大众传播媒介,它自始至终都必须以普通大众为服务宗旨。译制的目的就在于使其成为不同文化间进行有效交流的桥梁。一部来自异国他乡的优秀影视作品,如果因为文化的差异、语言的障碍,结果只能充当少数艺术家或者再包括一个以外语"过硬"为标志的文化程度较高的少数阶层的奢侈品,而把千千万万的普通大众拒之于门外,那么,这样的艺术,终究是遗憾的艺术;同时,它与创作者所应有的初衷也是相背离的。

李岚清同志十分赞称影片《居里夫人》的译制水平。他对翻译讲:"你翻译得很好。你感动了我,感动了导演,感动了演员,最后感动了广大观众。另外还有个专业性问题。你能译得通俗明白,做到这一点很不容易。比如测量放射性能量那一段,铀和钍包含在铀矿里的时候,读数是八,而分别测量后加起来只有四。这个差数在哪里? 这样译出来,人们很好理解。"①

从改革开放的现实需要来看,中国正在昂首迈向全面建设小康社会的崭新时代,在建设物质文明的同时,还要大力建设社会主义的精神文明。为了使译制片更为广泛地走向千家万户,从而帮助广大人民群众在欣赏艺术的同时更好地了解世界,提倡译制"通俗化",力求雅俗共赏,其现实意义就不言而喻了。

四、人物性格化原则

文学作品大都以塑造人物性格为特征。文学翻译的重要任务见于人物性格的再造。张友松先生谈翻译马克·吐温作品的体会时说,译者必须细心揣摩原作中描绘的各色各样的人物形象及其言谈举止,把自己溶化在作品的境界里,下笔时则力求使原著中的各种人物和自然景色活生生地呈现在读者眼前,使读者得到艺术的享受。②

动人的故事由活生生的人物的一言一行构筑起来,人物性格越鲜明,故事就越感人。鲜明的性格赋予了故事生活的气息,使每一幅画面生动而逼真,留给观众难忘的印象。准确把握人物性格是保证译制再创作实现生动传神的关键。译制者只有准确把握人物性格,才能在翻译、配音的创作过程中做到"对号入座",真正达到言如其人,观众闻其声便知其人的艺术境界。人物性格化恐怕是机器译制永远无法胜任的。

比如在美国影片《起锚》中,乔机智勇敢、快言快语、风趣幽默,而克劳伦斯则憨厚老实、说话推心置腹、诚恳真挚。热情开朗的苏珊言辞坦率而富有激情,而纯朴善良的布鲁克林姑娘则句句朴实、字字真诚。就连天真倔强的小唐纳德也"出言不凡",寥寥几句,却句句有棱角,使人听后不能轻易拿他"当儿戏"。

试对比下列对话原文和译文的语言特色。(乔和苏珊的对话)

> Joe：You're dressed up. You'll look like a million dollars. A girl like Sussy, I
> believe you'll kill him. Huh?

①　参见麻争旗:《新制译制片〈居里夫人〉之翻译及其艺术品格》,载于《现代传播——北京广播学院学报》1998年,第6期,第59页。

②　张友松:《文学翻译漫谈》,载于巴金等著《当代文学翻译百家谈》,北京大学出版社1989年版,第432页至433页。

乔：① 你着装起来，看上去就像一百万美元。像苏珊这样的姑娘，我相信，你会杀了他。哈？

② 你打扮好，一看就像是摇钱树。噢，相信我，你会迷倒他的。哈？

Joe：He wants somebody to think about, write to—you know to come home to.

乔：① 他想要个值得想念的，写信的，你知道——值得回家找的人。

② 他想找个值得想念的，鸿雁传情的——守在家里等待的。

再比如，影片《居里夫人》中的人物性格十分鲜明。居里夫人，聪颖倔强，脸上闪着火焰，眼里充满好奇和智慧，言语朴素而不平淡，铿锵有力却不咄咄逼人；居里博士，温和善良、热情诚挚，精辟的话语里充满了想象又富有哲理；老居里先生，豪爽耿直，说话直言快语，不给人一点情面；老居里夫人，慈祥厚道，是好心肠的贤妻良母；佩罗特教授，高瞻远瞩，寓意深刻，语重心长，正是他的一句教诲成了居里夫人乃至无数学子献身科学的座右铭；只有短暂出场的大科学家开尔文男爵，一位善良而纯朴的老人，纯朴得像天真的孩童……正是这些活生生的不同性格赋予了故事生活的气息，使每一幅画面生动而逼真，留给观众难忘的印象。

试对比下列原文与译文中人物语言的性格特点：

（居里夫人简称 Marie—玛丽；居里博士简称 Pierre—皮埃尔）

例1（在第 458 次实验失败后，皮埃尔欲劝玛丽放弃。）

Pierre：How much longer do you think you can drive yourself like this? And how much longer do you think I can stand by and watch you destroy yourself? The world has done without radium up to now. What does it matter if isn't isolated for another hundred years?

皮埃尔：你这样没命地干还能坚持多久？我能永远这样陪着你，眼巴巴看着你毁了自己吗？没有镭世界也存在到了现在。就算再过一百年还分离不出镭，又有什么关系呢？

Marie：I can't give it up. If it takes a hundred years it would be a pity. But I'm going to see how far I can go in my lifetime.

玛丽：我不能放弃。假如还需要一百年，那的确很遗憾。但我一定要看看，以我的毕生精力能不能完成。

例2（医生诊断玛丽的烧伤有可能引发癌症，皮埃尔万分担忧。）

Marie：Oh, Pierre, can't you see how—how unimportant little things like this are compared with what it might mean? It might prevent great sicknesses—even deaths—Pierr...

玛丽：噢，皮埃尔。你不明白吗？比起它可能产生的作用来说，我这点烧伤算得了什么？它有可能治疗疑难病，甚至绝症。皮埃尔……

例3（刚认识玛丽时，皮埃尔对女人的观点。）

Pierre：Always the continual struggle against woman. When we wish to give

all our thoughts to some work which estranges us from humanity, we
always have to struggle against woman.

皮埃尔：我们总是要不断地抵抗女人，因为我们要集中精力搞研究，这是远离尘
世的事业。所以我们总是要和女人作斗争。

Pierre：Woman loves life for the living of it. In the world of abstract research,
she's a danger and a distraction. She's the natural enemy of science.

皮埃尔：女人的天性就是爱生活。在抽象研究的领域里，女人是干扰物，是危险
品，女人是科学的天敌。

Pierre：Women and science are incompatible. Women of genius are rare. No
true scientist can have anything to do with women.

皮埃尔：女人和科学水火不相容。女人很少有天才。真正的科学家跟女人没什
么缘分。

例 4（皮埃尔向玛丽倾诉衷肠。）

Pierre：... It's an excellent combination. I might compare it with the chemical
formula NaCl，Sodium Chloride. It's a stable，necessary compound.
So，if we marry on this basis, our marriage would always be the same，
the temperature would be the same，the composition would be the
same...

皮埃尔：……你我是最完美的结合。拿一个化学式来打比方，比如氯化钠，是一
种稳定而必要的化合物。所以，如果我们按这种意义结婚，那么，我们的
结合是牢固的，温度保持不变，成分不会变化……

对比以上各例可以发现，原文中的人物语言带着鲜明的性格特征，而译文则以同样的风格再塑
了人物的鲜明性格。可见，翻译追求人物个性化，就是要字斟句酌，力图使其话语句句恰如其
分。这是使译文准确、生动的基本保证。

准确把握人物性格对影视剧本的翻译来说尤其重要，它是保证译制再创作实现生动传神
的关键。正如张友松先生所说："年龄、身份，习性和社会地位，文化水平等等各自不同的人物，
各有其特征，他们的外貌、语言、举动和表情，在译文中都要恰如其分地表达出来，才算是真正
地忠于原著，光在字面上死抠是不行的。"[①]

总之，翻译要整体把握人物性格、把握其语言特色，从而在译文中努力再创这些人物性格，
通过配音，最终实现不仅"形"似，而且"神"似，观众闻其声便知其人的艺术效果。这就是言如
其人，人物性格化的道理所在。

五、情感化原则

文学翻译家把翻译视为再创作，其原因之一在于译者情感的投入。张君川先生说，不论小
说还是剧本，都是诗，都是创作，首先必须爱之如命，甚至自己也有此创作欲望，拿它当自己的

① 张友松：《文学翻译漫谈》，载于巴金等著《当代文学翻译百家谈》，北京大学出版社 1989 年版，第 432 页至 433 页。

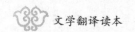

作品,才可下手翻译,不然译起来干巴巴的,失去诗意。艺术作品不是科学论文,要有丰富的思想感情与想象,译作亦应如此,才能感人。如果没有译者思想感情的参与,所译的作品就失去了灵魂。就以演剧打个比方:我们看剧本,脑中就生出舞台形象,就等于再创造,即就观众、读者来说,在看戏、看小说,也随了演出及作者再创造。译者又何尝可以例外呢?①

这就是"情感化"的原则,也就是说,翻译要努力"进入角色",设身处地,从人物内心深处把握、领会其言语的确切含义,从而使译文"言而由衷"、"有感而发",具有真情实感。

好的译制片,观众为剧情所吸引,几乎感觉不到是经过配译而成的。这其中自然以译文达到"真切感人"作为先决条件。如果翻译只停留在文字的浅层上,没有潜入其情感深层,那么,即使文字上说得过去,算得上"真实、通顺",甚至在字数、节奏等方面也无可挑剔,其结果也往往"貌合神离",难以求得"神似"。

试比较下列对话的两种不同译法(选自美国电视系列片《亡命追凶》中"目击者"一集):(金布尔把捡到的钱包送还马西娅,马西娅很感动,于是她也帮了金布尔的忙。)

Kimble:Why are you helping me?

金布尔:为什么帮助我?

Marcia:Don't get the wrong idea,Mr. Sanders. You returned my wallet. It had two weeks salary in it. To a working girl living dollar to dollar, losing it could be a disaster.

马西娅:你可别想错了,桑德斯先生。你送回我的钱包,里面有两周的工资呢!

① 一个靠工资生活的打工女来说,丢掉它会是一场灾难。

② 我还要靠这点薪水过日子,把它丢了,我会很惨的。

(金布尔不得不继续逃亡,临别时,马西娅恋恋不舍。)

Marcia:Well, another farewell scene. Don't you hate them?

马西娅:① 又一个离别的情景。你不讨厌它们?

② 呃,这是第二次分手。你讨厌分手吗?

Kimble:I don't like this one.

金布尔:① 我不喜欢这个。

② 我讨厌这一次。

Marcia:I can't coax you to stay. I'm shameless.

马西娅:① 我不能把你留住。我真不害臊。

② 我不会挽留人。我真不害臊。

Kimble:I'm not that man.

金布尔:① 我不是那个人。

② 我不值得。

Marcia:He must be somewhere... Whatever you're running from—or searching for—good luck.

---

① 张君川:《我的文艺翻译》,载于巴金等著《当代文学翻译百家谈》,北京大学出版社 1989 年版,第 443 页。

马西娅：① 他一定在某个地方……不管你是为何而逃跑——或者寻找什么——
　　　　　 祝你好运。
　　　　　② 是我没福气……不管你从哪儿来，或到哪儿去——祝你好运。

　　在上几列中，显然第二种译法更能表达人物的内心情感，比之第一种更有"戏"，更"传神"，更感人。所以说翻译不能只作"表面文章"，或者做文字游戏。那样的译文往往干枯乏味，很难准确传递人物言辞间所流露的思想感情，因而很难具有感人至深的魅力。

　　笔者认为，对影视剧脚本的翻译来说，"情感化"的原则，既是译者在创作过程中所追求的理想境界，也是下笔时锤炼文字、决定取舍的衡量尺度，同时也是鉴赏翻译水平的重要标准。影片《居里夫人》的感人魅力，不仅在于它赞颂了作为伟大科学家的无私献身精神，而且还在于它讴歌了作为平凡人的真实情感。准确自然地传递原作所蕴含的每一份感情，实为翻译的天职，这就是情感化原则的核心所在。

　　一位翻译家曾说，翻译是寂寞的行当。要论工作条件，一个角落放一张桌子足矣。然而翻译家却并不孤独，因为他总是在跟人家对话，跟作者对话，跟各个不同的人物对话，直至跟每一位观众（读者）对话。对影视剧脚本的翻译来说，这种对话更生动、更形象、更直观。在翻译的脑海里有一个大千世界，时而翻滚着惊心动魄的巨幅画卷，时而流淌着催人泪下的绵绵情丝。然而由于文化间的差异，"表面文章"往往很难传达那些细微而珍贵的真情实感。所以，翻译必须设身处地，进入人物内心深处，与之息息相通，从而思其所思，感其所感，进而言其所欲言。笔者在译《居里夫人》时近乎忘我，每遇动人之处往往情不自禁，随人物一同掉泪，由此深感情感化语言译制的灵魂。

试体会下列原文与译文中人物语言的情感成分：
例1（玛丽愉快地接受皮埃尔的求婚。）

　　Marie：I can imagine no respect or friendship greater than I have for you now.
　　　　　I can imagine no future so full of promise the one you offer.

　　玛丽：我想象不出还有什么能比得上我对你的尊敬和友谊。我想象不出什么样
　　　　　的未来能比你为我所描绘的更光明。

例2（新婚蜜月，玛丽满怀幸福。）

　　Marie：I wouldn't even know how to start，Pierre. I wouldn't know what to
　　　　　do. I'm very glad we're married to each other，Pierre.

　　玛丽：没有你，我甚至不知道从何入手。我不知道该怎么做。我真高兴，我们有
　　　　　这样的缘分，皮埃尔。

例3（镭的伟大发现里凝聚着爱的无私奉献。玛丽对皮埃尔一片深情。）

　　Marie：Because I'm so proud of you. I'm so proud that sometimes I think I'll
　　　　　burst. You're a very great man，Pierre. Not the way the word means，
　　　　　but just you，your kindness，your gentleness，and your wisdom. I love
　　　　　you，Pierre，so deeply. I never dreamed that. I'm so thankful，Pierre.
　　　　　That's what I wanted to tell you. That's what I hope you've always

known.

玛丽：我为你感到骄傲，有时骄傲得简直控制不住。你是一个伟大的人，皮埃尔，不是一般意义的伟大，我是指你的善良，你的温和文雅，你的智慧。我爱你，而且这么深。以前我没注意我对你这么感激。我想说的就是这些。我希望你永远知道。

例4（在玛丽的眼里，皮埃尔完美无缺。）

Pierre：Perhaps one day I'll get a new dress suit. You know, I've had mine since I got my doctor's degree. Looks bad on me, doesn't it?

皮埃尔：也许我该做一套新礼服穿。我这套是我获得博士学位时做的。很难看了，对吧？

Marie：No, Pierre! No! You look very handsome in anything.

玛丽：不，皮埃尔！不！你穿什么都非常英俊。

例5（五千多次实验之后居里夫妇误认为彻底失败，面对这一沉痛打击，皮埃尔借女儿缠着要妈妈讲故事之机，编讲了一个寓意深长的美好神话——美丽的公主和孤独的男士相爱，他们为造福人类共同探寻一件藏在神石里的珍宝。）

Pierre：One day... So, they worked very hard for a long, long time to try and secure the treasure from the stone—but they grew very tired, and at last, they knew that they would never be able to free the treasure from the enchantment of the stone. But they weren't sad about it, because they knew that no matter how many disappointments they had, they would always go on together having the courage to take many disappointments, because they were together. And they lived happily ever after.

皮埃尔：有一天……于是，他们苦干了好长好长时间，千方百计想把财宝从石头中取出来。他们非常疲劳。最后，他们发现他们永远不可能从那块神石中把财宝取出来。但他们并不难过，因为他们知道不管他们经历过多少次失望，他们将永远并肩前进。他们有勇气经受失望的打击，因为他们在一起。从此，他们生活得非常幸福。

例6（皮埃尔为玛丽挑选耳饰，向店主介绍她的有关特征。）

Pierre：And her hair is sort of gold, you know. Yes. And her eyes are grey—very calm and grey, and her coloring is very—very lovely, sort of—smooth skin, and nice delicate coloring and uh—well, I—I don't know whether it would be of any help to you, but I believe the lady is quite beautiful.

皮埃尔：呃，她的头发有一点金黄。是的。眼睛是淡蓝，淡蓝色，很宁静。她的肤色非常漂亮，非常漂亮，非常细嫩，而且非常光滑，呃，还有我，呃，我不知道对你有没有什么帮助，我，呃，我觉得这位女士非常漂亮。①

从以上各例中可以看出，居里夫妇的话语中没有海誓山盟更没有打情骂俏，然而就在这自然朴实的字里行间却洋溢着他们彼此深深的爱，那种人世间最真挚、最炽热、最崇高的爱。细细体味以上原文与译文的感情色彩可以发现，充满真情实感的语言是自然的、由衷的，是有感而发、发自内心的，往往并不是翻译刻意雕琢所能为之。要达到这一境界，翻译必须与人物进行感情沟通、成为情感知音。翻译就是以忘我的感情投入实现译文言而由衷、真实感人的艺术追求。张友松先生说，文学翻译工作者也像作家一样，需要运用形象思维，不可把翻译工作当做单纯的文字转移工作，译者如果只有笔杆子的活动，而没有心灵的活动，不把思想情感调动起来，那就传达不出作者的风格和原著的神韵，会糟蹋名著，贻误读者。②

总之，情感投入是影视译制的一条基本原则。影视译制的过程首先是欣赏，译制者须投入情感和想象，方能心领神会，进入原作意境，如果报以冷漠，那就很难为之感染、与之共鸣，谈不上真正理解。表达的过程更须调动情感、发挥想象，以道出真情，说出实话，最终实现传达神韵的境界。

结　语

总结以上五个方面，"口语化"要求译文具有生活气息、使对话像"话"；"人物性格化"要求言如其人，使话语带着人物个性；"情感化"要求语出有情，使言语真实感人；"口型化"是对译文在形式、结构等方面的严格规定；而"通俗化"则是在翻译已经承担的多重使命中又赋之予一个为观众着想的新内容。这五个方面可以说是影视剧脚本翻译最主要的特征，也是翻译在创作中所必须遵循的最基本原则。五个方面相辅相成，共同作用，翻译时不能有所偏废、顾此失彼。这是做好影视剧脚本翻译的基本保证，也是影视剧脚本翻译完成艺术再创造的基本审美追求。

影视文学的国际传播受到语言文化因素的严重制约。单是语言的障碍就使传播的有效性大打折扣，甚至使传播成为不可能。因此，影视文学译制是中外影视文学交流的关键环节，在技术和艺术两方面都有很高的要求，因而需要大量的专业人才。目前，国内译制人才匮乏，译制市场混乱，低劣译制品充斥市场。所以，加强译制工作，加强译制理论研究，对于提高译制质量、促进中外影视文学的有效交流具有十分重要的现实意义。

---

① 张子扬主编：《译制片剧本精选》，作家出版社 1998 年版，第 543 至 596 页。
② 张友松：《文学翻译漫谈》，载于巴金等著《当代文学翻译百家谈》，北京大学出版社 1989 年版，第 432 页至 433 页。

选文三 Politeness in Screen Translating

Basil Hatim & Ian Mason

导 言

本文选自 Lawrence Venuti, *The Translation Studies Reader*. New York: Routledge, 2000.

根据相关文献综述,选文首先归纳了字幕翻译者在工作过程中受到的四大类型的约束,诸如语音系统向书写系统转换的跨度、意义传递的空间、语句长度、声像同步等。哈蒂姆与梅森在较早的研究(1989)中已注意到字幕、配音翻译中的人际交往语用信息——即礼貌性,常遭"牺牲",本文是对前期研究的继续深化,分析指出礼貌性法则在影视翻译中遭受忽略可能带来的影响,为该领域的未来研究指明方向。借用布朗与列文森的礼貌准则及其对于"威胁面子行为"的相关论述,选文从社会文化和语言文化角度展开影视作品受众类型的分析,结合收集的相关个案数据,分别阐述具有积极意义和消极意义的礼貌性,详述表达不同意、意图和解或质疑的语言及语言外手段,强调语篇、语境在影视作品翻译中的重要性。

We now turn to an entirely different mode of translating, that of film subtitling, in order to show discourse processes of a similar kind at work. In this chapter, the emphasis will be on the pragmatic dimension of context and we shall see how the constraints of particular communicative tasks affect variously the textural devices employed both in original screen writing and in the writing of subtitles. It will immediately be realized that we are here confronted with mixed modes. Unlike the dubber, who translates speech into speech, the subtitler has to represent in the written mode what is spoken on the soundtrack of the film.

It would be superfluous here to enter into a detailed description of the task of the subtitler (for a full account of what is involved, see for example Vöge (1977), Titford (1982). For our purposes, it will suffice to summarize the main constraints on subtitling, which create particular kinds of difficulties for the translator. They are, broadly speaking, of four kinds:

(1) The shift in mode from speech to writing. This has the result that certain features of speech (non-standard dialect, emphatic devices such as intonation, code-switching and style-shifting, turn-taking) will not automatically be represented in the written form of the target text.

(2) Factors which govern the medium or channel in which meaning is to be conveyed. These are physical constraints of available space (generally up to

33, or in some cases 40 keyboard spaces per line; no more than two lines on screen)① and the pace of the sound-track dialogue (titles may remain on screen for a minimum of two and a maximum of seven seconds).

(3) The reduction of the source text as a consequence of (2) above. Because of this the translator has to reassess coherence strategies in order to maximize the retrievability of intended meaning from a more concise target language version. In face-to-face communication, the normal redundancy of speech gives hearers more than one chance of picking up intended meaning; in subtitling, the redundancy is inevitably reduced and chances of retrieving lost meaning are therefore fewer. Moreover, unlike other forms of written communication, this mode does not allow the reader to back-track for the purpose of retrieving meaning.

(4) The requirement of matching the visual image. As Chaume [1998] points out, the acoustic and visual images are inseparable in film and, in translating, coherence is required between the subtitled text and the moving image itself. Thus, matching the subtitle to what is actually visible on screen may at times create an additional constraint.

Some of the studies which have been carried out have concentrated on the effect of these constraints on the form of the translation. Goris (1993) and Lambert (1990) note the levelling effect of the mode-shift and, in particular, the way in which features of speech which are in any way non-standard tend to be eliminated. Lambert speaks of "un style zéro" and Goris, comparing user variation in subtitling and dubbing, observes that, in the latter, social dialect is under-represented in terms of prosodic features of speech but quite well represented lexically; in subtitling, on the other hand, neither prosodic features nor variant lexis appear to be represented.

Politeness

In an earlier study (Mason, 1989), we observed that one area of meaning which appeared consistently to be sacrificed in subtitling was that of interpersonal pragmatics and, in particular, **politeness** features. In what follows, we hope to illustrate how politeness is almost inevitably underrepresented in this mode of translating and to suggest what the effects of this might be. Additionally, we shall point to further research which might be carried out in this particular area of translation studies.

We use the term politeness in the sense intended by Brown and Levinson (1987), on which much of this chapter is based. It is important to establish immediately that the term is

---

① These norms appear to be generally observed in Europe and the Western world as a whole. It should be noted that, elsewhere, far greater intrusion of a text on screen may be tolerated.

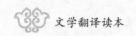

not used here in its conventional sense of displaying courtesy but rather it is intended to cover all aspects of language usage which serve to establish, maintain or modify interpersonal relationships between text producer and text receiver.

Brown and Levinson's theory rests on the assumption that all competent language users have the capacity of reasoning and have what is known as "face". Face is defined as:

> the public self-image that everyone lays claim to, consisting of two related aspects:
> (1) negative **face**: the basic claim to freedom of action and freedom from imposition;
> (2) positive **face**: positive self-image and the desire that this self-image be appreciated and approved of. (Brown and Levinson, 1987: 61)

Now, because language users are aware of each other's face, it will in general be in their mutual interest to maintain each other's face. So speakers will usually want to maintain addressees' face because they want addressees to maintain their face. Above all, speakers want to maintain their own face. They are, however, aware that some linguistic actions they may wish to perform (such as asking for a favour) intrinsically threaten face. These are referred to as **"face-threatening acts"** (FTAs). Normally, a speaker will want to minimize the face-threat to the hearer of an FTA (unless their desire to carry out an FTA with maximum efficiency—defined as "bald on-record"— outweighs their concern to preserve their hearer's or their own face). So, the more an act threatens the speaker's or the hearer's face, the more the speaker will want to select a strategy that minimizes the risk.

Strategies available to speakers for this purpose are (in order of increasing face-threat):

(1) *Don't carry out the FTA at all.*
(2) *Do carry out the FTA, but off-the-record*, i. e. allowing for a certain ambiguity of intention.
(3) *Do the FTA on-record with redressive action (negative politeness).* This will involve reassuring hearers that they are being respected by expressions of deference and formality, by hedging, maintaining distance, etc.
(4) *Do the FTA on-record with redressive action (positive politeness).* This will involve paying attention to hearers' positive face by, e. g. expressing agreement, sympathy or approval.
(5) *Do the FTA on-record, without redressive action, baldly.*

To illustrate this, let us imagine that A wants B to lend her money, in itself an FTA. Strategy 5 above would involve A making a direct request of the type: "lend me twenty pounds"— a threat to B because it seems to lack respect; and a threat to A because it is not good for her self-image. For both of these reasons, A is more likely to opt for a less face-threatening strategy. Strategy 4 might involve an utterance along the lines of: "We're old friends and I know I can rely on you. Please lend me... " The threat, although still direct, is slightly mitigated by the attention paid to B's self-image. Strategy 3 would involve expressions of the kind: "I hate to ask you this but could you possibly...?" Again, this is still a direct request for money, although the way it is put makes it slightly easier for B to refuse without losing face and without causing A to lose face. On the other hand, strategy 2 (e. g. "I'm desperately short of money. I wonder where I could get twenty pounds from. ") allows A to protest, if challenged by B, "Oh, but I wouldn't dream of asking you!"

Crucially, it should be added that the seriousness of an FTA is a cultural variable; it cannot be assumed that the same act would carry the same threat in different socio-cultural settings. Moreover, the weight of an FTA is subject to the variables of the social **distance** and relative **power** of speakers and addressees. A direct request for a favour is less face-threatening between friends than between people who are relative strangers to each other or whose relationship is hierarchical (employee to employer, for example). Thus, in languages which have distinct pronouns of address to encode addresser/addressee relationship (French *tu* and *vous*, for example), a switch from the use of one form to the other form may in itself constitute a potential FTA—to the addressee because the sudden reduction of the social distance between him or her and the speaker may be unwelcome; and to the speaker because he or she runs the risk of being rebuffed by non-reciprocal use by addressees. In addition, if a speaker who is in a hierarchically superior position to a hearer initiates the change, then threat to face may stem from the hearer's impression that this is an attempt to exercise power, i. e. encode the non-reciprocal relationship. Consequently, pronouns of address are often the site for complex negotiation of face.

Brown and Levinson present evidence from three unrelated social and linguistic cultures to show that, whereas the linguistic realization of politeness varies considerably, there is a remarkable uniformity of underlying strategy, which might suggest that politeness is a universal feature of natural language communication. From a translation point of view, what this might suggest is that the dynamics of politeness can be relayed trans-culturally but will require a degree of linguistic modification at the level of texture. [1] Relaying the significance of the shift from *vous* to *tu* mentioned above, for example, is a familiar problem for screen translators as well as translators of novels.

At the same time, as suggested above, the particular constraints under which the film subtitler works make it impossible for all of the meaning values perceived in the source language soundtrack to be relayed. Indeed, it would be fair to say that this is not even an aim of the subtitler, who seeks to provide a target language guide to what is going on in the source text. Meaning is then to be retrieved by cinema audiences by a process of matching this target text guide with visual perception of the action on screen, including paralinguistic

---

[1]　This is so because attention to face is what adds words to basic prepositional meaning. Brown and Levinson (1987: 57) observe, "... one recognizes what people are doing in verbal exchanges ... not so much in what they overtly claim to be doing as in the fine linguistic detail of their utterances (together with kinesic)".

features, body language, etc. Consequently, any phrase-by-phrase comparison of source text and target text for the purpose of translation criticism would be an idle exercise and our analysis below should not be construed as having any such intention. What is an altogether more legitimate subject of investigation, however, is to ascertain whether there is any consistent pattern in the kinds of values/signals/items, which are perforce omitted in translated dialogue. Such research would require the analysis of a wide variety of acts of subtitling of various kinds and in widely differing languages. Here, we can do no more than provide some initial evidence which would point in the direction such research might take.

Audience Design

Before proceeding to the analysis of our data, it is important to consider the nature of film dialogue. As with all works of fiction, the dialogue is "authentic" only in a special sense. Characters on screen address each other as if they were real persons while in reality, a script-writer is like a novelist, constructing discourse for the sake of the effect it will have on its receivers, in this case the cinema audience. Consequently, in the case of film dialogue, some refinement is needed to our key notions of text producer and text receiver. Thus, potentially

Text producer 1 = scriptwriter (film director, etc.)

Text producer 2 = character A on screen

Text receiver 1 = character B on screen

Text receiver 2 = cinema audience

(Text receiver 3 = other potential receivers)

Bell (1984) provides a taxonomy of categories of text receiver and shows how speech style is affected above all by what he calls **"audience design"**, that is, the extent to which speakers accommodate to their addressees. He argues convincingly that style is essentially a matter of speakers' response to their audience, who include four potential categories. **Addressees** are known to the speaker, ratified participants in the speech event and directly addressed; **auditors** are both known to the speaker and ratified participants but they are not being directly addressed; **overhearers** are known by the speaker to be present but are neither directly addressed nor ratified participants; finally, **eavesdroppers** are those of whose presence the speaker is unaware. Bell's hypothesis is that the text producer's style is affected most of all by addressees, to a lesser extent by auditors and less again by overhearers. (Evaesdroppers, being unknown, cannot, by definition, influence a speaker's style.) Adapting this classification now to film dialogue, we may say that characters on screen treat each other as addressees within a fictional world in which the cinema audience is like an eavesdropper. What we know, however, is that in reality the screenwriter intends the dialogue for a set of known, ratified but not directly addressed receivers—i. e. the cinema audience, who then according to the above classification may be considered to be auditors.

(Other categories of potential receivers, such as film festival juries, boards of censors, etc. may then be considered as overhearers.)

In the case of mass communication, furthermore, Bell argues that audience design is not so much a response to the audience (since the communicator cannot know exactly who is being addressed) but rather an initiative of the communicator, who forms a mental image of the kind of (socio-cultural) group he or she knows to be the likely receivers. He also suggests that this kind of communication inverts the normal hierarchy of audience roles, since "mass auditors are likely to be more important to a communicator than the immediate addressees" (Bell 1984:177). Thus, it could be said according to this hypothesis that the style of a film script is more subject to influence by the auditors than by the immediate addressees within the fictional dialogue. For example, in the data to be discussed below, a fictional character appearing on screen for the first time at a dinner-table conversation, begins:

> *Ce que je trouve navrant—et c'est ce que j'essaie de dire dans mon dernier livre—c'est que...*
>
> [What I find upsetting—and this is what I attempt to say in my latest book—is that...]

It seems plausible that what is primarily involved here is a scriptwriter's signal to mass auditors that the character who is being introduced is pompous or pretentious; secondarily, the fictional character is seeking to establish his intellectual authority with his interlocutors. In other words, the pretentious style is both addressee-designed and auditor-designed but, in terms of cinema as communication, the orientation towards the mass auditors is perhaps the overriding consideration.

The relevance of these audience-design distinctions to our consideration of the subtitler's task may now become apparent. As a translator, the subtitler is seeking to preserve the coherence of communication between addressees on screen at the same time as relaying a coherent discourse from screenwriter to mass auditors. Given the severe constraints of the task as detailed above, hard choices have to be made. Elements of meaning will, inevitably and knowingly, be sacrificed. On the basis of our observation, we wish to suggest that, typically, subtitlers make it their overriding priority to establish coherence for their receivers, i.e. the mass auditors, by ensuring easy readability and connectivity; their second priority would then be the addressee-design of the fictional characters on screen (particularly in terms of the inter-personal pragmatics involved). Specifically, there is systematic loss in subtitling of indicators of interlocutors accommodating to each other's "face-wants". In the remainder of this chapter, we shall illustrate such processes at work.

The Data

The examples of screen translating reproduced below are taken from the English-subtitled version of the French film *Un cœur en hiver* (Claude Sautet, 1992). This film was chosen for the following reasons. First, being a recent, widely-distributed, full-length feature film, the quality of subtitling is high. Second, a theme of the film is the establishment, maintenance and modification of personal relationships and the ways in which these are or are not made explicit in language. Thus, our central concern, which we described above as interpersonal pragmatics, is always to the fore in this film. Third, the film contains many sequences of verbal sparring, in which characters on screen seek to get the better of each other, impose their will or improve their image among others present (ef. the notions of face and threat to face, outlined above). This confronts us with an abundance of the politeness phenomena referred to earlier.

In the film, Stéphane, a violin-maker, is attracted to Camille, a musician who is involved in a close relationship with Stéphane's colleague, Maxime. Camille is attracted to Stéphane but the latter's reticence and unwillingness to commit himself is a growing problem between them.

The sequences from which our examples are taken are (Sample 5. 1) a rehearsal by Camille and two (male) fellow-musicians of a Ravel sonata, witnessed by Stéphane, who has improved the sound of Camille's violin. In the sequence, the dialogue is between Camille and Stéphane. Camille speaks first; (Sample 5. 2) a dinner-table conversation between guests, including Stéphane, Camille and Maxime, and their hosts.

Positive and Negative Politeness

Sample 5. 1

    —Ça vous convient?[①]   Like it?

    [Does that suit you?]

    —Oui, m...   Yes, but...

    [Yes, b...]

    —Dites.   Go on.

    [Say it]

    —Vous n'avez pas joué un peu vite?   You took it a bit fast.

    [Didn't you play rather fast?]

    —Si. Vous voulez l'entendre à sa vitesse.   Yes. You want to hear it at the right

                                    tempo?

    [Yes. You wish to hear it at its normal pace.]

    —Oui, siça ne...   If you wouldn't mind.

    [Yes, if it's not...]

---

  ① Literal translations are provided in square brackets, simply as a guide to the form of the ST; the subtitles are reproduced on the right-hand side of the page.

(Music)

—Alors?	Well?
[Well?]	
—C'est très beau.	It was beautiful.
[It's very beautiful.]	
(Pause)	
—Vous partez déjà?	Leaving already?
[You're leaving already?]	
—Oui.	Yes.
[Yes.]	
—Vous avez d'autres rendez-vous?	Other business?
[You have other appointments?]	

—Non mais j... je dois vous laisser travailler. Au revoir. No, I must let you work.
Goodbye.

[No but I... I must let you work. Goodbye.]

—Au revoir.	Goodbye.
[Goodbye.]	
(Other musicians)—Salut!	
—Salut!	
[Cheerio!]	

In Sample 5.1, what is really going on is apparent not so much from the prepositional meaning of what is said but from what is implicated in what is said. Camille is seeking to provoke Stéphane and get behind his defences. Her utterances constitute direct threats to his face. Stéphane, on the contrary, is self-effacing and defensive; his whole strategy is to avoid going on-record and his embarrassment is apparent not only in his speech but also in his facial expression. Camille's directness is also apparent in her gaze. To an extent, then, these paralinguistic features will convey the interpersonal meanings to the cinema audience without the need for them to be explicitly encoded in subtitles. But let us look more closely at what is going on here. Camille's initial question asks bluntly whether her rendering "suits" Stéphane (rather than simply whether he likes it). What is implicated in such an utterance is that Stéphane is the kind of person who requires things to suit him. This threatens his face in two ways. First, to accept the question as it stands implies acceptance of the implicature that he would wish it to "suit" him—which, in turn, commits him to something which is face-threatening to his interlocutor. Second, it commits him (a non-musician) to going on-record in expressing an opinion of a concert-violinist's work. In reply, Stéphane's strategy is consequently one of minimization of face-loss; he wishes to express a point of view (the music was played too fast) but he cannot afford either to agree or disagree with the question as put and so opts for a "yes, but" which is, even then, not fully stated but just alluded to (Oui, m...). Not content to allow Stéphane to be so evasive, Camille insists, with a bald, on-record imperative: "say it!" Now Stéphane can no longer avoid expressing an opinion. But his main concern is still to protect his own face. Again, he takes redressive action by putting his view in the form of a question, thus allowing himself the let-out "I didn't say it was too fast" and implicating "this is only my view: you're the expert". Not to be outdone, Camille replies as if Stéphane's view had been intended as an instruction. Her rejoinder *Vous voulez l'entendre à sa vitesse* ("You wish to hear it at its own tempo") is uttered with the intonation of a statement of confirmation, not with that of a question. Stéphane, again recognizing the face-threat involved in saying either "yes" or "no", is once more equivocal and hesitant: "Yes, if it's not... " It is as if he dare not finish his utterances for fear of going on-record. ①

In the remainder of the exchange, three things are evident. First, Camille's direct (bald, on-record) strategy continues, with short questions which function either as instructions (*Alors?* = "State an opinion") or as reproaches (*Vous partez déjà?* And *Vous avez d'autres rendez-vous?* may implicate "You're not really interested in me or my music"). Second, Stéphane's evasiveness is further served by his ambiguous reply *C'est très beau*, which can be understood either as "Your rendering was beautiful" or as "The music (but not necessarily your rendering of it) is beautiful". Again, he avoids committing himself any more than necessary. Finally, the artificial distance between Stéphane and Camille is thrown into sharp relief when their formal leave-taking (—*Au revoir*, —*au revoir*) is echoed in much less formal terms (*Salut!*) by the two other musicians, whose relations with Stéphane are apparently casual and unproblematic.

Thus far in our analysis, the textural encoding of politeness has included lexical choice, sentence form (imperative, interrogative), unfinished utterance, intonation, ambiguity of reference. These then are the linguistic features which constitute the best evidence of the management of the situation, the interpersonal dynamics and the progress of the conflictual verbal relationship. We now turn to the sequence of subtitles to consider the extent to which the implicatures are still retrievable from the target text. Unsurprisingly—and almost inevitably—a different picture emerges.

The preference for brevity and case of readability accounts for such translations of Camille's questions as "Like it?", "Leaving already?", "Other business?" Yet this concise style, omitting the subject pronoun, is conventionally associated in English with familiarity and solidarity (in terms of politeness theory, it is a way of minimizing face-threat by "claiming common ground")— the opposite of the strategy adopted by Camille, who, in the source text, does nothing to reduce threat to face. This different, altogether more conciliatory Camille also emerges in lexical selection (asking someone about "likes" is far less face-threatening than asking about what suits him; "Go on" is a conventional way of

---

① Among the off-record strategies listed by Brown and Levinson (1987:214) are: "Do the FTA but be indirect... *be incomplete*, use ellipsis" (emphasis added).

encouraging a speaker to say more, whereas "Say it!" is a direct challenge). Finally, the mode-shift from speech to writing requires choices to be made in punctuation. Camille's question delivered as a statement (*Vous voulez l'entendre à sa vitesse*) has become "You want to hear it at the right tempo?"— again suggesting a more conciliatory stance.

Turning now to Stéphane, we find that several of the politeness features observed above have disappeared. His off-record strategy of tentativeness, vagueness and ambiguity is not recoverable from the subtitles. *Oui m...* has become "Yes, but..."; *Oui siça ne...* has become "If you wouldn't mind" and the hesitation in *Non mais j... je dois vous laisser travailler* is, in translation, the more assertive "No, I must let you work". The verdict "It was beautiful" no longer allows the inference that the comment *C'est très beau* refers to Ravel rather than Camille. Likewise, the redressive action which mitigates the threat to face in *Vous n'avez pas joué un peu vite?* (see above) is no longer perceptible in the pronouncement "You took it a bit fast". In other words, the translated Stéphane is pursuing a different strategy. Finally, the opposition *Au revoir/salut!*, so important in the encoding of social relations that it must be supposed to be primarily a signal from the scriptwriter to the auditors, is not relayed; the audience relying on the translation is unaware of the stark contrast between Stéphane's and Camille's leave-taking and that of the two other musicians.

From the point of view of the verbal exchange in Sample 5.1 as a whole, it could be argued that enough is apparent from facial expression and gesture for all of these interpersonal dynamics to be retrieved without the need for them to be made explicit in the target text. There is no doubt some substance to such a claim and our analysis cannot do full justice to the visual image which the subtitles are intended to accompany. Nevertheless, if indicators of politeness in the target text are at variance with those suggested by the moving image, then a discordance is created which may need more processing time to resolve than the cinema audience has available to it. The problem is not so much that explicit markers of politeness are just absent from the translation; rather, that subtitling may create a substantially different interpersonal dynamics from that intended.

In Sample 5.1, the general brevity and spacing of the (source text) exchanges mean that the subtitler's task is not as constrained as it usually is when the density of source text dialogue requires to be significantly abridged in translation. Indeed, more space was theoretically available for the representation of Camille's and Stéphane's politeness features than was actually used, although subtitlers invariably opt for the briefest translation compatible with establishing coherence. We shall return to this point at the conclusion of this chapter. Now, let us proceed to Sample 5.2, where the dialogue is rapid and the translator's leeway consequently far less.

Sample 5.2

(Speakers are identified as follows: L=Louis, the host; X=an unnamed guest, who is a writer; C=Camille; M=Maxim, her partner; S=Stéphane)

X: Mais non, Camille, c'est　　　　　　　No, Camille, it's worse!

pire. Toutes ces foules
sans aucun repère qui
piétinent dans les musées.

Herds of people drifting around art
galleries...

[But no, Camille, it's worse.
All those drifting
crowds trampling in the museums.]

C: Mais si dans ces musées
au milieu de cette foule qui herd...
ne voit rien il n'y a qu'une
seule personne qui rencontrè...
une œuvre qui la touche,
qui va peut-être changer sa
vie, c'est déjà beaucoup, non?

But if, among that drifting

one person sees a
painting that moves him
and may change his life—
isn't that good?

[But if in those museums
amid that crowd which
sees nothing there is just
one person who finds a
work of art which moves
him/her, which may change
his/her life, that's already
a lot, isn't it?]

X: Mais ça c'est toujours
passé comme ça.

That's nothing new.

[But it has always
happened like that.]

C: Je ne crois pas.

I think it is.

[I don't think so.]

S: Au fond, vous êtes à peu
près d'accord. Vous
aussi vous parlez de la sensitive
sensibilité de l'individu
en face d'une masse qui
serait aveugle.

Basically, you agree.
You also talk about one
person in a dull
herd.

[Basically you more or less
agree. You too speak of
the sensitivity of
the individual confronted with
a blind crowd.]

C: Je n'ai pas dit ça.   I didn't say that.
    [I didn't say that.]
M: Non, ce que tu as dit, je   You said that, in any group,
    crois, c'est qu'à chances   a select few are more
    égales, il y aurait comme   likely to...
    une sélection des gens qui
    seraient destinés à...
    [No, what you said, I think, was
    that, all things being equal, there
    might be some kind of selection
    of those who might be destined to...]
C: Mais pas du tout. I did not!
    [But not at all.]
M: Tu as dit que certains   You said some people see
    voient des choses   what others don't.
    que d'autres ne voient pas.
    [You said that some see
    things that others do not.]
S: Oui, c'est ce que vous avez dit. That's what you said.
    [Yes, that's what you said.]
C: Oui mais... non. Enfin,   Yes... no!
    moi, je n'exclus personne.
    [Yes, but... no. Well,
    I exclude no-one.] I exclude nobody.
X: Mais moi non plus.   neither do I.
    [But neither do I.]
S: Bien sûr.   Of course.
    [Of course.]
L: Et toi, tu n'as pas d'avis And you? Have you no
    sur la question?   opinion?
    [And you, have you no
    opinion on the question?]
S: Non. [No.]
C: Aucun. [None.]   None?
L: Il est au-dessus du débat.   He's above it all.
    [He is above the discussion.]
S: Non, j'entends des   No, I hear conflicting
    arguments contradictoires   arguments, all valid.
    et tous valables.

[No, I hear arguments which are contradictory and all valid.]

C: Tout s'annule, c'est ça. On ne peut plus parler de rien. [Everything cancels everything else out, that's it. One can no longer talk about anything.]

They cancel each other out, so we may as well shut up?

S: C'est une tentation, en effet. Je n'ai pas votre bonne volonté. [It's a temptation, indeed. I do not have your good intentions.]

It's a tempting thought.

I lack your good intentions

L: Bien, nous respectons ton silence. [Good, we respect your silence.]

All right.

We'll respect your silence.

C: Evidemment si on parle, on s'expose à dire des conneries. Si on se tait, on ne risque rien, on est tranquille, on peut même paraître intelligent. [Of course if one speaks, one exposes oneself to talking rubbish. If one keeps quiet, one risks nothing, one is unconcerned, one may even appear intelligent.]

Of course

If we speak, we run the risk of being wrong.

It's easier to keep quiet and appear intelligent.

S: Peut-être simplement qu'on a peur. [Perhaps simply one is afraid.]

Maybe it's just fear.

In Sample 5.2, threats to face come thick and fast. At a dinner table discussion initiated by someone who holds controversial opinions and is unafraid to go onrecord with them at some length (X has expounded his views in the immediately preceding sequence), it becomes increasingly difficult to challenge these views without exposing oneself to attack. Camille, however, attempts this only to find herself flatly contradicted and then reinterpreted by others. Noticing that Stéphane is not similarly prepared to put himself on the line, she goes on to the attack. The subtitler's difficulties may be appreciated even from the script of the source text reproduced here. To this must be added, of course, the pace of the conversation on the sound-track, the need to represent each voice separately and identify it with a particular character on screen. If politeness features were difficult to relay in Sample 5. 1, they will be all the more difficult to accommodate in Sample 5. 2.

Rather than attempt a complete analysis of the interaction in this sequence, we propose to focus on selected features in order to add to what has already been said. They are ① Camille's disagreement with the writer "X"; ② Maxime's attempted reconciliation; and ③ Camille's challenge to Stéphane.

1 Disagreement

The counter-argumentative structure employed by Camille ("I agree... but") at the beginning of Sample 5. 2 is a conventional form of positive politeness, claiming common ground before committing the face-threatening act of disagreeing. (On the use of this text format and politeness in written texts, see Hatim and Mason, 1997: chap 8.) This is so conventional that, especially in spoken French, the first half of the structure is commonly omitted and utterances begin Mais... What is noticeable here, however, is the power differential referred to earlier. As a recognized writer, X has status within the situation and his opinions are valued. Camille, on the other hand, is relatively powerless in this situation (her recognized expertise lying elsewhere). Thus, she must pay full attention to her interlocutor's face (using the full counter-argumentative structure and putting her view as a question—*C'est déjà beaucoup*, *non?*) whereas he need make only the minimal ritual gesture (*Mais non*, *Camille*, *c'est pire* and *Mais ça c'est toujours passé comme ça*). In translation, X is even more direct, without a hint of positive politeness ("No, Camille, it's worse" and "That's nothing new"). In this sense, the translation, although it modifies the interpersonal relations, does so in the intended direction: the power differential between Camille and X is heightened.

2 Attempted reconciliation

Stéphane feels the need to reconcile the two opposing viewpoints. Yet it will be extremely face-threatening to suggest to two people who have gone on-record as having diametrically opposed views that they are, in fact, in agreement with each other. Consequently, Stéphane adopts the negative politeness strategy of hedging:

Au fond, *vous êtes* **à peu près** *d'accord* (emphasis added to show hedges)

as redressive action to his interlocutors' want to be unimpinged upon. By inserting these hedges, Stéphane also protects his own face by implicating "I didn't say that you agree in all respects". Camille, relatively powerless in her confrontation with X, is on the other hand far more confident of her position now: she can afford to be direct: *Je n'ai pas dit ça* ("I didn't say that"). This is, of course, a direct threat to face. Maxime seeks to retrieve the situation by hedging still more. First, he agrees: *Non* (=no, you didn't) and then goes on record in restating Stéphane's view but with redressive action: *ce que tu as dit*, **je crois** (=I may be wrong) *c'est qu'à* **chances égales** (= "*only in some circumstances*") il y **aurait** (= *hypothetical*) **comme** (="*not exactly*") une sélection des gens qui seraient (=*hypothetical*) destinés à... *Once again, we can see how it is in the textural detail that evidence of the maintenance and development of relations between characters is revealed. And once again, the subtitles reflect an entirely different politeness strategy:* "You said that, in any group, a select few are more likely to..." *Here, the translated Maxime appears altogether more defiant.*

3 Challenge

Among the interesting features of Camille's subsequent attack on Stéphane are use of intonation, irony and use of pronouns. It is worth noting that, when Stéphane admits to Louis that he has no opinion, Camille, as in the sequence in Sample 5.1, challenges him with what might seem to be a question ("None at all?") but is uttered with the intonation of a statement, creating an implicature along the lines of "You simply have no view". This is, of course, an altogether more face-threatening act than the "None?" of the subtitle. It provides an opportunity for Louis to accuse Stéphane of remaining aloof. The latter employs positive politeness in suggesting that the contradictory views he has heard are equally valid. To counter this, Camille employs irony (an off-record strategy listed by Brown and Levinson 1987:214):

Tout s'annule, c'est ça. On ne peut plus parler de rien.

The expression *c'est ça* ("that's it") is a strong signal of the ironic intention, indicating that the opinion being stated is not sincerely held and that the words used are intended to mimic or parody another person's words. In this way, Camille can strongly implicate that Stéphane's position is absurd ("no-one can talk about anything"). Interestingly, there is another instance of this use of irony (in a sequence of the conversation not reproduced in Sample 5.2) when X, feeling that he has been accused of being "traditional", exclaims:

La tradition, c'est ça, je suis réac [tradition! that's it, I'm reactionary]

This utterance is to be compared to the discussion [in Hatim and Mason 1997: Ch. 3] of the "hijacked" discourse. By hijacking the discourse of the political left (*réac* is a ritual term of abuse used to describe anyone with conservative views) and attaching it ironically to his opponent in argument, X can implicate "Your view is no more than the knee-jerk response of the extremist". This use of irony as an offrecord strategy by X and by Camille is scarcely retrievable from the subtitled versions ("Tradition? So I'm a reactionary?" and "They cancel each other out, so we may as well shut up?").

Our final point concerns the use of personal pronouns. The way in which speakers exploit personal reference for purposes of positive and negative politeness is analysed in Stewart (1992 and 1995). In addition to their core values, some pronouns can be used to refer to other individuals or groups. For example, "you" can refer to people in general ("generic reference", as in "On a clear day, you/ one can see the coast of France"). There is no space here for a complete analysis of pronominal use in *Un cœur en hiver*, including, for example, the mutual use of *tu* by most of the friends in the film, contrasting with the studied *vous* of Camille and Stéphane to each other—a feature which, as noted earlier, the subtitler cannot easily relay. But let us take one significant instance—the use of the French impersonal pronoun *on* ("one") by Camille. It is Stewart's (1995) insight that speakers exploit the ambiguity of reference of on for purposes of face-protection and redressive action. Camille's final attack on Stéphane is a case in point:

> *Evidemment si on parle, on s'expose à dire des canneries. Si on se tait, on ne risque rien, on est tranquille, on peut même paraître intelligent.*
>
> [Of course, if one speaks one exposes oneself to talking rubbish. If one keeps quiet, one risks nothing, one is unconcerned, one may even appear intelligent.]

The implicature is clear: Camille is referring to her own earlier willingness to go on record as disagreeing with the writer and to Stéphane's silence in the discussion. By using *on*, which can be used for self, other and generic reference, she avoids explicit self-reference and thus protects her own face from the threat of admitting that she might have been "talking rubbish". Conversely, by using the same pronoun to refer to Stéphane's silence, she can carry out the face-threatening act of accusing him but with the negative politeness strategy (strategy 3) of indirectness; that is, "if one keeps quiet, one can appear intelligent" has the potential meaning "if people keep quiet, they can appear intelligent". No-one would misunderstand who her real target is but, with her redressive action, Camille avoids a bald, on-record FTA which might provoke a confrontation (they are in company and, at this stage in the film, Camille has been acquainted with Stéphane only for a short time). That Stéphane himself does not mistake the target of the accusation is apparent from his defensive response: *Peut-être simplement qu'on a peur* ["Perhaps simply one is afraid"], which serves to protect his own face. How is all this to be relayed in translation? The pronoun "we" in "If we speak..." partly fulfils the same function as on but, if repeated several times, would sound unnatural in English. The translator is therefore forced into the use of impersonal expressions (Camille: "it's easier to keep quiet" and Stéphane: "it's just fear"). The politeness strategies—and consequently the interpersonal dynamics—of the exchange are only partly relayed.

There are many more points that could be made and readers may find other significant details in samples 5. 1 and 5. 2. Subtitlers may also object that it is quite unjust to subject to such scrutiny of detail a translation which is in any case intended to be partial and is normally "consumed" in real time. The objection would be valid if the objective had been to criticize subtitlers or subtitling. But, as has been made clear, given that some elements of meaning must be sacrificed, our interest lies in the kinds of meaning which tend to be omitted and in the effects such omission may have. We hope to have shown that, in sequences such as those analysed, it is difficult for the target language auditors to retrieve interpersonal meaning in its entirety. In some cases, they may even derive misleading impressions of characters' directness or indirectness. In order to test the generalizability of these limited findings to other films and other languages, far more empirical research would be needed. In particular, one could test source language and target language auditor impressions of characters' attitudes. Beyond this, our data provide some insight into the problems involved (in any mode of translating) in relaying interpersonal meaning generally and politeness in particular. Politeness will be referred to again (see Hatim and Mason 1997: chaps 7 and 8), from a cross-cultural perspective and applied to written text.

Indeed, there is overlap between what has been shown here and all that is said elsewhere in the book on the topic of pragmatic meaning in translation. In our discussion of subtitling, we have gone beyond the limits of this particular mode of translating and observed discourse at work.

选文四　In Search of a Theoretical Framework for the Study of Audiovisual Translation

Jorge Díaz Cintas

导　言

本文选自 Pilar Orero, *Topics in Audiovisual Translation*. Amsterdam & Philadelphia: Benjamins Publishing Company, 2004.

近年来,文学及文学翻译研究领域广泛采用多元系统理论和描述翻译学研究方法,展开对翻译历史、翻译现象以及翻译文本接受效度的研究。本文一反通常学界对影视作品译介研究的语言学、语用学研究路数,借鉴文化研究学派,展开对影视文学翻译的分析,以期探索影视译介研究的宏观理论框架。选文首先简明扼要地介绍了描述翻译学领域的相关源流及主要概念,对伊万·佐哈尔的多元系统理论展开细致入微的优劣评判。选文结合图里的翻译规范理论,以及影视作品译介流通与接受中赞助人的操纵及影响,分别分析影视作品翻译的"充分性"与"可接受性",并提出整体评价方案。选文结论明确提出,仅仅从语言学视角展开对字幕翻译、配音翻译的研究明显有失偏颇,认为只有将语言学理论与文化研究理论结合起来,对影视作品译介的研究才最为可行、可信。

1. Historical Approach

The main objective of this paper is to analyse the validity and functionality of a series of concepts that have been articulated within the theoretical framework loosely known as Descriptive Translation Studies (DTS) and apply them to the field of audiovisual translation (AVT). [①] In recent years, these concepts have been highly successful in research terms but could be perceived as somewhat restricted, being as they were conceived with literature and literary translation at their core.

One of the first hurdles in a study of this nature is defining what is understood by the umbrella terms Descriptive Translation Studies and Polysystem Theory. The selection of those scholars that might be included in this "school" is also another highly controversial concept. Although there are some nuances differentiating both currents of thought, the prevailing opinion in this paper is that both are entirely complementary. In fact, the cumulative term Descriptive Translation Studies is understood here as a wider classification that encompasses the Polysystem Theory.

In 1972, Holmes, a pioneer of Descriptive Translation Studies, coined the more general term Translation Studies as a discipline with two main objectives: "① to describe the phenomena of translating and translation(s) as they manifest themselves in the world of our experience, and ② to establish general principles by means of which these phenomena can be explained and predicted" (1994: 71). This conception gives rise to two different branches. An empirical one which he calls descriptive translation studies (DTS) or translation description (TD) and another of a more theoretical nature that he refers to as theoretical translation studies (ThTS) or translation theory (TTh). With these principles in mind, and aided by several conferences organised in the late 70s, [②] the discipline began to gain momentum and weight. Some of the scholars that in one way or another have subscribed and elaborated on these theoretical postulates are Toury, Even-Zohar, Lefevere, Hermans, Lambert, van den Broeck and Bassnett. Although, as Hermans (1999: 8) points out, Translation Studies has occasionally being taken to mean the specifically descriptive line of approach, its usage has recently evolved and Holmes's broad term is nowadays commonly used to refer to the entire field of study. In the following pages the term Translation Studies is employed when talking about the whole discipline, whereas Descriptive Translation Studies is a more concrete term and refers to a particular scholarly approach.

---

① For a debate on the terminology attached to the approach which forms the subject of this chapter, see Hermans (1999: 7 - 16).

② The conferences took place in Leuven (1976), Tel Aviv (1978), and Antwerp (1980).

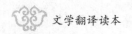

2. Concepts and Premises

It is not my intention to offer a detailed analysis of all the axial concepts around which this school of thought revolves, but rather to offer an overview with the aim of foregrounding their potential validity in the field of AVT research.

One of the first obstacles that must be overcome is the need to adapt most of their theoretical premises to the audiovisual world. Despite the fact that in his initial proposal Holmes spoke about translation in general—not only in the literary realm—and that most scholars are aware of the need to open up new research avenues in order to incorporate translation practices that have been traditionally neglected in academic exchanges, the truth is that DTS refers almost exclusively to the literary world. It is only in certain recent works that some references have been made to translation modes such as dubbing and subtitling (Bassnett 1998: 136). However, I would like to underline that these concepts are in essence operative and functional as heuristic tools in researching AVT. In some cases, as we will see, they even offer more possibilities to carry out analyses in new directions.

3. Polysystem

This is a term coined by Even-Zohar in a series of papers written in the 70s and published in English at the end of the decade (1978a and 1978b). It is used to refer to a group of semiotic systems that co-exist dynamically within a particular cultural sphere. It is characterised by continuous changes and internal oppositions, whose main aim is to occupy the centre position in the system, and it is regulated by socio-historic norms. The literary polysystem comprises a range of literatures, from the canonical to works and genres traditionally considered minor (children's literature, popular and romantic fiction, thrillers, etc.), as well as translated works. The concept is sufficiently flexible to allow us to also talk of a film polysystem in Spain or in any other country. The film polysystem is made up of the national products and the translated ones—dubbed or subtitled—and deals with the relationships that are established among all of them. This new approach to translation allows for the translated work to be studied as a product in itself that is integrated in the target polysystem. It also dispenses with the traditional perception of the inferior translated copy derived from a superior original to which it barely does justice (Hermans 1985). There is a shift of interest that departs from the study of translation as a process, translating, in order to centre on the analysis of translation as a product, translation. The newborn is thus fully embodied in its adoptive society and its positioning in this new culture requires the scholar to untangle and to interpret.

The advantages of this approach are manifold. Firstly, it blurs the boundaries between high and low culture, allowing the reclamation of social activities that have been traditionally marginalized in the academic exchanges, e. g. thrillers or, in our case, audiovisual translation as opposed to literary or poetry translation. Secondly, it helps to broaden the research horizon since it underlines the need to incorporate the translated works in the study of the cinematography of any country. This is an area of research that does not have to interest all scholars in AVT, but some knowledge of this discipline can help them enormously in their pursuits. This association between national production and translation affects not only the translators but also the academics involved in Film Studies that have usually ignored the role played by translation. Only recently have some scholars started to direct their attention towards translation, as evidenced by the introduction of modules in dubbing and subtitling, not only in translation degrees but also in other degrees such as Film and Television Studies, Journalism and Media Studies. Conferences centred on Film Studies are opening up to allow the inclusion of papers on film translation. [1] Some scholars are actively seeking to bridge the gap between Film and Translation Studies (Chaume 2000, 2003 and Remael 2000). And it is also very telling that some publishing companies are launching books on audiovisual translation as part of their cinema collections rather than their translation series. [2] These trends help translators and researchers to gain in prestige and become more visible in our society. Within this theoretical framework, translation—and translators to a certain extent— ceases to be a Cinderella of academia, and translated works shake off the mantle of a secondary, deficient product with which they have historically been burdened. The translated product is, in principle, at the same social and cultural level as the national ones.

Pioneering studies on dubbing and subtitling were flawed by approaches that were biased by the linguistic dimension. Socio-cultural, as well as professional factors that also have an impact on the final decision on how to translate an audiovisual product, were ignored or dealt with in a rather superficial manner. In this sense, the dynamics of the polysystem, characterised by the continuous confrontation among the different systems that form it, offer an ideal platform from which to launch an analytical assault at the dubbing versus subtitling debate. It certainly opens new possibilities of study by establishing a direct link between the national system (Spanish films) and the foreign system (translated films). What sort of relationships can be detected between the dialogue of dubbed/subtitled films and the dialogue of films shot originally in Spanish? Are there any other intersemiotic influences? Why are film remakes produced? What are their socio-cultural implications? What kind of hierarchy and power struggle takes place between original audiovisual products and foreign ones?

---

① *World Cinemas: Identity, Culture, Politics.* Conference held at the University of Leeds, United Kingdom, 25 – 27 June, 2002.

② Despite having a translation series, the Spanish publishing company Cátedra has a couple of volumes centred on dubbing and subtitling that are commercialised within its cinema collection *Signo e Imagen.* Something similar is happening with a new series of books on audiovisual translation published by the company Ariel in its collection *Ariel Cine* (see Díaz Cintas 2003).

The analytical guidelines that stem from the polysystem theory allow us to focus the dubbing versus subtitling confrontation from a stronger socio-cultural perspective. Instead of talking about exclusion, the complementarity between both modes of translation is foregrounded. And although the analysis of a translated film continues to be relevant, this approach opens up a new avenue of research with two main objectives. Firstly, to make clear the relationships that exist among all dubbed and subtitled films as a group of film texts structured and functioning as a system. Secondly, to study the associations that can be established between translated films and the national ones. Also, more research ought to be done into the similarities and/or discrepancies that exist between the different translation practices in different polysystems within the same society, e. g. film and literary polysystems.

One of the areas needing revision in the polysystem theory is relative to the concepts primary and secondary. Even-Zohar (1978a) uses these two concepts in a rather ambiguous manner to refer both to the position that products occupy in the polysystem as well as to the artistic power they hold in that polysystem. Primary practices are at the core of the polysystem creating new models and are "by and large an integral part of innovatory forces" (ibid.: 120). On the other hand, to occupy a secondary position means to be on the margins of the polysystem and not have any influence on other products. It also implies obedience to conservative conventions and to those forces which reinforce existing models. However, films that occupy a secondary position do not have to obey conservative forces and films that are in a primary position are not always innovative. Given the fact that in Spain USA translated films are more numerous than the national ones, attract larger numbers of spectators and generate more revenue, it seems legitimate to say that they occupy a primary position and the Spanish films a secondary position. However, what is not so evident is that the secondary ones, i. e. the Spanish films, have a more conservative character and that the primary ones, i. e. the USA films, an innovative one. This bipolarity without apparent nuances between primary and secondary positions seems to oversimplify a far richer and more complex reality. Consider, for instance, underground films in which many other factors are at play: budget, artistic intentions and equipment, for example. Besides, a film might well be primary and innovative from a formal point of view but secondary as far as the plot is concerned.

Another problem deserving a more detailed analysis is the establishing of the limits of the polysystem that we want to use in our field. The literary polysystem seems to encompass a body of work sulciently coherent and cohesive, but to talk about a film or cinematographic polysystem is too limited to films and neglects other products of the audiovisual world that are also translated such as TV series, documentaries, cartoons, soap operas, commercials or corporate videos. The ambivalence shown in our field by the use of terms of a more general nature such as "multimedia", "audiovisual" or "screen" translation serves only to place emphasis on the difficulty of solving this terminological conundrum.

4. Norms

The different norms postulated by Toury (1978, 1980 and 1995), and reworked by Hermans (1999), take on special importance in this theoretical framework. Norms are understood as a central element in the translation process and they account for the relationships that exist between the rules of the abstract and modelling society and the idiosyncrasies of each translator. These norms constitute the theoretical pillars on which the methodological principles rest. As translation scholars, our task consists of elucidating the similarities and differences between the criteria shared by the collective of users and the instructions that have been implemented by the translator in genuine cases and in a particular historical context. Thus, the study of norms will help to account for the policy that regulates the whole translation project—preliminary norm—as well as the relations that take place in the distribution of the linguistic material when moving from source to target language—operational norms, divided into matricial and textual norms. At a macro-structural level, these norms allow us to determine which are the distinctive characteristics that regulate the delivery of the dubbed or subtitled discourse, bearing in mind the many different constraints imposed by the medium. At a micro-structural level, they help us to observe the translator's behaviour in the linguistic mediation.

Norms are a very successful concept in the study of translation because they provide a clear objective to the research and direct the translation scholar to what needs to be found and analysed. Now the aim is to ascertain the norms that govern the translators' behaviour, bearing in mind that norms change and are not the same throughout history. It marks a departure from previous analytical studies focused on determining the degree of equivalence between source and target products. This new approach accepts translated texts without judging their solutions as correct or incorrect. It seeks to explain why a particular equivalence has been reached and what this means in the historical context in which the translation took place. There is a deliberate emphasis on the need to carry out more descriptive studies focused on the product, the function and the process (Holmes 1994: 71 - 73) with the intention of coming up with a clear map of the translation practice. Instead of throwing up abstract ideas unsupported by empirical data or making up ad hoc examples to illustrate a particular case in point that suits the researcher, what is now suggested is mapping what really happens in translation to avoid falling into absolute theorisation. Only from real examples that already exist can we draw conclusions that will help to further knowledge in translation studies. And these norms are precisely the tools that will help us in this task.

The changing and evolving nature of norms frees the scholar from the prescriptive principles that have characterised the postulates of previous theoretical constructs such as linguistics structuralism. The equivalence between source and target products is not absolute and depends on socio-historical variables. These norms also allow us to foreground aspects that belong to the supralinguistic (presentation of the translation, the author's canonical status, the time and place where the original and the translation were produced) as well as the metalinguistic (formulations that theorise about translation and translating, critical reviews) dimensions that had been previously ignored or, in the best cases, had received a rather superficial analysis. However productive this perception might be, the changing nature of norms also has a negative slant to it. Since they are forever changing, it is difficult to isolate them in our present day and, therefore, to analyse them. Their study in past periods would seem to be easier and more feasible because the scholar can take a look at them from a distance. In order to avoid an attitude that might lead us to ignore what is now happening, I would propose taking priority away from the historical dimension or, at least, playing it down.

Given that the emphasis tends to be placed on establishing which norms regulate the translator's behaviour in any particular socio-historical moment, it seems that this academic construct is more productive when the scholar carries out the contrastive analysis of several films or novels rather than just one. Some of the works carried out in this perspective tend to suffer from being over-ambitious. They try to cover all the works translated during several decades in a relatively large field of study, which inevitably raises certain problems. On the one hand, it seems to be an overly demanding enterprise, apparently only feasible for researchers with lots of spare time and energy. For those without the time, this research requires a group effort that, although desirable, is not always possible. In any case, it can stifle the initiative of the individual researcher. On the other hand, there is always the risk of having to generalise too much in the drive to determine the norms that have regulated translators' behaviour during a considerable long period of time. The researcher's conclusion may have to be very general so that the findings are encountered in all the products that are representative of that particular period. Even then, it might still be possible to note dissident behaviours that could call some of the findings into question.

A way to overcome this obstacle could be by searching for norms in bodies of data that are less expansive and more homogeneous and manageable. Here, AVT shows itself to be an area with many possibilities. The literary translator usually enjoys a degree of autonomy that is not so clear in the case of the audiovisual translator, whose product goes through different stages and hands before reaching the screen. Norms are on occasions applied by laboratories, production and distribution companies, dubbing actors and directors, technicians, adaptors, linguistic advisers or TV stations, and not so much by individual translators. In principle, then, certain normative behavioural patterns could be observed more easily if the researcher focused on the analysis of products that have been marketed, say, by a given TV channel or distribution company. The aforementioned deficiencies can be easily overcome and the concept of norm in the study of translation continues to be of paramount importance. To discover norms and to value them in the contexts in which they take and have taken place means to reveal how culture, the symbolic capital in Bourdieu's terminology, has been manipulated in favour of certain vested interests, be they economic, political or of any other kind.

5. Patronage

This concept helps to consolidate the study of extra-linguistic factors relating to the socio-economic and ideological imperatives that exist in all social interactions. Coined by Lefevere (1985), patronage is understood as the group of "powers (persons, institutions) which help or hinder the writing, reading and rewriting of literature" (ibid.: 227), and that "can be exerted by persons [...], groups of persons [...], a social class, a royal court, publishers [...] and, last but not least, the media" (ibid.: 228). Compared to the literary world, audiovisual products are a lot more exposed to commercial forces, a fact that opens up additional opportunities for manipulation and for avenues of research.

Patronage operates on three levels: ideological, economic and social status. In the case of AVT it opens the doors to the study of the state's interference through film censorship or cinema legislation (screen quotas, dubbing and subtitling licences, financial subsidies); the participation of higher bodies and authorities such as the European Union or more localised ones such as the Generalitat de Catalunya (Catalan Local Government); the role of the different TV channels and the dubbing and subtitling laboratories; and the importance of the educational centres like universities. It is also highly interesting to include the study of the decisive role played by the international distribution and production companies in any given country or linguistic region; the tension that arises between the needs and tastes of the audience and the commercial interests of the companies; the semi-accepted fallacy that what is translated is what the target spectator wants to consume and not what the companies want to sell. Until now, most of these factors have failed to receive an in-depth analysis. There is no doubt that a more systematic approach would lead to conclusions that could contribute to a better understanding of translation in its widest sense.

6. Adequacy and Acceptability

All translation process implies and reflects tensions between the two poles of a *continuum*. In one of the extremes we find adequacy, when the translated product adheres to the values and referents of the source product, and in the other acceptability, which means that the translation embraces the linguistic and cultural values of the target polysystem. Since no translation is completely adequate or acceptable, one of the researcher's tasks, helped by the norms, consists in discovering the sort of relation that gets established between the original and the translation. That is, to show if the translated product tends more to the pole of adequacy or acceptability. The latter will always imply a greater degree of acculturation and domestication in line with Venuti's postulates (1995) in this area. Domesticating and foreignizing are two concepts at the heart of literary translation theory that, given their emphasis on the linguistic dimension, can function with more or less success in the literary world. However, they are clearly insulcient when dealing with AVT in which the value of the image tends to take precedence over the word. For Venuti's concepts to be functional in our field, their re-elaboration is necessary. And the same is true with the concepts of acceptability and adequacy. Their opposition seems to suggest a bipolar conception that has been successfully argued by Zlateva (1990), when she maintains that the two poles are not necessarily at the extremes of a *continuum*. Using the translation of *Peter Pan* into Bulgarian as an example, she successfully highlights that a translation can be adequate and acceptable at the same time. A more functional definition of these two terms capable of accommodating the concept of error in translation could help to overcome this shortcoming (Díaz Cintas, 1997: 53 – 59).

7. General Evaluation

Descriptive Translation Studies avoids being prescriptive or normative in its postulates, hence the prominent use of the adjective "descriptive" as opposed to "prescriptive". However, if in the struggle to gain the central position in the polysystem, the ultimate objective of subtitling, or any other audiovisual translation mode, is the canonisation of its own discourse, then it seems imperative to formalise as well as harmonise the variables that define it. In our field, the time and spatial constraints in the presentation of subtitles imposed by the medium bring along an inescapable degree of prescriptivism. In order to entrench a stable and homogeneous discourse, it is imperative to reach a consensus among all parties involved in the polysystem. This would inevitably imply the following of a set of rules and norms that have to be essentially dogmatic. It is symptomatic, for example, that ESIST, European Association for Studies in Screen Translation (www. esist. org), has made one of its priorities the elaboration of a code of good practice in subtitling—this is nothing other than a prescriptive list of rules.

Another point that has been criticised is the aversion DTS has shown to the evaluation and analysis of translation errors. One of the reasons given is that what is important is the target product in itself and its positioning in the target culture. If the translated product has been commercialised in a given society it is therefore a valid product. The aim of the scholar is to study its articulation and positioning in the target polysystem and not its degree of equivalence with the original in terms of good or bad translation outcomes. However, as Malmkjær (2001: 35) points out, in cases in which a particular translation solution "strikes a reader not just as exiting (sic), innovative, unusual or unfortunate, but simply wrong", this target text oriented philosophy makes it difficult to justify any translation norms on theoretical or observational grounds.

Moreover, closing our eyes to this dimension to some extent separates—unnecessarily, I would argue—Descriptive Translation Studies from the educational world. This may be seen as a rather paradoxical occurrence, since academics from the field of DTS are the first not to want to create a schism between translation theory and practice. However, they seem to be happy for the creation of one between research and teaching. It also misses the possibility of an in-depth analysis that might examine whether there have been periods in which errors were worse, more numerous or of a different nature to the errors encountered nowadays; whether errors have something to do with the language we translate from; whether in the translation of films originally shot in minority languages, errors are due to a direct translation from the original or they have been transmitted through an English pivot translation; whether errors could be classified as natural or motivated, or whether they end up becoming accepted Anglicisms. Malmkjær's paper (2001) offers a valuable set of criteria that proves very useful as an attempt at incorporating the notion of error within this theoretical project.

However, I believe these are minor limitations that do not call into question the general validity of the whole framework. They simply bring to the fore the fact that there is room for improvement within DTS, just as there may be within other theoretical constructs. On the positive side, it enjoys a high degree of flexibility that makes it capable of incorporating alterations and new perspectives without jeopardising its essence. The advantages offered by this theoretical framework are without doubt superior to the limitations mentioned. If we want our area of research to be given the consideration it deserves, more analyses are needed with a more theoretical and less anecdotal approach. I personally believe that DTS offers an ideal platform from which to launch this approach. For translation scholars, this catalogue of concepts is a heuristic tool that opens up new avenues for study, strengthens the theoretical component and allows the researcher to come up with substantial analyses. Scholars then belong to a research community, minimising the risk of coming up with approximations that are too intuitive or too individual and subjective. To speak of polysystems, norms and patronage locates the academic within a theoretical framework that, if shared with other scholars, facilitates the debate and speeds up an exchange of ideas and information. To work within a school—that does not have to be static or rigid—helps to avoid a possible and menacing diaspora of knowledge. In 1996, Fawcett wondered if it was possible "to bring film translation under the sway of translation theories" (ibid.: 70). I firmly believe that DTS presents the scholar with a sulciently homogeneous and flexible theoretical framework that acts as a very valuable starting point for research in AVT. Works carried out in this field by Ballester Casado (1999, 2001), Díaz Cintas (1997), Gutiérrez Lanza (1999), Karamitroglou (2000), Remael (2000) and Sokoli (2000), among others, are clear examples.

To approach dubbing and subtitling from a mere linguistic perspective is clearly insufficient. By transcending the purely linguistic dimension, the postulates put forward by DTS have the advantage of placing translation researchers on a starting grid that allows them to channel their efforts into the object of study from a plural and interdisciplinary perspective. Translation is viewed as an act of intercultural communication, rather than simply interlinguistic, confirming Simon's prediction (1996: 134) that "it was only a question of time until cultural studies 'discovered' translation". A discovery that has come from the pen of authors sitting on the fence between Descriptive Translation Studies and Cultural Studies, such as Bassnett (1998).

The linguistic and cultural approaches should not be viewed as antagonistic paradigms but, rather, complementary. By focusing on our object of study from several angles we can only gain a better knowledge of translation and translating. It is only a logical development of Holmes's premonition (1994: 73) when in 1972 he stated that:

> The ultimate goal of the translation theorist in the broad sense must undoubtedly be to develop a full, inclusive theory accommodating so many elements that it can serve to explain and predict all phenomena falling within the terrain of translating and translation.

The problem only arises when priority is given to one of the two dimensions at the exclusion of the other. The ideal solution comes by integrating both approaches in what Munday (2001: 181 – 196) calls an inter-discipline, Translation Studies, which should play a more prominent and important role at universities and in the academic world. As translation scholars, we have a duty to avoid the risk of an irreconcilable split between the two paradigms: linguistic and cultural. One of the most lucid and perceptive observations in this respect comes from Harvey (2000: 466), when he states that "[t]ranslation is not just about texts: nor is it only about cultures and power. It is about the relation of the one to the other".

In an initial approach, it is reasonable to state that translation activity is primarily of a linguistic nature. However, it is no less true that the life of the translated product, as proposed by Benjamin with his concept of *Überleben* (1992 [1955]), does not finish with the translation, but starts with it. The analysis of the manifold relations that develop between the translated product and the recipient society can be as interesting and absorbing as the linguistic analysis. Borrowing Harvey's words (2000: 466), what the translation scholar needs is:

> A methodology that neither prioritizes broad concerns with power, ideology and patronage to the detriment of the need to examine representative examples of text, nor contents itself with detailed text-linguistic analysis while making do with sketchy and generalized notions of context.

Studies that combine the linguistic dimension with feminist (Simon, 1996; Flotow, 1997), post-colonial (Niranjana, 1992; Carbonell i Cortés, 1997), gender (Harvey, 2000) or power and culture perspectives (Álvarez and Vidal, 1996) are highly profitable from the point of view of research and as yet they have not made an appearance in audiovisual translation. I hope, however, that they will form the basis for future papers very soon.

【翻译鉴赏】

I Have As Much Soul As You (excerpted from *Jane Eyre*)

Jane: I thought you'd gone.

Rochester: I changed my mind or rather the Ingram family changed theirs. Why are you crying?

Jane: I was thinking about having to leave Thornfield.

Rochester: You've become quite attached to that foolish little Adele, haven't you? To that simple old Fairfax. You'd be sorry to part with them.

Jane: Yes, sir!

Rochester: It's always the way in this life. As sooner as have you got settled in a pleasant resting place, you're summoned to move on.

Jane: I told you, sir, I shall be ready when the order comes.

Rochester: It has come now!

Jane: Then it's settled?

Rochester: All settled! Even about your future situation.

Jane: You've found a place for me?

Rochester: Yes, Jane, I have... er... the west of Ireland. You'll like Ireland, I think. There are such warm-hearted people there.

Jane: It's a long way off, sir.

Rochester: From what, Jane?

Jane: From England and from Thornfield.

Rochester: Well?

Jane: And from you, sir.

Rochester: Yes, Jane, it's a long way. When you get there, I shall probably never see you again. We've been good friends, Jane, haven't we?

Jane: Yes, sir.

Rochester: Even good friends may be forced to part. Let's make the most of what time has left us. Let us sit here in peace. Even though we should be destined never to sit here again. Sometimes I have a queer feeling with regard to you, Jane. Especially when you're near me as now. As if I had a string somewhere under my left rib. Tightly and inextricably knotted to a similar string situated in a corresponding corner of your little frame. And if we should have to be parted, that cord of communion would be snapped. Kind of a nervous notion I should take to bleeding inwardly. As for you, you'd forget me.

Jane: That I never will, sir. You know that. I see the necessity of going, but it's like looking on the necessity of death.

Rochester: Where do you see that necessity?

Jane： In your bride.

Rochester：What bride? I have no bride.

Jane： But you will have!

Rochester：Yes，I will. I will.

Jane： You think I could stay here to become nothing to you? Do you think because I'm poor and obscure and plain that I'm soulless and heartless? I have as much soul as you and fully as much heart. And if God had gifted me with wealth and beauty, I should have made it as hard for you to leave me as it is now for me to leave you. There, I've spoken my heart，now let me go.

Rochester：Jane. Jane... you strange almost unearthly thing. It is you that I love as my own flesh.

Jane： Don't mock...

Rochester：I'm over with Blanche. It's you I want. Answer me, Jane, quickly. Say： "Edward, I'll marry you." Say it，Jane. Say it!

Jane： I want to read your face.

Rochester：Read quickly. Say, "Edward, I'll marry you."

Jane： Edward，I'll marry you.

Rochester：God pardon me.

【背景介绍】

《简·爱》是部脍炙人口的作品,是毋庸置疑的名著。英国19世纪著名的女作家夏洛蒂·勃朗特的代表作,当时人们普遍认为《简·爱》是夏洛蒂·勃朗特诗意生平的写照,是一部具有自传色彩的作品。作品被改版成电影,影片中简·爱的爱情表白成为众多英语爱好者的背诵精品。尤其是本文所选这一段"我们的精神是同等的",也被很多女性主义学者作为证明简·爱是女性主义者的宣言。

【词汇疏导】

1. Thornfield 桑费尔德,主人公罗切斯特居住的庄园

2. attach to 使依恋

3. part *vi.* 分开;分离

4. summon *vt.* 召唤;召集

5. be destined to 命定的;注定的

6. queer *a.* 奇怪的;奇特的

7. with regard to 关于……/对于……

8. rib *n.* 肋骨

9. inextricably *ad.* 逃不掉地

10. knot *vi.* 打结;(使)纠缠

11. situate *v.* 使位于;使处于

12. corresponding *a.* 符合的;一致的

13. frame *n.* 体格

14. cord *n.* 细绳;粗线

15. snap *v.* 咬断；拉断

16. notion *n.* 观念；想法

17. inwardly *ad.* 在内部；内里

18. obscure *a.* 无名的；微贱的

19. unearthly *a.* 非尘世的；神秘的

【译文】

我们的精神是同等的（节选自《简·爱》）

简：　　我以为你已经走了。

罗切斯特：我改主意了。或者说英格拉姆家改主意了。你怎么哭了？

简：　　我在想，我要离开桑菲尔德了。

罗切斯特：你很有些离不开那个小傻瓜阿黛勒了，是吗？还有那个头脑简单的老费尔法克斯太太。你因为要离开她们而伤心。

简：　　是的，先生！

罗切斯特：生活总是这样，你刚到一个令人愉快的休憩地，又有什么原因让你前行了。

简：　　我告诉过你，先生，我会随时准备接受您对我的吩咐。

罗切斯特：现在已经来了。

简：　　决定了？

罗切斯特：一切都定下来了。你将来的位置也定下来了。

简：　　你给我找了个地方？

罗切斯特：是的，简，我已经……唔……西爱尔兰。我想，你会喜欢爱尔兰，那儿的人都很热心。

简：　　路很远，先生。

罗切斯特：离哪儿远，简？

简：　　离英国和桑菲尔德。

罗切斯特：哦？

简：　　还有你，先生。

罗切斯特：对，简，是很远。你一旦到那，也许我再也见不到你了。我们已经是好朋友了，是吗，简？

简：　　是，先生。

罗切斯特：好朋友也会不得不分离。让我们好好利用剩下的时间。让我们在这儿安安静静坐一会儿，以后再也不会一起坐在这儿了。有时候我对你有一种奇怪的感觉，简。尤其是像你现在这样靠近我的时候。仿佛我左肋下的哪个地方有根弦，跟你那小小身躯里同样地方一根同样的弦难舍难分地紧紧纠结在一起。我们一旦分离，这根弦就会绷断。我有个奇怪的感觉，那时我体内会血流不止。至于你呢，你会把我忘得一干二净。

简：　　我决不会，先生。你知道，我看出非离别不可，可这就像看到了非死不可一样。

罗切斯特：你从哪儿看出非这样不可呢？

简：　　你的新娘。

罗切斯特：我的新娘？我没有新娘。

简：　　但你会有！

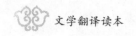

罗切斯特：对，我会，我会。

简：　　你以为我会留下来，做一个对你来说无足轻重的人吗？你以为，就因为我穷、低微、不美，我就没有心，没有灵魂吗？我也有一颗心，我们的精神是同等的。如果上帝赐予我美貌与财富的话，我也会让你难以离开我，就像我现在难以离开你一样。好了，我已经说出了我的心里话，让我走。

罗切斯特：简，简，你这小古怪，几乎不像人世中间的小东西。我爱你就像爱我自己。

简：　　别嘲笑……

罗切斯特：我和布兰奇结束了，你才是我想要的。回答我，简，快说，说："爱德华，我愿意嫁给你！"说，简，快说！

简：　　我想看清你的脸！

罗切斯特：快点说。说："爱德华，我愿意嫁给你！"

简：　　爱德华，我愿意嫁给你。

罗切斯特：上帝饶恕我。

《非诚勿扰》经典台词

　　你要想找一帅哥就别来了，你要想找一钱包就别见了，硕士学历以上的免谈，上海女人免谈，女企业家免谈（小商小贩除外），省得咱们互相都会失望。刘德华和阿汤哥那种财貌双全的郎君是不会来征你的婚的，当然我也没有做诺丁山的梦。您要真是一仙女我也接不住，没期待您长得跟画报封面一样看一眼就魂飞魄散。外表时尚，内心保守，身心都健康的一般人就行，要是多少还有点儿婉约那就更靠谱了。心眼儿别太多岁数别太小，允许时常有不切实际的想入非非，但三句话就能给轰回现实还不气恼顶多有点儿难为情地咧嘴一笑就该干吗干吗去了。我喜欢会叠衣服的女人，每次洗完烫平叠得都像刚从商店里买回来的一样。说得够具体了吧。

【背景介绍】

　　《非诚勿扰》是冯小刚"叛逃"贺岁喜剧四年后的回归之作，堪称 2008 年度最具亲和力和感染力的国产电影，作为一部"非典型冯氏喜剧"，摆脱了昔日那种小品化、拼贴化的特点，把希望与绝望、喜剧与优雅等多种矛盾元素合理地重叠在一起，一种新鲜的冯氏风格呼之欲出。电影通过给男主人公秦奋（葛优饰）征婚的形式，呈现了当下都市男女形形色色的生活方式和心理状态，糅合了众多笑点，关注时下热点、人生态度和逢场作戏，把光怪陆离的各种社会现象巧妙地融进影片中。影片以平民化的取材倾向，戏剧化的故事情节，游戏化的叙事方式，博得了广大观众的喜爱，幽默、调侃的影片中，精彩的人物语言是其最吸引观众的地方，其中的一些台词甚至成为令人津津乐道的年度时尚流行语。

【译文】

　　If you dream to find a very handsome guy, please do not come here, if you are looking for a man as your wallet, please do not meet me, whom do not want to enlist your marriage-hunting. If you hold a Master's degree or higher, not possible; girls born in Shanghai, not possible; female entrepreneurs (except small business hawker), not possible, so that we don't waste each other's hope. The wealthy and healthy Andy Liu or Tom Cruise kind, would not make an announcement looking for you. Of course, I do not expect to find Julia

Roberts. If you are really a fairy, I can't be your match. I do not expect you to look like a cover girl, just one look crushing people's souls. An average person, with outside stylishness and inside conservativeness, with fit body and mind, will just do, even better if you're beautifully shy. You need not to play too many tricks or be too young, from time to time, you're allowed to have unrealistic dreams, but a few words is enough to get you back into reality without getting you angry—a little embarrassed grin at most, and then do what you ought to do. I like a woman who knows how to fold clothes in a way that whenever you finish washing, ironing and folding them, they will look just like when you bought them from stores. It cannot be more specific than this, can it?

【译文评析】

[1] 原文一口气流畅道来，显示了京味汉语的调侃与戏谑，流水句为主；为体现原文的这一语言特点，译文较多使用短语以及断句，以再现主人公的思维之流。

[2] 汉语语境中大家都熟悉的"找一钱包"，意即：寻找经济来源，因为英语文化中不具备这一隐喻传统，不宜直译。

[3] "刘德华和阿汤哥那种财貌双全的郎君是不会来征你的婚的，当然我也没有做诺丁山的梦。"中两位世界级明星，对于英语世界的受众不会陌生，尤其是因在爱情大片《诺丁山》（又名《新娘百分百》）中的精湛表扬而获得公众一致好评的汤姆·克鲁索（内地观众多受港台片影响称之阿汤哥）。"财貌双全"是利用汉语谐音产生的幽默效果，译文通过尾韵进行积极补偿，以产生近似的节奏效果。"没有做诺丁山的梦"采取具体化翻译方法，译为 expect to find Julia Roberts，令人一听可知其意。

[4] "长得跟画报封面"与英文中的"封面女郎"直接对应。

【翻译试笔】

【英译汉】

Warning

（Excerpted from *George of the Jungle*）

Beatrice Stanhope:	George.
George of the Jungle:	Umhmm.
Beatrice:	I want... to talk. Would you mind stepping outside with me... (waiter passing her a cup of beer) thank you so much... (to George) for just a moment?
George:	Sure.
Lady:	Hello, Beatrice.
Beatrice:	Hello, hello. Well, we haven't been friends for very long, George, but I already think I know something about you.
George:	Oh?
Beatrice:	You are in love with my daughter.
George:	Oh, Mrs. Ursula, not so dumb...
Beatrice:	Charming. My concern, however, is that Ursula seems to reciprocate

your feelings and that does present a problem to me. You see you and Ursula together would be unbefitting her social stature. You see? Let me put it in a way you might understand, oh, where you come from zebras marry zebras, leopards marry leopards, stripes with stripes, spots with spots, well, Ursula is a stripe and you are a spot, one which I intend to have removed as soon as possible.

George：　So you know Ursula to love George.

Beatrice：　I would rather have my tongue nailed to this table every morning at breakfast.

George：　That hurt.

Beatrice：　Not as much as you will if you do anything to screw up my daughter's marriage to Lyle Van de Groot. When Lyle returns, this wedding will proceed as planned. If you do anything to upset that I will remove your reason for wearing a loin cloth.

Waiter：　Steak tartare, Mrs. Stanhope?

Beatrice：　Oh, no, no, thank you. I've had quite enough protein for today. Have a pleasant evening, Mr. Jungle.

【汉译英】

惊世之作

（根据池莉同名作品改编）

特写：一双手仔细地清洗一支旧的英雄牌吸水钢笔——洗净，擦干，组装，吸墨汁，关笔套，插入上衣口袋。

灰蒙蒙的上海，好像黑白电影。不修边幅的列可立骑着单车在拥挤的街道上。突然间，在短短的几秒钟内，路人们打起了雨伞，骑车的穿上了雨披。毛毛雨把上海染得五彩缤纷，洗得生气勃勃。

列可立的眼睛注意到马路上的细节（升格）：单车轮胎走过水塘，水溅到一个姑娘的小腿上；墙上还没干的广告滴着蓝色，汇入地上的雨水；小汽车窗里一张麻木不仁的脸。这些细节的递进似乎深刻而细腻，却又毫无意义。

列可立的画外音："这是我熟悉的城市和街道，熟悉得像自己的旧皮鞋，闭着眼睛就能穿进去。对于过分熟悉的东西我一般不留心，可是那天从开始就不寻常——虽然一切都跟以前一样。我似乎感受到某一种莫名的预感和神秘的暗示。"

列可立下车，锁车，然后走进中国银行。

银行里面比大街上暗好多，列可立在门口停下，让眼睛缓一缓，然后走到填表处。列可立掏出那支英雄牌钢笔填写存单。

他填完表刚要将笔放回，一个声音在他耳边说："先生，能借用您的笔吗？"列可立转头看见一位二十五，六的女孩儿。

他们互相看了一眼——比一般陌生人无意对上眼要长一些。然后她接下他的笔转身到柜台上去拿表格填。

他站在一旁，看她趴在桌上费劲地填表，像小学上做功课那样。

突然她抬起头，不好意思地问："大写的'二'字怎么写？"列可立写给她看。

她红着脸说，"我在这勾上多添了一撇，难怪不像了。"

列可立善解人意地说："很多这种结构的字都有这么一撇，所以容易混淆。"

陈荣波解气地说："就是。"

她把写错的存单在手里窝了窝，朝字纸篓随意扔过去。

这张存单掉在离列可立不到三步的地面上，然后缓缓舒开，迎向他的视线。于是，他在无意的低头动作中，把存单上的内容尽收眼底：

存款人姓名：陈荣波

存款人家住地址：上海市汇贤居一号楼八零五室

存款金额：拾万贰仟元

币种：美元

列可立盯着这张纸，目瞪口呆，头昏眼花。银行的人群声不见了，只听见他的心怦怦地跳，周围人群的钢笔在纸上摩擦出砂子刻划玻璃般的声音。

很长的几秒钟后，列可立鬼使神差地拾起那张存单，风似地溜走了。他拐到后厅，透过人群盯着这位叫陈荣波的女子。她正举着他的英雄钢笔东张西望，一脸迷惑。

列可立的心跳和呼吸慢慢均匀起来，他擦掉鼻尖上的汗，冷静地盯着陈荣波的一举一动：她把他的钢笔放进她的包；她排在队里百无聊赖地活动着脖子；她拿出存单仔细读一遍；她掏出一大沓美钞，动作慵懒地送进柜台；等的时候，她又四处张望地找借给她笔的列可立。

她好像看到他了，列可立躲闪到墙后。银行职员把存单交还给陈荣波，她不那么仔细地看了看，就把它塞进了皮包。她匆匆离开的时候在柜台防弹玻璃上照了照自己的脸蛋。

王教授家。

一架破单车被稀里哗啦地拆开。画外不停传来菜市场的喧闹。列可立蹲在一个极小的阳台上边做着手里的活儿边说：

"连他妈'贰'都不会写，倒有十多万美元。我们干一辈子都挣不到这样的钱。"

听他说话的人半躺在屋里的床上，床就在阳台的旁边。一架又小又破的电视机上放着英文盗版片。床上的是一位偏瘫的老人，嘴里嘟哝了个什么。

列可立接着说，"除了做鸡、做二奶她还能干什么？还是外国人的鸡，挣的是美元。"

床上的老人说话了，只有列可立听得懂。

列回答说："还没有，没见到什么有意思的招工广告。"话音未落，头顶上传来楼上摔门的声音，东西扔到地板上的声音，脚步声，尿尿声，抽水声。

他们俩都看着天花板。等了一会儿，老人问了个什么。

列回答说："我不给她签！不是我不想跟她离婚，什么'缺乏共同语言'，明明是嫌我没有工作，嫌我落魄。卓慧这种女人，面子里子她还都要。我要是有了这十万美金，她还会跟我闹离婚吗？算了，王教授，我不跟你说这些了，你整天躺在这儿听我们在你头顶上吵已经够烦的了。"

列可立回到小阳台上。他看着周围层层叠叠的旧公房，楼下窄马路上见不到头尾的露天菜场。

夜，列可立家。

列可立穿着背心短裤，戴着耳机听音乐。妻子卓慧进门他没听见。

卓慧冲着他骂："我拎着这么重的东西你也不起来帮我一下。你整天萎靡不振，里里外外

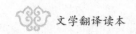

都让我一个人操心。"

戴着耳机的列可立不知道自己的声音有多大："什么？"

卓慧一把扯下他的耳机："你叫什么叫？"

列："我叫了吗？"

卓："你叫了！你干吗见我就有气？见我就这么凶？你让人怎么跟你过日子？还死活不肯承认家庭矛盾，真是的！"

列："你不要无事生非好不好？我没有气，也没有凶。我是戴着耳机没听见。"

列可立看见卓慧脱下的皮鞋一只东一只西，地上堆着各种塑料购物袋，他气就不打一处来："跟你说多少次了，我最讨厌你到处乱扔鞋！没看见我特地做了鞋柜放在门口吗？"

卓："你做了个破鞋柜就觉得了不起啦？满大街都是家具店，二十块钱就可以买一个鞋柜。现在是高科技时代了，你一个研究院毕业的工程师整天在家搞废铜烂铁破木板，也太没上进心了。比尔·盖茨就不用为自己做家具，他坐在那儿，动脑筋，设计电脑软件。现在他有的是钱，想买什么家具就买什么家具，家里有专业清洁人员保持整洁。用不着整天盯着人家鞋放哪儿。"

列可立重新戴上耳机，他走到门口那个做得十分漂亮和科学的鞋柜边，拿鞋，穿鞋，走出门。

夜。列可立家外的街道。

列走在楼下窄窄的马路上，菜场收了。马路两边躺满了乘凉的人，大部分已经睡着了，剩下有的在聊天，有的在下棋，有的在听无线电，有的把家里的电视搬到了街上。

晨，列可立家。

天蒙蒙亮，菜场已经十分活跃。摄影机升摇到列可立的小阳台上，他在自己用凳子和席子搭的床上熟睡。

太阳照到阳台上，列可立出了一头一脸的汗，还在熟睡。卓慧化了妆，拎着两只大包入画。

她一脸蔑视地看着列可立，"我去上班了，晚上我跟儿子都住我妈那儿。你整天吊儿郎当的，儿子跟着你就是学坏，你最好少影响他。离婚的事希望你认真考虑，拖下去对你我都没什么好处。"

见他没反应，转身就走了。

列可立挣扎着睁开眼，阳光太刺激，他赶紧用手挡。

下午，襄阳小学。

学校正放学，叽叽喳喳的男女学生跑出来。

列可立站在大门口看着、等着。

一个10岁的男孩儿低着头走出来，他在专心地玩游戏机。

列的目光跟着他。

另外两个比他大点的男孩儿嘻嘻哈哈地从他身后上来抢走了他的游戏机。他追上前去，要抢回他的游戏机，却被比他大的男孩推倒在地。那两大男孩儿又嘻嘻哈哈地跑走了。

列可立拔腿就追，抓住那个两个男孩儿。一手揪着一个领口，把他们揪了回来。

10岁的男孩儿有些欣喜地看着。

列说："把东西还给列海。好好跟他求饶，请他原谅你们。下次再敢动他一根毫毛我就没这么客气了。"

大男孩们把游戏机还给列海，低头说了声对不起。列问他儿子："可以放他们走吗？"

列海点头。

两个男孩儿撒腿就跑。

列可立搂住列海的肩问他："你没事吧？"

列海摇头。

列可立："我用单车送你回去吧。"

列海又摇头，"妈妈不许我跟你在一块儿，说会没出息。我自己坐公共汽车回去。"

列可立说："那我陪你去车站。"

列海想了想后点头。

夜，列可立家。

三四天没刮胡子没梳头的列可立在装修由单车改造的推车，地上摊满了图纸，工具，电焊器。推车造得很精致，简直是一件艺术品。

他站起来，仔仔细细地看他的劳动成果，然后不慌不忙地收拾工具，动作慢而精确，有点像机器人。他脸上的表情好像是在深思熟虑，也好像是在另一个空间。他慢慢抬头，夜空中一朵色彩神奇的云。

夜，汇贤居。

街道上人已经不多了，列可立戴着耳机踩着单车骑过不同的街道，然后他一拐弯停了下来。他从口袋里拿出陈荣波扔掉的存单，核对汇贤居的地址。没错，这里就是陈荣波住的地方。警卫正在关门——两扇巨大的黑色的雕花铁门，门的里面充满了绿树鲜花，院子深处有三栋高层的欧式公寓。

列可立看了看手表，刚过十二点。我们沿着列可立的视线爬到第一栋楼的第八层，有一扇窗还亮着灯。列可立久久地盯着这扇窗。

我们跟随他的视线从这栋楼转向周围的几栋楼——有类似的住宅，商业楼，还有一家医院，从医院又回到亮灯的窗户。

夜，医院/汇贤居。

列可立转身走向那家医院，大铁门已经锁了，一扇小门还开着，边上是门房办公室。列可立走到小门那儿往门房里看了一眼，值夜班的在看电视。列可立猫一样轻手轻脚地溜进了门。

他走进正对着汇贤居的那栋楼，厅里没有人，他按电梯，进了电梯他按第八层。到二层电梯停了，门开后进来一位小护士，她有点怀疑地看了列可立一眼，按了九层。列可立一动也不动地站着，眼睛盯着楼层数。小护士时不时地用余光警惕地瞄他。到五层电梯又停了，进来一位男的实习医生，他一进来就热情地跟小护士打招呼，聊天。八层终于到了，列可立下电梯时意识到他们两个都在看他。

列可立在走廊来回走了一下，然后进了男厕所，那儿的窗斜对汇贤居八层那扇亮着的窗。列可立的眼里闪烁着某一种冲动。

【参考译文】

警告

（选自电影《森林王子》）

比雅特莉斯·斯坦霍普：乔治。

森林王乔治：　　　　　　噢。

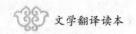

比雅特莉斯：	我想……谈一谈。你可以和我到外面去吗……（侍者递给他一杯啤酒）非常感谢……（面对乔治）就一会儿？
乔治：	当然。
女人：	你好,比雅特莉斯。
比雅特莉斯：	你好,你好。噢,我们认识不是很久,乔治,但我已经知道你的一些事情。
乔治：	哦?
比雅特莉斯：	你爱上我的女儿。
乔治：	噢,娥苏拉夫人,不至于那么笨……
比雅特莉斯：	很好,然而我所关心的是娥苏拉好像也喜欢你,那对我才是一个问题。你知道你和娥苏拉在一起不适合她的社会地位。你明白吗? 换句话说,你也许能明白,你来的地方,斑马配斑马,猎豹配猎豹,门当门,户对户,哦,娥苏拉和你门不当户不对,这个问题我想尽快地解决。
乔治：	那么你要娥苏拉爱乔治。
比雅特莉斯：	那我宁愿每天早餐都把舌头钉在这张桌子上。
乔治：	那样会痛的。
比雅特莉斯：	如果你做出什么事破坏我女儿和莱尔·冯·鲁特的婚礼,你会更痛。当莱尔回来后,婚礼会按计划举行。如果你捣乱的话,我会阉了你,这样就不用围遮羞布了。
侍者：	斯坦霍普夫人,要盐焗牛扒吗?
比雅特莉斯：	噢,不,谢谢,今天吃了够多的蛋白质了。森林先生,祝你有一个愉快的夜晚。

Staggerings

CLOSE-UP：An old Hero brand fountain pen：it is being carefully cleaned by a pair of hands—washed, wiped up, assembled, soaked up with ink, closed with the cap, finally, inserted into a jacket pocket.

EXT. STREET—DAY

Misty Shanghai looks like a black and white film. Raunchy LIE KELI is riding a bicycle in a crowded street. Suddenly, within a few seconds, foot passengers have opened umbrellas and bike riders have put on rain capes. Shanghai is dyed colorful and washed vigorous by a blast of drizzle.

LIE KELI turns his gaze to the details in the street (Zoom in)：a pair of bike wheels passes a small pond, spattering water to a girl's shank. Blue drops from a wet advertisement on the wall fall down, converging with rainwater on the ground. Behind a car's window there is a dull face. All these details going forward one by one seem profound and exquisite, but actually they are meaningless.

LIE KELI：(Voice-over) These are my familiar city and street, as familiar as my old leather shoes which I can easily put on even shut my eyes. I've never paid attention to those extremely familiar things. But that day is unusual from the dawn. Even though everything is same as before, I still feel a nameless hunch and a mystery omen.

LIE KELI gets off the bicycle, locks it up, and enters the door of Bank of China.

It is much darker inside the bank. LIE KELI stops at the door for a moment making his eyes relax. Then he approaches a form table. He draws out the Hero brand pen and begins to fill in a deposit form.

When he is going to put the pen back, a voice flies into his ears.

GIRL: (Off-screen) Excuse me, Mister. May I borrow your pen?

LIE KELI turns around and sees a girl in her mid-twenties.

They look at each other for a while, which is a little longer than ordinary seeing between strangers. Afterwards, she takes over his pen, turns around to the form table and gets a form to fill out.

He stands aside looking at her. The girl is bending over the table and filling out the form, just as a schoolgirl is doing her homework.

Suddenly she lifts up her head and asks him embarrassedly.

GIRL: How to write the capital character of the Chinese numeral "TWO"?

(LIE KELI writes it down and shows it to her.)

GIRL: (Blushingly) I made one more stroke on this tick, no wonder it looks strange.

LIE KELI: (Understandingly) Many characters of this structure have such a stroke. It's common to mix them up.

GIRL: (Venting the anger) Right!

She lightly rolls the mistaken deposit form in her hands and throws it towards a wastebasket randomly.

The deposit form falls down on the ground just three steps from LIE KELI. Then it is slowly stretching out and facing towards his sight. Bowing his head unintentionally, LIE KELI has a panoramic view on the content of the deposit form:

     Name of depositor: CHEN RONGBO

     Address of depositor: Aprt. 805, Buid. 1, Huixian Garden, Shanghai

     Amount of deposit: $102,000

     Currency: US Dollar

Staring at the paper, gape-mouthed LIE KELI feels a bit of dizziness. Noise in the bank has disappeared. What we can hear only is his heartbeat and the sound made by surrounding people using their pens on paper, like sands rubbing on glass.

A few seconds later, it seems quite long, LIE KELI, under the control of supernatural powers, picks up that deposit form and escapes like wind. Turning to the back hall, behind the crowd he secretly gazes the girl named CHEN RONGBO who is just holding his Hero pen and looking around in a puzzle.

LIE KELI's heartbeat and breath calm down slowly. He wipes off sweat on his nose tip and gazes on CHEN RONGBO carefully: she is putting he pen in her bag; standing in a queue with neck wearily turning; taking up the deposit form to read it again seriously. Finally, she is drawing out a pile of dollar bills and handing them into a counter, lazily. While waiting, she is looking around again to search LIE KELI who has lent her a pen.

It seems to LIE KELI that the girl has seen him! He dodges behind a wall. The bank clerk hands the bankbook to CHEN RONGBO. She looks at it halfheartedly and then puts it into her bag. She takes a look at her own face in the bulletproof glass of the bank counter while she is hurrying away.

INT. PROFESSOR WANG's HOME—DAY

A ragged bicycle is being broken down with a crash. Clamors of a food market ceaselessly come in from off-screen. Squatting in a very small balcony and doing the job in hands, LIE KELI talks to somebody.

LIE: Even can't write a fucking "TWO", can she have over 100,000 dollars. We can't make so much money for our lifetime.

The man listening to him is half lying on a bed inside the room. The bed is just near the balcony. An English-speaking pirate movie is going on a small and shabby TV set. The man on the bed is a paralyzed old man. He burbles something out of his mouth.

LIE: Besides being a hooker or a concubine, what else can she do? And a hooker for foreigners, makes dollars.

The old man on the bed talks, but only LIE can understand what he says.

LIE: Still not yet. I haven't found any interesting want ad.

Hardly has he finished his words when a bang of door-shutting from upstairs comes in. Then, different sounds on the top floor floats in one by one: something thrown on the floor, someone's walking, urinating, toilet flushing.

Both of them are looking at the ceiling. A moment later the old man asks him something.

LIE: I won't sign for her! It isn't that I don't want to divorce. What is "lack of common words"? Obviously she dislikes me for I don't have a job, for I look downhearted. The woman like ZHUO HUI wants everything, purse and face! If I had these 100,000 dollars, would she still struggle for a divorce with me?... Well, let it be. I won't say these trivial things to you, PROFESSOR WANG. You've been bothered a lot every day by our noise above while you're lying here.

LIE KELI goes back to the small balcony. He is looking at the old public buildings surrounding him ring upon ring, at the boundless open-air food market on a narrow road downstairs.

INT. LIE KELI's home—Night

Wearing a vest and short pants, LIE is listening to the music with an earphone. He has not heard that his wife, ZHUO HUI, was entering the room.

ZHUO HUI: (Scolding him) Why can't you stand up and help me when I'm carrying so heavy things? You are like a lazy dog every day. Let me worry about everything alone.

(With an earphone on his head, LIE KELI has not realized how loud his voice is.)

LIE: What?

ZHUO: (Tears down his earphone at a blow) What are you shouting for?

LIE: Have I shouted?

ZHUO: Yes, you have! Why are you so angry, so fierce as soon as you see me? How can I live with you? Anyway, you still don't admit family's conflict. Well, well, well!

LIE: Can't you make trouble out of nothing? I'm not angry at all! Not fierce, too! I've just not heard you for this earphone.

(Seeing Zhuo's shoes are scattered carelessly and plastic shopping bags are piled on the floor, LIE KELI gets angry.)

LIE: How many times should I tell you? You always throw out your shoes without care. That makes me sick! The shoes cabinet I specially made is just near the door. Can't you see it?

Zhuo: Is it amazing just for you made that rubbish shoes cabinet? There are furniture stores everywhere. If I want a cabinet, I only need to pay 20 Yuan. It's hi-tech era nowadays. An engineer out of a graduate school like you plays with metal and wood scraps every day at home! Why can't you have a little spirit? Bill Gates doesn't need to make furniture by himself. He sits there using his brains to design software. He has plenty of money. He can buy any furniture if he wants. His house is kept cleaning by professional cleaners. He never pays attention to where other people put their shoes.

LIE KELI wears the earphone again. He goes towards that refined and technically made shoes cabinet near the door, takes out his shoes, puts on them, and goes out.

EXT.　ROAD OUTSIDE LIE KELI's HOME—NIGHT

LIE is walking on that narrow road where the food market has been over. On both sides of the road people are lying and enjoying cool. Most of them have been asleep; some others are chatting, playing chess, or listening to the radio; some have even moved their TV-sets there.

INT.　LIE KELI's home—Morning

At daybreak the food market has already been quite lively. The camera cranes up to reveal LIE KELI's small balcony where he is deeply sleeping on a temporary bed put up by benches and a mat.

The sun is shining on the balcony. LIE KELI, whose head is all sweating, is still sleeping. Wearing her makeup and carrying two big bags, ZHUO HUI enters the screen.

ZHUO: (Looking at LIE KELI with scorn) I'm going to work now. The son and I will stay in my mother's home tonight. You are idle all day. If the son followed you, he'd certainly be ruined. You'd better not give him any influence. I hope you consider our divorce seriously. It's nothing good for either of us if it's always delaying.

Finding no reaction from him, she turns her steps out.

LIE KELI struggles to open his eyes. The sunlight is so stimulating that he quickly reaches out his hand to keep it out.

ExT. Xiangyang Primary School—Afternoon

The school is over just now. Boys and girls are chirpily running out.

LIE KELI stands at the school gate looking and waiting.

A ten-year-old boy comes out lowing the head and playing a portable game-player with undivided attention.

LIE's sight line follows him.

At this time, two other bigger boys come from behind, laughing and joking. They rob the smaller boy's game-player away. The smaller catches up with them and wants to get his game-player back. However, he is push over on the ground by the biggers. After that the two boys run away, leaving laughter behind.

LIE KELI springs into a chase and seizes the two boys in no time. He holds the boys back with each one's collar in a hand. The ten-year-old is surprised to look at this happening.

LIE: Return the player to LIE Hai! Beg him for mercy! If you dare hurt him a bit next time, I'll be not so polite.

(The bigger boys return the game-player to LIE Hai)

BOYS: (Hanging their heads) Sorry... sorry.

LIE: (To his son) Can we let them go?

(LIE Hai nods. The two boys run away quickly.)

LIE KELI: (Holding up LIE Hai's shoulders) Are you all right?

(LIE HAI nods.)

LIE KELI: Let me take you home with my bike.

LIE HAI: (Shaking his head again) Mama doesn't allow me being with you. She said I'd be good for nothing. I'll take the bus myself.

LIE KELI: Then I accompany you to the bus stop.

(LIE Hai thinks it over and nods.)

INT. LIE KELI's home—Night

LIE KELI, who hasn't shaved and combed for three or four days, is installing a handcart refitted by a bicycle. Drawings, tools and an electric welder are scattered on the floor. The handcart has been made so refined that it is simply an artwork.

He stands up, looking at his working achievement carefully. Then he begins to tidy up the tools. His action is slow and accurate, like a robot. The expression on his face tells us that he is in a deep consideration, or that he is in a different place. He lifts the head slowly, and sees a magical-colored cloud in the night sky.

EXT. HUIXIAN GARGEN—NIGHT

It is rather quiet in the street. LIE KELI is riding a bike with an earphone on his head through different streets. Finally, he turns around and halts. He draws out the deposit form thrown by CHEN RONGBO from his pocket, and checks up the address of the Huixian Garden.

Right! It is the very place where CHEN RONGBO lives. Entrance guards are closing the gate, which is a pair of big black iron gates with flowers engraved on the surface. Inside the gate there are lots of trees and flowers. In the depths of the courtyard we can see three European-style apartment buildings.

LIE KELI takes a look at his wristwatch. It is shortly past twelve. We follow LIE's sight line to the eighth floor of the first building. There is still a window with bright light. LIE KELI gazes on that window for a long time.

We follow his sight line from this building to surrounding buildings—they are similar apartment buildings, a commercial building, and a hospital. The sight line comes back again from the hospital to the window with bright light.

EXT. HOSPITAL/HUIXIAN GARDEN—NIGHT

LIE KELI turns around and walks towards that hospital. The iron gate of the hospital is locked, but a small door is still open. The gatehouse is beside the door, in which a night-shift watchman is watching TV. LIE glides into the door like a cat.

He goes into the building that is over against the Huixian Garden. The lobby is empty. He presses a button to call the elevator. After entering the elevator he presses the eighth floor. The elevator stops on the second floor and a young nurse comes in. The nurse casts a look at him suspiciously and presses the ninth floor. LIE KELI is standing there and gazing at the floor numbers without any movement. Between whiles the young nurse glances over him vigilantly. The elevator stops at the fifth floor again and a male intern gets in. The young doctor warmly greets the nurse and chats with her. The eighth floor is reached at last. Feeling the two are looking at him behind, LIE KELI gets off the elevator.

LIE KELI wanders in the corridor for a while and eventually enters the men's lavatory. The window in the men's room is obliquely against the bright-light window on the eighth floor of the Huixian Garden. An indescribable impulse glints in LIE KELI's eyes.

——选自 http://blog. sina. com. cn/s/blog_3f70d7 eao100096d. html

【延伸阅读】

[1] Cronin, M. *Translation and Globalization* [M]. London & New York：Routledge, 2003.

[2] Cronin, M. *Translation Goes to the Movies* [M]. London & New York：Routledge, 2009.

[3] Cintas, D. J. & Remael, A. *Audiovisual Translation：Subtitling* [M]. Manchester & Kinderhook：St. Jerome Publishing, 2007.

[4] Cintas, D. J. & Anderman, G. *Audiovisual Translation：Language Transfer on Screen* [C]. Hampshire：Palgrave Macmillan, 2009.

[5] Gambier, Y. & Gottlieb, H. *(Multi) Media Translation：Concepts, Practices and Research* [M]. Amsterdam/Philadelphia：John Benjamins Publishing Company, 2001.

[6] O'Hagan, M. & Ashworth, D. *Translation-Mediated Communication in a Digital World：Facing the Challenges of Globalization and Localization* [M]. Clevedon：

Multilingual Matters Limited，2002.

[7] Orero，P. *Topics in Audiovisual Translation*[C]. Amsterdam/Philadelphia：Benjamins Publishing Company，2004.

[8] Poyatos，F. *Nonverbal Communication Across Disciplines*. *Volume* 3：*Narrative Literature*，*Theater*，*Cinema*，*Translation*［M］. Amsterdam/Philadelphia：John Benjamins Publishing Company，2002.

[9] Pym，A. *The Moving Text*［M］. Amsterdam/Philadelphia：Benjamins Publishing Company，2004.

[10] Wood，M. The Languages of Cinema［A］. In Bermann，Sandra & Michael Wood （eds.），*Nation*，*Language*，*and the Ethics of Translation*[M]. Princeton & Oxford：Princeton University Press，2005.

[11] Zatlin，P. *Theatrical Translation and Film Adaptation*：*A Practitioner's View*［M］. Clevedon：Multilingual Matters Limited，2005.

[12] 段鸿欣. 人物对白的翻译在译制片和小说中的比较[A]. //张子扬. 电视节目论集[C]. 北京：作家出版社,1999.

[13] 段鸿欣. 西方经典电影(英汉对照本)[C]. 北京：西苑出版社,2005.

[14] 方华文. 世界上最精彩的电影对白(英汉对照)[C]. 合肥：安徽科学技术出版社,2009.

[15] 何宁. 英语电影片名翻译纵横谈[J]. 上海科技翻译,1998(3).

[16] 贺莺. 电影片名的翻译理论和方法[J]. 外语教学,2001(1).

[17] 麻争旗. 论影视翻译的基本原则[J]. 现代传播,1997(5).

[18] 麻争旗. 影视译制概论[M]. 北京：中国传媒大学出版社,2005.

[19] 孟广钧. 一部影片的翻译开创了一个片种——《普通一兵》剧本的诞生[A]. //郑鲁南. 一本书和一个世界. 北京：昆仑出版社,2008.

[20] 朴哲浩. 影视翻译研究[M]. 哈尔滨：黑龙江人民出版社,2008.

[21] 钱锋,刘爱萍. 英文名篇鉴赏金库：电影卷[C]. 天津：天津人民出版社,2005.

[22] 王鹏.《哈利·波特》与其汉语翻译[M]. 重庆：重庆大学出版社,2007.

[23] 徐学萍,朴哲浩. 影视作品主要特征探微——以影视翻译研究为视角[J]. 电影评介,2009(11).

[24] 杨和平. 当代中国译制[M]. 北京：中国传媒大学出版社,2010.

[25] 张春柏. 影视翻译初探[J]. 中国翻译,1998(2).

[26] 张仁凤,俞剑红. 英汉·汉英电影词典[C]. 北京：中国电影出版社,2000.

【问题与思考】

1. 影视翻译为文学翻译的一部分,与一般文学翻译的共同之处何在?

2. 影视语言的特性有哪些?

3. 影视剧本翻译的基本原则是什么?

4. 会话礼貌原则在电影脚本翻译中的使用契合度何在?

5. 文学翻译的"信达雅"准则,在影视翻译中三者之间关系如何?

6. 影视译制可以遵循的理论指导有哪些?

7. "多元系统理论"适用于影视翻译吗?
8. 请结合译制大片《哈利·波特》谈谈你对译制电影接受的看法。
9. 意识形态对于影视译制的干预具体表现在哪些地方?
10. 配音翻译与字幕翻译的区别与联系何在?

主要参考文献

[1] Bassnett, S. Transplanting the Seed: Poetry and Translation[A]. In Susan Bassnett & André Lefevere (eds.), *Constructing Cultures* (pp. 57 – 75)[M]. Shanghai: Shanghai Foreign Language Education Press, 2001.

[2] Bassnett, S. Translating Prose. //*Translation Studies* (3rd Edition)(pp. 114 – 123) [M]. London & New York: Routledge, 2002.

[3] Batteux, C. Principles of Literature[A]. In André Lefevere (ed.), *Translation/ History/ Culture*(pp. 116 – 120)[M]. London & New York: Routledge, 1992.

[4] Cintas, D. J. In Search of a Theoretical Framework for the Study of Audiovisual Translation[A]. In Pilar Orero (ed.), *Topics in Audiovisual Translation* (pp. 21 – 34) [M]. Amsterdam/Philadelphia: Benjamins Publishing Company, 2004.

[5] Hatim, B. & Mason, I. Politeness in Screen Translating[A]. In Lawrence Venuti (ed.), *The Translation Studies Reader* (pp. 430 – 445)[M]. New York: Routledge, 2000.

[6] Lefevere, A. Translating Literature/Translated Literature[A]. In Ortrun Zuber (ed.), *The Languages of Theatre* (pp. 153 – 161). Oxford & New York: Pergamon Press, 1980.

[7] Lefevere, A. Mother Courage's Cucumbers[A]. In Lawrence Venuti (ed.), *The Translation Studies Reader*(pp. 233 – 249)[M]. New York: Routledge, 2000.

[8] Newmark, P. The Translation of Metaphors. //*A Textbook of Translation* (pp. 104 – 113)[M]. Shanghai: Shanghai Foreign Language Education Press, 2001.

[9] Newmark, P. *A Textbook of Translation*[M]. Harlow: Pearson Education Ltd., 2003.

[10] Pound, E. Guido's Relations[A]. In Lawrence Venuti (ed.), *The Translation Studies Reader*(pp. 26 – 33)[M]. New York: Routledge, 2000.

[11] Şehnaz, T. G. Sherlock Holmes in the Interculture[A]. In Anthony, Pym, Miriam Shlesinger & Daniel Simeoni (eds.), *Beyond Descriptive Translation Studies* (pp. 133 – 151)[M]. Amsterdam/ Philadelphia: John Benjamins Publishing Company, 2008.

[12] Schleiermacher, F. On the Different Methods of Translating[A]. In André Lefevere (ed.), *Translation/ History/ Culture* (pp. 141 – 166)[M]. London & New York: Routledge, 1992.

[13] Snell-Hornby, M. Theatre and Opera Translation [A]. In Piotr Kuhiwczak & KarinLittau (eds.), *A Companion to Translation Studies* (pp. 106 – 119)[M]. Clevedon & Buffalo & Toronto: Multilingual Matters Ltd., 2006.

[14] Toury, G. Enhancing Cultural Changes by Means of Fictitious Translations[A]. In Eva Hung (ed.), *Translation and Cultural Change* (pp. 3 – 17)[M]. Amsterdam/

Philadelphia：John Benjamins Publishing Company，2005.

[15] Tucker，H. F. Metaphor，Translation，and Autoekphrasis in FitzGerald's Rubáiyát [J]. *Victorian Poetry*，2008(1)：69 – 85.

[16] Tytler，A. F. Essay on the Principles of Translation (extracts). In André Lefevere (ed.)，*Translation/ History/ Culture* (pp. 128 – 135) [M]. London & New York：Routledge，1992.

[17] 冯世则. 风格的翻译：必要、困难、可能与必然[A].//翻译匠语[M].上海：文汇出版社，2005.

[18] 傅浩. 二十世纪英语诗选[C].石家庄：河北教育出版社，2003.

[19] 黄维樑，江弱水. 余光中选集第五卷：译品集[C].合肥：安徽教育出版社，1999.

[20] 林语堂. 论译诗[A].//刘靖之. 翻译论集[C].香港：生活读书新知三联书店，1981.

[21] 刘炳善. 从翻译的角度看英国随笔. 译事随笔[M].北京：中国电影出版社，2000：pp. 126 – 134.

[22] 刘士聪. 汉英——英汉美文翻译与鉴赏[C].南京：译林出版社，2002.

[23] 刘士聪. 介绍一部中国散文经典译作——兼评 David Pollard 的汉英翻译艺术[J].中国翻译，2005(2).

[24] 吕叔湘. 中诗英译比录[M].北京：中华书局，2002.

[25] 罗新璋. 翻译论集[C].北京：商务印书馆，1984.

[26] 麻争旗. 影视剧脚本的翻译及审美特征[J].北京第二外国语学院学报，2003(2).

[27] 钱绍昌. 影视翻译——翻译园地中愈来愈重要的领域[J].中国翻译，2000(1).

[28] 钱钟书. 林纾的翻译[M].北京：商务印书馆，1981：pp. 18 – 51.

[29] 钱钟书. 围城(汉英对照)[M].珍妮·凯利，茅国权译.北京：人民文学出版社，2003.

[30] 申丹. 论西方现代文学文体学在小说翻译中的作用[J].外语与翻译，1998(4).

[31] 苏福忠. 说说朱生豪的翻译[J].读书，2004(5).

[32] 苏福忠. 译事余墨[M].北京：生活·读书·新知三联书店，2006.

[33] 孙致礼. 翻译：理论与实践探索[M].南京：译林出版社，1999.

[34] 杨平. 名作精译——《中国翻译》汉译英选萃[C].青岛：青岛出版社，2003.

[35] 杨武能. 三叶集——德语文学·文学翻译·比较文学[M].成都：巴蜀书社，2005.

[36] 杨宪益，戴乃迭. 关汉卿杂剧选[C].北京：外文出版社，2004.

[37] 余光中. 与王尔德拔河记——《不可儿戏》译后[A].余光中谈翻译[M].北京：中国对外翻译出版公司，2002.

[38] 余立三. 英汉翻译中修辞格的处理[A].//英汉修辞比较与翻译[M].北京：商务印书馆，1985.

[39] 张南峰. Delabastita 的双关语翻译理论在英汉翻译中的应用[J].中国翻译，2003(1).

[40] 张培基. 英译中国现代散文选(汉英对照)[C].上海：上海外语教育出版社，1999.

[41] 张英进. 从现代文体学看文学风格与翻译[J].外国语，1986(1).

[42] 郑海凌. 文学翻译的本质特征[J].中国翻译，1998(6).

[43] 郑延国. 妙手剪裁　风格再现——《老人与海》新译片断赏析[J].中国翻译，1990(3).

图书在版编目(CIP)数据

文学翻译读本 / 辛红娟主编. — 南京 :南京大学
出版社,2012.8

(大学本科翻译研究型系列读本 / 张柏然总主编)
ISBN 978 - 7 - 305 - 09830 - 7

Ⅰ. ①文… Ⅱ. ①辛… Ⅲ. ①文学翻译-高等学校-
教学参考资料 Ⅳ. ①I046

中国版本图书馆 CIP 数据核字(2012)第 068769 号

出版发行　南京大学出版社
社　　址　南京市汉口路 22 号　　　　邮　编　210093
网　　址　http://www. NjupCo. com
出 版 人　左　健
丛 书 名　大学本科翻译研究型系列读本
总 主 编　张柏然
书　　名　文学翻译读本
主　　编　辛红娟
责任编辑　刁晓静　　　　　　　　编辑热线　025 - 83685720

照　　排　南京南琳图文制作有限公司
印　　刷　南京玉河印刷厂
开　　本　787×1092　1/16　印张 29　字数 720 千
版　　次　2012 年 8 月第 1 版　2012 年 8 月第 1 次印刷
ISBN 978 - 7 - 305 - 09830 - 7
定　　价　58. 00 元

发行热线　025 - 83594756　83686452
电子邮箱　Press@NjupCo. com
　　　　　Sales@NjupCo. com(市场部)